HANS
CHRISTIAN
ANDERSEN
FAIRY TALES

ANTHOLOGY OF CLASSIC TALES

Foreword by Maria Tatar

FLAME TREE PUBLISHING

This is a FLAME TREE Book

Publisher & Creative Director: Nick Wells
Editorial Director: Catherine Taylor
Project Editor: Gillian Whitaker
Special thanks to Tim Leng

Publisher's Note: Due to the historical nature of the classic text, we're aware that there may be some language used which has the potential to cause offence to the modern reader. However, wishing overall to preserve the integrity of the text, rather than imposing contemporary sensibilities, we have left it unaltered.

FLAME TREE PUBLISHING
6 Melbray Mews, Fulham,
London SW6 3NS, United Kingdom
www.flametreepublishing.com

First published 2020

22 24 23 21
3 5 7 9 10 8 6 4 2

ISBN: 978-1-83964-165-7

The cover image is created by Flame Tree Studio

A copy of the CIP data for this book is available from the British Library.

Printed and bound in China

HANS
CHRISTIAN
ANDERSEN
FAIRY TALES
ANTHOLOGY OF CLASSIC TALES

Foreword by Maria Tatar

FLAME TREE PUBLISHING

Contents

Life & Death

The Heart's Desires

Marvels & Magics

Little Wonders

Foreword:
Hans Christian Andersen Fairy Tales

WHEN HANS CHRISTIAN ANDERSEN decided to write his autobiography, he instinctively and without hesitation gave it the title: *The Fairy Tale of My Life*. Nothing could have been more right, for Andersen's rapid rise from rags to riches reads exactly like a fairy tale. In 1819, at the age of fourteen, he left the Danish provinces with just a few coins in his pocket to seek what he called, in all seriousness, fame and fortune in Copenhagen. Like the simpletons of fairy tales, his winning naivete shaded into what proved to be real wisdom and true courage, for the determined boy, son of a washerwoman and shoemaker, quickly moved up the social and literary ladder to become what he himself had predicted would be Denmark's greatest poet.

How do we explain Andersen's enduring appeal and his continuing cultural relevance today? According to UNESCO, the United Nations Educational, Scientific and Cultural Organization, Andersen ranks among the ten most widely translated authors in the world, right alongside William Shakespeare and Karl Marx. We remember Andersen in part because of the beauty of his constructed images, which rival what we find in reality. In "The Fir Tree", the first story in this volume, the wonders of the natural world ("warm sunshine", "rosy clouds", and snow that is "white and glittering") are exceeded only by the "beautiful ornaments", "gilded apples and walnuts", and "lighted tapers" of the indoor Christmas tree. The Little Mermaid is dressed in "costly robes of silk and muslin", and she dances with slaves, "dressed in silk and gold", in scenes that surpass the beauty of her underwater habitat. Then there is the nightingale, in the tale of that title, a mechanical bird "covered all over with diamonds, rubies, and sapphires", seemingly more beautiful than the real nightingale, with its enchanting, improvised song.

In many ways, Andersen was ahead of his time, prefiguring the cult of beauty at the turn of the nineteenth century and preaching the doctrine of the redemptive power of art. Yet for all his absorption in surfaces and everything that glitters, sparkles and shines, Andersen was haunted by the twin spectres of suffering and mortality. And so, along with the doctrine of *l'art pour l'art*, Andersen gives us a poetics of ephemerality and pain, reminding us that beauty always makes demands on us and that its power is fugitive, destined to fade and die. Consider the Little Match Girl, and how she produces cheering warmth and luminous visions with each match she lights, only to see those beautiful hallucinations dissolve. Or Little Tuk, who dreams of palaces and kings, ships and pleasure gardens, birds of good omen and beautiful maidens only to find that everything vanishes – "it seemed to him like turning over the leaves of a book". Or the Little Mermaid, who trades her tail to become "the prettiest little human being" with unparalleled "floating gracefulness", but all the while feeling as if she is "treading upon sharp knives".

In many ways, Andersen inaugurated a new era in children's literature, turning away from the morals of nineteenth-century writers and promoting an ethics of empathy that remains a hallmark of children's literature today. He is supremely committed to creating beautiful images, using dazzling special effects and visual pyrotechnics, but his pictures are moving in the double sense of the term, animating us and also enabling us to see inside the minds of his characters, suffering with them at times, but above all empathizing with the pain they feel.

Although Andersen added the words "for children" (*fortalte for Børn*) to his early collections of fairy tales (which included "The Emperor's New Clothes" and "The Princess and the Pea"), he omitted that phrase from later titles. His 1844 collection, featuring "The Ugly Duckling" and "The Nightingale", appeared simply as *New Fairy Tales*. Just a few years later, in 1852, he began to use the Danish word for stories (*historier*) in his titles. He no doubt recognized that his narratives were less tied to the traditional tales he had once heard as a child in the spinning rooms of Odense than inspired by his powers of imagination – the ability, not just to bring inanimate objects to life, but also to enable his readers to feel the pleasures of extreme altruism and self-sacrifice and to recoil from the horrors of callousness and cruelty.

Andersen's stories may have migrated into new media for children (the Disney franchise comes to mind with its animated version of "The Little Mermaid" and with *Frozen*, inspired by "The Snow Queen"), but they have never lost their hold on adult readers. Today we can read Andersen in many new translations, but few take us back, as Mrs. Paull does in her 1872 translation, to the quaint charms of the nineteenth-century literary world and let us read Andersen as he was read by others before us, when he was first making his name in the Anglo-American world.

Maria Tatar
John L. Loeb Research Professor of
Germanic Languages & Literatures and Folklore & Mythology, Harvard University

Publisher's Note

Nearly all of the tales in this anthology derive from Mrs. Henry H. B. Paull's *Hans Andersen's Fairy Tales*, and have been carefully selected to present the reader with a satisfying collection of the most treasured narratives by that master of storytelling Hans Christian Andersen. Take yourself back to your childhood as you re-discover that classic "The Emperor's New Clothes" or the poignant "The Little Match-Seller", revel in the evocative "Little Tiny" ("Thumbelina") and read the original story of "The Little Mermaid", where you'll find more edge and depth than anything Disney can produce. In order to provide a pleasing experience, we have categorised the stories into thematic sections – this will perhaps guide your reading and reveal echoes and resonances that elevate your appreciation of the tales.

CLASSIC

HANS
CHRISTIAN
ANDERSEN
FAIRY TALES

ANTHOLOGY OF CLASSIC TALES

Foreword by Maria Tatar

FLAME TREE PUBLISHING

STORIES

Life & Death

The Fir Tree

FAR DOWN IN the forest, where the warm sun and the fresh air made a sweet resting-place, grew a pretty little fir-tree; and yet it was not happy, it wished so much to be tall like its companions – the pines and firs which grew around it. The sun shone, and the soft air fluttered its leaves, and the little peasant children passed by, prattling merrily, but the fir-tree heeded them not. Sometimes the children would bring a large basket of raspberries or strawberries, wreathed on a straw, and seat themselves near the fir-tree, and say, "Is it not a pretty little tree?" which made it feel more unhappy than before. And yet all this while the tree grew a notch or joint taller every year; for by the number of joints in the stem of a fir-tree we can discover its age. Still, as it grew, it complained, "Oh! how I wish I were as tall as the other trees, then I would spread out my branches on every side, and my top would over-look the wide world. I should have the birds building their nests on my boughs, and when the wind blew, I should bow with stately dignity like my tall companions." The tree was so discontented, that it took no pleasure in the warm sunshine, the birds, or the rosy clouds that floated over it morning and evening. Sometimes, in winter, when the snow lay white and glittering on the ground, a hare would come springing along, and jump right over the little tree; and then how mortified it would feel! Two winters passed, and when the third arrived, the tree had grown so tall that the hare was obliged to run round it. Yet it remained unsatisfied, and would exclaim, "Oh, if I could but keep on growing tall and old! There is nothing else worth caring for in the world!" In the autumn, as usual, the wood-cutters came and cut down several of the tallest trees, and the young fir-tree, which was now grown to its full height, shuddered as the noble trees fell to the earth with a crash. After the branches were lopped off, the trunks looked so slender and bare, that they could scarcely be recognized. Then they were placed upon wagons, and drawn by horses out of the forest. "Where were they going? What would become of them?" The young fir-tree wished very much to know; so in the spring, when the swallows and the storks came, it asked, "Do you know where those trees were taken? Did you meet them?"

The swallows knew nothing, but the stork, after a little reflection, nodded his head, and said, "Yes, I think I do. I met several new ships when I flew from Egypt, and they had fine masts that smelt like fir. I think these must have been the trees; I assure you they were stately, very stately."

"Oh, how I wish I were tall enough to go on the sea," said the fir-tree. "What is the sea, and what does it look like?"

"It would take too much time to explain," said the stork, flying quickly away.

"Rejoice in thy youth," said the sunbeam; "rejoice in thy fresh growth, and the young life that is in thee."

And the wind kissed the tree, and the dew watered it with tears; but the fir-tree regarded them not.

Christmas-time drew near, and many young trees were cut down, some even smaller and younger than the fir-tree who enjoyed neither rest nor peace with longing to leave its forest home. These young trees, which were chosen for their beauty, kept their branches, and were also laid on wagons and drawn by horses out of the forest.

"Where are they going?" asked the fir-tree. "They are not taller than I am: indeed, one is much less; and why are the branches not cut off? Where are they going?"

"We know, we know," sang the sparrows; "we have looked in at the windows of the houses in the town, and we know what is done with them. They are dressed up in the most splendid manner. We have seen them standing in the middle of a warm room, and adorned with all sorts of beautiful things, – honey cakes, gilded apples, playthings, and many hundreds of wax tapers."

"And then," asked the fir-tree, trembling through all its branches, "and then what happens?"

"We did not see any more," said the sparrows; "but this was enough for us."

"I wonder whether anything so brilliant will ever happen to me," thought the fir-tree. "It would be much better than crossing the sea. I long for it almost with pain. Oh! when will Christmas be here? I am now as tall and well grown as those which were taken away last year. Oh! that I were now laid on the wagon, or standing in the warm room, with all that brightness and splendor around me! Something better and more beautiful is to come after, or the trees would not be so decked out. Yes, what follows will be grander and more splendid. What can it be? I am weary with longing. I scarcely know how I feel."

"Rejoice with us," said the air and the sunlight. "Enjoy thine own bright life in the fresh air."

But the tree would not rejoice, though it grew taller every day; and, winter and summer, its dark-green foliage might be seen in the forest, while passers by would say, "What a beautiful tree!"

A short time before Christmas, the discontented fir-tree was the first to fall. As the axe cut through the stem, and divided the pith, the tree fell with a groan to the earth, conscious of pain and faintness, and forgetting all its anticipations of happiness, in sorrow at leaving its home in the forest. It knew that it should never again see its dear old companions, the trees, nor the little bushes and many-colored flowers that had grown by its side; perhaps not even the birds. Neither was the journey at all pleasant. The tree first recovered itself while being unpacked in the courtyard of a house, with several other trees; and it heard a man say, "We only want one, and this is the prettiest."

Then came two servants in grand livery, and carried the fir-tree into a large and beautiful apartment. On the walls hung pictures, and near the great stove stood great china vases, with lions on the lids. There were rocking chairs, silken sofas, large tables, covered with pictures, books, and playthings, worth a great deal of money, – at least, the children said so. Then the fir-tree was placed in a large tub, full of sand; but green baize hung all around it, so that no one could see it was a tub, and it stood on a very handsome carpet. How the fir-tree trembled! "What was going to happen to him now?" Some young ladies came, and the servants helped them to adorn the tree. On one branch they hung little bags cut out of colored paper, and each bag was filled with sweetmeats; from other branches hung gilded apples and walnuts, as if they had grown there; and above, and all round, were hundreds of red, blue, and white tapers, which were fastened on the branches. Dolls, exactly like real babies, were placed under the green leaves, – the tree had never seen such things before, – and at the very top was fastened a glittering star, made of tinsel. Oh, it was very beautiful!

"This evening," they all exclaimed, "how bright it will be!" "Oh, that the evening were come," thought the tree, "and the tapers lighted! then I shall know what else is going to happen. Will the trees of the forest come to see me? I wonder if the sparrows will peep in at the windows as they fly? shall I grow faster here, and keep on all these ornaments summer and winter?" But guessing was of very little use; it made his bark ache, and this pain is as bad for a slender fir-tree, as headache is for us. At last the tapers were lighted, and then what a glistening blaze of light the tree presented! It trembled so with joy in all its branches, that one of the candles fell among the green leaves and burnt some of them. "Help! help!" exclaimed the young ladies, but there was no danger, for they quickly extinguished the fire. After this, the tree tried not to tremble at all, though the fire frightened him; he was so anxious not to hurt any of the beautiful ornaments, even while their brilliancy dazzled him. And now the folding doors were thrown open, and a troop of children rushed in as if they intended to upset the tree; they were followed more silently by their elders. For a moment the little ones stood silent with astonishment, and then they shouted for joy, till the room rang, and they danced merrily round the tree, while one present after another was taken from it.

"What are they doing? What will happen next?" thought the fir. At last the candles burnt down to the branches and were put out. Then the children received permission to plunder the tree.

Oh, how they rushed upon it, till the branches cracked, and had it not been fastened with the glistening star to the ceiling, it must have been thrown down. The children then danced about with their pretty toys, and no one noticed the tree, except the children's maid who came and peeped among the branches to see if an apple or a fig had been forgotten.

"A story, a story," cried the children, pulling a little fat man towards the tree.

"Now we shall be in the green shade," said the man, as he seated himself under it, "and the tree will have the pleasure of hearing also, but I shall only relate one story; what shall it be? Ivede-Avede, or Humpty Dumpty, who fell down stairs, but soon got up again, and at last married a princess."

"Ivede-Avede," cried some. "Humpty Dumpty," cried others, and there was a fine shouting and crying out. But the fir-tree remained quite still, and thought to himself, "Shall I have anything to do with all this?" but he had already amused them as much as they wished. Then the old man told them the story of Humpty Dumpty, how he fell down stairs, and was raised up again, and married a princess. And the children clapped their hands and cried, "Tell another, tell another," for they wanted to hear the story of "Ivede-Avede;" but they only had "Humpty Dumpty." After this the fir-tree became quite silent and thoughtful; never had the birds in the forest told such tales as "Humpty Dumpty," who fell down stairs, and yet married a princess.

"Ah! yes, so it happens in the world," thought the fir-tree; he believed it all, because it was related by such a nice man. "Ah! well," he thought, "who knows? perhaps I may fall down too, and marry a princess;" and he looked forward joyfully to the next evening, expecting to be again decked out with lights and playthings, gold and fruit. "To-morrow I will not tremble," thought he; "I will enjoy all my splendor, and I shall hear the story of Humpty Dumpty again, and perhaps Ivede-Avede." And the tree remained quiet and thoughtful all night. In the morning the servants and the housemaid came in. "Now," thought the fir, "all my splendor is going to begin again." But they dragged him out of the room and up stairs to the garret, and threw him on the floor, in a dark corner, where no daylight shone, and there they left him. "What does this mean?" thought the tree, "what am I to do here? I can hear nothing in a place like this," and he had time enough to think, for days and nights passed and no one came near him, and when at last somebody did come, it was only to put away large boxes in a corner. So the tree was completely hidden from sight as if it had never existed. "It is winter now," thought the tree, "the ground is hard and covered with snow, so that people cannot plant me. I shall be sheltered here, I dare say, until spring comes. How thoughtful and kind everybody is to me! Still I wish this place were not so dark, as well as lonely, with not even a little hare to look at. How pleasant it was out in the forest while the snow lay on the ground, when the hare would run by, yes, and jump over me too, although I did not like it then. Oh! it is terrible lonely here."

"Squeak, squeak," said a little mouse, creeping cautiously towards the tree; then came another; and they both sniffed at the fir-tree and crept between the branches.

"Oh, it is very cold," said the little mouse, "or else we should be so comfortable here, shouldn't we, you old fir-tree?"

"I am not old," said the fir-tree, "there are many who are older than I am."

"Where do you come from? and what do you know?" asked the mice, who were full of curiosity. "Have you seen the most beautiful places in the world, and can you tell us all about them? and have you been in the storeroom, where cheeses lie on the shelf, and hams hang from the ceiling? One can run about on tallow candles there, and go in thin and come out fat."

"I know nothing of that place," said the fir-tree, "but I know the wood where the sun shines and the birds sing." And then the tree told the little mice all about its youth. They had never heard such an account in their lives; and after they had listened to it attentively, they said, "What a number of things you have seen? you must have been very happy."

"Happy!" exclaimed the fir-tree, and then as he reflected upon what he had been telling them, he said, "Ah, yes! after all those were happy days." But when he went on and related all about Christmas-eve, and how he had been dressed up with cakes and lights, the mice said, "How happy you must have been, you old fir-tree."

"I am not old at all," replied the tree, "I only came from the forest this winter, I am now checked in my growth."

"What splendid stories you can relate," said the little mice. And the next night four other mice came with them to hear what the tree had to tell. The more he talked the more he remembered, and then he thought to himself, "Those were happy days, but they may come again. Humpty Dumpty fell down stairs, and yet he married the princess; perhaps I may marry a princess too." And the fir-tree thought of the pretty little birch-tree that grew in the forest, which was to him a real beautiful princess.

"Who is Humpty Dumpty?" asked the little mice. And then the tree related the whole story; he could remember every single word, and the little mice was so delighted with it, that they were ready to jump to the top of the tree. The next night a great many more mice made their appearance, and on Sunday two rats came with them; but they said, it was not a pretty story at all, and the little mice were very sorry, for it made them also think less of it.

"Do you know only one story?" asked the rats.

"Only one," replied the fir-tree; "I heard it on the happiest evening of my life; but I did not know I was so happy at the time."

"We think it is a very miserable story," said the rats. "Don't you know any story about bacon, or tallow in the storeroom."

"No," replied the tree.

"Many thanks to you then," replied the rats, and they marched off.

The little mice also kept away after this, and the tree sighed, and said, "It was very pleasant when the merry little mice sat round me and listened while I talked. Now that is all passed too. However, I shall consider myself happy when some one comes to take me out of this place." But would this ever happen? Yes; one morning people came to clear out the garret, the boxes were packed away, and the tree was pulled out of the corner, and thrown roughly on the garret floor; then the servant dragged it out upon the staircase where the daylight shone. "Now life is beginning again," said the tree, rejoicing in the sunshine and fresh air. Then it was carried down stairs and taken into the courtyard so quickly, that it forgot to think of itself, and could only look about, there was so much to be seen. The court was close to a garden, where everything looked blooming. Fresh and fragrant roses hung over the little palings. The linden-trees were in blossom; while the swallows flew here and there, crying, "Twit, twit, twit, my mate is coming," – but it was not the fir-tree they meant. "Now I shall live," cried the tree, joyfully spreading out its branches; but alas! they were all withered and yellow, and it lay in a corner amongst weeds and nettles. The star of gold paper still stuck in the top of the tree and glittered in the sunshine. In the same courtyard two of the merry children were playing who had danced round the tree at Christmas, and had been so happy. The youngest saw the gilded star, and ran and pulled it off the tree. "Look what is sticking to the ugly old fir-tree," said the child, treading on the branches till they crackled under his boots. And the tree saw all the fresh bright flowers in the garden, and then looked at itself, and wished it had remained in the dark corner of the garret. It thought of its fresh youth in the forest, of the merry Christmas evening, and of the little mice who had listened to the story of "Humpty Dumpty." "Past! past!" said the old tree; "Oh, had I but enjoyed myself while I could have done so! but now it is too late." Then a lad came and chopped the tree into small pieces, till a large bundle lay in a heap on the ground. The pieces were placed in a fire under the copper, and they quickly blazed up brightly, while the tree sighed so deeply that each sigh was like a pistol-shot. Then the children, who were at play, came and seated themselves in front of the fire, and looked at it and cried, "Pop, pop." But at each "pop," which was a deep sigh, the tree was thinking of a summer day in the forest; and of Christmas evening, and of "Humpty Dumpty," the only story it had ever heard or knew how to relate, till at last it was consumed. The boys still played in the garden, and the youngest wore the golden star on his breast, with which the tree had been adorned during the happiest evening of its existence. Now all was past; the tree's life was past, and the story also, – for all stories must come to an end at last.

The Daisy

NOW LISTEN! IN the country, close by the high road, stood a farmhouse; perhaps you have passed by and seen it yourself. There was a little flower garden with painted wooden palings in front of it; close by was a ditch, on its fresh green bank grew a little daisy; the sun shone as warmly and brightly upon it as on the magnificent garden flowers, and therefore it thrived well. One morning it had quite opened, and its little snow-white petals stood round the yellow centre, like the rays of the sun. It did not mind that nobody saw it in the grass, and that it was a poor despised flower; on the contrary, it was quite happy, and turned towards the sun, looking upward and listening to the song of the lark high up in the air.

The little daisy was as happy as if the day had been a great holiday, but it was only Monday. All the children were at school, and while they were sitting on the forms and learning their lessons, it sat on its thin green stalk and learnt from the sun and from its surroundings how kind God is, and it rejoiced that the song of the little lark expressed so sweetly and distinctly its own feelings. With a sort of reverence the daisy looked up to the bird that could fly and sing, but it did not feel envious. "I can see and hear," it thought; "the sun shines upon me, and the forest kisses me. How rich I am!"

In the garden close by grew many large and magnificent flowers, and, strange to say, the less fragrance they had the haughtier and prouder they were. The peonies puffed themselves up in order to be larger than the roses, but size is not everything! The tulips had the finest colors, and they knew it well, too, for they were standing bolt upright like candles, that one might see them the better. In their pride they did not see the little daisy, which looked over to them and thought, "How rich and beautiful they are! I am sure the pretty bird will fly down and call upon them. Thank God, that I stand so near and can at least see all the splendor." And while the daisy was still thinking, the lark came flying down, crying "Tweet," but not to the peonies and tulips – no, into the grass to the poor daisy. Its joy was so great that it did not know what to think. The little bird hopped round it and sang, "How beautifully soft the grass is, and what a lovely little flower with its golden heart and silver dress is growing here." The yellow centre in the daisy did indeed look like gold, while the little petals shone as brightly as silver.

How happy the daisy was! No one has the least idea. The bird kissed it with its beak, sang to it, and then rose again up to the blue sky. It was certainly more than a quarter of an hour before the daisy recovered its senses. Half ashamed, yet glad at heart, it looked over to the other flowers in the garden; surely they had witnessed its pleasure and the honour that had been done to it; they understood its joy. But the tulips stood more stiffly than ever, their faces were pointed and red, because they were vexed. The peonies were sulky; it was well that they could not speak, otherwise they would have given the daisy a good lecture. The little flower could very well see that they were ill at ease, and pitied them sincerely.

Shortly after this a girl came into the garden, with a large sharp knife. She went to the tulips and began cutting them off, one after another. "Ugh!" sighed the daisy, "that is terrible; now they are done for."

The girl carried the tulips away. The daisy was glad that it was outside, and only a small flower – it felt very grateful. At sunset it folded its petals, and fell asleep, and dreamt all night of the sun and the little bird.

On the following morning, when the flower once more stretched forth its tender petals, like little arms, towards the air and light, the daisy recognized the bird's voice, but what it sang sounded so sad. Indeed the poor bird had good reason to be sad, for it had been caught and put into a cage close by the open window. It sang of the happy days when it could merrily fly about, of fresh green corn in the fields, and of the time when it could soar almost up to the clouds. The poor lark was most unhappy as a prisoner in a cage. The little daisy would have liked so much to help it, but what could be done? Indeed, that was very difficult for such a small flower to find out. It entirely forgot how beautiful everything around it was, how warmly the sun was shining, and how splendidly white its own petals were. It could only think of the poor captive bird, for which it could do nothing. Then two little boys came out of the garden; one of them had a large sharp knife, like that with which the girl had cut the tulips. They came straight towards the little daisy, which could not understand what they wanted.

"Here is a fine piece of turf for the lark," said one of the boys, and began to cut out a square round the daisy, so that it remained in the centre of the grass.

"Pluck the flower off" said the other boy, and the daisy trembled for fear, for to be pulled off meant death to it; and it wished so much to live, as it was to go with the square of turf into the poor captive lark's cage.

"No let it stay," said the other boy, "it looks so pretty."

And so it stayed, and was brought into the lark's cage. The poor bird was lamenting its lost liberty, and beating its wings against the wires; and the little daisy could not speak or utter a consoling word, much as it would have liked to do so. So the forenoon passed.

"I have no water," said the captive lark, "they have all gone out, and forgotten to give me anything to drink. My throat is dry and burning. I feel as if I had fire and ice within me, and the air is so oppressive. Alas! I must die, and part with the warm sunshine, the fresh green meadows, and all the beauty that God has created." And it thrust its beak into the piece of grass, to refresh itself a little. Then it noticed the little daisy, and nodded to it, and kissed it with its beak and said: "You must also fade in here, poor little flower. You and the piece of grass are all they have given me in exchange for the whole world, which I enjoyed outside. Each little blade of grass shall be a green tree for me, each of your white petals a fragrant flower. Alas! you only remind me of what I have lost."

"I wish I could console the poor lark," thought the daisy. It could not move one of its leaves, but the fragrance of its delicate petals streamed forth, and was much stronger than such flowers usually have: the bird noticed it, although it was dying with thirst, and in its pain tore up the green blades of grass, but did not touch the flower.

The evening came, and nobody appeared to bring the poor bird a drop of water; it opened its beautiful wings, and fluttered about in its anguish; a faint and mournful "Tweet, tweet," was all it could utter, then it bent its little head towards the flower, and its heart broke for want and longing. The flower could not, as on the previous evening, fold up its petals and sleep; it dropped sorrowfully. The boys only came the next morning; when they saw the dead bird, they began to cry bitterly, dug a nice grave for it, and adorned it with flowers. The bird's body was placed in a pretty red box; they wished to bury it with royal honours. While it was alive and sang they forgot it, and let it suffer want in the cage; now, they cried over it and covered it with flowers. The piece of turf, with the little daisy in it, was thrown out on the dusty highway. Nobody thought of the flower which had felt so much for the bird and had so greatly desired to comfort it.

The Storks

ON THE LAST house in a little village the storks had built a nest, and the mother stork sat in it with her four young ones, who stretched out their necks and pointed their black beaks, which had not yet turned red like those of the parent birds. A little way off, on the edge of the roof, stood the father stork, quite upright and stiff; not liking to be quite idle, he drew up one leg, and stood on the other, so still that it seemed almost as if he were carved in wood. "It must look very grand," thought he, "for my wife to have a sentry guarding her nest. They do not know that I am her husband; they will think I have been commanded to stand here, which is quite aristocratic;" and so he continued standing on one leg.

In the street below were a number of children at play, and when they caught sight of the storks, one of the boldest amongst the boys began to sing a song about them, and very soon he was joined by the rest. These are the words of the song, but each only sang what he could remember of them in his own way.

"Stork, stork, fly away,
Stand not on one leg, I pray,
See your wife is in her nest,
With her little ones at rest.
They will hang one,
And fry another;
They will shoot a third,
And roast his brother."

"Just hear what those boys are singing," said the young storks; "they say we shall be hanged and roasted."

"Never mind what they say; you need not listen," said the mother. "They can do no harm."

But the boys went on singing and pointing at the storks, and mocking at them, excepting one of the boys whose name was Peter; he said it was a shame to make fun of animals, and would not join with them at all. The mother stork comforted her young ones, and told them not to mind. "See," she said, "How quiet your father stands, although he is only on one leg."

"But we are very much frightened," said the young storks, and they drew back their heads into the nests.

The next day when the children were playing together, and saw the storks, they sang the song again –

"They will hang one,
And roast another."

"Shall we be hanged and roasted?" asked the young storks.

"No, certainly not," said the mother. "I will teach you to fly, and when you have learnt, we will fly into the meadows, and pay a visit to the frogs, who will bow themselves to us in the water, and cry 'Croak, croak,' and then we shall eat them up; that will be fun."

"And what next?" asked the young storks.

"Then," replied the mother, "all the storks in the country will assemble together, and go through their autumn manoeuvres, so that it is very important for every one to know how to fly properly. If they do not, the general will thrust them through with his beak, and kill them. Therefore you must take pains and learn, so as to be ready when the drilling begins."

"Then we may be killed after all, as the boys say; and hark! they are singing again."

"Listen to me, and not to them," said the mother stork. "After the great review is over, we shall fly away to warm countries far from hence, where there are mountains and forests. To Egypt, where we shall see three-cornered houses built of stone, with pointed tops that reach nearly to the clouds. They are called Pyramids, and are older than a stork could imagine; and in that country, there is a river that overflows its banks, and then goes back, leaving nothing but mire; there we can walk about, and eat frogs in abundance."

"Oh, o – h!" cried the young storks.

"Yes, it is a delightful place; there is nothing to do all day long but eat, and while we are so well off out there, in this country there will not be a single green leaf on the trees, and the weather will be so cold that the clouds will freeze, and fall on the earth in little white rags." The stork meant snow, but she could not explain it in any other way.

"Will the naughty boys freeze and fall in pieces?" asked the young storks.

"No, they will not freeze and fall into pieces," said the mother, "but they will be very cold, and be obliged to sit all day in a dark, gloomy room, while we shall be flying about in foreign lands, where there are blooming flowers and warm sunshine."

Time passed on, and the young storks grew so large that they could stand upright in the nest and look about them. The father brought them, every day, beautiful frogs, little snakes, and all kinds of stork-dainties that he could find. And then, how funny it was to see the tricks he would perform to amuse them. He would lay his head quite round over his tail, and clatter with his beak, as if it had been a rattle; and then he would tell them stories all about the marshes and fens.

"Come," said the mother one day, "Now you must learn to fly." And all the four young ones were obliged to come out on the top of the roof. Oh, how they tottered at first, and were obliged to balance themselves with their wings, or they would have fallen to the ground below.

"Look at me," said the mother, "you must hold your heads in this way, and place your feet so. Once, twice, once, twice – that is it. Now you will be able to take care of yourselves in the world."

Then she flew a little distance from them, and the young ones made a spring to follow her; but down they fell plump, for their bodies were still too heavy.

"I don't want to fly," said one of the young storks, creeping back into the nest. "I don't care about going to warm countries."

"Would you like to stay here and freeze when the winter comes?" said the mother, "or till the boys comes to hang you, or to roast you? – Well then, I'll call them."

"Oh no, no," said the young stork, jumping out on the roof with the others; and now they were all attentive, and by the third day could fly a little. Then they began to fancy they could soar, so they tried to do so, resting on their wings, but they soon found themselves falling, and had to flap their wings as quickly as possible. The boys came again in the street singing their song: –

"Stork, stork, fly away."

"Shall we fly down, and pick their eyes out?" asked the young storks.

"No; leave them alone," said the mother. "Listen to me; that is much more important. Now then. One-two-three. Now to the right. One-two-three. Now to the left, round the chimney. There now, that was very good. That last flap of the wings was so easy and graceful, that I shall give you permission to fly with me to-morrow to the marshes. There will be a number of very superior storks there with their families, and I expect you to show them that my children are the best brought up of any who may be present. You must strut about proudly – it will look well and make you respected."

"But may we not punish those naughty boys?" asked the young storks.

"No; let them scream away as much as they like. You can fly from them now up high amid the clouds, and will be in the land of the pyramids when they are freezing, and have not a green leaf on the trees or an apple to eat."

"We will revenge ourselves," whispered the young storks to each other, as they again joined the exercising.

Of all the boys in the street who sang the mocking song about the storks, not one was so determined to go on with it as he who first began it. Yet he was a little fellow not more than six years old. To the young storks he appeared at least a hundred, for he was so much bigger than their father and mother. To be sure, storks cannot be expected to know how old children and grown-up people are. So they determined to have their revenge on this boy, because he began the song first and would keep on with it. The young storks were very angry, and grew worse as they grew older; so at last their mother was obliged to promise that they should be revenged, but not until the day of their departure.

"We must see first, how you acquit yourselves at the grand review," said she. "If you get on badly there, the general will thrust his beak through you, and you will be killed, as the boys said, though not exactly in the same manner. So we must wait and see."

"You shall see," said the young birds, and then they took such pains and practised so well every day, that at last it was quite a pleasure to see them fly so lightly and prettily. As soon as the autumn arrived, all the storks began to assemble together before taking their departure for warm countries during the winter. Then the review commenced. They flew over forests and villages to show what they could do, for they had a long journey before them. The young storks performed their part so well that they received a mark of honor, with frogs and snakes as a present. These presents were the best part of the affair, for they could eat the frogs and snakes, which they very quickly did.

"Now let us have our revenge," they cried.

"Yes, certainly," cried the mother stork. "I have thought upon the best way to be revenged. I know the pond in which all the little children lie, waiting till the storks come to take them to their parents. The prettiest little babies lie there dreaming more sweetly than they will ever dream in the time to come. All parents are glad to have a little child, and children are so pleased with a little brother or sister. Now we will fly to the pond and fetch a little baby for each of the children who did not sing that naughty song to make game of the storks."

"But the naughty boy, who began the song first, what shall we do to him?" cried the young storks.

"There lies in the pond a little dead baby who has dreamed itself to death," said the mother. "We will take it to the naughty boy, and he will cry because we have brought him a little dead brother. But you have not forgotten the good boy who said it was a shame to laugh at animals: we will take him a little brother and sister too, because he was good. He is called Peter, and you shall all be called Peter in future."

So they all did what their mother had arranged, and from that day, even till now, all the storks have been called Peter.

The Money-Box

IN A NURSERY where a number of toys lay scattered about, a money-box stood on the top of a very high wardrobe. It was made of clay in the shape of a pig, and had been bought of the potter. In the back of the pig was a slit, and this slit had been enlarged with a knife, so that dollars, or crown pieces, might slip through; and, indeed there were two in the box, besides a number of pence. The money-pig was stuffed so full that it could no longer rattle, which is the highest state of perfection to which a money-pig can attain. There he stood upon the cupboard, high and lofty, looking down upon everything else in the room. He knew very well that he had enough inside him to buy up all the other toys, and this gave him a very good opinion of his own value. The rest thought of this fact also, although they did not express it, for there were so many other things to talk about. A large doll, still handsome, though rather old, for her neck had been mended, lay inside one of the drawers which was partly open. She called out to the others, "Let us have a game at being men and women, that is something worth playing at."

Upon this there was a great uproar; even the engravings, which hung in frames on the wall, turned round in their excitement, and showed that they had a wrong side to them, although they had not the least intention to expose themselves in this way, or to object to the game. It was late at night, but as the moon shone through the windows, they had light at a cheap rate. And as the game was now to begin, all were invited to take part in it, even the children's wagon, which certainly belonged to the coarser playthings. "Each has its own value," said the wagon; "we cannot all be noblemen; there must be some to do the work."

The money-pig was the only one who received a written invitation. He stood so high that they were afraid he would not accept a verbal message. But in his reply, he said, if he had to take a part, he must enjoy the sport from his own home; they were to arrange for him to do so; and so they did. The little toy theatre was therefore put up in such a way that the money-pig could look directly into it. Some wanted to begin with a comedy, and afterwards to have a tea party and a discussion for mental improvement, but they commenced with the latter first. The rocking-horse spoke of training and races; the wagon of railways and steam power, for these subjects belonged to each of their professions, and it was right they should talk of them. The clock talked politics – "tick, tick;" he professed to know what was the time of day, but there was a whisper that he did not go correctly. The bamboo cane stood by, looking stiff and proud: he was vain of his brass ferrule and silver top, and on the sofa lay two worked cushions, pretty but stupid. When the play at the little theatre began, the rest sat and looked on; they were requested to applaud and stamp, or crack, when they felt gratified with what they saw. But the riding-whip said he never cracked for old people, only for the young who were not yet married. "I crack for everybody," said the cracker.

"Yes, and a fine noise you make," thought the audience, as the play went on.

It was not worth much, but it was very well played, and all the characters turned their painted sides to the audience, for they were made only to be seen on one side. The acting was wonderful, excepting that sometimes they came out beyond the lamps, because the wires were a little too long. The doll, whose neck had been darned, was so excited that the place in her neck burst, and the money-pig declared he must do something for one of the players, as they had all pleased him so much. So he made up his mind to remember one of them in his will, as the one to be buried with him in the family vault, whenever that event should happen. They all enjoyed the comedy so much, that they gave up all thoughts of the tea party, and only carried out their idea of intellectual amusement, which they called playing at men and women; and there was nothing wrong about it, for it was only play. All the while, each one thought most of himself, or of what the money-pig could be thinking. His thoughts were on, as he supposed, a very distant time – of making his will, and of his burial, and of when it might all come to pass. Certainly sooner than he expected – for all at once down he came from the top of the press, fell on the ground, and was broken to pieces. Then the pennies hopped and danced about in the most amusing manner. The little ones twirled round like tops, and the large ones rolled away as far as they could, especially the one great silver crown piece who had often to go out into the world, and now he had his wish as well as all the rest of the money. The pieces of the money-pig were thrown into the dust-bin, and the next day there stood a new money-pig on the cupboard, but it had not a farthing in its inside yet, and therefore, like the old one, it could not rattle. This was the beginning with him, and we will make it the end of our story.

A Great Sorrow

The artist's burial site

THIS STORY REALLY consists of two parts. The first part might be left out, but it gives us a few particulars, and these are useful.

We were staying in the country at a gentleman's seat, where it happened that the master was absent for a few days. In the meantime, there arrived from the next town a lady; she had a pug dog with her, and came, she said, to dispose of shares in her tan-yard. She had her papers with her, and we advised her to put them in an envelope, and to write thereon the address of the proprietor of the estate, "General War-Commissary Knight," &c.

She listened to us attentively, seized the pen, paused, and begged us to repeat the direction slowly. We complied, and she wrote; but in the midst of the "General War-" she struck fast, sighed deeply, and said, "I am only a woman!" Her Puggie had seated itself on the ground while she wrote, and growled; for the dog had come with her for amusement and for the sake of its health; and then the bare floor ought not to be offered to a visitor. His outward appearance was characterized by a snub nose and a very fat back.

"He doesn't bite," said the lady; "he has no teeth. He is like one of the family, faithful and grumpy; but the latter is my grandchildren's fault, for they have teased him; they play at wedding, and want to give him the part of the bridesmaid, and that's too much for him, poor old fellow."

And she delivered her papers, and took Puggie upon her arm. And this is the first part of the story which might have been left out.

PUGGIE DIED!! That's the second part.

It was about a week afterwards we arrived in the town, and put up at the inn. Our windows looked into the tan-yard, which was divided into two parts by a partition of planks; in one half were many skins and hides, raw and tanned. Here was all the apparatus necessary to carry on a tannery, and it belonged to the widow. Puggie had died in the morning, and was to be buried in this part of the yard; the grandchildren of the widow (that is, of the tanner's widow, for Puggie had never been married) filled up the grave, and it was a beautiful grave – it must have been quite pleasant to lie there.

The grave was bordered with pieces of flower-pots and strewn over with sand; quite at the top they had stuck up half a beer bottle, with the neck upwards, and that was not at all allegorical.

The children danced round the grave, and the eldest of the boys among them, a practical youngster of seven years, made the proposition that there should be an exhibition of Puggie's burial-place for all who lived in the lane; the price of admission was to be a trouser button, for every boy would be sure to have one, and each might also give one for a little girl. This proposal was adopted by acclamation.

And all the children out of the lane – yes, even out of the little lane at the back – flocked to the place, and each gave a button. Many were noticed to go about on that afternoon with only one suspender; but then they had seen Puggie's grave, and the sight was worth much more.

But in front of the tan-yard, close to the entrance, stood a little girl clothed in rags, very pretty to look at, with curly hair, and eyes so blue and clear that it was a pleasure to look into them. The child said not a word, nor did she cry; but each time the little door was opened she gave a long, long look into the yard. She had not a button – that she knew right well, and therefore she remained standing sorrowfully outside, till all the others had seen the grave and had gone away; then she sat down, held her little brown hands before her eyes, and burst into tears; this girl alone had not seen Puggie's grave. It was a grief as great to her as any grown person can experience.

We saw this from above; and looked at from above, how many a grief of our own and of others can make us smile! That is the story, and whoever does not understand it may go and purchase a share in the tan-yard from the window.

The Angel

"WHENEVER A GOOD child dies, an angel of God comes down from heaven, takes the dead child in his arms, spreads out his great white wings, and flies with him over all the places which the child had loved during his life. Then he gathers a large handful of flowers, which he carries up to the Almighty, that they may bloom more brightly in heaven than they do on earth. And the Almighty presses the flowers to His heart, but He kisses the flower that pleases Him best, and it receives a voice, and is able to join the song of the chorus of bliss."

These words were spoken by an angel of God, as he carried a dead child up to heaven, and the child listened as if in a dream. Then they passed over well-known spots, where the little one had often played, and through beautiful gardens full of lovely flowers.

"Which of these shall we take with us to heaven to be transplanted there?" asked the angel.

Close by grew a slender, beautiful, rose-bush, but some wicked hand had broken the stem, and the half-opened rosebuds hung faded and withered on the trailing branches.

"Poor rose-bush!" said the child, "let us take it with us to heaven, that it may bloom above in God's garden."

The angel took up the rose-bush; then he kissed the child, and the little one half opened his eyes. The angel gathered also some beautiful flowers, as well as a few humble buttercups and heart's-ease.

"Now we have flowers enough," said the child; but the angel only nodded, he did not fly upward to heaven.

It was night, and quite still in the great town. Here they remained, and the angel hovered over a small, narrow street, in which lay a large heap of straw, ashes, and sweepings from the houses of people who had removed. There lay fragments of plates, pieces of plaster, rags, old hats, and other rubbish not pleasant to see. Amidst all this confusion, the angel pointed to the pieces of a broken flower-pot, and to a lump of earth which had fallen out of it. The earth had been kept from falling to pieces by the roots of a withered field-flower, which had been thrown amongst the rubbish.

"We will take this with us," said the angel, "I will tell you why as we fly along."

And as they flew the angel related the history.

"Down in that narrow lane, in a low cellar, lived a poor sick boy; he had been afflicted from his childhood, and even in his best days he could just manage to walk up and down the room on crutches once or twice, but no more. During some days in summer, the sunbeams would lie on the floor of the cellar for about half an hour. In this spot the poor sick boy would sit warming himself in the sunshine, and watching the red blood through his delicate fingers as he held them before his face. Then he would say he had been out, yet he knew nothing of the green forest in its spring verdure, till a neighbor's son brought him a green bough from a beech-tree. This he would place over his head, and fancy that he was in the beech-wood while the sun shone, and the birds carolled gayly. One spring day the neighbor's boy brought him some field-flowers, and among them was one to which the root still adhered. This he carefully planted in a flower-pot, and placed in a window-seat near his bed. And the flower had been planted by a fortunate hand, for it grew, put forth fresh shoots, and blossomed every year. It became a splendid flower-garden to the sick boy, and his little treasure upon earth. He watered it, and cherished it, and took care it should have the benefit of every sunbeam that found its way into the cellar, from the earliest morning ray to the evening sunset. The flower entwined itself even in his dreams – for him it bloomed, for him spread its perfume. And it gladdened his eyes, and to the flower he turned, even in death, when the Lord called him. He has been one year with God. During that time the flower has stood in the window, withered and forgotten, till at length cast out among the sweepings into the street, on the day of the lodgers' removal. And this poor flower, withered and faded as it is, we have added to our nosegay, because it gave more real joy than the most beautiful flower in the garden of a queen."

"But how do you know all this?" asked the child whom the angel was carrying to heaven.

"I know it," said the angel, "because I myself was the poor sick boy who walked upon crutches, and I know my own flower well."

Then the child opened his eyes and looked into the glorious happy face of the angel, and at the same moment they found themselves in that heavenly home where all is happiness and joy. And God pressed the dead child to His heart, and wings were given him so that he could fly with the angel, hand in hand. Then the Almighty pressed all the flowers to His heart; but He kissed the withered field-flower, and it received a voice. Then it joined in the song of the angels, who surrounded the throne, some near, and others in a distant circle, but all equally happy. They all joined in the chorus of praise, both great and small, – the good, happy child, and the poor field-flower, that once lay withered and cast away on a heap of rubbish in a narrow, dark street.

Heaven as truth; the value is in the joy given
without law there is no order

The Last Dream of the Old Oak

IN THE FOREST, high up on the steep shore, and not far from the open seacoast, stood a very old oak-tree. It was just three hundred and sixty-five years old, but that long time was to the tree as the same number of days might be to us; we wake by day and sleep by night, and then we have our dreams. It is different with the tree; it is obliged to keep awake through three seasons of the year, and does not get any sleep till winter comes. Winter is its time for rest; its night after the long day of spring, summer, and autumn. On many a warm summer, the Ephemera, the flies that exist for only a day, had fluttered about the old oak, enjoyed life and felt happy and if, for a moment, one of the tiny creatures rested on one of his large fresh leaves, the tree would always say, "Poor little creature! your whole life consists only of a single day. How very short. It must be quite melancholy."

"Melancholy! what do you mean?" the little creature would always reply. "Everything around me is so wonderfully bright and warm, and beautiful, that it makes me joyous."

"But only for one day, and then it is all over."

"Over!" repeated the fly; "what is the meaning of all over? Are you all over too?"

"No; I shall very likely live for thousands of your days, and my day is whole seasons long; indeed it is so long that you could never reckon it out."

"No? then I don't understand you. You may have thousands of my days, but I have thousands of moments in which I can be merry and happy. Does all the beauty of the world cease when you die?"

"No," replied the tree; "it will certainly last much longer, – infinitely longer than I can even think of." "Well, then," said the little fly, "we have the same time to live; only we reckon differently." And the little creature danced and floated in the air, rejoicing in her delicate wings of gauze and velvet, rejoicing in the balmy breezes, laden with the fragrance of clover-fields and wild roses, elder-blossoms and honeysuckle, from the garden hedges, wild thyme, primroses, and mint, and the scent of all these was so strong that the perfume almost intoxicated the little fly. The long and beautiful day had been so full of joy and sweet delights, that when the sun sank low it felt tired of all its happiness and enjoyment. Its wings could sustain it no longer, and gently and slowly it glided down upon the soft waving blades of grass, nodded its little head as well as it could nod, and slept peacefully and sweetly. The fly was dead.

"Poor little Ephemera!" said the oak; "what a terribly short life!" And so, on every summer day the dance was repeated, the same questions asked, and the same answers given. The same thing was continued through many generations of Ephemera; all of them felt equally merry and equally happy.

The oak remained awake through the morning of spring, the noon of summer, and the evening of autumn; its time of rest, its night drew nigh – winter was coming. Already the storms were singing, "Good-night, good-night." Here fell a leaf and there fell a leaf. "We will rock you and lull you. Go to sleep, go to sleep. We will sing you to sleep, and shake you to sleep, and it will do your old twigs good; they will even crackle with pleasure. Sleep sweetly, sleep sweetly, it is your three-hundred-and-sixty-fifth night. Correctly speaking, you are but a youngster in the world. Sleep sweetly, the clouds will drop snow upon you, which will be quite a cover-lid, warm and sheltering to your feet. Sweet sleep to you, and pleasant dreams." And there stood the oak, stripped of all its leaves, left to rest during the whole of a long winter, and to dream many dreams of events that had happened in its life, as in the dreams of men. The great tree had once been small; indeed, in its cradle it had been an acorn. According to human computation, it was now in the fourth century of its existence. It was the largest and best tree in the forest. Its summit towered above all the other trees, and could be seen far out at sea, so that it served as a landmark to the sailors. It had no idea how many eyes looked eagerly for it. In its topmost branches the wood-pigeon built her nest, and the cuckoo carried out his usual vocal performances, and his well-known notes echoed amid the boughs; and in autumn, when the leaves looked like beaten copper plates, the birds of passage would come and rest upon the branches before taking their flight across the sea. But now it was winter, the tree stood leafless, so that every one could see how crooked and bent were the branches that sprang forth from the trunk. Crows and rooks came by turns and sat on them, and talked of the hard times which were beginning, and how difficult it was in winter to obtain food.

It was just about holy Christmas time that the tree dreamed a dream. The tree had, doubtless, a kind of feeling that the festive time had arrived, and in his dream fancied he heard the bells ringing from all the churches round, and yet it seemed to him to be a beautiful summer's day, mild and warm. His mighty summits was crowned with spreading fresh green foliage; the sunbeams played among the leaves and branches, and the air was full of fragrance from herb and blossom; painted butterflies chased each other; the summer flies danced around him, as if the world had been created merely for them to dance and be merry in. All that had happened to the tree during every year of his life seemed to pass before him, as in a festive procession. He saw the knights of olden times and noble ladies ride by through the wood on their gallant steeds, with plumes waving in their hats, and falcons on their wrists. The hunting horn sounded, and the dogs barked. He saw hostile warriors, in colored dresses and glittering armor, with spear and halberd, pitching their tents, and anon striking them. The watchfires again blazed, and men sang and slept under the hospitable shelter of the tree. He saw lovers meet in quiet happiness near him in the moonshine, and carve the initials of their names in the grayish-green bark on his trunk. Once, but long years had intervened since then, guitars and Eolian harps had been hung on his boughs by merry travellers; now they seemed to hang there again, and he could hear their marvellous tones. The wood-pigeons cooed as if to explain the feelings of the tree, and the cuckoo called out to tell him how many summer days he had yet to live. Then it seemed as if new life was thrilling through every fibre of root and stem and leaf, rising even to the highest branches. The tree felt itself stretching and spreading out, while through the root beneath the earth ran the warm vigor of life. As he grew higher and still higher, with increased strength, his topmost boughs became broader and fuller; and in proportion to his growth, so was his self-satisfaction increased, and with it arose a joyous longing to grow higher and higher, to reach even to the warm, bright sun itself. Already had his topmost branches pierced the clouds, which floated beneath them like troops of birds of passage, or large white swans; every leaf seemed gifted with sight, as if it possessed eyes to see. The stars became visible in broad daylight, large and sparkling, like clear and gentle eyes. They recalled to the memory the well-known look in the eyes of a child, or in the eyes of lovers who had once met beneath the branches of the old oak. These were wonderful and happy moments for the old tree, full of peace and joy; and yet, amidst all this happiness, the tree felt a yearning, longing desire that all the other trees, bushes, herbs, and flowers beneath him, might be able also to rise higher, as he had done, and to see all this splendor, and experience the same happiness. The grand, majestic oak could not be quite happy in the midst of his enjoyment, while all the rest, both great and small, were not with him. And this feeling of yearning trembled through every branch, through every leaf, as warmly and fervently as if they had been the fibres of a human heart. The summit of the tree waved to and fro, and bent downwards as if in his silent longing he sought for something. Then there came to him the fragrance of thyme, followed by the more powerful scent of honeysuckle and violets; and he fancied he heard the note of the cuckoo. At length his longing was satisfied. Up through the clouds came the green summits of the forest trees, and beneath him, the oak saw them rising, and growing higher and higher. Bush and herb shot upward, and some even tore themselves up by the roots to rise more quickly. The birch-tree was the quickest of all. Like a lightning flash the slender stem shot upwards in a zigzag line, the branches spreading around it like green gauze and banners. Every native of the wood, even to the brown and feathery rushes, grew with the rest, while the birds ascended with the melody of song. On a blade of grass, that fluttered in the air like a long, green ribbon, sat a grasshopper, cleaning his wings with his legs. May beetles hummed, the bees murmured, the birds sang, each in his own way; the air was filled with the sounds of song and gladness.

"But where is the little blue flower that grows by the water?" asked the oak, "and the purple bell-flower, and the daisy?" You see the oak wanted to have them all with him.

"Here we are, we are here," sounded in voice and song.

"But the beautiful thyme of last summer, where is that? and the lilies-of-the-valley, which last year covered the earth with their bloom? and the wild apple-tree with its lovely blossoms, and all the glory of the wood, which has flourished year after year? even what may have but now sprouted forth could be with us here."

"We are here, we are here," sounded voices higher in the air, as if they had flown there beforehand.

"Why this is beautiful, too beautiful to be believed," said the oak in a joyful tone. "I have them all here, both great and small; not one has been forgotten. Can such happiness be imagined?" It seemed almost impossible.

"In heaven with the Eternal God, it can be imagined, and it is possible," sounded the reply through the air.

And the old tree, as it still grew upwards and onwards, felt that his roots were loosening themselves from the earth.

"It is right so, it is best," said the tree, "no fetters hold me now. I can fly up to the very highest point in light and glory. And all I love are with me, both small and great. All – all are here."

Such was the dream of the old oak: and while he dreamed, a mighty storm came rushing over land and sea, at the holy Christmas time. The sea rolled in great billows towards the shore. There was a cracking and crushing heard in the tree. The root was torn from the ground just at the moment when in his dream he fancied it was being loosened from the earth. He fell – his three hundred and sixty-five years were passed as the single day of the Ephemera. On the morning of Christmas-day, when the sun rose, the storm had ceased. From all the churches sounded the festive bells, and from every hearth, even of the smallest hut, rose the smoke into the blue sky, like the smoke from the festive thank-offerings on the Druids' altars. The sea gradually became calm, and on board a great ship that had withstood the tempest during the night, all the flags were displayed, as a token of joy and festivity. "The tree is down! The old oak, – our landmark on the coast!" exclaimed the sailors. "It must have fallen in the storm of last night. Who can replace it? Alas! no one." This was a funeral oration over the old tree; short, but well-meant. There it lay stretched on the snow-covered shore, and over it sounded the notes of a song from the ship – a song of Christmas joy, and of the redemption of the soul of man, and of eternal life through Christ's atoning blood.

> *"Sing aloud on the happy morn,*
> *All is fulfilled, for Christ is born;*
> *With songs of joy let us loudly sing,*
> *'Hallelujahs to Christ our King.'"*

Thus sounded the old Christmas carol, and every one on board the ship felt his thoughts elevated, through the song and the prayer, even as the old tree had felt lifted up in its last, its beautiful dream on that Christmas morn.

The Portuguese Duck

A DUCK ONCE arrived from Portugal, but there were some who said she came from Spain, which is almost the same thing. At all events, she was called the "Portuguese," and she laid eggs, was killed, and cooked, and there was an end of her. But the ducklings which crept forth from the eggs were also called "Portuguese," and about that there may be some question. But of all the family one only remained in the duckyard, which may be called a farmyard, as the chickens were admitted, and the cock strutted about in a very hostile manner. "He annoys me with his loud crowing," said the Portuguese duck; "but, still, he's a handsome bird, there's no denying that, although he's not a drake. He ought to moderate his voice, like those little birds who are singing in the lime-trees over there in our neighbor's garden, but that is an art only acquired in polite society. How sweetly they sing there; it is quite a pleasure to listen to them! I call it Portuguese singing. If I had only such a little singing-bird, I'd be kind and good as a mother to him, for it's in my nature, in my Portuguese blood."

While she was speaking, one of the little singing-birds came tumbling head over heels from the roof into the yard. The cat was after him, but he had escaped from her with a broken wing, and so came tumbling into the yard. "That's just like the cat, she's a villain," said the Portuguese duck. "I remember her ways when I had children of my own. How can such a creature be allowed to live, and wander about upon the roofs. I don't think they allow such things in Portugal." She pitied the little singing-bird, and so did all the other ducks who were not Portuguese.

"Poor little creature!" they said, one after another, as they came up. "We can't sing, certainly; but we have a sounding-board, or something of the kind, within us; we can feel that, though we don't talk about it."

"But I can talk," said the Portuguese duck; "and I'll do something for the little fellow; it's my duty;" and she stepped into the water-trough, and beat her wings upon the water so strongly that the bird was nearly drowned by a shower-bath; but the duck meant it kindly. "That is a good deed," she said; "I hope the others will take example by it."

"Tweet, tweet!" said the little bird, for one of his wings being broken, he found it difficult to shake himself; but he quite understood that the bath was meant kindly, and he said, "You are very kind-hearted, madam;" but he did not wish for a second bath.

"I have never thought about my heart," replied the Portuguese duck, "but I know that I love all my fellow-creatures, except the cat, and nobody can expect me to love her, for she ate up two of my ducklings. But pray make yourself at home; it is easy to make one's self comfortable. I am myself from a foreign country, as you may see by my feathery dress. My drake is a native of these parts; he's not of my race; but I am not proud on that account. If any one here can understand you, I may say positively I am that person."

"She's quite full of 'Portulak,'" said a little common duck, who was witty. All the common ducks considered the word "Portulak" a good joke, for it sounded like Portugal. They nudged each other, and said, "Quack! that was witty!"

Then the other ducks began to notice the little bird. "The Portuguese had certainly a great flow of language," they said to the little bird. "For our part we don't care to fill our beaks with such long words, but we sympathize with you quite as much. If we don't do anything else, we can walk about with you everywhere, and we think that is the best thing we can do."

"You have a lovely voice," said one of the eldest ducks; "it must be great satisfaction to you to be able to give so much pleasure as you do. I am certainly no judge of your singing so I keep my beak shut, which is better than talking nonsense, as others do."

"Don't plague him so," interposed the Portuguese duck; "he requires rest and nursing. My little singing-bird do you wish me to prepare another bath for you?"

"Oh, no! no! pray let me dry," implored the little bird.

"The water-cure is the only remedy for me, when I am not well," said the Portuguese. "Amusement, too, is very beneficial. The fowls from the neighborhood will soon be here to pay you a visit. There are two Cochin Chinese amongst them; they wear feathers on their legs, and are well educated. They have been brought from a great distance, and consequently I treat them with greater respect than I do the others."

Then the fowls arrived, and the cock was polite enough to-day to keep from being rude. "You are a real songster," he said, "you do as much with your little voice as it is possible to do; but there requires more noise and shrillness in any one who wishes it to be known who he is."

The two Chinese were quite enchanted with the appearance of the singing-bird. His feathers had been much ruffled by his bath, so that he seemed to them quite like a tiny Chinese fowl. "He's charming," they said to each other, and began a conversation with him in whispers, using the most aristocratic Chinese dialect: "We are of the same race as yourself," they said. "The ducks, even the Portuguese, are all aquatic birds, as you must have noticed. You do not know us yet, – very few know us, or give themselves the trouble to make our acquaintance, not even any of the fowls, though we are born to occupy a higher grade in society than most of them. But that does not disturb us, we quietly go on in our own way among the rest, whose ideas are certainly not ours; for we look at the bright side of things, and only speak what is good, although that is sometimes very difficult to find where none exists. Except ourselves and the cock there is not one in the yard who can be called talented or polite. It cannot even be said of the ducks, and we warn you, little bird, not to trust that one yonder, with the short tail feathers, for she is cunning; that curiously marked one, with the crooked stripes on her wings, is a mischief-maker, and never lets any one have the last word, though she is always in the wrong. That fat duck yonder speaks evil of every one, and that is against our principles. If we have nothing good to tell, we close our beaks. The Portuguese is the only one who has had any education, and with whom we can associate, but she is passionate, and talks too much about 'Portugal.'"

"I wonder what those two Chinese are whispering about," whispered one duck to another; "they are always doing it, and it annoys me. We never speak to them."

Now the drake came up, and he thought the little singing-bird was a sparrow. "Well, I don't understand the difference," he said; "it appears to me all the same. He's only a plaything, and if people will have playthings, why let them, I say."

"Don't take any notice of what he says," whispered the Portuguese; "he's very well in matters of business, and with him business is placed before everything. But now I shall lie down and have a little rest. It is a duty we owe to ourselves that we may be nice and fat when we come to be embalmed with sage and onions and apples." So she laid herself down in the sun and winked with one eye; she had a very comfortable place, and felt so comfortable that she fell asleep. The little singing-bird busied himself for some time with his broken wing, and at last he lay down, too, quite close to his protectress. The sun shone warm and bright, and he found out that it was a very good place. But the fowls of the neighborhood were all awake, and, to tell the truth, they paid a visit to the duckyard, simply and solely to find food for themselves. The Chinese were the first to leave, and the other fowls soon followed them.

The witty little duck said of the Portuguese, that the old lady was getting quite a "doting ducky," All the other ducks laughed at this. "Doting ducky," they whispered. "Oh, that's too 'witty!'" And then they repeated the former joke about "Portulak," and declared it was most amusing. Then they all lay down to have a nap.

They had been lying asleep for some time, when suddenly something was thrown into the yard for them to eat. It came down with such a bang, that the whole company started up and clapped their wings. The Portuguese awoke too, and rushed over to the other side: in so doing she trod upon the little singing-bird.

"Tweet," he cried; "you trod very hard upon me, madam."

"Well, then, why do you lie in my way?" she retorted, "you must not be so touchy. I have nerves of my own, but I do not cry 'tweet.'"

"Don't be angry," said the little bird; "the 'tweet' slipped out of my beak unawares."

The Portuguese did not listen to him, but began eating as fast as she could, and made a good meal. When she had finished, she lay down again, and the little bird, who wished to be amiable, began to sing, –

> *"Chirp and twitter,*
> *The dew-drops glitter,*
> *In the hours of sunny spring,*
> *I'll sing my best,*
> *Till I go to rest,*
> *With my head behind my wing."*

"Now I want rest after my dinner," said the Portuguese; "you must conform to the rules of the house while you are here. I want to sleep now."

The little bird was quite taken aback, for he meant it kindly. When madam awoke afterwards, there he stood before her with a little corn he had found, and laid it at her feet; but as she had not slept well, she was naturally in a bad temper. "Give that to a chicken," she said, "and don't be always standing in my way."

"Why are you angry with me?" replied the little singing-bird, "what have I done?"

"Done!" repeated the Portuguese duck, "your mode of expressing yourself is not very polite. I must call your attention to that fact."

"It was sunshine here yesterday," said the little bird, "but to-day it is cloudy and the air is close."

"You know very little about the weather, I fancy," she retorted, "the day is not over yet. Don't stand there, looking so stupid."

"But you are looking at me just as the wicked eyes looked when I fell into the yard yesterday."

"Impertinent creature!" exclaimed the Portuguese duck: "would you compare me with the cat – that beast of prey? There's not a drop of malicious blood in me. I've taken your part, and now I'll teach you better manners." So saying, she made a bite at the little singing-bird's head, and he fell dead on the ground. "Now whatever is the meaning of this?" she said; "could he not bear even such a little peck as I gave him? Then certainly he was not made for this world. I've been like a mother to him, I know that, for I've a good heart."

Then the cock from the neighboring yard stuck his head in, and crowed with steam-engine power.

"You'll kill me with your crowing," she cried, "it's all your fault. He's lost his life, and I'm very near losing mine."

"There's not much of him lying there," observed the cock.

"Speak of him with respect," said the Portuguese duck, "for he had manners and education, and he could sing. He was affectionate and gentle, and that is as rare a quality in animals as in those who call themselves human beings."

Then all the ducks came crowding round the little dead bird. Ducks have strong passions, whether they feel envy or pity. There was nothing to envy here, so they all showed a great deal of pity, even the two Chinese. "We shall never have another singing-bird again amongst us; he was almost a Chinese," they whispered, and then they wept with such a noisy, clucking sound, that all the other fowls clucked too, but the ducks went about with redder eyes afterwards. "We have hearts of our own," they said, "nobody can deny that."

"Hearts!" repeated the Portuguese, "indeed you have, almost as tender as the ducks in Portugal."

"Let us think of getting something to satisfy our hunger," said the drake, "that's the most important business. If one of our toys is broken, why we have plenty more."

The Snow Man

"IT IS SO delightfully cold," said the Snow Man, "that it makes my whole body crackle. This is just the kind of wind to blow life into one. How that great red thing up there is staring at me!" He meant the sun, who was just setting. "It shall not make me wink. I shall manage to keep the pieces."

He had two triangular pieces of tile in his head, instead of eyes; his mouth was made of an old broken rake, and was, of course, furnished with teeth. He had been brought into existence amidst the joyous shouts of boys, the jingling of sleigh-bells, and the slashing of whips. The sun went down, and the full moon rose, large, round, and clear, shining in the deep blue.

"There it comes again, from the other side," said the Snow Man, who supposed the sun was showing himself once more. "Ah, I have cured him of staring, though; now he may hang up there, and shine, that I may see myself. If I only knew how to manage to move away from this place, – I should so like to move. If I could, I would slide along yonder on the ice, as I have seen the boys do; but I don't understand how; I don't even know how to run."

"Away, away," barked the old yard-dog. He was quite hoarse, and could not pronounce "Bow wow" properly. He had once been an indoor dog, and lay by the fire, and he had been hoarse ever since. "The sun will make you run some day. I saw him, last winter, make your predecessor run, and his predecessor before him. Away, away, they all have to go."

"I don't understand you, comrade," said the Snow Man. "Is that thing up yonder to teach me to run? I saw it running itself a little while ago, and now it has come creeping up from the other side."

"You know nothing at all," replied the yard-dog; "but then, you've only lately been patched up. What you see yonder is the moon, and the one before it was the sun. It will come again to-morrow, and most likely teach you to run down into the ditch by the well; for I think the weather is going to change. I can feel such pricks and stabs in my left leg; I am sure there is going to be a change."

"I don't understand him," said the Snow Man to himself; "but I have a feeling that he is talking of something very disagreeable. The one who stared so just now, and whom he calls the sun, is not my friend; I can feel that too."

"Away, away," barked the yard-dog, and then he turned round three times, and crept into his kennel to sleep.

There was really a change in the weather. Towards morning, a thick fog covered the whole country round, and a keen wind arose, so that the cold seemed to freeze one's bones; but when the sun rose, the sight was splendid. Trees and bushes were covered with hoar frost, and looked like a forest of white coral; while on every twig glittered frozen dew-drops. The many delicate forms concealed in summer by luxuriant foliage, were now clearly defined, and looked like glittering lace-work. From every twig glistened a white radiance. The birch, waving in the wind, looked full of life, like trees in summer; and its appearance was wondrously beautiful. And where the sun shone, how everything glittered and sparkled, as if diamond dust had been strewn about; while the snowy carpet of the earth appeared as if covered with diamonds, from which countless lights gleamed, whiter than even the snow itself.

"This is really beautiful," said a young girl, who had come into the garden with a young man; and they both stood still near the Snow Man, and contemplated the glittering scene. "Summer cannot show a more beautiful sight," she exclaimed, while her eyes sparkled.

"And we can't have such a fellow as this in the summer time," replied the young man, pointing to the Snow Man; "he is capital."

The girl laughed, and nodded at the Snow Man, and then tripped away over the snow with her friend. The snow creaked and crackled beneath her feet, as if she had been treading on starch.

"Who are these two?" asked the Snow Man of the yard-dog. "You have been here longer than I have; do you know them?"

"Of course I know them," replied the yard-dog; "she has stroked my back many times, and he has given me a bone of meat. I never bite those two."

"But what are they?" asked the Snow Man.

"They are lovers," he replied; "they will go and live in the same kennel by-and-by, and gnaw at the same bone. Away, away!"

"Are they the same kind of beings as you and I?" asked the Snow Man.

"Well, they belong to the same master," retorted the yard-dog. "Certainly people who were only born yesterday know very little. I can see that in you. I have age and experience. I know every one here in the house, and I know there was once a time when I did not lie out here in the cold, fastened to a chain. Away, away!"

"The cold is delightful," said the Snow Man; "but do tell me tell me; only you must not clank your chain so; for it jars all through me when you do that."

"Away, away!" barked the yard-dog; "I'll tell you; they said I was a pretty little fellow once; then I used to lie in a velvet-covered chair, up at the master's house, and sit in the mistress's lap. They used to kiss my nose, and wipe my paws with an embroidered handkerchief, and I was called 'Ami, dear Ami, sweet Ami.' But after a while I grew too big for them, and they sent me away to the housekeeper's room; so I came to live on the lower story. You can look into the room from where you stand, and see where I was master once; for I was indeed master to the housekeeper. It was certainly a smaller room than those up stairs; but I was more comfortable; for I was not being continually taken hold of and pulled about by the children as I had been. I received quite as good food, or even better. I had my own cushion, and there was a stove – it is the finest thing in the world at this season of the year. I used to go under the stove, and lie down quite beneath it. Ah, I still dream of that stove. Away, away!"

"Does a stove look beautiful?" asked the Snow Man, "is it at all like me?"

"It is just the reverse of you," said the dog; "it's as black as a crow, and has a long neck and a brass knob; it eats firewood, so that fire spurts out of its mouth. We should keep on one side, or under it, to be comfortable. You can see it through the window, from where you stand."

Then the Snow Man looked, and saw a bright polished thing with a brazen knob, and fire gleaming from the lower part of it. The Snow Man felt quite a strange sensation come over him; it was very odd, he knew not what it meant, and he could not account for it. But there are people who are not men of snow, who understand what it is. "And why did you leave her?" asked the Snow Man, for it seemed to him that the stove must be of the female sex. "How could you give up such a comfortable place?"

"I was obliged," replied the yard-dog. "They turned me out of doors, and chained me up here. I had bitten the youngest of my master's sons in the leg, because he kicked away the bone I was gnawing. 'Bone for bone,' I thought; but they were so angry, and from that time I have been fastened with a chain, and lost my bone. Don't you hear how hoarse I am. Away, away! I can't talk any more like other dogs. Away, away, that is the end of it all."

But the Snow Man was no longer listening. He was looking into the housekeeper's room on the lower storey; where the stove stood on its four iron legs, looking about the same size as the Snow Man himself. "What a strange crackling I feel within me," he said. "Shall I ever get in there? It is an innocent wish, and innocent wishes are sure to be fulfilled. I must go in there and lean against her, even if I have to break the window."

"You must never go in there," said the yard-dog, "for if you approach the stove, you'll melt away, away."

"I might as well go," said the Snow Man, "for I think I am breaking up as it is."

During the whole day the Snow Man stood looking in through the window, and in the twilight hour the room became still more inviting, for from the stove came a gentle glow, not like the sun or the moon; no, only the bright light which gleams from a stove when it has been well fed. When the door of the stove was opened, the flames darted out of its mouth; this is customary with all stoves. The light of the flames fell directly on the face and breast of the Snow Man with a ruddy gleam. "I can endure it no longer," said he; "how beautiful it looks when it stretches out its tongue?"

The night was long, but did not appear so to the Snow Man, who stood there enjoying his own reflections, and crackling with the cold. In the morning, the window-panes of the housekeeper's room were covered with ice. They were the most beautiful ice-flowers any Snow Man could desire, but they concealed the stove. These window-panes would not thaw, and he could see nothing of the stove, which he pictured to himself, as if it had been a lovely human being. The snow crackled and the wind whistled around him; it was just the kind of frosty weather a Snow Man might thoroughly enjoy. But he did not enjoy it; how, indeed, could he enjoy anything when he was "stove sick?"

"That is terrible disease for a Snow Man," said the yard-dog; "I have suffered from it myself, but I got over it. Away, away," he barked and then he added, "the weather is going to change." And the weather did change; it began to thaw. As the warmth increased, the Snow Man decreased. He said nothing and made no complaint, which is a sure sign. One morning he broke, and sunk down altogether; and, behold, where he had stood, something like a broomstick remained sticking up in the ground. It was the pole round which the boys had built him up. "Ah, now I understand why he had such a great longing for the stove," said the yard-dog. "Why, there's the shovel that is used for cleaning out the stove, fastened to the pole." The Snow Man had a stove scraper in his body; that was what moved him so. "But it's all over now. Away, away." And soon the winter passed. "Away, away," barked the hoarse yard-dog. But the girls in the house sang,

"Come from your fragrant home, green thyme;
Stretch your soft branches, willow-tree;
The months are bringing the sweet spring-time,
When the lark in the sky sings joyfully.
Come gentle sun, while the cuckoo sings,
And I'll mock his note in my wanderings."

And nobody thought any more of the Snow Man.

The Farm-Yard Cock and the Weather-Cock

THERE WERE TWO cocks – one on the dung-hill, the other on the roof. They were both arrogant, but which of the two rendered most service? Tell us your opinion – we'll keep to ours just the same though.

The poultry yard was divided by some planks from another yard in which there was a dung-hill, and on the dung-hill lay and grew a large cucumber which was conscious of being a hot-bed plant.

"One is born to that," said the cucumber to itself. "Not all can be born cucumbers; there must be other things, too. The hens, the ducks, and all the animals in the next yard are creatures too. Now I have a great opinion of the yard cock on the plank; he is certainly of much more importance than the weather-cock who is placed so high and can't even creak, much less crow. The latter has neither hens nor chicks, and only thinks of himself and perspires verdigris. No, the yard cock is really a cock! His step is a dance! His crowing is music, and wherever he goes one knows what a trumpeter is like! If he would only come in here! Even if he ate me up stump, stalk, and all, and I had to dissolve in his body, it would be a happy death," said the cucumber.

In the night there was a terrible storm. The hens, chicks, and even the cock sought shelter; the wind tore down the planks between the two yards with a crash; the tiles came tumbling down, but the weather-cock sat firm. He did not even turn round, for he could not; and yet he was young and freshly cast, but prudent and sedate. He had been born old, and did not at all resemble the birds flying in the air – the sparrows, and the swallows; no, he despised them, these mean little piping birds, these common whistlers. He admitted that the pigeons, large and white and shining like mother-o'-pearl, looked like a kind of weather-cock; but they were fat and stupid, and all their thoughts and endeavours were directed to filling themselves with food, and besides, they were tiresome things to converse with. The birds of passage had also paid the weather-cock a visit and told him of foreign countries, of airy caravans and robber stories that made one's hair stand on end. All this was new and interesting; that is, for the first time, but afterwards, as the weather-cock found out, they repeated themselves and always told the same stories, and that's very tedious, and there was no one with whom one could associate, for one and all were stale and small-minded.

"The world is no good!" he said. "Everything in it is so stupid."

The weather-cock was puffed up, and that quality would have made him interesting in the eyes of the cucumber if it had known it, but it had eyes only for the yard cock, who was now in the yard with it.

The wind had blown the planks, but the storm was over.

"What do you think of that crowing?" said the yard cock to the hens and chickens. "It was a little rough – it wanted elegance."

And the hens and chickens came up on the dung-hill, and the cock strutted about like a lord.

"Garden plant!" he said to the cucumber, and in that one word his deep learning showed itself, and it forgot that he was pecking at her and eating it up. "A happy death!"

The hens and the chickens came, for where one runs the others run too; they clucked, and chirped, and looked at the cock, and were proud that he was of their kind.

"Cock-a-doodle-doo!" he crowed, "the chickens will grow up into great hens at once, if I cry it out in the poultry-yard of the world!"

And hens and chicks clucked and chirped, and the cock announced a great piece of news.

"A cock can lay an egg! And do you know what's in that egg? A basilisk. No one can stand the sight of such a thing; people know that, and now you know it too – you know what is in me, and what a champion of all cocks I am!"

With that the yard cock flapped his wings, made his comb swell up, and crowed again; and they all shuddered, the hens and the little chicks – but they were very proud that one of their number was such a champion of all cocks. They clucked and chirped till the weather-cock heard; he heard it; but he did not stir.

"Everything is very stupid," the weather-cock said to himself. "The yard cock lays no eggs, and I am too lazy to do so; if I liked, I could lay a wind-egg. But the world is not worth even a wind-egg. Everything is so stupid! I don't want to sit here any longer."

With that the weather-cock broke off; but he did not kill the yard cock, although the hens said that had been his intention. And what is the moral? "Better to crow than to be puffed up and break off!"

The Little Match-Seller

IT WAS TERRIBLY cold and nearly dark on the last evening of the old year, and the snow was falling fast. In the cold and the darkness, a poor little girl, with bare head and naked feet, roamed through the streets. It is true she had on a pair of slippers when she left home, but they were not of much use. They were very large, so large, indeed, that they had belonged to her mother, and the poor little creature had lost them in running across the street to avoid two carriages that were rolling along at a terrible rate. One of the slippers she could not find, and a boy seized upon the other and ran away with it, saying that he could use it as a cradle, when he had children of his own. So the little girl went on with her little naked feet, which were quite red and blue with the cold. In an old apron she carried a number of matches, and had a bundle of them in her hands. No one had bought anything of her the whole day, nor had anyone given her even a penny. Shivering with cold and hunger, she crept along; poor little child, she looked the picture of misery. The snowflakes fell on her long, fair hair, which hung in curls on her shoulders, but she regarded them not.

Lights were shining from every window, and there was a savory smell of roast goose, for it was New-year's eve – yes, she remembered that. In a corner, between two houses, one of which projected beyond the other, she sank down and huddled herself together. She had drawn her little feet under her, but she could not keep off the cold; and she dared not go home, for she had sold no matches, and could not take home even a penny of money. Her father would certainly beat her; besides, it was almost as cold at home as here, for they had only the roof to cover them, through which the wind howled, although the largest holes had been stopped up with straw and rags. Her little hands were almost frozen with the cold. Ah! perhaps a burning match might be some good, if she could draw it from the bundle and strike it against the wall, just to warm her fingers. She drew one out – "scratch!" how it sputtered as it burnt! It gave a warm, bright light, like a little candle, as she held her hand over it. It was really a wonderful light. It seemed to the little girl that she was sitting by a large iron stove, with polished brass feet and a brass ornament. How the fire burned! and seemed so beautifully warm that the child stretched out her feet as if to warm them, when, lo! the flame of the match went out, the stove vanished, and she had only the remains of the half-burnt match in her hand.

She rubbed another match on the wall. It burst into a flame, and where its light fell upon the wall it became as transparent as a veil, and she could see into the room. The table was covered with a snowy white table-cloth, on which stood a splendid dinner service, and a steaming roast goose, stuffed with apples and dried plums. And what was still more wonderful, the goose jumped down from the dish and waddled across the floor, with a knife and fork in its breast, to the little girl. Then the match went out, and there remained nothing but the thick, damp, cold wall before her.

She lighted another match, and then she found herself sitting under a beautiful Christmas-tree. It was larger and more beautifully decorated than the one which she had seen through the glass door at the rich merchant's. Thousands of tapers were burning upon the green branches, and colored pictures, like those she had seen in the show-windows, looked down upon it all. The little one stretched out her hand towards them, and the match went out.

The Christmas lights rose higher and higher, till they looked to her like the stars in the sky. Then she saw a star fall, leaving behind it a bright streak of fire. "Someone is dying," thought the little girl, for her old grandmother, the only one who had ever loved her, and who was now dead, had told her that when a star falls, a soul was going up to God.

She again rubbed a match on the wall, and the light shone round her; in the brightness stood her old grandmother, clear and shining, yet mild and loving in her appearance. "Grandmother," cried the little one, "O take me with you; I know you will go away when the match burns out; you will vanish like the warm stove, the roast goose, and the large, glorious Christmas-tree." And she made haste to light the whole bundle of matches, for she wished to keep her grandmother there. And the matches glowed with a light that was brighter than the noon-day, and her grandmother had never appeared so large or so beautiful. She took the little girl in her arms, and they both flew upwards in brightness and joy far above the earth, where there was neither cold nor hunger nor pain, for they were with God.

In the dawn of morning there lay the poor little one, with pale cheeks and smiling mouth, leaning against the wall; she had been frozen to death on the last evening of the year; and the New-year's sun rose and shone upon a little corpse! The child still sat, in the stiffness of death, holding the matches in her hand, one bundle of which was burnt. "She tried to warm herself," said some. No one imagined what beautiful things she had seen, nor into what glory she had entered with her grandmother, on New-year's day.

The Buckwheat

VERY OFTEN, AFTER a violent thunder-storm, a field of buckwheat appears blackened and singed, as if a flame of fire had passed over it. The country people say that this appearance is caused by lightning; but I will tell you what the sparrow says, and the sparrow heard it from an old willow-tree which grew near a field of buckwheat, and is there still. It is a large venerable tree, though a little crippled by age. The trunk has been split, and out of the crevice grass and brambles grow. The tree bends for-ward slightly, and the branches hang quite down to the ground just like green hair. Corn grows in the surrounding fields, not only rye and barley, but oats, – pretty oats that, when ripe, look like a number of little golden canary-birds sitting on a bough. The corn has a smiling look and the heaviest and richest ears bend their heads low as if in pious humility. Once there was also a field of buckwheat, and this field was exactly opposite to old willow-tree. The buckwheat did not bend like the other grain, but erected its head proudly and stiffly on the stem. "I am as valuable as any other corn," said he, "and I am much handsomer; my flowers are as beautiful as the bloom of the apple blossom, and it is a pleasure to look at us. Do you know of anything prettier than we are, you old willow-tree?"

And the willow-tree nodded his head, as if he would say, "Indeed I do."

But the buckwheat spread itself out with pride, and said, "Stupid tree; he is so old that grass grows out of his body."

There arose a very terrible storm. All the field-flowers folded their leaves together, or bowed their little heads, while the storm passed over them, but the buckwheat stood erect in its pride. "Bend your head as we do," said the flowers.

"I have no occasion to do so," replied the buckwheat.

"Bend your head as we do," cried the ears of corn; "the angel of the storm is coming; his wings spread from the sky above to the earth beneath. He will strike you down before you can cry for mercy."

"But I will not bend my head," said the buckwheat.

"Close your flowers and bend your leaves," said the old willow-tree. "Do not look at the lightning when the cloud bursts; even men cannot do that. In a flash of lightning heaven opens, and we can look in; but the sight will strike even human beings blind. What then must happen to us, who only grow out of the earth, and are so inferior to them, if we venture to do so?"

"Inferior, indeed!" said the buckwheat. "Now I intend to have a peep into heaven." Proudly and boldly he looked up, while the lightning flashed across the sky as if the whole world were in flames.

When the dreadful storm had passed, the flowers and the corn raised their drooping heads in the pure still air, refreshed by the rain, but the buckwheat lay like a weed in the field, burnt to blackness by the lightning. The branches of the old willow-tree rustled in the wind, and large water-drops fell from his green leaves as if the old willow were weeping. Then the sparrows asked why he was weeping, when all around him seemed so cheerful. "See," they said, "how the sun shines, and the clouds float in the blue sky.

Do you not smell the sweet perfume from flower and bush? Wherefore do you weep, old willow-tree?" Then the willow told them of the haughty pride of the buckwheat, and of the punishment which followed in consequence.

This is the story told me by the sparrows one evening when I begged them to relate some tale to me.

Little Claus and Big Claus

IN A VILLAGE there once lived two men who had the same name. They were both called Claus. One of them had four horses, but the other had only one; so to distinguish them, people called the owner of the four horses, "Great Claus," and he who had only one, "Little Claus." Now we shall hear what happened to them, for this is a true story.

Through the whole week, Little Claus was obliged to plough for Great Claus, and lend him his one horse; and once a week, on a Sunday, Great Claus lent him all his four horses. Then how Little Claus would smack his whip over all five horses, they were as good as his own on that one day. The sun shone brightly, and the church bells were ringing merrily as the people passed by, dressed in their best clothes, with their prayer-books under their arms. They were going to hear the clergyman preach. They looked at Little Claus ploughing with his five horses, and he was so proud that he smacked his whip, and said, "Gee-up, my five horses."

"You must not say that," said Big Claus; "for only one of them belongs to you." But Little Claus soon forgot what he ought to say, and when any one passed he would call out, "Gee-up, my five horses!"

"Now I must beg you not to say that again," said Big Claus; "for if you do, I shall hit your horse on the head, so that he will drop dead on the spot, and there will be an end of him."

"I promise you I will not say it any more," said the other; but as soon as people came by, nodding to him, and wishing him "Good day," he became so pleased, and thought how grand it looked to have five horses ploughing in his field, that he cried out again, "Gee-up, all my horses!"

"I'll gee-up your horses for you," said Big Claus; and seizing a hammer, he struck the one horse of Little Claus on the head, and he fell dead instantly.

"Oh, now I have no horse at all," said Little Claus, weeping. But after a while he took off the dead horse's skin, and hung the hide to dry in the wind. Then he put the dry skin into a bag, and, placing it over his shoulder, went out into the next town to sell the horse's skin. He had a very long way to go, and had to pass through a dark, gloomy forest. Presently a storm arose, and he lost his way, and before he discovered the right path, evening came on, and it was still a long way to the town, and too far to return home before night. Near the road stood a large farmhouse. The shutters outside the windows were closed, but lights shone through the crevices at the top. "I might get permission to stay here for the night," thought Little Claus; so he went up to the door and knocked. The farmer's wife opened the door; but when she heard what he wanted, she told him to go away, as her husband would not allow her to admit strangers. "Then I shall be obliged to lie out here," said Little Claus to himself, as the farmer's wife shut the door in his face. Near to the farmhouse stood a large haystack, and between it and the house was a small shed, with a thatched roof. "I can lie up there," said Little Claus, as he saw the roof; "it will make a famous bed, but I hope the stork will not fly down and bite my legs;" for on it stood a living stork, whose nest was in the roof. So Little Claus climbed to the roof of the shed, and while he turned himself to get comfortable, he discovered that the wooden shutters, which were closed, did not reach to the tops of the windows of the farmhouse, so that he could see into a room, in which a large table was laid out with wine, roast meat, and a splendid fish. The farmer's wife and the sexton were sitting at the table together; and she filled his glass, and helped him plenteously to fish, which appeared to be his favorite dish. "If I could only get some, too," thought Little Claus; and then, as he stretched his neck towards the window he spied a large, beautiful pie, – indeed they had a glorious feast before them.

At this moment he heard some one riding down the road, towards the farmhouse. It was the farmer returning home. He was a good man, but still he had a very strange prejudice, – he could not bear the sight of a sexton. If one appeared before him, he would put himself in a terrible rage. In consequence of this dislike, the sexton had gone to visit the farmer's wife during her husband's absence from home, and the good woman had placed before him the best she had in the house to eat. When she heard the farmer coming she was frightened, and begged the sexton to hide himself in a large empty chest that stood in the room. He did so, for he knew her husband could not endure the sight of a sexton. The woman then quickly put away the wine, and hid all the rest of the nice things in the oven; for if her husband had seen them he would have asked what they were brought out for.

"Oh, dear," sighed Little Claus from the top of the shed, as he saw all the good things disappear.

"Is any one up there?" asked the farmer, looking up and discovering Little Claus. "Why are you lying up there? Come down, and come into the house with me." So Little Claus came down and told the farmer how he had lost his way and begged for a night's lodging.

"All right," said the farmer; "but we must have something to eat first."

The woman received them both very kindly, laid the cloth on a large table, and placed before them a dish of porridge. The farmer was very hungry, and ate his porridge with a good appetite, but Little Claus could not help thinking of the nice roast meat, fish and pies, which he knew were in the oven. Under the table, at his feet, lay the sack containing the horse's skin, which he intended to sell at the next town. Now Little Claus did not relish the porridge at all, so he trod with his foot on the sack under the table, and the dry skin squeaked quite loud. "Hush!" said Little Claus to his sack, at the same time treading upon it again, till it squeaked louder than before.

"Hallo! what have you got in your sack!" asked the farmer.

"Oh, it is a conjuror," said Little Claus; "and he says we need not eat porridge, for he has conjured the oven full of roast meat, fish, and pie."

"Wonderful!" cried the farmer, starting up and opening the oven door; and there lay all the nice things hidden by the farmer's wife, but which he supposed had been conjured there by the wizard under the table. The woman dared not say anything; so she placed the things before them, and they both ate of the fish, the meat, and the pastry.

Then Little Claus trod again upon his sack, and it squeaked as before. "What does he say now?" asked the farmer.

"He says," replied Little Claus, "that there are three bottles of wine for us, standing in the corner, by the oven."

So the woman was obliged to bring out the wine also, which she had hidden, and the farmer drank it till he became quite merry. He would have liked such a conjuror as Little Claus carried in his sack. "Could he conjure up the evil one?" asked the farmer. "I should like to see him now, while I am so merry."

"Oh, yes!" replied Little Claus, "my conjuror can do anything I ask him, – can you not?" he asked, treading at the same time on the sack till it squeaked. "Do you hear? he answers 'Yes,' but he fears that we shall not like to look at him."

"Oh, I am not afraid. What will he be like?"

"Well, he is very much like a sexton."

"Ha!" said the farmer, "then he must be ugly. Do you know I cannot endure the sight of a sexton. However, that doesn't matter, I shall know who it is; so I shall not mind. Now then, I have got up my courage, but don't let him come too near me."

"Stop, I must ask the conjuror," said Little Claus; so he trod on the bag, and stooped his ear down to listen.

"What does he say?"

"He says that you must go and open that large chest which stands in the corner, and you will see the evil one crouching down inside; but you must hold the lid firmly, that he may not slip out."

"Will you come and help me hold it?" said the farmer, going towards the chest in which his wife had hidden the sexton, who now lay inside, very much frightened. The farmer opened the lid a very little way, and peeped in.

"Oh," cried he, springing backwards, "I saw him, and he is exactly like our sexton. How dreadful it is!" So after that he was obliged to drink again, and they sat and drank till far into the night.

"You must sell your conjuror to me," said the farmer; "ask as much as you like, I will pay it; indeed I would give you directly a whole bushel of gold."

"No, indeed, I cannot," said Little Claus; "only think how much profit I could make out of this conjuror."

"But I should like to have him," said the farmer, still continuing his entreaties.

"Well," said Little Claus at length, "you have been so good as to give me a night's lodging, I will not refuse you; you shall have the conjuror for a bushel of money, but I will have quite full measure."

"So you shall," said the farmer; "but you must take away the chest as well. I would not have it in the house another hour; there is no knowing if he may not be still there."

So Little Claus gave the farmer the sack containing the dried horse's skin, and received in exchange a bushel of money – full measure. The farmer also gave him a wheelbarrow on which to carry away the chest and the gold.

"Farewell," said Little Claus, as he went off with his money and the great chest, in which the sexton lay still concealed. On one side of the forest was a broad, deep river, the water flowed so rapidly that very few were able to swim against the stream. A new bridge had lately been built across it, and in the middle of this bridge Little Claus stopped, and said, loud enough to be heard by the sexton, "Now what shall I do with this stupid chest; it is as heavy as if it were full of stones: I shall be tired if I roll it any farther, so I may as well throw it in the river; if it swims after me to my house, well and good, and if not, it will not much matter."

So he seized the chest in his hand and lifted it up a little, as if he were going to throw it into the water.

"No, leave it alone," cried the sexton from within the chest; "let me out first."

"Oh," exclaimed Little Claus, pretending to be frightened, "he is in there still, is he? I must throw him into the river, that he may be drowned."

"Oh, no; oh, no," cried the sexton; "I will give you a whole bushel full of money if you will let me go."

"Why, that is another matter," said Little Claus, opening the chest. The sexton crept out, pushed the empty chest into the water, and went to his house, then he measured out a whole bushel full of gold for Little Claus, who had already received one from the farmer, so that now he had a barrow full.

"I have been well paid for my horse," said he to himself when he reached home, entered his own room, and emptied all his money into a heap on the floor. "How vexed Great Claus will be when he finds out how rich I have become all through my one horse; but I shall not tell him exactly how it all happened." Then he sent a boy to Great Claus to borrow a bushel measure.

"What can he want it for?" thought Great Claus; so he smeared the bottom of the measure with tar, that some of whatever was put into it might stick there and remain. And so it happened; for when the measure returned, three new silver florins were sticking to it.

"What does this mean?" said Great Claus; so he ran off directly to Little Claus, and asked, "Where did you get so much money?"

"Oh, for my horse's skin, I sold it yesterday."

"It was certainly well paid for then," said Great Claus; and he ran home to his house, seized a hatchet, and knocked all his four horses on the head, flayed off their skins, and took them to the town to sell. "Skins, skins, who'll buy skins?" he cried, as he went through the streets. All the shoemakers and tanners came running, and asked how much he wanted for them.

"A bushel of money, for each," replied Great Claus.

"Are you mad?" they all cried; "do you think we have money to spend by the bushel?"

"Skins, skins," he cried again, "who'll buy skins?" but to all who inquired the price, his answer was, "a bushel of money."

"He is making fools of us," said they all; then the shoemakers took their straps, and the tanners their leather aprons, and began to beat Great Claus.

"Skins, skins!" they cried, mocking him; "yes, we'll mark your skin for you, till it is black and blue."

"Out of the town with him," said they. And Great Claus was obliged to run as fast as he could, he had never before been so thoroughly beaten.

"Ah," said he, as he came to his house; "Little Claus shall pay me for this; I will beat him to death."

Meanwhile the old grandmother of Little Claus died. She had been cross, unkind, and really spiteful to him; but he was very sorry, and took the dead woman and laid her in his warm bed to see if he could bring her to life again. There he determined that she should lie the whole night, while he seated himself in a chair in a corner of the room as he had often done before. During the night, as he sat there, the door opened, and in came Great Claus with a hatchet. He knew well where Little Claus's bed stood; so he went right up to it, and struck the old grandmother on the head. thinking it must be Little Claus.

"There," cried he, "now you cannot make a fool of me again;" and then he went home.

"That is a very wicked man," thought Little Claus; "he meant to kill me. It is a good thing for my old grandmother that she was already dead, or he would have taken her life." Then he dressed his old grandmother in her best clothes, borrowed a horse of his neighbor, and harnessed it to a cart. Then he placed the old woman on the back seat, so that she might not fall out as he drove, and rode away through the wood. By sunrise they reached a large inn, where Little Claus stopped and went to get something to eat. The landlord was a rich man, and a good man too; but as passionate as if he had been made of pepper and snuff.

"Good morning," said he to Little Claus; "you are come betimes to-day."

"Yes," said Little Claus; "I am going to the town with my old grandmother; she is sitting at the back of the wagon, but I cannot bring her into the room. Will you take her a glass of mead? but you must speak very loud, for she cannot hear well."

"Yes, certainly I will," replied the landlord; and, pouring out a glass of mead, he carried it out to the dead grandmother, who sat upright in the cart. "Here is a glass of mead from your grandson," said the landlord. The dead woman did not answer a word, but sat quite still. "Do you not hear?" cried the landlord as loud as he could; "here is a glass of mead from your grandson."

Again and again he bawled it out, but as she did not stir he flew into a passion, and threw the glass of mead in her face; it struck her on the nose, and she fell backwards out of the cart, for she was only seated there, not tied in.

"Hallo!" cried Little Claus, rushing out of the door, and seizing hold of the landlord by the throat; "you have killed my grandmother; see, here is a great hole in her forehead."

"Oh, how unfortunate," said the landlord, wringing his hands. "This all comes of my fiery temper. Dear Little Claus, I will give you a bushel of money; I will bury your grandmother as if she were my own; only keep silent, or else they will cut off my head, and that would be disagreeable."

So it happened that Little Claus received another bushel of money, and the landlord buried his old grandmother as if she had been his own. When Little Claus reached home again, he immediately sent a boy to Great Claus, requesting him to lend him a bushel measure. "How is this?" thought Great Claus; "did I not kill him? I must go and see for myself." So he went to Little Claus, and took the bushel measure with him. "How did you get all this money?" asked Great Claus, staring with wide open eyes at his neighbor's treasures.

"You killed my grandmother instead of me," said Little Claus; "so I have sold her for a bushel of money."

"That is a good price at all events," said Great Claus. So he went home, took a hatchet, and killed his old grandmother with one blow. Then he placed her on a cart, and drove into the town to the apothecary, and asked him if he would buy a dead body.

"Whose is it, and where did you get it?" asked the apothecary.

"It is my grandmother," he replied; "I killed her with a blow, that I might get a bushel of money for her."

"Heaven preserve us!" cried the apothecary, "you are out of your mind. Don't say such things, or you will lose your head." And then he talked to him seriously about the wicked deed he had done, and told him that such a wicked man would surely be punished. Great Claus got so frightened that he rushed out of the surgery, jumped into the cart, whipped up his horses, and drove home quickly. The apothecary and all the people thought him mad, and let him drive where he liked.

"You shall pay for this," said Great Claus, as soon as he got into the highroad, "that you shall, Little Claus." So as soon as he reached home he took the largest sack he could find and went over to Little Claus. "You have played me another trick," said he. "First, I killed all my horses, and then my old grandmother, and it is all your fault; but you shall not make a fool of me any more." So he laid hold of Little Claus round the body, and pushed him into the sack, which he took on his shoulders, saying, "Now I'm going to drown you in the river."

He had a long way to go before he reached the river, and Little Claus was not a very light weight to carry. The road led by the church, and as they passed he could hear the organ playing and the people singing beautifully. Great Claus put down the sack close to the church-door, and thought he might as well go in and hear a psalm before he went any farther. Little Claus could not possibly get out of the sack, and all the people were in church; so in he went.

"Oh dear, oh dear," sighed Little Claus in the sack, as he turned and twisted about; but he found he could not loosen the string with which it was tied. Presently an old cattle driver, with snowy hair, passed by, carrying a large staff in his hand, with which he drove a large herd of cows and oxen before him. They stumbled against the sack in which lay Little Claus, and turned it over. "Oh dear," sighed Little Claus, "I am very young, yet I am soon going to heaven."

"And I, poor fellow," said the drover, "I who am so old already, cannot get there."

"Open the sack," cried Little Claus; "creep into it instead of me, and you will soon be there."

"With all my heart," replied the drover, opening the sack, from which sprung Little Claus as quickly as possible. "Will you take care of my cattle?" said the old man, as he crept into the bag.

"Yes," said Little Claus, and he tied up the sack, and then walked off with all the cows and oxen.

When Great Claus came out of church, he took up the sack, and placed it on his shoulders. It appeared to have become lighter, for the old drover was not half so heavy as Little Claus.

"How light he seems now," said he. "Ah, it is because I have been to a church." So he walked on to the river, which was deep and broad, and threw the sack containing the old drover into the water, believing it to be Little Claus. "There you may lie!" he exclaimed; "you will play me no more tricks now." Then he turned to go home, but when he came to a place where two roads crossed, there was Little Claus driving the cattle. "How is this?" said Great Claus. "Did I not drown you just now?"

"Yes," said Little Claus; "you threw me into the river about half an hour ago."

"But wherever did you get all these fine beasts?" asked Great Claus.

"These beasts are sea-cattle," replied Little Claus. "I'll tell you the whole story, and thank you for drowning me; I am above you now, I am really very rich. I was frightened, to be sure, while I lay tied up in the sack, and the wind whistled in my ears when you threw me into the river from the bridge, and I sank to the bottom immediately; but I did not hurt myself, for I fell upon beautifully soft grass which grows down there; and in a moment, the sack opened, and the sweetest little maiden came towards me. She had snow-white robes, and a wreath of green leaves on her wet hair. She took me by the hand, and said, 'So you are come, Little Claus, and here are some cattle for you to begin with. About a mile farther on the road, there is another herd for you.' Then I saw that the river formed a great highway for the people who live in the sea. They were walking and driving here and there from the sea to the land at the, spot where the river terminates. The bed of the river was covered with the loveliest flowers and sweet fresh grass. The fish swam past me as rapidly as the birds do here in the air. How handsome all the people were, and what fine cattle were grazing on the hills and in the valleys!"

"But why did you come up again," said Great Claus, "if it was all so beautiful down there? I should not have done so?"

"Well," said Little Claus, "it was good policy on my part; you heard me say just now that I was told by the sea-maiden to go a mile farther on the road, and I should find a whole herd of cattle. By the road she meant the river, for she could not travel any other way; but I knew the winding of the river, and how it bends, sometimes to the right and sometimes to the left, and it seemed a long way, so I chose a shorter one; and, by coming up to the land, and then driving across the fields back again to the river, I shall save half a mile, and get all my cattle more quickly."

"What a lucky fellow you are!" exclaimed Great Claus. "Do you think I should get any sea-cattle if I went down to the bottom of the river?"

"Yes, I think so," said Little Claus; "but I cannot carry you there in a sack, you are too heavy. However if you will go there first, and then creep into a sack, I will throw you in with the greatest pleasure."

"Thank you," said Great Claus; "but remember, if I do not get any sea-cattle down there I shall come up again and give you a good thrashing."

"No, now, don't be too fierce about it!" said Little Claus, as they walked on towards the river. When they approached it, the cattle, who were very thirsty, saw the stream, and ran down to drink.

"See what a hurry they are in," said Little Claus, "they are longing to get down again."

"Come, help me, make haste," said Great Claus; "or you'll get beaten." So he crept into a large sack, which had been lying across the back of one of the oxen.

"Put in a stone," said Great Claus, "or I may not sink."

"Oh, there's not much fear of that," he replied; still he put a large stone into the bag, and then tied it tightly, and gave it a push.

"Plump!" In went Great Claus, and immediately sank to the bottom of the river.

"I'm afraid he will not find any cattle," said Little Claus, and then he drove his own beasts homewards.

She Was Good for Nothing

THE MAYOR STOOD at the open window. He looked smart, for his shirt-frill, in which he had stuck a breast-pin, and his ruffles, were very fine. He had shaved his chin uncommonly smooth, although he had cut himself slightly, and had stuck a piece of newspaper over the place. "Hark 'ee, youngster!" cried he.

The boy to whom he spoke was no other than the son of a poor washer-woman, who was just going past the house. He stopped, and respectfully took off his cap. The peak of this cap was broken in the middle, so that he could easily roll it up and put it in his pocket. He stood before the mayor in his poor but clean and well-mended clothes, with heavy wooden shoes on his feet, looking as humble as if it had been the king himself.

"You are a good and civil boy," said the mayor. "I suppose your mother is busy washing the clothes down by the river, and you are going to carry that thing to her that you have in your pocket. It is very bad for your mother. How much have you got in it?"

"Only half a quartern," stammered the boy in a frightened voice.

"And she has had just as much this morning already?"

"No, it was yesterday," replied the boy.

"Two halves make a whole," said the mayor. "She's good for nothing. What a sad thing it is with these people. Tell your mother she ought to be ashamed of herself. Don't you become a drunkard, but I expect you will though. Poor child! there, go now."

The boy went on his way with his cap in his hand, while the wind fluttered his golden hair till the locks stood up straight. He turned round the corner of the street into the little lane that led to the river, where his mother stood in the water by her washing bench, beating the linen with a heavy wooden bar. The floodgates at the mill had been drawn up, and as the water rolled rapidly on, the sheets were dragged along by the stream, and nearly overturned the bench, so that the washer-woman was obliged to lean against it to keep it steady. "I have been very nearly carried away," she said; "it is a good thing that you are come, for I want something to strengthen me. It is cold in the water, and I have stood here six hours. Have you brought anything for me?"

The boy drew the bottle from his pocket, and the mother put it to her lips, and drank a little.

"Ah, how much good that does, and how it warms me," she said; "it is as good as a hot meal, and not so dear. Drink a little, my boy; you look quite pale; you are shivering in your thin clothes, and autumn has really come. Oh, how cold the water is! I hope I shall not be ill. But no, I must not be afraid of that. Give me a little more, and you may have a sip too, but only a sip; you must not get used to it, my poor, dear child." She stepped up to the bridge on which the boy stood as she spoke, and came on shore. The water dripped from the straw mat which she had bound round her body, and from her gown. "I work hard and suffer pain with my poor hands," said she, "but I do it willingly, that I may be able to bring you up honestly and truthfully, my dear boy."

At the same moment, a woman, rather older than herself, came towards them. She was a miserable-looking object, lame of one leg, and with a large false curl hanging down over one of her eyes, which was blind. This curl was intended to conceal the blind eye, but it made the defect only more visible. She was a friend of the laundress, and was called, among the neighbors, "Lame Martha, with the curl." "Oh, you poor thing; how you do work, standing there in the water!" she exclaimed. "You really do need something to give you a little warmth, and yet spiteful people cry out about the few drops you take." And then Martha repeated to the laundress, in a very few minutes, all that the mayor had said to her boy, which she had overheard; and she felt very angry that any man could speak, as he had done, of a mother to her own child, about the few drops she had taken; and she was still more angry because, on that very day, the mayor was going to have a dinner-party, at which there would be wine, strong, rich wine, drunk by the bottle. "Many will take more than they ought, but they don't call that drinking! They are all right, you are good for nothing indeed!" cried Martha indignantly.

"And so he spoke to you in that way, did he, my child?" said the washer-woman, and her lips trembled as she spoke. "He says you have a mother who is good for nothing. Well, perhaps he is right, but he should not have said it to my child. How much has happened to me from that house!"

"Yes," said Martha; "I remember you were in service there, and lived in the house when the mayor's parents were alive; how many years ago that is. Bushels of salt have been eaten since then, and people may well be thirsty," and Martha smiled. "The mayor's great dinner-party to-day ought to have been put off, but the news came too late. The footman told me the dinner was already cooked, when a letter came to say that the mayor's younger brother in Copenhagen is dead."

"Dead!" cried the laundress, turning pale as death.

"Yes, certainly," replied Martha; "but why do you take it so much to heart? I suppose you knew him years ago, when you were in service there?"

"Is he dead?" she exclaimed. "Oh, he was such a kind, good-hearted man, there are not many like him," and the tears rolled down her cheeks as she spoke. Then she cried, "Oh, dear me; I feel quite ill: everything is going round me, I cannot bear it. Is the bottle empty?" and she leaned against the plank.

"Dear me, you are ill indeed," said the other woman. "Come, cheer up; perhaps it will pass off. No, indeed, I see you are really ill; the best thing for me to do is to lead you home."

"But my washing yonder?"

"I will take care of that. Come, give me your arm. The boy can stay here and take care of the linen, and I'll come back and finish the washing; it is but a trifle."

The limbs of the laundress shook under her, and she said, "I have stood too long in the cold water, and I have had nothing to eat the whole day since the morning. O kind Heaven, help me to get home; I am in a burning fever. Oh, my poor child," and she burst into tears. And he, poor boy, wept also, as he sat alone by the river, near to and watching the damp linen.

The two women walked very slowly. The laundress slipped and tottered through the lane, and round the corner, into the street where the mayor lived; and just as she reached the front of his house, she sank down upon the pavement. Many persons came round her, and Lame Martha ran into the house for help. The mayor and his guests came to the window.

"Oh, it is the laundress," said he; "she has had a little drop too much. She is good for nothing. It is a sad thing for her pretty little son. I like the boy very well; but the mother is good for nothing."

After a while the laundress recovered herself, and they led her to her poor dwelling, and put her to bed. Kind Martha warmed a mug of beer for her, with butter and sugar – she considered this the best medicine – and then hastened to the river, washed and rinsed, badly enough, to be sure, but she did her best. Then she drew the linen ashore, wet as it was, and laid it in a basket. Before evening, she was sitting in the poor little room with the laundress. The mayor's cook had given her some roasted potatoes and a beautiful piece of fat for the sick woman. Martha and the boy enjoyed these good things very much; but the sick woman could only say that the smell was very nourishing, she thought. By-and-by the boy was put to bed, in the same bed as the one in which his mother lay; but he slept at her feet, covered with an old quilt made of blue and white patchwork. The laundress felt a little better by this time. The warm beer had strengthened her, and the smell of the good food had been pleasant to her.

"Many thanks, you good soul," she said to Martha. "Now the boy is asleep, I will tell you all. He is soon asleep. How gentle and sweet he looks as he lies there with his eyes closed! He does not know how his mother has suffered; and Heaven grant he never may know it. I was in service at the counsellor's, the father of the mayor, and it happened that the youngest of his sons, the student, came home. I was a young wild girl then, but honest; that I can declare in the sight of Heaven. The student was merry and gay, brave and affectionate; every drop of blood in him was good and honorable; a better man never lived on earth. He was the son of the house, and I was only a maid; but he loved me truly and honorably, and he told his mother of it. She was to him as an angel upon earth; she was so wise and loving. He went to travel, and before he started he placed a gold ring on my finger; and as soon as he was out of the house, my mistress sent for me. Gently and earnestly she drew me to her, and spake as if an angel were speaking. She showed me clearly, in spirit and in truth, the difference there was between him and me. 'He is pleased now,' she said, 'with your pretty face; but good looks do not last long. You have not been educated like he has. You are not equals in mind and rank, and therein lies the misfortune. I esteem the poor,' she added. 'In the sight of God, they may occupy a higher place than many of the rich; but here upon earth we must beware of entering upon a false track, lest we are overturned in our plans, like a carriage that travels by a dangerous road. I know a worthy man, an artisan, who wishes to marry you. I mean Eric, the glovemaker. He is a widower, without children, and in a good position. Will you think it over?' Every word she said pierced my heart like a knife; but I knew she was right, and the thought pressed heavily upon me. I kissed her hand, and wept bitter tears, and I wept still more when I went to my room, and threw myself on the bed. I passed through a dreadful night; God knows what I suffered, and how I struggled. The following Sunday I went to the house of God to pray for light to direct my path. It seemed like a providence that as I stepped out of church Eric came towards me; and then there remained not a doubt in my mind. We were suited to each other in rank and circumstances. He was, even then, a man of good means. I went up to him, and took his hand, and said, 'Do you still feel the same for me?' 'Yes; ever and always,' said he. 'Will you, then, marry a maiden who honors and esteems you, although she cannot offer you her love? but that may come.' 'Yes, it will come,' said he; and we joined our hands together, and I went home to my mistress. The gold ring which her son had given me I wore next to my heart. I could not place it on my finger during the daytime, but only in the evening, when I went to bed. I kissed the ring till my lips almost bled, and then I gave it to my mistress, and told her that the banns were to be put up for me and the glovemaker the following week. Then my mistress threw her arms round me, and kissed me. She did not say that I was 'good for nothing;' very likely I was better then than I am now; but the misfortunes of this world, were unknown to me then. At Michaelmas we were married, and for the first year everything went well with us. We had a journeyman and an apprentice, and you were our servant, Martha."

"Ah, yes, and you were a dear, good mistress," said Martha, "I shall never forget how kind you and your husband were to me."

"Yes, those were happy years when you were with us, although we had no children at first. The student I never met again. Yet I saw him once, although he did not see me. He came to his mother's funeral. I saw him, looking pale as death, and deeply troubled, standing at her grave; for she was his mother. Sometime after, when his father died, he was in foreign lands, and did not come home. I know that he never married, I believe he became a lawyer. He had forgotten me, and even had we met he would not have known me, for I have lost all my good looks, and perhaps that is all for the best." And then she spoke of the dark days of trial, when misfortune had fallen upon them.

"We had five hundred dollars," she said, "and there was a house in the street to be sold for two hundred, so we thought it would be worth our while to pull it down and build a new one in its place; so it was bought. The builder and carpenter made an estimate that the new house would cost ten hundred and twenty dollars to build. Eric had credit, so he borrowed the money in the chief town. But the captain, who was bringing it to him, was shipwrecked, and the money lost. Just about this time, my dear sweet boy, who lies sleeping there, was born, and my husband was attacked with a severe lingering illness. For three quarters of a year I was obliged to dress and undress him. We were backward in our payments, we borrowed more money, and all that we had was lost and sold, and then my husband died. Since then I have worked, toiled, and striven for the sake of the child. I have scrubbed and washed both coarse and fine linen, but I have not been able to make myself better off; and it was God's will. In His own time He will take me to Himself, but I know He will never forsake my boy." Then she fell asleep. In the morning she felt much refreshed, and strong enough, as she thought, to go on with her work. But as soon as she stepped into the cold water, a sudden faintness seized her; she clutched at the air convulsively with her hand, took one step forward, and fell. Her head rested on dry land, but her feet were in the water; her wooden shoes, which were only tied on by a wisp of straw, were carried away by the stream, and thus she was found by Martha when she came to bring her some coffee.

In the meantime a messenger had been sent to her house by the mayor, to say that she must come to him immediately, as he had something to tell her. It was too late; a surgeon had been sent for to open a vein in her arm, but the poor woman was dead.

"She has drunk herself to death," said the cruel mayor. In the letter, containing the news of his brother's death, it was stated that he had left in his will a legacy of six hundred dollars to the glovemaker's widow, who had been his mother's maid, to be paid with discretion, in large or small sums to the widow or her child.

"There was something between my brother and her, I remember," said the mayor; "it is a good thing that she is out of the way, for now the boy will have the whole. I will place him with honest people to bring him up, that he may become a respectable working man." And the blessing of God rested upon these words. The mayor sent for the boy to come to him, and promised to take care of him, but most cruelly added that it was a good thing that his mother was dead, for "she was good for nothing." They carried her to the churchyard, the churchyard in which the poor were buried. Martha strewed sand on the grave and planted a rose-tree upon it, and the boy stood by her side.

"Oh, my poor mother!" he cried, while the tears rolled down his cheeks. "Is it true what they say, that she was good for nothing?"

"No, indeed, it is not true," replied the old servant, raising her eyes to heaven; "she was worth a great deal; I knew it years ago, and since the last night of her life I am more certain of it than ever. I say she was a good and worthy woman, and God, who is in heaven, knows I am speaking the truth, though the world may say, even now she was good for nothing."

What the Old Man Does Is Always Right

I WILL TELL you a story that was told me when I was a little boy. Every time I thought of this story, it seemed to me more and more charming; for it is with stories as it is with many people – they become better as they grow older.

I have no doubt that you have been in the country, and seen a very old farmhouse, with a thatched roof, and mosses and small plants growing wild upon it. There is a stork's nest on the ridge of the gable, for we cannot do without the stork. The walls of the house are sloping, and the windows are low, and only one of the latter is made to open. The baking-oven sticks out of the wall like a great knob. An elder-tree hangs over the palings; and beneath its branches, at the foot of the paling, is a pool of water, in which a few ducks are disporting themselves. There is a yard-dog too, who barks at all corners. Just such a farmhouse as this stood in a country lane; and in it dwelt an old couple, a peasant and his wife. Small as their possessions were, they had one article they could not do without, and that was a horse, which contrived to live upon the grass which it found by the side of the high road. The old peasant rode into the town upon this horse, and his neighbors often borrowed it of him, and paid for the loan of it by rendering some service to the old couple. After a time they thought it would be as well to sell the horse, or exchange it for something which might be more useful to them. But what might this something be?

"You'll know best, old man," said the wife. "It is fair-day to-day; so ride into town, and get rid of the horse for money, or make a good exchange; whichever you do will be right to me, so ride to the fair."

And she fastened his neckerchief for him; for she could do that better than he could, and she could also tie it very prettily in a double bow. She also smoothed his hat round and round with the palm of her hand, and gave him a kiss. Then he rode away upon the horse that was to be sold or bartered for something else. Yes, the old man knew what he was about. The sun shone with great heat, and not a cloud was to be seen in the sky. The road was very dusty; for a number of people, all going to the fair, were driving, riding, or walking upon it. There was no shelter anywhere from the hot sunshine. Among the rest a man came trudging along, and driving a cow to the fair. The cow was as beautiful a creature as any cow could be.

"She gives good milk, I am certain," said the peasant to himself. "That would be a very good exchange: the cow for the horse. Hallo there! you with the cow," he said. "I tell you what; I dare say a horse is of more value than a cow; but I don't care for that, – a cow will be more useful to me; so, if you like, we'll exchange."

"To be sure I will," said the man.

Accordingly the exchange was made; and as the matter was settled, the peasant might have turned back; for he had done the business he came to do. But, having made up his mind to go to the fair, he determined to do so, if only to have a look at it; so on he went to the town with his cow. Leading the animal, he strode on sturdily, and, after a short time, overtook a man who was driving a sheep. It was a good fat sheep, with a fine fleece on its back.

"I should like to have that fellow," said the peasant to himself. "There is plenty of grass for him by our palings, and in the winter we could keep him in the room with us. Perhaps it would be more profitable to have a sheep than a cow. Shall I exchange?"

The man with the sheep was quite ready, and the bargain was quickly made. And then our peasant continued his way on the high-road with his sheep. Soon after this, he overtook another man, who had come into the road from a field, and was carrying a large goose under his arm.

"What a heavy creature you have there!" said the peasant; "it has plenty of feathers and plenty of fat, and would look well tied to a string, or paddling in the water at our place. That would be very useful to my old woman; she could make all sorts of profits out of it. How often she has said, 'If now we only had a goose!' Now here is an opportunity, and, if possible, I will get it for her. Shall we exchange? I will give you my sheep for your goose, and thanks into the bargain."

The other had not the least objection, and accordingly the exchange was made, and our peasant became possessor of the goose. By this time he had arrived very near the town. The crowd on the high road had been gradually increasing, and there was quite a rush of men and cattle. The cattle walked on the path and by the palings, and at the turnpike-gate they even walked into the toll-keeper's potato-field, where one fowl was strutting about with a string tied to its leg, for fear it should take fright at the crowd, and run away and get lost. The tail-feathers of the fowl were very short, and it winked with both its eyes, and looked very cunning, as it said "Cluck, cluck." What were the thoughts of the fowl as it said this I cannot tell you; but directly our good man saw it, he thought, "Why that's the finest fowl I ever saw in my life; it's finer than our parson's brood hen, upon my word. I should like to have that fowl. Fowls can always pick up a few grains that lie about, and almost keep themselves. I think it would be a good exchange if I could get it for my goose. Shall we exchange?" he asked the toll-keeper.

"Exchange," repeated the man; "well, it would not be a bad thing."

And so they made an exchange, – the toll-keeper at the turnpike-gate kept the goose, and the peasant carried off the fowl. Now he had really done a great deal of business on his way to the fair, and he was hot and tired. He wanted something to eat, and a glass of ale to refresh himself; so he turned his steps to an inn. He was just about to enter when the ostler came out, and they met at the door. The ostler was carrying a sack. "What have you in that sack?" asked the peasant.

"Rotten apples," answered the ostler; "a whole sackful of them. They will do to feed the pigs with."

"Why that will be terrible waste," he replied; "I should like to take them home to my old woman. Last year the old apple-tree by the grass-plot only bore one apple, and we kept it in the cupboard till it was quite withered and rotten. It was always property, my old woman said; and here she would see a great deal of property – a whole sackful; I should like to show them to her."

"What will you give me for the sackful?" asked the ostler.

"What will I give? Well, I will give you my fowl in exchange."

So he gave up the fowl, and received the apples, which he carried into the inn parlor. He leaned the sack carefully against the stove, and then went to the table. But the stove was hot, and he had not thought of that. Many guests were present – horse dealers, cattle drovers, and two Englishmen. The Englishmen were so rich that their pockets quite bulged out and seemed ready to burst; and they could bet too, as you shall hear. "Hiss-s-s, hiss-s-s." What could that be by the stove? The apples were beginning to roast. "What is that?" asked one.

"Why, do you know" – said our peasant. And then he told them the whole story of the horse, which he had exchanged for a cow, and all the rest of it, down to the apples.

"Well, your old woman will give it you well when you get home," said one of the Englishmen. "Won't there be a noise?"

"What! Give me what?" said the peasant. "Why, she will kiss me, and say, 'what the old man does is always right.'"

"Let us lay a wager on it," said the Englishmen. "We'll wager you a ton of coined gold, a hundred pounds to the hundred-weight."

"No; a bushel will be enough," replied the peasant. "I can only set a bushel of apples against it, and I'll throw myself and my old woman into the bargain; that will pile up the measure, I fancy."

"Done! taken!" and so the bet was made.

Then the landlord's coach came to the door, and the two Englishmen and the peasant got in, and away they drove, and soon arrived and stopped at the peasant's hut. "Good evening, old woman." "Good evening, old man." "I've made the exchange."

"Ah, well, you understand what you're about," said the woman. Then she embraced him, and paid no attention to the strangers, nor did she notice the sack.

"I got a cow in exchange for the horse."

"Thank Heaven," said she. "Now we shall have plenty of milk, and butter, and cheese on the table. That was a capital exchange."

"Yes, but I changed the cow for a sheep."

"Ah, better still!" cried the wife. "You always think of everything; we have just enough pasture for a sheep. Ewe's milk and cheese, woollen jackets and stockings! The cow could not give all these, and her hair only falls off. How you think of everything!"

"But I changed away the sheep for a goose."

"Then we shall have roast goose to eat this year. You dear old man, you are always thinking of something to please me. This is delightful. We can let the goose walk about with a string tied to her leg, so she will be fatter still before we roast her."

"But I gave away the goose for a fowl."

"A fowl! Well, that was a good exchange," replied the woman. "The fowl will lay eggs and hatch them, and we shall have chickens; we shall soon have a poultry-yard. Oh, this is just what I was wishing for."

"Yes, but I exchanged the fowl for a sack of shrivelled apples."

"What! I really must give you a kiss for that!" exclaimed the wife. "My dear, good husband, now I'll tell you something. Do you know, almost as soon as you left me this morning, I began to think of what I could give you nice for supper this evening, and then I thought of fried eggs and bacon, with sweet herbs; I had eggs and bacon, but I wanted the herbs; so I went over to the schoolmaster's: I knew they had plenty of herbs, but the schoolmistress is very mean, although she can smile so sweetly. I begged her to lend me a handful of herbs. 'Lend!' she exclaimed, 'I have nothing to lend; nothing at all grows in our garden, not even a shrivelled apple; I could not even lend you a shrivelled apple, my dear woman.' But now I can lend her ten, or a whole sackful, which I'm very glad of; it makes me laugh to think about it;" and then she gave him a hearty kiss.

"Well, I like all this," said both the Englishmen; "always going down the hill, and yet always merry; it's worth the money to see it." So they paid a hundred-weight of gold to the peasant, who, whatever he did, was not scolded but kissed.

Yes, it always pays best when the wife sees and maintains that her husband knows best, and whatever he does is right.

That is a story which I heard when I was a child; and now you have heard it too, and know that "What the old man does is always right."

The Story of a Mother

A MOTHER SAT by her little child; she was very sad, for she feared it would die. It was quite pale, and its little eyes were closed, and sometimes it drew a heavy deep breath, almost like a sigh; and then the mother gazed more sadly than ever on the poor little creature. Some one knocked at the door, and a poor old man walked in. He was wrapped in something that looked like a great horse-cloth; and he required it truly to keep him warm, for it was cold winter; the country everywhere lay covered with snow and ice, and the wind blew so sharply that it cut one's face. The little child had dozed off to sleep for a moment, and the mother, seeing that the old man shivered with the cold, rose and placed a small mug of beer on the stove to warm for him. The old man sat and rocked the cradle; and the mother seated herself on a chair near him, and looked at her sick child who still breathed heavily, and took hold of its little hand.

"You think I shall keep him, do you not?" she said. "Our all-merciful God will surely not take him away from me."

The old man, who was indeed Death himself, nodded his head in a peculiar manner, which might have signified either Yes, or No; and the mother cast down her eyes, while the tears rolled down her cheeks. Then her head became heavy, for she had not closed her eyes for three days and nights, and she slept, but only for a moment. Shivering with cold, she started up and looked round the room. The old man was gone, and her child – it was gone too! – the old man had taken it with him. In the corner of the room the old clock began to strike; "whirr" went the chains, the heavy weight sank to the ground, and the clock stopped; and the poor mother rushed out of the house calling for her child. Out in the snow sat a woman in long black garments, and she said to the mother, "Death has been with you in your room. I saw him hastening away with your little child; he strides faster than the wind, and never brings back what he has taken away."

"Only tell me which way he has gone," said the mother; "tell me the way, I will find him."

"I know the way," said the woman in the black garments; "but before I tell you, you must sing to me all the songs that you have sung to your child; I love these songs, I have heard them before. I am Night, and I saw your tears flow as you sang."

"I will sing them all to you," said the mother; "but do not detain me now. I must overtake him, and find my child."

But Night sat silent and still. Then the mother wept and sang, and wrung her hands. And there were many songs, and yet even more tears; till at length Night said, "Go to the right, into the dark forest of fir-trees; for I saw Death take that road with your little child."

Within the wood the mother came to cross roads, and she knew not which to take. Just by stood a thorn-bush; it had neither leaf nor flower, for it was the cold winter time, and icicles hung on the branches. "Have you not seen Death go by, with my little child?" she asked.

"Yes," replied the thorn-bush; "but I will not tell you which way he has taken until you have warmed me in your bosom. I am freezing to death here, and turning to ice."

Then she pressed the bramble to her bosom quite close, so that it might be thawed, and the thorns pierced her flesh, and great drops of blood flowed; but the bramble shot forth fresh green leaves, and they became flowers on the cold winter's night, so warm is the heart of a sorrowing mother. Then the bramble-bush told her the path she must take. She came at length to a great lake, on which there was neither ship nor boat to be seen. The lake was not frozen sufficiently for her to pass over on the ice, nor was it open enough for her to wade through; and yet she must cross it, if she wished to find her child. Then she laid herself down to drink up the water of the lake, which was of course impossible for any human being to do; but the bereaved mother thought that perhaps a miracle might take place to help her. "You will never succeed in this," said the lake; "let us make an agreement together which will be better. I love to collect pearls, and your eyes are the purest I have ever seen. If you will weep those eyes away in tears into my waters, then I will take you to the large hothouse where Death dwells and rears flowers and trees, every one of which is a human life."

"Oh, what would I not give to reach my child!" said the weeping mother; and as she still continued to weep, her eyes fell into the depths of the lake, and became two costly pearls.

Then the lake lifted her up, and wafted her across to the opposite shore as if she were on a swing, where stood a wonderful building many miles in length. No one could tell whether it was a mountain covered with forests and full of caves, or whether it had been built. But the poor mother could not see, for she had wept her eyes into the lake. "Where shall I find Death, who went away with my little child?" she asked.

"He has not arrived here yet," said an old gray-haired woman, who was walking about, and watering Death's hothouse. "How have you found your way here? and who helped you?"

"God has helped me," she replied. "He is merciful; will you not be merciful too? Where shall I find my little child?"

"I did not know the child," said the old woman; "and you are blind. Many flowers and trees have faded to-night, and Death will soon come to transplant them. You know already that every human being has a life-tree or a life-flower, just as may be ordained for him. They look like other plants; but they have hearts that beat. Children's hearts also beat: from that you may perhaps be able to recognize your child. But what will you give me, if I tell you what more you will have to do?"

"I have nothing to give," said the afflicted mother; "but I would go to the ends of the earth for you."

"I can give you nothing to do for me there," said the old woman; "but you can give me your long black hair. You know yourself that it is beautiful, and it pleases me. You can take my white hair in exchange, which will be something in return."

"Do you ask nothing more than that?" said she. "I will give it to you with pleasure."

And she gave up her beautiful hair, and received in return the white locks of the old woman. Then they went into Death's vast hothouse, where flowers and trees grew together in wonderful profusion. Blooming hyacinths, under glass bells, and peonies, like strong trees. There grew water-plants, some quite fresh, and others looking sickly, which had water-snakes twining round them, and black crabs clinging to their stems. There stood noble palm-trees, oaks, and plantains, and beneath them bloomed thyme and parsley. Each tree and flower had a name; each represented a human life, and belonged to men still living, some in China, others in Greenland, and in all parts of the world. Some large trees had been planted in little pots, so that they were cramped for room, and seemed about to burst the pot to pieces; while many weak little flowers were growing in rich soil, with moss all around them, carefully tended and cared for. The sorrowing mother bent over the little plants, and heard the human heart beating in each, and recognized the beatings of her child's heart among millions of others.

"That is it," she cried, stretching out her hand towards a little crocus-flower which hung down its sickly head.

"Do not touch the flower," exclaimed the old woman; "but place yourself here; and when Death comes – I expect him every minute – do not let him pull up that plant, but threaten him that if he does you will serve the other flowers in the same manner. This will make him afraid; for he must account to God for each of them. None can be uprooted, unless he receives permission to do so."

There rushed through the hothouse a chill of icy coldness, and the blind mother felt that Death had arrived.

"How did you find your way hither?" asked he; "how could you come here faster than I have?"

"I am a mother," she answered.

And Death stretched out his hand towards the delicate little flower; but she held her hands tightly round it, and held it fast at same time, with the most anxious care, lest she should touch one of the leaves. Then Death breathed upon her hands, and she felt his breath colder than the icy wind, and her hands sank down powerless.

"You cannot prevail against me," said Death.

"But a God of mercy can," said she.

"I only do His will," replied Death. "I am his gardener. I take all His flowers and trees, and transplant them into the gardens of Paradise in an unknown land. How they flourish there, and what that garden resembles, I may not tell you."

"Give me back my child," said the mother, weeping and imploring; and she seized two beautiful flowers in her hands, and cried to Death, "I will tear up all your flowers, for I am in despair."

"Do not touch them," said Death. "You say you are unhappy; and would you make another mother as unhappy as yourself?"

"Another mother!" cried the poor woman, setting the flowers free from her hands.

"There are your eyes," said Death. "I fished them up out of the lake for you. They were shining brightly; but I knew not they were yours. Take them back – they are clearer now than before – and then look into the deep well which is close by here. I will tell you the names of the two flowers which you wished to pull up; and you will see the whole future of the human beings they represent, and what you were about to frustrate and destroy."

Then she looked into the well; and it was a glorious sight to behold how one of them became a blessing to the world, and how much happiness and joy it spread around. But she saw that the life of the other was full of care and poverty, misery and woe.

"Both are the will of God," said Death.

"Which is the unhappy flower, and which is the blessed one?" she said.

"That I may not tell you," said Death; "but thus far you may learn, that one of the two flowers represents your own child. It was the fate of your child that you saw, – the future of your own child."

Then the mother screamed aloud with terror, "Which of them belongs to my child? Tell me that. Deliver the unhappy child. Release it from so much misery. Rather take it away. Take it to the kingdom of God. Forget my tears and my entreaties; forget all that I have said or done."

"I do not understand you," said Death. "Will you have your child back? or shall I carry him away to a place that you do not know?"

Then the mother wrung her hands, fell on her knees, and prayed to God, "Grant not my prayers, when they are contrary to Thy will, which at all times must be the best. Oh, hear them not;" and her head sank on her bosom.

Then Death carried away her child to the unknown land.

Ib and Little Christina

IN THE FOREST that extends from the banks of the Gudenau, in North Jutland, a long way into the country, and not far from the clear stream, rises a great ridge of land, which stretches through the wood like a wall. Westward of this ridge, and not far from the river, stands a farmhouse, surrounded by such poor land that the sandy soil shows itself between the scanty ears of rye and wheat which grow in it. Some years have passed since the people who lived here cultivated these fields; they kept three sheep, a pig, and two oxen; in fact they maintained themselves very well, they had quite enough to live upon, as people generally have who are content with their lot. They even could have afforded to keep two horses, but it was a saying among the farmers in those parts, "The horse eats himself up;" that is to say, he eats as much as he earns. Jeppe Jans cultivated his fields in summer, and in the winter he made wooden shoes. He also had an assistant, a lad who understood as well as he himself did how to make wooden shoes strong, but light, and in the fashion. They carved shoes and spoons, which paid well; therefore no one could justly call Jeppe Jans and his family poor people. Little Ib, a boy of seven years old and the only child, would sit by, watching the workmen, or cutting a stick, and sometimes his finger instead of the stick. But one day Ib succeeded so well in his carving that he made two pieces of wood look really like two little wooden shoes, and he determined to give them as a present to Little Christina.

"And who was Little Christina?" She was the boatman's daughter, graceful and delicate as the child of a gentleman; had she been dressed differently, no one would have believed that she lived in a hut on the neighboring heath with her father. He was a widower, and earned his living by carrying firewood in his large boat from the forest to the eel-pond and eel-weir, on the estate of Silkborg, and sometimes even to the distant town of Randers. There was no one under whose care he could leave Little Christina; so she was almost always with him in his boat, or playing in the wood among the blossoming heath, or picking the ripe wild berries. Sometimes, when her father had to go as far as the town, he would take Little Christina, who was a year younger than Ib, across the heath to the cottage of Jeppe Jans, and leave her there. Ib and Christina agreed together in everything; they divided their bread and berries when they were hungry; they were partners in digging their little gardens; they ran, and crept, and played about everywhere. Once they wandered a long way into the forest, and even ventured together to climb the high ridge. Another time they found a few snipes' eggs in the wood, which was a great event. Ib had never been on the heath where Christina's father lived, nor on the river; but at last came an opportunity. Christina's father invited him to go for a sail in his boat; and the evening before, he accompanied the boatman across the heath to his house. The next morning early, the two children were placed on the top of a high pile of firewood in the boat, and sat eating bread and wild strawberries, while Christina's father and his man drove the boat forward with poles. They floated on swiftly, for the tide was in their favor, passing over lakes, formed by the stream in its course; sometimes they seemed quite enclosed by reeds and water-plants, yet there was always room for them to pass out, although the old trees overhung the water and the old oaks stretched out their bare branches, as if they had turned up their sleeves and wished to show their knotty, naked arms. Old alder-trees, whose roots were loosened from the banks, clung with their fibres to the bottom of the stream, and the tops of the branches above the water looked like little woody islands. The water-lilies waved themselves to and fro on the river, everything made the excursion beautiful, and at last they came to the great eel-weir, where the water rushed through the flood-gates; and the children thought this a beautiful sight. In those days there was no factory nor any town house, nothing but the great farm, with its scanty-bearing fields, in which could be seen a few herd of cattle, and one or two farm laborers. The rushing of the water through the sluices, and the scream of the wild ducks, were almost the only signs of active life at Silkborg. After the firewood had been unloaded, Christina's father bought a whole bundle of eels and a sucking-pig, which were all placed in a basket in the stern of the boat. Then they returned again up the stream; and as the wind was favorable, two sails were hoisted, which carried the boat on as well as if two horses had been harnessed to it. As they sailed on, they came by chance to the place where the boatman's assistant lived, at a little distance from the bank of the river. The boat was moored; and the two men, after desiring the children to sit still, both went on shore. they obeyed this order for a very short time, and then forgot it altogether. First they peeped into the basket containing the eels and the sucking-pig; then they must needs pull out the pig and take it in their hands, and feel it, and touch it; and as they both wanted to hold it at the same time, the consequence was that they let it fall into the water, and the pig sailed away with the stream.

Here was a terrible disaster. Ib jumped ashore, and ran a little distance from the boat.

"Oh, take me with you," cried Christina; and she sprang after him. In a few minutes they found themselves deep in a thicket, and could no longer see the boat or the shore. They ran on a little farther, and then Christina fell down, and began to cry.

Ib helped her up, and said, "Never mind; follow me. Yonder is the house." But the house was not yonder; and they wandered still farther, over the dry rustling leaves of the last year, and treading on fallen branches that crackled under their little feet; then they heard a loud, piercing cry, and they stood still to listen. Presently the scream of an eagle sounded through the wood; it was an ugly cry, and it frightened the children; but before them, in the thickest part of the forest, grew the most beautiful blackberries, in wonderful quantities. They looked so inviting that the children could not help stopping; and they remained there so long eating, that their mouths and cheeks became quite black with the juice.

Presently they heard the frightful scream again, and Christina said, "We shall get into trouble about that pig."

"Oh, never mind," said Ib; "we will go home to my father's house. It is here in the wood." So they went on, but the road led them out of the way; no house could be seen, it grew dark, and the children were afraid. The solemn stillness that reigned around them was now and then broken by the shrill cries of the great horned owl and other birds that they knew nothing of. At last they both lost themselves in the thicket; Christina began to cry, and then Ib cried too; and, after weeping and lamenting for some time, they stretched themselves down on the dry leaves and fell asleep.

The sun was high in the heavens when the two children woke. They felt cold; but not far from their resting-place, on a hill, the sun was shining through the trees. They thought if they went there they should be warm, and Ib fancied he should be able to see his father's house from such a high spot. But they were far away from home now, in quite another part of the forest. They clambered to the top of the rising ground, and found themselves on the edge of a declivity, which sloped down to a clear transparent lake. Great quantities of fish could be seen through the clear water, sparkling in the sun's rays; they were quite surprised when they came so suddenly upon such an unexpected sight.

Close to where they stood grew a hazel-bush, covered with beautiful nuts. They soon gathered some, cracked them, and ate the fine young kernels, which were only just ripe. But there was another surprise and fright in store for them. Out of the thicket stepped a tall old woman, her face quite brown, and her hair of a deep shining black; the whites of her eyes glittered like a Moor's; on her back she carried a bundle, and in her hand a knotted stick. She was a gypsy. The children did not at first understand what she said. She drew out of her pocket three large nuts, in which she told them were hidden the most beautiful and lovely things in the world, for they were wishing nuts. Ib looked at her, and as she spoke so kindly, he took courage, and asked her if she would give him the nuts; and the woman gave them to him, and then gathered some more from the bushes for herself, quite a pocket full. Ib and Christina looked at the wishing nuts with wide open eyes.

"Is there in this nut a carriage, with a pair of horses?" asked Ib.

"Yes, there is a golden carriage, with two golden horses," replied the woman.

"Then give me that nut," said Christina; so Ib gave it to her, and the strange woman tied up the nut for her in her handkerchief.

Ib held up another nut. "Is there, in this nut, a pretty little neckerchief like the one Christina has on her neck?" asked Ib.

"There are ten neckerchiefs in it," she replied, "as well as beautiful dresses, stockings, and a hat and veil."

"Then I will have that one also," said Christina; "and it is a pretty one too." And then Ib gave her the second nut.

The third was a little black thing. "You may keep that one," said Christina; "it is quite as pretty."

"What is in it?" asked Ib.

"The best of all things for you," replied the gypsy. So Ib held the nut very tight.

Then the woman promised to lead the children to the right path, that they might find their way home: and they went forward certainly in quite another direction to the one they meant to take; therefore no one ought to speak against the woman, and say that she wanted to steal the children. In the wild wood-path they met a forester who knew Ib, and, by his help, Ib and Christina reached home, where they found every one had been very anxious about them. They were pardoned and forgiven, although they really had both done wrong, and deserved to get into trouble; first, because they had let the sucking-pig fall into the water; and, secondly, because they had run away. Christina was taken back to her father's house on the heath, and Ib remained in the farm-house on the borders of the wood, near the great land ridge.

The first thing Ib did that evening was to take out of his pocket the little black nut, in which the best thing of all was said to be enclosed. He laid it carefully between the door and the door-post, and then shut the door so that the nut cracked directly. But there was not much kernel to be seen; it was what we should call hollow or worm-eaten, and looked as if it had been filled with tobacco or rich black earth. "It is just what I expected!" exclaimed Ib. "How should there be room in a little nut like this for the best thing of all? Christina will find her two nuts just the same; there will be neither fine clothes or a golden carriage in them."

Winter came; and the new year, and indeed many years passed away; until Ib was old enough to be confirmed, and, therefore, he went during a whole winter to the clergyman of the nearest village to be prepared.

One day, about this time, the boatman paid a visit to Ib's parents, and told them that Christina was going to service, and that she had been remarkably fortunate in obtaining a good place, with most respectable people. "Only think," he said, "She is going to the rich innkeeper's, at the hotel in Herning, many miles west from here. She is to assist the landlady in the housekeeping; and, if afterwards she behaves well and remains to be confirmed, the people will treat her as their own daughter."

So Ib and Christina took leave of each other. People already called them "the betrothed," and at parting the girl showed Ib the two nuts, which she had taken care of ever since the time that they lost themselves in the wood; and she told him also that the little wooden shoes he once carved for her when he was a boy, and gave her as a present, had been carefully kept in a drawer ever since. And so they parted.

After Ib's confirmation, he remained at home with his mother, for he had become a clever shoemaker, and in summer managed the farm for her quite alone. His father had been dead some time, and his mother kept no farm servants. Sometimes, but very seldom, he heard of Christina, through a postillion or eel-seller who was passing. But she was well off with the rich innkeeper; and after being confirmed she wrote a letter to her father, in which was a kind message to Ib and his mother. In this letter, she mentioned that her master and mistress had made her a present of a beautiful new dress, and some nice under-clothes. This was, of course, pleasant news.

One day, in the following spring, there came a knock at the door of the house where Ib's old mother lived; and when they opened it, lo and behold, in stepped the boatman and Christina. She had come to pay them a visit, and to spend the day. A carriage had to come from the Herning hotel to the next village, and she had taken the opportunity to see her friends once more. She looked as elegant as a real lady, and wore a pretty dress, beautifully made on purpose for her. There she stood, in full dress, while Ib wore only his working clothes. He could not utter a word; he could only seize her hand and hold it fast in his own, but he felt too happy and glad to open his lips. Christina, however, was quite at her ease; she talked and talked, and kissed him in the most friendly manner. Even afterwards, when they were left alone, and she asked, "Did you know me again, Ib?" he still stood holding her hand, and said at last, "You are become quite a grand lady, Christina, and I am only a rough working man; but I have often thought of you and of old times." Then they wandered up the great ridge, and looked across the stream to the heath, where the little hills were covered with the flowering broom. Ib said nothing; but before the time came for them to part, it became quite clear to him that Christina must be his wife: had they not even in childhood been called the betrothed? To him it seemed as if they were really engaged to each other, although not a word had been spoken on the subject. They had only a few more hours to remain together, for Christina was obliged to return that evening to the neighboring village, to be ready for the carriage which was to start the next morning early for Herning. Ib and her father accompanied her to the village. It was a fine moonlight evening; and when they arrived, Ib stood holding Christina's hand in his, as if he could not let her go. His eyes brightened, and the words he uttered came with hesitation from his lips, but from the deepest recesses of his heart:

"Christina, if you have not become too grand, and if you can be contented to live in my mother's house as my wife, we will be married some day. But we can wait for a while."

"Oh yes," she replied; "Let us wait a little longer, Ib. I can trust you, for I believe that I do love you. But let me think it over." Then he kissed her lips; and so they parted.

On the way home, Ib told the boatman that he and Christina were as good as engaged to each other; and the boatman found out that he had always expected it would be so, and went home with Ib that evening, and remained the night in the farmhouse; but nothing further was said of the engagement. During the next year, two letters passed between Ib and Christina. They were signed, "Faithful till death;" but at the end of that time, one day the boatman came over to see Ib, with a kind greeting from Christina. He had something else to say, which made him hesitate in a strange manner. At last it came out that Christina, who had grown a very pretty girl, was more lucky than ever. She was courted and admired by every one; but her master's son, who had been home on a visit, was so much pleased with Christina that he wished to marry her. He had a very good situation in an office at Copenhagen, and as she had also taken a liking for him, his parents were not unwilling to consent. But Christina, in her heart, often thought of Ib, and knew how much he thought of her; so she felt inclined to refuse this good fortune, added the boatman. At first Ib said not a word, but he became as white as the wall, and shook his head gently, and then he spoke, – "Christina must not refuse this good fortune."

"Then will you write a few words to her?" said the boatman.

Ib sat down to write, but he could not get on at all. The words were not what he wished to say, so he tore up the page. The following morning, however, a letter lay ready to be sent to Christina, and the following is what he wrote: –

"The letter written by you to your father I have read, and see from it that you are prosperous in everything, and that still better fortune is in store for you. Ask your own heart, Christina, and think over carefully what awaits you if you take me for your husband, for I possess very little in the world. Do not think of me or of my position; think only of your own welfare. You are bound to me by no promises; and if in your heart you have given me one, I release you from it. May every blessing and happiness be poured out upon you, Christina. Heaven will give me the heart's consolation.

Ever your sincere friend, IB."

This letter was sent, and Christina received it in due time. In the course of the following November, her banns were published in the church on the heath, and also in Copenhagen, where the bridegroom lived. She was taken to Copenhagen under the protection of her future mother-in-law, because the bridegroom could not spare time from his numerous occupations for a journey so far into Jutland. On the journey, Christina met her father at one of the villages through which they passed, and here he took leave of her. Very little was said about the matter to Ib, and he did not refer to it; his mother, however, noticed that he had grown very silent and pensive. Thinking as he did of old times, no wonder the three nuts came into his mind which the gypsy woman had given him when a child, and of the two which he had given to Christina. These wishing nuts, after all, had proved true fortune-tellers. One had contained a gilded carriage and noble horses, and the other beautiful clothes; all of these Christina would now have in her new home at Copenhagen. Her part had come true. And for him the nut had contained only black earth. The gypsy woman had said it was the best for him. Perhaps it was, and this also would be fulfilled. He understood the gypsy woman's meaning now. The black earth – the dark grave – was the best thing for him now.

Again years passed away; not many, but they seemed long years to Ib. The old innkeeper and his wife died one after the other; and the whole of their property, many thousand dollars, was inherited by their son. Christina could have the golden carriage now, and plenty of fine clothes. During the two long years which followed, no letter came from Christina to her father; and when at last her father received one from her, it did not speak of prosperity or happiness. Poor Christina! Neither she nor her husband understood how to economize or save, and the riches brought no blessing with them, because they had not asked for it.

Years passed; and for many summers the heath was covered with bloom; in winter the snow rested upon it, and the rough winds blew across the ridge under which stood Ib's sheltered home. One spring day the sun shone brightly, and he was guiding the plough across his field. The ploughshare struck against something which he fancied was a firestone, and then he saw glittering in the earth a splinter of shining metal which the plough had cut from something which gleamed brightly in the furrow. He searched, and found a large golden armlet of superior workmanship, and it was evident that the plough had disturbed a Hun's grave. He searched further, and found more valuable treasures, which Ib showed to the clergyman, who explained their value to him. Then he went to the magistrate, who informed the president of the museum of the discovery, and advised Ib to take the treasures himself to the president.

"You have found in the earth the best thing you could find," said the magistrate.

"The best thing," thought Ib; "the very best thing for me, – and found in the earth! Well, if it really is so, then the gypsy woman was right in her prophecy."

So Ib went in the ferry-boat from Aarhus to Copenhagen. To him who had only sailed once or twice on the river near his own home, this seemed like a voyage on the ocean; and at length he arrived at Copenhagen. The value of the gold he had found was paid to him; it was a large sum – six hundred dollars. Then Ib of the heath went out, and wandered about in the great city.

On the evening before the day he had settled to return with the captain of the passage-boat, Ib lost himself in the streets, and took quite a different turning to the one he wished to follow. He wandered on till he found himself in a poor street of the suburb called Christian's Haven. Not a creature could be seen. At last a very little girl came out of one of the wretched-looking houses, and Ib asked her to tell him the way to the street he wanted; she looked up timidly at him, and began to cry bitterly. He asked her what was the matter; but what she said he could not understand. So he went along the street with her; and as they passed under a lamp, the light fell on the little girl's face. A strange sensation came over Ib, as he caught sight of it. The living, breathing embodiment of Little Christina stood before him, just as he remembered her in the days of her childhood. He followed the child to the wretched house, and ascended the narrow, crazy staircase which led to a little garret in the roof. The air in the room was heavy and stifling, no light was burning, and from one corner came sounds of moaning and sighing. It was the mother of the child who lay there on a miserable bed. With the help of a match, Ib struck a light, and approached her.

"Can I be of any service to you?" he asked. "This little girl brought me up here; but I am a stranger in this city. Are there no neighbors or any one whom I can call?"

Then he raised the head of the sick woman, and smoothed her pillow. He started as he did so. It was Christina of the heath! No one had mentioned her name to Ib for years; it would have disturbed his peace of mind, especially as the reports respecting her were not good. The wealth which her husband had inherited from his parents had made him proud and arrogant. He had given up his certain appointment, and travelled for six months in foreign lands, and, on his return, had lived in great style, and got into terrible debt. For a time he had trembled on the high pedestal on which he had placed himself, till at last he toppled over, and ruin came. His numerous merry companions, and the visitors at his table, said it served him right, for he had kept house like a madman. One morning his corpse was found in the canal. The cold hand of death had already touched the heart of Christina. Her youngest child, looked for in the midst of prosperity, had sunk into the grave when only a few weeks old; and at last Christina herself became sick unto death, and lay, forsaken and dying, in a miserable room, amid poverty she might have borne in her younger days, but which was now more painful to her from the luxuries to which she had lately been accustomed. It was her eldest child, also a Little Christina, whom Ib had followed to her home, where she suffered hunger and poverty with her mother.

"It makes me unhappy to think that I shall die, and leave this poor child," sighed she. "Oh, what will become of her?" She could say no more.

Then Ib brought out another match, and lighted a piece of candle which he found in the room, and it threw a glimmering light over the wretched dwelling. Ib looked at the little girl, and thought of Christina in her young days. For her sake, could he not love this child, who was a stranger to him? As he thus reflected, the dying woman opened her eyes, and gazed at him. Did she recognize him? He never knew; for not another word escaped her lips.

In the forest by the river Gudenau, not far from the heath, and beneath the ridge of land, stood the little farm, newly painted and whitewashed. The air was heavy and dark; there were no blossoms on the heath; the autumn winds whirled the yellow leaves towards the boatman's hut, in which strangers dwelt; but the little farm stood safely sheltered beneath the tall trees and the high ridge. The turf blazed brightly on the hearth, and within was sunlight, the sparkling light from the sunny eyes of a child; the birdlike tones from the rosy lips ringing like the song of a lark in spring. All was life and joy. Little Christina sat on Ib's knee. Ib was to her both father and mother; her own parents had vanished from her memory, as a dream-picture vanishes alike from childhood and age. Ib's house was well and prettily furnished; for he was a prosperous man now, while the mother of the little girl rested in the churchyard at Copenhagen, where she had died in poverty. Ib had money now – money which had come to him out of the black earth; and he had Christina for his own, after all.

The Jewish Maiden

IN A CHARITY school, among the children, sat a little Jewish girl. She was a good, intelligent child, and very quick at her lessons; but the Scripture-lesson class she was not allowed to join, for this was a Christian school. During the hour of this lesson, the Jewish girl was allowed to learn her geography, or to work her sum for the next day; and when her geography lesson was perfect, the book remained open before her, but she read not another word, for she sat silently listening to the words of the Christian teacher. He soon became aware that the little one was paying more attention to what he said than most of the other children. "Read your book, Sarah," he said to her gently.

But again and again he saw her dark, beaming eyes fixed upon him; and once, when he asked her a question, she could answer him even better than the other children. She had not only heard, but understood his words, and pondered them in her heart. Her father, a poor but honest man, had placed his daughter at the school on the conditions that she should not be instructed in the Christian faith. But it might have caused confusion, or raised discontent in the minds of the other children if she had been sent out of the room, so she remained; and now it was evident this could not go on. The teacher went to her father, and advised him to remove his daughter from the school, or to allow her to become a Christian. "I cannot any longer be an idle spectator of those beaming eyes, which express such a deep and earnest longing for the words of the gospel," said he.

Then the father burst into tears. "I know very little of the law of my fathers," said he; "but Sarah's mother was firm in her belief as a daughter of Israel, and I vowed to her on her deathbed that our child should never be baptized. I must keep my vow: it is to me even as a covenant with God Himself." And so the little Jewish girl left the Christian school.

Years rolled by. In one of the smallest provincial towns, in a humble household, lived a poor maiden of the Jewish faith, as a servant. Her hair was black as ebony, her eye dark as night, yet full of light and brilliancy so peculiar to the daughters of the east. It was Sarah. The expression in the face of the grown-up maiden was still the same as when, a child, she sat on the schoolroom form listening with thoughtful eyes to the words of the Christian teacher. Every Sunday there sounded forth from a church close by the tones of an organ and the singing of the congregation. The Jewish girl heard them in the house where, industrious and faithful in all things, she performed her household duties. "Thou shalt keep the Sabbath holy," said the voice of the law in her heart; but her Sabbath was a working day among the Christians, which was a great trouble to her. And then as the thought arose in her mind, "Does God reckon by days and hours?" her conscience felt satisfied on this question, and she found it a comfort to her, that on the Christian Sabbath she could have an hour for her own prayers undisturbed. The music and singing of the congregation sounded in her ears while at work in her kitchen, till the place itself became sacred to her. Then she would read in the Old Testament, that treasure and comfort to her people, and it was indeed the only Scriptures she could read. Faithfully in her inmost thoughts had she kept the words of her father to her teacher when she left the school, and the vow he had made to her dying mother that she should never receive Christian baptism. The New Testament must remain to her a sealed book, and yet she knew a great deal of its teaching, and the sound of the gospel truths still lingered among the recollections of her childhood.

One evening she was sitting in a corner of the dining-room, while her master read aloud. It was not the gospel he read, but an old story-book; therefore she might stay and listen to him. The story related that a Hungarian knight, who had been taken prisoner by a Turkish pasha, was most cruelly treated by him. He caused him to be yoked with his oxen to the plough, and driven with blows from the whip till the blood flowed, and he almost sunk with exhaustion and pain. The faithful wife of the knight at home gave up all her jewels, mortgaged her castle and land, and his friends raised large sums to make up the ransom demanded for his release, which was most enormously high. It was collected at last, and the knight released from slavery and misery. Sick and exhausted, he reached home.

Ere long came another summons to a struggle with the foes of Christianity. The still living knight heard the sound; he could endure no more, he had neither peace nor rest. He caused himself to be lifted on his war-horse; the color came into his cheeks, and his strength returned to him again as he went forth to battle and to victory. The very same pasha who had yoked him to the plough, became his prisoner, and was dragged to a dungeon in the castle. But an hour had scarcely passed, when the knight stood before the captive pasha, and inquired, "What do you suppose awaiteth thee?"

"I know," replied the pasha; "retribution."

"Yes, the retribution of a Christian," replied the knight. "The teaching of Christ, the Teacher, commands us to forgive our enemies, to love our neighbors; for God is love. Depart in peace: return to thy home. I give thee back to thy loved ones. But in future be mild and humane to all who are in trouble."

Then the prisoner burst into tears, and exclaimed, "Oh how could I imagine such mercy and forgiveness! I expected pain and torment. It seemed to me so sure that I took poison, which I secretly carried about me; and in a few hours its effects will destroy me. I must die! Nothing can save me! But before I die, explain to me the teaching which is so full of love and mercy, so great and God-like. Oh, that I may hear his teaching, and die a Christian!" And his prayer was granted.

This was the legend which the master read out of the old story-book. Every one in the house who was present listened, and shared the pleasure; but Sarah, the Jewish girl, sitting so still in a corner, felt her heart burn with excitement. Great tears came into her shining dark eyes; and with the same gentle piety with which she had once listened to the gospel while sitting on the form at school, she felt its grandeur now, and the tears rolled down her cheeks. Then the last words of her dying mother rose before her, "Let not my child become a Christian;" and with them sounded in her heart the words of the law, "Honor thy father and thy mother."

"I am not admitted among the Christians," she said; "they mock me as a Jewish girl; the neighbors' boys did so last Sunday when I stood looking in through the open church door at the candles burning on the altar, and listening to the singing. Ever since I sat on the school-bench I have felt the power of Christianity; a power which, like a sunbeam, streams into my heart, however closely I may close my eyes against it. But I will not grieve thee, my mother, in thy grave. I will not be unfaithful to my father's vow. I will not read the Bible of the Christian. I have the God of my fathers, and in Him I will trust."

And again years passed by. Sarah's master died, and his widow found herself in such reduced circumstances that she wished to dismiss her servant maid; but Sarah refused to leave the house, and she became a true support in time of trouble, and kept the household together by working till late at night, with her busy hands, to earn their daily bread. Not a relative came forward to assist them, and the widow was confined to a sick bed for months and grew weaker from day to day. Sarah worked hard, but contrived to spare time to amuse her and watch by the sick bed. She was gentle and pious, an angel of blessing in that house of poverty.

"My Bible lies on the table yonder," said the sick woman one day to Sarah. "Read me something from it; the night appears so long, and my spirit thirsts to hear the word of God."

And Sarah bowed her head. She took the book, and folded her hand over the Bible of the Christians, and at last opened it, and read to the sick woman. Tears stood in her eyes as she read, and they shone with brightness, for in her heart it was light.

"Mother," she murmured, "thy child may not receive Christian baptism, nor be admitted into the congregation of Christian people. Thou hast so willed it, and I will respect thy command. We are therefore still united here on earth; but in the next world there will be a higher union, even with God Himself, who leads and guides His people till death. He came down from heaven to earth to suffer for us, that we should bring forth the fruits of repentance. I understand it now. I know not how I learnt this truth, unless it is through the name of Christ." Yet she trembled as she pronounced the holy name. She struggled against these convictions of the truth of Christianity for some days, till one evening while watching her mistress she was suddenly taken very ill; her limbs tottered under her, and she sank fainting by the bedside of the sick woman.

"Poor Sarah," said the neighbors; "she is overcome with hard work and night watching." And then they carried her to the hospital for the sick poor. There she died; and they bore her to her resting-place in the earth, but not to the churchyard of the Christians. There was no place for the Jewish girl; but they dug a grave for her outside the wall. And God's sun, which shines upon the graves of the churchyard of the Christians, also throws its beams on the grave of the Jewish maiden beyond the wall. And when the psalms of the Christians sound across the churchyard, their echo reaches her lonely resting-place; and she who sleeps there will be counted worthy at the resurrection, through the name of Christ the Lord, who said to His disciples, "John baptized you with water, but I will baptize you with the Holy Ghost."

The Old Bachelor's Nightcap

THERE IS A street in Copenhagen with a very strange name. It is called "Hysken" street. Where the name came from, and what it means is very uncertain. It is said to be German, but that is unjust to the Germans, for it would then be called "Hauschen," not "Hysken." "Hauschen," means a little house; and for many years it consisted only of a few small houses, which were scarcely larger than the wooden booths we see in the market-places at fair time. They were perhaps a little higher, and had windows; but the panes consisted of horn or bladder-skins, for glass was then too dear to have glazed windows in every house. This was a long time ago, so long indeed that our grandfathers, and even great-grandfathers, would speak of those days as "olden times;" indeed, many centuries have passed since then.

The rich merchants in Bremen and Lubeck, who carried on trade in Copenhagen, did not reside in the town themselves, but sent their clerks, who dwelt in the wooden booths in the Hauschen street, and sold beer and spices. The German beer was very good, and there were many sorts – from Bremen, Prussia, and Brunswick – and quantities of all sorts of spices, saffron, aniseed, ginger, and especially pepper; indeed, pepper was almost the chief article sold here; so it happened at last that the German clerks in Denmark got their nickname of "pepper gentry." It had been made a condition with these clerks that they should not marry; so that those who lived to be old had to take care of themselves, to attend to their own comforts, and even to light their own fires, when they had any to light. Many of them were very aged; lonely old boys, with strange thoughts and eccentric habits. From this, all unmarried men, who have attained a certain age, are called, in Denmark, "pepper gentry;" and this must be remembered by all those who wish to understand the story. These "pepper gentlemen," or, as they are called in England, "old bachelors," are often made a butt of ridicule; they are told to put on their nightcaps, draw them over their eyes, and go to sleep. The boys in Denmark make a song of it, thus: –

> *"Poor old bachelor, cut your wood,*
> *Such a nightcap was never seen;*
> *Who would think it was ever clean?*
> *Go to sleep, it will do you good."*

So they sing about the "pepper gentleman;" so do they make sport of the poor old bachelor and his nightcap, and all because they really know nothing of either. It is a cap that no one need wish for, or laugh at. And why not? Well, we shall hear in the story.

In olden times, Hauschen Street was not paved, and passengers would stumble out of one hole into another, as they generally do in unfrequented highways; and the street was so narrow, and the booths leaning against each other were so close together, that in the summer time a sail would be stretched across the street from one booth to another opposite. At these times the odor of the pepper, saffron, and ginger became more powerful than ever. Behind the counter, as a rule, there were no young men. The clerks were almost all old boys; but they did not dress as we are accustomed to see old men represented, wearing wigs, nightcaps, and knee-breeches, and with coat and waistcoat buttoned up to the chin. We have seen the portraits of our great-grandfathers dressed in this way; but the "pepper gentlemen" had no money to spare to have their portraits taken, though one of them would have made a very interesting picture for us now, if taken as he appeared standing behind his counter, or going to church, or on holidays. On these occasions, they wore high-crowned, broad-brimmed hats, and sometimes a younger clerk would stick a feather in his. The woollen shirt was concealed by a broad, linen collar; the close jacket was buttoned up to the chin, and the cloak hung loosely over it; the trousers were tucked into the broad, tipped shoes, for the clerks wore no stockings. They generally stuck a table-knife and spoon in their girdles, as well as a larger knife, as a protection to themselves; and such a weapon was often very necessary.

After this fashion was Anthony dressed on holidays and festivals, excepting that, instead of a high-crowned hat, he wore a kind of bonnet, and under it a knitted cap, a regular nightcap, to which he was so accustomed that it was always on his head; he had two, nightcaps I mean, not heads. Anthony was one of the oldest of the clerks, and just the subject for a painter. He was as thin as a lath, wrinkled round the mouth and eyes, had long, bony fingers, bushy, gray eyebrows, and over his left eye hung a thick tuft of hair, which did not look handsome, but made his appearance very remarkable. People knew that he came from Bremen; it was not exactly his home, although his master resided there. His ancestors were from Thuringia, and had lived in the town of Eisenach, close by Wartburg. Old Anthony seldom spoke of this place, but he thought of it all the more.

The old clerks of Hauschen Street very seldom met together; each one remained in his own booth, which was closed early enough in the evening, and then it looked dark and dismal out in the street. Only a faint glimmer of light struggled through the horn panes in the little window on the roof, while within sat the old clerk, generally on his bed, singing his evening hymn in a low voice; or he would be moving about in his booth till late in the night, busily employed in many things. It certainly was not a very lively existence. To be a stranger in a strange land is a bitter lot; no one notices you unless you happen to stand in their way. Often, when it was dark night outside, with rain or snow falling, the place looked quite deserted and gloomy. There were no lamps in the street, excepting a very small one, which hung at one end of the street, before a picture of the Virgin, which had been painted on the wall. The dashing of the water against the bulwarks of a neighboring castle could plainly be heard. Such evenings are long and dreary, unless people can find something to do; and so Anthony found it. There were not always things to be packed or unpacked, nor paper bags to be made, nor the scales to be polished. So Anthony invented employment; he mended his clothes and patched his boots, and when he at last went to bed, – his nightcap, which he had worn from habit, still remained on his head; he had only to pull it down a little farther over his forehead. Very soon, however, it would be pushed up again to see if the light was properly put out; he would touch it, press the wick together, and at last pull his nightcap over his eyes and lie down again on the other side. But often there would arise in his mind a doubt as to whether every coal had been quite put out in the little fire-pan in the shop below. If even a tiny spark had remained it might set fire to something, and cause great damage. Then he would rise from his bed, creep down the ladder – for it could scarcely be called a flight of stairs – and when he reached the fire-pan not a spark could be seen; so he had just to go back again to bed. But often, when he had got half way back, he would fancy the iron shutters of the door were not properly fastened, and his thin legs would carry him down again. And when at last he crept into bed, he would be so cold that his teeth chattered in his head. He would draw the coverlet closer round him, pull his nightcap over his eyes, and try to turn his thoughts from trade, and from the labors of the day, to olden times. But this was scarcely an agreeable entertainment; for thoughts of olden memories raise the curtains from the past, and sometimes pierce the heart with painful recollections till the agony brings tears to the waking eyes. And so it was with Anthony; often the scalding tears, like pearly drops, would fall from his eyes to the coverlet and roll on the floor with a sound as if one of his heartstrings had broken. Sometimes, with a lurid flame, memory would light up a picture of life which had never faded from his heart. If he dried his eyes with his nightcap, then the tear and the picture would be crushed; but the source of the tears remained and welled up again in his heart. The pictures did not follow one another in order, as the circumstances they represented had occurred; very often the most painful would come together, and when those came which were most full of joy, they had always the deepest shadow thrown upon them.

The beech woods of Denmark are acknowledged by every one to be very beautiful, but more beautiful still in the eyes of old Anthony were the beech woods in the neighborhood of Wartburg. More grand and venerable to him seemed the old oaks around the proud baronial castle, where the creeping plants hung over the stony summits of the rocks; sweeter was the perfume there of the apple-blossom than in all the land of Denmark. How vividly were represented to him, in a glittering tear that rolled down his cheek, two children at play – a boy and a girl. The boy had rosy cheeks, golden ringlets, and clear, blue eyes; he was the son of Anthony, a rich merchant; it was himself. The little girl had brown eyes and black hair, and was clever and courageous; she was the mayor's daughter, Molly. The children were playing with an apple; they shook the apple, and heard the pips rattling in it. Then they cut it in two, and each of them took half. They also divided the pips and ate all but one, which the little girl proposed should be placed in the ground.

"You will see what will come out," she said; "something you don't expect. A whole apple-tree will come out, but not directly." Then they got a flower-pot, filled it with earth, and were soon both very busy and eager about it. The boy made a hole in the earth with his finger, and the little girl placed the pip in the hole, and then they both covered it over with earth.

"Now you must not take it out to-morrow to see if it has taken root," said Molly; "no one ever should do that. I did so with my flowers, but only twice; I wanted to see if they were growing. I didn't know any better then, and the flowers all died."

Little Anthony kept the flower-pot, and every morning during the whole winter he looked at it, but there was nothing to be seen but black earth. At last, however, the spring came, and the sun shone warm again, and then two little green leaves sprouted forth in the pot.

"They are Molly and me," said the boy. "How wonderful they are, and so beautiful!"

Very soon a third leaf made its appearance.

"Who does that stand for?" thought he, and then came another and another. Day after day, and week after week, till the plant became quite a tree. And all this about the two children was mirrored to old Anthony in a single tear, which could soon be wiped away and disappear, but might come again from its source in the heart of the old man.

In the neighborhood of Eisenach stretches a ridge of stony mountains, one of which has a rounded outline, and shows itself above the rest without tree, bush, or grass on its barren summits. It is called the "Venus Mountain," and the story goes that the "Lady Venus," one of the heathen goddesses, keeps house there. She is also called "Lady Halle," as every child round Eisenach well knows. She it was who enticed the noble knight, Tannhauser, the minstrel, from the circle of singers at Wartburg into her mountain.

Little Molly and Anthony often stood by this mountain, and one day Molly said, "Do you dare to knock and say, 'Lady Halle, Lady Halle, open the door: Tannhauser is here!'" But Anthony did not dare. Molly, however, did, though she only said the words, "Lady Halle, Lady Halle," loudly and distinctly; the rest she muttered so much under her breath that Anthony felt certain she had really said nothing; and yet she looked quite bold and saucy, just as she did sometimes when she was in the garden with a number of other little girls; they would all stand round him together, and want to kiss him, because he did not like to be kissed, and pushed them away. Then Molly was the only one who dared to resist him. "I may kiss him," she would say proudly, as she threw her arms round his neck; she was vain of her power over Anthony, for he would submit quietly and think nothing of it. Molly was very charming, but rather bold; and how she did tease!

They said Lady Halle was beautiful, but her beauty was that of a tempting fiend. Saint Elizabeth, the tutelar saint of the land, the pious princess of Thuringia, whose good deeds have been immortalized in so many places through stories and legends, had greater beauty and more real grace. Her picture hung in the chapel, surrounded by silver lamps; but it did not in the least resemble Molly.

The apple-tree, which the two children had planted, grew year after year, till it became so large that it had to be transplanted into the garden, where the dew fell and the sun shone warmly. And there it increased in strength so much as to be able to withstand the cold of winter; and after passing through the severe weather, it seemed to put forth its blossoms in spring for very joy that the cold season had gone. In autumn it produced two apples, one for Molly and one for Anthony; it could not well do less. The tree after this grew very rapidly, and Molly grew with the tree. She was as fresh as an apple-blossom, but Anthony was not to behold this flower for long. All things change; Molly's father left his old home, and Molly went with him far away. In our time, it would be only a journey of a few hours, but then it took more than a day and a night to travel so far eastward from Eisenbach to a town still called Weimar, on the borders of Thuringia. And Molly and Anthony both wept, but these tears all flowed together into one tear which had the rosy shimmer of joy. Molly had told him that she loved him – loved him more than all the splendors of Weimar.

One, two, three years went by, and during the whole time he received only two letters. One came by the carrier, and the other a traveller brought. The way was very long and difficult, with many turnings and windings through towns and villages. How often had Anthony and Molly heard the story of Tristan and Isolda, and Anthony had thought the story applied to him, although Tristan means born in sorrow, which Anthony certainly was not; nor was it likely he would ever say of Molly as Tristan said of Isolda, "She has forgotten me." But in truth, Isolda had not forgotten him, her faithful friend; and when both were laid in their graves, one, on each side of the church, the linden-trees that grew by each grave spread over the roof, and, bending towards each other, mingled their blossoms together. Anthony thought it a very beautiful but mournful story; yet he never feared anything so sad would happen to him and Molly, as he passed the spot, whistling the air of a song, composed by the minstrel Walter, called the "Willow bird," beginning –

"Under the linden-trees,
Out on the heath."

One stanza pleased him exceedingly –

"Through the forest, and in the vale,
Sweetly warbles the nightingale."

This song was often in his mouth, and he sung or whistled it on a moonlight night, when he rode on horseback along the deep, hollow way, on his road to Weimar, to visit Molly. He wished to arrive unexpectedly, and so indeed he did. He was received with a hearty welcome, and introduced to plenty of grand and pleasant company, where overflowing winecups were passed about. A pretty room and a good bed were provided for him, and yet his reception was not what he had expected and dreamed it would be. He could not comprehend his own feelings nor the feelings of others; but it is easily understood how a person can be admitted into a house or a family without becoming one of them. We converse in company with those we meet, as we converse with our fellow-travellers in a stage-coach, on a journey; we know nothing of them, and perhaps all the while we are incommoding one another, and each is wishing himself or his neighbor away. Something of this kind Anthony felt when Molly talked to him of old times.

"I am a straightforward girl," she said, "and I will tell you myself how it is. There have been great changes since we were children together; everything is different, both inwardly and outwardly. We cannot control our wills, nor the feelings of our hearts, by the force of custom. Anthony, I would not, for the world, make an enemy of you when I am far away. Believe me, I entertain for you the kindest wishes in my heart; but to feel for you what I now know can be felt for another man, can never be. You must try and reconcile yourself to this. Farewell, Anthony."

Anthony also said, "Farewell." Not a tear came into his eye; he felt he was no longer Molly's friend. Hot iron and cold iron alike take the skin from our lips, and we feel the same sensation if we kiss either; and Anthony's kiss was now the kiss of hatred, as it had once been the kiss of love. Within four-and-twenty hours Anthony was back again to Eisenach, though the horse that he rode was entirely ruined.

"What matters it?" said he; "I am ruined also. I will destroy everything that can remind me of her, or of Lady Halle, or Lady Venus, the heathen woman. I will break down the apple-tree, and tear it up by the roots; never more shall it blossom or bear fruit."

The apple-tree was not broken down; for Anthony himself was struck with a fever, which caused him to break down, and confined him to his bed. But something occurred to raise him up again. What was it? A medicine was offered to him, which he was obliged to take: a bitter remedy, at which the sick body and the oppressed spirit alike shuddered. Anthony's father lost all his property, and, from being known as one of the richest merchants, he became very poor. Dark days, heavy trials, with poverty at the door, came rolling into the house upon them like the waves of the sea. Sorrow and suffering deprived Anthony's father of his strength, so that he had something else to think of besides nursing his love-sorrows and his anger against Molly. He had to take his father's place, to give orders, to act with energy, to help, and, at last, to go out into the world and earn his bread. Anthony went to Bremen, and there he learnt what poverty and hard living really were. These things often harden the character, but sometimes soften the heart, even too much.

How different the world, and the people in it, appeared to Anthony now, to what he had thought in his childhood! What to him were the minstrel's songs? An echo of the past, sounds long vanished. At times he would think in this way; yet again and again the songs would sound in his soul, and his heart become gentle and pious.

"God's will is the best," he would then say. "It was well that I was not allowed to keep my power over Molly's heart, and that she did not remain true to me. How I should have felt it now, when fortune has deserted me! She left me before she knew of the change in my circumstances, or had a thought of what was before me. That is a merciful providence for me. All has happened for the best. She could not help it, and yet I have been so bitter, and in such enmity against her."

Years passed by: Anthony's father died, and strangers lived in the old house. He had seen it once again since then. His rich master sent him journeys on business, and on one occasion his way led him to his native town of Eisenach. The old Wartburg castle stood unchanged on the rock where the monk and the nun were hewn out of the stone. The great oaks formed an outline to the scene which he so well remembered in his childhood. The Venus mountain stood out gray and bare, overshadowing the valley beneath. He would have been glad to call out "Lady Halle, Lady Halle, unlock the mountain. I would fain remain here always in my native soil." That was a sinful thought, and he offered a prayer to drive it away. Then a little bird in the thicket sang out clearly, and old Anthony thought of the minstrel's song. How much came back to his remembrance as he looked through the tears once more on his native town! The old house was still standing as in olden times, but the garden had been greatly altered; a pathway led through a portion of the ground, and outside the garden, and beyond the path, stood the old apple-tree, which he had not broken down, although he talked of doing so in his trouble. The sun still threw its rays upon the tree, and the refreshing dew fell upon it as of old; and it was so overloaded with fruit that the branches bent towards the earth with the weight. "That flourishes still," said he, as he gazed. One of the branches of the tree had, however, been broken: mischievous hands must have done this in passing, for the tree now stood in a public thoroughfare. "The blossoms are often plucked," said Anthony; "the fruit is stolen and the branches broken without a thankful thought of their profusion and beauty. It might be said of a tree, as it has been said of some men – it was not predicted at his cradle that he should come to this. How brightly began the history of this tree, and what is it now? Forsaken and forgotten, in a garden by a hedge in a field, and close to a public road. There it stands, unsheltered, plundered, and broken. It certainly has not yet withered; but in the course of years the number of blossoms from time to time will grow less, and at last it was cease altogether to bear fruit; and then its history will be over."

Such were Anthony's thoughts as he stood under the tree, and during many a long night as he lay in his lonely chamber in the wooden house in Hauschen Street, Copenhagen, in the foreign land to which the rich merchant of Bremen, his employer, had sent him on condition that he should never marry. "Marry! ha, ha!" and he laughed bitterly to himself at the thought.

Winter one year set in early, and it was freezing hard. Without, a snowstorm made every one remain at home who could do so. Thus it happened that Anthony's neighbors, who lived opposite to him, did not notice that his house remained unopened for two days, and that he had not showed himself during that time, for who would go out in such weather unless he were obliged to do so. They were gray, gloomy days, and in the house whose windows were not glass, twilight and dark nights reigned in turns. During these two days old Anthony had not left his bed, he had not the strength to do so. The bitter weather had for some time affected his limbs. There lay the old bachelor, forsaken by all, and unable to help himself. He could scarcely reach the water jug that he had placed by his bed, and the last drop was gone. It was not fever, nor sickness, but old age, that had laid him low. In the little corner, where his bed lay, he was over-shadowed as it were by perpetual night. A little spider, which he could however not see, busily and cheerfully spun its web above him, so that there should be a kind of little banner waving over the old man, when his eyes closed. The time passed slowly and painfully. He had no tears to shed, and he felt no pain; no thought of Molly came into his mind. He felt as if the world was now nothing to him, as if he were lying beyond it, with no one to think of him. Now and then he felt slight sensations of hunger and thirst; but no one came to him, no one tended him. He thought of all those who had once suffered from starvation, of Saint Elizabeth, who once wandered on the earth, the saint of his home and his childhood, the noble Duchess of Thuringia, that highly esteemed lady who visited the poorest villages, bringing hope and relief to the sick inmates. The recollection of her pious deeds was as light to the soul of poor Anthony. He thought of her as she went about speaking words of comfort, binding up the wounds of the afflicted and feeding the hungry, although often blamed for it by her stern husband. He remembered a story told of her, that on one occasion, when she was carrying a basket full of wine and provisions, her husband, who had watched her footsteps, stepped forward and asked her angrily what she carried in her basket, whereupon, with fear and trembling, she answered, "Roses, which I have plucked from the garden." Then he tore away the cloth which covered the basket, and what could equal the surprise of the pious woman, to find that by a miracle, everything in her basket – the wine, the bread – had all been changed into roses.

In this way the memory of the kind lady dwelt in the calm mind of Anthony. She was as a living reality in his little dwelling in the Danish land. He uncovered his face that he might look into her gentle eyes, while everything around him changed from its look of poverty and want, to a bright rose tint. The fragrance of roses spread through the room, mingled with the sweet smell of apples. He saw the branches of an apple-tree spreading above him. It was the tree which he and Molly had planted together. The fragrant leaves of the tree fell upon him and cooled his burning brow; upon his parched lips they seemed like refreshing bread and wine; and as they rested on his breast, a peaceful calm stole over him, and he felt inclined to sleep. "I shall sleep now," he whispered to himself. "Sleep will do me good. In the morning I shall be upon my feet again, strong and well. Glorious! wonderful! That apple-tree, planted in love, now appears before me in heavenly beauty." And he slept.

The following day, the third day during which his house had been closed, the snow-storm ceased. Then his opposite neighbor stepped over to the house in which old Anthony lived, for he had not yet showed himself. There he lay stretched on his bed, dead, with his old nightcap tightly clasped in his two hands. The nightcap, however, was not placed on his head in his coffin; he had a clean white one on then. Where now were the tears he had shed? What had become of those wonderful pearls? They were in the nightcap still. Such tears as these cannot be washed out, even when the nightcap is forgotten. The old thoughts and dreams of a bachelor's nightcap still remain. Never wish for such a nightcap. It would make your forehead hot, cause your pulse to beat with agitation, and conjure up dreams which would appear realities.

The first who wore old Anthony's cap felt the truth of this, though it was half a century afterwards. That man was the mayor himself, who had already made a comfortable home for his wife and eleven children, by his industry. The moment he put the cap on he dreamed of unfortunate love, of bankruptcy, and of dark days. "Hallo! how the nightcap burns!" he exclaimed, as he tore it from his bead. Then a pearl rolled out, and then another, and another, and they glittered and sounded as they fell. "What can this be? Is it paralysis, or something dazzling my eyes?" They were the tears which old Anthony had shed half a century before.

To every one who afterwards put this cap on his head, came visions and dreams which agitated him not a little. His own history was changed into that of Anthony till it became quite a story, and many stories might be made by others, so we will leave them to relate their own. We have told the first; and our last word is, don't wish for a "bachelor's nightcap."

The Emperor's New Clothes

MANY, MANY YEARS ago lived an emperor, who thought so much of new clothes that he spent all his money in order to obtain them; his only ambition was to be always well dressed. He did not care for his soldiers, and the theatre did not amuse him; the only thing, in fact, he thought anything of was to drive out and show a new suit of clothes. He had a coat for every hour of the day; and as one would say of a king "He is in his cabinet," so one could say of him, "The emperor is in his dressing-room."

The great city where he resided was very gay; every day many strangers from all parts of the globe arrived. One day two swindlers came to this city; they made people believe that they were weavers, and declared they could manufacture the finest cloth to be imagined. Their colors and patterns, they said, were not only exceptionally beautiful, but the clothes made of their material possessed the wonderful quality of being invisible to any man who was unfit for his office or unpardonably stupid.

"That must be wonderful cloth," thought the emperor. "If I were to be dressed in a suit made of this cloth I should be able to find out which men in my empire were unfit for their places, and I could distinguish the clever from the stupid. I must have this cloth woven for me without delay." And he gave a large sum of money to the swindlers, in advance, that they should set to work without any loss of time. They set up two looms, and pretended to be very hard at work, but they did nothing whatever on the looms. They asked for the finest silk and the most precious gold-cloth; all they got they did away with, and worked at the empty looms till late at night.

"I should very much like to know how they are getting on with the cloth," thought the emperor. But he felt rather uneasy when he remembered that he who was not fit for his office could not see it. Personally, he was of opinion that he had nothing to fear, yet he thought it advisable to send somebody else first to see how matters stood. Everybody in the town knew what a remarkable quality the stuff possessed, and all were anxious to see how bad or stupid their neighbors were.

"I shall send my honest old minister to the weavers," thought the emperor. "He can judge best how the stuff looks, for he is intelligent, and nobody understands his office better than he."

The good old minister went into the room where the swindlers sat before the empty looms. "Heaven preserve us!" he thought, and opened his eyes wide, "I cannot see anything at all," but he did not say so. Both swindlers requested him to come near, and asked him if he did not admire the exquisite pattern and the beautiful colors, pointing to the empty looms. The poor old minister tried his very best, but he could see nothing, for there was nothing to be seen. "Oh dear," he thought, "can I be so stupid? I should never have thought so, and nobody must know it! Is it possible that I am not fit for my office? No, no, I cannot say that I was unable to see the cloth."

"Now, have you got nothing to say?" said one of the swindlers, while he pretended to be busily weaving.

"Oh, it is very pretty, exceedingly beautiful," replied the old minister looking through his glasses. "What a beautiful pattern, what brilliant colors! I shall tell the emperor that I like the cloth very much."

"We are pleased to hear that," said the two weavers, and described to him the colors and explained the curious pattern. The old minister listened attentively, that he might relate to the emperor what they said; and so he did.

Now the swindlers asked for more money, silk and gold-cloth, which they required for weaving. They kept everything for themselves, and not a thread came near the loom, but they continued, as hitherto, to work at the empty looms.

Soon afterwards the emperor sent another honest courtier to the weavers to see how they were getting on, and if the cloth was nearly finished. Like the old minister, he looked and looked but could see nothing, as there was nothing to be seen.

"Is it not a beautiful piece of cloth?" asked the two swindlers, showing and explaining the magnificent pattern, which, however, did not exist.

"I am not stupid," said the man. "It is therefore my good appointment for which I am not fit. It is very strange, but I must not let any one know it;" and he praised the cloth, which he did not see, and expressed his joy at the beautiful colors and the fine pattern. "It is very excellent," he said to the emperor.

Everybody in the whole town talked about the precious cloth. At last the emperor wished to see it himself, while it was still on the loom. With a number of courtiers, including the two who had already been there, he went to the two clever swindlers, who now worked as hard as they could, but without using any thread.

"Is it not magnificent?" said the two old statesmen who had been there before. "Your Majesty must admire the colors and the pattern." And then they pointed to the empty looms, for they imagined the others could see the cloth.

"What is this?" thought the emperor, "I do not see anything at all. That is terrible! Am I stupid? Am I unfit to be emperor? That would indeed be the most dreadful thing that could happen to me."

"Really," he said, turning to the weavers, "your cloth has our most gracious approval;" and nodding contentedly he looked at the empty loom, for he did not like to say that he saw nothing. All his attendants, who were with him, looked and looked, and although they could not see anything more than the others, they said, like the emperor, "It is very beautiful." And all advised him to wear the new magnificent clothes at a great procession which was soon to take place. "It is magnificent, beautiful, excellent," one heard them say; everybody seemed to be delighted, and the emperor appointed the two swindlers "Imperial Court weavers."

The whole night previous to the day on which the procession was to take place, the swindlers pretended to work, and burned more than sixteen candles. People should see that they were busy to finish the emperor's new suit. They pretended to take the cloth from the loom, and worked about in the air with big scissors, and sewed with needles without thread, and said at last: "The emperor's new suit is ready now."

The emperor and all his barons then came to the hall; the swindlers held their arms up as if they held something in their hands and said: "These are the trousers!" "This is the coat!" and "Here is the cloak!" and so on. "They are all as light as a cobweb, and one must feel as if one had nothing at all upon the body; but that is just the beauty of them."

"Indeed!" said all the courtiers; but they could not see anything, for there was nothing to be seen.

"Does it please your Majesty now to graciously undress," said the swindlers, "that we may assist your Majesty in putting on the new suit before the large looking-glass?"

The emperor undressed, and the swindlers pretended to put the new suit upon him, one piece after another; and the emperor looked at himself in the glass from every side.

"How well they look! How well they fit!" said all. "What a beautiful pattern! What fine colors! That is a magnificent suit of clothes!"

The master of the ceremonies announced that the bearers of the canopy, which was to be carried in the procession, were ready.

"I am ready," said the emperor. "Does not my suit fit me marvelously?" Then he turned once more to the looking-glass, that people should think he admired his garments.

The chamberlains, who were to carry the train, stretched their hands to the ground as if they lifted up a train, and pretended to hold something in their hands; they did not like people to know that they could not see anything.

The emperor marched in the procession under the beautiful canopy, and all who saw him in the street and out of the windows exclaimed: "Indeed, the emperor's new suit is incomparable! What a long train he has! How well it fits him!" Nobody wished to let others know he saw nothing, for then he would have been unfit for his office or too stupid. Never emperor's clothes were more admired.

"But he has nothing on at all," said a little child at last. "Good heavens! listen to the voice of an innocent child," said the father, and one whispered to the other what the child had said. "But he has nothing on at all," cried at last the whole people. That made a deep impression upon the emperor, for it seemed to him that they were right; but he thought to himself, "Now I must bear up to the end." And the chamberlains walked with still greater dignity, as if they carried the train which did not exist.

Anne Lisbeth

ANNE LISBETH WAS a beautiful young woman, with a red and white complexion, glittering white teeth, and clear soft eyes; and her footstep was light in the dance, but her mind was lighter still. She had a little child, not at all pretty; so he was put out to be nursed by a laborer's wife, and his mother went to the count's castle. She sat in splendid rooms, richly decorated with silk and velvet; not a breath of air was allowed to blow upon her, and no one was allowed to speak to her harshly, for she was nurse to the count's child. He was fair and delicate as a prince, and beautiful as an angel; and how she loved this child! Her own boy was provided for by being at the laborer's where the mouth watered more frequently than the pot boiled, and where in general no one was at home to take care of the child. Then he would cry, but what nobody knows nobody cares for; so he would cry till he was tired, and then fall asleep; and while we are asleep we can feel neither hunger nor thirst. Ah, yes; sleep is a capital invention.

As years went on, Anne Lisbeth's child grew apace like weeds, although they said his growth had been stunted. He had become quite a member of the family in which he dwelt; they received money to keep him, so that his mother got rid of him altogether. She had become quite a lady; she had a comfortable home of her own in the town; and out of doors, when she went for a walk, she wore a bonnet; but she never walked out to see the laborer: that was too far from the town, and, indeed, she had nothing to go for, the boy now belonged to these laboring people. He had food, and he could also do something towards earning his living; he took care of Mary's red cow, for he knew how to tend cattle and make himself useful.

The great dog by the yard gate of a nobleman's mansion sits proudly on the top of his kennel when the sun shines, and barks at every one that passes; but if it rains, he creeps into his house, and there he is warm and dry. Anne Lisbeth's boy also sat in the sunshine on the top of the fence, cutting out a little toy. If it was spring-time, he knew of three strawberry-plants in blossom, which would certainly bear fruit. This was his most hopeful thought, though it often came to nothing. And he had to sit out in the rain in the worst weather, and get wet to the skin, and let the cold wind dry the clothes on his back afterwards. If he went near the farmyard belonging to the count, he was pushed and knocked about, for the men and the maids said he was so horrible ugly; but he was used to all this, for nobody loved him. This was how the world treated Anne Lisbeth's boy, and how could it be otherwise. It was his fate to be beloved by no one. Hitherto he had been a land crab; the land at last cast him adrift. He went to sea in a wretched vessel, and sat at the helm, while the skipper sat over the grog-can. He was dirty and ugly, half-frozen and half-starved; he always looked as if he never had enough to eat, which was really the case.

Late in the autumn, when the weather was rough, windy, and wet, and the cold penetrated through the thickest clothing, especially at sea, a wretched boat went out to sea with only two men on board, or, more correctly, a man and a half, for it was the skipper and his boy. There had only been a kind of twilight all day, and it soon grew quite dark, and so bitterly cold, that the skipper took a dram to warm him. The bottle was old, and the glass too. It was perfect in the upper part, but the foot was broken off, and it had therefore been fixed upon a little carved block of wood, painted blue. A dram is a great comfort, and two are better still, thought the skipper, while the boy sat at the helm, which he held fast in his hard seamed hands. He was ugly, and his hair was matted, and he looked crippled and stunted; they called him the field-laborer's boy, though in the church register he was entered as Anne Lisbeth's son. The wind cut through the rigging, and the boat cut through the sea. The sails, filled by the wind, swelled out and carried them along in wild career. It was wet and rough above and below, and might still be worse. Hold! what is that? What has struck the boat? Was it a waterspout, or a heavy sea rolling suddenly upon them?

"Heaven help us!" cried the boy at the helm, as the boat heeled over and lay on its beam ends. It had struck on a rock, which rose from the depths of the sea, and sank at once, like an old shoe in a puddle. "It sank at once with mouse and man," as the saying is. There might have been mice on board, but only one man and a half, the skipper and the laborer's boy. No one saw it but the skimming sea-gulls and the fishes beneath the water; and even they did not see it properly, for they darted back with terror as the boat filled with water and sank. There it lay, scarcely a fathom below the surface, and those two were provided for, buried, and forgotten. The glass with the foot of blue wood was the only thing that did not sink, for the wood floated and the glass drifted away to be cast upon the shore and broken; where and when, is indeed of no consequence. It had served its purpose, and it had been loved, which Anne Lisbeth's boy had not been. But in heaven no soul will be able to say, "Never loved."

Anne Lisbeth had now lived in the town many years; she was called "Madame," and felt dignified in consequence; she remembered the old, noble days, in which she had driven in the carriage, and had associated with countess and baroness. Her beautiful, noble child had been a dear angel, and possessed the kindest heart; he had loved her so much, and she had loved him in return; they had kissed and loved each other, and the boy had been her joy, her second life. Now he was fourteen years of age, tall, handsome, and clever. She had not seen him since she carried him in her arms; neither had she been for years to the count's palace; it was quite a journey thither from the town.

"I must make one effort to go," said Anne Lisbeth, "to see my darling, the count's sweet child, and press him to my heart. Certainly he must long to see me, too, the young count; no doubt he thinks of me and loves me, as in those days when he would fling his angel-arms round my neck, and lisp 'Anne Liz.' It was music to my ears. Yes, I must make an effort to see him again." She drove across the country in a grazier's cart, and then got out, and continued her journey on foot, and thus reached the count's castle. It was as great and magnificent as it had always been, and the garden looked the same as ever; all the servants were strangers to her, not one of them knew Anne Lisbeth, nor of what consequence she had once been there; but she felt sure the countess would soon let them know it, and her darling boy, too: how she longed to see him!

Now that Anne Lisbeth was at her journey's end, she was kept waiting a long time; and for those who wait, time passes slowly. But before the great people went in to dinner, she was called in and spoken to very graciously. She was to go in again after dinner, and then she would see her sweet boy once more. How tall, and slender, and thin he had grown; but the eyes and the sweet angel mouth were still beautiful. He looked at her, but he did not speak, he certainly did not know who she was. He turned round and was going away, but she seized his hand and pressed it to her lips.

"Well, well," he said; and with that he walked out of the room. He who filled her every thought! he whom she loved best, and who was her whole earthly pride!

Anne Lisbeth went forth from the castle into the public road, feeling mournful and sad; he whom she had nursed day and night, and even now carried about in her dreams, had been cold and strange, and had not a word or thought respecting her. A great black raven darted down in front of her on the high road, and croaked dismally.

"Ah," said she, "what bird of ill omen art thou?" Presently she passed the laborer's hut; his wife stood at the door, and the two women spoke to each other.

"You look well," said the woman; "you're fat and plump; you are well off."

"Oh yes," answered Anne Lisbeth.

"The boat went down with them," continued the woman; "Hans the skipper and the boy were both drowned; so there's an end of them. I always thought the boy would be able to help me with a few dollars. He'll never cost you anything more, Anne Lisbeth."

"So they were drowned," repeated Anne Lisbeth; but she said no more, and the subject was dropped. She felt very low-spirited, because her count-child had shown no inclination to speak to her who loved him so well, and who had travelled so far to see him. The journey had cost money too, and she had derived no great pleasure from it. Still she said not a word of all this; she could not relieve her heart by telling the laborer's wife, lest the latter should think she did not enjoy her former position at the castle. Then the raven flew over her, screaming again as he flew.

"The black wretch!" said Anne Lisbeth, "he will end by frightening me today." She had brought coffee and chicory with her, for she thought it would be a charity to the poor woman to give them to her to boil a cup of coffee, and then she would take a cup herself.

The woman prepared the coffee, and in the meantime Anne Lisbeth seated her in a chair and fell asleep. Then she dreamed of something which she had never dreamed before; singularly enough she dreamed of her own child, who had wept and hungered in the laborer's hut, and had been knocked about in heat and in cold, and who was now lying in the depths of the sea, in a spot only known by God. She fancied she was still sitting in the hut, where the woman was busy preparing the coffee, for she could smell the coffee-berries roasting. But suddenly it seemed to her that there stood on the threshold a beautiful young form, as beautiful as the count's child, and this apparition said to her, "The world is passing away; hold fast to me, for you are my mother after all; you have an angel in heaven, hold me fast;" and the child-angel stretched out his hand and seized her. Then there was a terrible crash, as of a world crumbling to pieces, and the angel-child was rising from the earth, and holding her by the sleeve so tightly that she felt herself lifted from the ground; but, on the other hand, something heavy hung to her feet and dragged her down, and it seemed as if hundreds of women were clinging to her, and crying, "If thou art to be saved, we must be saved too. Hold fast, hold fast." And then they all hung on her, but there were too many; and as they clung the sleeve was torn, and Anne Lisbeth fell down in horror, and awoke. Indeed she was on the point of falling over in reality with the chair on which she sat; but she was so startled and alarmed that she could not remember what she had dreamed, only that it was something very dreadful.

They drank their coffee and had a chat together, and then Anne Lisbeth went away towards the little town where she was to meet the carrier, who was to drive her back to her own home. But when she came to him she found that he would not be ready to start till the evening of the next day. Then she began to think of the expense, and what the distance would be to walk. She remembered that the route by the sea-shore was two miles shorter than by the high road; and as the weather was clear, and there would be moonlight, she determined to make her way on foot, and to start at once, that she might reach home the next day.

The sun had set, and the evening bells sounded through the air from the tower of the village church, but to her it was not the bells, but the cry of the frogs in the marshes. Then they ceased, and all around became still; not a bird could be heard, they were all at rest, even the owl had not left her hiding place; deep silence reigned on the margin of the wood by the sea-shore. As Anne Lisbeth walked on she could hear her own footsteps in the sands; even the waves of the sea were at rest, and all in the deep waters had sunk into silence. There was quiet among the dead and the living in the deep sea. Anne Lisbeth walked on, thinking of nothing at all, as people say, or rather her thoughts wandered, but not away from her, for thought is never absent from us, it only slumbers. Many thoughts that have lain dormant are roused at the proper time, and begin to stir in the mind and the heart, and seem even to come upon us from above. It is written, that a good deed bears a blessing for its fruit; and it is also written, that the wages of sin is death. Much has been said and much written which we pass over or know nothing of. A light arises within us, and then forgotten things make themselves remembered; and thus it was with Anne Lisbeth. The germ of every vice and every virtue lies in our heart, in yours and in mine; they lie like little grains of seed, till a ray of sunshine, or the touch of an evil hand, or you turn the corner to the right or to the left, and the decision is made. The little seed is stirred, it swells and shoots up, and pours its sap into your blood, directing your course either for good or evil. Troublesome thoughts often exist in the mind, fermenting there, which are not realized by us while the senses are as it were slumbering; but still they are there. Anne Lisbeth walked on thus with her senses half asleep, but the thoughts were fermenting within her.

From one Shrove Tuesday to another, much may occur to weigh down the heart; it is the reckoning of a whole year; much may be forgotten, sins against heaven in word and thought, sins against our neighbor, and against our own conscience. We are scarcely aware of their existence; and Anne Lisbeth did not think of any of her errors. She had committed no crime against the law of the land; she was an honorable person, in a good position – that she knew.

She continued her walk along by the margin of the sea. What was it she saw lying there? An old hat; a man's hat. Now when might that have been washed overboard? She drew nearer, she stopped to look at the hat; "Ha! what was lying yonder?" She shuddered; yet it was nothing save a heap of grass and tangled seaweed flung across a long stone, but it looked like a corpse. Only tangled grass, and yet she was frightened at it. As she turned to walk away, much came into her mind that she had heard in her childhood: old superstitions of spectres by the sea-shore; of the ghosts of drowned but unburied people, whose corpses had been washed up on the desolate beach. The body, she knew, could do no harm to any one, but the spirit could pursue the lonely wanderer, attach itself to him, and demand to be carried to the churchyard, that it might rest in consecrated ground. "Hold fast! hold fast!" the spectre would cry; and as Anne Lisbeth murmured these words to herself, the whole of her dream was suddenly recalled to her memory, when the mother had clung to her, and uttered these words, when, amid the crashing of worlds, her sleeve had been torn, and she had slipped from the grasp of her child, who wanted to hold her up in that terrible hour. Her child, her own child, which she had never loved, lay now buried in the sea, and might rise up, like a spectre, from the waters, and cry, "Hold fast; carry me to consecrated ground!"

As these thoughts passed through her mind, fear gave speed to her feet, so that she walked faster and faster. Fear came upon her as if a cold, clammy hand had been laid upon her heart, so that she almost fainted. As she looked across the sea, all there grew darker; a heavy mist came rolling onwards, and clung to bush and tree, distorting them into fantastic shapes. She turned and glanced at the moon, which had risen behind her. It looked like a pale, rayless surface, and a deadly weight seemed to hang upon her limbs. "Hold," thought she; and then she turned round a second time to look at the moon. A white face appeared quite close to her, with a mist, hanging like a garment from its shoulders. "Stop! carry me to consecrated earth," sounded in her ears, in strange, hollow tones. The sound did not come from frogs or ravens; she saw no sign of such creatures. "A grave! dig me a grave!" was repeated quite loud. Yes, it was indeed the spectre of her child. The child that lay beneath the ocean, and whose spirit could have no rest until it was carried to the churchyard, and until a grave had been dug for it in consecrated ground. She would go there at once, and there she would dig. She turned in the direction of the church, and the weight on her heart seemed to grow lighter, and even to vanish altogether; but when she turned to go home by the shortest way, it returned. "Stop! stop!" and the words came quite clear, though they were like the croak of a frog, or the wail of a bird. "A grave! dig me a grave!"

The mist was cold and damp, her hands and face were moist and clammy with horror, a heavy weight again seized her and clung to her, her mind became clear for thoughts that had never before been there.

In these northern regions, a beech-wood often buds in a single night and appears in the morning sunlight in its full glory of youthful green. So, in a single instant, can the consciousness of the sin that has been committed in thoughts, words, and actions of our past life, be unfolded to us. When once the conscience is awakened, it springs up in the heart spontaneously, and God awakens the conscience when we least expect it. Then we can find no excuse for ourselves; the deed is there and bears witness against us. The thoughts seem to become words, and to sound far out into the world. We are horrified at the thought of what we have carried within us, and at the consciousness that we have not overcome the evil which has its origin in thoughtlessness and pride. The heart conceals within itself the vices as well as the virtues, and they grow in the shallowest ground. Anne Lisbeth now experienced in thought what we have clothed in words. She was overpowered by them, and sank down and crept along for some distance on the ground. "A grave! dig me a grave!" sounded again in her ears, and she would have gladly buried herself, if in the grave she could have found forgetfulness of her actions.

It was the first hour of her awakening, full of anguish and horror. Superstition made her alternately shudder with cold or burn with the heat of fever. Many things, of which she had feared even to speak, came into her mind. Silently, as the cloud-shadows in the moonshine, a spectral apparition flitted by her; she had heard of it before. Close by her galloped four snorting steeds, with fire flashing from their eyes and nostrils. They dragged a burning coach, and within it sat the wicked lord of the manor, who had ruled there a hundred years before. The legend says that every night, at twelve o'clock, he drove into his castleyard and out again. He was not as pale as dead men are, but black as a coal. He nodded, and pointed to Anne Lisbeth, crying out, "Hold fast! hold fast! and then you may ride again in a nobleman's carriage, and forget your child."

She gathered herself up, and hastened to the churchyard; but black crosses and black ravens danced before her eyes, and she could not distinguish one from the other. The ravens croaked as the raven had done which she saw in the daytime, but now she understood what they said. "I am the raven-mother; I am the raven-mother," each raven croaked, and Anne Lisbeth felt that the name also applied to her; and she fancied she should be transformed into a black bird, and have to cry as they cried, if she did not dig the grave. And she threw herself upon the earth, and with her hands dug a grave in the hard ground, so that the blood ran from her fingers. "A grave! dig me a grave!" still sounded in her ears; she was fearful that the cock might crow, and the first red streak appear in the east, before she had finished her work; and then she would be lost. And the cock crowed, and the day dawned in the east, and the grave was only half dug. An icy hand passed over her head and face, and down towards her heart. "Only half a grave," a voice wailed, and fled away. Yes, it fled away over the sea; it was the ocean spectre; and, exhausted and overpowered, Anne Lisbeth sunk to the ground, and her senses left her.

It was a bright day when she came to herself, and two men were raising her up; but she was not lying in the churchyard, but on the sea-shore, where she had dug a deep hole in the sand, and cut her hand with a piece of broken glass, whose sharp stem was stuck in a little block of painted wood. Anne Lisbeth was in a fever. Conscience had roused the memories of superstitions, and had so acted upon her mind, that she fancied she had only half a soul, and that her child had taken the other half down into the sea. Never would she be able to cling to the mercy of Heaven till she had recovered this other half which was now held fast in the deep water.

Anne Lisbeth returned to her home, but she was no longer the woman she had been. Her thoughts were like a confused, tangled skein; only one thread, only one thought was clear to her, namely that she must carry the spectre of the sea-shore to the churchyard, and dig a grave for him there; that by so doing she might win back her soul. Many a night she was missed from her home, and was always found on the sea-shore waiting for the spectre.

In this way a whole year passed; and then one night she vanished again, and was not to be found. The whole of the next day was spent in a useless search after her.

Towards evening, when the clerk entered the church to toll the vesper bell, he saw by the altar Anne Lisbeth, who had spent the whole day there. Her powers of body were almost exhausted, but her eyes flashed brightly, and on her cheeks was a rosy flush. The last rays of the setting sun shone upon her, and gleamed over the altar upon the shining clasps of the Bible, which lay open at the words of the prophet Joel, "Rend your hearts and not your garments, and turn unto the Lord."

"That was just a chance," people said; but do things happen by chance? In the face of Anne Lisbeth, lighted up by the evening sun, could be seen peace and rest. She said she was happy now, for she had conquered. The spectre of the shore, her own child, had come to her the night before, and had said to her, "Thou hast dug me only half a grave: but thou hast now, for a year and a day, buried me altogether in thy heart, and it is there a mother can best hide her child!" And then he gave her back her lost soul, and brought her into the church. "Now I am in the house of God," she said, "and in that house we are happy."

When the sun set, Anne Lisbeth's soul had risen to that region where there is no more pain; and Anne Lisbeth's troubles were at an end.

The Philosopher's Stone

FAR AWAY TOWARDS the east, in India, which seemed in those days the world's end, stood the Tree of the Sun; a noble tree, such as we have never seen, and perhaps never may see.

The summit of this tree spread itself for miles like an entire forest, each of its smaller branches forming a complete tree. Palms, beech-trees, pines, plane-trees, and various other kinds, which are found in all parts of the world, were here like small branches, shooting forth from the great tree; while the larger boughs, with their knots and curves, formed valleys and hills, clothed with velvety green and covered with flowers. Everywhere it was like a blooming meadow or a lovely garden. Here were birds from all quarters of the world assembled together; birds from the primeval forests of America, from the rose gardens of Damascus, and from the deserts of Africa, in which the elephant and the lion may boast of being the only rulers. Birds from the Polar regions came flying here, and of course the stork and the swallow were not absent. But the birds were not the only living creatures. There were stags, squirrels, antelopes, and hundreds of other beautiful and light-footed animals here found a home.

The summit of the tree was a wide-spreading garden, and in the midst of it, where the green boughs formed a kind of hill, stood a castle of crystal, with a view from it towards every quarter of heaven. Each tower was erected in the form of a lily, and within the stem was a winding staircase, through which one could ascend to the top and step out upon the leaves as upon balconies. The calyx of the flower itself formed a most beautiful, glittering, circular hall, above which no other roof arose than the blue firmament and the sun and stars.

Just as much splendor, but of another kind, appeared below, in the wide halls of the castle. Here, on the walls, were reflected pictures of the world, which represented numerous and varied scenes of everything that took place daily, so that it was useless to read the newspapers, and indeed there were none to be obtained in this spot. All was to be seen in living pictures by those who wished it, but all would have been too much for even the wisest man, and this man dwelt here. His name is very difficult; you would not be able to pronounce it, so it may be omitted. He knew everything that a man on earth can know or imagine. Every invention already in existence or yet to be, was known to him, and much more; still everything on earth has a limit. The wise king Solomon was not half so wise as this man. He could govern the powers of nature and held sway over potent spirits; even Death itself was obliged to give him every morning a list of those who were to die during the day. And King Solomon himself had to die at last, and this fact it was which so often occupied the thoughts of this great man in the castle on the Tree of the Sun. He knew that he also, however high he might tower above other men in wisdom, must one day die. He knew that his children would fade away like the leaves of the forest and become dust. He saw the human race wither and fall like leaves from the tree; he saw new men come to fill their places, but the leaves that fell off never sprouted forth again; they crumbled to dust or were absorbed into other plants.

"What happens to man," asked the wise man of himself, "when touched by the angel of death? What can death be? The body decays, and the soul. Yes; what is the soul, and whither does it go?"

"To eternal life," says the comforting voice of religion.

"But what is this change? Where and how shall we exist?"

"Above; in heaven," answers the pious man; "it is there we hope to go."

"Above!" repeated the wise man, fixing his eyes upon the moon and stars above him. He saw that to this earthly sphere above and below were constantly changing places, and that the position varied according to the spot on which a man found himself. He knew, also, that even if he ascended to the top of the highest mountain which rears its lofty summit on this earth, the air, which to us seems clear and transparent, would there be dark and cloudy; the sun would have a coppery glow and send forth no rays, and our earth would lie beneath him wrapped in an orange-colored mist. How narrow are the limits which confine the bodily sight, and how little can be seen by the eye of the soul. How little do the wisest among us know of that which is so important to us all.

In the most secret chamber of the castle lay the greatest treasure on earth – the Book of Truth. The wise man had read it through page after page. Every man may read in this book, but only in fragments. To many eyes the characters seem so mixed in confusion that the words cannot be distinguished. On certain pages the writing often appears so pale or so blurred that the page becomes a blank. The wiser a man becomes, the more he will read, and those who are wisest read most.

The wise man knew how to unite the sunlight and the moonlight with the light of reason and the hidden powers of nature; and through this stronger light, many things in the pages were made clear to him. But in the portion of the book entitled "Life after Death" not a single point could he see distinctly. This pained him. Should he never be able here on earth to obtain a light by which everything written in the Book of Truth should become clear to him? Like the wise King Solomon, he understood the language of animals, and could interpret their talk into song; but that made him none the wiser. He found out the nature of plants and metals, and their power in curing diseases and arresting death, but none to destroy death itself. In all created things within his reach he sought the light that should shine upon the certainty of an eternal life, but he found it not. The Book of Truth lay open before him, but, its pages were to him as blank paper. Christianity placed before him in the Bible a promise of eternal life, but he wanted to read it in his book, in which nothing on the subject appeared to be written.

He had five children; four sons, educated as the children of such a wise father should be, and a daughter, fair, gentle, and intelligent, but she was blind; yet this deprivation appeared as nothing to her; her father and brothers were outward eyes to her, and a vivid imagination made everything clear to her mental sight. The sons had never gone farther from the castle than the branches of the trees extended, and the sister had scarcely ever left home. They were happy children in that home of their childhood, the beautiful and fragrant Tree of the Sun. Like all children, they loved to hear stories related to them, and their father told them many things which other children would not have understood; but these were as clever as most grownup people are among us. He explained to them what they saw in the pictures of life on the castle walls – the doings of man, and the progress of events in all the lands of the earth; and the sons often expressed a wish that they could be present, and take a part in these great deeds. Then their father told them that in the world there was nothing but toil and difficulty: that it was not quite what it appeared to them, as they looked upon it in their beautiful home. He spoke to them of the true, the beautiful, and the good, and told them that these three held together in the world, and by that union they became crystallized into a precious jewel, clearer than a diamond of the first water – a jewel, whose splendor had a value even in the sight of God, in whose brightness all things are dim. This jewel was called the philosopher's stone. He told them that, by searching, man could attain to a knowledge of the existence of God, and that it was in the power of every man to discover the certainty that such a jewel as the philosopher's stone really existed. This information would have been beyond the perception of other children; but these children understood, and others will learn to comprehend its meaning after a time. They questioned their father about the true, the beautiful, and the good, and he explained it to them in many ways. He told them that God, when He made man out of the dust of the earth, touched His work five times, leaving five intense feelings, which we call the five senses. Through these, the true, the beautiful, and the good are seen, understood, and perceived, and through these they are valued, protected, and encouraged. Five senses have been given mentally and corporeally, inwardly and outwardly, to body and soul.

The children thought deeply on all these things, and meditated upon them day and night. Then the eldest of the brothers dreamt a splendid dream. Strange to say, not only the second brother but also the third and fourth brothers all dreamt exactly the same thing; namely, that each went out into the world to find the philosopher's stone. Each dreamt that he found it, and that, as he rode back on his swift horse, in the morning dawn, over the velvety green meadows, to his home in the castle of his father, that the stone gleamed from his forehead like a beaming light; and threw such a bright radiance upon the pages of the Book of Truth that every word was illuminated which spoke of the life beyond the grave. But the sister had no dream of going out into the wide world; it never entered her mind. Her world was her father's house.

"I shall ride forth into the wide world," said the eldest brother. "I must try what life is like there, as I mix with men. I will practise only the good and true; with these I will protect the beautiful. Much shall be changed for the better while I am there."

Now these thoughts were great and daring, as our thoughts generally are at home, before we have gone out into the world, and encountered its storms and tempests, its thorns and its thistles. In him, and in all his brothers, the five senses were highly cultivated, inwardly and outwardly; but each of them had one sense which in keenness and development surpassed the other four. In the case of the eldest, this pre-eminent sense was sight, which he hoped would be of special service. He had eyes for all times and all people; eyes that could discover in the depths of the earth hidden treasures, and look into the hearts of men, as through a pane of glass; he could read more than is often seen on the cheek that blushes or grows pale, in the eye that droops or smiles. Stags and antelopes accompanied him to the western boundary of his home, and there he found the wild swans. These he followed, and found himself far away in the north, far from the land of his father, which extended eastward to the ends of the earth. How he opened his eyes with astonishment! How many things were to be seen here! and so different to the mere representation of pictures such as those in his father's house. At first he nearly lost his eyes in astonishment at the rubbish and mockery brought forward to represent the beautiful; but he kept his eyes, and soon found full employment for them. He wished to go thoroughly and honestly to work in his endeavor to understand the true, the beautiful, and the good. But how were they represented in the world? He observed that the wreath which rightly belonged to the beautiful was often given the hideous; that the good was often passed by unnoticed, while mediocrity was applauded, when it should have been hissed. People look at the dress, not at the wearer; thought more of a name than of doing their duty; and trusted more to reputation than to real service. It was everywhere the same.

"I see I must make a regular attack on these things," said he; and he accordingly did not spare them. But while looking for the truth, came the evil one, the father of lies, to intercept him. Gladly would the fiend have plucked out the eyes of this Seer, but that would have been a too straightforward path for him; he works more cunningly. He allowed the young man to seek for, and discover, the beautiful and the good; but while he was contemplating them, the evil spirit blew one mote after another into each of his eyes; and such a proceeding would injure the strongest sight. Then he blew upon the motes, and they became beams, so that the clearness of his sight was gone, and the Seer was like a blind man in the world, and had no longer any faith in it. He had lost his good opinion of the world, as well as of himself; and when a man gives up the world, and himself too, it is all over with him.

"All over," said the wild swan, who flew across the sea to the east.

"All over," twittered the swallows, who were also flying eastward towards the Tree of the Sun. It was no good news which they carried home.

"I think the Seer has been badly served," said the second brother, "but the Hearer may be more successful."

This one possessed the sense of hearing to a very high degree: so acute was this sense, that it was said he could hear the grass grow. He took a fond leave of all at home, and rode away, provided with good abilities and good intentions. The swallows escorted him, and he followed the swans till he found himself out in the world, and far away from home. But he soon discovered that one may have too much of a good thing. His hearing was too fine. He not only heard the grass grow, but could hear every man's heart beat, whether in sorrow or in joy. The whole world was to him like a clockmaker's great workshop, in which all the clocks were going "tick, tick," and all the turret clocks striking "ding, dong." It was unbearable. For a long time his ears endured it, but at last all the noise and tumult became too much for one man to bear.

There were rascally boys of sixty years old – for years do not alone make a man – who raised a tumult, which might have made the Hearer laugh, but for the applause which followed, echoing through every street and house, and was even heard in country roads. Falsehood thrust itself forward and played the hypocrite; the bells on the fool's cap jingled, and declared they were church-bells, and the noise became so bad for the Hearer that he thrust his fingers into his ears. Still, he could hear false notes and bad singing, gossip and idle words, scandal and slander, groaning and moaning, without and within. "Heaven help us!" He thrust his fingers farther and farther into his ears, till at last the drums burst. And now he could hear nothing more of the true, the beautiful, and the good; for his hearing was to have been the means by which he hoped to acquire his knowledge. He became silent and suspicious, and at last trusted no one, not even himself, and no longer hoping to find and bring home the costly jewel, he gave it up, and gave himself up too, which was worse than all.

The birds in their flight towards the east, carried the tidings, and the news reached the castle in the Tree of the Sun.

"I will try now," said the third brother; "I have a keen nose." Now that was not a very elegant expression, but it was his way, and we must take him as he was. He had a cheerful temper, and was, besides, a real poet; he could make many things appear poetical, by the way in which he spoke of them, and ideas struck him long before they occurred to the minds of others. "I can smell," he would say; and he attributed to the sense of smelling, which he possessed in a high degree, a great power in the region of the beautiful. "I can smell," he would say, "and many places are fragrant or beautiful according to the taste of the frequenters. One man feels at home in the atmosphere of the tavern, among the flaring tallow candles, and when the smell of spirits mingles with the fumes of bad tobacco. Another prefers sitting amidst the overpowering scent of jasmine, or perfuming himself with scented olive oil. This man seeks the fresh sea breeze, while that one climbs the lofty mountain-top, to look down upon the busy life in miniature beneath him."

As he spoke in this way, it seemed as if he had already been out in the world, as if he had already known and associated with man. But this experience was intuitive – it was the poetry within him, a gift from Heaven bestowed on him in his cradle. He bade farewell to his parental roof in the Tree of the Sun, and departed on foot, from the pleasant scenes that surrounded his home. Arrived at its confines, he mounted on the back of an ostrich, which runs faster than a horse, and afterwards, when he fell in with the wild swans, he swung himself on the strongest of them, for he loved change, and away he flew over the sea to distant lands, where there were great forests, deep lakes, lofty mountains, and proud cities. Wherever he came it seemed as if sunshine travelled with him across the fields, for every flower, every bush, exhaled a renewed fragrance, as if conscious that a friend and protector was near; one who understood them, and knew their value. The stunted rose-bush shot forth twigs, unfolded its leaves, and bore the most beautiful roses; every one could see it, and even the black, slimy wood-snail noticed its beauty. "I will give my seal to the flower," said the snail, "I have trailed my slime upon it, I can do no more."

"Thus it always fares with the beautiful in this world," said the poet. And he made a song upon it, and sung it after his own fashion, but nobody listened. Then he gave a drummer twopence and a peacock's feather, and composed a song for the drum, and the drummer beat it through the streets of the town, and when the people heard it they said, "That is a capital tune." The poet wrote many songs about the true, the beautiful, and the good. His songs were listened to in the tavern, where the tallow candles flared, in the fresh clover field, in the forest, and on the high-seas; and it appeared as if this brother was to be more fortunate than the other two.

But the evil spirit was angry at this, so he set to work with soot and incense, which he can mix so artfully as to confuse an angel, and how much more easily a poor poet. The evil one knew how to manage such people. He so completely surrounded the poet with incense that the man lost his head, forgot his mission and his home, and at last lost himself and vanished in smoke.

But when the little birds heard of it, they mourned, and for three days they sang not one song. The black wood-snail became blacker still; not for grief, but for envy. "They should have offered me incense," he said, "for it was I who gave him the idea of the most famous of his songs – the drum song of 'The Way of the World;' and it was I who spat at the rose; I can bring a witness to that fact."

But no tidings of all this reached the poet's home in India. The birds had all been silent for three days, and when the time of mourning was over, so deep had been their grief, that they had forgotten for whom they wept. Such is the way of the world.

"Now I must go out into the world, and disappear like the rest," said the fourth brother. He was as good-tempered as the third, but no poet, though he could be witty.

The two eldest had filled the castle with joyfulness, and now the last brightness was going away. Sight and hearing have always been considered two of the chief senses among men, and those which they wish to keep bright; the other senses are looked upon as of less importance.

But the younger son had a different opinion; he had cultivated his taste in every way, and taste is very powerful. It rules over what goes into the mouth, as well as over all which is presented to the mind; and, consequently, this brother took upon himself to taste everything stored up in bottles or jars; this he called the rough part of his work. Every man's mind was to him as a vessel in which something was concocting; every land a kind of mental kitchen. "There are no delicacies here," he said; so he wished to go out into the world to find something delicate to suit his taste. "Perhaps fortune may be more favorable to me than it was to my brothers. I shall start on my travels, but what conveyance shall I choose? Are air balloons invented yet?" he asked of his father, who knew of all inventions that had been made, or would be made.

Air balloons had not then been invented, nor steam-ships, nor railways.

"Good," said he; "then I shall choose an air balloon; my father knows how they are to be made and guided. Nobody has invented one yet, and the people will believe that it is an aerial phantom. When I have done with the balloon I shall burn it, and for this purpose, you must give me a few pieces of another invention, which will come next; I mean a few chemical matches."

He obtained what he wanted, and flew away. The birds accompanied him farther than they had the other brothers. They were curious to know how this flight would end. Many more of them came swooping down; they thought it must be some new bird, and he soon had a goodly company of followers. They came in clouds till the air became darkened with birds as it was with the cloud of locusts over the land of Egypt.

And now he was out in the wide world. The balloon descended over one of the greatest cities, and the aeronaut took up his station at the highest point, on the church steeple. The balloon rose again into the air, which it ought not to have done; what became of it is not known, neither is it of any consequence, for balloons had not then been invented.

There he sat on the church steeple. The birds no longer hovered over him; they had got tired of him, and he was tired of them. All the chimneys in the town were smoking.

"There are altars erected to my honor," said the wind, who wished to say something agreeable to him as he sat there boldly looking down upon the people in the street. There was one stepping along, proud of his purse; another, of the key he carried behind him, though he had nothing to lock up; another took a pride in his moth-eaten coat; and another, in his mortified body. "Vanity, all vanity!" he exclaimed. "I must go down there by-and-by, and touch and taste; but I shall sit here a little while longer, for the wind blows pleasantly at my back. I shall remain here as long as the wind blows, and enjoy a little rest. It is comfortable to sleep late in the morning when one had a great deal to do," said the sluggard; "so I shall stop here as long as the wind blows, for it pleases me."

And there he stayed. But as he was sitting on the weather-cock of the steeple, which kept turning round and round with him, he was under the false impression that the same wind still blew, and that he could stay where he was without expense.

But in India, in the castle on the Tree of the Sun, all was solitary and still, since the brothers had gone away one after the other.

"Nothing goes well with them," said the father; "they will never bring the glittering jewel home, it is not made for me; they are all dead and gone." Then he bent down over the Book of Truth, and gazed on the page on which he should have read of the life after death, but for him there was nothing to be read or learned upon it.

His blind daughter was his consolation and joy; she clung to him with sincere affection, and for the sake of his happiness and peace she wished the costly jewel could be found and brought home.

With longing tenderness she thought of her brothers. Where were they? Where did they live? How she wished she might dream of them; but it was strange that not even in dreams could she be brought near to them. But at last one night she dreamt that she heard the voices of her brothers calling to her from the distant world, and she could not refrain herself, but went out to them, and yet it seemed in her dream that she still remained in her father's house. She did not see her brothers, but she felt as it were a fire burning in her hand, which, however, did not hurt her, for it was the jewel she was bringing to her father. When she awoke she thought for a moment that she still held the stone, but she only grasped the knob of her distaff.

During the long evenings she had spun constantly, and round the distaff were woven threads finer than the web of a spider; human eyes could never have distinguished these threads when separated from each other. But she had wetted them with her tears, and the twist was as strong as a cable. She rose with the impression that her dream must be a reality, and her resolution was taken.

It was still night, and her father slept; she pressed a kiss upon his hand, and then took her distaff and fastened the end of the thread to her father's house. But for this, blind as she was, she would never have found her way home again; to this thread she must hold fast, and trust not to others or even to herself. From the Tree of the Sun she broke four leaves; which she gave up to the wind and the weather, that they might be carried to her brothers as letters and a greeting, in case she did not meet them in the wide world. Poor blind child, what would become of her in those distant regions? But she had the invisible thread, to which she could hold fast; and she possessed a gift which all the others lacked. This was a determination to throw herself entirely into whatever she undertook, and it made her feel as if she had eyes even at the tips of her fingers, and could hear down into her very heart. Quietly she went forth into the noisy, bustling, wonderful world, and wherever she went the skies grew bright, and she felt the warm sunbeam, and a rainbow above in the blue heavens seemed to span the dark world. She heard the song of the birds, and smelt the scent of the orange groves and apple orchards so strongly that she seemed to taste it. Soft tones and charming songs reached her ear, as well as harsh sounds and rough words – thoughts and opinions in strange contradiction to each other. Into the deepest recesses of her heart penetrated the echoes of human thoughts and feelings. Now she heard the following words sadly sung, –

> *"Life is a shadow that flits away*
> *In a night of darkness and woe."*

But then would follow brighter thoughts:

> *"Life has the rose's sweet perfume*
> *With sunshine, light, and joy."*

And if one stanza sounded painfully –

"Each mortal thinks of himself alone,
Is a truth, alas, too clearly known;"

Then, on the other hand, came the answer –

"Love, like a mighty flowing stream,
Fills every heart with its radiant gleam."

She heard, indeed, such words as these –

"In the pretty turmoil here below,
All is a vain and paltry show."

Then came also words of comfort –

"Great and good are the actions done
By many whose worth is never known."

And if sometimes the mocking strain reached her –

"Why not join in the jesting cry,
That contemns all gifts from the throne on high?"

In the blind girl's heart a stronger voice repeated –

"To trust in thyself and God is best,
In His holy will forever to rest."

But the evil spirit could not see this and remain contented. He has more cleverness than ten thousand men, and he found means to compass his end. He betook himself to the marsh, and collected a few little bubbles of stagnant water. Then he uttered over them the echoes of lying words that they might become strong. He mixed up together songs of praise with lying epitaphs, as many as he could find, boiled them in tears shed by envy; put upon them rouge, which he had scraped from faded cheeks, and from these he produced a maiden, in form and appearance like the blind girl, the angel of completeness, as men called her. The evil one's plot was successful. The world knew not which was the true, and indeed how should the world know?

"To trust in thyself and God is best,
In his Holy will forever to rest."

So sung the blind girl in full faith. She had entrusted the four green leaves from the Tree of the Sun to the winds, as letters of greeting to her brothers, and she had full confidence that the leaves would reach them. She fully believed that the jewel which outshines all the glories of the world would yet be found, and that upon the forehead of humanity it would glitter even in the castle of her father. "Even in my father's house," she repeated. "Yes, the place in which this jewel is to be found is earth, and I shall bring more than the promise of it with me. I feel it glow and swell more and more in my closed hand. Every grain of truth which the keen wind carried up and whirled towards me I caught and treasured. I allowed it to be penetrated with the fragrance of the beautiful, of which there is so much in the world, even for the blind. I took the beatings of a heart engaged in a good action, and added them to my treasure. All that I can bring is but dust; still, it is a part of the jewel we seek, and there is plenty, my hand is quite full of it."

She soon found herself again at home; carried thither in a flight of thought, never having loosened her hold of the invisible thread fastened to her father's house. As she stretched out her hand to her father, the powers of evil dashed with the fury of a hurricane over the Tree of the Sun; a blast of wind rushed through the open doors, and into the sanctuary, where lay the Book of Truth.

"It will be blown to dust by the wind," said the father, as he seized the open hand she held towards him.

"No," she replied, with quiet confidence, "it is indestructible. I feel its beam warming my very soul."

Then her father observed that a dazzling flame gleamed from the white page on which the shining dust had passed from her hand. It was there to prove the certainty of eternal life, and on the book glowed one shining word, and only one, the word BELIEVE. And soon the four brothers were again with the father and daughter. When the green leaf from home fell on the bosom of each, a longing had seized them to return. They had arrived, accompanied by the birds of passage, the stag, the antelope, and all the creatures of the forest who wished to take part in their joy.

We have often seen, when a sunbeam burst through a crack in the door into a dusty room, how a whirling column of dust seems to circle round. But this was not poor, insignificant, common dust, which the blind girl had brought; even the rainbow's colors are dim when compared with the beauty which shone from the page on which it had fallen. The beaming word BELIEVE, from every grain of truth, had the brightness of the beautiful and the good, more bright than the mighty pillar of flame that led Moses and the children of Israel to the land of Canaan, and from the word BELIEVE arose the bridge of hope, reaching even to the unmeasurable Love in the realms of the infinite.

The Child in the Grave

IT WAS A VERY SAD DAY, and every heart in the house felt the deepest grief; for the youngest child, a boy of four years old, the joy and hope of his parents, was dead. Two daughters, the elder of whom was going to be confirmed, still remained: they were both good, charming girls; but the lost child always seems the dearest; and when it is youngest, and a son, it makes the trial still more heavy. The sisters mourned as young hearts can mourn, and were especially grieved at the sight of their parents' sorrow. The father's heart was bowed down, but the mother sunk completely under the deep grief. Day and night she had attended to the sick child, nursing and carrying it in her bosom, as a part of herself. She could not realize the fact that the child was dead, and must be laid in a coffin to rest in the ground. She thought God could not take her darling little one from her; and when it did happen notwithstanding her hopes and her belief, and there could be no more doubt on the subject, she said in her feverish agony, "God does not know it. He has hard-hearted ministering spirits on earth, who do according to their own will, and heed not a mother's prayers." Thus in her great grief she fell away from her faith in God, and dark thoughts arose in her mind respecting death and a future state. She tried to believe that man was but dust, and that with his life all existence ended. But these doubts were no support to her, nothing on which she could rest, and she sunk into the fathomless depths of despair. In her darkest hours she ceased to weep, and thought not of the young daughters who were still left to her. The tears of her husband fell on her forehead, but she took no notice of him; her thoughts were with her dead child; her whole existence seemed wrapped up in the remembrances of the little one and of every innocent word it had uttered.

The day of the little child's funeral came. For nights previously the mother had not slept, but in the morning twilight of this day she sunk from weariness into a deep sleep; in the mean time the coffin was carried into a distant room, and there nailed down, that she might not hear the blows of the hammer. When she awoke, and wanted to see her child, the husband, with tears, said, "We have closed the coffin; it was necessary to do so."

"When God is so hard to me, how can I expect men to be better?" she said with groans and tears.

The coffin was carried to the grave, and the disconsolate mother sat with her young daughters. She looked at them, but she saw them not; for her thoughts were far away from the domestic hearth. She gave herself up to her grief, and it tossed her to and fro, as the sea tosses a ship without compass or rudder. So the day of the funeral passed away, and similar days followed, of dark, wearisome pain. With tearful eyes and mournful glances, the sorrowing daughters and the afflicted husband looked upon her who would not hear their words of comfort; and, indeed, what comforting words could they speak, when they were themselves so full of grief? It seemed as if she would never again know sleep, and yet it would have been her best friend, one who would have strengthened her body and poured peace into her soul. They at last persuaded her to lie down, and then she would lie as still as if she slept.

One night, when her husband listened, as he often did, to her breathing, he quite believed that she had at length found rest and relief in sleep. He folded his arms and prayed, and soon sunk himself into healthful sleep; therefore he did not notice that his wife arose, threw on her clothes, and glided silently from the house, to go where her thoughts constantly lingered – to the grave of her child. She passed through the garden, to a path across a field that led to the churchyard. No one saw her as she walked, nor did she see any one; for her eyes were fixed upon the one object of her wanderings. It was a lovely starlight night in the beginning of September, and the air was mild and still. She entered the churchyard, and stood by the little grave, which looked like a large nosegay of fragrant flowers. She sat down, and bent her head low over the grave, as if she could see her child through the earth that covered him – her little boy, whose smile was so vividly before her, and the gentle expression of whose eyes, even on his sick-bed, she could not forget. How full of meaning that glance had been, as she leaned over him, holding in hers the pale hand which he had no longer strength to raise! As she had sat by his little cot, so now she sat by his grave; and here she could weep freely, and her tears fell upon it.

"Thou wouldst gladly go down and be with thy child," said a voice quite close to her, – a voice that sounded so deep and clear, that it went to her heart.

She looked up, and by her side stood a man wrapped in a black cloak, with a hood closely drawn over his face; but her keen glance could distinguish the face under the hood. It was stern, yet awakened confidence, and the eyes beamed with youthful radiance.

"Down to my child," she repeated; and tones of despair and entreaty sounded in the words.

"Darest thou to follow me?" asked the form. "I am Death."

She bowed her head in token of assent. Then suddenly it appeared as if all the stars were shining with the radiance of the full moon on the many-colored flowers that decked the grave. The earth that covered it was drawn back like a floating drapery. She sunk down, and the spectre covered her with a black cloak; night closed around her, the night of death. She sank deeper than the spade of the sexton could penetrate, till the churchyard became a roof above her. Then the cloak was removed, and she found herself in a large hall, of wide-spreading dimensions, in which there was a subdued light, like twilight, reigning, and in a moment her child appeared before her, smiling, and more beautiful than ever; with a silent cry she pressed him to her heart. A glorious strain of music sounded – now distant, now near. Never had she listened to such tones as these; they came from beyond a large dark curtain which separated the regions of death from the land of eternity.

"My sweet, darling mother," she heard the child say. It was the well-known, beloved voice; and kiss followed kiss, in boundless delight. Then the child pointed to the dark curtain. "There is nothing so beautiful on earth as it is here. Mother, do you not see them all? Oh, it is happiness indeed."

But the mother saw nothing of what the child pointed out, only the dark curtain. She looked with earthly eyes, and could not see as the child saw, – he whom God has called to be with Himself. She could hear the sounds of music, but she heard not the words, the Word in which she was to trust.

"I can fly now, mother," said the child; "I can fly with other happy children into the presence of the Almighty. I would fain fly away now; but if you weep for me as you are weeping now, you may never see me again. And yet I would go so gladly. May I not fly away? And you will come to me soon, will you not, dear mother?"

"Oh, stay, stay!" implored the mother; "only one moment more; only once more, that I may look upon thee, and kiss thee, and press thee to my heart."

Then she kissed and fondled her child. Suddenly her name was called from above; what could it mean? her name uttered in a plaintive voice.

"Hearest thou?" said the child. "It is my father who calls thee." And in a few moments deep sighs were heard, as of children weeping. "They are my sisters," said the child. "Mother, surely you have not forgotten them."

And then she remembered those she left behind, and a great terror came over her. She looked around her at the dark night. Dim forms flitted by. She seemed to recognize some of them, as they floated through the regions of death towards the dark curtain, where they vanished. Would her husband and her daughters flit past? No; their sighs and lamentations still sounded from above; and she had nearly forgotten them, for the sake of him who was dead.

"Mother, now the bells of heaven are ringing," said the child; "mother, the sun is going to rise."

An overpowering light streamed in upon her, the child had vanished, and she was being borne upwards. All around her became cold; she lifted her head, and saw that she was lying in the churchyard, on the grave of her child. The Lord, in a dream, had been a guide to her feet and a light to her spirit. She bowed her knees, and prayed for forgiveness. She had wished to keep back a soul from its immortal flight; she had forgotten her duties towards the living who were left her. And when she had offered this prayer, her heart felt lighter. The sun burst forth, over her head a little bird carolled his song, and the church-bells sounded for the early service. Everything around her seemed holy, and her heart was chastened. She acknowledged the goodness of God, she acknowledged the duties she had to perform, and eagerly she returned home. She bent over her husband, who still slept; her warm, devoted kiss awakened him, and words of heartfelt love fell from the lips of both. Now she was gentle and strong as a wife can be; and from her lips came the words of faith: "Whatever He doeth is right and best."

Then her husband asked, "From whence hast thou all at once derived such strength and comforting faith?"

And as she kissed him and her children, she said, "It came from God, through my child in the grave."

The Mail-Coach Passengers

IT WAS BITTERLY cold, the sky glittered with stars, and not a breeze stirred. "Bump" – an old pot was thrown at a neighbor's door; and "bang, bang," went the guns; for they were greeting the New Year. It was New Year's Eve, and the church clock was striking twelve. "Tan-ta-ra-ra, tan-ta-ra-ra," sounded the horn, and the mail-coach came lumbering up. The clumsy vehicle stopped at the gate of the town; all the places had been taken, for there were twelve passengers in the coach.

"Hurrah! hurrah!" cried the people in the town; for in every house the New Year was being welcomed; and as the clock struck, they stood up, the full glasses in their hands, to drink success to the new comer. "A happy New Year," was the cry; "a pretty wife, plenty of money, and no sorrow or care."

The wish passed round, and the glasses clashed together till they rang again; while before the town-gate the mail coach stopped with the twelve strange passengers. And who were these strangers? Each of them had his passport and his luggage with him; they even brought presents for me, and for you, and for all the people in the town. "Who were they? what did they want? and what did they bring with them?"

"Good-morning," they cried to the sentry at the town-gate.

"Good-morning," replied the sentry; for the clock had struck twelve. "Your name and profession?" asked the sentry of the one who alighted first from the carriage.

"See for yourself in the passport," he replied. "I am myself;" and a famous fellow he looked, arrayed in bear-skin and fur boots. "I am the man on whom many persons fix their hopes. Come to me to-morrow, and I'll give you a New Year's present. I throw shillings and pence among the people; I give balls, no less than thirty-one; indeed, that is the highest number I can spare for balls. My ships are often frozen in, but in my offices it is warm and comfortable. My name is JANUARY. I'm a merchant, and I generally bring my accounts with me."

Then the second alighted. He seemed a merry fellow. He was a director of a theatre, a manager of masked balls, and a leader of all the amusements we can imagine. His luggage consisted of a great cask.

"We'll dance the bung out of the cask at carnival time," said he; "I'll prepare a merry tune for you and for myself too. Unfortunately I have not long to live – the shortest time, in fact, of my whole family – only twenty-eight days. Sometimes they pop me in a day extra; but I trouble myself very little about that. Hurrah!"

"You must not shout so," said the sentry.

"Certainly I may shout," retorted the man; "I'm Prince Carnival, travelling under the name of FEBRUARY."

The third now got out. He looked a personification of fasting; but he carried his nose very high, for he was related to the "forty (k)nights," and was a weather prophet. But that is not a very lucrative office, and therefore he praised fasting. In his button-hole he carried a little bunch of violets, but they were very small.

"MARCH, March," the fourth called after him, slapping him on the shoulder, "don't you smell something? Make haste into the guard room; they're drinking punch there;

that's your favorite drink. I can smell it out here already. Forward, Master March." But it was not true; the speaker only wanted to remind him of his name, and to make an APRIL fool of him; for with that fun the fourth generally began his career. He looked very jovial, did little work, and had the more holidays. "If the world were only a little more settled," said he: "but sometimes I'm obliged to be in a good humor, and sometimes a bad one, according to circumstances; now rain, now sunshine. I'm kind of a house agent, also a manager of funerals. I can laugh or cry, according to circumstances. I have my summer wardrobe in this box here, but it would be very foolish to put it on now. Here I am. On Sundays I go out walking in shoes and white silk stockings, and a muff."

After him, a lady stepped out of the coach. She called herself Miss MAY. She wore a summer dress and overshoes; her dress was a light green, and she wore anemones in her hair. She was so scented with wild-thyme, that it made the sentry sneeze.

"Your health, and God bless you," was her salutation to him.

How pretty she was! and such a singer! not a theatre singer, nor a ballad singer; no, but a singer of the woods; for she wandered through the gay green forest, and had a concert there for her own amusement.

"Now comes the young lady," said those in the carriage; and out stepped a young dame, delicate, proud, and pretty. It was Mistress JUNE, in whose service people become lazy and fond of sleeping for hours. She gives a feast on the longest day of the year, that there may be time for her guests to partake of the numerous dishes at her table. Indeed, she keeps her own carriage; but still she travelled by the mail, with the rest, because she wished to show that she was not high-minded. But she was not without a protector; her younger brother, JULY, was with her. He was a plump young fellow, clad in summer garments and wearing a straw hat. He had but very little luggage with him, because it was so cumbersome in the great heat; he had, however, swimming-trousers with him, which are nothing to carry. Then came the mother herself, in crinoline, Madame AUGUST, a wholesale dealer in fruit, proprietress of a large number of fish ponds and a land cultivator. She was fat and heated, yet she could use her hands well, and would herself carry out beer to the laborers in the field. "In the sweat of the face shalt thou eat bread," said she; "it is written in the Bible." After work, came the recreations, dancing and playing in the greenwood, and the "harvest homes." She was a thorough housewife.

After her a man came out of the coach, who is a painter; he is the great master of colors, and is named SEPTEMBER. The forest, on his arrival, had to change its colors when he wished it; and how beautiful are the colors he chooses! The woods glow with hues of red and gold and brown. This great master painter could whistle like a blackbird. He was quick in his work, and soon entwined the tendrils of the hop plant around his beer jug. This was an ornament to the jug, and he has a great love for ornament. There he stood with his color pot in his hand, and that was the whole of his luggage. A landowner followed, who in the month for sowing seed attended to the ploughing and was fond of field sports. Squire OCTOBER brought his dog and his gun with him, and had nuts in his game bag. "Crack, crack." He had a great deal of luggage, even an English plough. He spoke of farming, but what he said could scarcely be heard for the coughing and gasping of his neighbor. It was NOVEMBER, who coughed violently as he got out. He had a cold, which caused him to use his pocket-handkerchief continually; and yet he said he was obliged to accompany servant girls to their new places, and initiate them into their winter service. He said he thought his cold would never leave him when he went out woodcutting, for he was a master sawyer, and had to supply wood to the whole parish.

He spent his evenings preparing wooden soles for skates, for he knew, he said, that in a few weeks these shoes would be wanted for the amusement of skating. At length the last passenger made her appearance, – old Mother DECEMBER, with her fire-stool. The dame was very old, but her eyes glistened like two stars. She carried on her arm a flower-pot, in which a little fir-tree was growing. "This tree I shall guard and cherish," she said, "that it may grow large by Christmas Eve, and reach from the ground to the ceiling, to be covered and adorned with flaming candles, golden apples, and little figures. The fire-stool will be as warm as a stove, and I shall then bring a story book out of my pocket, and read aloud till all the children in the room are quite quiet. Then the little figures on the tree will become lively, and the little waxen angel at the top spread out his wings of gold-leaf, and fly down from his green perch. He will kiss every one in the room, great and small; yes, even the poor children who stand in the passage, or out in the street singing a carol about the 'Star of Bethlehem.'"

"Well, now the coach may drive away," said the sentry; "we have the whole twelve. Let the horses be put up."

"First, let all the twelve come to me," said the captain on duty, "one after another. The passports I will keep here. Each of them is available for one month; when that has passed, I shall write the behavior of each on his passport. Mr. JANUARY, have the goodness to come here." And Mr. January stepped forward.

When a year has passed, I think I shall be able to tell you what the twelve passengers have brought to you, to me, and to all of us. Now I do not know, and probably even they don't know themselves, for we live in strange times.

Grandmother

GRANDMOTHER IS VERY old, her face is wrinkled, and her hair is quite white; but her eyes are like two stars, and they have a mild, gentle expression in them when they look at you, which does you good. She wears a dress of heavy, rich silk, with large flowers worked on it; and it rustles when she moves. And then she can tell the most wonderful stories. Grandmother knows a great deal, for she was alive before father and mother – that's quite certain. She has a hymn-book with large silver clasps, in which she often reads; and in the book, between the leaves, lies a rose, quite flat and dry; it is not so pretty as the roses which are standing in the glass, and yet she smiles at it most pleasantly, and tears even come into her eyes. "I wonder why grandmother looks at the withered flower in the old book that way? Do you know?" Why, when grandmother's tears fall upon the rose, and she is looking at it, the rose revives, and fills the room with its fragrance; the walls vanish as in a mist, and all around her is the glorious green wood, where in summer the sunlight streams through thick foliage; and grandmother, why she is young again, a charming maiden, fresh as a rose, with round, rosy cheeks, fair, bright ringlets, and a figure pretty and graceful; but the eyes, those mild, saintly eyes, are the same, – they have been left to grandmother. At her side sits a young man, tall and strong; he gives her a rose and she smiles. Grandmother cannot smile like that now. Yes, she is smiling at the memory of that day, and many thoughts and recollections of the past; but the handsome young man is gone, and the rose has withered in the old book, and grandmother is sitting there, again an old woman, looking down upon the withered rose in the book.

Grandmother is dead now. She had been sitting in her arm-chair, telling us a long, beautiful tale; and when it was finished, she said she was tired, and leaned her head back to sleep awhile. We could hear her gentle breathing as she slept; gradually it became quieter and calmer, and on her countenance beamed happiness and peace. It was as if lighted up with a ray of sunshine. She smiled once more, and then people said she was dead. She was laid in a black coffin, looking mild and beautiful in the white folds of the shrouded linen, though her eyes were closed; but every wrinkle had vanished, her hair looked white and silvery, and around her mouth lingered a sweet smile. We did not feel at all afraid to look at the corpse of her who had been such a dear, good grandmother. The hymn-book, in which the rose still lay, was placed under her head, for so she had wished it; and then they buried grandmother.

On the grave, close by the churchyard wall, they planted a rose-tree; it was soon full of roses, and the nightingale sat among the flowers, and sang over the grave. From the organ in the church sounded the music and the words of the beautiful psalms, which were written in the old book under the head of the dead one.

The moon shone down upon the grave, but the dead was not there; every child could go safely, even at night, and pluck a rose from the tree by the churchyard wall. The dead know more than we do who are living. They know what a terror would come upon us if such a strange thing were to happen, as the appearance of a dead person among us. They are better off than we are; the dead return no more. The earth has been heaped on the coffin, and it is earth only that lies within it. The leaves of the hymn-book are dust; and the rose, with all its recollections, has crumbled to dust also. But over the grave fresh roses bloom, the nightingale sings, and the organ sounds and there still lives a remembrance of old grandmother, with the loving, gentle eyes that always looked young. Eyes can never die. Ours will once again behold dear grandmother, young and beautiful as when, for the first time, she kissed the fresh, red rose, that is now dust in the grave.

Something

"I MEAN TO be somebody, and do something useful in the world," said the eldest of five brothers. "I don't care how humble my position is, so that I can only do some good, which will be something. I intend to be a brickmaker; bricks are always wanted, and I shall be really doing something."

"Your 'something' is not enough for me," said the second brother; "what you talk of doing is nothing at all, it is journeyman's work, or might even be done by a machine. No! I should prefer to be a builder at once, there is something real in that. A man gains a position, he becomes a citizen, has his own sign, his own house of call for his workmen: so I shall be a builder. If all goes well, in time I shall become a master, and have my own journeymen, and my wife will be treated as a master's wife. This is what I call something."

"I call it all nothing," said the third; "not in reality any position. There are many in a town far above a master builder in position. You may be an upright man, but even as a master you will only be ranked among common men. I know better what to do than that. I will be an architect, which will place me among those who possess riches and intellect, and who speculate in art. I shall certainly have to rise by my own endeavors from a bricklayer's laborer, or as a carpenter's apprentice – a lad wearing a paper cap, although I now wear a silk hat. I shall have to fetch beer and spirits for the journeymen, and they will call me 'thou,' which will be an insult. I shall endure it, however, for I shall look upon it all as a mere representation, a masquerade, a mummery, which to-morrow, that is, when I myself as a journeyman, shall have served my time, will vanish, and I shall go my way, and all that has passed will be nothing to me. Then I shall enter the academy, and get instructed in drawing, and be called an architect. I may even attain to rank, and have something placed before or after my name, and I shall build as others have done before me. By this there will be always 'something' to make me remembered, and is not that worth living for?"

"Not in my opinion," said the fourth; "I will never follow the lead of others, and only imitate what they have done. I will be a genius, and become greater than all of you together. I will create a new style of building, and introduce a plan for erecting houses suitable to the climate, with material easily obtained in the country, and thus suit national feeling and the developments of the age, besides building a storey for my own genius."

"But supposing the climate and the material are not good for much," said the fifth brother, "that would be very unfortunate for you, and have an influence over your experiments. Nationality may assert itself until it becomes affectation, and the developments of a century may run wild, as youth often does. I see clearly that none of you will ever really be anything worth notice, however you may now fancy it. But do as you like, I shall not imitate you. I mean to keep clear of all these things, and criticize what you do. In every action something imperfect may be discovered, something not right, which I shall make it my business to find out and expose; that will be something, I fancy." And he kept his word, and became a critic.

People said of this fifth brother, "There is something very precise about him; he has a good head-piece, but he does nothing." And on that very account they thought he must be something.

Now, you see, this is a little history which will never end; as long as the world exists, there will always be men like these five brothers. And what became of them? Were they each nothing or something? You shall hear; it is quite a history.

The eldest brother, he who fabricated bricks, soon discovered that each brick, when finished, brought him in a small coin, if only a copper one; and many copper pieces, if placed one upon another, can be changed into a shining shilling; and at whatever door a person knocks, who has a number of these in his hands, whether it be the baker's, the butcher's, or the tailor's, the door flies open, and he can get all he wants. So you see the value of bricks. Some of the bricks, however, crumbled to pieces, or were broken, but the elder brother found a use for even these.

On the high bank of earth, which formed a dyke on the sea-coast, a poor woman named Margaret wished to build herself a house, so all the imperfect bricks were given to her, and a few whole ones with them; for the eldest brother was a kind-hearted man, although he never achieved anything higher than making bricks. The poor woman built herself a little house – it was small and narrow, and the window was quite crooked, the door too low, and the straw roof might have been better thatched. But still it was a shelter, and from within you could look far over the sea, which dashed wildly against the sea-wall on which the little house was built. The salt waves sprinkled their white foam over it, but it stood firm, and remained long after he who had given the bricks to build it was dead and buried.

The second brother of course knew better how to build than poor Margaret, for he served an apprenticeship to learn it. When his time was up, he packed up his knapsack, and went on his travels, singing the journeyman's song, –

> "While young, I can wander without a care,
> And build new houses everywhere;
> Fair and bright are my dreams of home,
> Always thought of wherever I roam.
>
> Hurrah for a workman's life of glee!
> There's a loved one at home who thinks of me;
> Home and friends I can ne'er forget,
> And I mean to be a master yet."

And that is what he did. On his return home, he became a master builder, – built one house after another in the town, till they formed quite a street, which, when finished, became really an ornament to the town. These houses built a house for him in return, which was to be his own. But how can houses build a house? If the houses were asked, they could not answer; but the people would understand, and say, "Certainly the street built his house for him." It was not very large, and the floor was of lime; but when he danced with his bride on the lime-covered floor, it was to him white and shining, and from every stone in the wall flowers seemed to spring forth and decorate the room as with the richest tapestry. It was really a pretty house, and in it were a happy pair. The flag of the corporation fluttered before it, and the journeymen and apprentices shouted

"Hurrah." He had gained his position, he had made himself something, and at last he died, which was "something" too.

Now we come to the architect, the third brother, who had been first a carpenter's apprentice, had worn a cap, and served as an errand boy, but afterwards went to the academy, and risen to be an architect, a high and noble gentleman. Ah yes, the houses of the new street, which the brother who was a master builder erected, may have built his house for him, but the street received its name from the architect, and the handsomest house in the street became his property. That was something, and he was "something," for he had a list of titles before and after his name. His children were called "wellborn," and when he died, his widow was treated as a lady of position, and that was "something." His name remained always written at the corner of the street, and lived in every one's mouth as its name. Yes, this also was "something."

And what about the genius of the family – the fourth brother – who wanted to invent something new and original? He tried to build a lofty storey himself, but it fell to pieces, and he fell with it and broke his neck. However, he had a splendid funeral, with the city flags and music in the procession; flowers were strewn on the pavement, and three orations were spoken over his grave, each one longer than the other. He would have liked this very much during his life, as well as the poems about him in the papers, for he liked nothing so well as to be talked of. A monument was also erected over his grave. It was only another storey over him, but that was "something," Now he was dead, like the three other brothers.

The youngest – the critic – outlived them all, which was quite right for him. It gave him the opportunity of having the last word, which to him was of great importance. People always said he had a good head-piece. At last his hour came, and he died, and arrived at the gates of heaven. Souls always enter these gates in pairs; so he found himself standing and waiting for admission with another; and who should it be but old dame Margaret, from the house on the dyke! "It is evidently for the sake of contrast that I and this wretched soul should arrive here exactly at the same time," said the critic. "Pray who are you, my good woman?" said he; "do you want to get in here too?"

And the old woman curtsied as well as she could; she thought it must be St. Peter himself who spoke to her. "I am a poor old woman," she said, "without my family. I am old Margaret, that lived in the house on the dyke."

"Well, and what have you done – what great deed have you performed down below?"

"I have done nothing at all in the world that could give me a claim to have these doors open for me," she said. "It would be only through mercy that I can be allowed to slip in through the gate."

"In what manner did you leave the world?" he asked, just for the sake of saying something; for it made him feel very weary to stand there and wait.

"How I left the world?" she replied; "why, I can scarcely tell you. During the last years of my life I was sick and miserable, and I was unable to bear creeping out of bed suddenly into the frost and cold. Last winter was a hard winter, but I have got over it all now. There were a few mild days, as your honor, no doubt, knows. The ice lay thickly on the lake, as far one could see. The people came from the town, and walked upon it, and they say there were dancing and skating upon it, I believe, and a great feasting. The sound of beautiful music came into my poor little room where I lay. Towards evening, when the moon rose beautifully, though not yet in her full splendor, I glanced from my bed over the wide sea; and there, just where the sea and sky met, rose a curious white cloud. I lay looking at the cloud till I observed a little black spot in the middle of it, which gradually grew larger and larger, and then I knew what it meant – I am old and experienced; and although this token is not often seen, I knew it, and a shuddering seized me. Twice in my life had I seen this same thing, and I knew that there would be an awful storm, with a spring tide, which would overwhelm the poor people who were now out on the ice, drinking, dancing, and making merry. Young and old, the whole city, were there; who was to warn them, if no one noticed the sign, or knew what it meant as I did? I was so alarmed, that I felt more strength and life than I had done for some time. I got out of bed, and reached the window; I could not crawl any farther from weakness and exhaustion; but I managed to open the window. I saw the people outside running and jumping about on the ice; I saw the beautiful flags waving in the wind; I heard the boys shouting, 'Hurrah!' and the lads and lasses singing, and everything full of merriment and joy. But there was the white cloud with the black spot hanging over them. I cried out as loudly as I could, but no one heard me; I was too far off from the people. Soon would the storm burst, the ice break, and all who were on it be irretrievably lost. They could not hear me, and to go to them was quite out of my power. Oh, if I could only get them safe on land! Then came the thought, as if from heaven, that I would rather set fire to my bed, and let the house be burnt down, than that so many people should perish miserably. I got a light, and in a few moments the red flames leaped up as a beacon to them. I escaped fortunately as far as the threshold of the door; but there I fell down and remained: I could go no farther. The flames rushed out towards me, flickered on the window, and rose high above the roof. The people on the ice became aware of the fire, and ran as fast as possible to help a poor sick woman, who, as they thought, was being burnt to death. There was not one who did not run. I heard them coming, and I also at the same time was conscious of a rush of air and a sound like the roar of heavy artillery. The spring flood was lifting the ice covering, which brake into a thousand pieces. But the people had reached the sea-wall, where the sparks were flying round. I had saved them all; but I suppose I could not survive the cold and fright; so I came up here to the gates of paradise. I am told they are open to poor creatures such as I am, and I have now no house left on earth; but I do not think that will give me a claim to be admitted here."

Then the gates were opened, and an angel led the old woman in. She had dropped one little straw out of her straw bed, when she set it on fire to save the lives of so many. It had been changed into the purest gold – into gold that constantly grew and expanded into flowers and fruit of immortal beauty.

"See," said the angel, pointing to the wonderful straw, "this is what the poor woman has brought. What dost thou bring? I know thou hast accomplished nothing, not even made a single brick. Even if thou couldst return, and at least produce so much, very likely, when made, the brick would be useless, unless done with a good will, which is always something. But thou canst not return to earth, and I can do nothing for thee."

Then the poor soul, the old mother who had lived in the house on the dyke, pleaded for him. She said, "His brother made all the stone and bricks, and sent them to me to build my poor little dwelling, which was a great deal to do for a poor woman like me. Could not all these bricks and pieces be as a wall of stone to prevail for him? It is an act of mercy; he is wanting it now; and here is the very fountain of mercy."

"Then," said the angel, "thy brother, he who has been looked upon as the meanest of you all, he whose honest deeds to thee appeared so humble, – it is he who has sent you this heavenly gift. Thou shalt not be turned away. Thou shalt have permission to stand without the gate and reflect, and repent of thy life on earth; but thou shalt not be admitted here until thou hast performed one good deed of repentance, which will indeed for thee be something."

"I could have expressed that better," thought the critic; but he did not say it aloud, which for him was SOMETHING, after all.

A Cheerful Temper

FROM MY FATHER I received the best inheritance, namely a "good temper." "And who was my father?" That has nothing to do with the good temper; but I will say he was lively, good-looking round, and fat; he was both in appearance and character a complete contradiction to his profession. "And pray what was his profession and his standing in respectable society?" Well, perhaps, if in the beginning of a book these were written and printed, many, when they read it, would lay the book down and say, "It seems to me a very miserable title, I don't like things of this sort." And yet my father was not a skin-dresser nor an executioner; on the contrary, his employment placed him at the head of the grandest people of the town, and it was his place by right. He had to precede the bishop, and even the princes of the blood; he always went first, – he was a hearse driver! There, now, the truth is out. And I will own, that when people saw my father perched up in front of the omnibus of death, dressed in his long, wide, black cloak, and his black-edged, three-cornered hat on his head, and then glanced at his round, jocund face, round as the sun, they could not think much of sorrow or the grave. That face said, "It is nothing, it will all end better than people think." So I have inherited from him, not only my good temper, but a habit of going often to the churchyard, which is good, when done in a proper humor; and then also I take in the *Intelligencer*, just as he used to do.

I am not very young, I have neither wife nor children, nor a library, but, as I said, I read the *Intelligencer*, which is enough for me; it is to me a delightful paper, and so it was to my father. It is of great use, for it contains all that a man requires to know; the names of the preachers at the church, and the new books which are published; where houses, servants, clothes, and provisions may be obtained. And then what a number of subscriptions to charities, and what innocent verses! Persons seeking interviews and engagements, all so plainly and naturally stated. Certainly, a man who takes in the *Intelligencer* may live merrily and be buried contentedly, and by the end of his life will have such a capital stock of paper that he can lie on a soft bed of it, unless he prefers wood shavings for his resting-place. The newspaper and the churchyard were always exciting objects to me. My walks to the latter were like bathing-places to my good humor. Every one can read the newspaper for himself, but come with me to the churchyard while the sun shines and the trees are green, and let us wander among the graves. Each of them is like a closed book, with the back uppermost, on which we can read the title of what the book contains, but nothing more. I had a great deal of information from my father, and I have noticed a great deal myself. I keep it in my diary, in which I write for my own use and pleasure a history of all who lie here, and a few more beside.

Now we are in the churchyard. Here, behind the white iron railings, once a rose-tree grew; it is gone now, but a little bit of evergreen, from a neighboring grave, stretches out its green tendrils, and makes some appearance; there rests a very unhappy man, and yet while he lived he might be said to occupy a very good position. He had enough to live upon, and something to spare; but owing to his refined tastes the least thing in the world annoyed him. If he went to a theatre of an evening, instead of enjoying himself he would be quite annoyed if the machinist had put too strong a light into one side of the moon, or if the representations of the sky hung over the scenes when they ought to have hung behind them; or if a palm-tree was introduced into a scene representing the Zoological Gardens of Berlin, or a cactus in a view of Tyrol, or a beech-tree in the north of Norway. As if these things were of any consequence! Why did he not leave them alone? Who would trouble themselves about such trifles? especially at a comedy, where every one is expected to be amused. Then sometimes the public applauded too much, or too little, to please him. "They are like wet wood," he would say, looking round to see what sort of people were present, "this evening; nothing fires them." Then he would vex and fret himself because they did not laugh at the right time, or because they laughed in the wrong places; and so he fretted and worried himself till at last the unhappy man fretted himself into the grave.

Here rests a happy man, that is to say, a man of high birth and position, which was very lucky for him, otherwise he would have been scarcely worth notice. It is beautiful to observe how wisely nature orders these things. He walked about in a coat embroidered all over, and in the drawing-rooms of society looked just like one of those rich pearl-embroidered bell-pulls, which are only made for show; and behind them always hangs a good thick cord for use. This man also had a stout, useful substitute behind him, who did duty for him, and performed all his dirty work. And there are still, even now, these serviceable cords behind other embroidered bell-ropes. It is all so wisely arranged, that a man may well be in a good humor.

Here rests, – ah, it makes one feel mournful to think of him! – but here rests a man who, during sixty-seven years, was never remembered to have said a good thing; he lived only in the hope of having a good idea. At last he felt convinced, in his own mind, that he really had one, and was so delighted that he positively died of joy at the thought of having at last caught an idea. Nobody got anything by it; indeed, no one even heard what the good thing was. Now I can imagine that this same idea may prevent him from resting quietly in his grave; for suppose that to produce a good effect, it is necessary to bring out his new idea at breakfast, and that he can only make his appearance on earth at midnight, as ghosts are believed generally to do; why then this good idea would not suit the hour, and the man would have to carry it down again with him into the grave – that must be a troubled grave.

The woman who lies here was so remarkably stingy, that during her life she would get up in the night and mew, that her neighbors might think she kept a cat. What a miser she was!

Here rests a young lady, of a good family, who would always make her voice heard in society, and when she sang "Mi manca la voce" ("I have no voice"), it was the only true thing she ever said in her life.

Here lies a maiden of another description. She was engaged to be married, – but, her story is one of every-day life; we will leave her to rest in the grave.

Here rests a widow, who, with music in her tongue, carried gall in her heart. She used to go round among the families near, and search out their faults, upon which she preyed with all the envy and malice of her nature. This is a family grave. The members of this family held so firmly together in their opinions, that they would believe in no other. If the newspapers, or even the whole world, said of a certain subject, "It is so-and-so;" and a little schoolboy declared he had learned quite differently, they would take his assertion as the only true one, because he belonged to the family. And it is well known that if the yard-cock belonging to this family happened to crow at midnight, they would declare it was morning, although the watchman and all the clocks in the town were proclaiming the hour of twelve at night.

The great poet Goethe concludes his Faust with the words, "may be continued;" so might our wanderings in the churchyard be continued. I come here often, and if any of my friends, or those who are not my friends, are too much for me, I go out and choose a plot of ground in which to bury him or her. Then I bury them, as it were; there they lie, dead and powerless, till they come back new and better characters. Their lives and their deeds, looked at after my own fashion, I write down in my diary, as every one ought to do. Then, if any of our friends act absurdly, no one need to be vexed about it. Let them bury the offenders out of sight, and keep their good temper. They can also read the *Intelligencer*, which is a paper written by the people, with their hands guided. When the time comes for the history of my life, to be bound by the grave, then they will write upon it as my epitaph –

"The man with a cheerful temper."

And this is my story.

The Old Church Bell

IN THE COUNTRY of Wurtemburg, in Germany, where the acacias grow by the public road, where the apple-trees and the pear-trees in autumn bend to the earth with the weight of the precious fruit, lies the little town of Marbach. As is often the case with many of these towns, it is charmingly situated on the banks of the river Neckar, which rushes rapidly by, passing villages, old knights' castles, and green vineyards, till its waters mingle with those of the stately Rhine. It was late in the autumn; the vine-leaves still hung upon the branches of the vines, but they were already tinted with red and gold; heavy showers fell on the surrounding country, and the cold autumn wind blew sharp and strong. It was not at all pleasant weather for the poor. The days grew shorter and more gloomy, and, dark as it was out of doors in the open air, it was still darker within the small, old-fashioned houses of the village. The gable end of one of these houses faced the street, and with its small, narrow windows, presented a very mean appearance. The family who dwelt in it were also very poor and humble, but they treasured the fear of God in their innermost hearts. And now He was about to send them a child. It was the hour of the mother's sorrow, when there pealed forth from the church tower the sound of festive bells. In that solemn hour the sweet and joyous chiming filled the hearts of those in the humble dwelling with thankfulness and trust; and when, amidst these joyous sounds, a little son was born to them, the words of prayer and praise arose from their overflowing hearts, and their happiness seemed to ring out over town and country in the liquid tones of the church bells' chime. The little one, with its bright eyes and golden hair, had been welcomed joyously on that dark November day. Its parents kissed it lovingly, and the father wrote these words in the Bible, "On the tenth of November, 1759, God sent us a son." And a short time after, when the child had been baptized, the names he had received were added, "John Christopher Frederick."

And what became of the little lad? – the poor boy of the humble town of Marbach? Ah, indeed, there was no one who thought or supposed, not even the old church bell which had been the first to sound and chime for him, that he would be the first to sing the beautiful song of "The Bell." The boy grew apace, and the world advanced with him.

While he was yet a child, his parents removed from Marbach, and went to reside in another town; but their dearest friends remained behind at Marbach, and therefore sometimes the mother and her son would start on a fine day to pay a visit to the little town. The boy was at this time about six years old, and already knew a great many stories out of the Bible, and several religious psalms. While seated in the evening on his little cane-chair, he had often heard his father read from Gellert's fables, and sometimes from Klopstock's grand poem, "The Messiah." He and his sister, two years older than himself, had often wept scalding tears over the story of Him who suffered death on the cross for us all.

On his first visit to Marbach, the town appeared to have changed but very little, and it was not far enough away to be forgotten. The house, with its pointed gable, narrow windows, overhanging walls and stories, projecting one beyond another, looked just the same as in former times. But in the churchyard there were several new graves; and there also, in the grass, close by the wall, stood the old church bell! It had been taken down from its high position, in consequence of a crack in the metal which prevented it from ever chiming again, and a new bell now occupied its place. The mother and son were walking in the churchyard when they discovered the old bell, and they stood still to look at it. Then the mother reminded her little boy of what a useful bell this had been for many hundred years. It had chimed for weddings and for christenings; it had tolled for funerals, and to give the alarm in case of fire. With every event in the life of man the bell had made its voice heard. His mother also told him how the chiming of that old bell had once filled her heart with joy and confidence, and that in the midst of the sweet tones her child had been given to her. And the boy gazed on the large, old bell with the deepest interest. He bowed his head over it and kissed it, old, thrown away, and cracked as it was, and standing there amidst the grass and nettles. The boy never forgot what his mother told him, and the tones of the old bell reverberated in his heart till he reached manhood. In such sweet remembrance was the old bell cherished by the boy, who grew up in poverty to be tall and slender, with a freckled complexion and hair almost red; but his eyes were clear and blue as the deep sea, and what was his career to be? His career was to be good, and his future life enviable. We find him taking high honors at the military school in the division commanded by the member of a family high in position, and this was an honor, that is to say, good luck. He wore gaiters, stiff collars, and powdered hair, and by this he was recognized; and, indeed, he might be known by the word of command – "March! halt! front!"

The old church bell had long been quite forgotten, and no one imagined it would ever again be sent to the melting furnace to make it as it was before. No one could possibly have foretold this. Equally impossible would it have been to believe that the tones of the old bell still echoed in the heart of the boy from Marbach; or that one day they would ring out loud enough and strong enough to be heard all over the world. They had already been heard in the narrow space behind the school-wall, even above the deafening sounds of "March! halt! front!" They had chimed so loudly in the heart of the youngster, that he had sung them to his companions, and their tones resounded to the very borders of the country. He was not a free scholar in the military school, neither was he provided with clothes or food. But he had his number, and his own peg; for everything here was ordered like clockwork, which we all know is of the greatest utility – people get on so much better together when their position and duties are understood. It is by pressure that a jewel is stamped. The pressure of regularity and discipline here stamped the jewel, which in the future the world so well knew.

In the chief town of the province a great festival was being celebrated. The light streamed forth from thousands of lamps, and the rockets shot upwards towards the sky, filling the air with showers of colored fiery sparks. A record of this bright display will live in the memory of man, for through it the pupil in the military school was in tears and sorrow. He had dared to attempt to reach foreign territories unnoticed, and must therefore give up fatherland, mother, his dearest friends, all, or sink down into the stream of common life. The old church bell had still some comfort; it stood in the shelter of the church wall in Marbach, once so elevated, now quite forgotten. The wind roared around it, and could have readily related the story of its origin and of its sweet chimes, and the wind could also tell of him to whom he had brought fresh air when, in the woods of a neighboring country, he had sunk down exhausted with fatigue, with no other worldly possessions than hope for the future, and a written leaf from "Fiesco." The wind could have told that his only protector was an artist, who, by reading each leaf to him, made it plain; and that they amused themselves by playing at nine-pins together. The wind could also describe the pale fugitive, who, for weeks and months, lay in a wretched little road-side inn, where the landlord got drunk and raved, and where the merry-makers had it all their own way. And he, the pale fugitive, sang of the ideal.

For many heavy days and dark nights the heart must suffer to enable it to endure trial and temptation; yet, amidst it all, would the minstrel sing. Dark days and cold nights also passed over the old bell, and it noticed them not; but the bell in the man's heart felt it to be a gloomy time. What would become of this young man, and what would become of the old bell?

The old bell was, after a time, carried away to a greater distance than any one, even the warder in the bell tower, ever imagined; and the bell in the breast of the young man was heard in countries where his feet had never wandered. The tones went forth over the wide ocean to every part of the round world.

We will now follow the career of the old bell. It was, as we have said, carried far away from Marbach and sold as old copper; then sent to Bavaria to be melted down in a furnace. And then what happened?

In the royal city of Bavaria, many years after the bell had been removed from the tower and melted down, some metal was required for a monument in honor of one of the most celebrated characters which a German people or a German land could produce. And now we see how wonderfully things are ordered. Strange things sometimes happen in this world.

In Denmark, in one of those green islands where the foliage of the beech-woods rustles in the wind, and where many Huns' graves may be seen, was another poor boy born. He wore wooden shoes, and when his father worked in a ship-yard, the boy, wrapped up in an old worn-out shawl, carried his dinner to him every day. This poor child was now the pride of his country; for the sculptured marble, the work of his hands, had astonished the world. To him was offered the honor of forming from the clay, a model of the figure of him whose name, "John Christopher Frederick," had been written by his father in the Bible. The bust was cast in bronze, and part of the metal used for this purpose was the old church bell, whose tones had died away from the memory of those at home and elsewhere. The metal, glowing with heat, flowed into the mould, and formed the head and bust of the statue which was unveiled in the square in front of the old castle. The statue represented in living, breathing reality, the form of him who was born in poverty, the boy from Marbach, the pupil of the military school, the fugitive who struggled against poverty and oppression, from the outer world; Germany's great and immortal poet, who sung of Switzerland's deliverer, William Tell, and of the heaven-inspired Maid of Orleans.

It was a beautiful sunny day; flags were waving from tower and roof in royal Stuttgart, and the church bells were ringing a joyous peal. One bell was silent; but it was illuminated by the bright sunshine which streamed from the head and bust of the renowned figure, of which it formed a part. On this day, just one hundred years had passed since the day on which the chiming of the old church bell at Marbach had filled the mother's heart with trust and joy – the day on which her child was born in poverty, and in a humble home; the same who, in after-years, became rich, became the noble woman-hearted poet, a blessing to the world – the glorious, the sublime, the immortal bard, John Christoper Frederick Schiller!

Holger Danske

IN DENMARK THERE stands an old castle named Kronenburg, close by the Sound of Elsinore, where large ships, both English, Russian, and Prussian, pass by hundreds every day. And they salute the old castle with cannons, "Boom, boom," which is as if they said, "Good-day." And the cannons of the old castle answer "Boom," which means "Many thanks." In winter no ships sail by, for the whole Sound is covered with ice as far as the Swedish coast, and has quite the appearance of a high-road. The Danish and the Swedish flags wave, and Danes and Swedes say, "Good-day," and "Thank you" to each other, not with cannons, but with a friendly shake of the hand; and they exchange white bread and biscuits with each other, because foreign articles taste the best.

But the most beautiful sight of all is the old castle of Kronenburg, where Holger Danske sits in the deep, dark cellar, into which no one goes. He is clad in iron and steel, and rests his head on his strong arm; his long beard hangs down upon the marble table, into which it has become firmly rooted; he sleeps and dreams, but in his dreams he sees everything that happens in Denmark. On each Christmas-eve an angel comes to him and tells him that all he has dreamed is true, and that he may go to sleep again in peace, as Denmark is not yet in any real danger; but should danger ever come, then Holger Danske will rouse himself, and the table will burst asunder as he draws out his beard. Then he will come forth in his strength, and strike a blow that shall sound in all the countries of the world.

An old grandfather sat and told his little grandson all this about Holger Danske, and the boy knew that what his grandfather told him must be true. As the old man related this story, he was carving an image in wood to represent Holger Danske, to be fastened to the prow of a ship; for the old grandfather was a carver in wood, that is, one who carved figures for the heads of ships, according to the names given to them. And now he had carved Holger Danske, who stood there erect and proud, with his long beard, holding in one hand his broad battle-axe, while with the other he leaned on the Danish arms. The old grandfather told the little boy a great deal about Danish men and women who had distinguished themselves in olden times, so that he fancied he knew as much even as Holger Danske himself, who, after all, could only dream; and when the little fellow went to bed, he thought so much about it that he actually pressed his chin against the counterpane, and imagined that he had a long beard which had become rooted to it. But the old grandfather remained sitting at his work and carving away at the last part of it, which was the Danish arms. And when he had finished he looked at the whole figure, and thought of all he had heard and read, and what he had that evening related to his little grandson. Then he nodded his head, wiped his spectacles and put them on, and said, "Ah, yes; Holger Danske will not appear in my lifetime, but the boy who is in bed there may very likely live to see him when the event really comes to pass." And the old grandfather nodded again; and the more he looked at Holger Danske, the more satisfied he felt that he had carved a good image of him. It seemed to glow with the color of life; the armor glittered like iron and steel. The hearts in the Danish arms grew more and more red; while the lions, with gold crowns on their heads, were leaping up. "That is the most beautiful coat of arms in the world," said the old man. "The lions represent strength; and the hearts, gentleness and love." And as he gazed on the uppermost lion, he thought of King Canute, who chained great England to Denmark's throne; and he looked at the second lion, and thought of Waldemar, who untied Denmark and conquered the Vandals. The third lion reminded him of Margaret, who united Denmark, Sweden, and Norway. But when he gazed at the red hearts, their colors glowed more deeply, even as flames, and his memory followed each in turn. The first led him to a dark, narrow prison, in which sat a prisoner, a beautiful woman, daughter of Christian the Fourth, Eleanor Ulfeld, and the flame became a rose on her bosom, and its blossoms were not more pure than the heart of this noblest and best of all Danish women. "Ah, yes; that is indeed a noble heart in the Danish arms," said the grandfather. and his spirit followed the second flame, which carried him out to sea, where cannons roared and the ships lay shrouded in smoke, and the flaming heart attached itself to the breast of Hvitfeldt in the form of the ribbon of an order, as he blew himself and his ship into the air in order to save the fleet. And the third flame led him to Greenland's wretched huts, where the preacher, Hans Egede, ruled with love in every word and action. The flame was as a star on his breast, and added another heart to the Danish arms. And as the old grandfather's spirit followed the next hovering flame, he knew whither it would lead him. In a peasant woman's humble room stood Frederick the Sixth, writing his name with chalk on the beam. The flame trembled on his breast and in his heart, and it was in the peasant's room that his heart became one for the Danish arms. The old grandfather wiped his eyes, for he had known King Frederick, with his silvery locks and his honest blue eyes, and had lived for him, and he folded his hands and remained for some time silent. Then his daughter came to him and said it was getting late, that he ought to rest for a while, and that the supper was on the table.

"What you have been carving is very beautiful, grandfather," said she. "Holger Danske and the old coat of arms; it seems to me as if I have seen the face somewhere."

"No, that is impossible," replied the old grandfather; "but I have seen it, and I have tried to carve it in wood, as I have retained it in my memory. It was a long time ago, while the English fleet lay in the roads, on the second of April, when we showed that we were true, ancient Danes. I was on board the Denmark, in Steene Bille's squadron; I had a man by my side whom even the cannon balls seemed to fear. He sung old songs in a merry voice, and fired and fought as if he were something more than a man. I still remember his face, but from whence he came, or whither he went, I know not; no one knows. I have often thought it might have been Holger Danske himself, who had swam down to us from Kronenburg to help us in the hour of danger. That was my idea, and there stands his likeness."

The wooden figure threw a gigantic shadow on the wall, and even on part of the ceiling; it seemed as if the real Holger Danske stood behind it, for the shadow moved; but this was no doubt caused by the flame of the lamp not burning steadily. Then the daughter-in-law kissed the old grandfather, and led him to a large arm-chair by the table; and she, and her husband, who was the son of the old man and the father of the little boy who lay in bed, sat down to supper with him. And the old grandfather talked of the Danish lions and the Danish hearts, emblems of strength and gentleness, and explained quite clearly that there is another strength than that which lies in a sword, and he pointed to a shelf where lay a number of old books, and amongst them a collection of Holberg's plays, which are much read and are so clever and amusing that it is easy to fancy we have known the people of those days, who are described in them.

"He knew how to fight also," said the old man; "for he lashed the follies and prejudices of people during his whole life."

Then the grandfather nodded to a place above the looking-glass, where hung an almanac, with a representation of the Round Tower upon it, and said "Tycho Brahe was another of those who used a sword, but not one to cut into the flesh and bone, but to make the way of the stars of heaven clear, and plain to be understood. And then he whose father belonged to my calling, – yes, he, the son of the old image-carver, he whom we ourselves have seen, with his silvery locks and his broad shoulders, whose name is known in all lands; – yes, he was a sculptor, while I am only a carver. Holger Danske can appear in marble, so that people in all countries of the world may hear of the strength of Denmark. Now let us drink the health of Bertel."

But the little boy in bed saw plainly the old castle of Kronenburg, and the Sound of Elsinore, and Holger Danske, far down in the cellar, with his beard rooted to the table, and dreaming of everything that was passing above him.

And Holger Danske did dream of the little humble room in which the image-carver sat; he heard all that had been said, and he nodded in his dream, saying, "Ah, yes, remember me, you Danish people, keep me in your memory, I will come to you in the hour of need."

The bright morning light shone over Kronenburg, and the wind brought the sound of the hunting-horn across from the neighboring shores. The ships sailed by and saluted the castle with the boom of the cannon, and Kronenburg returned the salute, "Boom, boom." But the roaring cannons did not awake Holger Danske, for they meant only "Good morning," and "Thank you." They must fire in another fashion before he awakes; but wake he will, for there is energy yet in Holger Danske.

Children's Prattle

AT A RICH merchant's house there was a children's party, and the children of rich and great people were there. The merchant was a learned man, for his father had sent him to college, and he had passed his examination. His father had been at first only a cattle dealer, but always honest and industrious, so that he had made money, and his son, the merchant, had managed to increase his store. Clever as he was, he had also a heart; but there was less said of his heart than of his money. All descriptions of people visited at the merchant's house, well born, as well as intellectual, and some who possessed neither of these recommendations.

Now it was a children's party, and there was children's prattle, which always is spoken freely from the heart. Among them was a beautiful little girl, who was terribly proud; but this had been taught her by the servants, and not by her parents, who were far too sensible people.

Her father was groom of the Chambers, which is a high office at court, and she knew it. "I am a child of the court," she said; now she might just as well have been a child of the cellar, for no one can help his birth; and then she told the other children that she was well-born, and said that no one who was not well-born could rise in the world. It was no use to read and be industrious, for if a person was not well-born, he could never achieve anything. "And those whose names end with 'sen,'" said she, "can never be anything at all. We must put our arms akimbo, and make the elbow quite pointed, so as to keep these 'sen' people at a great distance." And then she stuck out her pretty little arms, and made the elbows quite pointed, to show how it was to be done; and her little arms were very pretty, for she was a sweet-looking child.

But the little daughter of the merchant became very angry at this speech, for her father's name was Petersen, and she knew that the name ended in "sen," and therefore she said as proudly as she could, "But my papa can buy a hundred dollars' worth of bonbons, and give them away to children. Can your papa do that?"

"Yes; and my papa," said the little daughter of the editor of a paper, "my papa can put your papa and everybody's papa into the newspaper. All sorts of people are afraid of him, my mamma says, for he can do as he likes with the paper." And the little maiden looked exceedingly proud, as if she had been a real princess, who may be expected to look proud.

But outside the door, which stood ajar, was a poor boy, peeping through the crack of the door. He was of such a lowly station that he had not been allowed even to enter the room. He had been turning the spit for the cook, and she had given him permission to stand behind the door and peep in at the well-dressed children, who were having such a merry time within; and for him that was a great deal. "Oh, if I could be one of them," thought he, and then he heard what was said about names, which was quite enough to make him more unhappy. His parents at home had not even a penny to spare to buy a newspaper, much less could they write in one; and worse than all, his father's name, and of course his own, ended in "sen," and therefore he could never turn out well, which was a very sad thought. But after all, he had been born into the world, and the station of life had been chosen for him, therefore he must be content.

And this is what happened on that evening.

Many years passed, and most of the children became grown-up persons.

There stood a splendid house in the town, filled with all kinds of beautiful and valuable objects. Everybody wished to see it, and people even came in from the country round to be permitted to view the treasures it contained.

Which of the children whose prattle we have described, could call this house his own? One would suppose it very easy to guess. No, no; it is not so very easy. The house belonged to the poor little boy who had stood on that night behind the door. He had really become something great, although his name ended in "sen," – for it was Thorwaldsen.

And the three other children – the children of good birth, of money, and of intellectual pride, – well, they were respected and honored in the world, for they had been well provided for by birth and position, and they had no cause to reproach themselves with what they had thought and spoken on that evening long ago, for, after all, it was mere "children's prattle."

The Old Grave-Stone

IN A HOUSE, with a large courtyard, in a provincial town, at that time of the year in which people say the evenings are growing longer, a family circle were gathered together at their old home. A lamp burned on the table, although the weather was mild and warm, and the long curtains hung down before the open windows, and without the moon shone brightly in the dark-blue sky.

But they were not talking of the moon, but of a large, old stone that lay below in the courtyard not very far from the kitchen door. The maids often laid the clean copper saucepans and kitchen vessels on this stone, that they might dry in the sun, and the children were fond of playing on it. It was, in fact, an old grave-stone.

"Yes," said the master of the house, "I believe the stone came from the graveyard of the old church of the convent which was pulled down, and the pulpit, the monuments, and the grave-stones sold. My father bought the latter; most of them were cut in two and used for paving-stones, but that one stone was preserved whole, and laid in the courtyard."

"Any one can see that it is a grave-stone," said the eldest of the children; "the representation of an hour-glass and part of the figure of an angel can still be traced, but the inscription beneath is quite worn out, excepting the name 'Preben,' and a large 'S' close by it, and a little farther down the name of 'Martha' can be easily read. But nothing more, and even that cannot be seen unless it has been raining, or when we have washed the stone."

"Dear me! how singular. Why that must be the grave-stone of Preben Schwane and his wife."

The old man who said this looked old enough to be the grandfather of all present in the room.

"Yes," he continued, "these people were among the last who were buried in the churchyard of the old convent. They were a very worthy old couple, I can remember them well in the days of my boyhood. Every one knew them, and they were esteemed by all. They were the oldest residents in the town, and people said they possessed a ton of gold, yet they were always very plainly dressed, in the coarsest stuff, but with linen of the purest whiteness. Preben and Martha were a fine old couple, and when they both sat on the bench, at the top of the steep stone steps, in front of their house, with the branches of the linden-tree waving above them, and nodded in a gentle, friendly way to passers by, it really made one feel quite happy. They were very good to the poor; they fed them and clothed them, and in their benevolence there was judgment as well as true Christianity. The old woman died first; that day is still quite vividly before my eyes. I was a little boy, and had accompanied my father to the old man's house. Martha had fallen into the sleep of death just as we arrived there. The corpse lay in a bedroom, near to the one in which we sat, and the old man was in great distress and weeping like a child. He spoke to my father, and to a few neighbors who were there, of how lonely he should feel now she was gone, and how good and true she, his dead wife, had been during the number of years that they had passed through life together, and how they had become acquainted, and learnt to love each other. I was, as I have said, a boy, and only stood by and listened to what the others said; but it filled me with a strange emotion to listen to the old man, and to watch how the color rose in his cheeks as he spoke of the days of their courtship, of how beautiful she was, and how many little tricks he had been guilty of, that he might meet her. And then he talked of his wedding-day; and his eyes brightened, and he seemed to be carried back, by his words, to that joyful time. And yet there she was, lying in the next room, dead – an old woman, and he was an old man, speaking of the days of hope, long passed away. Ah, well, so it is; then I was but a child, and now I am old, as old as Preben Schwane then was. Time passes away, and all things changed. I can remember quite well the day on which she was buried, and how Old Preben walked close behind the coffin.

"A few years before this time the old couple had had their grave-stone prepared, with an inscription and their names, but not the date. In the evening the stone was taken to the churchyard, and laid on the grave. A year later it was taken up, that Old Preben might be laid by the side of his wife. They did not leave behind them wealth, they left behind them far less than people had believed they possessed; what there was went to families distantly related to them, of whom, till then, no one had ever heard. The old house, with its balcony of wickerwork, and the bench at the top of the high steps, under the lime-tree, was considered, by the road-inspectors, too old and rotten to be left standing. Afterwards, when the same fate befell the convent church, and the graveyard was destroyed, the grave-stone of Preben and Martha, like everything else, was sold to whoever would buy it. And so it happened that this stone was not cut in two as many others had been, but now lies in the courtyard below, a scouring block for the maids, and a playground for the children. The paved street now passes over the resting place of Old Preben and his wife; no one thinks of them any more now."

And the old man who had spoken of all this shook his head mournfully, and said, "Forgotten! Ah, yes, everything will be forgotten!" And then the conversation turned on other matters.

But the youngest child in the room, a boy, with large, earnest eyes, mounted upon a chair behind the window curtains, and looked out into the yard, where the moon was pouring a flood of light on the old gravestone, – the stone that had always appeared to him so dull and flat, but which lay there now like a great leaf out of a book of history. All that the boy had heard of Old Preben and his wife seemed clearly defined on the stone, and as he gazed on it, and glanced at the clear, bright moon shining in the pure air, it was as if the light of God's countenance beamed over His beautiful world.

"Forgotten! Everything will be forgotten!" still echoed through the room, and in the same moment an invisible spirit whispered to the heart of the boy, "Preserve carefully the seed that has been entrusted to thee, that it may grow and thrive. Guard it well. Through thee, my child, shall the obliterated inscription on the old, weather-beaten grave-stone go forth to future generations in clear, golden characters. The old pair shall again wander through the streets arm-in-arm, or sit with their fresh, healthy cheeks on the bench under the lime-tree, and smile and nod at rich and poor. The seed of this hour shall ripen in the course of years into a beautiful poem. The beautiful and the good are never forgotten, they live always in story or in song."

The Loveliest Rose in the World

THERE LIVED ONCE a great queen, in whose garden were found at all seasons the most splendid flowers, and from every land in the world. She specially loved roses, and therefore she possessed the most beautiful varieties of this flower, from the wild hedge-rose, with its apple-scented leaves, to the splendid Provence rose. They grew near the shelter of the walls, wound themselves round columns and window-frames, crept along passages and over the ceilings of the halls. They were of every fragrance and color.

But care and sorrow dwelt within these halls; the queen lay upon a sick bed, and the doctors declared that she must die. "There is still one thing that could save her," said one of the wisest among them. "Bring her the loveliest rose in the world; one which exhibits the purest and brightest love, and if it is brought to her before her eyes close, she will not die."

Then from all parts came those who brought roses that bloomed in every garden, but they were not the right sort. The flower must be one from the garden of love; but which of the roses there showed forth the highest and purest love? The poets sang of this rose, the loveliest in the world, and each named one which he considered worthy of that title; and intelligence of what was required was sent far and wide to every heart that beat with love; to every class, age, and condition.

"No one has yet named the flower," said the wise man. "No one has pointed out the spot where it blooms in all its splendor. It is not a rose from the coffin of Romeo and Juliet, or from the grave of Walburg, though these roses will live in everlasting song. It is not one of the roses which sprouted forth from the blood-stained fame of Winkelreid. The blood which flows from the breast of a hero who dies for his country is sacred, and his memory is sweet, and no rose can be redder than the blood which flows from his veins. Neither is it the magic flower of Science, to obtain which wondrous flower a man devotes many an hour of his fresh young life in sleepless nights, in a lonely chamber."

"I know where it blooms," said a happy mother, who came with her lovely child to the bedside of the queen. "I know where the loveliest rose in the world is. It is seen on the blooming cheeks of my sweet child, when it expresses the pure and holy love of infancy; when refreshed by sleep it opens its eyes, and smiles upon me with childlike affection."

"This is a lovely rose," said the wise man; "but there is one still more lovely."

"Yes, one far more lovely," said one of the women. "I have seen it, and a loftier and purer rose does not bloom. But it was white, like the leaves of a blush-rose. I saw it on the cheeks of the queen. She had taken off her golden crown, and through the long, dreary night, she carried her sick child in her arms. She wept over it, kissed it, and prayed for it as only a mother can pray in that hour of her anguish."

"Holy and wonderful in its might is the white rose of grief, but it is not the one we seek."

"No; the loveliest rose in the world I saw at the Lord's table," said the good old bishop. "I saw it shine as if an angel's face had appeared. A young maiden knelt at the altar, and renewed the vows made at her baptism; and there were white roses and red roses on the blushing cheeks of that young girl. She looked up to heaven with all the purity and love of her young spirit, in all the expression of the highest and purest love."

"May she be blessed!" said the wise man: "but no one has yet named the loveliest rose in the world."

Then there came into the room a child – the queen's little son. Tears stood in his eyes, and glistened on his cheeks; he carried a great book and the binding was of velvet, with silver clasps. "Mother," cried the little boy; "only hear what I have read." And the child seated himself by the bedside, and read from the book of Him who suffered death on the cross to save all men, even who are yet unborn. He read, "Greater love hath no man than this," and as he read a roseate hue spread over the cheeks of the queen, and her eyes became so enlightened and clear, that she saw from the leaves of the book a lovely rose spring forth, a type of Him who shed His blood on the cross.

"I see it," she said. "He who beholds this, the loveliest rose on earth, shall never die."

A Leaf from Heaven

HIGH UP IN the clear, pure air flew an angel, with a flower plucked from the garden of heaven. As he was kissing the flower a very little leaf fell from it and sunk down into the soft earth in the middle of a wood. It immediately took root, sprouted, and sent out shoots among the other plants.

"What a ridiculous little shoot!" said one. "No one will recognize it; not even the thistle nor the stinging-nettle."

"It must be a kind of garden plant," said another; and so they sneered and despised the plant as a thing from a garden.

"Where are you coming?" said the tall thistles whose leaves were all armed with thorns. "It is stupid nonsense to allow yourself to shoot out in this way; we are not here to support you."

Winter came, and the plant was covered with snow, but the snow glittered over it as if it had sunshine beneath as well as above.

When spring came, the plant appeared in full bloom: a more beautiful object than any other plant in the forest. And now the professor of botany presented himself, one who could explain his knowledge in black and white. He examined and tested the plant, but it did not belong to his system of botany, nor could he possibly find out to what class it did belong. "It must be some degenerate species," said he; "I do not know it, and it is not mentioned in any system."

"Not known in any system!" repeated the thistles and the nettles.

The large trees which grew round it saw the plant and heard the remarks, but they said not a word either good or bad, which is the wisest plan for those who are ignorant.

There passed through the forest a poor innocent girl; her heart was pure, and her understanding increased by her faith. Her chief inheritance had been an old Bible, which she read and valued. From its pages she heard the voice of God speaking to her, and telling her to remember what was said of Joseph's brethren when persons wished to injure her. "They imagined evil in their hearts, but God turned it to good." If we suffer wrongfully, if we are misunderstood or despised, we must think of Him who was pure and holy, and who prayed for those who nailed Him to the cross, "Father forgive them, for they know not what they do."

The girl stood still before the wonderful plant, for the green leaves exhaled a sweet and refreshing fragrance, and the flowers glittered and sparkled in the sunshine like colored flames, and the harmony of sweet sounds lingered round them as if each concealed within itself a deep fount of melody, which thousands of years could not exhaust. With pious gratitude the girl looked upon this glorious work of God, and bent down over one of the branches, that she might examine the flower and inhale the sweet perfume. Then a light broke in on her mind, and her heart expanded. Gladly would she have plucked a flower, but she could not overcome her reluctance to break one off. She knew it would so soon fade; so she took only a single green leaf, carried it home, and laid it in her Bible, where it remained ever green, fresh, and unfading. Between the pages of the Bible it still lay when, a few weeks afterwards, that Bible was laid under the young girl's head in her coffin. A holy calm rested on her face, as if the earthly remains bore the impress of the truth that she now stood in the presence of God.

In the forest the wonderful plant still continued to bloom till it grew and became almost a tree, and all the birds of passage bowed themselves before it.

"That plant is a foreigner, no doubt," said the thistles and the burdocks. "We can never conduct ourselves like that in this country." And the black forest snails actually spat at the flower.

Then came the swineherd; he was collecting thistles and shrubs to burn them for the ashes. He pulled up the wonderful plant, roots and all, and placed it in his bundle. "This will be as useful as any," he said; so the plant was carried away.

Not long after, the king of the country suffered from the deepest melancholy. He was diligent and industrious, but employment did him no good. They read deep and learned books to him, and then the lightest and most trifling that could be found, but all to no purpose. Then they applied for advice to one of the wise men of the world, and he sent them a message to say that there was one remedy which would relieve and cure him, and that it was a plant of heavenly origin which grew in the forest in the king's own dominions. The messenger described the flower so that is appearance could not be mistaken.

Then said the swineherd, "I am afraid I carried this plant away from the forest in my bundle, and it has been burnt to ashes long ago. But I did not know any better."

"You did not know, any better! Ignorance upon ignorance indeed!"

The poor swineherd took these words to heart, for they were addressed to him; he knew not that there were others who were equally ignorant. Not even a leaf of the plant could be found. There was one, but it lay in the coffin of the dead; no one knew anything about it.

Then the king, in his melancholy, wandered out to the spot in the wood. "Here is where the plant stood," he said; "it is a sacred place." Then he ordered that the place should be surrounded with a golden railing, and a sentry stationed near it.

The botanical professor wrote a long treatise about the heavenly plant, and for this he was loaded with gold, which improved the position of himself and his family.

And this part is really the most pleasant part of the story. For the plant had disappeared, and the king remained as melancholy and sad as ever, but the sentry said he had always been so.

The Girl Who Trod on the Loaf

THERE WAS ONCE a girl who trod on a loaf to avoid soiling her shoes, and the misfortunes that happened to her in consequence are well known. Her name was Inge; she was a poor child, but proud and presuming, and with a bad and cruel disposition. When quite a little child she would delight in catching flies, and tearing off their wings, so as to make creeping things of them. When older, she would take cockchafers and beetles, and stick pins through them. Then she pushed a green leaf, or a little scrap of paper towards their feet, and when the poor creatures would seize it and hold it fast, and turn over and over in their struggles to get free from the pin, she would say, "The cockchafer is reading; see how he turns over the leaf." She grew worse instead of better with years, and, unfortunately, she was pretty, which caused her to be excused, when she should have been sharply reproved.

"Your headstrong will requires severity to conquer it," her mother often said to her. "As a little child you used to trample on my apron, but one day I fear you will trample on my heart." And, alas! this fear was realized.

Inge was taken to the house of some rich people, who lived at a distance, and who treated her as their own child, and dressed her so fine that her pride and arrogance increased.

When she had been there about a year, her patroness said to her, "You ought to go, for once, and see your parents, Inge."

So Inge started to go and visit her parents; but she only wanted to show herself in her native place, that the people might see how fine she was. She reached the entrance of the village, and saw the young laboring men and maidens standing together chatting, and her own mother amongst them. Inge's mother was sitting on a stone to rest, with a fagot of sticks lying before her, which she had picked up in the wood. Then Inge turned back; she who was so finely dressed she felt ashamed of her mother, a poorly clad woman, who picked up wood in the forest. She did not turn back out of pity for her mother's poverty, but from pride.

Another half-year went by, and her mistress said, "you ought to go home again, and visit your parents, Inge, and I will give you a large wheaten loaf to take to them, they will be glad to see you, I am sure."

So Inge put on her best clothes, and her new shoes, drew her dress up around her, and set out, stepping very carefully, that she might be clean and neat about the feet, and there was nothing wrong in doing so. But when she came to the place where the footpath led across the moor, she found small pools of water, and a great deal of mud, so she threw the loaf into the mud, and trod upon it, that she might pass without wetting her feet. But as she stood with one foot on the loaf and the other lifted up to step forward, the loaf began to sink under her, lower and lower, till she disappeared altogether, and only a few bubbles on the surface of the muddy pool remained to show where she had sunk. And this is the story.

But where did Inge go? She sank into the ground, and went down to the Marsh Woman, who is always brewing there.

The Marsh Woman is related to the elf maidens, who are well-known, for songs are sung and pictures painted about them. But of the Marsh Woman nothing is known, excepting that when a mist arises from the meadows, in summer time, it is because she is brewing beneath them. To the Marsh Woman's brewery Inge sunk down to a place which no one can endure for long. A heap of mud is a palace compared with the Marsh Woman's brewery; and as Inge fell she shuddered in every limb, and soon became cold and stiff as marble. Her foot was still fastened to the loaf, which bowed her down as a golden ear of corn bends the stem.

An evil spirit soon took possession of Inge, and carried her to a still worse place, in which she saw crowds of unhappy people, waiting in a state of agony for the gates of mercy to be opened to them, and in every heart was a miserable and eternal feeling of unrest. It would take too much time to describe the various tortures these people suffered, but Inge's punishment consisted in standing there as a statue, with her foot fastened to the loaf. She could move her eyes about, and see all the misery around her, but she could not turn her head; and when she saw the people looking at her she thought they were admiring her pretty face and fine clothes, for she was still vain and proud. But she had forgotten how soiled her clothes had become while in the Marsh Woman's brewery, and that they were covered with mud; a snake had also fastened itself in her hair, and hung down her back, while from each fold in her dress a great toad peeped out and croaked like an asthmatic poodle. Worse than all was the terrible hunger that tormented her, and she could not stoop to break off a piece of the loaf on which she stood. No; her back was too stiff, and her whole body like a pillar of stone. And then came creeping over her face and eyes flies without wings; she winked and blinked, but they could not fly away, for their wings had been pulled off; this, added to the hunger she felt, was horrible torture.

"If this lasts much longer," she said, "I shall not be able to bear it." But it did last, and she had to bear it, without being able to help herself.

A tear, followed by many scalding tears, fell upon her head, and rolled over her face and neck, down to the loaf on which she stood. Who could be weeping for Inge? She had a mother in the world still, and the tears of sorrow which a mother sheds for her child will always find their way to the child's heart, but they often increase the torment instead of being a relief. And Inge could hear all that was said about her in the world she had left, and every one seemed cruel to her. The sin she had committed in treading on the loaf was known on earth, for she had been seen by the cowherd from the hill, when she was crossing the marsh and had disappeared.

When her mother wept and exclaimed, "Ah, Inge! what grief thou hast caused thy mother," she would say, "Oh that I had never been born! My mother's tears are useless now."

And then the words of the kind people who had adopted her came to her ears, when they said, "Inge was a sinful girl, who did not value the gifts of God, but trampled them under her feet."

"Ah," thought Inge, "they should have punished me, and driven all my naughty tempers out of me."

A song was made about "The girl who trod on a loaf to keep her shoes from being soiled," and this song was sung everywhere. The story of her sin was also told to the little children, and they called her "wicked Inge," and said she was so naughty that she ought to be punished. Inge heard all this, and her heart became hardened and full of bitterness.

But one day, while hunger and grief were gnawing in her hollow frame, she heard a little, innocent child, while listening to the tale of the vain, haughty Inge, burst into tears and exclaim, "But will she never come up again?"

And she heard the reply, "No, she will never come up again."

"But if she were to say she was sorry, and ask pardon, and promise never to do so again?" asked the little one.

"Yes, then she might come; but she will not beg pardon," was the answer.

"Oh, I wish she would!" said the child, who was quite unhappy about it. "I should be so glad. I would give up my doll and all my playthings, if she could only come here again. Poor Inge! it is so dreadful for her."

These pitying words penetrated to Inge's inmost heart, and seemed to do her good. It was the first time any one had said, "Poor Inge!" without saying something about her faults. A little innocent child was weeping, and praying for mercy for her. It made her feel quite strange, and she would gladly have wept herself, and it added to her torment to find she could not do so. And while she thus suffered in a place where nothing changed, years passed away on earth, and she heard her name less frequently mentioned. But one day a sigh reached her ear, and the words, "Inge! Inge! what a grief thou hast been to me! I said it would be so." It was the last sigh of her dying mother.

After this, Inge heard her kind mistress say, "Ah, poor Inge! shall I ever see thee again? Perhaps I may, for we know not what may happen in the future." But Inge knew right well that her mistress would never come to that dreadful place.

Time-passed – a long bitter time – then Inge heard her name pronounced once more, and saw what seemed two bright stars shining above her. They were two gentle eyes closing on earth. Many years had passed since the little girl had lamented and wept about "poor Inge." That child was now an old woman, whom God was taking to Himself. In the last hour of existence the events of a whole life often appear before us; and this hour the old woman remembered how, when a child, she had shed tears over the story of Inge, and she prayed for her now. As the eyes of the old woman closed to earth, the eyes of the soul opened upon the hidden things of eternity, and then she, in whose last thoughts Inge had been so vividly present, saw how deeply the poor girl had sunk. She burst into tears at the sight, and in heaven, as she had done when a little child on earth, she wept and prayed for poor Inge. Her tears and her prayers echoed through the dark void that surrounded the tormented captive soul, and the unexpected mercy was obtained for it through an angel's tears. As in thought Inge seemed to act over again every sin she had committed on earth, she trembled, and tears she had never yet been able to weep rushed to her eyes. It seemed impossible that the gates of mercy could ever be opened to her; but while she acknowledged this in deep penitence, a beam of radiant light shot suddenly into the depths upon her. More powerful than the sunbeam that dissolves the man of snow which the children have raised, more quickly than the snowflake melts and becomes a drop of water on the warm lips of a child, was the stony form of Inge changed, and as a little bird she soared, with the speed of lightning, upward to the world of mortals. A bird that felt timid and shy to all things around it, that seemed to shrink with shame from meeting any living creature, and hurriedly sought to conceal itself in a dark corner of an old ruined wall; there it sat cowering and unable to utter a sound, for it was voiceless. Yet how quickly the little bird discovered the beauty of everything around it. The sweet, fresh air; the soft radiance of the moon, as its light spread over the earth; the fragrance which exhaled from bush and tree, made it feel happy as it sat there clothed in its fresh, bright plumage. All creation seemed to speak of beneficence and love. The bird wanted to give utterance to thoughts that stirred in his breast, as the cuckoo and the nightingale in the spring, but it could not. Yet in heaven can be heard the song of praise, even from a worm;

and the notes trembling in the breast of the bird were as audible to Heaven even as the psalms of David before they had fashioned themselves into words and song.

Christmas-time drew near, and a peasant who dwelt close by the old wall stuck up a pole with some ears of corn fastened to the top, that the birds of heaven might have feast, and rejoice in the happy, blessed time. And on Christmas morning the sun arose and shone upon the ears of corn, which were quickly surrounded by a number of twittering birds. Then, from a hole in the wall, gushed forth in song the swelling thoughts of the bird as he issued from his hiding place to perform his first good deed on earth, – and in heaven it was well known who that bird was.

The winter was very hard; the ponds were covered with ice, and there was very little food for either the beasts of the field or the birds of the air. Our little bird flew away into the public roads, and found here and there, in the ruts of the sledges, a grain of corn, and at the halting places some crumbs. Of these he ate only a few, but he called around him the other birds and the hungry sparrows, that they too might have food. He flew into the towns, and looked about, and wherever a kind hand had strewed bread on the window-sill for the birds, he only ate a single crumb himself, and gave all the rest to the rest of the other birds. In the course of the winter the bird had in this way collected many crumbs and given them to other birds, till they equalled the weight of the loaf on which Inge had trod to keep her shoes clean; and when the last bread-crumb had been found and given, the gray wings of the bird became white, and spread themselves out for flight.

"See, yonder is a sea-gull!" cried the children, when they saw the white bird, as it dived into the sea, and rose again into the clear sunlight, white and glittering. But no one could tell whither it went then although some declared it flew straight to the sun.

The Dumb Book

IN THE HIGH-ROAD which led through a wood stood a solitary farm-house; the road, in fact, ran right through its yard. The sun was shining and all the windows were open; within the house people were very busy. In the yard, in an arbour formed by lilac bushes in full bloom, stood an open coffin; thither they had carried a dead man, who was to be buried that very afternoon. Nobody shed a tear over him; his face was covered over with a white cloth, under his head they had placed a large thick book, the leaves of which consisted of folded sheets of blotting-paper, and withered flowers lay between them; it was the herbarium which he had gathered in various places and was to be buried with him, according to his own wish. Every one of the flowers in it was connected with some chapter of his life.

"Who is the dead man?" we asked.

"The old student," was the reply. "They say that he was once an energetic young man, that he studied the dead languages, and sang and even composed many songs; then something had happened to him, and in consequence of this he gave himself up to drink, body and mind. When at last he had ruined his health, they brought him into the country, where someone paid for his board and residence. He was gentle as a child as long as the sullen mood did not come over him; but when it came he was fierce, became as strong as a giant, and ran about in the wood like a chased deer. But when we succeeded in bringing him home, and prevailed upon him to open the book with the dried-up plants in it, he would sometimes sit for a whole day looking at this or that plant, while frequently the tears rolled over his cheeks. God knows what was in his mind; but he requested us to put the book into his coffin, and now he lies there. In a little while the lid will be placed upon the coffin, and he will have sweet rest in the grave!"

The cloth which covered his face was lifted up; the dead man's face expressed peace – a sunbeam fell upon it. A swallow flew with the swiftness of an arrow into the arbour, turning in its flight, and twittered over the dead man's head.

What a strange feeling it is – surely we all know it – to look through old letters of our young days; a different life rises up out of the past, as it were, with all its hopes and sorrows. How many of the people with whom in those days we used to be on intimate terms appear to us as if dead, and yet they are still alive – only we have not thought of them for such a long time, whom we imagined we should retain in our memories for ever, and share every joy and sorrow with them.

The withered oak leaf in the book here recalled the friend, the schoolfellow, who was to be his friend for life. He fixed the leaf to the student's cap in the green wood, when they vowed eternal friendship. Where does he dwell now? The leaf is kept, but the friendship does no longer exist. Here is a foreign hothouse plant, too tender for the gardens of the North. It is almost as if its leaves still smelt sweet! She gave it to him out of her own garden – a nobleman's daughter.

Here is a water-lily that he had plucked himself, and watered with salt tears – a lily of sweet water. And here is a nettle: what may its leaves tell us? What might he have thought when he plucked and kept it? Here is a little snowdrop out of the solitary wood; here is an evergreen from the flower-pot at the tavern; and here is a simple blade of grass.

The lilac bends its fresh fragrant flowers over the dead man's head; the swallow passes again – "twit, twit;" now the men come with hammer and nails, the lid is placed over the dead man, while his head rests on the dumb book – so long cherished, now closed for ever!

The Heart's Desires

The Top and Ball

A WHIPPING TOP and a little ball lay together in a box, among other toys, and the top said to the ball, "Shall we be married, as we live in the same box?"

But the ball, which wore a dress of morocco leather, and thought as much of herself as any other young lady, would not even condescend to reply.

The next day came the little boy to whom the playthings belonged, and he painted the top red and yellow, and drove a brass-headed nail into the middle, so that while the top was spinning round it looked splendid.

"Look at me," said the top to the ball. "What do you say now? Shall we be engaged to each other? We should suit so well; you spring, and I dance. No one could be happier than we should be."

"Indeed! do you think so? Perhaps you do not know that my father and mother were morocco slippers, and that I have a Spanish cork in my body."

"Yes; but I am made of mahogany," said the top. "The major himself turned me. He has a turning lathe of his own, and it is a great amusement to him."

"Can I believe it?" asked the ball.

"May I never be whipped again," said the top, "if I am not telling you the truth."

"You certainly know how to speak for yourself very well," said the ball; "but I cannot accept your proposal. I am almost engaged to a swallow. Every time I fly up in the air, he puts his head out of the nest, and says, 'Will you?' and I have said, 'Yes,' to myself silently, and that is as good as being half engaged; but I will promise never to forget you."

"Much good that will be to me," said the top; and they spoke to each other no more.

Next day the ball was taken out by the boy. The top saw it flying high in the air, like a bird, till it would go quite out of sight. Each time it came back, as it touched the earth, it gave a higher leap than before, either because it longed to fly upwards, or from having a Spanish cork in its body. But the ninth time it rose in the air, it remained away, and did not return. The boy searched everywhere for it, but he searched in vain, for it could not be found; it was gone.

"I know very well where she is," sighed the top; "she is in the swallow's nest, and has married the swallow."

The more the top thought of this, the more he longed for the ball. His love increased the more, just because he could not get her; and that she should have been won by another, was the worst of all. The top still twirled about and hummed, but he continued to think of the ball; and the more he thought of her, the more beautiful she seemed to his fancy.

Thus several years passed by, and his love became quite old. The top, also, was no longer young; but there came a day when he looked handsomer than ever; for he was gilded all over. He was now a golden top, and whirled and danced about till he hummed quite loud, and was something worth looking at; but one day he leaped too high, and then he, also, was gone. They searched everywhere, even in the cellar, but he was nowhere to be found. Where could he be? He had jumped into the dust-bin, where all sorts of rubbish were lying: cabbage-stalks, dust, and rain-droppings that had fallen down from the gutter under the roof.

"Now I am in a nice place," said he; "my gilding will soon be washed off here. Oh dear, what a set of rabble I have got amongst!" And then he glanced at a curious round thing like an old apple, which lay near a long, leafless cabbage-stalk. It was, however, not an apple, but an old ball, which had lain for years in the gutter, and was soaked through with water.

"Thank goodness, here comes one of my own class, with whom I can talk," said the ball, examining the gilded top. "I am made of morocco," she said. "I was sewn together by a young lady, and I have a Spanish cork in my body; but no one would think it, to look at me now. I was once engaged to a swallow; but I fell in here from the gutter under the roof, and I have lain here more than five years, and have been thoroughly drenched. Believe me, it is a long time for a young maiden."

The top said nothing, but he thought of his old love; and the more she said, the more clear it became to him that this was the same ball.

The servant then came to clean out the dust-bin.

"Ah," she exclaimed, "here is a gilt top." So the top was brought again to notice and honor, but nothing more was heard of the little ball. He spoke not a word about his old love; for that soon died away. When the beloved object has lain for five years in a gutter, and has been drenched through, no one cares to know her again on meeting her in a dust-bin.

The Little Mermaid

FAR OUT IN the ocean, where the water is as blue as the prettiest cornflower, and as clear as crystal, it is very, very deep; so deep, indeed, that no cable could fathom it: many church steeples, piled one upon another, would not reach from the ground beneath to the surface of the water above. There dwell the Sea King and his subjects. We must not imagine that there is nothing at the bottom of the sea but bare yellow sand. No, indeed; the most singular flowers and plants grow there; the leaves and stems of which are so pliant, that the slightest agitation of the water causes them to stir as if they had life. Fishes, both large and small, glide between the branches, as birds fly among the trees here upon land. In the deepest spot of all, stands the castle of the Sea King. Its walls are built of coral, and the long, gothic windows are of the clearest amber. The roof is formed of shells, that open and close as the water flows over them. Their appearance is very beautiful, for in each lies a glittering pearl, which would be fit for the diadem of a queen.

The Sea King had been a widower for many years, and his aged mother kept house for him. She was a very wise woman, and exceedingly proud of her high birth; on that account she wore twelve oysters on her tail; while others, also of high rank, were only allowed to wear six. She was, however, deserving of very great praise, especially for her care of the little sea-princesses, her grand-daughters. They were six beautiful children; but the youngest was the prettiest of them all; her skin was as clear and delicate as a rose-leaf, and her eyes as blue as the deepest sea; but, like all the others, she had no feet, and her body ended in a fish's tail. All day long they played in the great halls of the castle, or among the living flowers that grew out of the walls. The large amber windows were open, and the fish swam in, just as the swallows fly into our houses when we open the windows, excepting that the fishes swam up to the princesses, ate out of their hands, and allowed themselves to be stroked. Outside the castle there was a beautiful garden, in which grew bright red and dark blue flowers, and blossoms like flames of fire; the fruit glittered like gold, and the leaves and stems waved to and fro continually. The earth itself was the finest sand, but blue as the flame of burning sulphur. Over everything lay a peculiar blue radiance, as if it were surrounded by the air from above, through which the blue sky shone, instead of the dark depths of the sea. In calm weather the sun could be seen, looking like a purple flower, with the light streaming from the calyx. Each of the young princesses had a little plot of ground in the garden, where she might dig and plant as she pleased. One arranged her flower-bed into the form of a whale; another thought it better to make hers like the figure of a little mermaid; but that of the youngest was round like the sun, and contained flowers as red as his rays at sunset. She was a strange child, quiet and thoughtful; and while her sisters would be delighted with the wonderful things which they obtained from the wrecks of vessels, she cared for nothing but her pretty red flowers, like the sun, excepting a beautiful marble statue. It was the representation of a handsome boy, carved out of pure white stone, which had fallen to the bottom of the sea from a wreck. She planted by the statue a rose-colored weeping willow. It grew splendidly, and very soon hung its fresh branches over the statue, almost down to the blue sands. The shadow had a violet tint, and waved to and fro like the branches; it seemed as if the crown of the tree and the root were at play, and trying to kiss each other. Nothing gave her so much pleasure as to hear about the world above the sea. She made her old grandmother tell her all she knew of the ships and of the towns, the people and the animals. To her it seemed most wonderful and beautiful to hear that the flowers of the land should have fragrance, and not those below the sea; that the trees of the forest should be green; and that the fishes among the trees could sing so sweetly, that it was quite a pleasure to hear them. Her grandmother called the little birds fishes, or she would not have understood her; for she had never seen birds.

"When you have reached your fifteenth year," said the grand-mother, "you will have permission to rise up out of the sea, to sit on the rocks in the moonlight, while the great ships are sailing by; and then you will see both forests and towns."

In the following year, one of the sisters would be fifteen: but as each was a year younger than the other, the youngest would have to wait five years before her turn came to rise up from the bottom of the ocean, and see the earth as we do. However, each promised to tell the others what she saw on her first visit, and what she thought the most beautiful; for their grandmother could not tell them enough; there were so many things on which they wanted information. None of them longed so much for her turn to come as the youngest, she who had the longest time to wait, and who was so quiet and thoughtful. Many nights she stood by the open window, looking up through the dark blue water, and watching the fish as they splashed about with their fins and tails. She could see the moon and stars shining faintly; but through the water they looked larger than they do to our eyes. When something like a black cloud passed between her and them, she knew that it was either a whale swimming over her head, or a ship full of human beings, who never imagined that a pretty little mermaid was standing beneath them, holding out her white hands towards the keel of their ship.

As soon as the eldest was fifteen, she was allowed to rise to the surface of the ocean. When she came back, she had hundreds of things to talk about; but the most beautiful, she said, was to lie in the moonlight, on a sandbank, in the quiet sea, near the coast, and to gaze on a large town nearby, where the lights were twinkling like hundreds of stars; to listen to the sounds of the music, the noise of carriages, and the voices of human beings, and then to hear the merry bells peal out from the church steeples; and because she could not go near to all those wonderful things, she longed for them more than ever. Oh, did not the youngest sister listen eagerly to all these descriptions? and afterwards, when she stood at the open window looking up through the dark blue water, she thought of the great city, with all its bustle and noise, and even fancied she could hear the sound of the church bells, down in the depths of the sea.

In another year the second sister received permission to rise to the surface of the water, and to swim about where she pleased. She rose just as the sun was setting, and this, she said, was the most beautiful sight of all. The whole sky looked like gold, while violet and rose-colored clouds, which she could not describe, floated over her; and, still more rapidly than the clouds, flew a large flock of wild swans towards the setting sun, looking like a long white veil across the sea. She also swam towards the sun; but it sunk into the waves, and the rosy tints faded from the clouds and from the sea.

The third sister's turn followed; she was the boldest of them all, and she swam up a broad river that emptied itself into the sea. On the banks she saw green hills covered with beautiful vines; palaces and castles peeped out from amid the proud trees of the forest; she heard the birds singing, and the rays of the sun were so powerful that she was obliged often to dive down under the water to cool her burning face. In a narrow creek she found a whole troop of little human children, quite naked, and sporting about in the water; she wanted to play with them, but they fled in a great fright; and then a little black animal came to the water; it was a dog, but she did not know that, for she had never before seen one. This animal barked at her so terribly that she became frightened, and rushed back to the open sea. But she said she should never forget the beautiful forest, the green hills, and the pretty little children who could swim in the water, although they had not fish's tails.

The fourth sister was more timid; she remained in the midst of the sea, but she said it was quite as beautiful there as nearer the land. She could see for so many miles around her, and the sky above looked like a bell of glass. She had seen the ships, but at such a great distance that they looked like sea-gulls. The dolphins sported in the waves, and the great whales spouted water from their nostrils till it seemed as if a hundred fountains were playing in every direction.

The fifth sister's birthday occurred in the winter; so when her turn came, she saw what the others had not seen the first time they went up. The sea looked quite green, and large icebergs were floating about, each like a pearl, she said, but larger and loftier than the churches built by men. They were of the most singular shapes, and glittered like diamonds. She had seated herself upon one of the largest, and let the wind play with her long hair, and she remarked that all the ships sailed by rapidly, and steered as far away as they could from the iceberg, as if they were afraid of it. Towards evening, as the sun went down, dark clouds covered the sky, the thunder rolled and the lightning flashed, and the red light glowed on the icebergs as they rocked and tossed on the heaving sea. On all the ships the sails were reefed with fear and trembling, while she sat calmly on the floating iceberg, watching the blue lightning, as it darted its forked flashes into the sea.

When first the sisters had permission to rise to the surface, they were each delighted with the new and beautiful sights they saw; but now, as grown-up girls, they could go when they pleased, and they had become indifferent about it. They wished themselves back again in the water, and after a month had passed they said it was much more beautiful down below, and pleasanter to be at home. Yet often, in the evening hours, the five sisters would twine their arms round each other, and rise to the surface, in a row. They had more beautiful voices than any human being could have; and before the approach of a storm, and when they expected a ship would be lost, they swam before the vessel, and sang sweetly of the delights to be found in the depths of the sea, and begging the sailors not to fear if they sank to the bottom. But the sailors could not understand the song, they took it for the howling of the storm. And these things were never to be beautiful for them; for if the ship sank, the men were drowned, and their dead bodies alone reached the palace of the Sea King.

When the sisters rose, arm-in-arm, through the water in this way, their youngest sister would stand quite alone, looking after them, ready to cry, only that the mermaids have no tears, and therefore they suffer more. "Oh, were I but fifteen years old," said she: "I know that I shall love the world up there, and all the people who live in it."

At last she reached her fifteenth year. "Well, now, you are grown up," said the old dowager, her grandmother; "so you must let me adorn you like your other sisters;" and she placed a wreath of white lilies in her hair, and every flower leaf was half a pearl. Then the old lady ordered eight great oysters to attach themselves to the tail of the princess to show her high rank.

"But they hurt me so," said the little mermaid.

"Pride must suffer pain," replied the old lady. Oh, how gladly she would have shaken off all this grandeur, and laid aside the heavy wreath! The red flowers in her own garden would have suited her much better, but she could not help herself: so she said, "Farewell," and rose as lightly as a bubble to the surface of the water. The sun had just set as she raised her head above the waves; but the clouds were tinted with crimson and gold, and through the glimmering twilight beamed the evening star in all its beauty. The sea was calm, and the air mild and fresh. A large ship, with three masts, lay becalmed on the water, with only one sail set; for not a breeze stiffed, and the sailors sat idle on deck or amongst the rigging. There was music and song on board; and, as darkness came on, a hundred colored lanterns were lighted, as if the flags of all nations waved in the air. The little mermaid swam close to the cabin windows; and now and then, as the waves lifted her up, she could look in through clear glass window-panes, and see a number of well-dressed people within. Among them was a young prince, the most beautiful of all, with large black eyes; he was sixteen years of age, and his birthday was being kept with much rejoicing. The sailors were dancing on deck, but when the prince came out of the cabin, more than a hundred rockets rose in the air, making it as bright as day. The little mermaid was so startled that she dived under water; and when she again stretched out her head, it appeared as if all the stars of heaven were falling around her, she had never seen such fireworks before. Great suns spurted fire about, splendid fireflies flew into the blue air, and everything was reflected in the clear, calm sea beneath. The ship itself was so brightly illuminated that all the people, and even the smallest rope, could be distinctly and plainly seen. And how handsome the young prince looked, as he pressed the hands of all present and smiled at them, while the music resounded through the clear night air.

It was very late; yet the little mermaid could not take her eyes from the ship, or from the beautiful prince. The colored lanterns had been extinguished, no more rockets rose in the air, and the cannon had ceased firing; but the sea became restless, and a moaning, grumbling sound could be heard beneath the waves: still the little mermaid remained by the cabin window, rocking up and down on the water, which enabled her to look in. After a while, the sails were quickly unfurled, and the noble ship continued her passage; but soon the waves rose higher, heavy clouds darkened the sky, and lightning appeared in the distance. A dreadful storm was approaching; once more the sails were reefed, and the great ship pursued her flying course over the raging sea. The waves rose mountains high, as if they would have overtopped the mast; but the ship dived like a swan between them, and then rose again on their lofty, foaming crests. To the little mermaid this appeared pleasant sport; not so to the sailors. At length the ship groaned and creaked; the thick planks gave way under the lashing of the sea as it broke over the deck; the mainmast snapped asunder like a reed; the ship lay over on her side; and the water rushed in. The little mermaid now perceived that the crew were in danger; even she herself was obliged to be careful to avoid the beams and planks of the wreck which lay scattered on the water. At one moment it was so pitch dark that she could not see a single object, but a flash of lightning revealed the whole scene; she could see every one who had been on board excepting the prince; when the ship parted, she had seen him sink into the deep waves, and she was glad, for she thought he would now be with her; and then she remembered that human beings could not live in the water, so that when he got down to her father's palace he would be quite dead. But he must not die. So she swam about among the beams and planks which strewed the surface of the sea, forgetting that they could crush her to pieces. Then she dived deeply under the dark waters, rising and falling with the waves, till at length she managed to reach the young prince, who was fast losing the power of swimming in that stormy sea. His limbs were failing him, his beautiful eyes were closed, and he would have died had not the little mermaid come to his assistance. She held his head above the water, and let the waves drift them where they would.

In the morning the storm had ceased; but of the ship not a single fragment could be seen. The sun rose up red and glowing from the water, and its beams brought back the hue of health to the prince's cheeks; but his eyes remained closed. The mermaid kissed his high, smooth forehead, and stroked back his wet hair; he seemed to her like the marble statue in her little garden, and she kissed him again, and wished that he might live. Presently they came in sight of land; she saw lofty blue mountains, on which the white snow rested as if a flock of swans were lying upon them. Near the coast were beautiful green forests, and close by stood a large building, whether a church or a convent she could not tell. Orange and citron trees grew in the garden, and before the door stood lofty palms. The sea here formed a little bay, in which the water was quite still, but very deep; so she swam with the handsome prince to the beach, which was covered with fine, white sand, and there she laid him in the warm sunshine, taking care to raise his head higher than his body. Then bells sounded in the large white building, and a number of young girls came into the garden. The little mermaid swam out farther from the shore and placed herself between some high rocks that rose out of the water; then she covered her head and neck with the foam of the sea so that her little face might not be seen, and watched to see what would become of the poor prince. She did not wait long before she saw a young girl approach the spot where he lay. She seemed frightened at first, but only for a moment; then she fetched a number of people, and the mermaid saw that the prince came to life again, and smiled upon those who stood round him. But to her he sent no smile; he knew not that she had saved him. This made her very unhappy, and when he was led away into the great building, she dived down sorrowfully into the water, and returned to her father's castle. She had always been silent and thoughtful, and now she was more so than ever. Her sisters asked her what she had seen during her first visit to the surface of the water; but she would tell them nothing. Many an evening and morning did she rise to the place where she had left the prince. She saw the fruits in the garden ripen till they were gathered, the snow on the tops of the mountains melt away; but she never saw the prince, and therefore she returned home, always more sorrowful than before. It was her only comfort to sit in her own little garden, and fling her arm round the beautiful marble statue which was like the prince; but she gave up tending her flowers, and they grew in wild confusion over the paths, twining their long leaves and stems round the branches of the trees, so that the whole place became dark and gloomy. At length she could bear it no longer, and told one of her sisters all about it. Then the others heard the secret, and very soon it became known to two mermaids whose intimate friend happened to know who the prince was. She had also seen the festival on board ship, and she told them where the prince came from, and where his palace stood.

"Come, little sister," said the other princesses; then they entwined their arms and rose up in a long row to the surface of the water, close by the spot where they knew the prince's palace stood. It was built of bright yellow shining stone, with long flights of marble steps, one of which reached quite down to the sea. Splendid gilded cupolas rose over the roof, and between the pillars that surrounded the whole building stood life-like statues of marble. Through the clear crystal of the lofty windows could be seen noble rooms, with costly silk curtains and hangings of tapestry; while the walls were covered with beautiful paintings which were a pleasure to look at. In the centre of the largest saloon a fountain threw its sparkling jets high up into the glass cupola of the ceiling, through which the sun shone down upon the water and upon the beautiful plants growing round the basin of the fountain. Now that she knew where he lived, she spent many an evening and many a night on the water near the palace. She would swim much nearer the shore than any of the others ventured to do; indeed once she went quite up the narrow channel under the marble balcony, which threw a broad shadow on the water. Here she would sit and watch the young prince, who thought himself quite alone in the bright moonlight. She saw him many times of an evening sailing in a pleasant boat, with music playing and flags waving. She peeped out from among the green rushes, and if the wind caught her long silvery-white veil, those who saw it believed it to be a swan, spreading out its wings. On many a night, too, when the fishermen, with their torches, were out at sea, she heard them relate so many good things about the doings of the young prince, that she was glad she had saved his life when he had been tossed about half-dead on the waves. And she remembered that his head had rested on her bosom, and how heartily she had kissed him; but he knew nothing of all this, and could not even dream of her. She grew more and more fond of human beings, and wished more and more to be able to wander about with those whose world seemed to be so much larger than her own. They could fly over the sea in ships, and mount the high hills which were far above the clouds; and the lands they possessed, their woods and their fields, stretched far away beyond the reach of her sight. There was so much that she wished to know, and her sisters were unable to answer all her questions. Then she applied to her old grandmother, who knew all about the upper world, which she very rightly called the lands above the sea.

"If human beings are not drowned," asked the little mermaid, "can they live forever? do they never die as we do here in the sea?"

"Yes," replied the old lady, "they must also die, and their term of life is even shorter than ours. We sometimes live to three hundred years, but when we cease to exist here we only become the foam on the surface of the water, and we have not even a grave down here of those we love. We have not immortal souls, we shall never live again; but, like the green sea-weed, when once it has been cut off, we can never flourish more. Human beings, on the contrary, have a soul which lives forever, lives after the body has been turned to dust. It rises up through the clear, pure air beyond the glittering stars. As we rise out of the water, and behold all the land of the earth, so do they rise to unknown and glorious regions which we shall never see."

"Why have not we an immortal soul?" asked the little mermaid mournfully; "I would give gladly all the hundreds of years that I have to live, to be a human being only for one day, and to have the hope of knowing the happiness of that glorious world above the stars."

"You must not think of that," said the old woman; "we feel ourselves to be much happier and much better off than human beings."

"So I shall die," said the little mermaid, "and as the foam of the sea I shall be driven about never again to hear the music of the waves, or to see the pretty flowers nor the red sun. Is there anything I can do to win an immortal soul?"

"No," said the old woman, "unless a man were to love you so much that you were more to him than his father or mother; and if all his thoughts and all his love were fixed upon you, and the priest placed his right hand in yours, and he promised to be true to you here and hereafter, then his soul would glide into your body and you would obtain a share in the future happiness of mankind. He would give a soul to you and retain his own as well; but this can never happen. Your fish's tail, which amongst us is considered so beautiful, is thought on earth to be quite ugly; they do not know any better, and they think it necessary to have two stout props, which they call legs, in order to be handsome."

Then the little mermaid sighed, and looked sorrowfully at her fish's tail. "Let us be happy," said the old lady, "and dart and spring about during the three hundred years that we have to live, which is really quite long enough; after that we can rest ourselves all the better. This evening we are going to have a court ball."

It is one of those splendid sights which we can never see on earth. The walls and the ceiling of the large ball-room were of thick, but transparent crystal. May hundreds of colossal shells, some of a deep red, others of a grass green, stood on each side in rows, with blue fire in them, which lighted up the whole saloon, and shone through the walls, so that the sea was also illuminated. Innumerable fishes, great and small, swam past the crystal walls; on some of them the scales glowed with a purple brilliancy, and on others they shone like silver and gold. Through the halls flowed a broad stream, and in it danced the mermen and the mermaids to the music of their own sweet singing. No one on earth has such a lovely voice as theirs. The little mermaid sang more sweetly than them all. The whole court applauded her with hands and tails; and for a moment her heart felt quite gay, for she knew she had the loveliest voice of any on earth or in the sea. But she soon thought again of the world above her, for she could not forget the charming prince, nor her sorrow that she had not an immortal soul like his; therefore she crept away silently out of her father's palace, and while everything within was gladness and song, she sat in her own little garden sorrowful and alone. Then she heard the bugle sounding through the water, and thought – "He is certainly sailing above, he on whom my wishes depend, and in whose hands I should like to place the happiness of my life. I will venture all for him, and to win an immortal soul, while my sisters are dancing in my father's palace, I will go to the sea witch, of whom I have always been so much afraid, but she can give me counsel and help."

And then the little mermaid went out from her garden, and took the road to the foaming whirlpools, behind which the sorceress lived. She had never been that way before: neither flowers nor grass grew there; nothing but bare, gray, sandy ground stretched out to the whirlpool, where the water, like foaming mill-wheels, whirled round everything that it seized, and cast it into the fathomless deep. Through the midst of these crushing whirlpools the little mermaid was obliged to pass, to reach the dominions of the sea witch; and also for a long distance the only road lay right across a quantity of warm, bubbling mire, called by the witch her turfmoor. Beyond this stood her house, in the centre of a strange forest, in which all the trees and flowers were polypi, half animals and half plants; they looked like serpents with a hundred heads growing out of the ground. The branches were long slimy arms, with fingers like flexible worms, moving limb after limb from the root to the top. All that could be reached in the sea they seized upon, and held fast, so that it never escaped from their clutches. The little mermaid was so alarmed at what she saw, that she stood still, and her heart beat with fear, and she was very nearly turning back; but she thought of the prince, and of the human soul for which she longed, and her courage returned. She fastened her long flowing hair round her head, so that the polypi might not seize hold of it. She laid her hands together across her bosom, and then she darted forward as a fish shoots through the water, between the supple arms and fingers of the ugly polypi, which were stretched out on each side of her. She saw that each held in its grasp something it had seized with its numerous little arms, as if they were iron bands. The white skeletons of human beings who had perished at sea, and had sunk down into the deep waters, skeletons of land animals, oars, rudders, and chests of ships were lying tightly grasped by their clinging arms; even a little mermaid, whom they had caught and strangled; and this seemed the most shocking of all to the little princess.

She now came to a space of marshy ground in the wood, where large, fat water-snakes were rolling in the mire, and showing their ugly, drab-colored bodies. In the midst of this spot stood a house, built with the bones of shipwrecked human beings. There sat the sea witch, allowing a toad to eat from her mouth, just as people sometimes feed a canary with a piece of sugar. She called the ugly water-snakes her little chickens, and allowed them to crawl all over her bosom.

"I know what you want," said the sea witch; "it is very stupid of you, but you shall have your way, and it will bring you to sorrow, my pretty princess. You want to get rid of your fish's tail, and to have two supports instead of it, like human beings on earth, so that the young prince may fall in love with you, and that you may have an immortal soul." And then the witch laughed so loud and disgustingly, that the toad and the snakes fell to the ground, and lay there wriggling about. "You are but just in time," said the witch; "for after sunrise to-morrow I should not be able to help you till the end of another year. I will prepare a draught for you, with which you must swim to land tomorrow before sunrise, and sit down on the shore and drink it. Your tail will then disappear, and shrink up into what mankind calls legs, and you will feel great pain, as if a sword were passing through you. But all who see you will say that you are the prettiest little human being they ever saw. You will still have the same floating gracefulness of movement, and no dancer will ever tread so lightly; but at every step you take it will feel as if you were treading upon sharp knives, and that the blood must flow. If you will bear all this, I will help you."

"Yes, I will," said the little princess in a trembling voice, as she thought of the prince and the immortal soul.

"But think again," said the witch; "for when once your shape has become like a human being, you can no more be a mermaid. You will never return through the water to your sisters, or to your father's palace again; and if you do not win the love of the prince, so that he is willing to forget his father and mother for your sake, and to love you with his whole soul, and allow the priest to join your hands that you may be man and wife, then you will never have an immortal soul. The first morning after he marries another your heart will break, and you will become foam on the crest of the waves."

"I will do it," said the little mermaid, and she became pale as death.

"But I must be paid also," said the witch, "and it is not a trifle that I ask. You have the sweetest voice of any who dwell here in the depths of the sea, and you believe that you will be able to charm the prince with it also, but this voice you must give to me; the best thing you possess will I have for the price of my draught. My own blood must be mixed with it, that it may be as sharp as a two-edged sword."

"But if you take away my voice," said the little mermaid, "what is left for me?"

"Your beautiful form, your graceful walk, and your expressive eyes; surely with these you can enchain a man's heart. Well, have you lost your courage? Put out your little tongue that I may cut it off as my payment; then you shall have the powerful draught."

"It shall be," said the little mermaid.

Then the witch placed her cauldron on the fire, to prepare the magic draught.

"Cleanliness is a good thing," said she, scouring the vessel with snakes, which she had tied together in a large knot; then she pricked herself in the breast, and let the black blood drop into it. The steam that rose formed itself into such horrible shapes that no one could look at them without fear. Every moment the witch threw something else into the vessel, and when it began to boil, the sound was like the weeping of a crocodile. When at last the magic draught was ready, it looked like the clearest water. "There it is for you," said the witch. Then she cut off the mermaid's tongue, so that she became dumb, and would never again speak or sing. "If the polypi should seize hold of you as you return through the wood," said the witch, "throw over them a few drops of the potion, and their fingers will be torn into a thousand pieces." But the little mermaid had no occasion to do this, for the polypi sprang back in terror when they caught sight of the glittering draught, which shone in her hand like a twinkling star.

So she passed quickly through the wood and the marsh, and between the rushing whirlpools. She saw that in her father's palace the torches in the ballroom were extinguished, and all within asleep; but she did not venture to go in to them, for now she was dumb and going to leave them forever, she felt as if her heart would break. She stole into the garden, took a flower from the flower-beds of each of her sisters, kissed her hand a thousand times towards the palace, and then rose up through the dark blue waters. The sun had not risen when she came in sight of the prince's palace, and approached the beautiful marble steps, but the moon shone clear and bright. Then the little mermaid drank the magic draught, and it seemed as if a two-edged sword went through her delicate body: she fell into a swoon, and lay like one dead. When the sun arose and shone over the sea, she recovered, and felt a sharp pain; but just before her stood the handsome young prince. He fixed his coal-black eyes upon her so earnestly that she cast down her own, and then became aware that her fish's tail was gone, and that she had as pretty a pair of white legs and tiny feet as any little maiden could have; but she had no clothes, so she wrapped herself in her long, thick hair. The prince asked her who she was, and where she came from, and she looked at him mildly and sorrowfully with her deep blue eyes; but she could not speak. Every step she took was as the witch had said it would be, she felt as if treading upon the points of needles or sharp knives; but she bore it willingly, and stepped as lightly by the prince's side as a soap-bubble, so that he and all who saw her wondered at her graceful-swaying movements. She was very soon arrayed in costly robes of silk and muslin, and was the most beautiful creature in the palace; but she was dumb, and could neither speak nor sing.

Beautiful female slaves, dressed in silk and gold, stepped forward and sang before the prince and his royal parents: one sang better than all the others, and the prince clapped his hands and smiled at her. This was great sorrow to the little mermaid; she knew how much more sweetly she herself could sing once, and she thought, "Oh if he could only know that! I have given away my voice forever, to be with him."

The slaves next performed some pretty fairy-like dances, to the sound of beautiful music. Then the little mermaid raised her lovely white arms, stood on the tips of her toes, and glided over the floor, and danced as no one yet had been able to dance. At each moment her beauty became more revealed, and her expressive eyes appealed more directly to the heart than the songs of the slaves. Every one was enchanted, especially the prince, who called her his little foundling; and she danced again quite readily, to please him, though each time her foot touched the floor it seemed as if she trod on sharp knives.

The prince said she should remain with him always, and she received permission to sleep at his door, on a velvet cushion. He had a page's dress made for her, that she might accompany him on horseback. They rode together through the sweet-scented woods, where the green boughs touched their shoulders, and the little birds sang among the fresh leaves. She climbed with the prince to the tops of high mountains; and although her tender feet bled so that even her steps were marked, she only laughed, and followed him till they could see the clouds beneath them looking like a flock of birds travelling to distant lands. While at the prince's palace, and when all the household were asleep, she would go and sit on the broad marble steps; for it eased her burning feet to bathe them in the cold sea-water; and then she thought of all those below in the deep.

Once during the night her sisters came up arm-in-arm, singing sorrowfully, as they floated on the water. She beckoned to them, and then they recognized her, and told her how she had grieved them. After that, they came to the same place every night; and once she saw in the distance her old grandmother, who had not been to the surface of the sea for many years, and the old Sea King, her father, with his crown on his head. They stretched out their hands towards her, but they did not venture so near the land as her sisters did.

As the days passed, she loved the prince more fondly, and he loved her as he would love a little child, but it never came into his head to make her his wife; yet, unless he married her, she could not receive an immortal soul; and, on the morning after his marriage with another, she would dissolve into the foam of the sea.

"Do you not love me the best of them all?" the eyes of the little mermaid seemed to say, when he took her in his arms, and kissed her fair forehead.

"Yes, you are dear to me," said the prince; "for you have the best heart, and you are the most devoted to me; you are like a young maiden whom I once saw, but whom I shall never meet again. I was in a ship that was wrecked, and the waves cast me ashore near a holy temple, where several young maidens performed the service. The youngest of them found me on the shore, and saved my life. I saw her but twice, and she is the only one in the world whom I could love; but you are like her, and you have almost driven her image out of my mind. She belongs to the holy temple, and my good fortune has sent you to me instead of her; and we will never part."

"Ah, he knows not that it was I who saved his life," thought the little mermaid. "I carried him over the sea to the wood where the temple stands: I sat beneath the foam, and watched till the human beings came to help him. I saw the pretty maiden that he loves better than he loves me;" and the mermaid sighed deeply, but she could not shed tears. "He says the maiden belongs to the holy temple, therefore she will never return to the world. They will meet no more: while I am by his side, and see him every day. I will take care of him, and love him, and give up my life for his sake."

Very soon it was said that the prince must marry, and that the beautiful daughter of a neighboring king would be his wife, for a fine ship was being fitted out. Although the prince gave out that he merely intended to pay a visit to the king, it was generally supposed that he really went to see his daughter. A great company were to go with him.

The little mermaid smiled, and shook her head. She knew the prince's thoughts better than any of the others.

"I must travel," he had said to her; "I must see this beautiful princess; my parents desire it; but they will not oblige me to bring her home as my bride. I cannot love her; she is not like the beautiful maiden in the temple, whom you resemble. If I were forced to choose a bride, I would rather choose you, my dumb foundling, with those expressive eyes." And then he kissed her rosy mouth, played with her long waving hair, and laid his head on her heart, while she dreamed of human happiness and an immortal soul. "You are not afraid of the sea, my dumb child," said he, as they stood on the deck of the noble ship which was to carry them to the country of the neighboring king. And then he told her of storm and of calm, of strange fishes in the deep beneath them, and of what the divers had seen there; and she smiled at his descriptions, for she knew better than any one what wonders were at the bottom of the sea.

In the moonlight, when all on board were asleep, excepting the man at the helm, who was steering, she sat on the deck, gazing down through the clear water. She thought she could distinguish her father's castle, and upon it her aged grandmother, with the silver crown on her head, looking through the rushing tide at the keel of the vessel. Then her sisters came up on the waves, and gazed at her mournfully, wringing their white hands. She beckoned to them, and smiled, and wanted to tell them how happy and well off she was; but the cabin-boy approached, and when her sisters dived down he thought it was only the foam of the sea which he saw.

The next morning the ship sailed into the harbor of a beautiful town belonging to the king whom the prince was going to visit. The church bells were ringing, and from the high towers sounded a flourish of trumpets; and soldiers, with flying colors and glittering bayonets, lined the rocks through which they passed. Every day was a festival; balls and entertainments followed one another.

But the princess had not yet appeared. People said that she was being brought up and educated in a religious house, where she was learning every royal virtue. At last she came. Then the little mermaid, who was very anxious to see whether she was really beautiful, was obliged to acknowledge that she had never seen a more perfect vision of beauty. Her skin was delicately fair, and beneath her long dark eye-lashes her laughing blue eyes shone with truth and purity.

"It was you," said the prince, "who saved my life when I lay dead on the beach," and he folded his blushing bride in his arms. "Oh, I am too happy," said he to the little mermaid; "my fondest hopes are all fulfilled. You will rejoice at my happiness; for your devotion to me is great and sincere."

The little mermaid kissed his hand, and felt as if her heart were already broken. His wedding morning would bring death to her, and she would change into the foam of the sea. All the church bells rung, and the heralds rode about the town proclaiming the betrothal. Perfumed oil was burning in costly silver lamps on every altar. The priests waved the censers, while the bride and bridegroom joined their hands and received the blessing of the bishop. The little mermaid, dressed in silk and gold, held up the bride's train; but her ears heard nothing of the festive music, and her eyes saw not the holy ceremony; she thought of the night of death which was coming to her, and of all she had lost in the world. On the same evening the bride and bridegroom went on board ship; cannons were roaring, flags waving, and in the centre of the ship a costly tent of purple and gold had been erected. It contained elegant couches, for the reception of the bridal pair during the night. The ship, with swelling sails and a favorable wind, glided away smoothly and lightly over the calm sea. When it grew dark a number of colored lamps were lit, and the sailors danced merrily on the deck. The little mermaid could not help thinking of her first rising out of the sea, when she had seen similar festivities and joys; and she joined in the dance, poised herself in the air as a swallow when he pursues his prey, and all present cheered her with wonder. She had never danced so elegantly before. Her tender feet felt as if cut with sharp knives, but she cared not for it; a sharper pang had pierced through her heart. She knew this was the last evening she should ever see the prince, for whom she had forsaken her kindred and her home; she had given up her beautiful voice, and suffered unheard-of pain daily for him, while he knew nothing of it. This was the last evening that she would breathe the same air with him, or gaze on the starry sky and the deep sea; an eternal night, without a thought or a dream, awaited her: she had no soul and now she could never win one. All was joy and gayety on board ship till long after midnight; she laughed and danced with the rest, while the thoughts of death were in her heart. The prince kissed his beautiful bride, while she played with his raven hair, till they went arm-in-arm to rest in the splendid tent. Then all became still on board the ship; the helmsman, alone awake, stood at the helm. The little mermaid leaned her white arms on the edge of the vessel, and looked towards the east for the first blush of morning, for that first ray of dawn that would bring her death. She saw her sisters rising out of the flood: they were as pale as herself; but their long beautiful hair waved no more in the wind, and had been cut off.

"We have given our hair to the witch," said they, "to obtain help for you, that you may not die to-night. She has given us a knife: here it is, see it is very sharp. Before the sun rises you must plunge it into the heart of the prince; when the warm blood falls upon your feet they will grow together again, and form into a fish's tail, and you will be once more a mermaid, and return to us to live out your three hundred years before you die and change into the salt sea foam. Haste, then; he or you must die before sunrise. Our old grandmother moans so for you, that her white hair is falling off from sorrow, as ours fell under the witch's scissors. Kill the prince and come back; hasten: do you not see the first red streaks in the sky? In a few minutes the sun will rise, and you must die." And then they sighed deeply and mournfully, and sank down beneath the waves.

The little mermaid drew back the crimson curtain of the tent, and beheld the fair bride with her head resting on the prince's breast. She bent down and kissed his fair brow, then looked at the sky on which the rosy dawn grew brighter and brighter; then she glanced at the sharp knife, and again fixed her eyes on the prince, who whispered the name of his bride in his dreams. She was in his thoughts, and the knife trembled in the hand of the little mermaid: then she flung it far away from her into the waves; the water turned red where it fell, and the drops that spurted up looked like blood. She cast one more lingering, half-fainting glance at the prince, and then threw herself from the ship into the sea, and thought her body was dissolving into foam. The sun rose above the waves, and his warm rays fell on the cold foam of the little mermaid, who did not feel as if she were dying. She saw the bright sun, and all around her floated hundreds of transparent beautiful beings; she could see through them the white sails of the ship, and the red clouds in the sky; their speech was melodious, but too ethereal to be heard by mortal ears, as they were also unseen by mortal eyes. The little mermaid perceived that she had a body like theirs, and that she continued to rise higher and higher out of the foam. "Where am I?" asked she, and her voice sounded ethereal, as the voice of those who were with her; no earthly music could imitate it.

"Among the daughters of the air," answered one of them. "A mermaid has not an immortal soul, nor can she obtain one unless she wins the love of a human being. On the power of another hangs her eternal destiny. But the daughters of the air, although they do not possess an immortal soul, can, by their good deeds, procure one for themselves. We fly to warm countries, and cool the sultry air that destroys mankind with the pestilence. We carry the perfume of the flowers to spread health and restoration. After we have striven for three hundred years to all the good in our power, we receive an immortal soul and take part in the happiness of mankind. You, poor little mermaid, have tried with your whole heart to do as we are doing; you have suffered and endured and raised yourself to the spirit-world by your good deeds; and now, by striving for three hundred years in the same way, you may obtain an immortal soul."

The little mermaid lifted her glorified eyes towards the sun, and felt them, for the first time, filling with tears. On the ship, in which she had left the prince, there were life and noise; she saw him and his beautiful bride searching for her; sorrowfully they gazed at the pearly foam, as if they knew she had thrown herself into the waves. Unseen she kissed the forehead of the bride, and fanned the prince, and then mounted with the other children of the air to a rosy cloud that floated through the aether.

"After three hundred years, thus shall we float into the kingdom of heaven," said she. "And we may even get there sooner," whispered one of her companions. "Unseen we can enter the houses of men, where there are children, and for every day on which we find a good child, who is the joy of his parents and deserves their love, our time of probation is shortened. The child does not know, when we fly through the room, that we smile with joy at his good conduct, for we can count one year less of our three hundred years. But when we see a naughty or a wicked child, we shed tears of sorrow, and for every tear a day is added to our time of trial!"

The Travelling Companion

POOR JOHN WAS very sad; for his father was so ill, he had no hope of his recovery. John sat alone with the sick man in the little room, and the lamp had nearly burnt out; for it was late in the night.

"You have been a good son, John," said the sick father, "and God will help you on in the world." He looked at him, as he spoke, with mild, earnest eyes, drew a deep sigh, and died; yet it appeared as if he still slept.

John wept bitterly. He had no one in the wide world now; neither father, mother, brother, nor sister. Poor John! he knelt down by the bed, kissed his dead father's hand, and wept many, many bitter tears. But at last his eyes closed, and he fell asleep with his head resting against the hard bedpost. Then he dreamed a strange dream; he thought he saw the sun shining upon him, and his father alive and well, and even heard him laughing as he used to do when he was very happy. A beautiful girl, with a golden crown on her head, and long, shining hair, gave him her hand; and his father said, "See what a bride you have won. She is the loveliest maiden on the whole earth." Then he awoke, and all the beautiful things vanished before his eyes, his father lay dead on the bed, and he was all alone. Poor John!

During the following week the dead man was buried. The son walked behind the coffin which contained his father, whom he so dearly loved, and would never again behold. He heard the earth fall on the coffin-lid, and watched it till only a corner remained in sight, and at last that also disappeared. He felt as if his heart would break with its weight of sorrow, till those who stood round the grave sang a psalm, and the sweet, holy tones brought tears into his eyes, which relieved him. The sun shone brightly down on the green trees, as if it would say, "You must not be so sorrowful, John. Do you see the beautiful blue sky above you? Your father is up there, and he prays to the loving Father of all, that you may do well in the future."

"I will always be good," said John, "and then I shall go to be with my father in heaven. What joy it will be when we see each other again! How much I shall have to relate to him, and how many things he will be able to explain to me of the delights of heaven, and teach me as he once did on earth. Oh, what joy it will be!"

He pictured it all so plainly to himself, that he smiled even while the tears ran down his cheeks.

The little birds in the chestnut-trees twittered, "Tweet, tweet;" they were so happy, although they had seen the funeral; but they seemed as if they knew that the dead man was now in heaven, and that he had wings much larger and more beautiful than their own; and he was happy now, because he had been good here on earth, and they were glad of it. John saw them fly away out of the green trees into the wide world, and he longed to fly with them; but first he cut out a large wooden cross, to place on his father's grave; and when he brought it there in the evening, he found the grave decked out with gravel and flowers. Strangers had done this; they who had known the good old father who was now dead, and who had loved him very much.

Early the next morning, John packed up his little bundle of clothes, and placed all his money, which consisted of fifty dollars and a few shillings, in his girdle; with this he determined to try his fortune in the world. But first he went into the churchyard; and, by his father's grave, he offered up a prayer, and said, "Farewell."

As he passed through the fields, all the flowers looked fresh and beautiful in the warm sunshine, and nodded in the wind, as if they wished to say, "Welcome to the green wood, where all is fresh and bright."

Then John turned to have one more look at the old church, in which he had been christened in his infancy, and where his father had taken him every Sunday to hear the service and join in singing the psalms. As he looked at the old tower, he espied the ringer standing at one of the narrow openings, with his little pointed red cap on his head, and shading his eyes from the sun with his bent arm. John nodded farewell to him, and the little ringer waved his red cap, laid his hand on his heart, and kissed his hand to him a great many times, to show that he felt kindly towards him, and wished him a prosperous journey.

John continued his journey, and thought of all the wonderful things he should see in the large, beautiful world, till he found himself farther away from home than ever he had been before. He did not even know the names of the places he passed through, and could scarcely understand the language of the people he met, for he was far away, in a strange land. The first night he slept on a haystack, out in the fields, for there was no other bed for him; but it seemed to him so nice and comfortable that even a king need not wish for a better. The field, the brook, the haystack, with the blue sky above, formed a beautiful sleeping-room. The green grass, with the little red and white flowers, was the carpet; the elder-bushes and the hedges of wild roses looked like garlands on the walls; and for a bath he could have the clear, fresh water of the brook; while the rushes bowed their heads to him, to wish him good morning and good evening. The moon, like a large lamp, hung high up in the blue ceiling, and he had no fear of its setting fire to his curtains. John slept here quite safely all night; and when he awoke, the sun was up, and all the little birds were singing round him, "Good morning, good morning. Are you not up yet?"

It was Sunday, and the bells were ringing for church. As the people went in, John followed them; he heard God's word, joined in singing the psalms, and listened to the preacher. It seemed to him just as if he were in his own church, where he had been christened, and had sung the psalms with his father. Out in the churchyard were several graves, and on some of them the grass had grown very high. John thought of his father's grave, which he knew at last would look like these, as he was not there to weed and attend to it. Then he set to work, pulled up the high grass, raised the wooden crosses which had fallen down, and replaced the wreaths which had been blown away from their places by the wind, thinking all the time, "Perhaps some one is doing the same for my father's grave, as I am not there to do it."

Outside the church door stood an old beggar, leaning on his crutch. John gave him his silver shillings, and then he continued his journey, feeling lighter and happier than ever. Towards evening, the weather became very stormy, and he hastened on as quickly as he could, to get shelter; but it was quite dark by the time he reached a little lonely church which stood on a hill. "I will go in here," he said, "and sit down in a corner; for I am quite tired, and want rest."

So he went in, and seated himself; then he folded his hands, and offered up his evening prayer, and was soon fast asleep and dreaming, while the thunder rolled and the lightning flashed without. When he awoke, it was still night; but the storm had ceased, and the moon shone in upon him through the windows. Then he saw an open coffin standing in the centre of the church, which contained a dead man, waiting for burial. John was not at all timid; he had a good conscience, and he knew also that the dead can never injure any one. It is living wicked men who do harm to others. Two such wicked persons stood now by the dead man, who had been brought to the church to be buried. Their evil intentions were to throw the poor dead body outside the church door, and not leave him to rest in his coffin.

"Why do you do this?" asked John, when he saw what they were going to do;

"it is very wicked. Leave him to rest in peace, in Christ's name."

"Nonsense," replied the two dreadful men. "He has cheated us; he owed us money which he could not pay, and now he is dead we shall not get a penny; so we mean to have our revenge, and let him lie like a dog outside the church door."

"I have only fifty dollars," said John, "it is all I possess in the world, but I will give it to you if you will promise me faithfully to leave the dead man in peace. I shall be able to get on without the money; I have strong and healthy limbs, and God will always help me."

"Why, of course," said the horrid men, "if you will pay his debt we will both promise not to touch him. You may depend upon that;" and then they took the money he offered them, laughed at him for his good nature, and went their way.

Then he laid the dead body back in the coffin, folded the hands, and took leave of it; and went away contentedly through the great forest. All around him he could see the prettiest little elves dancing in the moonlight, which shone through the trees. They were not disturbed by his appearance, for they knew he was good and harmless among men. They are wicked people only who can never obtain a glimpse of fairies. Some of them were not taller than the breadth of a finger, and they wore golden combs in their long, yellow hair. They were rocking themselves two together on the large dew-drops with which the leaves and the high grass were sprinkled. Sometimes the dew-drops would roll away, and then they fell down between the stems of the long grass, and caused a great deal of laughing and noise among the other little people. It was quite charming to watch them at play. Then they sang songs, and John remembered that he had learnt those pretty songs when he was a little boy. Large speckled spiders, with silver crowns on their heads, were employed to spin suspension bridges and palaces from one hedge to another, and when the tiny drops fell upon them, they glittered in the moonlight like shining glass. This continued till sunrise. Then the little elves crept into the flower-buds, and the wind seized the bridges and palaces, and fluttered them in the air like cobwebs.

As John left the wood, a strong man's voice called after him, "Hallo, comrade, where are you travelling?"

"Into the wide world," he replied; "I am only a poor lad, I have neither father nor mother, but God will help me."

"I am going into the wide world also," replied the stranger; "shall we keep each other company?"

"With all my heart," he said, and so they went on together. Soon they began to like each other very much, for they were both good; but John found out that the stranger was much more clever than himself. He had travelled all over the world, and could describe almost everything. The sun was high in the heavens when they seated themselves under a large tree to eat their breakfast, and at the same moment an old woman came towards them. She was very old and almost bent double. She leaned upon a stick and carried on her back a bundle of firewood, which she had collected in the forest; her apron was tied round it, and John saw three great stems of fern and some willow twigs peeping out. just as she came close up to them, her foot slipped and she fell to the ground screaming loudly; poor old woman, she had broken her leg! John proposed directly that they should carry the old woman home to her cottage; but the stranger opened his knapsack and took out a box, in which he said he had a salve that would quickly make her leg well and strong again, so that she would be able to walk home herself, as if her leg had never been broken. And all that he would ask in return was the three fern stems which she carried in her apron.

"That is rather too high a price," said the old woman, nodding her head quite strangely. She did not seem at all inclined to part with the fern stems. However, it was not very agreeable to lie there with a broken leg, so she gave them to him; and such was the power of the ointment, that no sooner had he rubbed her leg with it than the old mother rose up and walked even better than she had done before. But then this wonderful ointment could not be bought at a chemist's.

"What can you want with those three fern rods?" asked John of his fellow-traveller.

"Oh, they will make capital brooms," said he; "and I like them because I have strange whims sometimes." Then they walked on together for a long distance.

"How dark the sky is becoming," said John; "and look at those thick, heavy clouds."

"Those are not clouds," replied his fellow-traveller; "they are mountains – large lofty mountains – on the tops of which we should be above the clouds, in the pure, free air. Believe me, it is delightful to ascend so high, tomorrow we shall be there." But the mountains were not so near as they appeared; they had to travel a whole day before they reached them, and pass through black forests and piles of rock as large as a town. The journey had been so fatiguing that John and his fellow-traveller stopped to rest at a roadside inn, so that they might gain strength for their journey on the morrow. In the large public room of the inn a great many persons were assembled to see a comedy performed by dolls. The showman had just erected his little theatre, and the people were sitting round the room to witness the performance. Right in front, in the very best place, sat a stout butcher, with a great bull-dog by his side who seemed very much inclined to bite. He sat staring with all his eyes, and so indeed did every one else in the room. And then the play began. It was a pretty piece, with a king and a queen in it, who sat on a beautiful throne, and had gold crowns on their heads. The trains to their dresses were very long, according to the fashion; while the prettiest of wooden dolls, with glass eyes and large mustaches, stood at the doors, and opened and shut them, that the fresh air might come into the room. It was a very pleasant play, not at all mournful; but just as the queen stood up and walked across the stage, the great bull-dog, who should have been held back by his master, made a spring forward, and caught the queen in the teeth by the slender wrist, so that it snapped in two. This was a very dreadful disaster. The poor man, who was exhibiting the dolls, was much annoyed, and quite sad about his queen; she was the prettiest doll he had, and the bull-dog had broken her head and shoulders off. But after all the people were gone away, the stranger, who came with John, said that he could soon set her to rights. And then he brought out his box and rubbed the doll with some of the salve with which he had cured the old woman when she broke her leg. As soon as this was done the doll's back became quite right again; her head and shoulders were fixed on, and she could even move her limbs herself: there was now no occasion to pull the wires, for the doll acted just like a living creature, excepting that she could not speak.

The man to whom the show belonged was quite delighted at having a doll who could dance of herself without being pulled by the wires; none of the other dolls could do this.

During the night, when all the people at the inn were gone to bed, some one was heard to sigh so deeply and painfully, and the sighing continued for so long a time, that every one got up to see what could be the matter. The showman went at once to his little theatre and found that it proceeded from the dolls, who all lay on the floor sighing piteously, and staring with their glass eyes; they all wanted to be rubbed with the ointment, so that, like the queen, they might be able to move of themselves. The queen threw herself on her knees, took off her beautiful crown, and, holding it in her hand, cried, "Take this from me, but do rub my husband and his courtiers."

The poor man who owned the theatre could scarcely refrain from weeping; he was so sorry that he could not help them. Then he immediately spoke to John's comrade, and promised him all the money he might receive at the next evening's performance, if he would only rub the ointment on four or five of his dolls. But the fellow-traveller said he did not require anything in return, excepting the sword which the showman wore by his side. As soon as he received the sword he anointed six of the dolls with the ointment, and they were able immediately to dance so gracefully that all the living girls in the room could not help joining in the dance. The coachman danced with the cook, and the waiters with the chambermaids, and all the strangers joined; even the tongs and the fire-shovel made an attempt, but they fell down after the first jump. So after all it was a very merry night. The next morning John and his companion left the inn to continue their journey through the great pine-forests and over the high mountains. They arrived at last at such a great height that towns and villages lay beneath them, and the church steeples looked like little specks between the green trees. They could see for miles round, far away to places they had never visited, and John saw more of the beautiful world than he had ever known before. The sun shone brightly in the blue firmament above, and through the clear mountain air came the sound of the huntsman's horn, and the soft, sweet notes brought tears into his eyes, and he could not help exclaiming, "How good and loving God is to give us all this beauty and loveliness in the world to make us happy!"

His fellow-traveller stood by with folded hands, gazing on the dark wood and the towns bathed in the warm sunshine. At this moment there sounded over their heads sweet music. They looked up, and discovered a large white swan hovering in the air, and singing as never bird sang before. But the song soon became weaker and weaker, the bird's head drooped, and he sunk slowly down, and lay dead at their feet.

"It is a beautiful bird," said the traveller, "and these large white wings are worth a great deal of money. I will take them with me. You see now that a sword will be very useful."

So he cut off the wings of the dead swan with one blow, and carried them away with him.

They now continued their journey over the mountains for many miles, till they at length reached a large city, containing hundreds of towers, that shone in the sunshine like silver. In the midst of the city stood a splendid marble palace, roofed with pure red gold, in which dwelt the king. John and his companion would not go into the town immediately; so they stopped at an inn outside the town, to change their clothes; for they wished to appear respectable as they walked through the streets. The landlord told them that the king was a very good man, who never injured any one: but as to his daughter, "Heaven defend us!"

She was indeed a wicked princess. She possessed beauty enough – nobody could be more elegant or prettier than she was; but what of that? for she was a wicked witch; and in consequence of her conduct many noble young princes had lost their lives. Any one was at liberty to make her an offer; were he a prince or a beggar, it mattered not to her. She would ask him to guess three things which she had just thought of, and if he succeed, he was to marry her, and be king over all the land when her father died; but if he could not guess these three things, then she ordered him to be hanged or to have his head cut off. The old king, her father, was very much grieved at her conduct, but he could not prevent her from being so wicked, because he once said he would have nothing more to do with her lovers; she might do as she pleased. Each prince who came and tried the three guesses, so that he might marry the princess, had been unable to find them out, and had been hanged or beheaded. They had all been warned in time, and might have left her alone, if they would. The old king became at last so distressed at all these dreadful circumstances, that for a whole day every year he and his soldiers knelt and prayed that the princess might become good; but she continued as wicked as ever. The old women who drank brandy would color it quite black before they drank it, to show how they mourned; and what more could they do?

"What a horrible princess!" said John; "she ought to be well flogged. If I were the old king, I would have her punished in some way."

Just then they heard the people outside shouting, "Hurrah!" and, looking out, they saw the princess passing by; and she was really so beautiful that everybody forgot her wickedness, and shouted "Hurrah!" Twelve lovely maidens in white silk dresses, holding golden tulips in their hands, rode by her side on coal-black horses. The princess herself had a snow-white steed, decked with diamonds and rubies. Her dress was of cloth of gold, and the whip she held in her hand looked like a sunbeam. The golden crown on her head glittered like the stars of heaven, and her mantle was formed of thousands of butterflies' wings sewn together. Yet she herself was more beautiful than all.

When John saw her, his face became as red as a drop of blood, and he could scarcely utter a word. The princess looked exactly like the beautiful lady with the golden crown, of whom he had dreamed on the night his father died. She appeared to him so lovely that he could not help loving her.

"It could not be true," he thought, "that she was really a wicked witch, who ordered people to be hanged or beheaded, if they could not guess her thoughts. Every one has permission to go and ask her hand, even the poorest beggar. I shall pay a visit to the palace," he said; "I must go, for I cannot help myself."

Then they all advised him not to attempt it; for he would be sure to share the same fate as the rest. His fellow-traveller also tried to persuade him against it; but John seemed quite sure of success. He brushed his shoes and his coat, washed his face and his hands, combed his soft flaxen hair, and then went out alone into the town, and walked to the palace.

"Come in," said the king, as John knocked at the door. John opened it, and the old king, in a dressing gown and embroidered slippers, came towards him. He had the crown on his head, carried his sceptre in one hand, and the orb in the other. "Wait a bit," said he, and he placed the orb under his arm, so that he could offer the other hand to John; but when he found that John was another suitor, he began to weep so violently, that both the sceptre and the orb fell to the floor, and he was obliged to wipe his eyes with his dressing gown. Poor old king! "Let her alone," he said; "you will fare as badly as all the others. Come, I will show you." Then he led him out into the princess's pleasure gardens, and there he saw a frightful sight. On every tree hung three or four king's sons who had wooed the princess, but had not been able to guess the riddles she gave them. Their skeletons rattled in every breeze, so that the terrified birds never dared to venture into the garden. All the flowers were supported by human bones instead of sticks, and human skulls in the flower-pots grinned horribly. It was really a doleful garden for a princess. "Do you see all this?" said the old king; "your fate will be the same as those who are here, therefore do not attempt it. You really make me very unhappy, – I take these things to heart so very much."

John kissed the good old king's hand, and said he was sure it would be all right, for he was quite enchanted with the beautiful princess. Then the princess herself came riding into the palace yard with all her ladies, and he wished her "Good morning." She looked wonderfully fair and lovely when she offered her hand to John, and he loved her more than ever. How could she be a wicked witch, as all the people asserted? He accompanied her into the hall, and the little pages offered them gingerbread nuts and sweetmeats, but the old king was so unhappy he could eat nothing, and besides, gingerbread nuts were too hard for him. It was decided that John should come to the palace the next day, when the judges and the whole of the counsellors would be present, to try if he could guess the first riddle. If he succeeded, he would have to come a second time; but if not, he would lose his life, – and no one had ever been able to guess even one. However, John was not at all anxious about the result of his trial; on the contrary, he was very merry. He thought only of the beautiful princess, and believed that in some way he should have help, but how he knew not, and did not like to think about it; so he danced along the high-road as he went back to the inn, where he had left his fellow-traveller waiting for him. John could not refrain from telling him how gracious the princess had been, and how beautiful she looked. He longed for the next day so much, that he might go to the palace and try his luck at guessing the riddles. But his comrade shook his head, and looked very mournful. "I do so wish you to do well," said he; "we might have continued together much longer, and now I am likely to lose you; you poor dear John! I could shed tears, but I will not make you unhappy on the last night we may be together. We will be merry, really merry this evening; to-morrow, after you are gone, shall be able to weep undisturbed."

It was very quickly known among the inhabitants of the town that another suitor had arrived for the princess, and there was great sorrow in consequence. The theatre remained closed, the women who sold sweetmeats tied crape round the sugar-sticks, and the king and the priests were on their knees in the church. There was a great lamentation, for no one expected John to succeed better than those who had been suitors before.

In the evening John's comrade prepared a large bowl of punch, and said, "Now let us be merry, and drink to the health of the princess." But after drinking two glasses, John became so sleepy, that he could not keep his eyes open, and fell fast asleep. Then his fellow-traveller lifted him gently out of his chair, and laid him on the bed; and as soon as it was quite dark, he took the two large wings which he had cut from the dead swan, and tied them firmly to his own shoulders. Then he put into his pocket the largest of the three rods which he had obtained from the old woman who had fallen and broken her leg. After this he opened the window, and flew away over the town, straight towards the palace, and seated himself in a corner, under the window which looked into the bedroom of the princess.

The town was perfectly still when the clocks struck a quarter to twelve. Presently the window opened, and the princess, who had large black wings to her shoulders, and a long white mantle, flew away over the city towards a high mountain. The fellow-traveller, who had made himself invisible, so that she could not possibly see him, flew after her through the air, and whipped the princess with his rod, so that the blood came whenever he struck her. Ah, it was a strange flight through the air! The wind caught her mantle, so that it spread out on all sides, like the large sail of a ship, and the moon shone through it. "How it hails, to be sure!" said the princess, at each blow she received from the rod; and it served her right to be whipped.

At last she reached the side of the mountain, and knocked. The mountain opened with a noise like the roll of thunder, and the princess went in. The traveller followed her; no one could see him, as he had made himself invisible. They went through a long, wide passage. A thousand gleaming spiders ran here and there on the walls, causing them to glitter as if they were illuminated with fire. They next entered a large hall built of silver and gold. Large red and blue flowers shone on the walls, looking like sunflowers in size, but no one could dare to pluck them, for the stems were hideous poisonous snakes, and the flowers were flames of fire, darting out of their jaws. Shining glow-worms covered the ceiling, and sky-blue bats flapped their transparent wings. Altogether the place had a frightful appearance. In the middle of the floor stood a throne supported by four skeleton horses, whose harness had been made by fiery-red spiders. The throne itself was made of milk-white glass, and the cushions were little black mice, each biting the other's tail. Over it hung a canopy of rose-colored spider's webs, spotted with the prettiest little green flies, which sparkled like precious stones. On the throne sat an old magician with a crown on his ugly head, and a sceptre in his hand. He kissed the princess on the forehead, seated her by his side on the splendid throne, and then the music commenced. Great black grasshoppers played the mouth organ, and the owl struck herself on the body instead of a drum. It was altogether a ridiculous concert. Little black goblins with false lights in their caps danced about the hall; but no one could see the traveller, and he had placed himself just behind the throne where he could see and hear everything. The courtiers who came in afterwards looked noble and grand; but any one with common sense could see what they really were, only broomsticks, with cabbages for heads. The magician had given them life, and dressed them in embroidered robes. It answered very well, as they were only wanted for show. After there had been a little dancing, the princess told the magician that she had a new suitor, and asked him what she could think of for the suitor to guess when he came to the castle the next morning.

"Listen to what I say," said the magician, "you must choose something very easy, he is less likely to guess it then. Think of one of your shoes, he will never imagine it is that. Then cut his head off; and mind you do not forget to bring his eyes with you to-morrow night, that I may eat them."

The princess curtsied low, and said she would not forget the eyes.

The magician then opened the mountain and she flew home again, but the traveller followed and flogged her so much with the rod, that she sighed quite deeply about the heavy hail-storm, and made as much haste as she could to get back to her bedroom through the window. The traveller then returned to the inn where John still slept, took off his wings and laid down on the bed, for he was very tired. Early in the morning John awoke, and when his fellow-traveller got up, he said that he had a very wonderful dream about the princess and her shoe, he therefore advised John to ask her if she had not thought of her shoe. Of course the traveller knew this from what the magician in the mountain had said.

"I may as well say that as anything," said John. "Perhaps your dream may come true; still I will say farewell, for if I guess wrong I shall never see you again."

Then they embraced each other, and John went into the town and walked to the palace. The great hall was full of people, and the judges sat in arm-chairs, with eider-down cushions to rest their heads upon, because they had so much to think of. The old king stood near, wiping his eyes with his white pocket-handkerchief. When the princess entered, she looked even more beautiful than she had appeared the day before, and greeted every one present most gracefully; but to John she gave her hand, and said, "Good morning to you."

Now came the time for John to guess what she was thinking of; and oh, how kindly she looked at him as she spoke. But when he uttered the single word shoe, she turned as pale as a ghost; all her wisdom could not help her, for he had guessed rightly. Oh, how pleased the old king was! It was quite amusing to see how he capered about. All the people clapped their hands, both on his account and John's, who had guessed rightly the first time. His fellow-traveller was glad also, when he heard how successful John had been. But John folded his hands, and thanked God, who, he felt quite sure, would help him again; and he knew he had to guess twice more. The evening passed pleasantly like the one preceding. While John slept, his companion flew behind the princess to the mountain, and flogged her even harder than before; this time he had taken two rods with him. No one saw him go in with her, and he heard all that was said. The princess this time was to think of a glove, and he told John as if he had again heard it in a dream. The next day, therefore, he was able to guess correctly the second time, and it caused great rejoicing at the palace. The whole court jumped about as they had seen the king do the day before, but the princess lay on the sofa, and would not say a single word. All now depended upon John. If he only guessed rightly the third time, he would marry the princess, and reign over the kingdom after the death of the old king: but if he failed, he would lose his life, and the magician would have his beautiful blue eyes. That evening John said his prayers and went to bed very early, and soon fell asleep calmly. But his companion tied on his wings to his shoulders, took three rods, and, with his sword at his side, flew to the palace. It was a very dark night, and so stormy that the tiles flew from the roofs of the houses, and the trees in the garden upon which the skeletons hung bent themselves like reeds before the wind. The lightning flashed, and the thunder rolled in one long-continued peal all night. The window of the castle opened, and the princess flew out. She was pale as death, but she laughed at the storm as if it were not bad enough. Her white mantle fluttered in the wind like a large sail, and the traveller flogged her with the three rods till the blood trickled down, and at last she could scarcely fly; she contrived, however, to reach the mountain. "What a hail-storm!" she said, as she entered; "I have never been out in such weather as this."

"Yes, there may be too much of a good thing sometimes," said the magician.

Then the princess told him that John had guessed rightly the second time, and if he succeeded the next morning, he would win, and she could never come to the mountain again, or practice magic as she had done, and therefore she was quite unhappy. "I will find out something for you to think of which he will never guess, unless he is a greater conjuror than myself. But now let us be merry."

Then he took the princess by both hands, and they danced with all the little goblins and Jack-o'-lanterns in the room. The red spiders sprang here and there on the walls quite as merrily, and the flowers of fire appeared as if they were throwing out sparks. The owl beat the drum, the crickets whistled and the grasshoppers played the mouth-organ. It was a very ridiculous ball. After they had danced enough, the princess was obliged to go home, for fear she should be missed at the palace. The magician offered to go with her, that they might be company to each other on the way. Then they flew away through the bad weather, and the traveller followed them, and broke his three rods across their shoulders. The magician had never been out in such a hail-storm as this. Just by the palace the magician stopped to wish the princess farewell, and to whisper in her ear, "To-morrow think of my head."

But the traveller heard it, and just as the princess slipped through the window into her bedroom, and the magician turned round to fly back to the mountain, he seized him by the long black beard, and with his sabre cut off the wicked conjuror's head just behind the shoulders, so that he could not even see who it was. He threw the body into the sea to the fishes, and after dipping the head into the water, he tied it up in a silk handkerchief, took it with him to the inn, and then went to bed. The next morning he gave John the handkerchief, and told him not to untie it till the princess asked him what she was thinking of. There were so many people in the great hall of the palace that they stood as thick as radishes tied together in a bundle. The council sat in their arm-chairs with the white cushions. The old king wore new robes, and the golden crown and sceptre had been polished up so that he looked quite smart. But the princess was very pale, and wore a black dress as if she were going to a funeral.

"What have I thought of?" asked the princess, of John. He immediately untied the handkerchief, and was himself quite frightened when he saw the head of the ugly magician. Every one shuddered, for it was terrible to look at; but the princess sat like a statue, and could not utter a single word. At length she rose and gave John her hand, for he had guessed rightly.

She looked at no one, but sighed deeply, and said, "You are my master now; this evening our marriage must take place."

"I am very pleased to hear it," said the old king. "It is just what I wish."

Then all the people shouted "Hurrah." The band played music in the streets, the bells rang, and the cake-women took the black crape off the sugar-sticks. There was universal joy. Three oxen, stuffed with ducks and chickens, were roasted whole in the market-place, where every one might help himself to a slice. The fountains spouted forth the most delicious wine, and whoever bought a penny loaf at the baker's received six large buns, full of raisins, as a present. In the evening the whole town was illuminated. The soldiers fired off cannons, and the boys let off crackers. There was eating and drinking, dancing and jumping everywhere. In the palace, the high-born gentlemen and beautiful ladies danced with each other, and they could be heard at a great distance singing the following song: –

> *"Here are maidens, young and fair,*
> *Dancing in the summer air;*
> *Like two spinning-wheels at play,*
> *Pretty maidens dance away-*
> *Dance the spring and summer through*
> *Till the sole falls from your shoe."*

But the princess was still a witch, and she could not love John. His fellow-traveller had thought of that, so he gave John three feathers out of the swan's wings, and a little bottle with a few drops in it. He told him to place a large bath full of water by the princess's bed, and put the feathers and the drops into it. Then, at the moment she was about to get into bed, he must give her a little push, so that she might fall into the water, and then dip her three times. This would destroy the power of the magician, and she would love him very much. John did all that his companion told him to do. The princess shrieked aloud when he dipped her under the water the first time, and struggled under his hands in the form of a great black swan with fiery eyes. As she rose the second time from the water, the swan had become white, with a black ring round its neck. John allowed the water to close once more over the bird, and at the same time it changed into a most beautiful princess. She was more lovely even than before, and thanked him, while her eyes sparkled with tears, for having broken the spell of the magician. The next day, the king came with the whole court to offer their congratulations, and stayed till quite late. Last of all came the travelling companion; he had his staff in his hand and his knapsack on his back. John kissed him many times and told him he must not go, he must remain with him, for he was the cause of all his good fortune. But the traveller shook his head, and said gently and kindly, "No: my time is up now; I have only paid my debt to you. Do you remember the dead man whom the bad people wished to throw out of his coffin? You gave all you possessed that he might rest in his grave; I am that man." As he said this, he vanished.

The wedding festivities lasted a whole month. John and his princess loved each other dearly, and the old king lived to see many a happy day, when he took their little children on his knees and let them play with his sceptre. And John became king over the whole country.

The Flying Trunk

THERE WAS ONCE a merchant who was so rich that he could have paved the whole street with gold, and would even then have had enough for a small alley. But he did not do so; he knew the value of money better than to use it in this way. So clever was he, that every shilling he put out brought him a crown; and so he continued till he died. His son inherited his wealth, and he lived a merry life with it; he went to a masquerade every night, made kites out of five pound notes, and threw pieces of gold into the sea instead of stones, making ducks and drakes of them. In this manner he soon lost all his money. At last he had nothing left but a pair of slippers, an old dressing-gown, and four shillings. And now all his friends deserted him, they could not walk with him in the streets; but one of them, who was very good-natured, sent him an old trunk with this message, "Pack up!" "Yes," he said, "it is all very well to say 'pack up,'" but he had nothing left to pack up, therefore he seated himself in the trunk. It was a very wonderful trunk; no sooner did any one press on the lock than the trunk could fly. He shut the lid and pressed the lock, when away flew the trunk up the chimney with the merchant's son in it, right up into the clouds. Whenever the bottom of the trunk cracked, he was in a great fright, for if the trunk fell to pieces he would have made a tremendous somerset over the trees. However, he got safely in his trunk to the land of Turkey. He hid the trunk in the wood under some dry leaves, and then went into the town: he could so this very well, for the Turks always go about dressed in dressing-gowns and slippers, as he was himself. He happened to meet a nurse with a little child. "I say, you Turkish nurse," cried he, "what castle is that near the town, with the windows placed so high?"

"The king's daughter lives there," she replied; "it has been prophesied that she will be very unhappy about a lover, and therefore no one is allowed to visit her, unless the king and queen are present."

"Thank you," said the merchant's son. So he went back to the wood, seated himself in his trunk, flew up to the roof of the castle, and crept through the window into the princess's room. She lay on the sofa asleep, and she was so beautiful that the merchant's son could not help kissing her. Then she awoke, and was very much frightened; but he told her he was a Turkish angel, who had come down through the air to see her, which pleased her very much. He sat down by her side and talked to her: he said her eyes were like beautiful dark lakes, in which the thoughts swam about like little mermaids, and he told her that her forehead was a snowy mountain, which contained splendid halls full of pictures. And then he related to her about the stork who brings the beautiful children from the rivers. These were delightful stories; and when he asked the princess if she would marry him, she consented immediately.

"But you must come on Saturday," she said; "for then the king and queen will take tea with me. They will be very proud when they find that I am going to marry a Turkish angel; but you must think of some very pretty stories to tell them, for my parents like to hear stories better than anything. My mother prefers one that is deep and moral; but my father likes something funny, to make him laugh."

"Very well," he replied; "I shall bring you no other marriage portion than a story," and so they parted. But the princess gave him a sword which was studded with gold coins, and these he could use.

Then he flew away to the town and bought a new dressing-gown, and afterwards returned to the wood, where he composed a story, so as to be ready for Saturday, which was no easy matter. It was ready however by Saturday, when he went to see the princess. The king, and queen, and the whole court, were at tea with the princess; and he was received with great politeness.

"Will you tell us a story?" said the queen, – "one that is instructive and full of deep learning."

"Yes, but with something in it to laugh at," said the king.

"Certainly," he replied, and commenced at once, asking them to listen attentively. "There was once a bundle of matches that were exceedingly proud of their high descent. Their genealogical tree, that is, a large pine-tree from which they had been cut, was at one time a large, old tree in the wood. The matches now lay between a tinder-box and an old iron saucepan, and were talking about their youthful days. 'Ah! then we grew on the green boughs, and were as green as they; every morning and evening we were fed with diamond drops of dew. Whenever the sun shone, we felt his warm rays, and the little birds would relate stories to us as they sung. We knew that we were rich, for the other trees only wore their green dress in summer, but our family were able to array themselves in green, summer and winter. But the wood-cutter came, like a great revolution, and our family fell under the axe. The head of the house obtained a situation as mainmast in a very fine ship, and can sail round the world when he will. The other branches of the family were taken to different places, and our office now is to kindle a light for common people. This is how such high-born people as we came to be in a kitchen.'

"'Mine has been a very different fate,' said the iron pot, which stood by the matches; 'from my first entrance into the world I have been used to cooking and scouring. I am the first in this house, when anything solid or useful is required. My only pleasure is to be made clean and shining after dinner, and to sit in my place and have a little sensible conversation with my neighbors. All of us, excepting the water-bucket, which is sometimes taken into the courtyard, live here together within these four walls. We get our news from the market-basket, but he sometimes tells us very unpleasant things about the people and the government. Yes, and one day an old pot was so alarmed, that he fell down and was broken to pieces. He was a liberal, I can tell you.'

"'You are talking too much,' said the tinder-box, and the steel struck against the flint till some sparks flew out, crying, 'We want a merry evening, don't we?'

"'Yes, of course,' said the matches, 'let us talk about those who are the highest born.'

"'No, I don't like to be always talking of what we are,' remarked the saucepan; 'let us think of some other amusement; I will begin. We will tell something that has happened to ourselves; that will be very easy, and interesting as well. On the Baltic Sea, near the Danish shore' –

"'What a pretty commencement!' said the plates; 'we shall all like that story, I am sure.'

"'Yes; well in my youth, I lived in a quiet family, where the furniture was polished, the floors scoured, and clean curtains put up every fortnight.'

"'What an interesting way you have of relating a story,' said the carpet-broom; 'it is easy to perceive that you have been a great deal in women's society, there is something so pure runs through what you say.'

"'That is quite true,' said the water-bucket; and he made a spring with joy, and splashed some water on the floor.

"Then the saucepan went on with his story, and the end was as good as the beginning.

"The plates rattled with pleasure, and the carpet-broom brought some green parsley out of the dust-hole and crowned the saucepan, for he knew it would vex the others; and he thought, 'If I crown him to-day he will crown me to-morrow.'

"'Now, let us have a dance,' said the fire-tongs; and then how they danced and stuck up one leg in the air. The chair-cushion in the corner burst with laughter when she saw it.

"'Shall I be crowned now?' asked the fire-tongs; so the broom found another wreath for the tongs.

"'They were only common people after all,' thought the matches. The tea-urn was now asked to sing, but she said she had a cold, and could not sing without boiling heat. They all thought this was affectation, and because she did not wish to sing excepting in the parlor, when on the table with the grand people.

"In the window sat an old quill-pen, with which the maid generally wrote. There was nothing remarkable about the pen, excepting that it had been dipped too deeply in the ink, but it was proud of that.

"'If the tea-urn won't sing,' said the pen, 'she can leave it alone; there is a nightingale in a cage who can sing; she has not been taught much, certainly, but we need not say anything this evening about that.'

"'I think it highly improper,' said the tea-kettle, who was kitchen singer, and half-brother to the tea-urn, 'that a rich foreign bird should be listened to here. Is it patriotic? Let the market-basket decide what is right.'

"'I certainly am vexed,' said the basket; 'inwardly vexed, more than any one can imagine. Are we spending the evening properly? Would it not be more sensible to put the house in order? If each were in his own place I would lead a game; this would be quite another thing.'

"'Let us act a play,' said they all. At the same moment the door opened, and the maid came in. Then not one stirred; they all remained quite still; yet, at the same time, there was not a single pot amongst them who had not a high opinion of himself, and of what he could do if he chose.

"'Yes, if we had chosen,' they each thought, 'we might have spent a very pleasant evening.'

"The maid took the matches and lighted them; dear me, how they sputtered and blazed up!

"'Now then,' they thought, 'every one will see that we are the first. How we shine; what a light we give!' Even while they spoke their light went out.

"What a capital story," said the queen, "I feel as if I were really in the kitchen, and could see the matches; yes, you shall marry our daughter."

"Certainly," said the king, "thou shalt have our daughter." The king said thou to him because he was going to be one of the family. The wedding-day was fixed, and, on the evening before, the whole city was illuminated. Cakes and sweetmeats were thrown among the people. The street boys stood on tiptoe and shouted "hurrah," and whistled between their fingers; altogether it was a very splendid affair.

"I will give them another treat," said the merchant's son. So he went and bought rockets and crackers, and all sorts of fire-works that could be thought of, packed them in his trunk, and flew up with it into the air. What a whizzing and popping they made as they went off! The Turks, when they saw such a sight in the air, jumped so high that their slippers flew about their ears. It was easy to believe after this that the princess was really going to marry a Turkish angel.

As soon as the merchant's son had come down in his flying trunk to the wood after the fireworks, he thought, "I will go back into the town now, and hear what they think of the entertainment." It was very natural that he should wish to know. And what strange things people did say, to be sure! every one whom he questioned had a different tale to tell, though they all thought it very beautiful.

"I saw the Turkish angel myself," said one; "he had eyes like glittering stars, and a head like foaming water."

"He flew in a mantle of fire," cried another, "and lovely little cherubs peeped out from the folds."

He heard many more fine things about himself, and that the next day he was to be married. After this he went back to the forest to rest himself in his trunk. It had disappeared! A spark from the fireworks which remained had set it on fire; it was burnt to ashes! So the merchant's son could not fly any more, nor go to meet his bride. She stood all day on the roof waiting for him, and most likely she is waiting there still; while he wanders through the world telling fairy tales, but none of them so amusing as the one he related about the matches.

The Shepherdess and the Sweep

HAVE YOU EVER seen an old wooden cupboard quite black with age, and ornamented with carved foliage and curious figures? Well, just such a cupboard stood in a parlor, and had been left to the family as a legacy by the great-grandmother. It was covered from top to bottom with carved roses and tulips; the most curious scrolls were drawn upon it, and out of them peeped little stags' heads, with antlers. In the middle of the cupboard door was the carved figure of a man most ridiculous to look at. He grinned at you, for no one could call it laughing. He had goat's legs, little horns on his head, and a long beard; the children in the room always called him, "Major general-field-sergeant-commander Billy-goat's-legs." It was certainly a very difficult name to pronounce, and there are very few who ever receive such a title, but then it seemed wonderful how he came to be carved at all; yet there he was, always looking at the table under the looking-glass, where stood a very pretty little shepherdess made of china. Her shoes were gilt, and her dress had a red rose or an ornament. She wore a hat, and carried a crook, that were both gilded, and looked very bright and pretty. Close by her side stood a little chimney-sweep, as black as coal, and also made of china. He was, however, quite as clean and neat as any other china figure; he only represented a black chimney-sweep, and the china workers might just as well have made him a prince, had they felt inclined to do so. He stood holding his ladder quite handily, and his face was as fair and rosy as a girl's; indeed, that was rather a mistake, it should have had some black marks on it. He and the shepherdess had been placed close together, side by side; and, being so placed, they became engaged to each other, for they were very well suited, being both made of the same sort of china, and being equally fragile. Close to them stood another figure, three times as large as they were, and also made of china. He was an old Chinaman, who could nod his head, and used to pretend that he was the grandfather of the shepherdess, although he could not prove it. He however assumed authority over her, and therefore when "Major-general-field-sergeant-commander Billy-goat's-legs" asked for the little shepherdess to be his wife, he nodded his head to show that he consented. "You will have a husband," said the old Chinaman to her, "who I really believe is made of mahogany. He will make you a lady of Major-general-field-sergeant-commander Billy-goat's-legs. He has the whole cupboard full of silver plate, which he keeps locked up in secret drawers."

"I won't go into the dark cupboard," said the little shepherdess. "I have heard that he has eleven china wives there already."

"Then you shall be the twelfth," said the old Chinaman. "To-night as soon as you hear a rattling in the old cupboard, you shall be married, as true as I am a Chinaman;" and then he nodded his head and fell asleep.

Then the little shepherdess cried, and looked at her sweetheart, the china chimney-sweep. "I must entreat you," said she, "to go out with me into the wide world, for we cannot stay here."

"I will do whatever you wish," said the little chimney-sweep; "let us go immediately: I think I shall be able to maintain you with my profession."

"If we were but safely down from the table!" said she; "I shall not be happy till we are really out in the world."

Then he comforted her, and showed her how to place her little foot on the carved edge and gilt-leaf ornaments of the table. He brought his little ladder to help her, and so they contrived to reach the floor. But when they looked at the old cupboard, they saw it was all in an uproar. The carved stags pushed out their heads, raised their antlers, and twisted their necks. The major-general sprung up in the air; and cried out to the old Chinaman, "They are running away! they are running away!" The two were rather frightened at this, so they jumped into the drawer of the window-seat. Here were three or four packs of cards not quite complete, and a doll's theatre, which had been built up very neatly. A comedy was being performed in it, and all the queens of diamonds, clubs, and hearts, and spades, sat in the first row fanning themselves with tulips, and behind them stood all the knaves, showing that they had heads above and below as playing cards generally have. The play was about two lovers, who were not allowed to marry, and the shepherdess wept because it was so like her own story. "I cannot bear it," said she, "I must get out of the drawer;" but when they reached the floor, and cast their eyes on the table, there was the old Chinaman awake and shaking his whole body, till all at once down he came on the floor, "plump." "The old Chinaman is coming," cried the little shepherdess in a fright, and down she fell on one knee.

"I have thought of something," said the chimney-sweep; "let us get into the great pot-pourri jar which stands in the corner; there we can lie on rose-leaves and lavender, and throw salt in his eyes if he comes near us."

"No, that will never do," said she, "because I know that the Chinaman and the pot-pourri jar were lovers once, and there always remains behind a feeling of good-will between those who have been so intimate as that. No, there is nothing left for us but to go out into the wide world."

"Have you really courage enough to go out into the wide world with me?" said the chimney-sweep; "have you thought how large it is, and that we can never come back here again?"

"Yes, I have," she replied.

When the chimney-sweep saw that she was quite firm, he said, "My way is through the stove and up the chimney. Have you courage to creep with me through the fire-box, and the iron pipe? When we get to the chimney I shall know how to manage very well. We shall soon climb too high for any one to reach us, and we shall come through a hole in the top out into the wide world." So he led her to the door of the stove.

"It looks very dark," said she; still she went in with him through the stove and through the pipe, where it was as dark as pitch.

"Now we are in the chimney," said he; "and look, there is a beautiful star shining above it." It was a real star shining down upon them as if it would show them the way. So they clambered, and crept on, and a frightful steep place it was; but the chimney-sweep helped her and supported her, till they got higher and higher. He showed her the best places on which to set her little china foot, so at last they reached the top of the chimney, and sat themselves down, for they were very tired, as may be supposed. The sky, with all its stars, was over their heads, and below were the roofs of the town. They could see for a very long distance out into the wide world, and the poor little shepherdess leaned her head on her chimney-sweep's shoulder, and wept till she washed the gilt off her sash; the world was so different to what she expected. "This is too much," she said; "I cannot bear it, the world is too large. Oh, I wish I were safe back on the table. again, under the looking glass; I shall never be happy till I am safe back again. Now I have followed you out into the wide world, you will take me back, if you love me."

Then the chimney-sweep tried to reason with her, and spoke of the old Chinaman, and of the Major-general-field-sergeant-commander Billy-goat's legs; but she sobbed so bitterly, and kissed her little chimney-sweep till he was obliged to do all she asked, foolish as it was. And so, with a great deal of trouble, they climbed down the chimney, and then crept through the pipe and stove, which were certainly not very pleasant places. Then they stood in the dark fire-box, and listened behind the door, to hear what was going on in the room. As it was all quiet, they peeped out. Alas! there lay the old Chinaman on the floor; he had fallen down from the table as he attempted to run after them, and was broken into three pieces; his back had separated entirely, and his head had rolled into a corner of the room. The major-general stood in his old place, and appeared lost in thought.

"This is terrible," said the little shepherdess. "My poor old grandfather is broken to pieces, and it is our fault. I shall never live after this;" and she wrung her little hands.

"He can be riveted," said the chimney-sweep; "he can be riveted. Do not be so hasty. If they cement his back, and put a good rivet in it, he will be as good as new, and be able to say as many disagreeable things to us as ever."

"Do you think so?" said she; and then they climbed up to the table, and stood in their old places.

"As we have done no good," said the chimney-sweep, "we might as well have remained here, instead of taking so much trouble."

"I wish grandfather was riveted," said the shepherdess. "Will it cost much, I wonder?"

And she had her wish. The family had the Chinaman's back mended, and a strong rivet put through his neck; he looked as good as new, but he could no longer nod his head.

"You have become proud since your fall broke you to pieces," said Major-general-field-sergeant-commander Billy-goat's-legs. "You have no reason to give yourself such airs. Am I to have her or not?"

The chimney-sweep and the little shepherdess looked piteously at the old Chinaman, for they were afraid he might nod; but he was not able: besides, it was so tiresome to be always telling strangers he had a rivet in the back of his neck.

And so the little china people remained together, and were glad of the grandfather's rivet, and continued to love each other till they were broken to pieces.

Under the Willow-tree

THE REGION ROUND the little town of Kjøge is very bleak and cold. The town lies on the sea shore, which is always beautiful; but here it might be more beautiful than it is, for on every side the fields are flat, and it is a long way to the forest. But when persons reside in a place and get used to it, they can always find something beautiful in it, – something for which they long, even in the most charming spot in the world which is not home. It must be owned that there are in the outskirts of the town some humble gardens on the banks of a little stream that runs on towards the sea, and in summer these gardens look very pretty. Such indeed was the opinion of two little children, whose parents were neighbors, and who played in these gardens, and forced their way from one garden to the other through the gooseberry-bushes that divided them. In one of the gardens grew an elder-tree, and in the other an old willow, under which the children were very fond of playing. They had permission to do so, although the tree stood close by the stream, and they might easily have fallen into the water; but the eye of God watches over the little ones, otherwise they would never be safe. At the same time, these children were very careful not to go too near the water; indeed, the boy was so afraid of it, that in the summer, while the other children were splashing about in the sea, nothing could entice him to join them. They jeered and laughed at him, and he was obliged to bear it all as patiently as he could. Once the neighbor's little girl, Joanna, dreamed that she was sailing in a boat, and the boy – Knud was his name – waded out in the water to join her, and the water came up to his neck, and at last closed over his head, and in a moment he had disappeared. When little Knud heard this dream, it seemed as if he could not bear the mocking and jeering again; how could he dare to go into the water now, after Joanna's dream! He never would do it, for this dream always satisfied him. The parents of these children, who were poor, often sat together while Knud and Joanna played in the gardens or in the road. Along this road – a row of willow-trees had been planted to separate it from a ditch on one side of it. They were not very handsome trees, for the tops had been cut off; however, they were intended for use, and not for show. The old willow-tree in the garden was much handsomer, and therefore the children were very fond of sitting under it. The town had a large market-place; and at the fair-time there would be whole rows, like streets, of tents and booths containing silks and ribbons, and toys and cakes, and everything that could be wished for. There were crowds of people, and sometimes the weather would be rainy, and splash with moisture the woollen jackets of the peasants; but it did not destroy the beautiful fragrance of the honey-cakes and gingerbread with which one booth was filled; and the best of it was, that the man who sold these cakes always lodged during the fair-time with little Knud's parents. So every now and then he had a present of gingerbread, and of course Joanna always had a share. And, more delightful still, the gingerbread seller knew all sorts of things to tell and could even relate stories about his own gingerbread. So one evening he told them a story that made such a deep impression on the children that they never forgot it; and therefore I think we may as well hear it too, for it is not very long.

"Once upon a time," said he, "there lay on my counter two gingerbread cakes, one in the shape of a man wearing a hat, the other of a maiden without a bonnet. Their faces were on the side that was uppermost, for on the other side they looked very different. Most people have a best side to their characters, which they take care to show to the world. On the left, just where the heart is, the gingerbread man had an almond stuck in to represent it, but the maiden was honey cake all over. They were placed on the counter as samples, and after lying there a long time they at last fell in love with each other; but neither of them spoke of it to the other, as they should have done if they expected anything to follow. 'He is a man, he ought to speak the first word,' thought the gingerbread maiden; but she felt quite happy – she was sure that her love was returned. But his thoughts were far more ambitious, as the thoughts of a man often are. He dreamed that he was a real street boy, that he possessed four real pennies, and that he had bought the gingerbread lady, and ate her up. And so they lay on the counter for days and weeks, till they grew hard and dry; but the thoughts of the maiden became ever more tender and womanly. 'Ah well, it is enough for me that I have been able to live on the same counter with him,' said she one day; when suddenly, 'crack,' and she broke in two. 'Ah,' said the gingerbread man to himself, 'if she had only known of my love, she would have kept together a little longer.' And here they both are, and that is their history," said the cake man. "You think the history of their lives and their silent love, which never came to anything, very remarkable; and there they are for you." So saying, he gave Joanna the gingerbread man, who was still quite whole – and to Knud the broken maiden; but the children had been so much impressed by the story, that they had not the heart to eat the lovers up.

The next day they went into the churchyard, and took the two cake figures with them, and sat down under the church wall, which was covered with luxuriant ivy in summer and winter, and looked as if hung with rich tapestry. They stuck up the two gingerbread figures in the sunshine among the green leaves, and then told the story, and all about the silent love which came to nothing, to a group of children. They called it, "love," because the story was so lovely, and the other children had the same opinion. But when they turned to look at the gingerbread pair, the broken maiden was gone! A great boy, out of wickedness, had eaten her up. At first the children cried about it; but afterwards, thinking very probably that the poor lover ought not to be left alone in the world, they ate him up too: but they never forgot the story.

The two children still continued to play together by the elder-tree, and under the willow; and the little maiden sang beautiful songs, with a voice that was as clear as a bell. Knud, on the contrary, had not a note of music in him, but knew the words of the songs, and that of course is something. The people of Kjøge, and even the rich wife of the man who kept the fancy shop, would stand and listen while Joanna was singing, and say, "She has really a very sweet voice."

Those were happy days; but they could not last forever. The neighbors were separated, the mother of the little girl was dead, and her father had thoughts of marrying again and of residing in the capital, where he had been promised a very lucrative appointment as messenger. The neighbors parted with tears, the children wept sadly; but their parents promised that they should write to each other at least once a year.

After this, Knud was bound apprentice to a shoemaker; he was growing a great boy, and could not be allowed to run wild any longer. Besides, he was going to be confirmed. Ah, how happy he would have been on that festal day in Copenhagen with little Joanna; but he still remained at Kjøge, and had never seen the great city, though the town is not five miles from it. But far across the bay, when the sky was clear, the towers of Copenhagen could be seen; and on the day of his confirmation he saw distinctly the golden cross on the principal church glittering in the sun. How often his thoughts were with Joanna! but did she think of him? Yes. About Christmas came a letter from her father to Knud's parents, which stated that they were going on very well in Copenhagen, and mentioning particularly that Joanna's beautiful voice was likely to bring her a brilliant fortune in the future. She was engaged to sing at a concert, and she had already earned money by singing, out of which she sent her dear neighbors at Kjøge a whole dollar, for them to make merry on Christmas eve, and they were to drink her health. She had herself added this in a postscript, and in the same postscript she wrote, "Kind regards to Knud."

The good neighbors wept, although the news was so pleasant; but they wept tears of joy. Knud's thoughts had been daily with Joanna, and now he knew that she also had thought of him; and the nearer the time came for his apprenticeship to end, the clearer did it appear to him that he loved Joanna, and that she must be his wife; and a smile came on his lips at the thought, and at one time he drew the thread so fast as he worked, and pressed his foot so hard against the knee strap, that he ran the awl into his finger; but what did he care for that? He was determined not to play the dumb lover as both the gingerbread cakes had done; the story was a good lesson to him.

At length he become a journeyman; and then, for the first time, he prepared for a journey to Copenhagen, with his knapsack packed and ready. A master was expecting him there, and he thought of Joanna, and how glad she would be to see him. She was now seventeen, and he nineteen years old. He wanted to buy a gold ring for her in Kjøge, but then he recollected how far more beautiful such things would be in Copenhagen. So he took leave of his parents, and on a rainy day, late in the autumn, wandered forth on foot from the town of his birth. The leaves were falling from the trees; and, by the time he arrived at his new master's in the great metropolis, he was wet through. On the following Sunday he intended to pay his first visit to Joanna's father. When the day came, the new journeyman's clothes were brought out, and a new hat, which he had brought in Kjøge. The hat became him very well, for hitherto he had only worn a cap. He found the house that he sought easily, but had to mount so many stairs that he became quite giddy; it surprised him to find how people lived over one another in this dreadful town.

On entering a room in which everything denoted prosperity, Joanna's father received him very kindly. The new wife was a stranger to him, but she shook hands with him, and offered him coffee.

"Joanna will be very glad to see you," said her father. "You have grown quite a nice young man, you shall see her presently; she is a good child, and is the joy of my heart, and, please God, she will continue to be so; she has her own room now, and pays us rent for it." And the father knocked quite politely at a door, as if he were a stranger, and then they both went in. How pretty everything was in that room! a more beautiful apartment could not be found in the whole town of Kjøge; the queen herself could scarcely be better accommodated. There were carpets, and rugs, and window curtains hanging to the ground. Pictures and flowers were scattered about. There was a velvet chair, and a looking-glass against the wall, into which a person might be in danger of stepping, for it was as large as a door. All this Knud saw at a glance, and yet, in truth, he saw nothing but Joanna. She was quite grown up, and very different from what Knud had fancied her, and a great deal more beautiful. In all Kjøge there was not a girl like her; and how graceful she looked, although her glance at first was odd, and not familiar; but for a moment only, then she rushed towards him as if she would have kissed him; she did not, however, although she was very near it. Yes, she really was joyful at seeing the friend of her childhood once more, and the tears even stood in her eyes. Then she asked so many questions about Knud's parents, and everything, even to the elder-tree and the willow, which she called "elder-mother and willow-father," as if they had been human beings; and so, indeed, they might be, quite as much as the gingerbread cakes. Then she talked about them, and the story of their silent love, and how they lay on the counter together and split in two; and then she laughed heartily; but the blood rushed into Knud's cheeks, and his heart beat quickly. Joanna was not proud at all; he noticed that through her he was invited by her parents to remain the whole evening with them, and she poured out the tea and gave him a cup herself; and afterwards she took a book and read aloud to them, and it seemed to Knud as if the story was all about himself and his love, for it agreed so well with his own thoughts. And then she sang a simple song, which, through her singing, became a true story, and as if she poured forth the feelings of her own heart.

"Oh," he thought, "she knows I am fond of her." The tears he could not restrain rolled down his cheeks, and he was unable to utter a single word; it seemed as if he had been struck dumb.

When he left, she pressed his hand, and said, "You have a kind heart, Knud: remain always as you are now." What an evening of happiness this had been; to sleep after it was impossible, and Knud did not sleep.

At parting, Joanna's father had said, "Now, you won't quite forget us; you must not let the whole winter go by without paying us another visit;" so that Knud felt himself free to go again the following Sunday evening, and so he did. But every evening after working hours – and they worked by candle-light then – he walked out into the town, and through the street in which Joanna lived, to look up at her window. It was almost always lighted up; and one evening he saw the shadow of her face quite plainly on the window blind; that was a glorious evening for him. His master's wife did not like his always going out in the evening, idling, wasting time, as she called it, and she shook her head.

But his master only smiled, and said, "He is a young man, my dear, you know."

"On Sunday I shall see her," said Knud to himself, "and I will tell her that I love her with my whole heart and soul, and that she must be my little wife. I know I am now only a poor journeyman shoemaker, but I will work and strive, and become a master in time. Yes, I will speak to her; nothing comes from silent love. I learnt that from the gingerbread-cake story."

Sunday came, but when Knud arrived, they were all unfortunately invited out to spend the evening, and were obliged to tell him so.

Joanna pressed his hand, and said, "Have you ever been to the theatre? you must go once; I sing there on Wednesday, and if you have time on that day, I will send you a ticket; my father knows where your master lives." How kind this was of her! And on Wednesday, about noon, Knud received a sealed packet with no address, but the ticket was inside; and in the evening Knud went, for the first time in his life, to a theatre. And what did he see? He saw Joanna, and how beautiful and charming she looked! He certainly saw her being married to a stranger, but that was all in the play, and only a pretence; Knud well knew that. She could never have the heart, he thought, to send him a ticket to go and see it, if it had been real. So he looked on, and when all the people applauded and clapped their hands, he shouted "hurrah." He could see that even the king smiled at Joanna, and seemed delighted with her singing. How small Knud felt; but then he loved her so dearly, and thought she loved him, and the man must speak the first word, as the gingerbread maiden had thought. Ah, how much there was for him in that childish story. As soon as Sunday arrived, he went again, and felt as if he were about to enter on holy ground. Joanna was alone to welcome him, nothing could be more fortunate.

"I am so glad you are come," she said. "I was thinking of sending my father for you, but I had a presentiment that you would be here this evening. The fact is, I wanted to tell you that I am going to France. I shall start on Friday. It is necessary for me to go there, if I wish to become a first-rate performer."

Poor Knud! it seemed to him as if the whole room was whirling round with him. His courage failed, and he felt as if his heart would burst. He kept down the tears, but it was easy to see how sorrowful he was.

"You honest, faithful soul," she exclaimed; and the words loosened Knud's tongue, and he told her how truly he had loved her, and that she must be his wife; and as he said this, he saw Joanna change color, and turn pale. She let his hand fall, and said, earnestly and mournfully, "Knud, do not make yourself and me unhappy. I will always be a good sister to you, one in whom you can trust; but I can never be anything more." And she drew her white hand over his burning forehead, and said, "God gives strength to bear a great deal, if we only strive ourselves to endure."

At this moment her stepmother came into the room, and Joanna said quickly, "Knud is so unhappy, because I am going away;" and it appeared as if they had only been talking of her journey. "Come, be a man" she added, placing her hand on his shoulder; "you are still a child, and you must be good and reasonable, as you were when we were both children, and played together under the willow-tree."

Knud listened, but he felt as if the world had slid out of its course. His thoughts were like a loose thread fluttering to and fro in the wind. He stayed, although he could not tell whether she had asked him to do so. But she was kind and gentle to him; she poured out his tea, and sang to him; but the song had not the old tone in it, although it was wonderfully beautiful, and made his heart feel ready to burst. And then he rose to go. He did not offer his hand, but she seized it, and said –

"Will you not shake hands with your sister at parting, my old playfellow?" and she smiled through the tears that were rolling down her cheeks. Again she repeated the word "brother," which was a great consolation certainly; and thus they parted.

She sailed to France, and Knud wandered about the muddy streets of Copenhagen. The other journeymen in the shop asked him why he looked so gloomy, and wanted him to go and amuse himself with them, as he was still a young man. So he went with them to a dancing-room. He saw many handsome girls there, but none like Joanna; and here, where he thought to forget her, she was more life-like before his mind than ever. "God gives us strength to bear much, if we try to do our best," she had said; and as he thought of this, a devout feeling came into his mind, and he folded his hands. Then, as the violins played and the girls danced round the room, he started; for it seemed to him as if he were in a place where he ought not to have brought Joanna, for she was here with him in his heart; and so he went out at once. As he went through the streets at a quick pace, he passed the house where she used to live; it was all dark, empty, and lonely. But the world went on its course, and Knud was obliged to go on too.

Winter came; the water was frozen, and everything seemed buried in a cold grave. But when spring returned, and the first steamer prepared to sail, Knud was seized with a longing to wander forth into the world, but not to France. So he packed his knapsack, and travelled through Germany, going from town to town, but finding neither rest or peace. It was not till he arrived at the glorious old town of Nuremberg that he gained the mastery over himself, and rested his weary feet; and here he remained.

Nuremberg is a wonderful old city, and looks as if it had been cut out of an old picture-book. The streets seem to have arranged themselves according to their own fancy, and as if the houses objected to stand in rows or rank and file. Gables, with little towers, ornamented columns, and statues, can be seen even to the city gate; and from the singular-shaped roofs, waterspouts, formed like dragons, or long lean dogs, extend far across to the middle of the street. Here, in the market-place, stood Knud, with his knapsack on his back, close to one of the old fountains which are so beautifully adorned with figures, scriptural and historical, and which spring up between the sparkling jets of water. A pretty servant-maid was just filling her pails, and she gave Knud a refreshing draught; she had a handful of roses, and she gave him one, which appeared to him like a good omen for the future. From a neighboring church came the sounds of music, and the familiar tones reminded him of the organ at home at Kjøge; so he passed into the great cathedral. The sunshine streamed through the painted glass windows, and between two lofty slender pillars. His thoughts became prayerful, and calm peace rested on his soul. He next sought and found a good master in Nuremberg, with whom he stayed and learnt the German language.

The old moat round the town had been converted into a number of little kitchen gardens; but the high walls, with their heavy-looking towers, are still standing. Inside these walls the ropemaker twisted his ropes along a walk built like a gallery, and in the cracks and crevices of the walls elderbushes grow and stretch their green boughs over the small houses which stand below. In one of these houses lived the master for whom Knud worked; and over the little garret window where he sat, the elder-tree waved its branches. Here he dwelt through one summer and winter, but when spring came again, he could endure it no longer. The elder was in blossom, and its fragrance was so homelike, that he fancied himself back again in the gardens of Kjøge. So Knud left his master, and went to work for another who lived farther in the town, where no elder grew. His workshop was quite close to one of the old stone bridges, near to a water-mill, round which the roaring stream rushed and foamed always, yet restrained by the neighboring houses, whose old, decayed balconies hung over, and seemed ready to fall into the water. Here grew no elder; here was not even a flower-pot, with its little green plant; but just opposite the workshop stood a great willow-tree, which seemed to hold fast to the house for fear of being carried away by the water. It stretched its branches over the stream just as those of the willow-tree in the garden at Kjøge had spread over the river. Yes, he had indeed gone from elder-mother to willow-father. There was a something about the tree here, especially in the moonlight nights, that went direct to his heart; yet it was not in reality the moonlight, but the old tree itself. However, he could not endure it: and why? Ask the willow, ask the blossoming elder! At all events, he bade farewell to Nuremberg and journeyed onwards. He never spoke of Joanna to any one; his sorrow was hidden in his heart. The old childish story of the two cakes had a deep meaning for him. He understood now why the gingerbread man had a bitter almond in his left side; his was the feeling of bitterness, and Joanna, so mild and friendly, was represented by the honeycake maiden. As he thought upon all this, the strap of his knapsack pressed across his chest so that he could hardly breathe; he loosened it, but gained no relief. He saw but half the world around him; the other half he carried with him in his inward thoughts; and this is the condition in which he left Nuremberg. Not till he caught sight of the lofty mountains did the world appear more free to him; his thoughts were attracted to outer objects, and tears came into his eyes. The Alps appeared to him like the wings of earth folded together; unfolded, they would display the variegated pictures of dark woods, foaming waters, spreading clouds, and masses of snow. "At the last day," thought he, "the earth will unfold its great wings, and soar upwards to the skies, there to burst like a soap-bubble in the radiant glance of the Deity. Oh," sighed he, "that the last day were come!"

Silently he wandered on through the country of the Alps, which seemed to him like a fruit garden, covered with soft turf. From the wooden balconies of the houses the young lacemakers nodded as he passed. The summits of the mountains glowed in the red evening sunset, and the green lakes beneath the dark trees reflected the glow. Then he thought of the sea coast by the bay Kjøge, with a longing in his heart that was, however, without pain. There, where the Rhine rolls onward like a great billow, and dissolves itself into snowflakes, where glistening clouds are ever changing as if here was the place of their creation, while the rainbow flutters about them like a many-colored ribbon, there did Knud think of the water-mill at Kjøge, with its rushing, foaming waters. Gladly would he have remained in the quiet Rhenish town, but there were too many elders and willow-trees.

So he travelled onwards, over a grand, lofty chain of mountains, over rugged, – rocky precipices, and along roads that hung on the mountain's side like a swallow's nest. The waters foamed in the depths below him. The clouds lay beneath him. He wandered on, treading upon Alpine roses, thistles, and snow, with the summer sun shining upon him, till at length he bid farewell to the lands of the north. Then he passed on under the shade of blooming chestnut-trees, through vineyards, and fields of Indian corn, till conscious that the mountains were as a wall between him and his early recollections; and he wished it to be so.

Before him lay a large and splendid city, called Milan, and here he found a German master who engaged him as a workman. The master and his wife, in whose workshop he was employed, were an old, pious couple; and the two old people became quite fond of the quiet journeyman, who spoke but little, but worked more, and led a pious, Christian life; and even to himself it seemed as if God had removed the heavy burden from his heart. His greatest pleasure was to climb, now and then, to the roof of the noble church, which was built of white marble. The pointed towers, the decorated and open cloisters, the stately columns, the white statues which smiled upon him from every corner and porch and arch, – all, even the church itself, seemed to him to have been formed from the snow of his native land. Above him was the blue sky; below him, the city and the wide-spreading plains of Lombardy; and towards the north, the lofty mountains, covered with perpetual snow. And then he thought of the church of Kjøge, with its red, ivy-clad walls, but he had no longing to go there; here, beyond the mountains, he would die and be buried.

Three years had passed away since he left his home; one year of that time he had dwelt at Milan.

One day his master took him into the town; not to the circus in which riders performed, but to the opera, a large building, itself a sight well worth seeing. The seven tiers of boxes, which reached from the ground to a dizzy height, near the ceiling, were hung with rich, silken curtains; and in them were seated elegantly-dressed ladies, with bouquets of flowers in their hands. The gentlemen were also in full dress, and many of them wore decorations of gold and silver. The place was so brilliantly lighted that it seemed like sunshine, and glorious music rolled through the building. Everything looked more beautiful than in the theatre at Copenhagen, but then Joanna had been there, and – could it be? Yes – it was like magic, – she was here also: for, when the curtain rose, there stood Joanna, dressed in silk and gold, and with a golden crown upon her head. She sang, he thought, as only an angel could sing; and then she stepped forward to the front and smiled, as only Joanna could smile, and looked directly at Knud. Poor Knud! he seized his master's hand, and cried out loud, "Joanna," but no one heard him, excepting his master, for the music sounded above everything.

"Yes, yes, it is Joanna," said his master; and he drew forth a printed bill, and pointed to her name, which was there in full. Then it was not a dream. All the audience applauded her, and threw wreaths of flowers at her; and every time she went away they called for her again, so that she was always coming and going. In the street the people crowded round her carriage, and drew it away themselves without the horses. Knud was in the foremost row, and shouted as joyously as the rest; and when the carriage stopped before a brilliantly lighted house, Knud placed himself close to the door of her carriage. It flew open, and she stepped out; the light fell upon her dear face, and he could see that she smiled as she thanked them, and appeared quite overcome. Knud looked straight in her face, and she looked at him, but she did not recognize him. A man, with a glittering star on his breast, gave her his arm, and people said the two were engaged to be married. Then Knud went home and packed up his knapsack; he felt he must return to the home of his childhood, to the elder-tree and the willow. "Ah, under that willow-tree!" A man may live a whole life in one single hour.

The old couple begged him to remain, but words were useless. In vain they reminded him that winter was coming, and that the snow had already fallen on the mountains. He said he could easily follow the track of the closely-moving carriages, for which a path must be kept clear, and with nothing but his knapsack on his back, and leaning on his stick, he could step along briskly. So he turned his steps to the mountains, ascended one side and descended the other, still going northward till his strength began to fail, and not a house or village could be seen. The stars shone in the sky above him, and down in the valley lights glittered like stars, as if another sky were beneath him; but his head was dizzy and his feet stumbled, and he felt ill. The lights in the valley grew brighter and brighter, and more numerous, and he could see them moving to and fro, and then he understood that there must be a village in the distance; so he exerted his failing strength to reach it, and at length obtained shelter in a humble lodging. He remained there that night and the whole of the following day, for his body required rest and refreshment, and in the valley there was rain and a thaw. But early in the morning of the third day, a man came with an organ and played one of the melodies of home; and after that Knud could remain there no longer, so he started again on his journey toward the north. He travelled for many days with hasty steps, as if he were trying to reach home before all whom he remembered should die; but he spoke to no one of this longing. No one would have believed or understood this sorrow of his heart, the deepest that can be felt by human nature. Such grief is not for the world; it is not entertaining even to friends, and poor Knud had no friends; he was a stranger, wandering through strange lands to his home in the north.

He was walking one evening through the public roads, the country around him was flatter, with fields and meadows, the air had a frosty feeling. A willow-tree grew by the roadside, everything reminded him of home. He felt very tired; so he sat down under the tree, and very soon began to nod, then his eyes closed in sleep. Yet still he seemed conscious that the willow-tree was stretching its branches over him; in his dreaming state the tree appeared like a strong, old man – the "willow-father" himself, who had taken his tired son up in his arms to carry him back to the land of home, to the garden of his childhood, on the bleak open shores of Kjøge. And then he dreamed that it was really the willow-tree itself from Kjøge, which had travelled out in the world to seek him, and now had found him and carried him back into the little garden on the banks of the streamlet; and there stood Joanna, in all her splendor, with the golden crown on her head, as he had last seen her, to welcome him back. And then there appeared before him two remarkable shapes, which looked much more like human beings than when he had seen them in his childhood; they were changed, but he remembered that they were the two gingerbread cakes, the man and the woman, who had shown their best sides to the world and looked so good.

"We thank you," they said to Knud, "for you have loosened our tongues; we have learnt from you that thoughts should be spoken freely, or nothing will come of them; and now something has come of our thoughts, for we are engaged to be married." Then they walked away, hand-in-hand, through the streets of Kjøge, looking very respectable on the best side, which they were quite right to show. They turned their steps to the church, and Knud and Joanna followed them, also walking hand-in-hand; there stood the church, as of old, with its red walls, on which the green ivy grew.

The great church door flew open wide, and as they walked up the broad aisle, soft tones of music sounded from the organ. "Our master first," said the gingerbread pair, making room for Knud and Joanna. As they knelt at the altar, Joanna bent her head over him, and cold, icy tears fell on his face from her eyes. They were indeed tears of ice, for her heart was melting towards him through his strong love, and as her tears fell on his burning cheeks he awoke. He was still sitting under the willow-tree in a strange land, on a cold winter evening, with snow and hail falling from the clouds, and beating upon his face.

"That was the most delightful hour of my life," said he, "although it was only a dream. Oh, let me dream again." Then he closed his eyes once more, and slept and dreamed.

Towards morning there was a great fall of snow; the wind drifted it over him, but he still slept on. The villagers came forth to go to church; by the roadside they found a workman seated, but he was dead! frozen to death under a willow-tree.

The Princess and the Pea

ONCE UPON A TIME there was a prince who wanted to marry a princess; but she would have to be a real princess. He travelled all over the world to find one, but nowhere could he get what he wanted. There were princesses enough, but it was difficult to find out whether they were real ones. There was always something about them that was not as it should be. So he came home again and was sad, for he would have liked very much to have a real princess.

One evening a terrible storm came on; there was thunder and lightning, and the rain poured down in torrents. Suddenly a knocking was heard at the city gate, and the old king went to open it.

It was a princess standing out there in front of the gate. But, good gracious! what a sight the rain and the wind had made her look. The water ran down from her hair and clothes; it ran down into the toes of her shoes and out again at the heels. And yet she said that she was a real princess.

"Well, we'll soon find that out," thought the old queen. But she said nothing, went into the bed-room, took all the bedding off the bedstead, and laid a pea on the bottom; then she took twenty mattresses and laid them on the pea, and then twenty eider-down beds on top of the mattresses.

On this the princess had to lie all night. In the morning she was asked how she had slept.

"Oh, very badly!" said she. "I have scarcely closed my eyes all night. Heaven only knows what was in the bed, but I was lying on something hard, so that I am black and blue all over my body. It's horrible!"

Now they knew that she was a real princess because she had felt the pea right through the twenty mattresses and the twenty eider-down beds.

Nobody but a real princess could be as sensitive as that.

So the prince took her for his wife, for now he knew that he had a real princess; and the pea was put in the museum, where it may still be seen, if no one has stolen it.

There, that is a true story.

The Shepherd's Story of the Bond of Friendship

THE LITTLE DWELLING in which we lived was of clay, but the door-posts were columns of fluted marble, found near the spot on which it stood. The roof sloped nearly to the ground. It was at this time dark, brown, and ugly, but had originally been formed of blooming olive and laurel branches, brought from beyond the mountains. The house was situated in a narrow gorge, whose rocky walls rose to a perpendicular height, naked and black, while round their summits clouds often hung, looking like white living figures. Not a singing bird was ever heard there, neither did men dance to the sound of the pipe. The spot was one sacred to olden times; even its name recalled a memory of the days when it was called "Delphi." Then the summits of the dark, sacred mountains were covered with snow, and the highest, mount Parnassus, glowed longest in the red evening light. The brook which rolled from it near our house, was also sacred. How well I can remember every spot in that deep, sacred solitude! A fire had been kindled in the midst of the hut, and while the hot ashes lay there red and glowing, the bread was baked in them. At times the snow would be piled so high around our hut as almost to hide it, and then my mother appeared most cheerful. She would hold my head between her hands, and sing the songs she never sang at other times, for the Turks, our masters, would not allow it. She sang, –

"On the summit of mount Olympus, in a forest of dwarf firs, lay an old stag. His eyes were heavy with tears, and glittering with colors like dewdrops; and there came by a roebuck, and said, 'What ailest thee, that thou weepest blue and red tears?' And the stag answered, 'The Turk has come to our city; he has wild dogs for the chase, a goodly pack.' 'I will drive them away across the islands!' cried the young roebuck; 'I will drive them away across the islands into the deep sea.' But before evening the roebuck was slain, and before night the hunted stag was dead."

And when my mother sang thus, her eyes would become moist; and on the long eyelashes were tears, but she concealed them and watched the black bread baking in the ashes. Then I would clench my fist, and cry, "We will kill these Turks!" But she repeated the words of the song, "I will drive them across the islands to the deep sea; but before evening came the roebuck was slain, and before the night the hunted stag was dead."

We had been lonely in our hut for several days and nights when my father came home. I knew he would bring me some shells from the gulf of Lepanto, or perhaps a knife with a shining blade. This time he brought, under his sheep-skin cloak, a little child, a little half-naked girl. She was wrapped in a fur; but when this was taken off, and she lay in my mother's lap, three silver coins were found fastened in her dark hair; they were all her possessions. My father told us that the child's parents had been killed by the Turks, and he talked so much about them that I dreamed of Turks all night. He himself had been wounded, and my mother bound up his arm. It was a deep wound, and the thick sheep-skin cloak was stiff with congealed blood. The little maiden was to be my sister. How pretty and bright she looked: even my mother's eyes were not more gentle than hers.

Anastasia, as she was called, was to be my sister, because her father had been united to mine by an old custom, which we still follow. They had sworn brotherhood in their youth, and the most beautiful and virtuous maiden in the neighborhood was chosen to perform the act of consecration upon this bond of friendship. So now this little girl was my sister. She sat in my lap, and I brought her flowers, and feathers from the birds of the mountain. We drank together of the waters of Parnassus, and dwelt for many years beneath the laurel roof of the hut, while, winter after winter, my mother sang her song of the stag who shed red tears. But as yet I did not understand that the sorrows of my own countrymen were mirrored in those tears.

One day there came to our hut Franks, men from a far country, whose dress was different to ours. They had tents and beds with them, carried by horses; and they were accompanied by more than twenty Turks, all armed with swords and muskets. These Franks were friends of the Pacha, and had letters from him, commanding an escort for them. They only came to see our mountain, to ascend Parnassus amid the snow and clouds, and to look at the strange black rocks which raised their steep sides near our hut. They could not find room in the hut, nor endure the smoke that rolled along the ceiling till it found its way out at the low door; so they pitched their tents on a small space outside our dwelling. Roasted lambs and birds were brought forth, and strong, sweet wine, of which the Turks are forbidden to partake.

When they departed, I accompanied them for some distance, carrying my little sister Anastasia, wrapped in a goat-skin, on my back. One of the Frankish gentlemen made me stand in front of a rock, and drew us both as we stood there, so that we looked like one creature. I did not think of it then, but Anastasia and I were really one. She was always sitting on my lap, or riding in the goat-skin on my back; and in my dreams she always appeared to me.

Two nights after this, other men, armed with knives and muskets, came into our tent. They were Albanians, brave men, my mother told me. They only stayed a short time. My sister Anastasia sat on the knee of one of them; and when they were gone, she had not three, but two silver coins in her hair – one had disappeared. They wrapped tobacco in strips of paper, and smoked it; and I remember they were uncertain as to the road they ought to take. But they were obliged to go at last, and my father went with them. Soon after, we heard the sound of firing. The noise continued, and presently soldiers rushed into our hut, and took my mother and myself and Anastasia prisoners. They declared that we had entertained robbers, and that my father had acted as their guide, and therefore we must now go with them. The corpses of the robbers, and my father's corpse, were brought into the hut. I saw my poor dead father, and cried till I fell asleep. When I awoke, I found myself in a prison; but the room was not worse than our own in the hut. They gave me onions and musty wine from a tarred cask; but we were not accustomed to much better fare at home. How long we were kept in prison, I do not know; but many days and nights passed by. We were set free about Easter-time. I carried Anastasia on my back, and we walked very slowly; for my mother was very weak, and it is a long way to the sea, to the Gulf of Lepanto.

On our arrival, we entered a church, in which there were beautiful pictures in golden frames. They were pictures of angels, fair and bright; and yet our little Anastasia looked equally beautiful, as it seemed to me. In the centre of the floor stood a coffin filled with roses. My mother told me it was the Lord Jesus Christ who was represented by these roses. Then the priest announced, "Christ is risen," and all the people greeted each other. Each one carried a burning taper in his hand, and one was given to me, as well as to little Anastasia. The music sounded, and the people left the church hand-in-hand, with joy and gladness. Outside, the women were roasting the paschal lamb. We were invited to partake; and as I sat by the fire, a boy, older than myself, put his arms round my neck, and kissed me, and said, "Christ is risen." And thus it was that for the first time I met Aphtanides.

My mother could make fishermen's nets, for which there was a great demand here in the bay; and we lived a long time by the side of the sea, the beautiful sea, that had a taste like tears, and in its colors reminded me of the stag that wept red tears; for sometimes its waters were red, and sometimes green or blue. Aphtanides knew how to manage our boat, and I often sat in it, with my little Anastasia, while it glided on through the water, swift as a bird flying through the air. Then, when the sun set, how beautifully, deeply blue, would be the tint on the mountains, one rising above the other in the far distance, and the summit of mount Parnassus rising above them all like a glorious crown. Its top glittered in the evening rays like molten gold, and it seemed as if the light came from within it; for long after the sun had sunk beneath the horizon, the mountain-top would glow in the clear, blue sky. The white aquatic birds skimmed the surface of the water in their flight, and all was calm and still as amid the black rocks at Delphi. I lay on my back in the boat, Anastasia leaned against me, while the stars above us glittered more brightly than the lamps in our church. They were the same stars, and in the same position over me as when I used to sit in front of our hut at Delphi, and I had almost begun to fancy I was still there, when suddenly there was a splash in the water – Anastasia had fallen in; but in a moment Aphtanides has sprung in after her, and was now holding her up to me. We dried her clothes as well as we were able, and remained on the water till they were dry; for we did not wish it to be known what a fright we had, nor the danger which our little adopted sister had incurred, in whose life Aphtanides had now a part.

The summer came, and the burning heat of the sun tinted the leaves of the trees with lines of gold. I thought of our cool mountain-home, and the fresh water that flowed near it; my mother, too, longed for if, and one evening we wandered towards home. How peaceful and silent it was as we walked on through the thick, wild thyme, still fragrant, though the sun had scorched the leaves. Not a single herdsman did we meet, not a solitary hut did we pass; everything appeared lonely and deserted – only a shooting star showed that in the heavens there was yet life. I know not whether the clear, blue atmosphere gleamed with its own light, or if the radiance came from the stars; but we could distinguish quite plainly the outline of the mountains. My mother lighted a fire, and roasted some roots she had brought with her, and I and my little sister slept among the bushes, without fear of the ugly smidraki, from whose throat issues fire, or of the wolf and the jackal; for my mother sat by us, and I considered her presence sufficient protection.

We reached our old home; but the cottage was in ruins, and we had to build a new one. With the aid of some neighbors, chiefly women, the walls were in a few days erected, and very soon covered with a roof of olive-branches. My mother obtained a living by making bottle-cases of bark and skins, and I kept the sheep belonging to the priests, who were sometimes peasants, while I had for my playfellows Anastasia and the turtles.

Once our beloved Aphtanides paid us a visit. He said he had been longing to see us so much; and he remained with us two whole happy days. A month afterwards he came again to wish us good-bye, and brought with him a large fish for my mother. He told us he was going in a ship to Corfu and Patras, and could relate a great many stories, not only about the fishermen who lived near the gulf of Lepanto, but also of kings and heroes who had once possessed Greece, just as the Turks possess it now.

I have seen a bud on a rose-bush gradually, in the course of a few weeks, unfold its leaves till it became a rose in all its beauty; and, before I was aware of it, I beheld it blooming in rosy loveliness. The same thing had happened to Anastasia. Unnoticed by me, she had gradually become a beautiful maiden, and I was now also a stout, strong youth. The wolf-skins that covered the bed in which my mother and Anastasia slept, had been taken from wolves which I had myself shot.

Years had gone by when, one evening, Aphtanides came in. He had grown tall and slender as a reed, with strong limbs, and a dark, brown skin. He kissed us all, and had so much to tell of what he had seen of the great ocean, of the fortifications at Malta, and of the marvellous sepulchres of Egypt, that I looked up to him with a kind of veneration. His stories were as strange as the legends of the priests of olden times.

"How much you know!" I exclaimed, "and what wonders you can relate?"

"I think what you once told me, the finest of all," he replied; "you told me of a thing that has never been out of my thoughts – of the good old custom of 'the bond of friendship,' – a custom I should like to follow. Brother, let you and I go to church, as your father and Anastasia's father once did. Your sister Anastasia is the most beautiful and most innocent of maidens, and she shall consecrate the deed. No people have such grand old customs as we Greeks."

Anastasia blushed like a young rose, and my mother kissed Aphtanides.

At about two miles from our cottage, where the earth on the hill is sheltered by a few scattered trees, stood the little church, with a silver lamp hanging before the altar. I put on my best clothes, and the white tunic fell in graceful folds over my hips. The red jacket fitted tight and close, the tassel on my Fez cap was of silver, and in my girdle glittered a knife and my pistols. Aphtanides was clad in the blue dress worn by the Greek sailors; on his breast hung a silver medal with the figure of the Virgin Mary, and his scarf was as costly as those worn by rich lords. Every one could see that we were about to perform a solemn ceremony. When we entered the little, unpretending church, the evening sunlight streamed through the open door on the burning lamp, and glittered on the golden picture frames. We knelt down together on the altar steps, and Anastasia drew near and stood beside us. A long, white garment fell in graceful folds over her delicate form, and on her white neck and bosom hung a chain entwined with old and new coins, forming a kind of collar. Her black hair was fastened into a knot, and confined by a headdress formed of gold and silver coins which had been found in an ancient temple. No Greek girl had more beautiful ornaments than these. Her countenance glowed, and her eyes were like two stars. We all three offered a silent prayer, and then she said to us, "Will you be friends in life and in death?"

"Yes," we replied.

"Will you each remember to say, whatever may happen, 'My brother is a part of myself; his secret is my secret, my happiness is his; self-sacrifice, patience, everything belongs to me as they do to him?'"

And we again answered, "Yes." Then she joined out hands and kissed us on the forehead, and we again prayed silently. After this a priest came through a door near the altar, and blessed us all three. Then a song was sung by other holy men behind the altar-screen, and the bond of eternal friendship was confirmed. When we arose, I saw my mother standing by the church door, weeping.

How cheerful everything seemed now in our little cottage by the Delphian springs! On the evening before his departure, Aphtanides sat thoughtfully beside me on the slopes of the mountain. His arm was flung around me, and mine was round his neck. We spoke of the sorrows of Greece, and of the men of the country who could be trusted. Every thought of our souls lay clear before us. Presently I seized his hand: "Aphtanides," I exclaimed, "there is one thing still that you must know, – one thing that till now has been a secret between myself and Heaven. My whole soul is filled with love, – with a love stronger than the love I bear to my mother and to thee."

"And whom do you love?" asked Aphtanides. And his face and neck grew red as fire.

"I love Anastasia," I replied.

Then his hand trembled in mine, and he became pale as a corpse. I saw it, I understood the cause, and I believe my hand trembled too. I bent towards him, I kissed his forehead, and whispered, "I have never spoken of this to her, and perhaps she does not love me. Brother, think of this; I have seen her daily, she has grown up beside me, and has become a part of my soul."

"And she shall be thine," he exclaimed; "thine! I may not wrong thee, nor will I do so. I also love her, but tomorrow I depart. In a year we will see each other again, but then you will be married; shall it not be so? I have a little gold of my own, it shall be yours. You must and shall take it."

We wandered silently homeward across the mountains. It was late in the evening when we reached my mother's door. Anastasia held the lamp as we entered; my mother was not there. She looked at Aphtanides with a sweet but mournful expression on her face. "To-morrow you are going to leave us," she said. "I am very sorry."

"Sorry!" he exclaimed, and his voice was troubled with a grief as deep as my own. I could not speak; but he seized her hand and said, "Our brother yonder loves you, and is he not dear to you? His very silence now proves his affection."

Anastasia trembled, and burst into tears. Then I saw no one, thought of none, but her. I threw my arms round her, and pressed my lips to hers. As she flung her arms round my neck, the lamp fell to the ground, and we were in darkness, dark as the heart of poor Aphtanides.

Before daybreak he rose, kissed us all, and said "Farewell," and went away. He had given all his money to my mother for us. Anastasia was betrothed to me, and in a few days afterwards she became my wife.

Beauty of Form and Beauty of Mind

THERE WAS ONCE a sculptor, named Alfred, who having won the large gold medal and obtained a travelling scholarship, went to Italy, and then came back to his native land. He was young at that time – indeed, he is young still, although he is ten years older than he was then. On his return, he went to visit one of the little towns in the island of Zealand. The whole town knew who the stranger was; and one of the richest men in the place gave a party in his honor, and all who were of any consequence, or who possessed some property, were invited. It was quite an event, and all the town knew of it, so that it was not necessary to announce it by beat of drum. Apprentice-boys, children of the poor, and even the poor people themselves, stood before the house, watching the lighted windows; and the watchman might easily fancy he was giving a party also, there were so many people in the streets. There was quite an air of festivity about it, and the house was full of it; for Mr. Alfred, the sculptor, was there. He talked and told anecdotes, and every one listened to him with pleasure, not unmingled with awe; but none felt so much respect for him as did the elderly widow of a naval officer. She seemed, so far as Mr. Alfred was concerned, to be like a piece of fresh blotting-paper that absorbed all he said and asked for more. She was very appreciative, and incredibly ignorant – a kind of female Gaspar Hauser.

"I should like to see Rome," she said; "it must be a lovely city, or so many foreigners would not be constantly arriving there. Now, do give me a description of Rome. How does the city look when you enter in at the gate?"

"I cannot very well describe it," said the sculptor; "but you enter on a large open space, in the centre of which stands an obelisk, which is a thousand years old."

"An organist!" exclaimed the lady, who had never heard the word 'obelisk.' Several of the guests could scarcely forbear laughing, and the sculptor would have had some difficulty in keeping his countenance, but the smile on his lips faded away; for he caught sight of a pair of dark-blue eyes close by the side of the inquisitive lady. They belonged to her daughter; and surely no one who had such a daughter could be silly. The mother was like a fountain of questions; and the daughter, who listened but never spoke, might have passed for the beautiful maid of the fountain. How charming she was! She was a study for the sculptor to contemplate, but not to converse with; for she did not speak, or, at least, very seldom.

"Has the pope a great family?" inquired the lady.

The young man answered considerately, as if the question had been a different one, "No; he does not come from a great family."

"That is not what I asked," persisted the widow; "I mean, has he a wife and children?"

"The pope is not allowed to marry," replied the gentleman.

"I don't like that," was the lady's remark.

She certainly might have asked more sensible questions; but if she had not been allowed to say just what she liked, would her daughter have been there, leaning so gracefully on her shoulder, and looking straight before her, with a smile that was almost mournful on her face?

Mr. Alfred again spoke of Italy, and of the glorious colors in Italian scenery; the purple hills, the deep blue of the Mediterranean, the azure of southern skies, whose brightness and glory could only be surpassed in the north by the deep-blue eyes of a maiden; and he said this with a peculiar intonation; but she who should have understood his meaning looked quite unconscious of it, which also was charming.

"Beautiful Italy!" sighed some of the guests.

"Oh, to travel there!" exclaimed others.

"Charming! Charming!" echoed from every voice.

"I may perhaps win a hundred thousand dollars in the lottery," said the naval officer's widow; "and if I do, we will travel – I and my daughter; and you, Mr. Alfred, must be our guide. We can all three travel together, with one or two more of our good friends." And she nodded in such a friendly way at the company, that each imagined himself to be the favored person who was to accompany them to Italy. "Yes, we must go," she continued; "but not to those parts where there are robbers. We will keep to Rome. In the public roads one is always safe."

The daughter sighed very gently; and how much there may be in a sigh, or attributed to it! The young man attributed a great deal of meaning to this sigh. Those deep-blue eyes, which had been lit up this evening in honor of him, must conceal treasures, treasures of heart and mind, richer than all the glories of Rome; and so when he left the party that night, he had lost it completely to the young lady. The house of the naval officer's widow was the one most constantly visited by Mr. Alfred, the sculptor. It was soon understood that his visits were not intended for that lady, though they were the persons who kept up the conversation. He came for the sake of the daughter. They called her Kæla. Her name was really Karen Malena, and these two names had been contracted into the one name Kæla. She was really beautiful; but some said she was rather dull, and slept late of a morning.

"She has been accustomed to that," her mother said. "She is a beauty, and they are always easily tired. She does sleep rather late; but that makes her eyes so clear."

What power seemed to lie in the depths of those dark eyes! The young man felt the truth of the proverb, "Still waters run deep:" and his heart had sunk into their depths. He often talked of his adventures, and the mamma was as simple and eager in her questions as on the first evening they met. It was a pleasure to hear Alfred describe anything. He showed them colored plates of Naples, and spoke of excursions to Mount Vesuvius, and the eruptions of fire from it. The naval officer's widow had never heard of them before.

"Good heavens!" she exclaimed. "So that is a burning mountain; but is it not very dangerous to the people who live near it?"

"Whole cities have been destroyed," he replied; "for instance, Herculaneum and Pompeii."

"Oh, the poor people! And you saw all that with your own eyes?"

"No; I did not see any of the eruptions which are represented in those pictures; but I will show you a sketch of my own, which represents an eruption I once saw."

He placed a pencil sketch on the table; and mamma, who had been over-powered with the appearance of the colored plates, threw a glance at the pale drawing and cried in astonishment, "What, did you see it throw up white fire?"

For a moment, Alfred's respect for Kæla's mamma underwent a sudden shock, and lessened considerably; but, dazzled by the light which surrounded Kæla, he soon found it quite natural that the old lady should have no eye for color. After all, it was of very little consequence; for Kæla's mamma had the best of all possessions; namely, Kæla herself.

Alfred and Kæla were betrothed, which was a very natural result; and the betrothal was announced in the newspaper of the little town. Mama purchased thirty copies of the paper, that she might cut out the paragraph and send it to friends and acquaintances. The betrothed pair were very happy, and the mother was happy too. She said it seemed like connecting herself with Thorwalsden.

"You are a true successor of Thorwalsden," she said to Alfred; and it seemed to him as if, in this instance, mamma had said a clever thing. Kæla was silent; but her eyes shone, her lips smiled, every movement was graceful, – in fact, she was beautiful; that cannot be repeated too often. Alfred decided to take a bust of Kæla as well as of her mother. They sat to him accordingly, and saw how he moulded and formed the soft clay with his fingers.

"I suppose it is only on our account that you perform this common-place work yourself, instead of leaving it to your servant to do all that sticking together."

"It is really necessary that I should mould the clay myself," he replied.

"Ah, yes, you are always so polite," said mamma, with a smile; and Kæla silently pressed his hand, all soiled as it was with the clay.

Then he unfolded to them both the beauties of Nature, in all her works; he pointed out to them how, in the scale of creation, inanimate matter was inferior to animate nature; the plant above the mineral, the animal above the plant, and man above them all. He strove to show them how the beauty of the mind could be displayed in the outward form, and that it was the sculptor's task to seize upon that beauty of expression, and produce it in his works. Kæla stood silent, but nodded in approbation of what he said, while mamma-in-law made the following confession: –

"It is difficult to follow you; but I go hobbling along after you with my thoughts, though what you say makes my head whirl round and round. Still I contrive to lay hold on some of it."

Kæla's beauty had a firm hold on Alfred; it filled his soul, and held a mastery over him. Beauty beamed from Kæla's every feature, glittered in her eyes, lurked in the corners of her mouth, and pervaded every movement of her agile fingers. Alfred, the sculptor, saw this. He spoke only to her, thought only of her, and the two became one; and so it may be said she spoke much, for he was always talking to her; and he and she were one. Such was the betrothal, and then came the wedding, with bride's-maids and wedding presents, all duly mentioned in the wedding speech. Mamma-in-law had set up Thorwalsden's bust at the end of the table, attired in a dressing-gown; it was her fancy that he should be a guest. Songs were sung, and cheers given; for it was a gay wedding, and they were a handsome pair. "Pygmalion loved his Galatea," said one of the songs.

"Ah, that is some of your mythologies," said mamma-in-law.

Next day the youthful pair started for Copenhagen, where they were to live; mamma-in-law accompanied them, to attend to the "coarse work," as she always called the domestic arrangements. Kæla looked like a doll in a doll's house, for everything was bright and new, and so fine. There they sat, all three; and as for Alfred, a proverb may describe his position – he looked like a swan amongst the geese. The magic of form had enchanted him; he had looked at the casket without caring to inquire what it contained, and that omission often brings the greatest unhappiness into married life. The casket may be injured, the gilding may fall off, and then the purchaser regrets his bargain. In a large party it is very disagreeable to find a button giving way, with no studs at hand to fall back upon; but it is worse still in a large company to be conscious that your wife and mother-in-law are talking nonsense, and that you cannot depend upon yourself to produce a little ready wit to carry off the stupidity of the whole affair.

The young married pair often sat together hand in hand; he would talk, but she could only now and then let fall a word in the same melodious voice, the same bell-like tones. It was a mental relief when Sophy, one of her friends, came to pay them a visit. Sophy was not pretty. She was, however, quite free from any physical deformity, although Kæla used to say she was a little crooked; but no eye, save an intimate acquaintance, would have noticed it. She was a very sensible girl, yet it never occurred to her that she might be a dangerous person in such a house. Her appearance created a new atmosphere in the doll's house, and air was really required, they all owned that. They felt the want of a change of air, and consequently the young couple and their mother travelled to Italy.

"Thank heaven we are at home again within our own four walls," said mamma-in-law and daughter both, on their return after a year's absence.

"There is no real pleasure in travelling," said mamma; "to tell the truth, it's very wearisome; I beg pardon for saying so. I was soon very tired of it, although I had my children with me; and, besides, it's very expensive work travelling, very expensive. And all those galleries one is expected to see, and the quantity of things you are obliged to run after! It must be done, for very shame; you are sure to be asked when you come back if you have seen everything, and will most likely be told that you've omitted to see what was best worth seeing of all. I got tired at last of those endless Madonnas; I began to think I was turning into a Madonna myself."

"And then the living, mamma," said Kæla.

"Yes, indeed," she replied, "no such a thing as a respectable meat soup – their cookery is miserable stuff."

The journey had also tired Kæla; but she was always fatigued, that was the worst of it. So they sent for Sophy, and she was taken into the house to reside with them, and her presence there was a great advantage. Mamma-in-law acknowledged that Sophy was not only a clever housewife, but well-informed and accomplished, though that could hardly be expected in a person of her limited means. She was also a generous-hearted, faithful girl; she showed that thoroughly while Kæla lay sick, fading away. When the casket is everything, the casket should be strong, or else all is over. And all was over with the casket, for Kæla died.

"She was beautiful," said her mother; "she was quite different from the beauties they call 'antiques,' for they are so damaged. A beauty ought to be perfect, and Kæla was a perfect beauty."

Alfred wept, and mamma wept, and they both wore mourning. The black dress suited mamma very well, and she wore mourning the longest. She had also to experience another grief in seeing Alfred marry again, marry Sophy, who was nothing at all to look at. "He's gone to the very extreme," said mamma-in-law; "he has gone from the most beautiful to the ugliest, and he has forgotten his first wife. Men have no constancy. My husband was a very different man, – but then he died before me."

"'Pygmalion loved his Galatea,' was in the song they sung at my first wedding," said Alfred; "I once fell in love with a beautiful statue, which awoke to life in my arms; but the kindred soul, which is a gift from heaven, the angel who can feel and sympathize with and elevate us, I have not found and won till now. You came, Sophy, not in the glory of outward beauty, though you are even fairer than is necessary. The chief thing still remains. You came to teach the sculptor that his work is but dust and clay only, an outward form made of a material that decays, and that what we should seek to obtain is the ethereal essence of mind and spirit. Poor Kæla! our life was but as a meeting by the way-side; in yonder world, where we shall know each other from a union of mind, we shall be but mere acquaintances."

"That was not a loving speech," said Sophy, "nor spoken like a Christian. In a future state, where there is neither marrying nor giving in marriage, but where, as you say, souls are attracted to each other by sympathy; there everything beautiful develops itself, and is raised to a higher state of existence: her soul will acquire such completeness that it may harmonize with yours, even more than mine, and you will then once more utter your first rapturous exclamation of your love, 'Beautiful, most beautiful!'"

The Ice Maiden

I
Little Rudy

WE WILL PAY a visit to Switzerland, and wander through that country of mountains, whose steep and rocky sides are overgrown with forest trees. Let us climb to the dazzling snow-fields at their summits, and descend again to the green meadows beneath, through which rivers and brooks rush along as if they could not quickly enough reach the sea and vanish. Fiercely shines the sun over those deep valleys, as well as upon the heavy masses of snow which lie on the mountains.

During the year these accumulations thaw or fall in the rolling avalance, or are piled up in shining glaciers. Two of these glaciers lie in the broad, rocky cliffs, between the Schreckhorn and the Wetterhorn, near the little town of Grindelwald. They are wonderful to behold, and therefore in the summer time strangers come here from all parts of the world to see them. They cross snow-covered mountains, and travel through the deep valleys, or ascend for hours, higher and still higher, the valleys appearing to sink lower and lower as they proceed, and become as small as if seen from an air balloon. Over the lofty summits of these mountains the clouds often hang like a dark veil; while beneath in the valley, where many brown, wooden houses are scattered about, the bright rays of the sun may be shining upon a little brilliant patch of green, making it appear almost transparent. The waters foam and dash along in the valleys beneath; the streams from above trickle and murmur as they fall down the rocky mountain's side, looking like glittering silver bands.

On both sides of the mountain-path stand these little wooden houses; and, as within, there are many children and many mouths to feed, each house has its own little potato garden. These children rush out in swarms, and surround travellers, whether on foot or in carriages. They are all clever at making a bargain. They offer for sale the sweetest little toy-houses, models of the mountain cottages in Switzerland. Whether it be rain or sunshine, these crowds of children are always to be seen with their wares.

About twenty years ago, there might be seen occasionally, standing at a short distance from the other children, a little boy, who was also anxious to sell his curious wares. He had an earnest, expressive countenance, and held the box containing his carved toys tightly with both hands, as if unwilling to part with it. His earnest look, and being also a very little boy, made him noticed by the strangers; so that he often sold the most, without knowing why. An hour's walk farther up the ascent lived his grandfather, who cut and carved the pretty little toy-houses; and in the old man's room stood a large press, full of all sorts of carved things – nut-crackers, knives and forks, boxes with beautifully carved foliage, leaping chamois. It contained everything that could delight the eyes of a child. But the boy, who was named Rudy, looked with still greater pleasure and longing at some old fire-arms which hung upon the rafters, under the ceiling of the room. His grandfather promised him that he should have them some day, but that he must first grow big and strong, and learn how to use them. Small as he was, the goats were placed in his care, and a good goat-keeper should also be a good climber, and such Rudy was; he sometimes, indeed, climbed higher than the goats, for he was fond of seeking for birds'-nests at the top of high trees; he was bold and daring, but was seldom seen to smile, excepting when he stood by the roaring cataract, or heard the descending roll of the avalanche. He never played with the other children, and was not seen with them, unless his grandfather sent him down to sell his curious workmanship. Rudy did not much like trade; he loved to climb the mountains, or to sit by his grandfather and listen to his tales of olden times, or of the people in Meyringen, the place of his birth.

"In the early ages of the world," said the old man, "these people could not be found in Switzerland. They are a colony from the north, where their ancestors still dwell, and are called Swedes."

This was something for Rudy to know, but he learnt more from other sources, particularly from the domestic animals who belonged to the house. One was a large dog, called Ajola, which had belonged to his father; and the other was a tom-cat. This cat stood very high in Rudy's favor, for he had taught him to climb.

"Come out on the roof with me," said the cat; and Rudy quite understood him, for the language of fowls, ducks, cats, and dogs, is as easily understood by a young child as his own native tongue. But it must be at the age when grandfather's stick becomes a neighing horse, with head, legs, and tail. Some children retain these ideas later than others, and they are considered backwards and childish for their age. People say so; but is it so?

"Come out on the roof with me, little Rudy," was the first thing he heard the cat say, and Rudy understood him. "What people say about falling down is all nonsense," continued the cat; "you will not fall, unless you are afraid. Come, now, set one foot here and another there, and feel your way with your fore-feet. Keep your eyes wide open, and move softly, and if you come to a hole jump over it, and cling fast as I do." And this was just what Rudy did. He was often on the sloping roof with the cat, or on the tops of high trees. But, more frequently, higher still on the ridges of the rocks where puss never came.

"Higher, higher!" cried the trees and the bushes, "see to what height we have grown, and how fast we hold, even to the narrow edges of the rocks."

Rudy often reached the top of the mountain before the sunrise, and there inhaled his morning draught of the fresh, invigorating mountain air, – God's own gift, which men call the sweet fragrance of plant and herb on the mountain-side, and the mint and wild thyme in the valleys. The overhanging clouds absorb all heaviness from the air, and the winds convey them away over the pine-tree summits. The spirit of fragrance, light and fresh, remained behind, and this was Rudy's morning draught. The sunbeams – those blessing-bringing daughters of the sun – kissed his cheeks. Vertigo might be lurking on the watch, but he dared not approach him. The swallows, who had not less than seven nests in his grandfather's house, flew up to him and his goats, singing, "We and you, you and we." They brought him greetings from his grandfather's house, even from two hens, the only birds of the household; but Rudy was not intimate with them.

Although so young and such a little fellow, Rudy had travelled a great deal. He was born in the canton of Valais, and brought to his grandfather over the mountains. He had walked to Staubbach – a little town that seems to flutter in the air like a silver veil – the glittering, snow-clad mountain Jungfrau. He had also been to the great glaciers; but this is connected with a sad story, for here his mother met her death, and his grandfather used to say that all Rudy's childish merriment was lost from that time. His mother had written in a letter, that before he was a year old he had laughed more than he cried; but after his fall into the snow-covered crevasse, his disposition had completely changed. The grandfather seldom spoke of this, but the fact was generally known. Rudy's father had been a postilion, and the large dog which now lived in his grandfather's cottage had always followed him on his journeys over the Simplon to the lake of Geneva. Rudy's relations, on his father's side, lived in the canton of Valais, in the valley of the Rhone. His uncle was a chamois hunter, and a well-known guide. Rudy was only a year old when his father died, and his mother was anxious to return with her child to her own relations, who lived in the Bernese Oberland. Her father dwelt at a few hours' distance from Grindelwald; he was a carver in wood, and gained so much by it that he had plenty to live upon. She set out homewards in the month of June, carrying her infant in her arms, and, accompanied by two chamois hunters, crossed the Gemmi on her way to Grindelwald. They had already left more than half the journey behind them. They had crossed high ridges, and traversed snow-fields; they could even see her native valley, with its familiar wooden cottages. They had only one more glacier to climb. Some newly fallen snow concealed a cleft which, though it did not extend to the foaming waters in the depths beneath, was still much deeper than the height of a man. The young woman, with the child in her arms, slipped upon it, sank in, and disappeared. Not a shriek, not a groan was heard; nothing but the whining of a little child. More than an hour elapsed before her two companions could obtain from the nearest house ropes and poles to assist in raising them; and it was with much exertion that they at last succeeded in raising from the crevasse what appeared to be two dead bodies. Every means was used to restore them to life. With the child they were successful, but not with the mother; so the old grandfather received his daughter's little son into his house an orphan, – a little boy who laughed more than he cried; but it seemed as if laughter had left him in the cold ice-world into which he had fallen, where, as the Swiss peasants say, the souls of the lost are confined till the judgment-day.

The glaciers appear as if a rushing stream had been frozen in its course, and pressed into blocks of green crystal, which, balanced one upon another, form a wondrous palace of crystal for the Ice Maiden – the queen of the glaciers. It is she whose mighty power can crush the traveller to death, and arrest the flowing river in its course. She is also a child of the air, and with the swiftness of the chamois she can reach the snow-covered mountain tops, where the boldest mountaineer has to cut footsteps in the ice to ascend. She will sail on a frail pine-twig over the raging torrents beneath, and spring lightly from one iceberg to another, with her long, snow-white hair flowing around her, and her dark-green robe glittering like the waters of the deep Swiss lakes. "Mine is the power to seize and crush," she cried. "Once a beautiful boy was stolen from me by man, – a boy whom I had kissed, but had not kissed to death. He is again among mankind, and tends the goats on the mountains. He is always climbing higher and higher, far away from all others, but not from me. He is mine; I will send for him." And she gave Vertigo the commission.

It was summer, and the Ice Maiden was melting amidst the green verdure, when Vertigo swung himself up and down. Vertigo has many brothers, quite a troop of them, and the Ice Maiden chose the strongest among them. They exercise their power in different ways, and everywhere. Some sit on the banisters of steep stairs, others on the outer rails of lofty towers, or spring like squirrels along the ridges of the mountains. Others tread the air as a swimmer treads the water, and lure their victims here and there till they fall into the deep abyss. Vertigo and the Ice Maiden clutch at human beings, as the polypus seizes upon all that comes within its reach. And now Vertigo was to seize Rudy.

"Seize him, indeed," cried Vertigo; "I cannot do it. That monster of a cat has taught him her tricks. That child of the human race has a power within him which keeps me at a distance; I cannot possibly reach the boy when he hangs from the branches of trees, over the precipice; or I would gladly tickle his feet, and send him heels over head through the air; but I cannot accomplish it."

"We must accomplish it," said the Ice Maiden; "either you or I must; and I will – I will!"

"No, no!" sounded through the air, like an echo on the mountain church bells chime. It was an answer in song, in the melting tones of a chorus from others of nature's spirits – good and loving spirits, the daughters of the sunbeam. They who place themselves in a circle every evening on the mountain peaks; there they spread out their rose-colored wings, which, as the sun sinks, become more flaming red, until the lofty Alps seem to burn with fire. Men call this the Alpine glow. After the sun has set, they disappear within the white snow on the mountain-tops, and slumber there till sunrise, when they again come forth. They have great love for flowers, for butterflies, and for mankind; and from among the latter they had chosen little Rudy. "You shall not catch him; you shall not seize him!" they sang.

"Greater and stronger than he have I seized!" said the Ice Maiden.

Then the daughters of the sun sang a song of the traveller, whose cloak had been carried away by the wind. "The wind took the covering, but not the man; it could even seize upon him, but not hold him fast. The children of strength are more powerful, more ethereal, even than we are. They can rise higher than our parent, the sun. They have the magic words that rule the wind and the waves, and compel them to serve and obey; and they can, at last, cast off the heavy, oppressive weight of mortality, and soar upwards." Thus sweetly sounded the bell-like tones of the chorus.

And each morning the sun's rays shone through the one little window of the grandfather's house upon the quiet child. The daughters of the sunbeam kissed him; they wished to thaw, and melt, and obliterate the ice kiss which the queenly maiden of the glaciers had given him as he lay in the lap of his dead mother, in the deep crevasse of ice from which he had been so wonderfully rescued.

II
The Journey to the New Home

Rudy was just eight years old, when his uncle, who lived on the other side of the mountain, wished to have the boy, as he thought he might obtain a better education with him, and learn something more. His grandfather thought the same, so he consented to let him go. Rudy had many to say farewell to, as well as his grandfather. First, there was Ajola, the old dog.

"Your father was the postilion, and I was the postilion's dog," said Ajola. "We have often travelled the same journey together; I knew all the dogs and men on this side of the mountain. It is not my habit to talk much; but now that we have so little time to converse together, I will say something more than usual. I will relate to you a story, which I have reflected upon for a long time. I do not understand it, and very likely you will not, but that is of no consequence. I have, however, learnt from it that in this world things are not equally divided, neither for dogs nor for men. All are not born to lie on the lap and to drink milk: I have never been petted in this way, but I have seen a little dog seated in the place of a gentleman or lady, and travelling inside a post-chaise. The lady, who was his mistress, or of whom he was master, carried a bottle of milk, of which the little dog now and then drank; she also offered him pieces of sugar to crunch. He sniffed at them proudly, but would not eat one, so she ate them herself. I was running along the dirty road by the side of the carriage as hungry as a dog could be, chewing the cud of my own thoughts, which were rather in confusion. But many other things seemed in confusion also. Why was not I lying on a lap and travelling in a coach? I could not tell; yet I knew I could not alter my own condition, either by barking or growling."

This was Ajola's farewell speech, and Rudy threw his arms round the dog's neck and kissed his cold nose. Then he took the cat in his arms, but he struggled to get free.

"You are getting too strong for me," he said; "but I will not use my claws against you. Clamber away over the mountains; it was I who taught you to climb. Do not fancy you are going to fall, and you will be quite safe." Then the cat jumped down and ran away; he did not wish Rudy to see that there were tears in his eyes.

The hens were hopping about the floor; one of them had no tail; a traveller, who fancied himself a sportsman, had shot off her tail, he had mistaken her for a bird of prey.

"Rudy is going away over the mountains," said one of the hens.

"He is always in such a hurry," said the other; "and I don't like taking leave," so they both hopped out.

But the goats said farewell; they bleated and wanted to go with him, they were so very sorry.

Just at this time two clever guides were going to cross the mountains to the other side of the Gemmi, and Rudy was to go with them on foot. It was a long walk for such a little boy, but he had plenty of strength and invincible courage. The swallows flew with him a little way, singing, "We and you – you and we." The way led across the rushing Lutschine, which falls in numerous streams from the dark clefts of the Grindelwald glaciers. Trunks of fallen trees and blocks of stone form bridges over these streams. After passing a forest of alders, they began to ascend, passing by some blocks of ice that had loosened themselves from the side of the mountain and lay across their path; they had to step over these ice-blocks or walk round them. Rudy crept here and ran there, his eyes sparkling with joy, and he stepped so firmly with his iron-tipped mountain shoe, that he left a mark behind him wherever he placed his foot.

The earth was black where the mountain torrents or the melted ice had poured upon it, but the bluish green, glassy ice sparkled and glittered. They had to go round little pools, like lakes, enclosed between large masses of ice; and, while thus wandering out of their path, they came near an immense stone, which lay balanced on the edge of an icy peak. The stone lost its balance just as they reached it, and rolled over into the abyss beneath, while the noise of its fall was echoed back from every hollow cliff of the glaciers.

They were always going upwards. The glaciers seemed to spread above them like a continued chain of masses of ice, piled up in wild confusion between bare and rugged rocks. Rudy thought for a moment of what had been told him, that he and his mother had once lain buried in one of these cold, heart-chilling fissures; but he soon banished such thoughts, and looked upon the story as fabulous, like many other stories which had been told him. Once or twice, when the men thought the way was rather difficult for such a little boy, they held out their hands to assist him; but he would not accept their assistance, for he stood on the slippery ice as firmly as if he had been a chamois. They came at length to rocky ground; sometimes stepping upon moss-covered stones, sometimes passing beneath stunted fir-trees, and again through green meadows. The landscape was always changing, but ever above them towered the lofty snow-clad mountains, whose names not only Rudy but every other child knew – "The Jungfrau," "The Monk and the Eiger."

Rudy had never been so far away before; he had never trodden on the wide-spreading ocean of snow that lay here with its immovable billows, from which the wind blows off the snowflake now and then, as it cuts the foam from the waves of the sea. The glaciers stand here so close together it might almost be said they are hand-in-hand; and each is a crystal palace for the Ice Maiden, whose power and will it is to seize and imprison the unwary traveller.

The sun shone warmly, and the snow sparkled as if covered with glittering diamonds. Numerous insects, especially butterflies and bees, lay dead in heaps on the snow. They had ventured too high, or the wind had carried them here and left them to die of cold.

Around the Wetterhorn hung a feathery cloud, like a woolbag, and a threatening cloud too, for as it sunk lower it increased in size, and concealed within was a "föhn," fearful in its violence should it break loose. This journey, with its varied incidents, – the wild paths, the night passed on the mountain, the steep rocky precipices, the hollow clefts, in which the rustling waters from time immemorial had worn away passages for themselves through blocks of stone, – all these were firmly impressed on Rudy's memory.

In a forsaken stone building, which stood just beyond the seas of snow, they one night took shelter. Here they found some charcoal and pine branches, so that they soon made a fire. They arranged couches to lie on as well as they could, and then the men seated themselves by the fire, took out their pipes, and began to smoke. They also prepared a warm, spiced drink, of which they partook and Rudy was not forgotten – he had his share. Then they began to talk of those mysterious beings with which the land of the Alps abounds; the hosts of apparitions which come in the night, and carry off the sleepers through the air, to the wonderful floating town of Venice; of the wild herds-man, who drives the black sheep across the meadows. These flocks are never seen, yet the tinkle of their little bells has often been heard, as well as their unearthly bleating. Rudy listened eagerly, but without fear, for he knew not what fear meant; and while he listened, he fancied he could hear the roaring of the spectral herd. It seemed to come nearer and roar louder, till the men heard it also and listened in silence, till, at length, they told Rudy that he must not dare to sleep. It was a "föhn," that violent storm-wind which rushes from the mountain to the valley beneath, and in its fury snaps asunder the trunks of large trees as if they were but slender reeds, and carries the wooden houses from one side of a river to the other as easily as we could move the pieces on a chess-board. After an hour had passed, they told Rudy that it was all over, and he might go to sleep; and, fatigued with his long walk, he readily slept at the word of command.

Very early the following morning they again set out. The sun on this day lighted up for Rudy new mountains, new glaciers, and new snow-fields. They had entered the Canton Valais, and found themselves on the ridge of the hills which can be seen from Grindelwald; but he was still far from his new home. They pointed out to him other clefts, other meadows, other woods and rocky paths, and other houses. Strange men made their appearance before him, and what men! They were misshapen, wretched-looking creatures, with yellow complexions; and on their necks were dark, ugly lumps of flesh, hanging down like bags. They were called cretins. They dragged themselves along painfully, and stared at the strangers with vacant eyes. The women looked more dreadful than the men. Poor Rudy! were these the sort of people he should see at his new home?

III
The Uncle

Rudy arrived at last at his uncle's house, and was thankful to find the people like those he had been accustomed to see. There was only one cretin amongst them, a poor idiot boy, one of those unfortunate beings who, in their neglected conditions, go from house to house, and are received and taken care of in different families, for a month or two at a time.

Poor Saperli had just arrived at his uncle's house when Rudy came. The uncle was an experienced hunter; he also followed the trade of a cooper; his wife was a lively little person, with a face like a bird, eyes like those of an eagle, and a long, hairy throat. Everything was new to Rudy – the fashion of the dress, the manners, the employments, and even the language; but the latter his childish ear would soon learn. He saw also that there was more wealth here, when compared with his former home at his grandfather's. The rooms were larger, the walls were adorned with the horns of the chamois, and brightly polished guns. Over the door hung a painting of the Virgin Mary, fresh alpine roses and a burning lamp stood near it. Rudy's uncle was, as we have said, one of the most noted chamois hunters in the whole district, and also one of the best guides. Rudy soon became the pet of the house; but there was another pet, an old hound, blind and lazy, who would never more follow the hunt, well as he had once done so. But his former good qualities were not forgotten, and therefore the animal was kept in the family and treated with every indulgence. Rudy stroked the old hound, but he did not like strangers, and Rudy was as yet a stranger; he did not, however, long remain so, he soon endeared himself to every heart, and became like one of the family.

"We are not very badly off, here in the canton Valais," said his uncle one day; "we have the chamois, they do not die so fast as the wild goats, and it is certainly much better here now than in former times. How highly the old times have been spoken of, but ours is better. The bag has been opened, and a current of air now blows through our once confined valley. Something better always makes its appearance when old, worn-out things fail."

When his uncle became communicative, he would relate stories of his youthful days, and farther back still of the warlike times in which his father had lived. Valais was then, as he expressed it, only a closed-up bag, quite full of sick people, miserable cretins; but the French soldiers came, and they were capital doctors, they soon killed the disease and the sick people, too. The French people knew how to fight in more ways than one, and the girls knew how to conquer too; and when he said this the uncle nodded at his wife, who was a French woman by birth, and laughed. The French could also do battle on the stones. "It was they who cut a road out of the solid rock over the Simplon – such a road, that I need only say to a child of three years old, 'Go down to Italy, you have only to keep in the high road,' and the child will soon arrive in Italy, if he followed my directions."

Then the uncle sang a French song, and cried, "Hurrah! long live Napoleon Bonaparte." This was the first time Rudy had ever heard of France, or of Lyons, that great city on the Rhone where his uncle had once lived. His uncle said that Rudy, in a very few years, would become a clever hunter, he had quite a talent for it; he taught the boy to hold a gun properly, and to load and fire it. In the hunting season he took him to the hills, and made him drink the warm blood of the chamois, which is said to prevent the hunter from becoming giddy; he taught him to know the time when, from the different mountains, the avalanche is likely to fall, namely, at noontide or in the evening, from the effects of the sun's rays; he made him observe the movements of the chamois when he gave a leap, so that he might fall firmly and lightly on his feet. He told him that when on the fissures of the rocks he could find no place for his feet, he must support himself on his elbows, and cling with his legs, and even lean firmly with his back, for this could be done when necessary. He told him also that the chamois are very cunning, they place lookers-out on the watch; but the hunter must be more cunning than they are, and find them out by the scent.

One day, when Rudy went out hunting with his uncle, he hung a coat and hat on an alpine staff, and the chamois mistook it for a man, as they generally do. The mountain path was narrow here; indeed it was scarcely a path at all, only a kind of shelf, close to the yawning abyss. The snow that lay upon it was partially thawed, and the stones crumbled beneath the feet. Every fragment of stone broken off struck the sides of the rock in its fall, till it rolled into the depths beneath, and sunk to rest. Upon this shelf Rudy's uncle laid himself down, and crept forward. At about a hundred paces behind him stood Rudy, upon the highest point of the rock, watching a great vulture hovering in the air; with a single stroke of his wing the bird might easily cast the creeping hunter into the abyss beneath, and make him his prey. Rudy's uncle had eyes for nothing but the chamois, who, with its young kid, had just appeared round the edge of the rock. So Rudy kept his eyes fixed on the bird, he knew well what the great creature wanted; therefore he stood in readiness to discharge his gun at the proper moment. Suddenly the chamois made a spring, and his uncle fired and struck the animal with the deadly bullet; while the young kid rushed away, as if for a long life he had been accustomed to danger and practised flight. The large bird, alarmed at the report of the gun, wheeled off in another direction, and Rudy's uncle was saved from danger, of which he knew nothing till he was told of it by the boy.

While they were both in pleasant mood, wending their way homewards, and the uncle whistling the tune of a song he had learnt in his young days, they suddenly heard a peculiar sound which seemed to come from the top of the mountain. They looked up, and saw above them, on the over-hanging rock, the snow-covering heave and lift itself as a piece of linen stretched on the ground to dry raises itself when the wind creeps under it. Smooth as polished marble slabs, the waves of snow cracked and loosened themselves, and then suddenly, with the rumbling noise of distant thunder, fell like a foaming cataract into the abyss. An avalanche had fallen, not upon Rudy and his uncle, but very near them. Alas, a great deal too near!

"Hold fast, Rudy!" cried his uncle; "hold fast, with all your might."

Then Rudy clung with his arms to the trunk of the nearest tree, while his uncle climbed above him, and held fast by the branches. The avalanche rolled past them at some distance; but the gust of wind that followed, like the storm-wings of the avalanche, snapped asunder the trees and bushes over which it swept, as if they had been but dry rushes, and threw them about in every direction. The tree to which Rudy clung was thus overthrown, and Rudy dashed to the ground. The higher branches were snapped off, and carried away to a great distance; and among these shattered branches lay Rudy's uncle, with his skull fractured. When they found him, his hand was still warm; but it would have been impossible to recognize his face. Rudy stood by, pale and trembling; it was the first shock of his life, the first time he had ever felt fear. Late in the evening he returned home with the fatal news, – to that home which was now to be so full of sorrow. His uncle's wife uttered not a word, nor shed a tear, till the corpse was brought in; then her agony burst forth. The poor cretin crept away to his bed, and nothing was seen of him during the whole of the following day. Towards evening, however, he came to Rudy, and said, "Will you write a letter for me? Saperli cannot write; Saperli can only take the letters to the post."

"A letter for you!" said Rudy; "who do you wish to write to?"

"To the Lord Christ," he replied.

"What do you mean?" asked Rudy.

Then the poor idiot, as the cretin was often called, looked at Rudy with a most touching expression in his eyes, clasped his hands, and said, solemnly and devoutly, "Saperli wants to send a letter to Jesus Christ, to pray Him to let Saperli die, and not the master of the house here."

Rudy pressed his hand, and replied, "A letter would not reach Him up above; it would not give him back whom we have lost."

It was not, however, easy for Rudy to convince Saperli of the impossibility of doing what he wished.

"Now you must work for us," said his foster-mother; and Rudy very soon became the entire support of the house.

IV
Babette

Who was the best marksman in the canton Valais? The chamois knew well. "Save yourselves from Rudy," they might well say. And who is the handsomest marksman? "Oh, it is Rudy," said the maidens; but they did not say, "Save yourselves from Rudy." Neither did anxious mothers say so; for he bowed to them as pleasantly as to the young girls. He was so brave and cheerful. His cheeks were brown, his teeth white, and his eyes dark and sparkling. He was now a handsome young man of twenty years. The most icy water could not deter him from swimming; he could twist and turn like a fish. None could climb like he, and he clung as firmly to the edges of the rocks as a limpet. He had strong muscular power, as could be seen when he leapt from rock to rock. He had learnt this first from the cat, and more lately from the chamois. Rudy was considered the best guide over the mountains; every one had great confidence in him. He might have made a great deal of money as guide. His uncle had also taught him the trade of a cooper; but he had no inclination for either; his delight was in chamois-hunting, which also brought him plenty of money. Rudy would be a very good match, as people said, if he would not look above his own station. He was also such a famous partner in dancing, that the girls often dreamt about him, and one and another thought of him even when awake.

"He kissed me in the dance," said Annette, the schoolmaster's daughter, to her dearest friend; but she ought not to have told this, even to her dearest friend. It is not easy to keep such secrets; they are like sand in a sieve; they slip out. It was therefore soon known that Rudy, so brave and so good as he was, had kissed some one while dancing, and yet he had never kissed her who was dearest to him.

"Ah, ah," said an old hunter, "he has kissed Annette, has he? he has begun with A, and I suppose he will kiss through the whole alphabet."

But a kiss in the dance was all the busy tongues could accuse him of. He certainly had kissed Annette, but she was not the flower of his heart.

Down in the valley, near Bex, among the great walnut-trees, by the side of a little rushing mountain-stream, lived a rich miller. His dwelling-house was a large building, three storeys high, with little turrets. The roof was covered with chips, bound together with tin plates, that glittered in sunshine and in the moonlight. The largest of the turrets had a weather-cock, representing an apple pierced by a glittering arrow, in memory of William Tell. The mill was a neat and well-ordered place, that allowed itself to be sketched and written about; but the miller's daughter did not permit any to sketch or write about her. So, at least, Rudy would have said, for her image was pictured in his heart; her eyes shone in it so brightly, that quite a flame had been kindled there; and, like all other fires, it had burst forth so suddenly, that the miller's daughter, the beautiful Babette, was quite unaware of it. Rudy had never spoken a word to her on the subject. The miller was rich, and, on that account, Babette stood very high, and was rather difficult to aspire to. But said Rudy to himself, "Nothing is too high for a man to reach: he must climb with confidence in himself, and he will not fail." He had learnt this lesson in his youthful home.

It happened once that Rudy had some business to settle at Bex. It was a long journey at that time, for the railway had not been opened. From the glaciers of the Rhone, at the foot of the Simplon, between its ever-changing mountain summits, stretches the valley of the canton Valais. Through it runs the noble river of the Rhone, which often overflows its banks, covering fields and highways, and destroying everything in its course. Near the towns of Sion and St. Maurice, the valley takes a turn, and bends like an elbow, and behind St. Maurice becomes so narrow that there is only space enough for the bed of the river and a narrow carriage-road. An old tower stands here, as if it were guardian to the canton Valais, which ends at this point; and from it we can look across the stone bridge to the toll-house on the other side, where the canton Vaud commences. Not far from this spot stands the town of Bex, and at every step can be seen an increase of fruitfulness and verdure. It is like entering a grove of chestnut and walnut-trees. Here and there the cypress and pomegranate blossoms peep forth; and it is almost as warm as an Italian climate. Rudy arrived at Bex, and soon finished the business which had brought him there, and then walked about the town; but not even the miller's boy could be seen, nor any one belonging to the mill, not to mention Babette. This did not please him at all. Evening came on. The air was filled with the perfume of the wild thyme and the blossoms of the lime-trees, and the green woods on the mountains seemed to be covered with a shining veil, blue as the sky. Over everything reigned a stillness, not of sleep or of death, but as if Nature were holding her breath, that her image might be photographed on the blue vault of heaven. Here and there, amidst the trees of the silent valley, stood poles which supported the wires of the electric telegraph. Against one of these poles leaned an object so motionless that it might have been mistaken for the trunk of a tree; but it was Rudy, standing there as still as at that moment was everything around him. He was not asleep, neither was he dead; but just as the various events in the world – matters of momentous importance to individuals – were flying through the telegraph wires, without the quiver of a wire or the slightest tone, so, through the mind of Rudy, thoughts of overwhelming importance were passing, without an outward sign of emotion. The happiness of his future life depended upon the decision of his present reflections. His eyes were fixed on one spot in the distance – a light that twinkled through the foliage from the parlor of the miller's house, where Babette dwelt. Rudy stood so still, that it might have been supposed he was watching for a chamois; but he was in reality like a chamois, who will stand for a moment, looking as if it were chiselled out of the rock, and then, if only a stone rolled by, would suddenly bound forward with a spring, far away from the hunter. And so with Rudy: a sudden roll of his thoughts roused him from his stillness, and made him bound forward with determination to act.

"Never despair!" cried he. "A visit to the mill, to say good evening to the miller, and good evening to little Babette, can do no harm. No one ever fails who has confidence in himself. If I am to be Babette's husband, I must see her some time or other."

Then Rudy laughed joyously, and took courage to go to the mill. He knew what he wanted; he wanted to marry Babette. The clear water of the river rolled over its yellow bed, and willows and lime-trees were reflected in it, as Rudy stepped along the path to the miller's house. But, as the children sing –

> *"There was no one at home in the house,*
> *Only a kitten at play."*

The cat standing on the steps put up its back and cried "mew." But Rudy had no inclination for this sort of conversation; he passed on, and knocked at the door. No one heard him, no one opened the door. "Mew," said the cat again; and had Rudy been still a child, he would have understood this language, and known that the cat wished to tell him there was no one at home. So he was obliged to go to the mill and make inquiries, and there he heard that the miller had gone on a journey to Interlachen, and taken Babette with him, to the great shooting festival, which began that morning, and would continue for eight days, and that people from all the German settlements would be there.

Poor Rudy! we may well say. It was not a fortunate day for his visit to Bex. He had just to return the way he came, through St. Maurice and Sion, to his home in the valley. But he did not despair. When the sun rose the next morning, his good spirits had returned; indeed he had never really lost them. "Babette is at Interlachen," said Rudy to himself, "many days' journey from here. It is certainly a long way for any one who takes the high-road, but not so far if he takes a short cut across the mountain, and that just suits a chamois-hunter. I have been that way before, for it leads to the home of my childhood, where, as a little boy, I lived with my grandfather. And there are shooting matches at Interlachen. I will go, and try to stand first in the match. Babette will be there, and I shall be able to make her acquaintance."

Carrying his light knapsack, which contained his Sunday clothes, on his back, and with his musket and his game-bag over his shoulder, Rudy started to take the shortest way across the mountain. Still it was a great distance. The shooting matches were to commence on that day, and to continue for a whole week. He had been told also that the miller and Babette would remain that time with some relatives at Interlachen. So over the Gemmi Rudy climbed bravely, and determined to descend the side of the Grindelwald. Bright and joyous were his feelings as he stepped lightly onwards, inhaling the invigorating mountain air. The valley sunk as he ascended, the circle of the horizon expanded. One snow-capped peak after another rose before him, till the whole of the glittering Alpine range became visible. Rudy knew each ice-clad peak, and he continued his course towards the Schreckhorn, with its white powdered stone finger raised high in the air. At length he had crossed the highest ridges, and before him lay the green pasture lands sloping down towards the valley, which was once his home. The buoyancy of the air made his heart light. Hill and valley were blooming in luxuriant beauty, and his thoughts were youthful dreams, in which old age or death were out of the question. Life, power, and enjoyment were in the future, and he felt free and light as a bird. And the swallows flew round him, as in the days of his childhood, singing "We and you – you and we." All was overflowing with joy. Beneath him lay the meadows, covered with velvety green, with the murmuring river flowing through them, and dotted here and there were small wooden houses. He could see the edges of the glaciers, looking like green glass against the soiled snow, and the deep chasms beneath the loftiest glacier. The church bells were ringing, as if to welcome him to his home with their sweet tones. His heart beat quickly, and for a moment he seemed to have forgotten Babette, so full were his thoughts of old recollections. He was, in imagination, once more wandering on the road where, when a little boy, he, with other children, came to sell their curiously carved toy houses. Yonder, behind the fir-trees, still stood his grandfather's house, his mother's father, but strangers dwelt in it now. Children came running to him, as he had once done, and wished to sell their wares. One of them offered him an Alpine rose. Rudy took the rose as a good omen, and thought of Babette. He quickly crossed the bridge where the two rivers flow into each other. Here he found a walk over-shadowed with large walnut-trees, and their thick foliage formed a pleasant shade. Very soon he perceived in the distance, waving flags, on which glittered a white cross on a red ground – the standard of the Danes as well as of the Swiss – and before him lay Interlachen.

"It is really a splendid town, like none other that I have ever seen," said Rudy to himself. It was indeed a Swiss town in its holiday dress. Not like the many other towns, crowded with heavy stone houses, stiff and foreign looking. No; here it seemed as if the wooden houses on the hills had run into the valley, and placed themselves in rows and ranks by the side of the clear river, which rushes like an arrow in its course. The streets were rather irregular, it is true, but still this added to their picturesque appearance. There was one street which Rudy thought the prettiest of them all; it had been built since he had visited the town when a little boy. It seemed to him as if all the neatest and most curiously carved toy houses which his grandfather once kept in the large cupboard at home, had been brought out and placed in this spot, and that they had increased in size since then, as the old chestnut trees had done. The houses were called hotels; the woodwork on the windows and balconies was curiously carved. The roofs were gayly painted, and before each house was a flower garden, which separated it from the macadamized high-road. These houses all stood on the same side of the road, so that the fresh, green meadows, in which were cows grazing, with bells on their necks, were not hidden. The sound of these bells is often heard amidst Alpine scenery. These meadows were encircled by lofty hills, which receded a little in the centre, so that the most beautifully formed of Swiss mountains – the snow-crowned Jungfrau – could be distinctly seen glittering in the distance. A number of elegantly dressed gentlemen and ladies from foreign lands, and crowds of country people from the neighboring cantons, were assembled in the town. Each marksman wore the number of hits he had made twisted in a garland round his hat. Here were music and singing of all descriptions: hand-organs, trumpets, shouting, and noise. The houses and bridges were adorned with verses and inscriptions. Flags and banners were waving. Shot after shot was fired, which was the best music to Rudy's ears.

And amidst all this excitement he quite forgot Babette, on whose account only he had come. The shooters were thronging round the target, and Rudy was soon amongst them. But when he took his turn to fire, he proved himself the best shot, for he always struck the bull's-eye.

"Who may that young stranger be?" was the inquiry on all sides. "He speaks French as it is spoken in the Swiss cantons."

"And makes himself understood very well when he speaks German," said some.

"He lived here, when a child, with his grandfather, in a house on the road to Grindelwald," remarked one of the sportsmen.

And full of life was this young stranger; his eyes sparkled, his glance was steady, and his arm sure, therefore he always hit the mark. Good fortune gives courage, and Rudy was always courageous. He soon had a circle of friends gathered round him. Every one noticed him, and did him homage. Babette had quite vanished from his thoughts, when he was struck on the shoulder by a heavy hand, and a deep voice said to him in French, "You are from the canton Valais."

Rudy turned round, and beheld a man with a ruddy, pleasant face, and a stout figure. It was the rich miller from Bex. His broad, portly person, hid the slender, lovely Babette; but she came forward and glanced at him with her bright, dark eyes. The rich miller was very much flattered at the thought that the young man, who was acknowledged to be the best shot, and was so praised by every one, should be from his own canton. Now was Rudy really fortunate: he had travelled all this way to this place, and those he had forgotten were now come to seek him. When country people go far from home, they often meet with those they know, and improve their acquaintance. Rudy, by his shooting, had gained the first place in the shooting-match, just as the miller at home at Bex stood first, because of his money and his mill. So the two men shook hands, which they had never done before. Babette, too, held out her hand to Rudy frankly, and he pressed it in his, and looked at her so earnestly, that she blushed deeply. The miller talked of the long journey they had travelled, and of the many towns they had seen. It was his opinion that he had really made as great a journey as if he had travelled in a steamship, a railway carriage, or a post-chaise.

"I came by a much shorter way," said Rudy; "I came over the mountains. There is no road so high that a man may not venture upon it."

"Ah, yes; and break your neck," said the miller; "and you look like one who will break his neck some day, you are so daring."

"Oh, nothing ever happens to a man if he has confidence in himself," replied Rudy.

The miller's relations at Interlachen, with whom the miller and Babette were staying, invited Rudy to visit them, when they found he came from the same canton as the miller. It was a most pleasant visit. Good fortune seemed to follow him, as it does those who think and act for themselves, and who remember the proverb, "Nuts are given to us, but they are not cracked for us." And Rudy was treated by the miller's relations almost like one of the family, and glasses of wine were poured out to drink to the welfare of the best shooter. Babette clinked glasses with Rudy, and he returned thanks for the toast. In the evening they all took a delightful walk under the walnut-trees, in front of the stately hotels; there were so many people, and such crowding, that Rudy was obliged to offer his arm to Babette. Then he told her how happy it made him to meet people from the canton Vaud, – for Vaud and Valais were neighboring cantons. He spoke of this pleasure so heartily that Babette could not resist giving his arm a slight squeeze; and so they walked on together, and talked and chatted like old acquaintances. Rudy felt inclined to laugh sometimes at the absurd dress and walk of the foreign ladies; but Babette did not wish to make fun of them, for she knew there must be some good, excellent people amongst them; she, herself, had a godmother, who was a high-born English lady. Eighteen years before, when Babette was christened, this lady was staying at Bex, and she stood godmother for her, and gave her the valuable brooch she now wore in her bosom.

Her godmother had twice written to her, and this year she was expected to visit Interlachen with her two daughters; "but they are old-maids," added Babette, who was only eighteen: "they are nearly thirty." Her sweet little mouth was never still a moment, and all that she said sounded in Rudy's ears as matters of the greatest importance, and at last he told her what he was longing to tell. How often he had been at Bex, how well he knew the mill, and how often he had seen Babette, when most likely she had not noticed him; and lastly, that full of many thoughts which he could not tell her, he had been to the mill on the evening when she and her father has started on their long journey, but not too far for him to find a way to overtake them. He told her all this, and a great deal more; he told her how much he could endure for her; and that it was to see her, and not the shooting-match, which had brought him to Interlachen. Babette became quite silent after hearing all this; it was almost too much, and it troubled her.

And while they thus wandered on, the sun sunk behind the lofty mountains. The Jungfrau stood out in brightness and splendor, as a back-ground to the green woods of the surrounding hills. Every one stood still to look at the beautiful sight, Rudy and Babette among them.

"Nothing can be more beautiful than this," said Babette.

"Nothing!" replied Rudy, looking at Babette.

"To-morrow I must return home," remarked Rudy a few minutes afterwards.

"Come and visit us at Bex," whispered Babette; "my father will be pleased to see you."

V
On the Way Home

Oh, what a number of things Rudy had to carry over the mountains, when he set out to return home! He had three silver cups, two handsome pistols, and a silver coffee-pot. This latter would be useful when he began housekeeping. But all these were not the heaviest weight he had to bear; something mightier and more important he carried with him in his heart, over the high mountains, as he journeyed homeward.

The weather was dismally dark, and inclined to rain; the clouds hung low, like a mourning veil on the tops of the mountains, and shrouded their glittering peaks. In the woods could be heard the sound of the axe and the heavy fall of the trunks of the trees, as they rolled down the slopes of the mountains. When seen from the heights, the trunks of these trees looked like slender stems; but on a nearer inspection they were found to be large and strong enough for the masts of a ship. The river murmured monotonously, the wind whistled, and the clouds sailed along hurriedly.

Suddenly there appeared, close by Rudy's side, a young maiden; he had not noticed her till she came quite near to him. She was also going to ascend the mountain. The maiden's eyes shone with an unearthly power, which obliged you to look into them; they were strange eyes, – clear, deep, and unfathomable.

"Hast thou a lover?" asked Rudy; all his thoughts were naturally on love just then.

"I have none," answered the maiden, with a laugh; it was as if she had not spoken the truth.

"Do not let us go such a long way round," said she. "We must keep to the left; it is much shorter."

"Ah, yes," he replied; "and fall into some crevasse. Do you pretend to be a guide, and not know the road better than that?"

"I know every step of the way," said she; "and my thoughts are collected, while yours are down in the valley yonder. We should think of the Ice Maiden while we are up here; men say she is not kind to their race."

"I fear her not," said Rudy. "She could not keep me when I was a child; I will not give myself up to her now I am a man."

Darkness came on, the rain fell, and then it began to snow, and the whiteness dazzled the eyes.

"Give me your hand," said the maiden; "I will help you to mount." And he felt the touch of her icy fingers.

"You help me," cried Rudy; "I do not yet require a woman to help me to climb." And he stepped quickly forwards away from her.

The drifting snow-shower fell like a veil between them, the wind whistled, and behind him he could hear the maiden laughing and singing, and the sound was most strange to hear.

"It certainly must be a spectre or a servant of the Ice Maiden," thought Rudy, who had heard such things talked about when he was a little boy, and had stayed all night on the mountain with the guides.

The snow fell thicker than ever, the clouds lay beneath him; he looked back, there was no one to be seen, but he heard sounds of mocking laughter, which were not those of a human voice.

When Rudy at length reached the highest part of the mountain, where the path led down to the valley of the Rhone, the snow had ceased, and in the clear heavens he saw two bright stars twinkling. They reminded him of Babette and of himself, and of his future happiness, and his heart glowed at the thought.

VI
The Visit to the Mill

"What beautiful things you have brought home!" said his old foster-mother; and her strange-looking eagle-eyes sparkled, while she wriggled and twisted her skinny neck more quickly and strangely than ever. "You have brought good luck with you, Rudy. I must give you a kiss, my dear boy."

Rudy allowed himself to be kissed; but it could be seen by his countenance that he only endured the infliction as a homely duty.

"How handsome you are, Rudy!" said the old woman.

"Don't flatter," said Rudy, with a laugh; but still he was pleased.

"I must say once more," said the old woman, "that you are very lucky."

"Well, in that I believe you are right," said he, as he thought of Babette. Never had he felt such a longing for that deep valley as he now had. "They must have returned home by this time," said he to himself, "it is already two days over the time which they fixed upon. I must go to Bex."

So Rudy set out to go to Bex; and when he arrived there, he found the miller and his daughter at home. They received him kindly, and brought him many greetings from their friends at Interlachen. Babette did not say much. She seemed to have become quite silent; but her eyes spoke, and that was quite enough for Rudy. The miller had generally a great deal to talk about, and seemed to expect that every one should listen to his jokes, and laugh at them; for was not he the rich miller? But now he was more inclined to hear Rudy's adventures while hunting and travelling, and to listen to his descriptions of the difficulties the chamois-hunter has to overcome on the mountain-tops, or of the dangerous snow-drifts which the wind and weather cause to cling to the edges of the rocks, or to lie in the form of a frail bridge over the abyss beneath. The eyes of the brave Rudy sparkled as he described the life of a hunter, or spoke of the cunning of the chamois and their wonderful leaps; also of the powerful fohn and the rolling avalanche. He noticed that the more he described, the more interested the miller became, especially when he spoke of the fierce vulture and of the royal eagle. Not far from Bex, in the canton Valais, was an eagle's nest, more curiously built under a high, over-hanging rock. In this nest was a young eagle; but who would venture to take it? A young Englishman had offered Rudy a whole handful of gold, if he would bring him the young eagle alive.

"There is a limit to everything," was Rudy's reply. "The eagle could not be taken; it would be folly to attempt it."

The wine was passed round freely, and the conversation kept up pleasantly; but the evening seemed too short for Rudy, although it was midnight when he left the miller's house, after this his first visit.

While the lights in the windows of the miller's house still twinkled through the green foliage, out through the open skylight came the parlor-cat on to the roof, and along the water-pipe walked the kitchen-cat to meet her.

"What is the news at the mill?" asked the parlor-cat. "Here in the house there is secret love-making going on, which the father knows nothing about. Rudy and Babette have been treading on each other's paws, under the table, all the evening. They trod on my tail twice, but I did not mew; that would have attracted notice."

"Well, I should have mewed," said the kitchen-cat.

"What might suit the kitchen would not suit the parlor," said the other. "I am quite curious to know what the miller will say when he finds out this engagement."

Yes, indeed; what would the miller say? Rudy himself was anxious to know that; but to wait till the miller heard of it from others was out of the question. Therefore, not many days after this visit, he was riding in the omnibus that runs between the two cantons, Valais and Vaud. These cantons are separated by the Rhone, over which is a bridge that unites them. Rudy, as usual, had plenty of courage, and indulged in pleasant thoughts of the favorable answer he should receive that evening. And when the omnibus returned, Rudy was again seated in it, going homewards; and at the same time the parlor-cat at the miller's house ran out quickly, crying, –

"Here, you from the kitchen, what do you think? The miller knows all now. Everything has come to a delightful end. Rudy came here this evening, and he and Babette had much whispering and secret conversation together. They stood in the path near the miller's room. I lay at their feet; but they had no eyes or thoughts for me.

"'I will go to your father at once,' said he; 'it is the most honorable way.'

"'Shall I go with you?' asked Babette; 'it will give you courage.'

"'I have plenty of courage,' said Rudy; 'but if you are with me, he must be friendly, whether he says Yes or No.'"

"So they turned to go in, and Rudy trod heavily on my tail; he certainly is very clumsy. I mewed; but neither he nor Babette had any ears for me. They opened the door, and entered together. I was before them, and jumped on the back of a chair. I hardly know what Rudy said; but the miller flew into a rage, and threatened to kick him out of the house. He told him he might go to the mountains, and look after the chamois, but not after our little Babette."

"And what did they say? Did they speak?" asked the kitchen-cat.

"What did they say! why, all that people generally do say when they go a-wooing – 'I love her, and she loves me; and when there is milk in the can for one, there is milk in the can for two.'"

"'But she is so far above you,' said the miller; 'she has heaps of gold, as you know. You should not attempt to reach her.'

"'There is nothing so high that a man cannot reach, if he will,' answered Rudy; for he is a brave youth.

"'Yet you could not reach the young eagle,' said the miller, laughing. 'Babette is higher than the eagle's nest.'

"'I will have them both,' said Rudy.

"'Very well; I will give her to you when you bring me the young eaglet alive,' said the miller; and he laughed till the tears stood in his eyes. "But now I thank you for this visit, Rudy; and if you come to-morrow, you will find nobody at home. Good-bye, Rudy.'

"Babette also wished him farewell; but her voice sounded as mournful as the mew of a little kitten that has lost its mother.

"'A promise is a promise between man and man,' said Rudy. 'Do not weep, Babette; I shall bring the young eagle.'

"'You will break your neck, I hope,' said the miller, 'and we shall be relieved from your company.'

"I call that kicking him out of the house," said the parlor-cat. "And now Rudy is gone, and Babette sits and weeps, while the miller sings German songs that he learnt on his journey; but I do not trouble myself on the matter, – it would be of no use."

"Yet, for all that, it is a very strange affair," said the kitchen-cat.

VII
The Eagle's Nest

From the mountain-path came a joyous sound of some person whistling, and it betokened good humor and undaunted courage. It was Rudy, going to meet his friend Vesinaud. "You must come and help," said he. "I want to carry off the young eaglet from the top of the rock. We will take young Ragli with us."

"Had you not better first try to take down the moon? That would be quite as easy a task," said Vesinaud. "You seem to be in good spirits."

"Yes, indeed I am. I am thinking of my wedding. But to be serious, I will tell you all about it, and how I am situated."

Then he explained to Vesinaud and Ragli what he wished to do, and why.

"You are a daring fellow," said they; "but it is no use; you will break your neck."

"No one falls, unless he is afraid," said Rudy.

So at midnight they set out, carrying with them poles, ladders, and ropes. The road lay amidst brushwood and underwood, over rolling stones, always upwards higher and higher in the dark night. Waters roared beneath them, or fell in cascades from above.

Humid clouds were driving through the air as the hunters reached the precipitous ledge of the rock. It was even darker here, for the sides of the rocks almost met, and the light penetrated only through a small opening at the top. At a little distance from the edge could be heard the sound of the roaring, foaming waters in the yawning abyss beneath them. The three seated themselves on a stone, to await in stillness the dawn of day, when the parent eagle would fly out, as it would be necessary to shoot the old bird before they could think of gaining possession of the young one. Rudy sat motionless, as if he had been part of the stone on which he sat. He held his gun ready to fire, with his eyes fixed steadily on the highest point of the cliff, where the eagle's nest lay concealed beneath the overhanging rock.

The three hunters had a long time to wait. At last they heard a rustling, whirring sound above them, and a large hovering object darkened the air. Two guns were ready to aim at the dark body of the eagle as it rose from the nest. Then a shot was fired; for an instant the bird fluttered its wide-spreading wings, and seemed as if it would fill up the whole of the chasm, and drag down the hunters in its fall. But it was not so; the eagle sunk gradually into the abyss beneath, and the branches of trees and bushes were broken by its weight. Then the hunters roused themselves: three of the longest ladders were brought and bound together; the topmost ring of these ladders would just reach the edge of the rock which hung over the abyss, but no farther. The point beneath which the eagle's nest lay sheltered was much higher, and the sides of the rock were as smooth as a wall. After consulting together, they determined to bind together two more ladders, and to hoist them over the cavity, and so form a communication with the three beneath them, by binding the upper ones to the lower. With great difficulty they contrived to drag the two ladders over the rock, and there they hung for some moments, swaying over the abyss; but no sooner had they fastened them together, than Rudy placed his foot on the lowest step.

It was a bitterly cold morning; clouds of mist were rising from beneath, and Rudy stood on the lower step of the ladder as a fly rests on a piece of swinging straw, which a bird may have dropped from the edge of the nest it was building on some tall factory chimney; but the fly could fly away if the straw were shaken, Rudy could only break his neck. The wind whistled around him, and beneath him the waters of the abyss, swelled by the thawing of the glaciers, those palaces of the Ice Maiden, foamed and roared in their rapid course. When Rudy began to ascend, the ladder trembled like the web of the spider, when it draws out the long, delicate threads; but as soon as he reached the fourth of the ladders, which had been bound together, he felt more confidence, – he knew that they had been fastened securely by skilful hands. The fifth ladder, that appeared to reach the nest, was supported by the sides of the rock, yet it swung to and fro, and flapped about like a slender reed, and as if it had been bound by fishing lines. It seemed a most dangerous undertaking to ascend it, but Rudy knew how to climb; he had learnt that from the cat, and he had no fear. He did not observe Vertigo, who stood in the air behind him, trying to lay hold of him with his outstretched polypous arms.

When at length he stood on the topmost step of the ladder, he found that he was still some distance below the nest, and not even able to see into it. Only by using his hands and climbing could he possibly reach it. He tried the strength of the stunted trees, and the thick underwood upon which the nest rested, and of which it was formed, and finding they would support his weight, he grasped them firmly, and swung himself up from the ladder till his head and breast were above the nest, and then what an overpowering stench came from it, for in it lay the putrid remains of lambs, chamois, and birds. Vertigo, although he could not reach him, blew the poisonous vapor in his face, to make him giddy and faint; and beneath, in the dark, yawning deep, on the rushing waters, sat the Ice Maiden, with her long, pale, green hair falling around her, and her death-like eyes fixed upon him, like the two barrels of a gun. "I have thee now," she cried.

In a corner of the eagle's nest sat the young eaglet, a large and powerful bird, though still unable to fly. Rudy fixed his eyes upon it, held on by one hand with all his strength, and with the other threw a noose round the young eagle. The string slipped to its legs. Rudy tightened it, and thus secured the bird alive. Then flinging the sling over his shoulder, so that the creature hung a good way down behind him, he prepared to descend with the help of a rope, and his foot soon touched safely the highest step of the ladder. Then Rudy, remembering his early lesson in climbing, "Hold fast, and do not fear," descended carefully down the ladders, and at last stood safely on the ground with the young living eaglet, where he was received with loud shouts of joy and congratulations.

VIII
What Fresh News the Parlor-Cat Had to Tell

"Where is what you asked for," said Rudy, as he entered the miller's house at Bex, and placed on the floor a large basket. He removed the lid as he spoke, and a pair of yellow eyes, encircled by a black ring, stared forth with a wild, fiery glance, that seemed ready to burn and destroy all that came in its way. Its short, strong beak was open, ready to bite, and on its red throat were short feathers, like stubble.

"The young eaglet!" cried the miller.

Babette screamed, and started back, while her eyes wandered from Rudy to the bird in astonishment.

"You are not to be discouraged by difficulties, I see," said the miller.

"And you will keep your word," replied Rudy. "Each has his own characteristic, whether it is honor or courage."

"But how is it you did not break your neck?" asked the miller.

"Because I held fast," answered Rudy; "and I mean to hold fast to Babette."

"You must get her first," said the miller, laughing; and Babette thought this a very good sign.

"We must take the bird out of the basket," said she. "It is getting into a rage; how its eyes glare. How did you manage to conquer it?"

Then Rudy had to describe his adventure, and the miller's eyes opened wide as he listened.

"With your courage and your good fortune you might win three wives," said the miller.

"Oh, thank you," cried Rudy.

"But you have not won Babette yet," said the miller, slapping the young Alpine hunter on the shoulder playfully.

"Have you heard the fresh news at the mill?" asked the parlor-cat of the kitchen-cat. "Rudy has brought us the young eagle, and he is to take Babette in exchange. They kissed each other in the presence of the old man, which is as good as an engagement. He was quite civil about it; drew in his claws, and took his afternoon nap, so that the two were left to sit and wag their tails as much as they pleased. They have so much to talk about that it will not be finished till Christmas." Neither was it finished till Christmas.

The wind whirled the faded, fallen leaves; the snow drifted in the valleys, as well as upon the mountains, and the Ice Maiden sat in the stately palace which, in winter time, she generally occupied. The perpendicular rocks were covered with slippery ice, and where in summer the stream from the rocks had left a watery veil, icicles large and heavy hung from the trees, while the snow-powdered fir-trees were decorated with fantastic garlands of crystal. The Ice Maiden rode on the howling wind across the deep valleys, the country, as far as Bex, was covered with a carpet of snow, so that the Ice Maiden could follow Rudy, and see him, when he visited the mill; and while in the room at the miller's house, where he was accustomed to spend so much of his time with Babette. The wedding was to take place in the following summer, and they heard enough of it, for so many of their friends spoke of the matter.

Then came sunshine to the mill. The beautiful Alpine roses bloomed, and joyous, laughing Babette, was like the early spring, which makes all the birds sing of summer time and bridal days.

"How those two do sit and chatter together," said the parlor-cat; "I have had enough of their mewing."

IX
The Ice Maiden

The walnut and chestnut trees, which extend from the bridge of St. Maurice, by the river Rhone, to the shores of the lake of Geneva, were already covered with the delicate green garlands of early spring, just bursting into bloom, while the Rhone rushed wildly from its source among the green glaciers which form the ice palace of the Ice Maiden. She sometimes allows herself to be carried by the keen wind to the lofty snow-fields, where she stretches herself in the sunshine on the soft snowy-cushions. From thence she throws her far-seeing glance into the deep valley beneath, where human beings are busily moving about like ants on a stone in the sun. "Spirits of strength, as the children of the sun call you," cried the Ice Maiden, "ye are but worms! Let but a snow-ball roll, and you and your houses and your towns are crushed and swept away." And she raised her proud head, and looked around her with eyes that flashed death from their glance. From the valley came a rumbling sound; men were busily at work blasting the rocks to form tunnels, and laying down roads for the railway. "They are playing at work underground, like moles," said she. "They are digging passages beneath the earth, and the noise is like the reports of cannons. I shall throw down my palaces, for the clamor is louder than the roar of thunder." Then there ascended from the valley a thick vapor, which waved itself in the air like a fluttering veil. It rose, as a plume of feathers, from a steam engine, to which, on the lately-opened railway, a string of carriages was linked, carriage to carriage, looking like a winding serpent. The train shot past with the speed of an arrow. "They play at being masters down there, those spirits of strength!" exclaimed the Ice Maiden; "but the powers of nature are still the rulers." And she laughed and sang till her voice sounded through the valley, and people said it was the rolling of an avalanche. But the children of the sun sang in louder strains in praise of the mind of man, which can span the sea as with a yoke, can level mountains, and fill up valleys. It is the power of thought which gives man the mastery over nature.

Just at this moment there came across the snow-field, where the Ice Maiden sat, a party of travellers. They had bound themselves fast to each other, so that they looked like one large body on the slippery plains of ice encircling the deep abyss.

"Worms!" exclaimed the Ice Maiden. "You, the lords of the powers of nature!" And she turned away and looked maliciously at the deep valley where the railway train was rushing by. "There they sit, these thoughts!" she exclaimed. "There they sit in their power over nature's strength. I see them all. One sits proudly apart, like a king; others sit together in a group; yonder, half of them are asleep; and when the steam dragon stops, they will get out and go their way. The thoughts go forth into the world," and she laughed.

"There goes another avalanche," said those in the valley beneath.

"It will not reach us," said two who sat together behind the steam dragon. "Two hearts and one beat," as people say. They were Rudy and Babette, and the miller was with them. "I am like the luggage," said he; "I am here as a necessary appendage."

"There sit those two," said the Ice Maiden. "Many a chamois have I crushed. Millions of Alpine roses have I snapped and broken off; not a root have I spared. I know them all, and their thoughts, those spirits of strength!" and again she laughed.

"There rolls another avalanche," said those in the valley.

X
The Godmother

At Montreux, one of the towns which encircle the northeast part of the lake of Geneva, lived Babette's godmother, the noble English lady, with her daughters and a young relative. They had only lately arrived, yet the miller had paid them a visit, and informed them of Babette's engagement to Rudy. The whole story of their meeting at Interlachen, and his brave adventure with the eaglet, were related to them, and they were all very much interested, and as pleased about Rudy and Babette as the miller himself. The three were invited to come to Montreux; it was but right for Babette to become acquainted with her godmother, who wished to see her very much. A steam-boat started from the town of Villeneuve, at one end of the lake of Geneva, and arrived at Bernex, a little town beyond Montreux, in about half an hour. And in this boat, the miller, with his daughter and Rudy, set out to visit her godmother. They passed the coast which has been so celebrated in song. Here, under the walnut-trees, by the deep blue lake, sat Byron, and wrote his melodious verses about the prisoner confined in the gloomy castle of Chillon. Here, where Clarens, with its weeping-willows, is reflected in the clear water, wandered Rousseau, dreaming of Heloise. The river Rhone glides gently by beneath the lofty snow-capped hills of Savoy, and not far from its mouth lies a little island in the lake, so small that, seen from the shore, it looks like a ship. The surface of the island is rocky; and about a hundred years ago, a lady caused the ground to be covered with earth, in which three acacia-trees were planted, and the whole enclosed with stone walls. The acacia-trees now overshadow every part of the island. Babette was enchanted with the spot; it seemed to her the most beautiful object in the whole voyage, and she thought how much she should like to land there. But the steam-ship passed it by, and did not stop till it reached Bernex. The little party walked slowly from this place to Montreux, passing the sun-lit walls with which the vineyards of the little mountain town of Montreux are surrounded, and peasants' houses, overshadowed by fig-trees, with gardens in which grow the laurel and the cypress.

Halfway up the hill stood the boarding-house in which Babette's godmother resided. She was received most cordially; her godmother was a very friendly woman, with a round, smiling countenance. When a child, her head must have resembled one of Raphael's cherubs; it was still an angelic face, with its white locks of silvery hair. The daughters were tall, elegant, slender maidens.

The young cousin, whom they had brought with them, was dressed in white from head to foot; he had golden hair and golden whiskers, large enough to be divided amongst three gentlemen; and he began immediately to pay the greatest attention to Babette.

Richly bound books, note-paper, and drawings, lay on the large table. The balcony window stood open, and from it could be seen the beautiful wide extended lake, the water so clear and still, that the mountains of Savoy, with their villages, woods, and snow-crowned peaks, were clearly reflected in it.

Rudy, who was usually so lively and brave, did not in the least feel himself at home; he acted as if he were walking on peas, over a slippery floor. How long and wearisome the time appeared; it was like being in a treadmill. And then they went out for a walk, which was very slow and tedious. Two steps forward and one backwards had Rudy to take to keep pace with the others. They walked down to Chillon, and went over the old castle on the rocky island. They saw the implements of torture, the deadly dungeons, the rusty fetters in the rocky walls, the stone benches for those condemned to death, the trap-doors through which the unhappy creatures were hurled upon iron spikes, and impaled alive. They called looking at all these a pleasure. It certainly was the right place to visit. Byron's poetry had made it celebrated in the world. Rudy could only feel that it was a place of execution. He leaned against the stone framework of the window, and gazed down into the deep, blue water, and over to the little island with the three acacias, and wished himself there, away and free from the whole chattering party. But Babette was most unusually lively and good-tempered.

"I have been so amused," she said.

The cousin had found her quite perfect.

"He is a perfect fop," said Rudy; and this was the first time Rudy had said anything that did not please Babette.

The Englishman had made her a present of a little book, in remembrance of their visit to Chillon. It was Byron's poem, "The Prisoner of Chillon," translated into French, so that Babette could read it.

"The book may be very good," said Rudy; "but that finely combed fellow who gave it to you is not worth much."

"He looks something like a flour-sack without any flour," said the miller, laughing at his own wit. Rudy laughed, too, for so had he appeared to him.

XI
The Cousin

When Rudy went a few days after to pay a visit to the mill, he found the young Englishman there. Babette was just thinking of preparing some trout to set before him. She understood well how to garnish the dish with parsley, and make it look quite tempting. Rudy thought all this quite unnecessary. What did the Englishman want there? What was he about? Why should he be entertained, and waited upon by Babette? Rudy was jealous, and that made Babette happy. It amused her to discover all the feelings of his heart; the strong points and weak ones. Love was to her as yet only a pastime, and she played with Rudy's whole heart. At the same time it must be acknowledged that her fortune, her whole life, her inmost thoughts, her best and most noble feelings in this world were all for him. Still the more gloomy he looked, the more her eyes laughed. She could almost have kissed the fair Englishman, with the golden whiskers, if by so doing she could have put Rudy in a rage, and made him run out of the house. That would have proved how much he loved her. All this was not right in Babette, but she was only nineteen years of age, and she did not reflect on what she did, neither did she think that her conduct would appear to the young Englishman as light, and not even becoming the modest and much-loved daughter of the miller.

The mill at Bex stood in the highway, which passed under the snow-clad mountains, and not far from a rapid mountain-stream, whose waters seemed to have been lashed into a foam like soap-suds. This stream, however, did not pass near enough to the mill, and therefore the mill-wheel was turned by a smaller stream which tumbled down the rocks on the opposite side, where it was opposed by a stone mill-dam, and obtained greater strength and speed, till it fell into a large basin, and from thence through a channel to the mill-wheel. This channel sometimes overflowed, and made the path so slippery that any one passing that way might easily fall in, and be carried towards the mill wheel with frightful rapidity. Such a catastrophe nearly happened to the young Englishman. He had dressed himself in white clothes, like a miller's man, and was climbing the path to the miller's house, but he had never been taught to climb, and therefore slipped, and nearly went in head-foremost. He managed, however, to scramble out with wet sleeves and bespattered trousers. Still, wet and splashed with mud, he contrived to reach Babette's window, to which he had been guided by the light that shone from it. Here he climbed the old linden-tree that stood near it, and began to imitate the voice of an owl, the only bird he could venture to mimic. Babette heard the noise, and glanced through the thin window curtain; but when she saw the man in white, and guessed who he was, her little heart beat with terror as well as anger. She quickly put out the light, felt if the fastening of the window was secure, and then left him to howl as long as he liked. How dreadful it would be, thought Babette, if Rudy were here in the house. But Rudy was not in the house. No, it was much worse, he was outside, standing just under the linden-tree. He was speaking loud, angry words. He could fight, and there might be murder! Babette opened the window in alarm, and called Rudy's name; she told him to go away, she did not wish him to remain there.

"You do not wish me to stay," cried he; "then this is an appointment you expected – this good friend whom you prefer to me. Shame on you, Babette!"

"You are detestable!" exclaimed Babette, bursting into tears. "Go away. I hate you."

"I have not deserved this," said Rudy, as he turned away, his cheeks burning, and his heart like fire.

Babette threw herself on the bed, and wept bitterly. "So much as I loved thee, Rudy, and yet thou canst think ill of me."

Thus her anger broke forth; it relieved her, however: otherwise she would have been more deeply grieved; but now she could sleep soundly, as youth only can sleep.

XII
Evil Powers

Rudy left Bex, and took his way home along the mountain path. The air was fresh, but cold; for here amidst the deep snow, the Ice Maiden reigned. He was so high up that the large trees beneath him, with their thick foliage, appeared like garden plants, and the pines and bushes even less. The Alpine roses grew near the snow, which lay in detached stripes, and looked like linen laid out to bleach. A blue gentian grew in his path, and he crushed it with the butt end of his gun. A little higher up, he espied two chamois. Rudy's eyes glistened, and his thoughts flew at once in a different direction; but he was not near enough to take a sure aim. He ascended still higher, to a spot where a few rough blades of grass grew between the blocks of stone and the chamois passed quietly on over the snow-fields. Rudy walked hurriedly, while the clouds of mist gathered round him. Suddenly he found himself on the brink of a precipitous rock. The rain was falling in torrents. He felt a burning thirst, his head was hot, and his limbs trembled with cold. He seized his hunting-flask, but it was empty; he had not thought of filling it before ascending the mountain. He had never been ill in his life, nor ever experienced such sensations as those he now felt. He was so tired that he could scarcely resist lying down at his full length to sleep, although the ground was flooded with the rain. Yet when he tried to rouse himself a little, every object around him danced and trembled before his eyes.

Suddenly he observed in the doorway of a hut newly built under the rock, a young maiden. He did not remember having seen this hut before, yet there it stood; and he thought, at first, that the young maiden was Annette, the schoolmaster's daughter, whom he had once kissed in the dance. The maiden was not Annette; yet it seemed as if he had seen her somewhere before, perhaps near Grindelwald, on the evening of his return home from Interlachen, after the shooting-match.

"How did you come here?" he asked.

"I am at home," she replied; "I am watching my flocks."

"Your flocks!" he exclaimed; "where do they find pasture? There is nothing here but snow and rocks."

"Much you know of what grows here," she replied, laughing. "not far beneath us there is beautiful pasture-land. My goats go there. I tend them carefully; I never miss one. What is once mine remains mine."

"You are bold," said Rudy.

"And so are you," she answered.

"Have you any milk in the house?" he asked; "if so, give me some to drink; my thirst is intolerable."

"I have something better than milk," she replied, "which I will give you. Some travellers who were here yesterday with their guide left behind them a half a flask of wine, such as you have never tasted. They will not come back to fetch it, I know, and I shall not drink it; so you shall have it."

Then the maiden went to fetch the wine, poured some into a wooden cup, and offered it to Rudy.

"How good it is!" said he; "I have never before tasted such warm, invigorating wine." And his eyes sparkled with new life; a glow diffused itself over his frame; it seemed as if every sorrow, every oppression were banished from his mind, and a fresh, free nature were stirring within him. "You are surely Annette, the schoolmaster's daughter," cried he; "will you give me a kiss?"

"Yes, if you will give me that beautiful ring which you wear on your finger."

"My betrothal ring?" he replied.

"Yes, just so," said the maiden, as she poured out some more wine, and held it to his lips. Again he drank, and a living joy streamed through every vein.

"The whole world is mine, why therefore should I grieve?" thought he. "Everything is created for our enjoyment and happiness. The stream of life is a stream of happiness; let us flow on with it to joy and felicity."

Rudy gazed on the young maiden; it was Annette, and yet it was not Annette; still less did he suppose it was the spectral phantom, whom he had met near Grindelwald. The maiden up here on the mountain was fresh as the new fallen snow, blooming as an Alpine rose, and as nimble-footed as a young kid. Still, she was one of Adam's race, like Rudy. He flung his arms round the beautiful being, and gazed into her wonderfully clear eyes, – only for a moment; but in that moment words cannot express the effect of his gaze. Was it the spirit of life or of death that overpowered him? Was he rising higher, or sinking lower and lower into the deep, deadly abyss? He knew not; but the walls of ice shone like blue-green glass; innumerable clefts yawned around him, and the water-drops tinkled like the chiming of church bells, and shone clearly as pearls in the light of a pale-blue flame. The Ice Maiden, for she it was, kissed him, and her kiss sent a chill as of ice through his whole frame. A cry of agony escaped from him; he struggled to get free, and tottered from her. For a moment all was dark before his eyes, but when he opened them again it was light, and the Alpine maiden had vanished. The powers of evil had played their game; the sheltering hut was no more to be seen. The water trickled down the naked sides of the rocks, and snow lay thickly all around. Rudy shivered with cold; he was wet through to the skin; and his ring was gone, – the betrothal ring that Babette had given him. His gun lay near him in the snow; he took it up and tried to discharge it, but it missed fire. Heavy clouds lay on the mountain clefts, like firm masses of snow. Upon one of these Vertigo sat, lurking after his powerless prey, and from beneath came a sound as if a piece of rock had fallen from the cleft, and was crushing everything that stood in its way or opposed its course.

But, at the miller's, Babette sat alone and wept. Rudy had not been to see her for six days. He who was in the wrong, and who ought to ask her forgiveness; for did she not love him with her whole heart?

XIII
At the Mill

What strange creatures human beings are," said the parlor-cat to the kitchen-cat; "Babette and Rudy have fallen out with each other. She sits and cries, and he thinks no more about her."

"That does not please me to hear," said the kitchen-cat.

"Nor me either," replied the parlor-cat; "but I do not take it to heart. Babette may fall in love with the red whiskers, if she likes, but he has not been here since he tried to get on the roof."

The powers of evil carry on their game both around us and within us. Rudy knew this, and thought a great deal about it. What was it that had happened to him on the mountain? Was it really a ghostly apparition, or a fever dream? Rudy knew nothing of fever, or any other ailment. But, while he judged Babette, he began to examine his own conduct. He had allowed wild thoughts to chase each other in his heart, and a fierce tornado to break loose. Could he confess to Babette, indeed, every thought which in the hour of temptation might have led him to wrong doing? He had lost her ring, and that very loss had won him back to her. Could she expect him to confess? He felt as if his heart would break while he thought of it, and while so many memories lingered on his mind. He saw her again, as she once stood before him, a laughing, spirited child; many loving words, which she had spoken to him out of the fulness of her love, came like a ray of sunshine into his heart, and soon it was all sunshine as he thought of Babette. But she must also confess she was wrong; that she should do.

He went to the mill – he went to confession. It began with a kiss, and ended with Rudy being considered the offender. It was such a great fault to doubt Babette's truth – it was most abominable of him. Such mistrust, such violence, would cause them both great unhappiness. This certainly was very true, she knew that; and therefore Babette preached him a little sermon, with which she was herself much amused, and during the preaching of which she looked quite lovely. She acknowledged, however, that on one point Rudy was right. Her godmother's nephew was a fop: she intended to burn the book which he had given her, so that not the slightest thing should remain to remind her of him.

"Well, that quarrel is all over," said the kitchen-cat. "Rudy is come back, and they are friends again, which they say is the greatest of all pleasures."

"I heard the rats say one night," said the kitchen-cat, "that the greatest pleasure in the world was to eat tallow candles and to feast on rancid bacon. Which are we to believe, the rats or the lovers?"

"Neither of them," said the parlor-cat; "it is always the safest plan to believe nothing you hear."

The greatest happiness was coming for Rudy and Babette. The happy day, as it is called, that is, their wedding-day, was near at hand. They were not to be married at the church at Bex, nor at the miller's house; Babette's godmother wished the nuptials to be solemnized at Montreux, in the pretty little church in that town. The miller was very anxious that this arrangement should be agreed to. He alone knew what the newly-married couple would receive from Babette's godmother, and he knew also that it was a wedding present well worth a concession. The day was fixed, and they were to travel as far as Villeneuve the evening before, to be in time for the steamer which sailed in the morning for Montreux, and the godmother's daughters were to dress and adorn the bride.

"Here in this house there ought to be a wedding-day kept," said the parlor-cat, "or else I would not give a mew for the whole affair."

"There is going to be great feasting," replied the kitchen-cat. "Ducks and pigeons have been killed, and a whole roebuck hangs on the wall. It makes me lick my lips when I think of it."

"To-morrow morning they will begin the journey."

Yes, to-morrow! And this evening, for the last time, Rudy and Babette sat in the miller's house as an engaged couple. Outside, the Alps glowed in the evening sunset, the evening bells chimed, and the children of the sunbeam sang, "Whatever happens is best."

XIV
Night Visions

THE sun had gone down, and the clouds lay low on the valley of the Rhone. The wind blew from the south across the mountains; it was an African wind, a wind which scattered the clouds for a moment, and then suddenly fell. The broken clouds hung in fantastic forms upon the wood-covered hills by the rapid Rhone. They assumed the shapes of antediluvian animals, of eagles hovering in the air, of frogs leaping over a marsh, and then sunk down upon the rushing stream and appeared to sail upon it, although floating in the air. An uprooted fir-tree was being carried away by the current, and marking out its path by eddying circles on the water. Vertigo and his sisters were dancing upon it, and raising these circles on the foaming river. The moon lighted up the snow on the mountain-tops, shone on the dark woods, and on the drifting clouds those fantastic forms which at night might be taken for spirits of the powers of nature. The mountain-dweller saw them through the panes of his little window. They sailed in hosts before the Ice Maiden as she came out of her palace of ice. Then she seated herself on the trunk of the fir-tree as on a broken skiff, and the water from the glaciers carried her down the river to the open lake.

"The wedding guests are coming," sounded from air and sea. These were the sights and sounds without; within there were visions, for Babette had a wonderful dream. She dreamt that she had been married to Rudy for many years, and that, one day when he was out chamois hunting, and she alone in their dwelling at home, the young Englishman with the golden whiskers sat with her. His eyes were quite eloquent, and his words possessed a magic power; he offered her his hand, and she was obliged to follow him. They went out of the house and stepped downwards, always downwards, and it seemed to Babette as if she had a weight on her heart which continually grew heavier. She felt she was committing a sin against Rudy, a sin against God. Suddenly she found herself forsaken, her clothes torn by the thorns, and her hair gray; she looked upwards in her agony, and there, on the edge of the rock, she espied Rudy. She stretched out her arms to him, but she did not venture to call him or to pray; and had she called him, it would have been useless, for it was not Rudy, only his hunting coat and hat hanging on an alpenstock, as the hunters sometimes arrange them to deceive the chamois. "Oh!" she exclaimed in her agony; "oh, that I had died on the happiest day of my life, my wedding-day. O my God, it would have been a mercy and a blessing had Rudy travelled far away from me, and I had never known him. None know what will happen in the future." And then, in ungodly despair, she cast herself down into the deep rocky gulf. The spell was broken; a cry of terror escaped her, and she awoke.

The dream was over; it had vanished. But she knew she had dreamt something frightful about the young Englishman, yet months had passed since she had seen him or even thought of him. Was he still at Montreux, and should she meet him there on her wedding day? A slight shadow passed over her pretty mouth as she thought of this, and she knit her brows; but the smile soon returned to her lip, and joy sparkled in her eyes, for this was the morning of the day on which she and Rudy were to be married, and the sun was shining brightly. Rudy was already in the parlor when she entered it, and they very soon started for Villeneuve. Both of them were overflowing with happiness, and the miller was in the best of tempers, laughing and merry; he was a good, honest soul, and a kind father.

"Now we are masters of the house," said the parlor-cat.

XV
The Conclusion

It was early in the afternoon, and just at dinner-time, when the three joyous travellers reached Villeneuve. After dinner, the miller placed himself in the arm-chair, smoked his pipe, and had a little nap. The bridal pair went arm-in-arm out through the town and along the high road, at the foot of the wood-covered rocks, and by the deep, blue lake.

The gray walls, and the heavy clumsy-looking towers of the gloomy castle of Chillon, were reflected in the clear flood. The little island, on which grew the three acacias, lay at a short distance, looking like a bouquet rising from the lake. "How delightful it must be to live there," said Babette, who again felt the greatest wish to visit the island; and an opportunity offered to gratify her wish at once, for on the shore lay a boat, and the rope by which it was moored could be very easily loosened. They saw no one near, so they took possession of it without asking permission of any one, and Rudy could row very well. The oars divided the pliant water like the fins of a fish – that water which, with all its yielding softness, is so strong to bear and to carry, so mild and smiling when at rest, and yet so terrible in its destroying power. A white streak of foam followed in the wake of the boat, which, in a few minutes, carried them both to the little island, where they went on shore; but there was only just room enough for two to dance. Rudy swung Babette round two or three times; and then, hand-in-hand, they sat down on a little bench under the drooping acacia-tree, and looked into each other's eyes, while everything around them glowed in the rays of the setting sun.

The fir-tree forests on the mountains were covered with a purple hue like the heather bloom; and where the woods terminated, and the rocks became prominent, they looked almost transparent in the rich crimson glow of the evening sky. The surface of the lake was like a bed of pink rose-leaves.

As the evening advanced, the shadows fell upon the snow-capped mountains of Savoy painting them in colors of deep blue, while their topmost peaks glowed like red lava; and for a moment this light was reflected on the cultivated parts of the mountains, making them appear as if newly risen from the lap of earth, and giving to the snow-crested peak of the Dent du Midi the appearance of the full moon as it rises above the horizon.

Rudy and Babette felt that they had never seen the Alpine glow in such perfection before. "How very beautiful it is, and what happiness to be here!" exclaimed Babette.

"Earth has nothing more to bestow upon me," said Rudy; "an evening like this is worth a whole life. Often have I realized my good fortune, but never more than in this moment. I feel that if my existence were to end now, I should still have lived a happy life. What a glorious world this is; one day ends, and another begins even more beautiful than the last. How infinitely good God is, Babette!"

"I have such complete happiness in my heart," said she.

"Earth has no more to bestow," answered Rudy. And then came the sound of the evening bells, borne upon the breeze over the mountains of Switzerland and Savoy, while still, in the golden splendor of the west, stood the dark blue mountains of Jura.

"God grant you all that is brightest and best!" exclaimed Babette.

"He will," said Rudy. "He will to-morrow. To-morrow you will be wholly mine, my own sweet wife."

"The boat!" cried Babette, suddenly. The boat in which they were to return had broken loose, and was floating away from the island.

"I will fetch it back," said Rudy; throwing off his coat and boots, he sprang into the lake, and swam with strong efforts towards it.

The dark-blue water, from the glaciers of the mountains, was icy cold and very deep. Rudy gave but one glance into the water beneath; but in that one glance he saw a gold ring rolling, glittering, and sparkling before him. His engaged ring came into his mind; but this was larger, and spread into a glittering circle, in which appeared a clear glacier. Deep chasms yawned around it, the water-drops glittered as if lighted with blue flame, and tinkled like the chiming of church bells. In one moment he saw what would require many words to describe. Young hunters, and young maidens – men and women who had sunk in the deep chasms of the glaciers – stood before him here in lifelike forms, with eyes open and smiles on their lips; and far beneath them could be heard the chiming of the church bells of buried villages, where the villagers knelt beneath the vaulted arches of churches in which ice-blocks formed the organ pipes, and the mountain stream the music.

On the clear, transparent ground sat the Ice Maiden. She raised herself towards Rudy, and kissed his feet; and instantly a cold, deathly chill, like an electric shock, passed through his limbs. Ice or fire! It was impossible to tell, the shock was so instantaneous.

"Mine! mine!" sounded around him, and within him; "I kissed thee when thou wert a little child. I once kissed thee on the mouth, and now I have kissed thee from heel to toe; thou art wholly mine." And then he disappeared in the clear, blue water.

All was still. The church bells were silent; the last tone floated away with the last red glimmer on the evening clouds. "Thou art mine," sounded from the depths below: but from the heights above, from the eternal world, also sounded the words, "Thou art mine!" Happy was he thus to pass from life to life, from earth to heaven. A chord was loosened, and tones of sorrow burst forth. The icy kiss of death had overcome the perishable body; it was but the prelude before life's real drama could begin, the discord which was quickly lost in harmony. Do you think this a sad story? Poor Babette! for her it was unspeakable anguish.

The boat drifted farther and farther away. No one on the opposite shore knew that the betrothed pair had gone over to the little island. The clouds sunk as the evening drew on, and it became dark. Alone, in despair, she waited and trembled. The weather became fearful; flash after flash lighted up the mountains of Jura, Savoy, and Switzerland, while peals of thunder, that lasted for many minutes, rolled over her head. The lightning was so vivid that every single vine stem could be seen for a moment as distinctly as in the sunlight at noon-day; and then all was veiled in darkness. It flashed across the lake in winding, zigzag lines, lighting it up on all sides; while the echoes of the thunder grew louder and stronger. On land, the boats were all carefully drawn up on the beach, every living thing sought shelter, and at length the rain poured down in torrents.

"Where can Rudy and Babette be in this awful weather?" said the miller.

Poor Babette sat with her hands clasped, and her head bowed down, dumb with grief; she had ceased to weep and cry for help.

"In the deep water!" she said to herself; "far down he lies, as if beneath a glacier."

Deep in her heart rested the memory of what Rudy had told her of the death of his mother, and of his own recovery, even after he had been taken up as dead from the cleft in the glacier.

"Ah," she thought, "the Ice Maiden has him at last."

Suddenly there came a flash of lightning, as dazzling as the rays of the sun on the white snow. The lake rose for a moment like a shining glacier; and before Babette stood the pallid, glittering, majestic form of the Ice Maiden, and at her feet lay Rudy's corpse.

"Mine!" she cried, and again all was darkness around the heaving water.

"How cruel," murmured Babette; "why should he die just as the day of happiness drew near? Merciful God, enlighten my understanding, shed light upon my heart; for I cannot comprehend the arrangements of Thy providence, even while I bow to the decree of Thy almighty wisdom and power." And God did enlighten her heart.

A sudden flash of thought, like a ray of mercy, recalled her dream of the preceding night; all was vividly represented before her. She remembered the words and wishes she had then expressed, that what was best for her and for Rudy she might piously submit to.

"Woe is me," she said; "was the germ of sin really in my heart? was my dream a glimpse into the course of my future life, whose thread must be violently broken to rescue me from sin? Oh, miserable creature that I am!"

Thus she sat lamenting in the dark night, while through the deep stillness the last words of Rudy seemed to ring in her ears. "This earth has nothing more to bestow." Words, uttered in the fulness of joy, were again heard amid the depths of sorrow.

Years have passed since this sad event happened. The shores of the peaceful lake still smile in beauty. The vines are full of luscious grapes. Steamboats, with waving flags, pass swiftly by. Pleasure-boats, with their swelling sails, skim lightly over the watery mirror, like white butterflies. The railway is opened beyond Chillon, and goes far into the deep valley of the Rhone. At every station strangers alight with red-bound guide-books in their hands, in which they read of every place worth seeing. They visit Chillon, and observe on the lake the little island with the three acacias, and then read in their guide-book the story of the bridal pair who, in the year 1856, rowed over to it. They read that the two were missing till the next morning, when some people on the shore heard the despairing cries of the bride, and went to her assistance, and by her were told of the bridegroom's fate.

But the guide-book does not speak of Babette's quiet life afterwards with her father, not at the mill – strangers dwell there now – but in a pretty house in a row near the station. On many an evening she sits at her window, and looks out over the chestnut-trees to the snow-capped mountains on which Rudy once roamed. She looks at the Alpine glow in the evening sky, which is caused by the children of the sun retiring to rest on the mountain-tops; and again they breathe their song of the traveller whom the whirlwind could deprive of his cloak but not of his life. There is a rosy tint on the mountain snow, and there are rosy gleams in each heart in which dwells the thought, "God permits nothing to happen, which is not the best for us." But this is not often revealed to all, as it was revealed to Babette in her wonderful dream.

The Brave Tin Soldier

THERE WERE ONCE five-and-twenty tin soldiers, who were all brothers, for they had been made out of the same old tin spoon. They shouldered arms and looked straight before them, and wore a splendid uniform, red and blue. The first thing in the world they ever heard were the words, "Tin soldiers!" uttered by a little boy, who clapped his hands with delight when the lid of the box, in which they lay, was taken off. They were given him for a birthday present, and he stood at the table to set them up. The soldiers were all exactly alike, excepting one, who had only one leg; he had been left to the last, and then there was not enough of the melted tin to finish him, so they made him to stand firmly on one leg, and this caused him to be very remarkable.

The table on which the tin soldiers stood, was covered with other playthings, but the most attractive to the eye was a pretty little paper castle. Through the small windows the rooms could be seen. In front of the castle a number of little trees surrounded a piece of looking-glass, which was intended to represent a transparent lake. Swans, made of wax, swam on the lake, and were reflected in it. All this was very pretty, but the prettiest of all was a tiny little lady, who stood at the open door of the castle; she, also, was made of paper, and she wore a dress of clear muslin, with a narrow blue ribbon over her shoulders just like a scarf. In front of these was fixed a glittering tinsel rose, as large as her whole face. The little lady was a dancer, and she stretched out both her arms, and raised one of her legs so high, that the tin soldier could not see it at all, and he thought that she, like himself, had only one leg. "That is the wife for me," he thought; "but she is too grand, and lives in a castle, while I have only a box to live in, five-and-twenty of us altogether, that is no place for her. Still I must try and make her acquaintance." Then he laid himself at full length on the table behind a snuff-box that stood upon it, so that he could peep at the little delicate lady, who continued to stand on one leg without losing her balance. When evening came, the other tin soldiers were all placed in the box, and the people of the house went to bed. Then the playthings began to have their own games together, to pay visits, to have sham fights, and to give balls. The tin soldiers rattled in their box; they wanted to get out and join the amusements, but they could not open the lid. The nut-crackers played at leap-frog, and the pencil jumped about the table. There was such a noise that the canary woke up and began to talk, and in poetry too. Only the tin soldier and the dancer remained in their places. She stood on tiptoe, with her legs stretched out, as firmly as he did on his one leg. He never took his eyes from her for even a moment. The clock struck twelve, and, with a bounce, up sprang the lid of the snuff-box; but, instead of snuff, there jumped up a little black goblin; for the snuff-box was a toy puzzle.

"Tin soldier," said the goblin, "don't wish for what does not belong to you."

But the tin soldier pretended not to hear.

"Very well; wait till to-morrow, then," said the goblin.

When the children came in the next morning, they placed the tin soldier in the window. Now, whether it was the goblin who did it, or the draught, is not known, but the window flew open, and out fell the tin soldier, heels over head, from the third story, into the street beneath. It was a terrible fall; for he came head downwards, his helmet and his bayonet stuck in between the flagstones, and his one leg up in the air. The servant maid and the little boy went down stairs directly to look for him; but he was nowhere to be seen, although once they nearly trod upon him. If he had called out, "Here I am," it would have been all right, but he was too proud to cry out for help while he wore a uniform.

Presently it began to rain, and the drops fell faster and faster, till there was a heavy shower. When it was over, two boys happened to pass by, and one of them said, "Look, there is a tin soldier. He ought to have a boat to sail in."

So they made a boat out of a newspaper, and placed the tin soldier in it, and sent him sailing down the gutter, while the two boys ran by the side of it, and clapped their hands. Good gracious, what large waves arose in that gutter! and how fast the stream rolled on! for the rain had been very heavy. The paper boat rocked up and down, and turned itself round sometimes so quickly that the tin soldier trembled; yet he remained firm; his countenance did not change; he looked straight before him, and shouldered his musket. Suddenly the boat shot under a bridge which formed a part of a drain, and then it was as dark as the tin soldier's box.

"Where am I going now?" thought he. "This is the black goblin's fault, I am sure. Ah, well, if the little lady were only here with me in the boat, I should not care for any darkness."

Suddenly there appeared a great water-rat, who lived in the drain.

"Have you a passport?" asked the rat, "give it to me at once." But the tin soldier remained silent and held his musket tighter than ever. The boat sailed on and the rat followed it. How he did gnash his teeth and cry out to the bits of wood and straw, "Stop him, stop him; he has not paid toll, and has not shown his pass." But the stream rushed on stronger and stronger. The tin soldier could already see daylight shining where the arch ended. Then he heard a roaring sound quite terrible enough to frighten the bravest man. At the end of the tunnel the drain fell into a large canal over a steep place, which made it as dangerous for him as a waterfall would be to us. He was too close to it to stop, so the boat rushed on, and the poor tin soldier could only hold himself as stiffly as possible, without moving an eyelid, to show that he was not afraid. The boat whirled round three or four times, and then filled with water to the very edge; nothing could save it from sinking. He now stood up to his neck in water, while deeper and deeper sank the boat, and the paper became soft and loose with the wet, till at last the water closed over the soldier's head. He thought of the elegant little dancer whom he should never see again, and the words of the song sounded in his ears –

"Farewell, warrior! ever brave,
Drifting onward to thy grave."

Then the paper boat fell to pieces, and the soldier sank into the water and immediately afterwards was swallowed up by a great fish. Oh how dark it was inside the fish! A great deal darker than in the tunnel, and narrower too, but the tin soldier continued firm, and lay at full length shouldering his musket. The fish swam to and fro, making the most wonderful movements, but at last he became quite still. After a while, a flash of lightning seemed to pass through him, and then the daylight approached, and a voice cried out, "I declare here is the tin soldier." The fish had been caught, taken to the market and sold to the cook, who took him into the kitchen and cut him open with a large knife. She picked up the soldier and held him by the waist between her finger and thumb, and carried him into the room. They were all anxious to see this wonderful soldier who had travelled about inside a fish; but he was not at all proud. They placed him on the table, and – how many curious things do happen in the world! – there he was in the very same room from the window of which he had fallen, there were the same children, the same playthings, standing on the table, and the pretty castle with the elegant little dancer at the door; she still balanced herself on one leg, and held up the other, so she was as firm as himself. It touched the tin soldier so much to see her that he almost wept tin tears, but he kept them back. He only looked at her and they both remained silent. Presently one of the little boys took up the tin soldier, and threw him into the stove. He had no reason for doing so, therefore it must have been the fault of the black goblin who lived in the snuff-box. The flames lighted up the tin soldier, as he stood, the heat was very terrible, but whether it proceeded from the real fire or from the fire of love he could not tell. Then he could see that the bright colors were faded from his uniform, but whether they had been washed off during his journey or from the effects of his sorrow, no one could say. He looked at the little lady, and she looked at him. He felt himself melting away, but he still remained firm with his gun on his shoulder. Suddenly the door of the room flew open and the draught of air caught up the little dancer, she fluttered like a sylph right into the stove by the side of the tin soldier, and was instantly in flames and was gone. The tin soldier melted down into a lump, and the next morning, when the maid servant took the ashes out of the stove, she found him in the shape of a little tin heart. But of the little dancer nothing remained but the tinsel rose, which was burnt black as a cinder.

The Wild Swans

FAR AWAY IN the land to which the swallows fly when it is winter, dwelt a king who had eleven sons, and one daughter, named Eliza. The eleven brothers were princes, and each went to school with a star on his breast, and a sword by his side. They wrote with diamond pencils on gold slates, and learnt their lessons so quickly and read so easily that every one might know they were princes. Their sister Eliza sat on a little stool of plate-glass, and had a book full of pictures, which had cost as much as half a kingdom. Oh, these children were indeed happy, but it was not to remain so always. Their father, who was king of the country, married a very wicked queen, who did not love the poor children at all. They knew this from the very first day after the wedding. In the palace there were great festivities, and the children played at receiving company; but instead of having, as usual, all the cakes and apples that were left, she gave them some sand in a tea-cup, and told them to pretend it was cake. The week after, she sent little Eliza into the country to a peasant and his wife, and then she told the king so many untrue things about the young princes, that he gave himself no more trouble respecting them.

"Go out into the world and get your own living," said the queen. "Fly like great birds, who have no voice." But she could not make them ugly as she wished, for they were turned into eleven beautiful wild swans. Then, with a strange cry, they flew through the windows of the palace, over the park, to the forest beyond. It was early morning when they passed the peasant's cottage, where their sister Eliza lay asleep in her room. They hovered over the roof, twisted their long necks and flapped their wings, but no one heard them or saw them, so they were at last obliged to fly away, high up in the clouds; and over the wide world they flew till they came to a thick, dark wood, which stretched far away to the seashore. Poor little Eliza was alone in her room playing with a green leaf, for she had no other playthings, and she pierced a hole through the leaf, and looked through it at the sun, and it was as if she saw her brothers' clear eyes, and when the warm sun shone on her cheeks, she thought of all the kisses they had given her. One day passed just like another; sometimes the winds rustled through the leaves of the rose-bush, and would whisper to the roses, "Who can be more beautiful than you!" But the roses would shake their heads, and say, "Eliza is." And when the old woman sat at the cottage door on Sunday, and read her hymn-book, the wind would flutter the leaves, and say to the book, "Who can be more pious than you?" and then the hymn-book would answer "Eliza." And the roses and the hymn-book told the real truth. At fifteen she returned home, but when the queen saw how beautiful she was, she became full of spite and hatred towards her. Willingly would she have turned her into a swan, like her brothers, but she did not dare to do so yet, because the king wished to see his daughter. Early one morning the queen went into the bath-room; it was built of marble, and had soft cushions, trimmed with the most beautiful tapestry. She took three toads with her, and kissed them, and said to one, "When Eliza comes to the bath, seat yourself upon her head, that she may become as stupid as you are." Then she said to another, "Place yourself on her forehead, that she may become as ugly as you are, and that her father may not know her." "Rest on her heart," she whispered to the third, "then she will have evil inclinations, and suffer in consequence." So she put the toads into the clear water, and they turned green immediately. She next called Eliza, and helped her to undress and get into the bath. As Eliza dipped her head under the water, one of the toads sat on her hair, a second on her forehead, and a third on her breast, but she did not seem to notice them, and when she rose out of the water, there were three red poppies floating upon it. Had not the creatures been venomous or been kissed by the witch, they would have been changed into red roses. At all events they became flowers, because they had rested on Eliza's head, and on her heart. She was too good and too innocent for witchcraft to have any power over her. When the wicked queen saw this, she rubbed her face with walnut-juice, so that she was quite brown; then she tangled her beautiful hair and smeared it with disgusting ointment, till it was quite impossible to recognize the beautiful Eliza.

When her father saw her, he was much shocked, and declared she was not his daughter. No one but the watch-dog and the swallows knew her; and they were only poor animals, and could say nothing. Then poor Eliza wept, and thought of her eleven brothers, who were all away. Sorrowfully, she stole away from the palace, and walked, the whole day, over fields and moors, till she came to the great forest. She knew not in what direction to go; but she was so unhappy, and longed so for her brothers, who had been, like herself, driven out into the world, that she was determined to seek them. She had been but a short time in the wood when night came on, and she quite lost the path; so she laid herself down on the soft moss, offered up her evening prayer, and leaned her head against the stump of a tree. All nature was still, and the soft, mild air fanned her forehead. The light of hundreds of glow-worms shone amidst the grass and the moss, like green fire; and if she touched a twig with her hand, ever so lightly, the brilliant insects fell down around her, like shooting-stars.

All night long she dreamt of her brothers. She and they were children again, playing together. She saw them writing with their diamond pencils on golden slates, while she looked at the beautiful picture-book which had cost half a kingdom. They were not writing lines and letters, as they used to do; but descriptions of the noble deeds they had performed, and of all they had discovered and seen. In the picture-book, too, everything was living. The birds sang, and the people came out of the book, and spoke to Eliza and her brothers; but, as the leaves turned over, they darted back again to their places, that all might be in order.

When she awoke, the sun was high in the heavens; yet she could not see him, for the lofty trees spread their branches thickly over her head; but his beams were glancing through the leaves here and there, like a golden mist. There was a sweet fragrance from the fresh green verdure, and the birds almost perched upon her shoulders. She heard water rippling from a number of springs, all flowing in a lake with golden sands. Bushes grew thickly round the lake, and at one spot an opening had been made by a deer, through which Eliza went down to the water. The lake was so clear that, had not the wind rustled the branches of the trees and the bushes, so that they moved, they would have appeared as if painted in the depths of the lake; for every leaf was reflected in the water, whether it stood in the shade or the sunshine. As soon as Eliza saw her own face, she was quite terrified at finding it so brown and ugly; but when she wetted her little hand, and rubbed her eyes and forehead, the white skin gleamed forth once more; and, after she had undressed, and dipped herself in the fresh water, a more beautiful king's daughter could not be found in the wide world. As soon as she had dressed herself again, and braided her long hair, she went to the bubbling spring, and drank some water out of the hollow of her hand. Then she wandered far into the forest, not knowing whither she went. She thought of her brothers, and felt sure that God would not forsake her. It is God who makes the wild apples grow in the wood, to satisfy the hungry, and He now led her to one of these trees, which was so loaded with fruit, that the boughs bent beneath the weight. Here she held her noonday repast, placed props under the boughs, and then went into the gloomiest depths of the forest. It was so still that she could hear the sound of her own footsteps, as well as the rustling of every withered leaf which she crushed under her feet. Not a bird was to be seen, not a sunbeam could penetrate through the large, dark boughs of the trees. Their lofty trunks stood so close together, that, when she looked before her, it seemed as if she were enclosed within trellis-work. Such solitude she had never known before. The night was very dark. Not a single glow-worm glittered in the moss.

Sorrowfully she laid herself down to sleep; and, after a while, it seemed to her as if the branches of the trees parted over her head, and that the mild eyes of angels looked down upon her from heaven. When she awoke in the morning, she knew not whether she had dreamt this, or if it had really been so. Then she continued her wandering; but she had not gone many steps forward, when she met an old woman with berries in her basket, and she gave her a few to eat. Then Eliza asked her if she had not seen eleven princes riding through the forest.

"No," replied the old woman, "But I saw yesterday eleven swans, with gold crowns on their heads, swimming on the river close by." Then she led Eliza a little distance farther to a sloping bank, and at the foot of it wound a little river. The trees on its banks stretched their long leafy branches across the water towards each other, and where the growth prevented them from meeting naturally, the roots had torn themselves away from the ground, so that the branches might mingle their foliage as they hung over the water. Eliza bade the old woman farewell, and walked by the flowing river, till she reached the shore of the open sea. And there, before the young maiden's eyes, lay the glorious ocean, but not a sail appeared on its surface, not even a boat could be seen. How was she to go farther? She noticed how the countless pebbles on the sea-shore had been smoothed and rounded by the action of the water. Glass, iron, stones, everything that lay there mingled together, had taken its shape from the same power, and felt as smooth, or even smoother than her own delicate hand. "The water rolls on without weariness," she said, "till all that is hard becomes smooth; so will I be unwearied in my task. Thanks for your lessons, bright rolling waves; my heart tells me you will lead me to my dear brothers." On the foam-covered sea-weeds, lay eleven white swan feathers, which she gathered up and placed together. Drops of water lay upon them; whether they were dew-drops or tears no one could say. Lonely as it was on the sea-shore, she did not observe it, for the ever-moving sea showed more changes in a few hours than the most varying lake could produce during a whole year. If a black heavy cloud arose, it was as if the sea said, "I can look dark and angry too;" and then the wind blew, and the waves turned to white foam as they rolled. When the wind slept, and the clouds glowed with the red sunlight, then the sea looked like a rose leaf. But however quietly its white glassy surface rested, there was still a motion on the shore, as its waves rose and fell like the breast of a sleeping child. When the sun was about to set, Eliza saw eleven white swans with golden crowns on their heads, flying towards the land, one behind the other, like a long white ribbon. Then Eliza went down the slope from the shore, and hid herself behind the bushes. The swans alighted quite close to her and flapped their great white wings. As soon as the sun had disappeared under the water, the feathers of the swans fell off, and eleven beautiful princes, Eliza's brothers, stood near her. She uttered a loud cry, for, although they were very much changed, she knew them immediately. She sprang into their arms, and called them each by name. Then, how happy the princes were at meeting their little sister again, for they recognized her, although she had grown so tall and beautiful. They laughed, and they wept, and very soon understood how wickedly their mother had acted to them all. "We brothers," said the eldest, "fly about as wild swans, so long as the sun is in the sky; but as soon as it sinks behind the hills, we recover our human shape. Therefore must we always be near a resting place for our feet before sunset; for if we should be flying towards the clouds at the time we recovered our natural shape as men, we should sink deep into the sea. We do not dwell here, but in a land just as fair, that lies beyond the ocean, which we have to cross for a long distance; there is no island in our passage upon which we could pass, the night; nothing but a little rock rising out of the sea, upon which we can scarcely stand with safety, even closely crowded together. If the sea is rough, the foam dashes over us, yet we thank God even for this rock; we have passed whole nights upon it, or we should never have reached our beloved fatherland, for our flight across the sea occupies two of the longest days in the year. We have permission to visit our home once in every year, and to remain eleven days, during which we fly across the forest to look once more at the palace where our father dwells, and where we were born, and at the church, where our mother lies buried. Here it seems as if the very trees and bushes were related to us. The wild horses leap over the plains as we have seen them in our childhood. The charcoal burners sing the old songs, to which we have danced as children. This is our fatherland, to which we are drawn by loving ties; and here we have found you, our dear little sister. Two days longer we can remain here, and then must we fly away to a beautiful land which is not our home; and how can we take you with us? We have neither ship nor boat."

"How can I break this spell?" said their sister. And then she talked about it nearly the whole night, only slumbering for a few hours. Eliza was awakened by the rustling of the swans' wings as they soared above. Her brothers were again changed to swans, and they flew in circles wider and wider, till they were far away; but one of them, the youngest swan, remained behind, and laid his head in his sister's lap, while she stroked his wings; and they remained together the whole day. Towards evening, the rest came back, and as the sun went down they resumed their natural forms. "To-morrow," said one, "we shall fly away, not to return again till a whole year has passed. But we cannot leave you here. Have you courage to go with us? My arm is strong enough to carry you through the wood; and will not all our wings be strong enough to fly with you over the sea?"

"Yes, take me with you," said Eliza. Then they spent the whole night in weaving a net with the pliant willow and rushes. It was very large and strong. Eliza laid herself down on the net, and when the sun rose, and her brothers again became wild swans, they took up the net with their beaks, and flew up to the clouds with their dear sister, who still slept. The sunbeams fell on her face, therefore one of the swans soared over her head, so that his broad wings might shade her. They were far from the land when Eliza woke. She thought she must still be dreaming, it seemed so strange to her to feel herself being carried so high in the air over the sea. By her side lay a branch full of beautiful ripe berries, and a bundle of sweet roots; the youngest of her brothers had gathered them for her, and placed them by her side. She smiled her thanks to him; she knew it was the same who had hovered over her to shade her with his wings. They were now so high, that a large ship beneath them looked like a white sea-gull skimming the waves. A great cloud floating behind them appeared like a vast mountain, and upon it Eliza saw her own shadow and those of the eleven swans, looking gigantic in size. Altogether it formed a more beautiful picture than she had ever seen; but as the sun rose higher, and the clouds were left behind, the shadowy picture vanished away. Onward the whole day they flew through the air like a winged arrow, yet more slowly than usual, for they had their sister to carry. The weather seemed inclined to be stormy, and Eliza watched the sinking sun with great anxiety, for the little rock in the ocean was not yet in sight. It appeared to her as if the swans were making great efforts with their wings. Alas! she was the cause of their not advancing more quickly. When the sun set, they would change to men, fall into the sea and be drowned. Then she offered a prayer from her inmost heart, but still no appearance of the rock. Dark clouds came nearer, the gusts of wind told of a coming storm, while from a thick, heavy mass of clouds the lightning burst forth flash after flash. The sun had reached the edge of the sea, when the swans darted down so swiftly, that Eliza's head trembled; she believed they were falling, but they again soared onward. Presently she caught sight of the rock just below them, and by this time the sun was half hidden by the waves. The rock did not appear larger than a seal's head thrust out of the water. They sunk so rapidly, that at the moment their feet touched the rock, it shone only like a star, and at last disappeared like the last spark in a piece of burnt paper. Then she saw her brothers standing closely round her with their arms linked together. There was but just room enough for them, and not the smallest space to spare. The sea dashed against the rock, and covered them with spray. The heavens were lighted up with continual flashes, and peal after peal of thunder rolled. But the sister and brothers sat holding each other's hands, and singing hymns, from which they gained hope and courage. In the early dawn the air became calm and still, and at sunrise the swans flew away from the rock with Eliza. The sea was still rough, and from their high position in the air, the white foam on the dark green waves looked like millions of swans swimming on the water. As the sun rose higher, Eliza saw before her, floating on the air, a range of mountains, with shining masses of ice on their summits. In the centre, rose a castle apparently a mile long, with rows of columns, rising one above another, while, around it, palm-trees waved and flowers bloomed as large as mill wheels. She asked if this was the land to which they were hastening. The swans shook their heads, for what she beheld were the beautiful ever-changing cloud palaces of the "Fata Morgana," into which no mortal can enter. Eliza was still gazing at the scene, when mountains, forests, and castles melted away, and twenty stately churches rose in their stead, with high towers and pointed gothic windows. Eliza even fancied she could hear the tones of the organ, but it was the music of the murmuring sea which she heard. As they drew nearer to the churches, they also changed into a fleet of ships, which seemed to be sailing beneath her; but as she looked again, she found it was only a sea mist gliding over the ocean. So there continued to pass before her eyes a constant change of scene, till at last she saw the real land to which they were bound, with its blue mountains, its cedar forests, and its cities and palaces. Long before the sun went down, she sat on a rock, in front of a large cave, on the floor of which the over-grown yet delicate green creeping plants looked like an embroidered carpet. "Now we shall expect to hear what you dream of to-night," said the youngest brother, as he showed his sister her bedroom.

"Heaven grant that I may dream how to save you," she replied. And this thought took such hold upon her mind that she prayed earnestly to God for help, and even in her sleep she continued to pray. Then it appeared to her as if she were flying high in the air, towards the cloudy palace of the "Fata Morgana," and a fairy came out to meet her, radiant and beautiful in appearance, and yet very much like the old woman who had given her berries in the wood, and who had told her of the swans with golden crowns on their heads. "Your brothers can be released," said she, "if you have only courage and perseverance. True, water is softer than your own delicate hands, and yet it polishes stones into shapes; it feels no pain as your fingers would feel, it has no soul, and cannot suffer such agony and torment as you will have to endure. Do you see the stinging nettle which I hold in my hand? Quantities of the same sort grow round the cave in which you sleep, but none will be of any use to you unless they grow upon the graves in a churchyard. These you must gather even while they burn blisters on your hands. Break them to pieces with your hands and feet, and they will become flax, from which you must spin and weave eleven coats with long sleeves; if these are then thrown over the eleven swans, the spell will be broken. But remember, that from the moment you commence your task until it is finished, even should it occupy years of your life, you must not speak. The first word you utter will pierce through the hearts of your brothers like a deadly dagger. Their lives hang upon your tongue. Remember all I have told you." And as she finished speaking, she touched her hand lightly with the nettle, and a pain, as of burning fire, awoke Eliza.

It was broad daylight, and close by where she had been sleeping lay a nettle like the one she had seen in her dream. She fell on her knees and offered her thanks to God. Then she went forth from the cave to begin her work with her delicate hands. She groped in amongst the ugly nettles, which burnt great blisters on her hands and arms, but she determined to bear it gladly if she could only release her dear brothers. So she bruised the nettles with her bare feet and spun the flax. At sunset her brothers returned and were very much frightened when they found her dumb. They believed it to be some new sorcery of their wicked step-mother. But when they saw her hands they understood what she was doing on their behalf, and the youngest brother wept, and where his tears fell the pain ceased, and the burning blisters vanished. She kept to her work all night, for she could not rest till she had released her dear brothers. During the whole of the following day, while her brothers were absent, she sat in solitude, but never before had the time flown so quickly. One coat was already finished and she had begun the second, when she heard the huntsman's horn, and was struck with fear. The sound came nearer and nearer, she heard the dogs barking, and fled with terror into the cave. She hastily bound together the nettles she had gathered into a bundle and sat upon them. Immediately a great dog came bounding towards her out of the ravine, and then another and another; they barked loudly, ran back, and then came again. In a very few minutes all the huntsmen stood before the cave, and the handsomest of them was the king of the country. He advanced towards her, for he had never seen a more beautiful maiden.

"How did you come here, my sweet child?" he asked. But Eliza shook her head. She dared not speak, at the cost of her brothers' lives. And she hid her hands under her apron, so that the king might not see how she must be suffering.

"Come with me," he said; "here you cannot remain. If you are as good as you are beautiful, I will dress you in silk and velvet, I will place a golden crown upon your head, and you shall dwell, and rule, and make your home in my richest castle." And then he lifted her on his horse. She wept and wrung her hands, but the king said, "I wish only for your happiness. A time will come when you will thank me for this." And then he galloped away over the mountains, holding her before him on this horse, and the hunters followed behind them. As the sun went down, they approached a fair royal city, with churches, and cupolas. On arriving at the castle the king led her into marble halls, where large fountains played, and where the walls and the ceilings were covered with rich paintings. But she had no eyes for all these glorious sights, she could only mourn and weep. Patiently she allowed the women to array her in royal robes, to weave pearls in her hair, and draw soft gloves over her blistered fingers. As she stood before them in all her rich dress, she looked so dazzlingly beautiful that the court bowed low in her presence. Then the king declared his intention of making her his bride, but the archbishop shook his head, and whispered that the fair young maiden was only a witch who had blinded the king's eyes and bewitched his heart. But the king would not listen to this; he ordered the music to sound, the daintiest dishes to be served, and the loveliest maidens to dance. After-wards he led her through fragrant gardens and lofty halls, but not a smile appeared on her lips or sparkled in her eyes. She looked the very picture of grief. Then the king opened the door of a little chamber in which she was to sleep; it was adorned with rich green tapestry, and resembled the cave in which he had found her. On the floor lay the bundle of flax which she had spun from the nettles, and under the ceiling hung the coat she had made. These things had been brought away from the cave as curiosities by one of the huntsmen.

"Here you can dream yourself back again in the old home in the cave," said the king; "here is the work with which you employed yourself. It will amuse you now in the midst of all this splendor to think of that time."

When Eliza saw all these things which lay so near her heart, a smile played around her mouth, and the crimson blood rushed to her cheeks. She thought of her brothers, and their release made her so joyful that she kissed the king's hand. Then he pressed her to his heart. Very soon the joyous church bells announced the marriage feast, and that the beautiful dumb girl out of the wood was to be made the queen of the country. Then the archbishop whispered wicked words in the king's ear, but they did not sink into his heart. The marriage was still to take place, and the archbishop himself had to place the crown on the bride's head; in his wicked spite, he pressed the narrow circlet so tightly on her forehead that it caused her pain. But a heavier weight encircled her heart – sorrow for her brothers. She felt not bodily pain. Her mouth was closed; a single word would cost the lives of her brothers. But she loved the kind, handsome king, who did everything to make her happy more and more each day; she loved him with all her heart, and her eyes beamed with the love she dared not speak. Oh! if she had only been able to confide in him and tell him of her grief. But dumb she must remain till her task was finished. Therefore at night she crept away into her little chamber, which had been decked out to look like the cave, and quickly wove one coat after another. But when she began the seventh she found she had no more flax. She knew that the nettles she wanted to use grew in the churchyard, and that she must pluck them herself. How should she get out there? "Oh, what is the pain in my fingers to the torment which my heart endures?" said she. "I must venture, I shall not be denied help from heaven." Then with a trembling heart, as if she were about to perform a wicked deed, she crept into the garden in the broad moonlight, and passed through the narrow walks and the deserted streets, till she reached the churchyard. Then she saw on one of the broad tombstones a group of ghouls. These hideous creatures took off their rags, as if they intended to bathe, and then clawing open the fresh graves with their long, skinny fingers, pulled out the dead bodies and ate the flesh! Eliza had to pass close by them, and they fixed their wicked glances upon her, but she prayed silently, gathered the burning nettles, and carried them home with her to the castle. One person only had seen her, and that was the archbishop – he was awake while everybody was asleep. Now he thought his opinion was evidently correct. All was not right with the queen. She was a witch, and had bewitched the king and all the people. Secretly he told the king what he had seen and what he feared, and as the hard words came from his tongue, the carved images of the saints shook their heads as if they would say. "It is not so. Eliza is innocent."

But the archbishop interpreted it in another way; he believed that they witnessed against her, and were shaking their heads at her wickedness. Two large tears rolled down the king's cheeks, and he went home with doubt in his heart, and at night he pretended to sleep, but there came no real sleep to his eyes, for he saw Eliza get up every night and disappear in her own chamber. From day to day his brow became darker, and Eliza saw it and did not understand the reason, but it alarmed her and made her heart tremble for her brothers. Her hot tears glittered like pearls on the regal velvet and diamonds, while all who saw her were wishing they could be queens. In the mean time she had almost finished her task; only one coat of mail was wanting, but she had no flax left, and not a single nettle. Once more only, and for the last time, must she venture to the churchyard and pluck a few handfuls. She thought with terror of the solitary walk, and of the horrible ghouls, but her will was firm, as well as her trust in Providence. Eliza went, and the king and the archbishop followed her. They saw her vanish through the wicket gate into the churchyard, and when they came nearer they saw the ghouls sitting on the tombstone, as Eliza had seen them, and the king turned away his head, for he thought she was with them – she whose head had rested on his breast that very evening. "The people must condemn her," said he, and she was very quickly condemned by every one to suffer death by fire. Away from the gorgeous regal halls was she led to a dark, dreary cell, where the wind whistled through the iron bars. Instead of the velvet and silk dresses, they gave her the coats of mail which she had woven to cover her, and the bundle of nettles for a pillow; but nothing they could give her would have pleased her more. She continued her task with joy, and prayed for help, while the street-boys sang jeering songs about her, and not a soul comforted her with a kind word. Towards evening, she heard at the grating the flutter of a swan's wing, it was her youngest brother – he had found his sister, and she sobbed for joy, although she knew that very likely this would be the last night she would have to live. But still she could hope, for her task was almost finished, and her brothers were come. Then the archbishop arrived, to be with her during her last hours, as he had promised the king. But she shook her head, and begged him, by looks and gestures, not to stay; for in this night she knew she must finish her task, otherwise all her pain and tears and sleepless nights would have been suffered in vain. The archbishop withdrew, uttering bitter words against her; but poor Eliza knew that she was innocent, and diligently continued her work.

The little mice ran about the floor, they dragged the nettles to her feet, to help as well as they could; and the thrush sat outside the grating of the window, and sang to her the whole night long, as sweetly as possible, to keep up her spirits.

It was still twilight, and at least an hour before sunrise, when the eleven brothers stood at the castle gate, and demanded to be brought before the king. They were told it could not be, it was yet almost night, and as the king slept they dared not disturb him.

They threatened, they entreated. Then the guard appeared, and even the king himself, inquiring what all the noise meant. At this moment the sun rose. The eleven brothers were seen no more, but eleven wild swans flew away over the castle.

And now all the people came streaming forth from the gates of the city, to see the witch burnt. An old horse drew the cart on which she sat. They had dressed her in a garment of coarse sackcloth. Her lovely hair hung loose on her shoulders, her cheeks were deadly pale, her lips moved silently, while her fingers still worked at the green flax. Even on the way to death, she would not give up her task. The ten coats of mail lay at her feet, she was working hard at the eleventh, while the mob jeered her and said, "See the witch, how she mutters! She has no hymn-book in her hand. She sits there with her ugly sorcery. Let us tear it in a thousand pieces."

And then they pressed towards her, and would have destroyed the coats of mail, but at the same moment eleven wild swans flew over her, and alighted on the cart. Then they flapped their large wings, and the crowd drew on one side in alarm.

"It is a sign from heaven that she is innocent," whispered many of them; but they ventured not to say it aloud.

As the executioner seized her by the hand, to lift her out of the cart, she hastily threw the eleven coats of mail over the swans, and they immediately became eleven handsome princes; but the youngest had a swan's wing, instead of an arm; for she had not been able to finish the last sleeve of the coat.

"Now I may speak," she exclaimed. "I am innocent."

Then the people, who saw what happened, bowed to her, as before a saint; but she sank lifeless in her brothers' arms, overcome with suspense, anguish, and pain.

"Yes, she is innocent," said the eldest brother; and then he related all that had taken place; and while he spoke there rose in the air a fragrance as from millions of roses. Every piece of faggot in the pile had taken root, and threw out branches, and appeared a thick hedge, large and high, covered with roses; while above all bloomed a white and shining flower, that glittered like a star. This flower the king plucked, and placed in Eliza's bosom, when she awoke from her swoon, with peace and happiness in her heart. And all the church bells rang of themselves, and the birds came in great troops. And a marriage procession returned to the castle, such as no king had ever before seen.

The Tinder-Box

A SOLDIER CAME marching along the high road: "Left, right – left, right." He had his knapsack on his back, and a sword at his side; he had been to the wars, and was now returning home.

As he walked on, he met a very frightful-looking old witch in the road. Her under-lip hung quite down on her breast, and she stopped and said, "Good evening, soldier; you have a very fine sword, and a large knapsack, and you are a real soldier; so you shall have as much money as ever you like."

"Thank you, old witch," said the soldier.

"Do you see that large tree," said the witch, pointing to a tree which stood beside them. "Well, it is quite hollow inside, and you must climb to the top, when you will see a hole, through which you can let yourself down into the tree to a great depth. I will tie a rope round your body, so that I can pull you up again when you call out to me."

"But what am I to do, down there in the tree?" asked the soldier.

"Get money," she replied; "for you must know that when you reach the ground under the tree, you will find yourself in a large hall, lighted up by three hundred lamps; you will then see three doors, which can be easily opened, for the keys are in all the locks. On entering the first of the chambers, to which these doors lead, you will see a large chest, standing in the middle of the floor, and upon it a dog seated, with a pair of eyes as large as teacups. But you need not be at all afraid of him; I will give you my blue checked apron, which you must spread upon the floor, and then boldly seize hold of the dog, and place him upon it. You can then open the chest, and take from it as many pence as you please, they are only copper pence; but if you would rather have silver money, you must go into the second chamber. Here you will find another dog, with eyes as big as mill-wheels; but do not let that trouble you. Place him upon my apron, and then take what money you please. If, however, you like gold best, enter the third chamber, where there is another chest full of it. The dog who sits on this chest is very dreadful; his eyes are as big as a tower, but do not mind him. If he also is placed upon my apron, he cannot hurt you, and you may take from the chest what gold you will."

"This is not a bad story," said the soldier; "but what am I to give you, you old witch? for, of course, you do not mean to tell me all this for nothing."

"No," said the witch; "but I do not ask for a single penny. Only promise to bring me an old tinder-box, which my grandmother left behind the last time she went down there."

"Very well; I promise. Now tie the rope round my body."

"Here it is," replied the witch; "and here is my blue checked apron."

As soon as the rope was tied, the soldier climbed up the tree, and let himself down through the hollow to the ground beneath; and here he found, as the witch had told him, a large hall, in which many hundred lamps were all burning. Then he opened the first door. "Ah!" there sat the dog, with the eyes as large as teacups, staring at him.

"You're a pretty fellow," said the soldier, seizing him, and placing him on the witch's apron, while he filled his pockets from the chest with as many pieces as they would hold.

Then he closed the lid, seated the dog upon it again, and walked into another chamber, And, sure enough, there sat the dog with eyes as big as mill-wheels.

"You had better not look at me in that way," said the soldier; "you will make your eyes water;" and then he seated him also upon the apron, and opened the chest. But when he saw what a quantity of silver money it contained, he very quickly threw away all the coppers he had taken, and filled his pockets and his knapsack with nothing but silver.

Then he went into the third room, and there the dog was really hideous; his eyes were, truly, as big as towers, and they turned round and round in his head like wheels.

"Good morning," said the soldier, touching his cap, for he had never seen such a dog in his life. But after looking at him more closely, he thought he had been civil enough, so he placed him on the floor, and opened the chest. Good gracious, what a quantity of gold there was! enough to buy all the sugar-sticks of the sweet-stuff women; all the tin soldiers, whips, and rocking-horses in the world, or even the whole town itself There was, indeed, an immense quantity. So the soldier now threw away all the silver money he had taken, and filled his pockets and his knapsack with gold instead; and not only his pockets and his knapsack, but even his cap and boots, so that he could scarcely walk.

He was really rich now; so he replaced the dog on the chest, closed the door, and called up through the tree, "Now pull me out, you old witch."

"Have you got the tinder-box?" asked the witch.

"No; I declare I quite forgot it." So he went back and fetched the tinderbox, and then the witch drew him up out of the tree, and he stood again in the high road, with his pockets, his knapsack, his cap, and his boots full of gold.

"What are you going to do with the tinder-box?" asked the soldier.

"That is nothing to you," replied the witch; "you have the money, now give me the tinder-box."

"I tell you what," said the soldier, "if you don't tell me what you are going to do with it, I will draw my sword and cut off your head."

"No," said the witch.

The soldier immediately cut off her head, and there she lay on the ground. Then he tied up all his money in her apron. and slung it on his back like a bundle, put the tinderbox in his pocket, and walked off to the nearest town. It was a very nice town, and he put up at the best inn, and ordered a dinner of all his favorite dishes, for now he was rich and had plenty of money.

The servant, who cleaned his boots, thought they certainly were a shabby pair to be worn by such a rich gentleman, for he had not yet bought any new ones. The next day, however, he procured some good clothes and proper boots, so that our soldier soon became known as a fine gentleman, and the people visited him, and told him all the wonders that were to be seen in the town, and of the king's beautiful daughter, the princess.

"Where can I see her?" asked the soldier.

"She is not to be seen at all," they said; "she lives in a large copper castle, surrounded by walls and towers. No one but the king himself can pass in or out, for there has been a prophecy that she will marry a common soldier, and the king cannot bear to think of such a marriage."

"I should like very much to see her," thought the soldier; but he could not obtain permission to do so. However, he passed a very pleasant time; went to the theatre, drove in the king's garden, and gave a great deal of money to the poor, which was very good of him; he remembered what it had been in olden times to be without a shilling. Now he was rich, had fine clothes, and many friends, who all declared he was a fine fellow and a real gentleman, and all this gratified him exceedingly. But his money would not last forever; and as he spent and gave away a great deal daily, and received none, he found himself at last with only two shillings left. So he was obliged to leave his elegant rooms, and live in a little garret under the roof, where he had to clean his own boots, and even mend them with a large needle. None of his friends came to see him, there were too many stairs to mount up. One dark evening, he had not even a penny to buy a candle; then all at once he remembered that there was a piece of candle stuck in the tinder-box, which he had brought from the old tree, into which the witch had helped him.

He found the tinder-box, but no sooner had he struck a few sparks from the flint and steel, than the door flew open and the dog with eyes as big as teacups, whom he had seen while down in the tree, stood before him, and said, "What orders, master?"

"Hallo," said the soldier; "well this is a pleasant tinderbox, if it brings me all I wish for."

"Bring me some money," said he to the dog.

He was gone in a moment, and presently returned, carrying a large bag of coppers in his month. The soldier very soon discovered after this the value of the tinder-box. If he struck the flint once, the dog who sat on the chest of copper money made his appearance; if twice, the dog came from the chest of silver; and if three times, the dog with eyes like towers, who watched over the gold. The soldier had now plenty of money; he returned to his elegant rooms, and reappeared in his fine clothes, so that his friends knew him again directly, and made as much of him as before.

After a while he began to think it was very strange that no one could get a look at the princess. "Every one says she is very beautiful," thought he to himself; "but what is the use of that if she is to be shut up in a copper castle surrounded by so many towers. Can I by any means get to see her. Stop! where is my tinder-box?" Then he struck a light, and in a moment the dog, with eyes as big as teacups, stood before him.

"It is midnight," said the soldier, "yet I should very much like to see the princess, if only for a moment."

The dog disappeared instantly, and before the soldier could even look round, he returned with the princess. She was lying on the dog's back asleep, and looked so lovely, that every one who saw her would know she was a real princess. The soldier could not help kissing her, true soldier as he was. Then the dog ran back with the princess; but in the morning, while at breakfast with the king and queen, she told them what a singular dream she had had during the night, of a dog and a soldier, that she had ridden on the dog's back, and been kissed by the soldier.

"That is a very pretty story, indeed," said the queen. So the next night one of the old ladies of the court was set to watch by the princess's bed, to discover whether it really was a dream, or what else it might be.

The soldier longed very much to see the princess once more, so he sent for the dog again in the night to fetch her, and to run with her as fast as ever he could. But the old lady put on water boots, and ran after him as quickly as he did, and found that he carried the princess into a large house. She thought it would help her to remember the place if she made a large cross on the door with a piece of chalk. Then she went home to bed, and the dog presently returned with the princess. But when he saw that a cross had been made on the door of the house, where the soldier lived, he took another piece of chalk and made crosses on all the doors in the town, so that the lady-in-waiting might not be able to find out the right door.

Early the next morning the king and queen accompanied the lady and all the officers of the household, to see where the princess had been.

"Here it is," said the king, when they came to the first door with a cross on it.

"No, my dear husband, it must be that one," said the queen, pointing to a second door having a cross also.

"And here is one, and there is another!" they all exclaimed; for there were crosses on all the doors in every direction.

So they felt it would be useless to search any farther. But the queen was a very clever woman; she could do a great deal more than merely ride in a carriage. She took her large gold scissors, cut a piece of silk into squares, and made a neat little bag. This bag she filled with buckwheat flour, and tied it round the princess's neck; and then she cut a small hole in the bag, so that the flour might be scattered on the ground as the princess went along. During the night, the dog came again and carried the princess on his back, and ran with her to the soldier, who loved her very much, and wished that he had been a prince, so that he might have her for a wife. The dog did not observe how the flour ran out of the bag all the way from the castle wall to the soldier's house, and even up to the window, where he had climbed with the princess. Therefore in the morning the king and queen found out where their daughter had been, and the soldier was taken up and put in prison. Oh, how dark and disagreeable it was as he sat there, and the people said to him, "To-morrow you will be hanged." It was not very pleasant news, and besides, he had left the tinder-box at the inn. In the morning he could see through the iron grating of the little window how the people were hastening out of the town to see him hanged; he heard the drums beating, and saw the soldiers marching. Every one ran out to look at them. and a shoemaker's boy, with a leather apron and slippers on, galloped by so fast, that one of his slippers flew off and struck against the wall where the soldier sat looking through the iron grating. "Hallo, you shoemaker's boy, you need not be in such a hurry," cried the soldier to him. "There will be nothing to see till I come; but if you will run to the house where I have been living, and bring me my tinder-box, you shall have four shillings, but you must put your best foot foremost."

The shoemaker's boy liked the idea of getting the four shillings, so he ran very fast and fetched the tinder-box, and gave it to the soldier. And now we shall see what happened. Outside the town a large gibbet had been erected, round which stood the soldiers and several thousands of people. The king and the queen sat on splendid thrones opposite to the judges and the whole council. The soldier already stood on the ladder; but as they were about to place the rope around his neck, he said that an innocent request was often granted to a poor criminal before he suffered death. He wished very much to smoke a pipe, as it would be the last pipe he should ever smoke in the world. The king could not refuse this request, so the soldier took his tinder-box, and struck fire, once, twice, thrice, – and there in a moment stood all the dogs; – the one with eyes as big as teacups, the one with eyes as large as mill-wheels, and the third, whose eyes were like towers. "Help me now, that I may not be hanged," cried the soldier.

And the dogs fell upon the judges and all the councillors; seized one by the legs, and another by the nose, and tossed them many feet high in the air, so that they fell down and were dashed to pieces.

"I will not be touched," said the king. But the largest dog seized him, as well as the queen, and threw them after the others. Then the soldiers and all the people were afraid, and cried, "Good soldier, you shall be our king, and you shall marry the beautiful princess."

So they placed the soldier in the king's carriage, and the three dogs ran on in front and cried "Hurrah!" and the little boys whistled through their fingers, and the soldiers presented arms. The princess came out of the copper castle, and became queen, which was very pleasing to her. The wedding festivities lasted a whole week, and the dogs sat at the table, and stared with all their eyes.

A Story from the Sand-Hills

THIS STORY IS from the sand-dunes or sand-hills of Jutland, but it does not begin there in the North, but far away in the South, in Spain. The wide sea is the highroad from nation to nation; journey in thought, then, to sunny Spain. It is warm and beautiful there; the fiery pomegranate flowers peep from among dark laurels; a cool refreshing breeze from the mountains blows over the orange gardens, over the Moorish halls with their golden cupolas and colored walls. Children go through the streets in procession with candles and waving banners, and the sky, lofty and clear with its glittering stars, rises above them. Sounds of singing and castanets can be heard, and youths and maidens dance upon the flowering acacia trees, while even the beggar sits upon a block of marble, refreshing himself with a juicy melon, and dreamily enjoying life. It all seems like a beautiful dream.

Here dwelt a newly married couple who completely gave themselves up to the charm of life; indeed they possessed every good thing they could desire – health and happiness, riches and honour.

"We are as happy as human beings can be," said the young couple from the depths of their hearts. They had indeed only one step higher to mount on the ladder of happiness – they hoped that God would give them a child, a son like them in form and spirit. The happy little one was to be welcomed with rejoicing, to be cared for with love and tenderness, and enjoy every advantage of wealth and luxury that a rich and influential family can give. So the days went by like a joyous festival.

"Life is a gracious gift from God, almost too great a gift for us to appreciate!" said the young wife. "Yet they say that fulness of joy for ever and ever can only be found in the future life. I cannot realise it!"

"The thought arises, perhaps, from the arrogance of men," said the husband. "It seems a great pride to believe that we shall live for ever, that we shall be as gods! Were not these the words of the serpent, the father of lies?"

"Surely you do not doubt the existence of a future life?" exclaimed the young wife. It seemed as if one of the first shadows passed over her sunny thoughts.

"Faith realises it, and the priests tell us so," replied her husband; "but amid all my happiness I feel that it is arrogant to demand a continuation of it – another life after this. Has not so much been given us in this world that we ought to be, we must be, contented with it?"

"Yes, it has been given to us," said the young wife, "but this life is nothing more than one long scene of trial and hardship to many thousands. How many have been cast into this world only to endure poverty, shame, illness, and misfortune? If there were no future life, everything here would be too unequally divided, and God would not be the personification of justice."

"The beggar there," said her husband, "has joys of his own which seem to him great, and cause him as much pleasure as a king would find in the magnificence of his palace. And then do you not think that the beast of burden, which suffers blows and hunger, and works itself to death, suffers just as much from its miserable fate? The dumb creature might demand a future life also, and declare the law unjust that excludes it from the advantages of the higher creation."

"Christ said: 'In my father's house are many mansions,'" she answered. "Heaven is as boundless as the love of our Creator; the dumb animal is also His creature, and I firmly believe that no life will be lost, but each will receive as much happiness as he can enjoy, which will be sufficient for him."

"This world is sufficient for me," said the husband, throwing his arm round his beautiful, sweet-tempered wife. He sat by her side on the open balcony, smoking a cigarette in the cool air, which was loaded with the sweet scent of carnations and orange blossoms. Sounds of music and the clatter of castanets came from the road beneath, the stars shone above then, and two eyes full of affection – those of his wife – looked upon him with the expression of undying love. "Such a moment," he said, "makes it worth while to be born, to die, and to be annihilated!" He smiled – the young wife raised her hand in gentle reproof, and the shadow passed away from her mind, and they were happy – quite happy.

Everything seemed to work together for their good. They advanced in honour, in prosperity, and in happiness. A change came certainly, but it was only a change of place and not of circumstances.

The young man was sent by his Sovereign as ambassador to the Russian Court. This was an office of high dignity, but his birth and his acquirements entitled him to the honour. He possessed a large fortune, and his wife had brought him wealth equal to his own, for she was the daughter of a rich and respected merchant. One of this merchant's largest and finest ships was to be sent that year to Stockholm, and it was arranged that the dear young couple, the daughter and the son-in-law, should travel in it to St. Petersburg. All the arrangements on board were princely and silk and luxury on every side.

In an old war song, called "The King of England's Son," it says:

> *"Farewell, he said, and sailed away.*
> *And many recollect that day.*
> *The ropes were of silk, the anchor of gold,*
> *And everywhere riches and wealth untold."*

These words would aptly describe the vessel from Spain, for here was the same luxury, and the same parting thought naturally arose:

> *"God grant that we once more may meet*
> *In sweet unclouded peace and joy."*

There was a favourable wind blowing as they left the Spanish coast, and it would be but a short journey, for they hoped to reach their destination in a few weeks; but when they came out upon the wide ocean the wind dropped, the sea became smooth and shining, and the stars shone brightly. Many festive evenings were spent on board. At last the travellers began to wish for wind, for a favourable breeze; but their wish was useless – not a breath of air stirred, or if it did arise it was contrary. Weeks passed by in this way, two whole months, and then at length a fair wind blew from the south-west. The ship sailed on the high seas between Scotland and Jutland; then the wind increased, just as it did in the old song of "The King of England's Son."

"'Mid storm and wind, and pelting hail,
Their efforts were of no avail.
The golden anchor forth they threw;
Towards Denmark the west wind blew."

This all happened a long time ago; King Christian VII, who sat on the Danish throne, was still a young man. Much has happened since then, much has altered or been changed. Sea and moorland have been turned into green meadows, stretches of heather have become arable land, and in the shelter of the peasant's cottages, apple-trees and rose-bushes grow, though they certainly require much care, as the sharp west wind blows upon them. In West Jutland one may go back in thought to old times, farther back than the days when Christian VII ruled. The purple heather still extends for miles, with its barrows and aerial spectacles, intersected with sandy uneven roads, just as it did then; towards the west, where broad streams run into the bays, are marshes and meadows encircled by lofty, sandy hills, which, like a chain of Alps, raise their pointed summits near the sea; they are only broken by high ridges of clay, from which the sea, year by year, bites out great mouthfuls, so that the overhanging banks fall down as if by the shock of an earthquake. Thus it is there today and thus it was long ago, when the happy pair were sailing in the beautiful ship.

It was a Sunday, towards the end of September; the sun was shining, and the chiming of the church bells in the Bay of Nissum was carried along by the breeze like a chain of sounds. The churches there are almost entirely built of hewn blocks of stone, each like a piece of rock. The North Sea might foam over them and they would not be disturbed. Nearly all of them are without steeples, and the bells are hung outside between two beams. The service was over, and the congregation passed out into the churchyard, where not a tree or bush was to be seen; no flowers were planted there, and they had not placed a single wreath upon any of the graves. It is just the same now. Rough mounds show where the dead have been buried, and rank grass, tossed by the wind, grows thickly over the whole churchyard; here and there a grave has a sort of monument, a block of half-decayed wood, rudely cut in the shape of a coffin; the blocks are brought from the forest of West Jutland, but the forest is the sea itself, and the inhabitants find beams, and planks, and fragments which the waves have cast upon the beach. One of these blocks had been placed by loving hands on a child's grave, and one of the women who had come out of the church walked up to it; she stood there, her eyes resting on the weather-beaten memorial, and a few moments afterwards her husband joined her. They were both silent, but he took her hand, and they walked together across the purple heath, over moor and meadow towards the sandhills. For a long time they went on without speaking.

"It was a good sermon to-day," the man said at last. "If we had not God to trust in, we should have nothing."

"Yes," replied the woman, "He sends joy and sorrow, and He has a right to send them. To-morrow our little son would have been five years old if we had been permitted to keep him."

"It is no use fretting, wife," said the man. "The boy is well provided for. He is where we hope and pray to go to."

They said nothing more, but went out towards their houses among the sand-hills. All at once, in front of one of the houses where the sea grass did not keep the sand down with its twining roots, what seemed to be a column of smoke rose up. A gust of wind rushed between the hills, hurling the particles of sand high into the air; another gust, and the strings of fish hung up to dry flapped and beat violently against the walls of the cottage; then everything was quiet once more, and the sun shone with renewed heat.

The man and his wife went into the cottage. They had soon taken off their Sunday clothes and come out again, hurrying over the dunes which stood there like great waves of sand suddenly arrested in their course, while the sandweeds and dune grass with its bluish stalks spread a changing color over them. A few neighbors also came out, and helped each other to draw the boats higher up on the beach. The wind now blew more keenly, it was chilly and cold, and when they went back over the sand-hills, sand and little sharp stones blew into their faces. The waves rose high, crested with white foam, and the wind cut off their crests, scattering the foam far and wide.

Evening came; there was a swelling roar in the air, a wailing or moaning like the voices of despairing spirits, that sounded above the thunder of the waves. The fisherman's little cottage was on the very margin, and the sand rattled against the window panes; every now and then a violent gust of wind shook the house to its foundation. It was dark, but about midnight the moon would rise. Later on the air became clearer, but the storm swept over the perturbed sea with undiminished fury; the fisher folks had long since gone to bed, but in such weather there was no chance of closing an eye. Presently there was a tapping at the window; the door was opened, and a voice said:

"There's a large ship stranded on the farthest reef."

In a moment the fisher people sprung from their beds and hastily dressed themselves. The moon had risen, and it was light enough to make the surrounding objects visible to those who could open their eyes in the blinding clouds of sand; the violence of the wind was terrible, and it was only possible to pass among the sand-hills if one crept forward between the gusts; the salt spray flew up from the sea like down, and the ocean foamed like a roaring cataract towards the beach. Only a practised eye could discern the vessel out in the offing; she was a fine brig, and the waves now lifted her over the reef, three or four cables' length out of the usual channel. She drove towards the shore, struck on the second reef, and remained fixed.

It was impossible to render assistance; the sea rushed in upon the vessel, making a clean breach over her. Those on shore thought they heard cries for help from those on board, and could plainly distinguish the busy but useless efforts made by the stranded sailors. Now a wave came rolling onward. It fell with enormous force on the bowsprit, tearing it from the vessel, and the stern was lifted high above the water. Two people were seen to embrace and plunge together into the sea, and the next moment one of the largest waves that rolled towards the sand-hills threw a body on the beach. It was a woman; the sailors said that she was quite dead, but the women thought they saw signs of life in her, so the stranger was carried across the sand-hills to the fisherman's cottage. How beautiful and fair she was! She must be a great lady, they said.

They laid her upon the humble bed; there was not a yard of linen on it, only a woollen coverlet to keep the occupant warm.

Life returned to her, but she was delirious, and knew nothing of what had happened or where she was; and it was better so, for everything she loved and valued lay buried in the sea. The same thing happened to her ship as to the one spoken of in the song about "The King of England's Son."

> *"Alas! how terrible to see*
> *The gallant bark sink rapidly."*

Fragments of the wreck and pieces of wood were washed ashore; they were all that remained of the vessel. The wind still blew violently on the coast.

For a few moments the strange lady seemed to rest; but she awoke in pain, and uttered cries of anguish and fear. She opened her wonderfully beautiful eyes, and spoke a few words, but nobody understood her. – And lo! as a reward for the sorrow and suffering she had undergone, she held in her arms a new-born babe. The child that was to have rested upon a magnificent couch, draped with silken curtains, in a luxurious home; it was to have been welcomed with joy to a life rich in all the good things of this world; and now Heaven had ordained that it should be born in this humble retreat, that it should not even receive a kiss from its mother, for when the fisherman's wife laid the child upon the mother's bosom, it rested on a heart that beat no more – she was dead.

The child that was to have been reared amid wealth and luxury was cast into the world, washed by the sea among the sand-hills to share the fate and hardships of the poor.

Here we are reminded again of the song about "The King of England's Son," for in it mention is made of the custom prevalent at the time, when knights and squires plundered those who had been saved from shipwreck. The ship had stranded some distance south of Nissum Bay, and the cruel, inhuman days, when, as we have just said, the inhabitants of Jutland treated the shipwrecked people so crudely were past, long ago. Affectionate sympathy and self-sacrifice for the unfortunate existed then, just as it does in our own time in many a bright example. The dying mother and the unfortunate child would have found kindness and help wherever they had been cast by the winds, but nowhere would it have been more sincere than in the cottage of the poor fisherman's wife, who had stood, only the day before, beside her child's grave, who would have been five years old that day if God had spared it to her.

No one knew who the dead stranger was, they could not even form a conjecture; the fragments of wreckage gave no clue to the matter.

No tidings reached Spain of the fate of the daughter and son-in-law. They did not arrive at their destination, and violent storms had raged during the past weeks. At last the verdict was given: "Foundered at sea – all lost." But in the fisherman's cottage among the sand-hills near Huusby, there lived a little scion of the rich Spanish family.

Where Heaven sends food for two, a third can manage to find a meal, and in the depth of the sea there is many a dish of fish for the hungry.

They called the boy Jørgen.

"It must certainly be a Jewish child, its skin is so dark," the people said.

"It might be an Italian or a Spaniard," remarked the clergyman.

But to the fisherman's wife these nations seemed all the same, and she consoled herself with the thought that the child was baptized as a Christian.

The boy throve; the noble blood in his veins was warm, and he became strong on his homely fare. He grew apace in the humble cottage, and the Danish dialect spoken by the West Jutes became his language. The pomegranate seed from Spain became a hardy plant on the coast of West Jutland. Thus may circumstances alter the course of a man's life! To this home he clung with deep-rooted affection; he was to experience cold and hunger, and the misfortunes and hardships that surround the poor; but he also tasted of their joys.

Childhood has bright days for every one, and the memory of them shines through the whole after-life. The boy had many sources of pleasure and enjoyment; the coast for miles and miles was full of playthings, for it was a mosaic of pebbles, some red as coral or yellow as amber, and others again white and rounded like birds' eggs and smoothed and prepared by the sea. Even the bleached fishes' skeletons, the water plants dried by the wind, and seaweed, white and shining long linen-like bands waving between the stones – all these seemed made to give pleasure and occupation for the boy's thoughts, and he had an intelligent mind; many great talents lay dormant in him. How readily he remembered stories and songs that he heard, and how dexterous he was with his fingers! With stones and mussel-shells he could put together pictures and ships with which one could decorate the room; and he could make wonderful things from a stick, his foster-mother said, although he was still so young and little. He had a sweet voice, and every melody seemed to flow naturally from his lips. And in his heart were hidden chords, which might have sounded far out into the world if he had been placed anywhere else than in the fisherman's hut by the North Sea.

One day another ship was wrecked on the coast, and among other things a chest filled with valuable flower bulbs was washed ashore. Some were put into saucepans and cooked, for they were thought to be fit to eat, and others lay and shrivelled in the sand – they did not accomplish their purpose, or unfold their magnificent colors. Would Jørgen fare better? The flower bulbs had soon played their part, but he had years of apprenticeship before him. Neither he nor his friends noticed in what a monotonous, uniform way one day followed another, for there was always plenty to do and see. The ocean itself was a great lesson-book, and it unfolded a new leaf each day of calm or storm – the crested wave or the smooth surface.

The visits to the church were festive occasions, but among the fisherman's house one was especially looked forward to; this was, in fact, the visit of the brother of Jørgen's foster-mother, the eel-breeder from Fjaltring, near Bovbjerg. He came twice a year in a cart, painted red with blue and white tulips upon it, and full of eels; it was covered and locked like a box, two dun oxen drew it, and Jørgen was allowed to guide them.

The eel-breeder was a witty fellow, a merry guest, and brought a measure of brandy with him. They all received a small glassful or a cupful if there were not enough glasses; even Jørgen had about a thimbleful, that he might digest the fat eel, as the eel-breeder said; he always told one story over and over again, and if his hearers laughed he would immediately repeat it to them. Jørgen while still a boy, and also when he was older, used phrases from the eel-breeder's story on various occasions, so it will be as well for us to listen to it. It runs thus:

"The eels went into the bay, and the young ones begged leave to go a little farther out. 'Don't go too far,' said their mother; 'the ugly eel-spearer might come and snap you all up.' But they went too far, and of eight daughters only three came back to the mother, and these wept and said, 'We only went a little way out, and the ugly eel-spearer came immediately and stabbed five of our sisters to death.' 'They'll come back again,' said the mother eel. 'Oh, no,' exclaimed the daughters, 'for he skinned them, cut them in two, and fried them.' 'Oh, they'll come back again,' the mother eel persisted. 'No,' replied the daughters, 'for he ate them up.' 'They'll come back again,' repeated the mother eel. 'But he drank brandy after them,' said the daughters. 'Ah, then they'll never come back,' said the mother, and she burst out crying, 'it's the brandy that buries the eels.'"

"And therefore," said the eel-breeder in conclusion, "it is always the proper thing to drink brandy after eating eels."

This story was the tinsel thread, the most humorous recollection of Jørgen's life. He also wanted to go a little way farther out and up the bay – that is to say, out into the world in a ship – but his mother said, like the eel-breeder, "There are so many bad people – eel spearers!" He wished to go a little way past the sand-hills, out into the dunes, and at last he did: four happy days, the brightest of his childhood, fell to his lot, and the whole beauty and splendor of Jutland, all the happiness and sunshine of his home, were concentrated in these. He went to a festival, but it was a burial feast.

A rich relation of the fisherman's family had died; the farm was situated far eastward in the country and a little towards the north. Jørgen's foster parents went there, and he also went with them from the dunes, over heath and moor, where the Skjærumaa takes its course through green meadows and contains many eels; mother eels live there with their daughters, who are caught and eaten up by wicked people. But do not men sometimes act quite as cruelly towards their own fellow-men? Was not the knight Sir Bugge murdered by wicked people? And though he was well spoken of, did he not also wish to kill the architect who built the castle for him, with its thick walls and tower, at the point where the Skjærumaa falls into the bay? Jørgen and his parents now stood there; the wall and the ramparts still remained, and red crumbling fragments lay scattered around. Here it was that Sir Bugge, after the architect had left him, said to one of his men, "Go after him and say, 'Master, the tower shakes.' If he turns round, kill him and take away the money I paid him, but if he does not turn round let him go in peace." The man did as he was told; the architect did not turn round, but called back "The tower does not shake in the least, but one day a man will come from the west in a blue cloak – he will cause it to shake!" And so indeed it happened a hundred years later, for the North Sea broke in and cast down the tower; but Predbjørn Gyldenstjerne, the man who then possessed the castle, built a new castle higher up at the end of the meadow, and that one is standing to this day, and is called Nørre-Vosborg.

Jørgen and his foster parents went past this castle. They had told him its story during the long winter evenings, and now he saw the stately edifice, with its double moat, and trees and bushes; the wall, covered with ferns, rose within the moat, but the lofty lime-trees were the most beautiful of all; they grew up to the highest windows, and the air was full of their sweet fragrance. In a north-west corner of the garden stood a great bush full of blossom, like winter snow amid the summer's green; it was a juniper bush, the first that Jørgen had ever seen in bloom. He never forgot it, nor the lime-trees; the child's soul treasured up these memories of beauty and fragrance to gladden the old man.

From Nørre-Vosborg, where the juniper blossomed, the journey became more pleasant, for they met some other people who were also going to the funeral and were riding in waggons. Our travellers had to sit all together on a little box at the back of the waggon, but even this, they thought, was better than walking. So they continued their journey across the rugged heath. The oxen which drew the waggon stopped every now and then, where a patch of fresh grass appeared amid the heather. The sun shone with considerable heat, and it was wonderful to behold how in the far distance something like smoke seemed to be rising; yet this smoke was clearer than the air; it was transparent, and looked like rays of light rolling and dancing afar over the heath.

"That is Lokeman driving his sheep," said some one.

And this was enough to excite Jørgen's imagination. He felt as if they were now about to enter fairyland, though everything was still real. How quiet it was! The heath stretched far and wide around them like a beautiful carpet. The heather was in blossom, and the juniper-bushes and fresh oak saplings rose like bouquets from the earth. An inviting place for a frolic, if it had not been for the number of poisonous adders of which the travellers spoke; they also mentioned that the place had formerly been infested with wolves, and that the district was still called Wolfsborg for this reason. The old man who was driving the oxen told them that in the lifetime of his father the horses had many a hard battle with the wild beasts that were now exterminated. One morning, when he himself had gone out to bring in the horses, he found one of them standing with its forefeet on a wolf it had killed, but the savage animal had torn and lacerated the brave horse's legs.

The journey over the heath and the deep sand was only too quickly at an end. They stopped before the house of mourning, where they found plenty of guests within and without. Waggon after waggon stood side by side, while the horses and oxen had been turned out to graze on the scanty pasture. Great sand-hills like those at home by the North Sea rose behind the house and extended far and wide. How had they come here, so many miles inland? They were as large and high as those on the coast, and the wind had carried them there; there was also a legend attached to them.

Psalms were sung, and a few of the old people shed tears; with this exception, the guests were cheerful enough, it seemed to Jørgen, and there was plenty to eat and drink. There were eels of the fattest, requiring brandy to bury them, as the eel-breeder said; and certainly they did not forget to carry out his maxim here.

Jørgen went in and out the house; and on the third day he felt as much at home as he did in the fisherman's cottage among the sand-hills, where he had passed his early days. Here on the heath were riches unknown to him until now; for flowers, blackberries, and bilberries were to be found in profusion, so large and sweet that when they were crushed beneath the tread of passers-by the heather was stained with their red juice. Here was a barrow and yonder another. Then columns of smoke rose into the still air; it was a heath fire, they told him – how brightly it blazed in the dark evening!

The fourth day came, and the funeral festivities were at an end; they were to go back from the land-dunes to the sand-dunes.

"Ours are better," said the old fisherman, Jørgen's foster-father; "these have no strength."

And they spoke of the way in which the sand-dunes had come inland, and it seemed very easy to understand. This is how they explained it:

A dead body had been found on the coast, and the peasants buried it in the churchyard. From that time the sand began to fly about and the sea broke in with violence. A wise man in the district advised them to open the grave and see if the buried man was not lying sucking his thumb, for if so he must be a sailor, and the sea would not rest until it had got him back. The grave was opened, and he really was found with his thumb in his mouth. So they laid him upon a cart, and harnessed two oxen to it; and the oxen ran off with the sailor over heath and moor to the ocean, as if they had been stung by an adder. Then the sand ceased to fly inland, but the hills that had been piled up still remained.

All this Jørgen listened to and treasured up in his memory of the happiest days of his childhood – the days of the burial feast.

How delightful it was to see fresh places and to mix with strangers! And he was to go still farther, for he was not yet fourteen years old when he went out in a ship to see the world. He encountered bad weather, heavy seas, unkindness, and hard men – such were his experiences, for he became ship-boy. Cold nights, bad living, and blows had to be endured; then he felt his noble Spanish blood boil within him, and bitter, angry, words rose to his lips, but he gulped them down; it was better, although he felt as the eel must feel when it is skinned, cut up, and put into the frying-pan.

"I shall get over it," said a voice within him.

He saw the Spanish coast, the native land of his parents. He even saw the town where they had lived in joy and prosperity, but he knew nothing of his home or his relations, and his relations knew just as little about him.

The poor ship boy was not permitted to land, but on the last day of their stay he managed to get ashore. There were several purchases to be made, and he was sent to carry them on board.

Jørgen stood there in his shabby clothes which looked as if they had been washed in the ditch and dried in the chimney; he, who had always dwelt among the sand-hills, now saw a great city for the first time. How lofty the houses seemed, and what a number of people there were in the streets! some pushing this way, some that – a perfect maelstrom of citizens and peasants, monks and soldiers – the jingling of bells on the trappings of asses and mules, the chiming of church bells, calling, shouting, hammering and knocking – all going on at once. Every trade was located in the basement of the houses or in the side thoroughfares; and the sun shone with such heat, and the air was so close, that one seemed to be in an oven full of beetles, cockchafers, bees and flies, all humming and buzzing together. Jørgen scarcely knew where he was or which way he went. Then he saw just in front of him the great doorway of a cathedral; the lights were gleaming in the dark aisles, and the fragrance of incense was wafted towards him. Even the poorest beggar ventured up the steps into the sanctuary. Jørgen followed the sailor he was with into the church, and stood in the sacred edifice. Colored pictures gleamed from their golden background, and on the altar stood the figure of the Virgin with the child Jesus, surrounded by lights and flowers; priests in festive robes were chanting, and choir boys in dazzling attire swung silver censers. What splendor and magnificence he saw there! It streamed in upon his soul and overpowered him: the church and the faith of his parents surrounded him, and touched a chord in his heart that caused his eyes to overflow with tears.

They went from the church to the market-place. Here a quantity of provisions were given him to carry. The way to the harbour was long; and weary and overcome with various emotions, he rested for a few moments before a splendid house, with marble pillars, statues, and broad steps. Here he rested his burden against the wall. Then a porter in livery came out, lifted up a silver-headed cane, and drove him away – him, the grandson of that house. But no one knew that, and he just as little as any one. Then he went on board again, and once more encountered rough words and blows, much work and little sleep – such was his experience of life. They say it is good to suffer in one's young days, if age brings something to make up for it.

His period of service on board the ship came to an end, and the vessel lay once more at Ringkjøbing in Jutland. He came ashore, and went home to the sand-dunes near Huusby; but his foster-mother had died during his absence.

A hard winter followed this summer. Snow-storms swept over land and sea, and there was difficulty in getting from one place to another. How unequally things are distributed in this world! Here there was bitter cold and snow-storms, while in Spain there was burning sunshine and oppressive heat. Yet, when a clear frosty day came, and Jørgen saw the swans flying in numbers from the sea towards the land, across to Nørre-Vosborg, it seemed to him that people could breathe more freely here; the summer also in this part of the world was splendid. In imagination he saw the heath blossom and become purple with rich juicy berries, and the elder-bushes and lime-trees at Nørre Vosborg in flower. He made up his mind to go there again.

Spring came, and the fishing began. Jørgen was now an active helper in this, for he had grown during the last year, and was quick at work. He was full of life, and knew how to swim, to tread water, and to turn over and tumble in the strong tide. They often warned him to beware of the sharks, which seize the best swimmer, draw him down, and devour him; but such was not to be Jørgen's fate.

At a neighbor's house in the dunes there was a boy named Martin, with whom Jørgen was on very friendly terms, and they both took service in the same ship to Norway, and also went together to Holland. They never had a quarrel, but a person can be easily excited to quarrel when he is naturally hot tempered, for he often shows it in many ways; and this is just what Jørgen did one day when they fell out about the merest trifle. They were sitting behind the cabin door, eating from a delft plate, which they had placed between them. Jørgen held his pocket-knife in his hand and raised it towards Martin, and at the same time became ashy pale, and his eyes had an ugly look. Martin only said, "Ah! ah! you are one of that sort, are you? Fond of using the knife!"

The words were scarcely spoken, when Jørgen's hand sank down. He did not answer a syllable, but went on eating, and afterwards returned to his work. When they were resting again he walked up to Martin and said:

"Hit me in the face! I deserve it. But sometimes I feel as if I had a pot in me that boils over."

"There, let the thing rest," replied Martin.

And after that they were almost better friends than ever; when afterwards they returned to the dunes and began telling their adventures, this was told among the rest. Martin said that Jørgen was certainly passionate, but a good fellow after all.

They were both young and healthy, well-grown and strong; but Jørgen was the cleverer of the two.

In Norway the peasants go into the mountains and take the cattle there to find pasture. On the west coast of Jutland huts have been erected among the sand-hills; they are built of pieces of wreck, and thatched with turf and heather; there are sleeping places round the walls, and here the fishermen live and sleep during the early spring. Every fisherman has a female helper, or manager as she is called, who baits his hooks, prepares warm beer for him when he comes ashore, and gets the dinner cooked and ready for him by the time he comes back to the hut tired and hungry. Besides this the managers bring up the fish from the boats, cut them open, prepare them, and have generally a great deal to do.

Jørgen, his father, and several other fishermen and their managers inhabited the same hut; Martin lived in the next one.

One of the girls, whose name was Else, had known Jørgen from childhood; they were glad to see each other, and were of the same opinion on many points, but in appearance they were entirely opposite; for he was dark, and she was pale, and fair, and had flaxen hair, and eyes as blue as the sea in sunshine.

As they were walking together one day, Jørgen held her hand very firmly in his, and she said to him:

"Jørgen, I have something I want to say to you; let me be your manager, for you are like a brother to me; but Martin, whose housekeeper I am – he is my lover – but you need not tell this to the others."

It seemed to Jørgen as if the loose sand was giving way under his feet. He did not speak a word, but nodded his head, and that meant "yes." It was all that was necessary; but he suddenly felt in his heart that he hated Martin, and the more he thought the more he felt convinced that Martin had stolen away from him the only being he ever loved, and that this was Else: he had never thought of Else in this way before, but now it all became plain to him.

When the sea is rather rough, and the fishermen are coming home in their great boats, it is wonderful to see how they cross the reefs. One of them stands upright in the bow of the boat, and the others watch him sitting with the oars in their hands. Outside the reef it looks as if the boat was not approaching land but going back to sea; then the man who is standing up gives them the signal that the great wave is coming which is to float them across the reef. The boat is lifted high into the air, so that the keel is seen from the shore; the next moment nothing can be seen, mast, keel, and people are all hidden – it seems as though the sea had devoured them; but in a few moments they emerge like a great sea animal climbing up the waves, and the oars move as if the creature had legs. The second and third reef are passed in the same manner; then the fishermen jump into the water and push the boat towards the shore – every wave helps them – and at length they have it drawn up, beyond the reach of the breakers.

A wrong order given in front of the reef – the slightest hesitation – and the boat would be lost,

"Then it would be all over with me and Martin too!"

This thought passed through Jørgen's mind one day while they were out at sea, where his foster-father had been taken suddenly ill. The fever had seized him. They were only a few oars' strokes from the reef, and Jørgen sprang from his seat and stood up in the bow.

"Father-let me come!" he said, and he glanced at Martin and across the waves; every oar bent with the exertions of the rowers as the great wave came towards them, and he saw his father's pale face, and dared not obey the evil impulse that had shot through his brain. The boat came safely across the reef to land; but the evil thought remained in his heart, and roused up every little fibre of bitterness which he remembered between himself and Martin since they had known each other. But he could not weave the fibres together, nor did he endeavour to do so. He felt that Martin had robbed him, and this was enough to make him hate his former friend. Several of the fishermen saw this, but Martin did not – he remained as obliging and talkative as ever, in fact he talked rather too much.

Jørgen's foster-father took to his bed, and it became his death-bed, for he died a week afterwards; and now Jørgen was heir to the little house behind the sand-hills. It was small, certainly, but still it was something, and Martin had nothing of the kind.

"You will not go to sea again, Jørgen, I suppose," observed one of the old fishermen. "You will always stay with us now."

But this was not Jørgen's intention; he wanted to see something of the world. The eel-breeder of Fjaltring had an uncle at Old Skagen, who was a fisherman, but also a prosperous merchant with ships upon the sea; he was said to be a good old man, and it would not be a bad thing to enter his service. Old Skagen lies in the extreme north of

Jutland, as far away from the Huusby dunes as one can travel in that country; and this is just what pleased Jørgen, for he did not want to remain till the wedding of Martin and Else, which would take place in a week or two.

The old fisherman said it was foolish to go away, for now that Jørgen had a home Else would very likely be inclined to take him instead of Martin.

Jørgen gave such a vague answer that it was not easy to make out what he meant – the old man brought Else to him, and she said:

"You have a home now; you ought to think of that."

And Jørgen thought of many things.

The sea has heavy waves, but there are heavier waves in the human heart. Many thoughts, strong and weak, rushed through Jørgen's brain, and he said to Else:

"If Martin had a house like mine, which of us would you rather have?"

"But Martin has no house and cannot get one."

"Suppose he had one?"

"Well, then I would certainly take Martin, for that is what my heart tells me; but one cannot live upon love."

Jørgen turned these things over in his mind all night. Something was working within him, he hardly knew what it was, but it was even stronger than his love for Else; and so he went to Martin's, and what he said and did there was well considered. He let the house to Martin on most liberal terms, saying that he wished to go to sea again, because he loved it. And Else kissed him when she heard of it, for she loved Martin best.

Jørgen proposed to start early in the morning, and on the evening before his departure, when it was already getting rather late, he felt a wish to visit Martin once more. He started, and among the dunes met the old fisherman, who was angry at his leaving the place. The old man made jokes about Martin, and declared there must be some magic about that fellow, of whom the girls were so fond.

Jørgen did not pay any attention to his remarks, but said good-bye to the old man and went on towards the house where Martin dwelt. He heard loud talking inside; Martin was not alone, and this made Jørgen waver in his determination, for he did not wish to see Else again. On second thoughts, he decided that it was better not to hear any more thanks from Martin, and so he turned back.

On the following morning, before the sun rose, he fastened his knapsack on his back, took his wooden provision box in his hand, and went away among the sand-hills towards the coast path. This way was more pleasant than the heavy sand road, and besides it was shorter; and he intended to go first to Fjaltring, near Bovbjerg, where the eel-breeder lived, to whom he had promised a visit.

The sea lay before him, clear and blue, and the mussel shells and pebbles, the playthings of his childhood, crunched over his feet. While he thus walked on his nose suddenly began to bleed; it was a trifling occurrence, but trifles sometimes are of great importance. A few large drops of blood fell upon one of his sleeves. He wiped them off and stopped the bleeding, and it seemed to him as if this had cleared and lightened his brain. The sea-cale bloomed here and there in the sand as he passed. He broke off a spray and stuck it in his hat; he determined to be merry and light-hearted, for he was going out into the wide world – "a little way out, beyond the bay," as the young eels had said. "Beware of bad people who will catch you, and skin you, and put you in the frying-pan!" he repeated in his mind, and smiled, for he thought he should find his way through the world – good courage is a strong weapon!

The sun was high in the heavens when he approached the narrow entrance to Nissum Bay. He looked back and saw a couple of horsemen galloping a long distance behind him, and there were other people with them. But this did not concern him.

The ferry-boat was on the opposite side of the bay. Jørgen called to the ferry-man, and the latter came over with his boat. Jørgen stepped in; but before he had got half-way across, the men whom he had seen riding so hastily, came up, hailed the ferry-man, and commanded him to return in the name of the law. Jørgen did not understand the reason of this, but he thought it would be best to turn back, and therefore he himself took an oar and returned. As soon as the boat touched the shore, the men sprang on board, and before he was aware of it, they had bound his hands with a rope.

"This wicked deed will cost you your life," they said. "It is a good thing we have caught you."

He was accused of nothing less than murder. Martin had been found dead, with his throat cut. One of the fishermen, late on the previous evening, had met Jørgen going towards Martin's house; this was not the first time Jørgen had raised his knife against Martin, so they felt sure that he was the murderer. The prison was in a town at a great distance, and the wind was contrary for going there by sea; but it would not take half an hour to get across the bay, and another quarter of an hour would bring them to Nørre-Vosborg, the great castle with ramparts and moat. One of Jørgen's captors was a fisherman, a brother of the keeper of the castle, and he said it might be managed that Jørgen should be placed for the present in the dungeon at Vosborg, where Long Martha the gipsy had been shut up till her execution. They paid no attention to Jørgen's defence; the few drops of blood on his shirt-sleeve bore heavy witness against him. But he was conscious of his innocence, and as there was no chance of clearing himself at present he submitted to his fate.

The party landed just at the place where Sir Bugge's castle had stood, and where Jørgen had walked with his foster-parents after the burial feast, during the four happiest days of his childhood. He was led by the well-known path, over the meadow to Vosborg; once more the elders were in bloom and the lofty lime-trees gave forth sweet fragrance, and it seemed as if it were but yesterday that he had last seen the spot. In each of the two wings of the castle there was a staircase which led to a place below the entrance, from whence there is access to a low, vaulted cellar. In this dungeon Long Martha had been imprisoned, and from here she was led away to the scaffold. She had eaten the hearts of five children, and had imagined that if she could obtain two more she would be able to fly and make herself invisible. In the middle of the roof of the cellar there was a little narrow air-hole, but no window. The flowering lime trees could not breathe refreshing fragrance into that abode, where everything was dark and mouldy. There was only a rough bench in the cell; but a good conscience is a soft pillow, and therefore Jørgen could sleep well.

The thick oaken door was locked, and secured on the outside by an iron bar; but the goblin of superstition can creep through a keyhole into a baron's castle just as easily as it can into a fisherman's cottage, and why should he not creep in here, where Jørgen sat thinking of Long Martha and her wicked deeds? Her last thoughts on the night before her execution had filled this place, and the magic that tradition asserted to have been practised here, in Sir Svanwedel's time, came into Jørgen's mind, and made him shudder; but a sunbeam, a refreshing thought from without, penetrated his heart even here – it was the remembrance of the flowering elder and the sweet smelling lime-trees.

He was not left there long. They took him away to the town of Ringkjøbing, where he was imprisoned with equal severity.

Those times were not like ours. The common people were treated harshly; and it was just after the days when farms were converted into knights' estates, when coachmen and servants were often made magistrates, and had power to sentence a poor man, for a small offence, to lose his property and to corporeal punishment. Judges of this kind were still to be found; and in Jutland, so far from the capital, and from the enlightened, well-meaning, head of the Government, the law was still very loosely administered sometimes – the smallest grievance Jørgen could expect was that his case should be delayed.

His dwelling was cold and comfortless; and how long would he be obliged to bear all this? It seemed his fate to suffer misfortune and sorrow innocently. He now had plenty of time to reflect on the difference of fortune on earth, and to wonder why this fate had been allotted to him; yet he felt sure that all would be made clear in the next life, the existence that awaits us when this life is over. His faith had grown strong in the poor fisherman's cottage; the light which had never shone into his father's mind, in all the richness and sunshine of Spain, was sent to him to be his comfort in poverty and distress, a sign of that mercy of God which never fails.

The spring storms began to blow. The rolling and moaning of the North Sea could be heard for miles inland when the wind was blowing, and then it sounded like the rushing of a thousand waggons over a hard road with a mine underneath. Jørgen heard these sounds in his prison, and it was a relief to him. No music could have touched his heart as did these sounds of the sea – the rolling sea, the boundless sea, on which a man can be borne across the world before the wind, carrying his own house with him wherever he goes, just as the snail carries its home even into a strange country.

He listened eagerly to its deep murmur and then the thought arose – "Free! free! How happy to be free, even barefooted and in ragged clothes!" Sometimes, when such thoughts crossed his mind, the fiery nature rose within him, and he beat the wall with his clenched fists.

Weeks, months, a whole year had gone by, when Niels the thief, called also a horse-dealer, was arrested; and now better times came, and it was seen that Jørgen had been wrongly accused.

On the afternoon before Jørgen's departure from home, and before the murder, Niels the thief, had met Martin at a beer-house in the neighborhood of Ringkjøbing. A few glasses were drank, not enough to cloud the brain, but enough to loosen Martin's tongue. He began to boast and to say that he had obtained a house and intended to marry, and when Niels asked him where he was going to get the money, he slapped his pocket proudly and said:

"The money is here, where it ought to be."

This boast cost him his life; for when he went home Niels followed him, and cut his throat, intending to rob the murdered man of the gold, which did not exist.

All this was circumstantially explained; but it is enough for us to know that Jørgen was set free. But what compensation did he get for having been imprisoned a whole year, and shut out from all communication with his fellow creatures? They told him he was fortunate in being proved innocent, and that he might go. The burgomaster gave him two dollars for travelling expenses, and many citizens offered him provisions and beer – there were still good people; they were not all hard and pitiless. But the best thing of all was that the merchant Brønne, of Skagen, into whose service Jørgen had proposed entering the year before, was just at that time on business in the town of Ringkjøbing. Brønne heard the whole story; he was kind-hearted, and understood what Jørgen must have felt and suffered. Therefore he made up his mind to make it up to the poor lad, and convince him that there were still kind folks in the world.

So Jørgen went forth from prison as if to paradise, to find freedom, affection, and trust. He was to travel this path now, for no goblet of life is all bitterness; no good man would pour out such a draught for his fellow-man, and how should He do it, Who is love personified?

"Let everything be buried and forgotten," said Brønne, the merchant. "Let us draw a thick line through last year: we will even burn the almanack. In two days we will start for dear, friendly, peaceful Skagen. People call it an out-of-the-way corner; but it is a good warm chimney-corner, and its windows open toward every part of the world."

What a journey that was: It was like taking fresh breath out of the cold dungeon air into the warm sunshine. The heather bloomed in pride and beauty, and the shepherd-boy sat on a barrow and blew his pipe, which he had carved for himself out of a sheep bone. Fata Morgana, the beautiful aerial phenomenon of the wilderness, appeared with hanging gardens and waving forests, and the wonderful cloud called "Lokeman driving his sheep" also was seen.

Up towards Skagen they went, through the land of the Wendels, whence the men with long beards (the Longobardi or Lombards) had emigrated in the reign of King Snio, when all the children and old people were to have been killed, till the noble Dame Gambaruk proposed that the young people should emigrate. Jørgen knew all this, he had some little knowledge; and although he did not know the land of the Lombards beyond the lofty Alps, he had an idea that it must be there, for in his boyhood he had been in the south, in Spain. He thought of the plenteousness of the southern fruit, of the red pomegranate flowers, of the humming, buzzing, and toiling in the great beehive of a city he had seen; but home is the best place after all, and Jørgen's home was Denmark.

At last they arrived at "Vendilskaga," as Skagen is called in old Norwegian and Icelandic writings. At that time Old Skagen, with the eastern and western town, extended for miles, with sand hills and arable land as far as the lighthouse near "Grenen." Then, as now, the houses were strewn among the wind-raised sand-hills – a wilderness in which the wind sports with the sand, and where the voice of the sea-gull and wild swan strikes harshly on the ear.

In the south-west, a mile from "Grenen," lies Old Skagen; merchant Brønne dwelt here, and this was also to be Jørgen's home for the future. The dwelling-house was tarred, and all the small out-buildings had been put together from pieces of wreck. There was no fence, for indeed there was nothing to fence in except the long rows of fishes which were hung upon lines, one above the other, to dry in the wind. The entire coast was strewn with spoiled herrings, for there were so many of these fish that a net was scarcely thrown into the sea before it was filled. They were caught by carloads, and many of them were either thrown back into the sea or left to lie on the beach.

The old man's wife and daughter and his servants also came to meet him with great rejoicing. There was a great squeezing of hands, and talking and questioning. And the daughter, what a sweet face and bright eyes she had!

The inside of the house was comfortable and roomy. Fritters, that a king would have looked upon as a dainty dish, were placed on the table, and there was wine from the Skagen vineyard – that is, the sea; for there the grapes come ashore ready pressed and prepared in barrels and in bottles.

When the mother and daughter heard who Jørgen was, and how innocently he had suffered, they looked at him in a still more friendly way; and pretty Clara's eyes had a look of especial interest as she listened to his story. Jørgen found a happy home in Old Skagen. It did his heart good, for it had been sorely tried. He had drunk the bitter goblet of love which softens or hardens the heart, according to circumstances. Jørgen's heart was still soft – it was young, and therefore it was a good thing that Miss Clara was going in three weeks' time to Christiansand in Norway, in her father's ship, to visit an aunt and to stay there the whole winter.

On the Sunday before she went away they all went to church, to the Holy Communion. The church was large and handsome, and had been built centuries before by Scotchmen and Dutchmen; it stood some little way out of the town. It was rather ruinous certainly, and the road to it was heavy, through deep sand, but the people gladly surmounted these difficulties to get to the house of God, to sing psalms and to hear the sermon. The sand had heaped itself up round the walls of the church, but the graves were kept free from it.

It was the largest church north of the Limfjorden. The Virgin Mary, with a golden crown on her head and the child Jesus in her arms, stood lifelike on the altar; the holy Apostles had been carved in the choir, and on the walls there were portraits of the old burgomasters and councillors of Skagen; the pulpit was of carved work. The sun shone brightly into the church, and its radiance fell on the polished brass chandelier and on the little ship that hung from the vaulted roof.

Jørgen felt overcome by a holy, childlike feeling, like that which possessed him, when, as a boy, he stood in the splendid Spanish cathedral. But here the feeling was different, for he felt conscious of being one of the congregation.

After the sermon followed Holy Communion. He partook of the bread and wine, and it so happened that he knelt by the side of Miss Clara; but his thoughts were so fixed upon heaven and the Holy Sacrament that he did not notice his neighbor until he rose from his knees, and then he saw tears rolling down her cheeks.

She left Skagen and went to Norway two days later. He remained behind, and made himself useful on the farm and at the fishery. He went out fishing, and in those days fish were more plentiful and larger than they are now. The shoals of the mackerel glittered in the dark nights, and indicated where they were swimming; the gurnards snarled, and the crabs gave forth pitiful yells when they were chased, for fish are not so mute as people say.

Every Sunday Jørgen went to church; and when his eyes rested on the picture of the Virgin Mary over the altar as he sat there, they often glided away to the spot where they had knelt side by side.

Autumn came, and brought rain and snow with it; the water rose up right into the town of Skagen, the sand could not suck it all in, one had to wade through it or go by boat. The storms threw vessel after vessel on the fatal reefs; there were snow-storm and sand-storms; the sand flew up to the houses, blocking the entrances, so that people had to creep up through the chimneys; that was nothing at all remarkable here. It was pleasant and cheerful indoors, where peat fuel and fragments of wood from the wrecks blazed and crackled upon the hearth. Merchant Brønne read aloud, from an old chronicle, about Prince Hamlet of Denmark, who had come over from England, landed near Bovbjerg, and fought a battle; close by Ramme was his grave, only a few miles from the place where the eel-breeder lived; hundreds of barrow rose there from the heath, forming as it were an enormous churchyard. Merchant Brønne had himself been at Hamlet's grave; they spoke about old times, and about their neighbors, the English and the Scotch, and Jørgen sang the air of "The King of England's Son," and of his splendid ship and its outfit.

> *"In the hour of peril when most men fear,*
> *He clasped the bride that he held so dear,*
> *And proved himself the son of a King;*
> *Of his courage and valor let us sing."*

This verse Jørgen sang with so much feeling that his eyes beamed, and they were black and sparkling since his infancy.

There was wealth, comfort, and happiness even among the domestic animals, for they were all well cared for, and well kept. The kitchen looked bright with its copper and tin utensils, and white plates, and from the rafters hung hams, beef, and winter stores in plenty. This can still be seen in many rich farms on the west coast of Jutland: plenty to eat and drink, clean, prettily decorated rooms, active minds, cheerful tempers, and hospitality can be found there, as in an Arab's tent.

Jørgen had never spent such a happy time since the famous burial feast, and yet Miss Clara was absent, except in the thoughts and memory of all.

In April a ship was to start for Norway, and Jørgen was to sail in it. He was full of life and spirits, and looked so sturdy and well that Dame Brønne said it did her good to see him.

"And it does one good to look at you also, old wife," said the merchant. "Jørgen has brought fresh life into our winter evenings, and into you too, mother. You look younger than ever this year, and seem well and cheerful. But then you were once the prettiest girl in Viborg, and that is saying a great deal, for I have always found the Viborg girls the prettiest of any."

Jørgen said nothing, but he thought of a certain maiden of Skagen, whom he was soon to visit. The ship set sail for Christiansand in Norway, and as the wind was favourable it soon arrived there.

One morning merchant Brønne went out to the lighthouse, which stands a little way out of Old Skagen, not far from "Grenen." The light was out, and the sun was already high in the heavens, when he mounted the tower. The sand-banks extend a whole mile from the shore, beneath the water, outside these banks; many ships could be seen that day, and with the aid of his telescope the old man thought he descried his own ship, the Karen Brønne. Yes! certainly, there she was, sailing homewards with Clara and Jørgen on board.

Clara sat on deck, and saw the sand-hills gradually appearing in the distance; the church and lighthouse looked like a heron and a swan rising from the blue waters. If the wind held good they might reach home in about an hour. So near they were to home and all its joys – so near to death and all its terrors! A plank in the ship gave way, and the water rushed in; the crew flew to the pumps, and did their best to stop the leak. A signal of distress was hoisted, but they were still fully a mile from the shore. Some fishing boats were in sight, but they were too far off to be of any use. The wind blew towards the land, the tide was in their favour, but it was all useless; the ship could not be saved.

Jørgen threw his right arm round Clara, and pressed her to him. With what a look she gazed up into his face, as with a prayer to God for help he breasted the waves, which rushed over the sinking ship! She uttered a cry, but she felt safe and certain that he would not leave her to sink. And in this hour of terror and danger Jørgen felt as the king's son did, as told in the old song:

> *"In the hour of peril when most men fear,*
> *He clasped the bride that he held so dear."*

How glad he felt that he was a good swimmer! He worked his way onward with his feet and one arm, while he held the young girl up firmly with the other. He rested on the waves, he trod the water – in fact, did everything he could think of, in order not to fatigue himself, and to reserve strength enough to reach land. He heard Clara sigh, and felt her shudder convulsively, and he pressed her more closely to him. Now and then a wave rolled over them, the current lifted them; the water, although deep, was so clear that for a moment he imagined he saw the shoals of mackerel glittering, or Leviathan himself ready to swallow them. Now the clouds cast a shadow over the water, then again came the playing sunbeams; flocks of loudly screaming birds passed over him, and the plump and lazy wild ducks which allow themselves to be drifted by the waves rose up terrified at the sight of the swimmer. He began to feel his strength decreasing, but he was only a few cable lengths' distance from the shore, and help was coming, for a boat was approaching him. At this moment he distinctly saw a white staring figure under the water – a wave lifted him up, and he came nearer to the figure – he felt a violent shock, and everything became dark around him.

On the sand reef lay the wreck of a ship, which was covered with water at high tide; the white figure head rested against the anchor, the sharp iron edge of which rose just above the surface. Jørgen had come in contact with this; the tide had driven him against it with great force. He sank down stunned with the blow, but the next wave lifted him and the young girl up again. Some fishermen, coming with a boat, seized them and dragged them into it. The blood streamed down over Jørgen's face; he seemed dead, but still held the young girl so tightly that they were obliged to take her from him by force. She was pale and lifeless; they laid her in the boat, and rowed as quickly as possible to the shore. They tried every means to restore Clara to life, but it was all of no avail. Jørgen had been swimming for some distance with a corpse in his arms, and had exhausted his strength for one who was dead.

Jørgen still breathed, so the fishermen carried him to the nearest house upon the sand-hills, where a smith and general dealer lived who knew something of surgery, and bound up Jørgen's wounds in a temporary way until a surgeon could be obtained from the nearest town the next day. The injured man's brain was affected, and in his delirium he uttered wild cries; but on the third day he lay quiet and weak upon his bed; his life seemed to hang by a thread, and the physician said it would be better for him if this thread broke. "Let us pray that God may take him," he said, "for he will never be the same man again."

But life did not depart from him – the thread would not break, but the thread of memory was severed; the thread of his mind had been cut through, and what was still more grievous, a body remained – a living healthy body that wandered about like a troubled spirit.

Jørgen remained in merchant Brønne's house. "He was hurt while endeavouring to save our child," said the old man, "and now he is our son." People called Jørgen insane but that was not exactly the correct term. He was like an instrument in which the strings are loose and will give no sound; only occasionally they regained their power for a few minutes, and then they sounded as they used to do. He would sing snatches of songs or old melodies, pictures of the past would rise before him, and then disappear in the mist, as it were, but as a general rule he sat staring into vacancy, without a thought. We may conjecture that he did not suffer, but his dark eyes lost their brightness, and looked like clouded glass.

"Poor mad Jørgen," said the people. And this was the end of a life whose infancy was to have been surrounded with wealth and splendor had his parents lived! All his great mental abilities had been lost, nothing but hardship, sorrow, and disappointment had been his fate. He was like a rare plant, torn from its native soil, and tossed upon the beach to wither there. And was this one of God's creatures, fashioned in His own likeness, to have no better fate? Was he to be only the plaything of fortune? No! the all-loving Creator would certainly repay him in the life to come for what he had suffered and lost here. "The Lord is good to all; and His mercy is over all His works." The pious old wife of the merchant repeated these words from the Psalms of David in patience and hope, and the prayer of her heart was that Jørgen might soon be called away to enter into eternal life.

In the churchyard where the walls were surrounded with sand Clara lay buried. Jørgen did not seem to know this; it did not enter his mind, which could only retain fragments of the past. Every Sunday he went to church with the old people, and sat there silently, staring vacantly before him. One day, when the Psalms were being sung, he sighed deeply, and his eyes became bright; they were fixed upon a place near the altar where he had knelt with his friend who was dead. He murmured her name, and became deadly pale, and tears rolled down his cheeks. They led him out of church; he told those standing round him that he was well, and had never been ill; he, who had been so grievously afflicted, the outcast, thrown upon the world, could not remember his sufferings. The Lord our Creator is wise and full of loving kindness – who can doubt it?

In Spain, where balmy breezes blow over the Moorish cupolas and gently stir the orange and myrtle groves, where singing and the sound of the castanets are always heard, the richest merchant in the place, a childless old man, sat in a luxurious house, while children marched in procession through the streets with waving flags and lighted tapers. If he had been able to press his children to his heart, his daughter, or her child, that had, perhaps never seen the light of day, far less the kingdom of heaven, how much of his wealth would he not have given! "Poor child!" Yes, poor child – a child still, yet more than thirty years old, for Jørgen had arrived at this age in Old Skagen.

The shifting sands had covered the graves in the courtyard, quite up to the church walls, but still, the dead must be buried among their relatives and the dear ones who had gone before them. Merchant Brønne and his wife now rested with their children under the white sand.

It was in the spring – the season of storms. The sand from the dunes was whirled up in clouds; the sea was rough, and flocks of birds flew like clouds in the storm, screaming across the sand-hills. Shipwreck followed upon shipwreck on the reefs between Old Skagen and the Huusby dunes.

One evening Jørgen sat in his room alone: all at once his mind seemed to become clearer, and a restless feeling came over him, such as had often, in his younger days, driven him out to wander over the sand-hills or on the heath. "Home, home!" he cried. No one heard him. He went out and walked towards the dunes. Sand and stones blew into his face, and whirled round him; he went in the direction of the church. The sand was banked up the walls, half covering the windows, but it had been cleared away in front of the door, and the entrance was free and easy to open, so Jørgen went into the church.

The storm raged over the town of Skagen; there had not been such a terrible tempest within the memory of the inhabitants, nor such a rough sea. But Jørgen was in the temple of God, and while the darkness of night reigned outside, a light arose in his soul that was never to depart from it; the heavy weight that pressed on his brain burst asunder. He fancied he heard the organ, but it was only the storm and the moaning of the sea. He sat down on one of the seats, and lo! the candles were lighted one by one, and there was brightness and grandeur such as he had only seen in the Spanish cathedral. The portraits of the old citizens became alive, stepped down from the walls against which they had hung for centuries, and took seats near the church door. The gates flew open, and all the dead people from the churchyard came in, and filled the church, while beautiful music sounded. Then the melody of the psalm burst forth, like the sound of the waters, and Jørgen saw that his foster parents from the Huusby dunes were there, also old merchant Brønne with his wife and their daughter Clara, who gave him her hand. They both went up to the altar where they had knelt before, and the priest joined their hands and united them for life. Then music was heard again; it was wonderfully sweet, like a child's voice, full of joy and expectation, swelling to the powerful tones of a full organ, sometimes soft and sweet, then like the sounds of a tempest, delightful and elevating to hear, yet strong enough to burst the stone tombs of the dead. Then the little ship that hung from the roof of the choir was let down and looked wonderfully large and beautiful with its silken sails and rigging:

> *"The ropes were of silk, the anchor of gold,*
> *And everywhere riches and pomp untold,"*

as the old song says.

The young couple went on board, accompanied by the whole congregation, for there was room and enjoyment for them all. Then the walls and arches of the church were covered with flowering junipers and lime trees breathing forth fragrance; the branches waved, creating a pleasant coolness; they bent and parted, and the ship sailed between them through the air and over the sea. Every candle in the church became a star, and the wind sang a hymn in which they all joined. "Through love to glory, no life is lost, the future is full of blessings and happiness. Hallelujah!" These were the last words Jørgen uttered in this world, for the thread that bound his immortal soul was severed, and nothing but the dead body lay in the dark church, while the storm raged outside, covering it with loose sand.

The next day was Sunday, and the congregation and their pastor went to the church. The road had always been heavy, but now it was almost unfit for use, and when they at last arrived at the church, a great heap of sand lay piled up in front of them. The whole church was completely buried in sand. The clergyman offered a short prayer, and said that God had closed the door of His house here, and that the congregation must go and build a new one for Him somewhere else. So they sung a hymn in the open air, and went home again.

Jørgen could not be found anywhere in the town of Skagen, nor on the dunes, though they searched for him everywhere. They came to the conclusion that one of the great waves, which had rolled far up on the beach, had carried him away; but his body lay buried in a great sepulchre – the church itself. The Lord had thrown down a covering for his grave during the storm, and the heavy mound of sand lies upon it to this day. The drifting sand had covered the vaulted roof of the church, the arched cloisters, and the stone aisles. The white thorn and the dog rose now blossom above the place where the church lies buried, but the spire, like an enormous monument over a grave, can be seen for miles round. No king has a more splendid memorial. Nothing disturbs the peaceful sleep of the dead. I was the first to hear this story, for the storm sung it to me among the sand-hills.

Marvels & Magics

The Red Shoes

ONCE UPON A time there was little girl, pretty and dainty. But in summer time she was obliged to go barefooted because she was poor, and in winter she had to wear large wooden shoes, so that her little instep grew quite red.

In the middle of the village lived an old shoemaker's wife; she sat down and made, as well as she could, a pair of little shoes out of some old pieces of red cloth. They were clumsy, but she meant well, for they were intended for the little girl, whose name was Karen.

Karen received the shoes and wore them for the first time on the day of her mother's funeral. They were certainly not suitable for mourning; but she had no others, and so she put her bare feet into them and walked behind the humble coffin.

Just then a large old carriage came by, and in it sat an old lady; she looked at the little girl, and taking pity on her, said to the clergyman, "Look here, if you will give me the little girl, I will take care of her."

Karen believed that this was all on account of the red shoes, but the old lady thought them hideous, and so they were burnt. Karen herself was dressed very neatly and cleanly; she was taught to read and to sew, and people said that she was pretty. But the mirror told her, "You are more than pretty – you are beautiful."

One day the Queen was travelling through that part of the country, and had her little daughter, who was a princess, with her. All the people, amongst them Karen too, streamed towards the castle, where the little princess, in fine white clothes, stood before the window and allowed herself to be stared at. She wore neither a train nor a golden crown, but beautiful red morocco shoes; they were indeed much finer than those which the shoemaker's wife had sewn for little Karen. There is really nothing in the world that can be compared to red shoes!

Karen was now old enough to be confirmed; she received some new clothes, and she was also to have some new shoes. The rich shoemaker in the town took the measure of her little foot in his own room, in which there stood great glass cases full of pretty shoes and white slippers. It all looked very lovely, but the old lady could not see very well, and therefore did not get much pleasure out of it. Amongst the shoes stood a pair of red ones, like those which the princess had worn. How beautiful they were! and the shoemaker said that they had been made for a count's daughter, but that they had not fitted her.

"I suppose they are of shiny leather?" asked the old lady. "They shine so."

"Yes, they do shine," said Karen. They fitted her, and were bought. But the old lady knew nothing of their being red, for she would never have allowed Karen to be confirmed in red shoes, as she was now to be.

Everybody looked at her feet, and the whole of the way from the church door to the choir it seemed to her as if even the ancient figures on the monuments, in their stiff collars and long black robes, had their eyes fixed on her red shoes. It was only of these that she thought when the clergyman laid his hand upon her head and spoke of the holy baptism, of the covenant with God, and told her that she was now to be a grown-up

Christian. The organ pealed forth solemnly, and the sweet children's voices mingled with that of their old leader; but Karen thought only of her red shoes. In the afternoon the old lady heard from everybody that Karen had worn red shoes. She said that it was a shocking thing to do, that it was very improper, and that Karen was always to go to church in future in black shoes, even if they were old.

On the following Sunday there was Communion. Karen looked first at the black shoes, then at the red ones – looked at the red ones again, and put them on.

The sun was shining gloriously, so Karen and the old lady went along the footpath through the corn, where it was rather dusty.

At the church door stood an old crippled soldier leaning on a crutch; he had a wonderfully long beard, more red than white, and he bowed down to the ground and asked the old lady whether he might wipe her shoes. Then Karen put out her little foot too. "Dear me, what pretty dancing-shoes!" said the soldier. "Sit fast, when you dance," said he, addressing the shoes, and slapping the soles with his hand.

The old lady gave the soldier some money and then went with Karen into the church.

And all the people inside looked at Karen's red shoes, and all the figures gazed at them; when Karen knelt before the altar and put the golden goblet to her mouth, she thought only of the red shoes. It seemed to her as though they were swimming about in the goblet, and she forgot to sing the psalm, forgot to say the "Lord's Prayer."

Now every one came out of church, and the old lady stepped into her carriage. But just as Karen was lifting up her foot to get in too, the old soldier said: "Dear me, what pretty dancing shoes!" and Karen could not help it, she was obliged to dance a few steps; and when she had once begun, her legs continued to dance. It seemed as if the shoes had got power over them. She danced round the church corner, for she could not stop; the coachman had to run after her and seize her. He lifted her into the carriage, but her feet continued to dance, so that she kicked the good old lady violently. At last they took off her shoes, and her legs were at rest.

At home the shoes were put into the cupboard, but Karen could not help looking at them.

Now the old lady fell ill, and it was said that she would not rise from her bed again. She had to be nursed and waited upon, and this was no one's duty more than Karen's. But there was a grand ball in the town, and Karen was invited. She looked at the red shoes, saying to herself that there was no sin in doing that; she put the red shoes on, thinking there was no harm in that either; and then she went to the ball; and commenced to dance.

But when she wanted to go to the right, the shoes danced to the left, and when she wanted to dance up the room, the shoes danced down the room, down the stairs through the street, and out through the gates of the town. She danced, and was obliged to dance, far out into the dark wood. Suddenly something shone up among the trees, and she believed it was the moon, for it was a face. But it was the old soldier with the red beard; he sat there nodding his head and said: "Dear me, what pretty dancing shoes!"

She was frightened, and wanted to throw the red shoes away; but they stuck fast. She tore off her stockings, but the shoes had grown fast to her feet. She danced and was obliged to go on dancing over field and meadow, in rain and sunshine, by night and by day – but by night it was most horrible.

She danced out into the open churchyard; but the dead there did not dance. They had something better to do than that. She wanted to sit down on the pauper's grave where the bitter fern grows; but for her there was neither peace nor rest. And as she danced past the open church door she saw an angel there in long white robes, with wings reaching from his shoulders down to the earth; his face was stern and grave, and in his hand he held a broad shining sword.

"Dance you shall," said he, "dance in your red shoes till you are pale and cold, till your skin shrivels up and you are a skeleton! Dance you shall, from door to door, and where proud and wicked children live you shall knock, so that they may hear you and fear you! Dance you shall, dance!"

"Mercy!" cried Karen. But she did not hear what the angel answered, for the shoes carried her through the gate into the fields, along highways and byways, and unceasingly she had to dance.

One morning she danced past a door that she knew well; they were singing a psalm inside, and a coffin was being carried out covered with flowers. Then she knew that she was forsaken by every one and damned by the angel of God.

She danced, and was obliged to go on dancing through the dark night. The shoes bore her away over thorns and stumps till she was all torn and bleeding; she danced away over the heath to a lonely little house. Here, she knew, lived the executioner; and she tapped with her finger at the window and said:

"Come out, come out! I cannot come in, for I must dance."

And the executioner said: "I don't suppose you know who I am. I strike off the heads of the wicked, and I notice that my axe is tingling to do so."

"Don't cut off my head!" said Karen, "for then I could not repent of my sin. But cut off my feet with the red shoes."

And then she confessed all her sin, and the executioner struck off her feet with the red shoes; but the shoes danced away with the little feet across the field into the deep forest.

And he carved her a pair of wooden feet and some crutches, and taught her a psalm which is always sung by sinners; she kissed the hand that guided the axe, and went away over the heath.

"Now, I have suffered enough for the red shoes," she said; "I will go to church, so that people can see me." And she went quickly up to the church-door; but when she came there, the red shoes were dancing before her, and she was frightened, and turned back.

During the whole week she was sad and wept many bitter tears, but when Sunday came again she said: "Now I have suffered and striven enough. I believe I am quite as good as many of those who sit in church and give themselves airs." And so she went boldly on; but she had not got farther than the churchyard gate when she saw the red shoes dancing along before her. Then she became terrified, and turned back and repented right heartily of her sin.

She went to the parsonage, and begged that she might be taken into service there. She would be industrious, she said, and do everything that she could; she did not mind about the wages as long as she had a roof over her, and was with good people. The pastor's wife had pity on her, and took her into service. And she was industrious and thoughtful. She sat quiet and listened when the pastor read aloud from the Bible in the evening. All the children liked her very much, but when they spoke about dress and grandeur and beauty she would shake her head.

On the following Sunday they all went to church, and she was asked whether she wished to go too; but, with tears in her eyes, she looked sadly at her crutches. And then the others went to hear God's Word, but she went alone into her little room; this was only large enough to hold the bed and a chair. Here she sat down with her hymn-book, and as she was reading it with a pious mind, the wind carried the notes of the organ over to her from the church, and in tears she lifted up her face and said: "O God! help me!"

Then the sun shone so brightly, and right before her stood an angel of God in white robes; it was the same one whom she had seen that night at the church-door. He no longer carried the sharp sword, but a beautiful green branch, full of roses; with this he touched the ceiling, which rose up very high, and where he had touched it there shone a golden star. He touched the walls, which opened wide apart, and she saw the organ which was pealing forth; she saw the pictures of the old pastors and their wives, and the congregation sitting in the polished chairs and singing from their hymn-books. The church itself had come to the poor girl in her narrow room, or the room had gone to the church. She sat in the pew with the rest of the pastor's household, and when they had finished the hymn and looked up, they nodded and said, "It was right of you to come, Karen."

"It was mercy," said she.

The organ played and the children's voices in the choir sounded soft and lovely. The bright warm sunshine streamed through the window into the pew where Karen sat, and her heart became so filled with it, so filled with peace and joy, that it broke. Her soul flew on the sunbeams to Heaven, and no one was there who asked after the Red Shoes.

Ole-Luk-Oie, the Dream-God

THERE IS NOBODY in the world who knows so many stories as Ole-Luk-Oie, or who can relate them so nicely. In the evening, while the children are seated at the table or in their little chairs, he comes up the stairs very softly, for he walks in his socks, then he opens the doors without the slightest noise, and throws a small quantity of very fine dust in their eyes, just enough to prevent them from keeping them open, and so they do not see him. Then he creeps behind them, and blows softly upon their necks, till their heads begin to droop. But Ole-Luk-Oie does not wish to hurt them, for he is very fond of children, and only wants them to be quiet that he may relate to them pretty stories, and they never are quiet until they are in bed and asleep. As soon as they are asleep, Ole-Luk-Oie seats himself upon the bed. He is nicely dressed; his coat is made of silken stuff; it is impossible to say of what color, for it changes from green to red, and from red to blue as he turns from side to side. Under each arm he carries an umbrella; one of them, with pictures on the inside, he spreads over the good children, and then they dream the most beautiful stories the whole night. But the other umbrella has no pictures, and this he holds over the naughty children so that they sleep heavily, and wake in the morning without having dreamed at all.

Now we shall hear how Ole-Luk-Oie came every night during a whole week to the little boy named Hjalmar, and what he told him. There were seven stories, as there are seven days in the week.

Monday

"Now pay attention," said Ole-Luk-Oie, in the evening, when Hjalmar was in bed, "and I will decorate the room."

Immediately all the flowers in the flower-pots became large trees, with long branches reaching to the ceiling, and stretching along the walls, so that the whole room was like a greenhouse. All the branches were loaded with flowers, each flower as beautiful and as fragrant as a rose; and, had any one tasted them, he would have found them sweeter even than jam. The fruit glittered like gold, and there were cakes so full of plums that they were nearly bursting. It was incomparably beautiful. At the same time sounded dismal moans from the table-drawer in which lay Hjalmar's school books.

"What can that be now?" said Ole-Luk-Oie, going to the table and pulling out the drawer.

It was a slate, in such distress because of a false number in the sum, that it had almost broken itself to pieces. The pencil pulled and tugged at its string as if it were a little dog that wanted to help, but could not.

And then came a moan from Hjalmar's copy-book. Oh, it was quite terrible to hear! On each leaf stood a row of capital letters, every one having a small letter by its side. This formed a copy; under these were other letters, which Hjalmar had written: they fancied they looked like the copy, but they were mistaken; for they were leaning on one side as if they intended to fall over the pencil-lines.

"See, this is the way you should hold yourselves," said the copy. "Look here, you should slope thus, with a graceful curve."

"Oh, we are very willing to do so, but we cannot," said Hjalmar's letters; "we are so wretchedly made."

"You must be scratched out, then," said Ole-Luk-Oie.

"Oh, no!" they cried, and then they stood up so gracefully it was quite a pleasure to look at them.

"Now we must give up our stories, and exercise these letters," said Ole-Luk-Oie; "One, two – one, two – " So he drilled them till they stood up gracefully, and looked as beautiful as a copy could look. But after Ole-Luk-Oie was gone, and Hjalmar looked at them in the morning, they were as wretched and as awkward as ever.

Tuesday

As soon as Hjalmar was in bed, Ole-Luk-Oie touched, with his little magic wand, all the furniture in the room, which immediately began to chatter, and each article only talked of itself.

Over the chest of drawers hung a large picture in a gilt frame, representing a landscape, with fine old trees, flowers in the grass, and a broad stream, which flowed through the wood, past several castles, far out into the wild ocean. Ole-Luk-Oie touched the picture with his magic wand, and immediately the birds commenced singing, the branches of the trees rustled, and the clouds moved across the sky, casting their shadows on the landscape beneath them. Then Ole-Luk-Oie lifted little Hjalmar up to the frame, and placed his feet in the picture, just on the high grass, and there he stood with the sun shining down upon him through the branches of the trees. He ran to the water, and seated himself in a little boat which lay there, and which was painted red and white. The sails glittered like silver, and six swans, each with a golden circlet round its neck, and a bright blue star on its forehead, drew the boat past the green wood, where the trees talked of robbers and witches, and the flowers of beautiful little elves and fairies, whose histories the butterflies had related to them. Brilliant fish, with scales like silver and gold, swam after the boat, sometimes making a spring and splashing the water round them, while birds, red and blue, small and great, flew after him in two long lines. The gnats danced round them, and the cockchafers cried "Buz, buz." They all wanted to follow Hjalmar, and all had some story to tell him. It was a most pleasant sail. Sometimes the forests were thick and dark, sometimes like a beautiful garden, gay with sunshine and flowers; then he passed great palaces of glass and of marble, and on the balconies stood princesses, whose faces were those of little girls whom Hjalmar knew well, and had often played with. One of them held out her hand, in which was a heart made of sugar, more beautiful than any confectioner ever sold. As Hjalmar sailed by, he caught hold of one side of the sugar heart, and held it fast, and the princess held fast also, so that it broke in two pieces. Hjalmar had one piece, and the princess the other, but Hjalmar's was the largest. At each castle stood little princes acting as sentinels. They presented arms, and had golden swords, and made it rain plums and tin soldiers, so that they must have been real princes.

Hjalmar continued to sail, sometimes through woods, sometimes as it were through large halls, and then by large cities. At last he came to the town where his nurse lived, who had carried him in her arms when he was a very little boy, and had always been kind to him. She nodded and beckoned to him, and then sang the little verses she had herself composed and set to him, –

> *"How oft my memory turns to thee,*
> *My own Hjalmar, ever dear!*
> *When I could watch thy infant glee,*
> *Or kiss away a pearly tear.*
> *'Twas in my arms thy lisping tongue*
> *First spoke the half-remembered word,*
> *While o'er thy tottering steps I hung,*
> *My fond protection to afford.*
> *Farewell! I pray the Heavenly Power*
> *To keep thee till thy dying hour."*

And all the birds sang the same tune, the flowers danced on their stems, and the old trees nodded as if Ole-Luk-Oie had been telling them stories as well.

Wednesday

How the rain did pour down! Hjalmar could hear it in his sleep;. and when Ole-Luk-Oie opened the window, the water flowed quite up to the window-sill. It had the appearance of a large lake outside, and a beautiful ship lay close to the house.

"Wilt thou sail with me to-night, little Hjalmar?" said Ole-Luk-Oie; "then we shall see foreign countries, and thou shalt return here in the morning."

All in a moment, there stood Hjalmar, in his best clothes, on the deck of the noble ship; and immediately the weather became fine. They sailed through the streets, round by the church, and on every side rolled the wide, great sea. They sailed till the land disappeared, and then they saw a flock of storks, who had left their own country, and were travelling to warmer climates. The storks flew one behind the other, and had already been a long, long time on the wing. One of them seemed so tired that his wings could scarcely carry him. He was the last of the row, and was soon left very far behind. At length he sunk lower and lower, with outstretched wings, flapping them in vain, till his feet touched the rigging of the ship, and he slided from the sails to the deck, and stood before them. Then a sailor-boy caught him, and put him in the hen-house, with the fowls, the ducks, and the turkeys, while the poor stork stood quite bewildered amongst them.

"Just look at that fellow," said the chickens.

Then the turkey-cock puffed himself out as large as he could, and inquired who he was; and the ducks waddled backwards, crying, "Quack, quack."

Then the stork told them all about warm Africa, of the pyramids, and of the ostrich, which, like a wild horse, runs across the desert. But the ducks did not understand what he said, and quacked amongst themselves, "We are all of the same opinion; namely, that he is stupid."

"Yes, to be sure, he is stupid," said the turkey-cock; and gobbled.

Then the stork remained quite silent, and thought of his home in Africa.

"Those are handsome thin legs of yours," said the turkey-cock. "What do they cost a yard?"

"Quack, quack, quack," grinned the ducks; but, the stork pretended not to hear.

"You may as well laugh," said the turkey; "for that remark was rather witty, or perhaps it was above you. Ah, ah, is he not clever? He will be a great amusement to us while he remains here." And then he gobbled, and the ducks quacked, "Gobble, gobble; Quack, quack."

What a terrible uproar they made, while they were having such fun among themselves!

Then Hjalmar went to the hen-house; and, opening the door, called to the stork. Then he hopped out on the deck. He had rested himself now, and he looked happy, and seemed as if he nodded to Hjalmar, as if to thank him. Then he spread his wings, and flew away to warmer countries, while the hens clucked, the ducks quacked, and the turkey-cock turned quite scarlet in the head.

"To-morrow you shall be made into soup," said Hjalmar to the fowls; and then he awoke, and found himself lying in his little bed.

It was a wonderful journey which Ole-Luk-Oie had made him take this night.

Thursday

"What do you think I have got here?" said Ole-Luk-Oie, "Do not be frightened, and you shall see a little mouse." And then he held out his hand to him, in which lay a lovely little creature. "It has come to invite you to a wedding. Two little mice are going to enter into the marriage state tonight. They reside under the floor of your mother's store-room, and that must be a fine dwelling-place."

"But how can I get through the little mouse-hole in the floor?" asked Hjalmar.

"Leave me to manage that," said Ole-Luk-Oie. "I will soon make you small enough." And then he touched Hjalmar with his magic wand, whereupon he became less and less, until at last he was not longer than a little finger. "Now you can borrow the dress of the tin soldier. I think it will just fit you. It looks well to wear a uniform when you go into company."

"Yes, certainly," said Hjalmar; and in a moment he was dressed as neatly as the neatest of all tin soldiers.

"Will you be so good as to seat yourself in your mamma's thimble," said the little mouse, "that I may have the pleasure of drawing you to the wedding."

"Will you really take so much trouble, young lady?" said Hjalmar. And so in this way he rode to the mouse's wedding.

First they went under the floor, and then passed through a long passage, which was scarcely high enough to allow the thimble to drive under, and the whole passage was lit up with the phosphorescent light of rotten wood.

"Does it not smell delicious?" asked the mouse, as she drew him along. "The wall and the floor have been smeared with bacon-rind; nothing can be nicer."

Very soon they arrived at the bridal hall. On the right stood all the little lady-mice, whispering and giggling, as if they were making game of each other. To the left were the gentlemen-mice, stroking their whiskers with their fore-paws; and in the centre of the hall could be seen the bridal pair, standing side by side, in a hollow cheese-rind, and kissing each other, while all eyes were upon them; for they had already been betrothed, and were soon to be married. More and more friends kept arriving, till the mice were nearly treading each other to death; for the bridal pair now stood in the doorway, and none could pass in or out.

The room had been rubbed over with bacon-rind, like the passage, which was all the refreshment offered to the guests. But for dessert they produced a pea, on which a mouse belonging to the bridal pair had bitten the first letters of their names. This was something quite uncommon. All the mice said it was a very beautiful wedding, and that they had been very agreeably entertained.

After this, Hjalmar returned home. He had certainly been in grand society; but he had been obliged to creep under a room, and to make himself small enough to wear the uniform of a tin soldier.

Friday

It is incredible how many old people there are who would be glad to have me at night," said Ole-Luk-Oie, "especially those who have done something wrong. 'Good little Ole,' say they to me, 'we cannot close our eyes, and we lie awake the whole night and see all our evil deeds sitting on our beds like little imps, and sprinkling us with hot water. Will you come and drive them away, that we may have a good night's rest?' and then they sigh so deeply and say, 'We would gladly pay you for it. Good-night, Ole-Luk, the money lies on the window.' But I never do anything for gold." "What shall we do to-night?" asked Hjalmar. "I do not know whether you would care to go to another wedding," he replied, "although it is quite a different affair to the one we saw last night. Your sister's large doll, that is dressed like a man, and is called Herman, intends to marry the doll Bertha. It is also the dolls' birthday, and they will receive many presents."

"Yes, I know that already," said Hjalmar, "my sister always allows her dolls to keep their birthdays or to have a wedding when they require new clothes; that has happened already a hundred times, I am quite sure."

"Yes, so it may; but to-night is the hundred and first wedding, and when that has taken place it must be the last, therefore this is to be extremely beautiful. Only look."

Hjalmar looked at the table, and there stood the little card-board doll's house, with lights in all the windows, and drawn up before it were the tin soldiers presenting arms. The bridal pair were seated on the floor, leaning against the leg of the table, looking very thoughtful, and with good reason. Then Ole-Luk-Oie dressed up in grandmother's black gown married them.

As soon as the ceremony was concluded, all the furniture in the room joined in singing a beautiful song, which had been composed by the lead pencil, and which went to the melody of a military tattoo.

> *"What merry sounds are on the wind,*
> *As marriage rites together bind*
> *A quiet and a loving pair,*
> *Though formed of kid, yet smooth and fair!*
> *Hurrah! If they are deaf and blind,*
> *We'll sing, though weather prove unkind."*

And now came the present; but the bridal pair had nothing to eat, for love was to be their food.

"Shall we go to a country house, or travel?" asked the bridegroom.

Then they consulted the swallow who had travelled so far, and the old hen in the yard, who had brought up five broods of chickens.

And the swallow talked to them of warm countries, where the grapes hang in large clusters on the vines, and the air is soft and mild, and about the mountains glowing with colors more beautiful than we can think of.

"But they have no red cabbage like we have," said the hen, "I was once in the country with my chickens for a whole summer, there was a large sand-pit, in which we could walk about and scratch as we liked. Then we got into a garden in which grew red cabbage; oh, how nice it was, I cannot think of anything more delicious."

"But one cabbage stalk is exactly like another," said the swallow; "and here we have often bad weather."

"Yes, but we are accustomed to it," said the hen.

"But it is so cold here, and freezes sometimes."

"Cold weather is good for cabbages," said the hen; "besides we do have it warm here sometimes. Four years ago, we had a summer that lasted more than five weeks, and it was so hot one could scarcely breathe. And then in this country we have no poisonous animals, and we are free from robbers. He must be wicked who does not consider our country the finest of all lands. He ought not to be allowed to live here." And then the hen wept very much and said, "I have also travelled. I once went twelve miles in a coop, and it was not pleasant travelling at all."

"The hen is a sensible woman," said the doll Bertha. "I don't care for travelling over mountains, just to go up and come down again. No, let us go to the sand-pit in front of the gate, and then take a walk in the cabbage garden."

And so they settled it.

Saturday

"Am I to hear any more stories?" asked little Hjalmar, as soon as Ole-Luk-Oie had sent him to sleep.

"We shall have no time this evening," said he, spreading out his prettiest umbrella over the child. "Look at these Chinese," and then the whole umbrella appeared like a large china bowl, with blue trees and pointed bridges, upon which stood little Chinamen nodding their heads. "We must make all the world beautiful for to-morrow morning," said Ole-Luk-Oie, "for it will be a holiday, it is Sunday. I must now go to the church steeple and see if the little sprites who live there have polished the bells, so that they may sound sweetly. Then I must go into the fields and see if the wind has blown the dust from the grass and the leaves, and the most difficult task of all which I have to do, is to take down all the stars and brighten them up. I have to number them first before I put them in my apron, and also to number the places from which I take them, so that they may go back into the right holes, or else they would not remain, and we should have a number of falling stars, for they would all tumble down one after the other."

"Hark ye! Mr. Luk-Oie," said an old portrait which hung on the wall of Hjalmar's bedroom. "Do you know me? I am Hjalmar's great-grandfather. I thank you for telling the boy stories, but you must not confuse his ideas. The stars cannot be taken down from the sky and polished; they are spheres like our earth, which is a good thing for them."

"Thank you, old great-grandfather," said Ole-Luk-Oie. "I thank you; you may be the head of the family, as no doubt you are, but I am older than you. I am an ancient heathen. The old Romans and Greeks named me the Dream-god. I have visited the noblest houses, and continue to do so; still I know how to conduct myself both to high and low, and now you may tell the stories yourself." and so Ole-Luk-Oie walked off, taking his umbrellas with him.

"Well, well, one is never to give an opinion, I suppose," grumbled the portrait. And it woke Hjalmar.

Sunday

"Good evening," said Ole-Luk-Oie.

Hjalmar nodded, and then sprang out of bed, and turned his great-grandfather's portrait to the wall, so that it might not interrupt them as it had done yesterday. "Now," said he, "you must tell me some stories about five green peas that lived in one pod; or of the chickseed that courted the chickweed; or of the darning needle, who acted so proudly because she fancied herself an embroidery needle."

"You may have too much of a good thing," said Ole-Luk-Oie. "You know that I like best to show you something, so I will show you my brother. He is also called Ole-Luk-Oie but he never visits any one but once, and when he does come, he takes him away on his horse, and tells him stories as they ride along. He knows only two stories. One of these is so wonderfully beautiful, that no one in the world can imagine anything at all like it; but the other is just as ugly and frightful, so that it would be impossible to describe it." Then Ole-Luk-Oie lifted Hjalmar up to the window. "There now, you can see my brother, the other Ole-Luk-Oie; he is also called Death. You perceive he is not so bad as they represent him in picture books; there he is a skeleton, but now his coat is embroidered with silver, and he wears the splendid uniform of a hussar, and a mantle of black velvet flies behind him, over the horse. Look, how he gallops along." Hjalmar saw that as this Ole-Luk-Oie rode on, he lifted up old and young, and carried them away on his horse. Some he seated in front of him, and some behind, but always inquired first, "How stands the mark-book?"

"Good," they all answered.

"Yes, but let me see for myself," he replied; and they were obliged to give him the books. Then all those who had "Very good," or "Exceedingly good," came in front of the horse, and heard the beautiful story; while those who had "Middling," or "Tolerably good," in their books, were obliged to sit behind, and listen to the frightful tale. They trembled and cried, and wanted to jump down from the horse, but they could not get free, for they seemed fastened to the seat.

"Why, Death is a most splendid Luk-Oie," said Hjalmar. "I am not in the least afraid of him."

"You need have no fear of him," said Ole-Luk-Oie, "if you take care and keep a good conduct book."

"Now I call that very instructive," murmured the great-grandfather's portrait. "It is useful sometimes to express an opinion;" so he was quite satisfied.

These are some of the doings and sayings of Ole-Luk-Oie. I hope he may visit you himself this evening, and relate some more.

Little Tuk

YES, THEY CALLED him Little Tuk, but it was not his real name; he had called himself so before he could speak plainly, and he meant it for Charles. It was all very well for those who knew him, but not for strangers.

Little Tuk was left at home to take care of his little sister, Gustava, who was much younger than himself, and he had to learn his lessons at the same time, and the two things could not very well be performed together. The poor boy sat there with his sister on his lap, and sung to her all the songs he knew, and now and then he looked into his geography lesson that lay open before him. By the next morning he had to learn by heart all the towns in Zealand, and all that could be described of them.

His mother came home at last, and took little Gustava in her arms. Then Tuk ran to the window, and read so eagerly that he nearly read his eyes out; for it had become darker and darker every minute, and his mother had no money to buy a light.

"There goes the old washerwoman up the lane," said the mother, as she looked out of the window; "the poor woman can hardly drag herself along, and now she had to drag a pail of water from the well. Be a good boy, Tuk, and run across and help the old woman, won't you?"

So Tuk ran across quickly, and helped her, but when he came back into the room it was quite dark, and there was not a word said about a light, so he was obliged to go to bed on his little truckle bedstead, and there he lay and thought of his geography lesson, and of Zealand, and of all the master had told him. He ought really to have read it over again, but he could not for want of light. So he put the geography book under his pillow, for he had heard that this was a great help towards learning a lesson, but not always to be depended upon. He still lay thinking and thinking, when all at once it seemed as if some one kissed him on his eyes and mouth. He slept and yet he did not sleep; and it appeared as if the old washerwoman looked at him with kind eyes and said, "It would be a great pity if you did not know your lesson to-morrow morning; you helped me, and now I will help you, and Providence will always keep those who help themselves;" and at the same time the book under Tuk's pillow began to move about. "Cluck, cluck, cluck," cried a hen as she crept towards him. "I am a hen from Kjøge," and then she told him how many inhabitants the town contained, and about a battle that had been fought there, which really was not worth speaking of.

"Crack, crack," down fell something. It was a wooden bird, the parrot which is used as a target as Præstø. He said there were as many inhabitants in that town as he had nails in his body. He was very proud, and said, "Thorwalsden lived close to me, and here I am now, quite comfortable."

But now little Tuk was no longer in bed; all in a moment he found himself on horseback. Gallop, gallop, away he went, seated in front of a richly-attired knight, with a waving plume, who held him on the saddle, and so they rode through the wood by the old town of Wordingburg, which was very large and busy. The king's castle was surrounded by lofty towers, and radiant light streamed from all the windows. Within there were songs and dancing; King Waldemar and the young gayly-dressed ladies of the court were dancing together. Morning dawned, and as the sun rose, the whole city and the king's castle sank suddenly down together. One tower after another fell, till at last only one remained standing on the hill where the castle had formerly been.

The town now appeared small and poor, and the school-boys read in their books, which they carried under their arms, that it contained two thousand inhabitants; but this was a mere boast, for it did not contain so many.

And again little Tuk lay in his bed, scarcely knowing whether he was dreaming or not, for some one stood by him.

"Tuk! little Tuk!" said a voice. It was a very little person who spoke. He was dressed as a sailor, and looked small enough to be a middy, but he was not one. "I bring you many greetings from Corsøe. It is a rising town, full of life. It has steamships and mail-coaches. In times past they used to call it ugly, but that is no longer true. I lie on the sea-shore," said Corsøe; "I have high-roads and pleasure-gardens; I have given birth to a poet who was witty and entertaining, which they are not all. I once wanted to fit out a ship to sail round the world, but I did not accomplish it, though most likely I might have done so. But I am fragrant with perfume, for close to my gates most lovely roses bloom."

Then before the eyes of little Tuk appeared a confusion of colors, red and green; but it cleared off, and he could distinguish a cliff close to the bay, the slopes of which were quite overgrown with verdure, and on its summit stood a fine old church with pointed towers. Springs of water flowed out of the cliff in thick waterspouts, so that there was a continual splashing. Close by sat an old king with a golden crown on his white head. This was King Hroar of the Springs and near the springs stood the town of Roeskilde, as it is called. Then all the kings and queens of Denmark went up the ascent to the old church, hand in hand, with golden crowns on their heads, while the organ played and the fountains sent forth jets of water.

Little Tuk saw and heard it all. "Don't forget the names of these towns," said King Hroar.

All at once everything vanished; but where! It seemed to him like turning over the leaves of a book. And now there stood before him an old peasant woman, who had come from Sorø where the grass grows in the market-place. She had a green linen apron thrown over her head and shoulders, and it was quite wet, as if it had been raining heavily. "Yes, that it has," said she, and then, just as she was going to tell him a great many pretty stories from Holberg's comedies, and about Waldemar and Absalom, she suddenly shrunk up together, and wagged her head as if she were a frog about to spring. "Croak," she cried; "it is always wet, and as quiet as death in Sorø." Then little Tuk saw she was changed into a frog. "Croak," and again she was an old woman. "One must dress according to the weather," said she. "It is wet, and my town is just like a bottle. By the cork we must go in, and by the cork we must come out again. In olden times I had beautiful fish, and now I have fresh, rosy-cheeked boys in the bottom of the bottle, and they learn wisdom, Hebrew and Greek."

"Croak." How it sounded like the cry of the frogs on the moor, or like the creaking of great boots when some one is marching, – always the same tone, so monotonous and wearing, that little Tuk at length fell fast asleep, and then the sound could not annoy him. But even in this sleep came a dream or something like it. His little sister Gustava, with her blue eyes, and fair curly hair, had grown up a beautiful maiden all at once, and without having wings she could fly. And they flew together over Zealand, over green forests and blue lakes.

"Hark, so you hear the cock crow, little Tuk. 'Cock-a-doodle-doo.' The fowls are flying out of Kjøge. You shall have a large farm-yard. You shall never suffer hunger or want. The bird of good omen shall be yours, and you shall become a rich and happy man; your house shall rise up like King Waldemar's towers, and shall be richly adorned with marble statues, like those at Præstø. Understand me well; your name shall travel with fame round the world like the ship that was to sail from Corsøe, and at Roeskilde, – Don't forget the names of the towns, as King Hroar said, – you shall speak well and clearly little Tuk, and when at last you lie in your grave you shall sleep peacefully, as – "

"As if I lay in Sorø," said little Tuk awaking. It was bright daylight, and he could not remember his dream, but that was not necessary, for we are not to know what will happen to us in the future. Then he sprang out of bed quickly, and read over his lesson in the book, and knew it all at once quite correctly. The old washerwoman put her head in at the door, and nodded to him quite kindly, and said, "Many thanks, you good child, for your help yesterday. I hope all your beautiful dreams will come true."

Little Tuk did not at all know what he had dreamt, but One above did.

Elder-Tree Mother

THERE WAS ONCE a little boy who had caught cold; he had gone out and got wet feet. Nobody had the least idea how it had happened; the weather was quite dry. His mother undressed him, put him to bed, and ordered the teapot to be brought in, that she might make him a good cup of tea from the elder-tree blossoms, which is so warming. At the same time, the kind-hearted old man who lived by himself in the upper storey of the house came in; he led a lonely life, for he had no wife and children; but he loved the children of others very much, and he could tell so many fairy tales and stories, that it was a pleasure to hear him.

"Now, drink your tea," said the mother; "perhaps you will hear a story."

"Yes, if I only knew a fresh one," said the old man, and nodded smilingly. "But how did the little fellow get his wet feet?" he then asked.

"That," replied the mother, "nobody can understand."

"Will you tell me a story?" asked the boy.

"Yes, if you can tell me as nearly as possible how deep is the gutter in the little street where you go to school."

"Just half as high as my top-boots," replied the boy; "but then I must stand in the deepest holes."

"There, now we know where you got your wet feet," said the old man. "I ought to tell you a story, but the worst of it is, I do not know any more."

"You can make one up," said the little boy. "Mother says you can tell a fairy tale about anything you look at or touch."

"That is all very well, but such tales or stories are worth nothing! No, the right ones come by themselves and knock at my forehead saying: 'Here I am.'"

"Will not one knock soon?" asked the boy; and the mother smiled while she put elder-tree blossoms into the teapot and poured boiling water over them. "Pray, tell me a story."

"Yes, if stories came by themselves; they are so proud, they only come when they please. – But wait," he said suddenly, "there is one. Look at the teapot; there is a story in it now."

And the little boy looked at the teapot; the lid rose up gradually, the elder-tree blossoms sprang forth one by one, fresh and white; long boughs came forth; even out of the spout they grew up in all directions, and formed a bush – nay, a large elder tree, which stretched its branches up to the bed and pushed the curtains aside; and there were so many blossoms and such a sweet fragrance! In the midst of the tree sat a kindly-looking old woman with a strange dress; it was as green as the leaves, and trimmed with large white blossoms, so that it was difficult to say whether it was real cloth, or the leaves and blossoms of the elder-tree.

"What is this woman's name?" asked the little boy.

"Well, the Romans and Greeks used to call her a Dryad," said the old man; "but we do not understand that. Out in the sailors' quarter they give her a better name; there she is called elder-tree mother. Now, you must attentively listen to her and look at the beautiful elder-tree.

"Just such a large tree, covered with flowers, stands out there; it grew in the corner of an humble little yard; under this tree sat two old people one afternoon in the beautiful sunshine. He was an old, old sailor, and she his old wife; they had already great-grandchildren, and were soon to celebrate their golden wedding, but they could not remember the date, and the elder-tree mother was sitting in the tree and looked as pleased as this one here. 'I know very well when the golden wedding is to take place,' she said; but they did not hear it – they were talking of bygone days.

"'Well, do you remember?' said the old sailor, 'when we were quite small and used to run about and play – it was in the very same yard where we now are – we used to put little branches into the ground and make a garden.'

"'Yes,' said the old woman, 'I remember it very well; we used to water the branches, and one of them, an elder-tree branch, took root, and grew and became the large tree under which we are now sitting as old people.'

"'Certainly, you are right,' he said; 'and in yonder corner stood a large water-tub; there I used to sail my boat, which I had cut out myself – it sailed so well; but soon I had to sail somewhere else.'

"'But first we went to school to learn something,' she said, 'and then we were confirmed; we both wept on that day, but in the afternoon we went out hand in hand, and ascended the high round tower and looked out into the wide world right over Copenhagen and the sea; then we walked to Fredericksburg, where the king and the queen were sailing about in their magnificent boat on the canals.'

"'But soon I had to sail about somewhere else, and for many years I was travelling about far away from home.'

"'And I often cried about you, for I was afraid lest you were drowned and lying at the bottom of the sea. Many a time I got up in the night and looked if the weathercock had turned; it turned often, but you did not return. I remember one day distinctly: the rain was pouring down in torrents; the dust-man had come to the house where I was in service; I went down with the dust-bin and stood for a moment in the doorway, and looked at the dreadful weather. Then the postman gave me a letter; it was from you. Heavens! how that letter had travelled about. I tore it open and read it; I cried and laughed at the same time, and was so happy! Therein was written that you were staying in the hot countries, where the coffee grows. These must be marvellous countries. You said a great deal about them, and I read all while the rain was pouring down and I was standing there with the dust-bin. Then suddenly some one put his arm round my waist –'

"'Yes, and you gave him a hearty smack on the cheek,' said the old man.

"'I did not know that it was you – you had come as quickly as your letter; and you looked so handsome, and so you do still. You had a large yellow silk handkerchief in your pocket and a shining hat on. You looked so well, and the weather in the street was horrible!'

"'Then we married,' he said. 'Do you remember how we got our first boy, and then Mary, Niels, Peter, John, and Christian?'

'Oh yes; and now they have all grown up, and have become useful members of society, whom everybody cares for.'

"'And their children have had children again,' said the old sailor. 'Yes, these are children's children, and they are strong and healthy. If I am not mistaken, our wedding took place at this season of the year.'

"'Yes, to-day is your golden wedding-day,' said the little elder-tree mother, stretching her head down between the two old people, who thought that she was their neighbor who was nodding to them; they looked at each other and clasped hands. Soon afterwards the children and grandchildren came, for they knew very well that it was the golden wedding-day; they had already wished them joy and happiness in the morning, but the old people had forgotten it, although they remembered things so well that had passed many, many years ago. The elder-tree smelt strongly, and the setting sun illuminated the faces of the two old people, so that they looked quite rosy; the youngest of the grandchildren danced round them, and cried merrily that there would be a feast in the evening, for they were to have hot potatoes; and the elder mother nodded in the tree and cried 'Hooray' with the others."

"But that was no fairy tale," said the little boy who had listened to it.

"You will presently understand it," said the old man who told the story. "Let us ask little elder-tree mother about it."

"That was no fairy tale," said the little elder-tree mother; "but now it comes! Real life furnishes us with subjects for the most wonderful fairy tales; for otherwise my beautiful elder-bush could not have grown forth out of the teapot."

And then she took the little boy out of bed and placed him on her bosom; the elder branches, full of blossoms, closed over them; it was as if they sat in a thick leafy bower which flew with them through the air; it was beautiful beyond all description. The little elder-tree mother had suddenly become a charming young girl, but her dress was still of the same green material, covered with white blossoms, as the elder-tree mother had worn; she had a real elder blossom on her bosom, and a wreath of the same flowers was wound round her curly golden hair; her eyes were so large and so blue that it was wonderful to look at them. She and the boy kissed each other, and then they were of the same age and felt the same joys. They walked hand in hand out of the bower, and now stood at home in a beautiful flower garden. Near the green lawn the father's walking-stick was tied to a post. There was life in this stick for the little ones, for as soon as they seated themselves upon it the polished knob turned into a neighing horse's head, a long black mane was fluttering in the wind, and four strong slender legs grew out. The animal was fiery and spirited; they galloped round the lawn. "Hooray! now we shall ride far away, many miles!" said the boy; "we shall ride to the nobleman's estate where we were last year." And they rode round the lawn again, and the little girl, who, as we know, was no other than the little elder-tree mother, continually cried, "Now we are in the country! Do you see the farmhouse there, with the large baking stove, which projects like a gigantic egg out of the wall into the road? The elder-tree spreads its branches over it, and the cock struts about and scratches for the hens. Look how proud he is! Now we are near the church; it stands on a high hill, under the spreading oak trees; one of them is half dead! Now we are at the smithy, where the fire roars and the half-naked men beat with their hammers so that the sparks fly far and wide. Let's be off to the beautiful farm!" And they passed by everything the little girl, who was sitting behind on the stick, described, and the boy saw it, and yet they only went round the lawn. Then they played in a sidewalk, and marked out a little garden on the ground; she took elder-blossoms out of her hair and planted them, and they grew exactly like those the old people planted when they were children, as we have heard before. They walked about hand in hand, just as the old couple had done when they were little, but they did not go to the round tower nor to the Fredericksburg garden. No; the little girl seized the boy round the waist, and then they flew far into the country. It was spring and it became summer, it was autumn and it became winter, and thousands of pictures reflected themselves in the boy's eyes and heart, and the little girl always sang again, "You will never forget that!" And during their whole flight the elder-tree smelt so sweetly; he noticed the roses and the fresh beeches, but the elder-tree smelt much stronger, for the flowers were fixed on the little girl's bosom, against which the boy often rested his head during the flight.

"It is beautiful here in spring," said the little girl, and they were again in the green beechwood, where the thyme breathed forth sweet fragrance at their feet, and the pink anemones looked lovely in the green moss. "Oh! that it were always spring in the fragrant beechwood!"

"Here it is splendid in summer!" she said, and they passed by old castles of the age of chivalry. The high walls and indented battlements were reflected in the water of the ditches, on which swans were swimming and peering into the old shady avenues. The corn waved in the field like a yellow sea. Red and yellow flowers grew in the ditches, wild hops and convolvuli in full bloom in the hedges. In the evening the moon rose, large and round, and the hayricks in the meadows smelt sweetly. "One can never forget it!"

"Here it is beautiful in autumn!" said the little girl, and the atmosphere seemed twice as high and blue, while the wood shone with crimson, green, and gold. The hounds were running off, flocks of wild fowl flew screaming over the barrows, while the bramble bushes twined round the old stones. The dark-blue sea was covered with white-sailed ships, and in the barns sat old women, girls, and children picking hops into a large tub; the young ones sang songs, and the old people told fairy tales about goblins and sorcerers. It could not be more pleasant anywhere.

"Here it's agreeable in winter!" said the little girl, and all the trees were covered with hoar-frost, so that they looked like white coral. The snow creaked under one's feet, as if one had new boots on. One shooting star after another traversed the sky. In the room the Christmas tree was lit, and there were song and merriment. In the peasant's cottage the violin sounded, and games were played for apple quarters; even the poorest child said, "It is beautiful in winter!"

And indeed it was beautiful! And the little girl showed everything to the boy, and the elder-tree continued to breathe forth sweet perfume, while the red flag with the white cross was streaming in the wind; it was the flag under which the old sailor had served. The boy became a youth; he was to go out into the wide world, far away to the countries where the coffee grows. But at parting the little girl took an elder-blossom from her breast and gave it to him as a keepsake. He placed it in his prayer-book, and when he opened it in distant lands it was always at the place where the flower of remembrance was lying; and the more he looked at it the fresher it became, so that he could almost smell the fragrance of the woods at home. He distinctly saw the little girl, with her bright blue eyes, peeping out from behind the petals, and heard her whispering, "Here it is beautiful in spring, in summer, in autumn, and in winter," and hundreds of pictures passed through his mind.

Thus many years rolled by. He had now become an old man, and was sitting, with his old wife, under an elder-tree in full bloom. They held each other by the hand exactly as the great-grandfather and the great-grandmother had done outside, and, like them, they talked about bygone days and of their golden wedding. The little girl with the blue eyes and elder-blossoms in her hair was sitting high up in the tree, and nodded to them, saying, "To-day is the golden wedding!" And then she took two flowers out of her wreath and kissed them. They glittered at first like silver, then like gold, and when she placed them on the heads of the old people each flower became a golden crown. There they both sat like a king and queen under the sweet-smelling tree, which looked exactly like an elder-tree, and he told his wife the story of the elder-tree mother as it had been told him when he was a little boy. They were both of opinion that the story contained many points like their own, and these similarities they liked best.

"Yes, so it is," said the little girl in the tree. "Some call me Little Elder-tree Mother; others a Dryad; but my real name is 'Remembrance.' It is I who sit in the tree which grows and grows. I can remember things and tell stories! But let's see if you have still got your flower."

And the old man opened his prayer-book; the elder-blossom was still in it, and as fresh as if it had only just been put in. Remembrance nodded, and the two old people, with the golden crowns on their heads, sat in the glowing evening sun. They closed their eyes and – and –

Well, now the story is ended! The little boy in bed did not know whether he had dreamt it or heard it told; the teapot stood on the table, but no elder-tree was growing out of it, and the old man who had told the story was on the point of leaving the room, and he did go out.

"How beautiful it was!" said the little boy. "Mother, I have been to warm countries!"

"I believe you," said the mother; "if one takes two cups of hot elder-tea it is quite natural that one gets into warm countries!" And she covered him up well, so that he might not take cold. "You have slept soundly while I was arguing with the old man whether it was a story or a fairy tale!"

"And what has become of the little elder-tree mother?" asked the boy.

"She is in the teapot," said the mother; "and there she may remain."

The Snow Queen

Story the First
Which Describes a Looking-Glass and the Broken Fragments.

YOU MUST ATTEND to the commencement of this story, for when we get to the end we shall know more than we do now about a very wicked hobgoblin; he was one of the very worst, for he was a real demon. One day, when he was in a merry mood, he made a looking-glass which had the power of making everything good or beautiful that was reflected in it almost shrink to nothing, while everything that was worthless and bad looked increased in size and worse than ever. The most lovely landscapes appeared like boiled spinach, and the people became hideous, and looked as if they stood on their heads and had no bodies. Their countenances were so distorted that no one could recognize them, and even one freckle on the face appeared to spread over the whole of the nose and mouth. The demon said this was very amusing. When a good or pious thought passed through the mind of any one it was misrepresented in the glass; and then how the demon laughed at his cunning invention. All who went to the demon's school – for he kept a school – talked everywhere of the wonders they had seen, and declared that people could now, for the first time, see what the world and mankind were really like. They carried the glass about everywhere, till at last there was not a land nor a people who had not been looked at through this distorted mirror. They wanted even to fly with it up to heaven to see the angels, but the higher they flew the more slippery the glass became, and they could scarcely hold it, till at last it slipped from their hands, fell to the earth, and was broken into millions of pieces. But now the looking-glass caused more unhappiness than ever, for some of the fragments were not so large as a grain of sand, and they flew about the world into every country. When one of these tiny atoms flew into a person's eye, it stuck there unknown to him, and from that moment he saw everything through a distorted medium, or could see only the worst side of what he looked at, for even the smallest fragment retained the same power which had belonged to the whole mirror. Some few persons even got a fragment of the looking-glass in their hearts, and this was very terrible, for their hearts became cold like a lump of ice. A few of the pieces were so large that they could be used as window-panes; it would have been a sad thing to look at our friends through them. Other pieces were made into spectacles; this was dreadful for those who wore them, for they could see nothing either rightly or justly. At all this the wicked demon laughed till his sides shook – it tickled him so to see the mischief he had done. There were still a number of these little fragments of glass floating about in the air, and now you shall hear what happened with one of them.

Second Story
A Little Boy and a Little Girl

In a large town, full of houses and people, there is not room for everybody to have even a little garden, therefore they are obliged to be satisfied with a few flowers in flower-pots.

In one of these large towns lived two poor children who had a garden something larger and better than a few flower-pots. They were not brother and sister, but they loved each other almost as much as if they had been. Their parents lived opposite to each other in two garrets, where the roofs of neighboring houses projected out towards each other and the water-pipe ran between them. In each house was a little window, so that any one could step across the gutter from one window to the other. The parents of these children had each a large wooden box in which they cultivated kitchen herbs for their own use, and a little rose-bush in each box, which grew splendidly. Now after a while the parents decided to place these two boxes across the water-pipe, so that they reached from one window to the other and looked like two banks of flowers. Sweet-peas drooped over the boxes, and the rose-bushes shot forth long branches, which were trained round the windows and clustered together almost like a triumphal arch of leaves and flowers. The boxes were very high, and the children knew they must not climb upon them, without permission, but they were often, however, allowed to step out together and sit upon their little stools under the rose-bushes, or play quietly. In winter all this pleasure came to an end, for the windows were sometimes quite frozen over. But then they would warm copper pennies on the stove, and hold the warm pennies against the frozen pane; there would be very soon a little round hole through which they could peep, and the soft bright eyes of the little boy and girl would beam through the hole at each window as they looked at each other. Their names were Kay and Gerda. In summer they could be together with one jump from the window, but in winter they had to go up and down the long staircase, and out through the snow before they could meet.

"See there are the white bees swarming," said Kay's old grandmother one day when it was snowing.

"Have they a queen bee?" asked the little boy, for he knew that the real bees had a queen.

"To be sure they have," said the grandmother. "She is flying there where the swarm is thickest. She is the largest of them all, and never remains on the earth, but flies up to the dark clouds. Often at midnight she flies through the streets of the town, and looks in at the windows, then the ice freezes on the panes into wonderful shapes, that look like flowers and castles."

"Yes, I have seen them," said both the children, and they knew it must be true.

"Can the Snow Queen come in here?" asked the little girl.

"Only let her come," said the boy, "I'll set her on the stove and then she'll melt."

Then the grandmother smoothed his hair and told him some more tales. One evening, when little Kay was at home, half undressed, he climbed on a chair by the window and peeped out through the little hole. A few flakes of snow were falling, and one of them, rather larger than the rest, alighted on the edge of one of the flower boxes. This snow-flake grew larger and larger, till at last it became the figure of a woman, dressed in garments of white gauze, which looked like millions of starry snow-flakes linked together. She was fair and beautiful, but made of ice – shining and glittering ice. Still she was alive and her eyes sparkled like bright stars, but there was neither peace nor rest in their glance. She nodded towards the window and waved her hand. The little boy was frightened and sprang from the chair; at the same moment it seemed as if a large bird flew by the window. On the following day there was a clear frost, and very soon came the spring. The sun shone; the young green leaves burst forth; the swallows built their nests; windows were opened, and the children sat once more in the garden on the roof, high above all the other rooms. How beautiful the roses blossomed this summer. The little girl had learnt a hymn in which roses were spoken of, and then she thought of their own roses, and she sang the hymn to the little boy, and he sang too: –

"Roses bloom and cease to be,
But we shall the Christ-child see."

Then the little ones held each other by the hand, and kissed the roses, and looked at the bright sunshine, and spoke to it as if the Christ-child were there. Those were splendid summer days. How beautiful and fresh it was out among the rose-bushes, which seemed as if they would never leave off blooming. One day Kay and Gerda sat looking at a book full of pictures of animals and birds, and then just as the clock in the church tower struck twelve, Kay said, "Oh, something has struck my heart!" and soon after, "There is something in my eye."

The little girl put her arm round his neck, and looked into his eye, but she could see nothing.

"I think it is gone," he said. But it was not gone; it was one of those bits of the looking-glass – that magic mirror, of which we have spoken – the ugly glass which made everything great and good appear small and ugly, while all that was wicked and bad became more visible, and every little fault could be plainly seen. Poor little Kay had also received a small grain in his heart, which very quickly turned to a lump of ice. He felt no more pain, but the glass was there still. "Why do you cry?" said he at last; "it makes you look ugly. There is nothing the matter with me now. Oh, see!" he cried suddenly, "that rose is worm-eaten, and this one is quite crooked. After all they are ugly roses, just like the box in which they stand," and then he kicked the boxes with his foot, and pulled off the two roses.

"Kay, what are you doing?" cried the little girl; and then, when he saw how frightened she was, he tore off another rose, and jumped through his own window away from little Gerda.

When she afterwards brought out the picture book, he said, "It was only fit for babies in long clothes," and when grandmother told any stories, he would interrupt her with "but;" or, when he could manage it, he would get behind her chair, put on a pair of spectacles, and imitate her very cleverly, to make people laugh. By-and-by he began to mimic the speech and gait of persons in the street. All that was peculiar or disagreeable in a person he would imitate directly, and people said, "That boy will be very clever; he has a remarkable genius." But it was the piece of glass in his eye, and the coldness in his heart, that made him act like this. He would even tease little Gerda, who loved him with all her heart. His games, too, were quite different; they were not so childish. One winter's day, when it snowed, he brought out a burning-glass, then he held out the tail of his blue coat, and let the snow-flakes fall upon it. "Look in this glass, Gerda," said he; and she saw how every flake of snow was magnified, and looked like a beautiful flower or a glittering star. "Is it not clever?" said Kay, "and much more interesting than looking at real flowers. There is not a single fault in it, and the snow-flakes are quite perfect till they begin to melt."

Soon after Kay made his appearance in large thick gloves, and with his sledge at his back. He called up stairs to Gerda, "I've got to leave to go into the great square, where the other boys play and ride." And away he went.

In the great square, the boldest among the boys would often tie their sledges to the country people's carts, and go with them a good way. This was capital. But while they were all amusing themselves, and Kay with them, a great sledge came by; it was painted white, and in it sat some one wrapped in a rough white fur, and wearing a white cap. The sledge drove twice round the square, and Kay fastened his own little sledge to it, so that when it went away, he followed with it. It went faster and faster right through the next street, and then the person who drove turned round and nodded pleasantly to Kay, just as if they were acquainted with each other, but whenever Kay wished to loosen his little sledge the driver nodded again, so Kay sat still, and they drove out through the town gate. Then the snow began to fall so heavily that the little boy could not see a hand's breadth before him, but still they drove on; then he suddenly loosened the cord so that the large sled might go on without him, but it was of no use, his little carriage held fast, and away they went like the wind. Then he called out loudly, but nobody heard him, while the snow beat upon him, and the sledge flew onwards. Every now and then it gave a jump as if it were going over hedges and ditches. The boy was frightened, and tried to say a prayer, but he could remember nothing but the multiplication table.

The snow-flakes became larger and larger, till they appeared like great white chickens. All at once they sprang on one side, the great sledge stopped, and the person who had driven it rose up. The fur and the cap, which were made entirely of snow, fell off, and he saw a lady, tall and white, it was the Snow Queen.

"We have driven well," said she, "but why do you tremble? here, creep into my warm fur." Then she seated him beside her in the sledge, and as she wrapped the fur round him he felt as if he were sinking into a snow drift.

"Are you still cold," she asked, as she kissed him on the forehead. The kiss was colder than ice; it went quite through to his heart, which was already almost a lump of ice; he felt as if he were going to die, but only for a moment; he soon seemed quite well again, and did not notice the cold around him.

"My sledge! don't forget my sledge," was his first thought, and then he looked and saw that it was bound fast to one of the white chickens, which flew behind him with the sledge at its back. The Snow Queen kissed little Kay again, and by this time he had forgotten little Gerda, his grandmother, and all at home.

"Now you must have no more kisses," she said, "or I should kiss you to death."

Kay looked at her, and saw that she was so beautiful, he could not imagine a more lovely and intelligent face; she did not now seem to be made of ice, as when he had seen her through his window, and she had nodded to him. In his eyes she was perfect, and she did not feel at all afraid. He told her he could do mental arithmetic, as far as fractions, and that he knew the number of square miles and the number of inhabitants in the country. And she always smiled so that he thought he did not know enough yet, and she looked round the vast expanse as she flew higher and higher with him upon a black cloud, while the storm blew and howled as if it were singing old songs. They flew over woods and lakes, over sea and land; below them roared the wild wind; the wolves howled and the snow crackled; over them flew the black screaming crows, and above all shone the moon, clear and bright, – and so Kay passed through the long winter's night, and by day he slept at the feet of the Snow Queen.

Third Story
The Flower Garden of the Woman Who Could Conjure

But how fared little Gerda during Kay's absence? What had become of him, no one knew, nor could any one give the slightest information, excepting the boys, who said that he had tied his sledge to another very large one, which had driven through the street, and out at the town gate. Nobody knew where it went; many tears were shed for him, and little Gerda wept bitterly for a long time. She said she knew he must be dead; that he was drowned in the river which flowed close by the school. Oh, indeed those long winter days were very dreary. But at last spring came, with warm sunshine. "Kay is dead and gone," said little Gerda.

"I don't believe it," said the sunshine.

"He is dead and gone," she said to the sparrows.

"We don't believe it," they replied; and at last little Gerda began to doubt it herself. "I will put on my new red shoes," she said one morning, "those that Kay has never seen, and then I will go down to the river, and ask for him." It was quite early when she kissed her old grandmother, who was still asleep; then she put on her red shoes, and went quite alone out of the town gates toward the river. "Is it true that you have taken my little playmate away from me?" said she to the river. "I will give you my red shoes if you will give him back to me." And it seemed as if the waves nodded to her in a strange manner. Then she took off her red shoes, which she liked better than anything else, and threw them both into the river, but they fell near the bank, and the little waves carried them back to the land, just as if the river would not take from her what she loved best, because they could not give her back little Kay. But she thought the shoes had not been thrown out far enough. Then she crept into a boat that lay among the reeds, and threw the shoes again from the farther end of the boat into the water, but it was not fastened. And her movement sent it gliding away from the land. When she saw this she hastened to reach the end of the boat, but before she could so it was more than a yard from the bank, and drifting away faster than ever. Then little Gerda was very much frightened, and began to cry, but no one heard her except the sparrows, and they could not carry her to land, but they flew along by the shore, and sang, as if to comfort her, "Here we are! Here we are!" The boat floated with the stream; little Gerda sat quite still with only her stockings on her feet; the red shoes floated after her, but she could not reach them because the boat kept so much in advance. The banks on each side of the river were very pretty. There were beautiful flowers, old trees, sloping fields, in which cows and sheep were grazing, but not a man to be seen. Perhaps the river will carry me to little Kay, thought Gerda, and then she became more cheerful, and raised her head, and looked at the beautiful green banks; and so the boat sailed on for hours. At length she came to a large cherry orchard, in which stood a small red house with strange red and blue windows. It had also a thatched roof, and outside were two wooden soldiers, that presented arms to her as she sailed past. Gerda called out to them, for she thought they were alive, but of course they did not answer; and as the boat drifted nearer to the shore, she saw what they really were. Then Gerda called still louder, and there came a very old woman out of the house, leaning on a crutch. She wore a large hat to shade her from the sun, and on it were painted all sorts of pretty flowers. "You poor little child," said the old woman, "how did you manage to come all this distance into the wide world on such a rapid rolling stream?" And then the old woman walked in the water, seized the boat with her crutch, drew it to land, and lifted Gerda out. And Gerda was glad to feel herself on dry ground, although she was rather afraid of the strange old woman. "Come and tell me who you are," said she, "and how came you here."

Then Gerda told her everything, while the old woman shook her head, and said, "Hem-hem;" and when she had finished, Gerda asked if she had not seen little Kay, and the old woman told her he had not passed by that way, but he very likely would come. So she told Gerda not to be sorrowful, but to taste the cherries and look at the flowers; they were better than any picture-book, for each of them could tell a story. Then she took Gerda by the hand and led her into the little house, and the old woman closed the door. The windows were very high, and as the panes were red, blue, and yellow, the daylight shone through them in all sorts of singular colors. On the table stood beautiful cherries, and Gerda had permission to eat as many as she would. While she was eating them the old woman combed out her long flaxen ringlets with a golden comb, and the glossy curls hung down on each side of the little round pleasant face, which looked fresh and blooming as a rose. "I have long been wishing for a dear little maiden like you," said the old woman, "and now you must stay with me, and see how happily we shall live together." And while she went on combing little Gerda's hair, she thought less and less about her adopted brother Kay, for the old woman could conjure, although she was not a wicked witch; she conjured only a little for her own amusement, and now, because she wanted to keep Gerda. Therefore she went into the garden, and stretched out her crutch towards all the rose-trees, beautiful though they were; and they immediately sunk into the dark earth, so that no one could tell where they had once stood. The old woman was afraid that if little Gerda saw roses she would think of those at home, and then remember little Kay, and run away. Then she took Gerda into the flower-garden. How fragrant and beautiful it was! Every flower that could be thought of for every season of the year was here in full bloom; no picture-book could have more beautiful colors. Gerda jumped for joy, and played till the sun went down behind the tall cherry-trees; then she slept in an elegant bed with red silk pillows, embroidered with colored violets; and then she dreamed as pleasantly as a queen on her wedding day. The next day, and for many days after, Gerda played with the flowers in the warm sunshine. She knew every flower, and yet, although there were so many of them, it seemed as if one were missing, but which it was she could not tell. One day, however, as she sat looking at the old woman's hat with the painted flowers on it, she saw that the prettiest of them all was a rose. The old woman had forgotten to take it from her hat when she made all the roses sink into the earth. But it is difficult to keep the thoughts together in everything; one little mistake upsets all our arrangements.

"What, are there no roses here?" cried Gerda; and she ran out into the garden, and examined all the beds, and searched and searched. There was not one to be found. Then she sat down and wept, and her tears fell just on the place where one of the rose-trees had sunk down. The warm tears moistened the earth, and the rose-tree sprouted up at once, as blooming as when it had sunk; and Gerda embraced it and kissed the roses, and thought of the beautiful roses at home, and, with them, of little Kay.

"Oh, how I have been detained!" said the little maiden, "I wanted to seek for little Kay. Do you know where he is?" she asked the roses; "do you think he is dead?"

And the roses answered, "No, he is not dead. We have been in the ground where all the dead lie; but Kay is not there."

"Thank you," said little Gerda, and then she went to the other flowers, and looked into their little cups, and asked, "Do you know where little Kay is?" But each flower, as it stood in the sunshine, dreamed only of its own little fairy tale of history. Not one knew anything of Kay. Gerda heard many stories from the flowers, as she asked them one after another about him.

And what, said the tiger-lily? "Hark, do you hear the drum? – 'turn, turn,' – there are only two notes, always, 'turn, turn.' Listen to the women's song of mourning! Hear the cry of the priest! In her long red robe stands the Hindoo widow by the funeral pile. The flames rise around her as she places herself on the dead body of her husband; but the Hindoo woman is thinking of the living one in that circle; of him, her son, who lighted those flames. Those shining eyes trouble her heart more painfully than the flames which will soon consume her body to ashes. Can the fire of the heart be extinguished in the flames of the funeral pile?"

"I don't understand that at all," said little Gerda.

"That is my story," said the tiger-lily.

What, says the convolvulus? "Near yonder narrow road stands an old knight's castle; thick ivy creeps over the old ruined walls, leaf over leaf, even to the balcony, in which stands a beautiful maiden. She bends over the balustrades, and looks up the road. No rose on its stem is fresher than she; no apple-blossom, wafted by the wind, floats more lightly than she moves. Her rich silk rustles as she bends over and exclaims, 'Will he not come?'

"Is it Kay you mean?" asked Gerda.

"I am only speaking of a story of my dream," replied the flower.

What, said the little snow-drop? "Between two trees a rope is hanging; there is a piece of board upon it; it is a swing. Two pretty little girls, in dresses white as snow, and with long green ribbons fluttering from their hats, are sitting upon it swinging. Their brother who is taller than they are, stands in the swing; he has one arm round the rope, to steady himself; in one hand he holds a little bowl, and in the other a clay pipe; he is blowing bubbles. As the swing goes on, the bubbles fly upward, reflecting the most beautiful varying colors. The last still hangs from the bowl of the pipe, and sways in the wind. On goes the swing; and then a little black dog comes running up. He is almost as light as the bubble, and he raises himself on his hind legs, and wants to be taken into the swing; but it does not stop, and the dog falls; then he barks and gets angry. The children stoop towards him, and the bubble bursts. A swinging plank, a light sparkling foam picture, – that is my story."

"It may be all very pretty what you are telling me," said little Gerda, "but you speak so mournfully, and you do not mention little Kay at all."

What do the hyacinths say? "There were three beautiful sisters, fair and delicate. The dress of one was red, of the second blue, and of the third pure white. Hand in hand they danced in the bright moonlight, by the calm lake; but they were human beings, not fairy elves. The sweet fragrance attracted them, and they disappeared in the wood; here the fragrance became stronger. Three coffins, in which lay the three beautiful maidens, glided from the thickest part of the forest across the lake. The fire-flies flew lightly over them, like little floating torches. Do the dancing maidens sleep, or are they dead? The scent of the flower says that they are corpses. The evening bell tolls their knell."

"You make me quite sorrowful," said little Gerda; "your perfume is so strong, you make me think of the dead maidens. Ah! is little Kay really dead then? The roses have been in the earth, and they say no."

"Cling, clang," tolled the hyacinth bells. "We are not tolling for little Kay; we do not know him. We sing our song, the only one we know."

Then Gerda went to the buttercups that were glittering amongst the bright green leaves.

"You are little bright suns," said Gerda; "tell me if you know where I can find my play-fellow."

And the buttercups sparkled gayly, and looked again at Gerda. What song could the buttercups sing? It was not about Kay.

"The bright warm sun shone on a little court, on the first warm day of spring. His bright beams rested on the white walls of the neighboring house; and close by bloomed the first yellow flower of the season, glittering like gold in the sun's warm ray. An old woman sat in her arm chair at the house door, and her granddaughter, a poor and pretty servant-maid came to see her for a short visit. When she kissed her grandmother there was gold everywhere: the gold of the heart in that holy kiss; it was a golden morning; there was gold in the beaming sunlight, gold in the leaves of the lowly flower, and on the lips of the maiden. There, that is my story," said the buttercup.

"My poor old grandmother!" sighed Gerda; "she is longing to see me, and grieving for me as she did for little Kay; but I shall soon go home now, and take little Kay with me. It is no use asking the flowers; they know only their own songs, and can give me no information."

And then she tucked up her little dress, that she might run faster, but the narcissus caught her by the leg as she was jumping over it; so she stopped and looked at the tall yellow flower, and said, "Perhaps you may know something."

Then she stooped down quite close to the flower, and listened; and what did he say?

"I can see myself, I can see myself," said the narcissus. "Oh, how sweet is my perfume! Up in a little room with a bow window, stands a little dancing girl, half undressed; she stands sometimes on one leg, and sometimes on both, and looks as if she would tread the whole world under her feet. She is nothing but a delusion. She is pouring water out of a tea-pot on a piece of stuff which she holds in her hand; it is her bodice. 'Cleanliness is a good thing,' she says. Her white dress hangs on a peg; it has also been washed in the tea-pot, and dried on the roof. She puts it on, and ties a saffron-colored handkerchief round her neck, which makes the dress look whiter. See how she stretches out her legs, as if she were showing off on a stem. I can see myself, I can see myself."

"What do I care for all that," said Gerda, "you need not tell me such stuff." And then she ran to the other end of the garden. The door was fastened, but she pressed against the rusty latch, and it gave way. The door sprang open, and little Gerda ran out with bare feet into the wide world. She looked back three times, but no one seemed to be following her. At last she could run no longer, so she sat down to rest on a great stone, and when she looked round she saw that the summer was over, and autumn very far advanced. She had known nothing of this in the beautiful garden, where the sun shone and the flowers grew all the year round.

"Oh, how I have wasted my time?" said little Gerda; "it is autumn. I must not rest any longer," and she rose up to go on. But her little feet were wounded and sore, and everything around her looked so cold and bleak. The long willow-leaves were quite yellow. The dew-drops fell like water, leaf after leaf dropped from the trees, the sloe-thorn alone still bore fruit, but the sloes were sour, and set the teeth on edge. Oh, how dark and weary the whole world appeared!

Fourth Story
The Prince and Princess

Gerda was obliged to rest again, and just opposite the place where she sat, she saw a great crow come hopping across the snow toward her. He stood looking at her for some time, and then he wagged his head and said, "Caw, caw; good-day, good-day." He pronounced the words as plainly as he could, because he meant to be kind to the little girl; and then he asked her where she was going all alone in the wide world.

The word alone Gerda understood very well, and knew how much it expressed. So then she told the crow the whole story of her life and adventures, and asked him if he had seen little Kay.

The crow nodded his head very gravely, and said, "Perhaps I have – it may be."

"No! Do you think you have?" cried little Gerda, and she kissed the crow, and hugged him almost to death with joy.

"Gently, gently," said the crow. "I believe I know. I think it may be little Kay; but he has certainly forgotten you by this time for the princess."

"Does he live with a princess?" asked Gerda.

"Yes, listen," replied the crow, "but it is so difficult to speak your language. If you understand the crows' language then I can explain it better. Do you?"

"No, I have never learnt it," said Gerda, "but my grandmother understands it, and used to speak it to me. I wish I had learnt it."

"It does not matter," answered the crow; "I will explain as well as I can, although it will be very badly done;" and he told her what he had heard. "In this kingdom where we now are," said he, "there lives a princess, who is so wonderfully clever that she has read all the newspapers in the world, and forgotten them too, although she is so clever. A short time ago, as she was sitting on her throne, which people say is not such an agreeable seat as is often supposed, she began to sing a song which commences in these words:

'Why should I not be married?'

'Why not indeed?' said she, and so she determined to marry if she could find a husband who knew what to say when he was spoken to, and not one who could only look grand, for that was so tiresome. Then she assembled all her court ladies together at the beat of the drum, and when they heard of her intentions they were very much pleased. 'We are so glad to hear it,' said they, 'we were talking about it ourselves the other day.' You may believe that every word I tell you is true," said the crow, "for I have a tame sweetheart who goes freely about the palace, and she told me all this."

Of course his sweetheart was a crow, for "birds of a feather flock together," and one crow always chooses another crow.

"Newspapers were published immediately, with a border of hearts, and the initials of the princess among them. They gave notice that every young man who was handsome was free to visit the castle and speak with the princess; and those who could reply loud enough to be heard when spoken to, were to make themselves quite at home at the palace; but the one who spoke best would be chosen as a husband for the princess. Yes, yes, you may believe me, it is all as true as I sit here," said the crow. "The people came in crowds. There was a great deal of crushing and running about, but no one succeeded either on the first or second day. They could all speak very well while they were outside in the streets, but when they entered the palace gates, and saw the guards in silver uniforms, and the footmen in their golden livery on the staircase, and the great halls lighted up, they became quite confused. And when they stood before the throne on which the princess sat, they could do nothing but repeat the last words she had said; and she had no particular wish to hear her own words over again. It was just as if they had all taken something to make them sleepy while they were in the palace, for they did not recover themselves nor speak till they got back again into the street. There was quite a long line of them reaching from the town-gate to the palace. I went myself to see them," said the crow. "They were hungry and thirsty, for at the palace they did not get even a glass of water. Some of the wisest had taken a few slices of bread and butter with them, but they did not share it with their neighbors; they thought if they went in to the princess looking hungry, there would be a better chance for themselves."

"But Kay! tell me about little Kay!" said Gerda, "was he amongst the crowd?"

"Stop a bit, we are just coming to him. It was on the third day, there came marching cheerfully along to the palace a little personage, without horses or carriage, his eyes sparkling like yours; he had beautiful long hair, but his clothes were very poor."

"That was Kay!" said Gerda joyfully. "Oh, then I have found him;" and she clapped her hands.

"He had a little knapsack on his back," added the crow.

"No, it must have been his sledge," said Gerda; "for he went away with it."

"It may have been so," said the crow; "I did not look at it very closely. But I know from my tame sweetheart that he passed through the palace gates, saw the guards in their silver uniform, and the servants in their liveries of gold on the stairs, but he was not in the least embarrassed. 'It must be very tiresome to stand on the stairs,' he said. 'I prefer to go in.' The rooms were blazing with light. Councillors and ambassadors walked about with bare feet, carrying golden vessels; it was enough to make any one feel serious. His boots creaked loudly as he walked, and yet he was not at all uneasy."

"It must be Kay," said Gerda, "I know he had new boots on, I have heard them creak in grandmother's room."

"They really did creak," said the crow, "yet he went boldly up to the princess herself, who was sitting on a pearl as large as a spinning wheel, and all the ladies of the court were present with their maids, and all the cavaliers with their servants; and each of the maids had another maid to wait upon her, and the cavaliers' servants had their own servants, as well as a page each. They all stood in circles round the princess, and the nearer they stood to the door, the prouder they looked. The servants' pages, who always wore slippers, could hardly be looked at, they held themselves up so proudly by the door."

"It must be quite awful," said little Gerda, "but did Kay win the princess?"

"If I had not been a crow," said he, "I would have married her myself, although I am engaged. He spoke just as well as I do, when I speak the crows' language, so I heard from my tame sweetheart. He was quite free and agreeable and said he had not come to woo the princess, but to hear her wisdom; and he was as pleased with her as she was with him."

"Oh, certainly that was Kay," said Gerda, "he was so clever; he could work mental arithmetic and fractions. Oh, will you take me to the palace?"

"It is very easy to ask that," replied the crow, "but how are we to manage it? However, I will speak about it to my tame sweetheart, and ask her advice; for I must tell you it will be very difficult to gain permission for a little girl like you to enter the palace."

"Oh, yes; but I shall gain permission easily," said Gerda, "for when Kay hears that I am here, he will come out and fetch me in immediately."

"Wait for me here by the palings," said the crow, wagging his head as he flew away.

It was late in the evening before the crow returned. "Caw, caw," he said, "she sends you greeting, and here is a little roll which she took from the kitchen for you; there is plenty of bread there, and she thinks you must be hungry. It is not possible for you to enter the palace by the front entrance. The guards in silver uniform and the servants in gold livery would not allow it. But do not cry, we will manage to get you in; my sweetheart knows a little back-staircase that leads to the sleeping apartments, and she knows where to find the key."

Then they went into the garden through the great avenue, where the leaves were falling one after another, and they could see the light in the palace being put out in the same manner. And the crow led little Gerda to the back door, which stood ajar. Oh! how little Gerda's heart beat with anxiety and longing; it was just as if she were going to do something wrong, and yet she only wanted to know where little Kay was. "It must be he," she thought, "with those clear eyes, and that long hair." She could fancy she saw him smiling at her, as he used to at home, when they sat among the roses. He would certainly be glad to see her, and to hear what a long distance she had come for his sake, and to know how sorry they had been at home because he did not come back. Oh what joy and yet fear she felt! They were now on the stairs, and in a small closet at the top a lamp was burning. In the middle of the floor stood the tame crow, turning her head from side to side, and gazing at Gerda, who curtseyed as her grandmother had taught her to do.

"My betrothed has spoken so very highly of you, my little lady," said the tame crow, "your life-history, Vita, as it may be called, is very touching. If you will take the lamp I will walk before you. We will go straight along this way, then we shall meet no one."

"It seems to me as if somebody were behind us," said Gerda, as something rushed by her like a shadow on the wall, and then horses with flying manes and thin legs, hunters, ladies and gentlemen on horseback, glided by her, like shadows on the wall.

"They are only dreams," said the crow, "they are coming to fetch the thoughts of the great people out hunting."

"All the better, for we shall be able to look at them in their beds more safely. I hope that when you rise to honor and favor, you will show a grateful heart."

"You may be quite sure of that," said the crow from the forest.

They now came into the first hall, the walls of which were hung with rose-colored satin, embroidered with artificial flowers. Here the dreams again flitted by them but so quickly that Gerda could not distinguish the royal persons. Each hall appeared more splendid than the last, it was enough to bewilder any one. At length they reached a bedroom. The ceiling was like a great palm-tree, with glass leaves of the most costly crystal, and over the centre of the floor two beds, each resembling a lily, hung from a stem of gold. One, in which the princess lay, was white, the other was red; and in this Gerda had to seek for little Kay. She pushed one of the red leaves aside, and saw a little brown neck. Oh, that must be Kay! She called his name out quite loud, and held the lamp over him. The dreams rushed back into the room on horseback. He woke, and turned his head round, it was not little Kay! The prince was only like him in the neck, still he was young and pretty. Then the princess peeped out of her white-lily bed, and asked what was the matter. Then little Gerda wept and told her story, and all that the crows had done to help her.

"You poor child," said the prince and princess; then they praised the crows, and said they were not angry for what they had done, but that it must not happen again, and this time they should be rewarded.

"Would you like to have your freedom?" asked the princess, "or would you prefer to be raised to the position of court crows, with all that is left in the kitchen for yourselves?"

Then both the crows bowed, and begged to have a fixed appointment, for they thought of their old age, and said it would be so comfortable to feel that they had provision for their old days, as they called it. And then the prince got out of his bed, and gave it up to Gerda, – he could do no more; and she lay down. She folded her little hands, and thought, "How good everyone is to me, men and animals too;" then she closed her eyes and fell into a sweet sleep. All the dreams came flying back again to her, and they looked like angels, and one of them drew a little sledge, on which sat Kay, and nodded to her. But all this was only a dream, and vanished as soon as she awoke.

The following day she was dressed from head to foot in silk and velvet, and they invited her to stay at the palace for a few days, and enjoy herself, but she only begged for a pair of boots, and a little carriage, and a horse to draw it, so that she might go into the wide world to seek for Kay. And she obtained, not only boots, but also a muff, and she was neatly dressed; and when she was ready to go, there, at the door, she found a coach made of pure gold, with the coat-of-arms of the prince and princess shining upon it like a star, and the coachman, footman, and outriders all wearing golden crowns on their heads. The prince and princess themselves helped her into the coach, and wished her success. The forest crow, who was now married, accompanied her for the first three miles; he sat by Gerda's side, as he could not bear riding backwards. The tame crow stood in the door-way flapping her wings. She could not go with them, because she had been suffering from headache ever since the new appointment, no doubt from eating too much. The coach was well stored with sweet cakes, and under the seat were fruit and gingerbread nuts. "Farewell, farewell," cried the prince and princess, and little Gerda wept, and the crow wept; and then, after a few miles, the crow also said "Farewell," and this was the saddest parting. However, he flew to a tree, and stood flapping his black wings as long as he could see the coach, which glittered in the bright sunshine.

Fifth Story
Little Robber-Girl

The coach drove on through a thick forest, where it lighted up the way like a torch, and dazzled the eyes of some robbers, who could not bear to let it pass them unmolested.

"It is gold! it is gold!" cried they, rushing forward, and seizing the horses. Then they struck the little jockeys, the coachman, and the footman dead, and pulled little Gerda out of the carriage.

"She is fat and pretty, and she has been fed with the kernels of nuts," said the old robber-woman, who had a long beard and eyebrows that hung over her eyes. "She is as good as a little lamb; how nice she will taste!" and as she said this, she drew forth a shining knife, that glittered horribly. "Oh!" screamed the old woman the same moment; for her own daughter, who held her back, had bitten her in the ear. She was a wild and naughty girl, and the mother called her an ugly thing, and had not time to kill Gerda.

"She shall play with me," said the little robber-girl; "she shall give me her muff and her pretty dress, and sleep with me in my bed." And then she bit her mother again, and made her spring in the air, and jump about; and all the robbers laughed, and said, "See how she is dancing with her young cub."

"I will have a ride in the coach," said the little robber-girl; and she would have her own way; for she was so self-willed and obstinate.

She and Gerda seated themselves in the coach, and drove away, over stumps and stones, into the depths of the forest. The little robber-girl was about the same size as Gerda, but stronger; she had broader shoulders and a darker skin; her eyes were quite black, and she had a mournful look. She clasped little Gerda round the waist, and said, –

"They shall not kill you as long as you don't make us vexed with you. I suppose you are a princess."

"No," said Gerda; and then she told her all her history, and how fond she was of little Kay.

The robber-girl looked earnestly at her, nodded her head slightly, and said, "They shan't kill you, even if I do get angry with you; for I will do it myself." And then she wiped Gerda's eyes, and stuck her own hands in the beautiful muff which was so soft and warm.

The coach stopped in the courtyard of a robber's castle, the walls of which were cracked from top to bottom. Ravens and crows flew in and out of the holes and crevices, while great bulldogs, either of which looked as if it could swallow a man, were jumping about; but they were not allowed to bark. In the large and smoky hall a bright fire was burning on the stone floor. There was no chimney; so the smoke went up to the ceiling, and found a way out for itself. Soup was boiling in a large cauldron, and hares and rabbits were roasting on the spit.

"You shall sleep with me and all my little animals to-night," said the robber-girl, after they had had something to eat and drink. So she took Gerda to a corner of the hall, where some straw and carpets were laid down. Above them, on laths and perches, were more than a hundred pigeons, who all seemed to be asleep, although they moved slightly when the two little girls came near them. "These all belong to me," said the robber-girl; and she seized the nearest to her, held it by the feet, and shook it till it flapped its wings. "Kiss it," cried she, flapping it in Gerda's face. "There sit the wood-pigeons," continued she, pointing to a number of laths and a cage which had been fixed into the walls, near one of the openings. "Both rascals would fly away directly, if they were not closely locked up. And here is my old sweetheart 'Ba;'" and she dragged out a reindeer by the horn; he wore a bright copper ring round his neck, and was tied up. "We are obliged to hold him tight too, or else he would run away from us also. I tickle his neck every evening with my sharp knife, which frightens him very much." And then the robber-girl drew a long knife from a chink in the wall, and let it slide gently over the reindeer's neck. The poor animal began to kick, and the little robber-girl laughed, and pulled down Gerda into bed with her.

"Will you have that knife with you while you are asleep?" asked Gerda, looking at it in great fright.

"I always sleep with the knife by me," said the robber-girl. "No one knows what may happen. But now tell me again all about little Kay, and why you went out into the world."

Then Gerda repeated her story over again, while the wood-pigeons in the cage over her cooed, and the other pigeons slept. The little robber-girl put one arm across Gerda's neck, and held the knife in the other, and was soon fast asleep and snoring. But Gerda could not close her eyes at all; she knew not whether she was to live or die. The robbers sat round the fire, singing and drinking, and the old woman stumbled about. It was a terrible sight for a little girl to witness.

Then the wood-pigeons said, "Coo, coo; we have seen little Kay. A white fowl carried his sledge, and he sat in the carriage of the Snow Queen, which drove through the wood while we were lying in our nest. She blew upon us, and all the young ones died excepting us two. Coo, coo."

"What are you saying up there?" cried Gerda. "Where was the Snow Queen going? Do you know anything about it?"

"She was most likely travelling to Lapland, where there is always snow and ice. Ask the reindeer that is fastened up there with a rope."

"Yes, there is always snow and ice," said the reindeer; "and it is a glorious place; you can leap and run about freely on the sparkling ice plains. The Snow Queen has her summer tent there, but her strong castle is at the North Pole, on an island called Spitzbergen."

"Oh, Kay, little Kay!" sighed Gerda.

"Lie still," said the robber-girl, "or I shall run my knife into your body."

In the morning Gerda told her all that the wood-pigeons had said; and the little robber-girl looked quite serious, and nodded her head, and said, "That is all talk, that is all talk. Do you know where Lapland is?" she asked the reindeer.

"Who should know better than I do?" said the animal, while his eyes sparkled. "I was born and brought up there, and used to run about the snow-covered plains."

"Now listen," said the robber-girl; "all our men are gone away, – only mother is here, and here she will stay; but at noon she always drinks out of a great bottle, and afterwards sleeps for a little while; and then, I'll do something for you." Then she jumped out of bed, clasped her mother round the neck, and pulled her by the beard, crying, "My own little nanny goat, good morning." Then her mother filliped her nose till it was quite red; yet she did it all for love.

When the mother had drunk out of the bottle, and was gone to sleep, the little robber-maiden went to the reindeer, and said, "I should like very much to tickle your neck a few times more with my knife, for it makes you look so funny; but never mind, – I will untie your cord, and set you free, so that you may run away to Lapland; but you must make good use of your legs, and carry this little maiden to the castle of the Snow Queen, where her play-fellow is. You have heard what she told me, for she spoke loud enough, and you were listening."

Then the reindeer jumped for joy; and the little robber-girl lifted Gerda on his back, and had the forethought to tie her on, and even to give her her own little cushion to sit on.

"Here are your fur boots for you," said she; "for it will be very cold; but I must keep the muff; it is so pretty. However, you shall not be frozen for the want of it; here are my mother's large warm mittens; they will reach up to your elbows. Let me put them on. There, now your hands look just like my mother's."

But Gerda wept for joy.

"I don't like to see you fret," said the little robber-girl; "you ought to look quite happy now; and here are two loaves and a ham, so that you need not starve." These were fastened on the reindeer, and then the little robber-maiden opened the door, coaxed in all the great dogs, and then cut the string with which the reindeer was fastened, with her sharp knife, and said, "Now run, but mind you take good care of the little girl." And then Gerda stretched out her hand, with the great mitten on it, towards the little robber-girl, and said, "Farewell," and away flew the reindeer, over stumps and stones, through the great forest, over marshes and plains, as quickly as he could. The wolves howled, and the ravens screamed; while up in the sky quivered red lights like flames of fire. "There are my old northern lights," said the reindeer; "see how they flash." And he ran on day and night still faster and faster, but the loaves and the ham were all eaten by the time they reached Lapland.

Sixth Story
The Lapland Woman and the Finland Woman

They stopped at a little hut; it was very mean looking; the roof sloped nearly down to the ground, and the door was so low that the family had to creep in on their hands and knees, when they went in and out. There was no one at home but an old Lapland woman, who was cooking fish by the light of a train-oil lamp. The reindeer told her all about Gerda's story, after having first told his own, which seemed to him the most important, but Gerda was so pinched with the cold that she could not speak. "Oh, you poor things," said the Lapland woman, "you have a long way to go yet. You must travel more than a hundred miles farther, to Finland. The Snow Queen lives there now, and she burns Bengal lights every evening. I will write a few words on a dried stock-fish, for I have no paper, and you can take it from me to the Finland woman who lives there; she can give you better information than I can." So when Gerda was warmed, and had taken something to eat and drink, the woman wrote a few words on the dried fish, and told Gerda to take great care of it. Then she tied her again on the reindeer, and he set off at full speed. Flash, flash, went the beautiful blue northern lights in the air the whole night long. And at length they reached Finland, and knocked at the chimney of the Finland woman's hut, for it had no door above the ground. They crept in, but it was so terribly hot inside that that woman wore scarcely any clothes; she was small and very dirty looking. She loosened little Gerda's dress, and took off the fur boots and the mittens, or Gerda would have been unable to bear the heat; and then she placed a piece of ice on the reindeer's head, and read what was written on the dried fish. After she had read it three times, she knew it by heart, so she popped the fish into the soup saucepan, as she knew it was good to eat, and she never wasted anything. The reindeer told his own story first, and then little Gerda's, and the Finlander twinkled with her clever eyes, but she said nothing. "You are so clever," said the reindeer; "I know you can tie all the winds of the world with a piece of twine. If a sailor unties one knot, he has a fair wind; when he unties the second, it blows hard; but if the third and fourth are loosened, then comes a storm, which will root up whole forests. Cannot you give this little maiden something which will make her as strong as twelve men, to overcome the Snow Queen?"

"The Power of twelve men!" said the Finland woman; "that would be of very little use." But she went to a shelf and took down and unrolled a large skin, on which were inscribed wonderful characters, and she read till the perspiration ran down from her forehead. But the reindeer begged so hard for little Gerda, and Gerda looked at the Finland woman with such beseeching tearful eyes, that her own eyes began to twinkle again; so she drew the reindeer into a corner, and whispered to him while she laid a fresh piece of ice on his head, "Little Kay is really with the Snow Queen, but he finds everything there so much to his taste and his liking, that he believes it is the finest place in the world; but this is because he has a piece of broken glass in his heart, and a little piece of glass in his eye. These must be taken out, or he will never be a human being again, and the Snow Queen will retain her power over him."

"But can you not give little Gerda something to help her to conquer this power?"

"I can give her no greater power than she has already," said the woman; "don't you see how strong that is? How men and animals are obliged to serve her, and how well she has got through the world, barefooted as she is. She cannot receive any power from me greater than she now has, which consists in her own purity and innocence of heart. If she cannot herself obtain access to the Snow Queen, and remove the glass fragments from little Kay, we can do nothing to help her. Two miles from here the Snow Queen's garden begins; you can carry the little girl so far, and set her down by the large bush which stands in the snow, covered with red berries. Do not stay gossiping, but come back here as quickly as you can." Then the Finland woman lifted little Gerda upon the reindeer, and he ran away with her as quickly as he could.

"Oh, I have forgotten my boots and my mittens," cried little Gerda, as soon as she felt the cutting cold, but the reindeer dared not stop, so he ran on till he reached the bush with the red berries; here he set Gerda down, and he kissed her, and the great bright tears trickled over the animal's cheeks; then he left her and ran back as fast as he could.

There stood poor Gerda, without shoes, without gloves, in the midst of cold, dreary, ice-bound Finland. She ran forwards as quickly as she could, when a whole regiment of snow-flakes came round her; they did not, however, fall from the sky, which was quite clear and glittering with the northern lights. The snow-flakes ran along the ground, and the nearer they came to her, the larger they appeared. Gerda remembered how large and beautiful they looked through the burning-glass. But these were really larger, and much more terrible, for they were alive, and were the guards of the Snow Queen, and had the strangest shapes. Some were like great porcupines, others like twisted serpents with their heads stretching out, and some few were like little fat bears with their hair bristled; but all were dazzlingly white, and all were living snow-flakes. Then little Gerda repeated the Lord's Prayer, and the cold was so great that she could see her own breath come out of her mouth like steam as she uttered the words. The steam appeared to increase, as she continued her prayer, till it took the shape of little angels who grew larger the moment they touched the earth. They all wore helmets on their heads, and carried spears and shields. Their number continued to increase more and more; and by the time Gerda had finished her prayers, a whole legion stood round her. They thrust their spears into the terrible snow-flakes, so that they shivered into a hundred pieces, and little Gerda could go forward with courage and safety. The angels stroked her hands and feet, so that she felt the cold less, and she hastened on to the Snow Queen's castle.

But now we must see what Kay is doing. In truth he thought not of little Gerda, and never supposed she could be standing in the front of the palace.

Seventh Story
Of the Palace of the Snow Queen and What Happened There At Last

The walls of the palace were formed of drifted snow, and the windows and doors of the cutting winds. There were more than a hundred rooms in it, all as if they had been formed with snow blown together. The largest of them extended for several miles; they were all lighted up by the vivid light of the aurora, and they were so large and empty, so icy cold and glittering! There were no amusements here, not even a little bear's ball, when the storm might have been the music, and the bears could have danced on their hind legs, and shown their good manners. There were no pleasant games of snap-dragon, or touch, or even a gossip over the tea-table, for the young-lady foxes. Empty, vast, and cold were the halls of the Snow Queen. The flickering flame of the northern lights could be plainly seen, whether they rose high or low in the heavens, from every part of the castle. In the midst of its empty, endless hall of snow was a frozen lake, broken on its surface into a thousand forms; each piece resembled another, from being in itself perfect as a work of art, and in the centre of this lake sat the Snow Queen, when she was at home. She called the lake "The Mirror of Reason," and said that it was the best, and indeed the only one in the world.

Little Kay was quite blue with cold, indeed almost black, but he did not feel it; for the Snow Queen had kissed away the icy shiverings, and his heart was already a lump of ice. He dragged some sharp, flat pieces of ice to and fro, and placed them together in all kinds of positions, as if he wished to make something out of them; just as we try to form various figures with little tablets of wood which we call "a Chinese puzzle." Kay's fingers were very artistic; it was the icy game of reason at which he played, and in his eyes the figures were very remarkable, and of the highest importance; this opinion was owing to the piece of glass still sticking in his eye. He composed many complete figures, forming different words, but there was one word he never could manage to form, although he wished it very much. It was the word "Eternity." The Snow Queen had said to him, "When you can find out this, you shall be your own master, and I will give you the whole world and a new pair of skates." But he could not accomplish it.

"Now I must hasten away to warmer countries," said the Snow Queen. "I will go and look into the black craters of the tops of the burning mountains, Etna and Vesuvius, as they are called, – I shall make them look white, which will be good for them, and for the lemons and the grapes." And away flew the Snow Queen, leaving little Kay quite alone in the great hall which was so many miles in length; so he sat and looked at his pieces of ice, and was thinking so deeply, and sat so still, that any one might have supposed he was frozen.

Just at this moment it happened that little Gerda came through the great door of the castle. Cutting winds were raging around her, but she offered up a prayer and the winds sank down as if they were going to sleep; and she went on till she came to the large empty hall, and caught sight of Kay; she knew him directly; she flew to him and threw her arms round his neck, and held him fast, while she exclaimed, "Kay, dear little Kay, I have found you at last."

But he sat quite still, stiff and cold.

Then little Gerda wept hot tears, which fell on his breast, and penetrated into his heart, and thawed the lump of ice, and washed away the little piece of glass which had stuck there. Then he looked at her, and she sang –

"Roses bloom and cease to be,
But we shall the Christ-child see."

Then Kay burst into tears, and he wept so that the splinter of glass swam out of his eye. Then he recognized Gerda, and said, joyfully, "Gerda, dear little Gerda, where have you been all this time, and where have I been?" And he looked all around him, and said, "How cold it is, and how large and empty it all looks," and he clung to Gerda, and she laughed and wept for joy. It was so pleasing to see them that the pieces of ice even danced about; and when they were tired and went to lie down, they formed themselves into the letters of the word which the Snow Queen had said he must find out before he could be his own master, and have the whole world and a pair of new skates. Then Gerda kissed his cheeks, and they became blooming; and she kissed his eyes, and they shone like her own; she kissed his hands and his feet, and then he became quite healthy and cheerful. The Snow Queen might come home now when she pleased, for there stood his certainty of freedom, in the word she wanted, written in shining letters of ice.

Then they took each other by the hand, and went forth from the great palace of ice. They spoke of the grandmother, and of the roses on the roof, and as they went on the winds were at rest, and the sun burst forth. When they arrived at the bush with red berries, there stood the reindeer waiting for them, and he had brought another young reindeer with him, whose udders were full, and the children drank her warm milk and kissed her on the mouth. Then they carried Kay and Gerda first to the Finland woman, where they warmed themselves thoroughly in the hot room, and she gave them directions about their journey home. Next they went to the Lapland woman, who had made some new clothes for them, and put their sleighs in order. Both the reindeer ran by their side, and followed them as far as the boundaries of the country, where the first green leaves were budding. And here they took leave of the two reindeer and the Lapland woman, and all said – Farewell. Then the birds began to twitter, and the forest too was full of green young leaves; and out of it came a beautiful horse, which Gerda remembered, for it was one which had drawn the golden coach. A young girl was riding upon it, with a shining red cap on her head, and pistols in her belt. It was the little robber-maiden, who had got tired of staying at home; she was going first to the north, and if that did not suit her, she meant to try some other part of the world. She knew Gerda directly, and Gerda remembered her: it was a joyful meeting.

"You are a fine fellow to go gadding about in this way," said she to little Kay, "I should like to know whether you deserve that any one should go to the end of the world to find you."

But Gerda patted her cheeks, and asked after the prince and princess.

"They are gone to foreign countries," said the robber-girl.

"And the crow?" asked Gerda.

"Oh, the crow is dead," she replied; "his tame sweetheart is now a widow, and wears a bit of black worsted round her leg. She mourns very pitifully, but it is all stuff. But now tell me how you managed to get him back."

Then Gerda and Kay told her all about it.

"Snip, snap, snare! it's all right at last," said the robber-girl.

Then she took both their hands, and promised that if ever she should pass through the town, she would call and pay them a visit. And then she rode away into the wide world. But Gerda and Kay went hand-in-hand towards home; and as they advanced, spring appeared more lovely with its green verdure and its beautiful flowers. Very soon they recognized the large town where they lived, and the tall steeples of the churches, in which the sweet bells were ringing a merry peal as they entered it, and found their way to their grandmother's door. They went upstairs into the little room, where all looked just as it used to do. The old clock was going "tick, tick," and the hands pointed to the time of day, but as they passed through the door into the room they perceived that they were both grown up, and become a man and woman. The roses out on the roof were in full bloom, and peeped in at the window; and there stood the little chairs, on which they had sat when children; and Kay and Gerda seated themselves each on their own chair, and held each other by the hand, while the cold empty grandeur of the Snow Queen's palace vanished from their memories like a painful dream. The grandmother sat in God's bright sunshine, and she read aloud from the Bible, "Except ye become as little children, ye shall in no wise enter into the kingdom of God." And Kay and Gerda looked into each other's eyes, and all at once understood the words of the old song,

> *"Roses bloom and cease to be,*
> *But we shall the Christ-child see."*

And they both sat there, grown up, yet children at heart; and it was summer, – warm, beautiful summer.

The Story of the Year

IT WAS NEAR the end of January, and a terrible fall of snow was pelting down, and whirling through the streets and lanes; the windows were plastered with snow on the outside, snow fell in masses from the roofs. Every one seemed in a great hurry; they ran, they flew, fell into each other's arms, holding fast for a moment as long as they could stand safely. Coaches and horses looked as if they had been frosted with sugar. The footmen stood with their backs against the carriages, so as to turn their faces from the wind. The foot passengers kept within the shelter of the carriages, which could only move slowly on in the deep snow. At last the storm abated, and a narrow path was swept clean in front of the houses; when two persons met in this path they stood still, for neither liked to take the first step on one side into the deep snow to let the other pass him. There they stood silent and motionless, till at last, as if by tacit consent, they each sacrificed a leg and buried it in the deep snow. Towards evening, the weather became calm. The sky, cleared from the snow, looked more lofty and transparent, while the stars shone with new brightness and purity. The frozen snow crackled under foot, and was quite firm enough to bear the sparrows, who hopped upon it in the morning dawn. They searched for food in the path which had been swept, but there was very little for them, and they were terribly cold. "Tweet, tweet," said one to another; "they call this a new year, but I think it is worse than the last. We might just as well have kept the old year; I'm quite unhappy, and I have a right to be so."

"Yes, you have; and yet the people ran about and fired off guns, to usher in the new year," said a little shivering sparrow. "They threw things against the doors, and were quite beside themselves with joy, because the old year had disappeared. I was glad too, for I expected we should have some warm days, but my hopes have come to nothing. It freezes harder than ever; I think mankind have made a mistake in reckoning time."

"That they have," said a third, an old sparrow with a white poll; "they have something they call a calendar; it's an invention of their own, and everything must be arranged according to it, but it won't do. When spring comes, then the year begins. It is the voice of nature, and I reckon by that."

"But when will spring come?" asked the others.

"It will come when the stork returns, but he is very uncertain, and here in the town no one knows anything about it. In the country they have more knowledge; shall we fly away there and wait? we shall be nearer to spring then, certainly."

"That may be all very well," said another sparrow, who had been hopping about for a long time, chirping, but not saying anything of consequence, "but I have found a few comforts here in town which, I'm afraid, I should miss out in the country. Here in this neighborhood, there lives a family of people who have been so sensible as to place three or four flower-pots against the wall in the court-yard, so that the openings are all turned inward, and the bottom of each points outward. In the latter a hole has been cut large enough for me to fly in and out. I and my husband have built a nest in one of these pots, and all our young ones, who have now flown away, were brought up there. The people who live there of course made the whole arrangement that they might have the pleasure of seeing us, or they would not have done it. It pleased them also to strew bread-crumbs for us, and so we have food, and may consider ourselves provided for. So I think my husband and I will stay where we are; although we are not very happy, but we shall stay."

"And we will fly into the country," said the others, "to see if spring is coming." And away they flew.

In the country it was really winter, a few degrees colder than in the town. The sharp winds blew over the snow-covered fields. The farmer, wrapped in warm clothing, sat in his sleigh, and beat his arms across his chest to keep off the cold. The whip lay on his lap. The horses ran till they smoked. The snow crackled, the sparrows hopped about in the wheel-ruts, and shivered, crying, "Tweet, tweet; when will spring come? It is very long in coming."

"Very long indeed," sounded over the field, from the nearest snow-covered hill. It might have been the echo which people heard, or perhaps the words of that wonderful old man, who sat high on a heap of snow, regardless of wind or weather. He was all in white; he had on a peasant's coarse white coat of frieze. He had long white hair, a pale face, and large clear blue eyes. "Who is that old man?" asked the sparrows.

"I know who he is," said an old raven, who sat on the fence, and was condescending enough to acknowledge that we are all equal in the sight of Heaven, even as little birds, and therefore he talked with the sparrows, and gave them the information they wanted. "I know who the old man is," he said. "It is Winter, the old man of last year; he is not dead yet, as the calendar says, but acts as guardian to little Prince Spring who is coming. Winter rules here still. Ugh! the cold makes you shiver, little ones, does it not?"

"There! Did I not tell you so?" said the smallest of the sparrows. "The calendar is only an invention of man, and is not arranged according to nature. They should leave these things to us; we are created so much more clever than they are."

One week passed, and then another. The forest looked dark, the hard-frozen lake lay like a sheet of lead. The mountains had disappeared, for over the land hung damp, icy mists. Large black crows flew about in silence; it was as if nature slept. At length a sunbeam glided over the lake, and it shone like burnished silver. But the snow on the fields and the hills did not glitter as before. The white form of Winter sat there still, with his un-wandering gaze fixed on the south. He did not perceive that the snowy carpet seemed to sink as it were into the earth; that here and there a little green patch of grass appeared, and that these patches were covered with sparrows.

"Tee-wit, tee-wit; is spring coming at last?"

Spring! How the cry resounded over field and meadow, and through the dark-brown woods, where the fresh green moss still gleamed on the trunks of the trees, and from the south came the two first storks flying through the air, and on the back of each sat a lovely little child, a boy and a girl. They greeted the earth with a kiss, and wherever they placed their feet white flowers sprung up from beneath the snow. Hand in hand they approached the old ice-man, Winter, embraced him and clung to his breast; and as they did so, in a moment all three were enveloped in a thick, damp mist, dark and heavy, that closed over them like a veil. The wind arose with mighty rustling tone, and cleared away the mist. Then the sun shone out warmly. Winter had vanished away, and the beautiful children of Spring sat on the throne of the year.

"This is really a new year," cried all the sparrows, "now we shall get our rights, and have some return for what we suffered in winter."

Wherever the two children wandered, green buds burst forth on bush and tree, the grass grew higher, and the corn-fields became lovely in delicate green.

The little maiden strewed flowers in her path. She held her apron before her: it was full of flowers; it was as if they sprung into life there, for the more she scattered around her, the more flowers did her apron contain. Eagerly she showered snowy blossoms over apple and peach-trees, so that they stood in full beauty before even their green leaves had burst from the bud. Then the boy and the girl clapped their hands, and troops of birds came flying by, no one knew from whence, and they all twittered and chirped, singing "Spring has come!" How beautiful everything was! Many an old dame came forth from her door into the sunshine, and shuffled about with great delight, glancing at the golden flowers which glittered everywhere in the fields, as they used to do in her young days. The world grew young again to her, as she said, "It is a blessed time out here to-day." The forest already wore its dress of dark-green buds. The thyme blossomed in fresh fragrance. Primroses and anemones sprung forth, and violets bloomed in the shade, while every blade of grass was full of strength and sap. Who could resist sitting down on such a beautiful carpet? and then the young children of Spring seated themselves, holding each other's hands, and sang, and laughed, and grew. A gentle rain fell upon them from the sky, but they did not notice it, for the rain-drops were their own tears of joy. They kissed each other, and were betrothed; and in the same moment the buds of the trees unfolded, and when the sun rose, the forest was green. Hand in hand the two wandered beneath the fresh pendant canopy of foliage, while the sun's rays gleamed through the opening of the shade, in changing and varied colors. The delicate young leaves filled the air with refreshing odor. Merrily rippled the clear brooks and rivulets between the green, velvety rushes, and over the many-colored pebbles beneath. All nature spoke of abundance and plenty. The cuckoo sang, and the lark carolled, for it was now beautiful spring. The careful willows had, however, covered their blossoms with woolly gloves; and this carefulness is rather tedious. Days and weeks went by, and the heat increased. Warm air waved the corn as it grew golden in the sun. The white northern lily spread its large green leaves over the glossy mirror of the woodland lake, and the fishes sought the shadows beneath them. In a sheltered part of the wood, the sun shone upon the walls of a farm-house, brightening the blooming roses, and ripening the black juicy berries, which hung on the loaded cherry-trees, with his hot beams. Here sat the lovely wife of Summer, the same whom we have seen as a child and a bride; her eyes were fixed on dark gathering clouds, which in wavy outlines of black and indigo were piling themselves up like mountains, higher and higher. They came from every side, always increasing like a rising, rolling sea. Then they swooped towards the forest, where every sound had been silenced as if by magic, every breath hushed, every bird mute. All nature stood still in grave suspense. But in the lanes and the highways, passengers on foot or in carriages were hurrying to find a place of shelter. Then came a flash of light, as if the sun had rushed forth from the sky, flaming, burning, all-devouring, and darkness returned amid a rolling crash of thunder. The rain poured down in streams, – now there was darkness, then blinding light, – now thrilling silence, then deafening din. The young brown reeds on the moor waved to and fro in feathery billows; the forest boughs were hidden in a watery mist, and still light and darkness followed each other, still came the silence after the roar, while the corn and the blades of grass lay beaten down and swamped, so that it seemed impossible they could ever raise themselves again. But after a while the rain began to fall gently, the sun's rays pierced the clouds, and the water-drops glittered like pearls on leaf and stem. The birds sang, the fishes leaped up to the surface of the water, the gnats danced in the sunshine, and yonder, on a rock by the heaving salt sea, sat Summer himself, a strong man with sturdy limbs and long, dripping hair. Strengthened by the cool bath, he sat in the warm sunshine, while all around him renewed nature bloomed strong, luxuriant, and beautiful: it was summer, warm, lovely summer. Sweet and pleasant was the fragrance wafted from the clover-field, where the bees swarmed round the ruined tower, the bramble twined itself over the old altar, which, washed by the rain, glittered in the sunshine; and thither flew the queen bee with her swarm, and prepared wax and honey. But Summer and his bosom-wife saw it with different eyes, to them the altar-table was covered with the offerings of nature. The evening sky shone like gold, no church dome could ever gleam so brightly, and between the golden evening and the blushing morning there was moonlight. It was indeed summer. And days and weeks passed, the bright scythes of the reapers glittered in the corn-fields, the branches of the apple-trees bent low, heavy with the red and golden fruit. The hop, hanging in clusters, filled the air with sweet fragrance, and beneath the hazel-bushes, where the nuts hung in great bunches, rested a man and a woman – Summer and his grave consort.

"See," she exclaimed, "what wealth, what blessings surround us. Everything is home-like and good, and yet, I know not why, I long for rest and peace; I can scarcely express what I feel. They are already ploughing the fields again; more and more the people wish for gain. See, the storks are flocking together, and following the plough at a short distance. They are the birds from Egypt, who carried us through the air. Do you remember how we came as children to this land of the north; we brought with us flowers and bright sunshine, and green to the forests, but the wind has been rough with them, and they are now become dark and brown, like the trees of the south, but they do not, like them, bear golden fruit."

"Do you wish to see golden fruit?" said the man, "then rejoice," and he lifted his arm. The leaves of the forest put on colors of red and gold, and bright tints covered the woodlands. The rose-bushes gleamed with scarlet hips, and the branches of the elder-trees hung down with the weight of the full, dark berries. The wild chestnuts fell ripe from their dark, green shells, and in the forests the violets bloomed for the second time. But the queen of the year became more and more silent and pale.

"It blows cold," she said, "and night brings the damp mist; I long for the land of my childhood." Then she saw the storks fly away every one, and she stretched out her hands towards them. She looked at the empty nests; in one of them grew a long-stalked corn flower, in another the yellow mustard seed, as if the nest had been placed there only for its comfort and protection, and the sparrows were flying round them all.

"Tweet, where has the master of the nest gone?" cried one, "I suppose he could not bear it when the wind blew, and therefore he has left this country. I wish him a pleasant journey."

The forest leaves became more and more yellow, leaf after leaf fell, and the stormy winds of Autumn howled. The year was now far advanced, and upon the fallen, yellow leaves, lay the queen of the year, looking up with mild eyes at a gleaming star, and her husband stood by her. A gust of wind swept through the foliage, and the leaves fell in a shower. The summer queen was gone, but a butterfly, the last of the year, flew through the cold air. Damp fogs came, icy winds blew, and the long, dark nights of winter approached.

The ruler of the year appeared with hair white as snow, but he knew it not; he thought snow-flakes falling from the sky covered his head, as they decked the green fields with a thin, white covering of snow. And then the church bells rang out for Christmas time.

"The bells are ringing for the new-born year," said the ruler, "soon will a new ruler and his bride be born, and. I shall go to rest with my wife in yonder light-giving star."

In the fresh, green fir-wood, where the snow lay all around, stood the angel of Christmas, and consecrated the young trees that were to adorn his feast.

"May there be joy in the rooms, and under the green boughs," said the old ruler of the year. In a few weeks he had become a very old man, with hair as white as snow. "My resting-time draws near; the young pair of the year will soon claim my crown and sceptre."

"But the night is still thine," said the angel of Christmas, "for power, but not for rest. Let the snow lie warmly upon the tender seed. Learn to endure the thought that another is worshipped whilst thou art still lord. Learn to endure being forgotten while yet thou livest. The hour of thy freedom will come when Spring appears."

"And when will Spring come?" asked Winter.

"It will come when the stork returns."

And with white locks and snowy beard, cold, bent, and hoary, but strong as the wintry storm, and firm as the ice, old Winter sat on the snowdrift-covered hill, looking towards the south, where Winter had sat before, and gazed. The ice glittered, the snow crackled, the skaters skimmed over the polished surface of the lakes; ravens and crows formed a pleasing contrast to the white ground, and not a breath of wind stirred, and in the still air old Winter clenched his fists, and the ice lay fathoms deep between the lands. Then came the sparrows again out of the town, and asked, "Who is that old man?" The raven sat there still, or it might be his son, which is the same thing, and he said to them, –

"It is Winter, the old man of the former year; he is not dead, as the calendar says, but he is guardian to the spring, which is coming."

"When will Spring come?" asked the sparrows, "for we shall have better times then, and a better rule. The old times are worth nothing."

And in quiet thought old Winter looked at the leafless forest, where the graceful form and bends of each tree and branch could be seen; and while Winter slept, icy mists came from the clouds, and the ruler dreamt of his youthful days and of his manhood, and in the morning dawn the whole forest glittered with hoar frost, which the sun shook from the branches, – and this was the summer dream of Winter.

"When will Spring come?" asked the sparrows. "Spring!" Again the echo sounded from the hills on which the snow lay. The sunshine became warmer, the snow melted, and the birds twittered, "Spring is coming!" And high in the air flew the first stork, and the second followed; a lovely child sat on the back of each, and they sank down on the open field, kissed the earth, and kissed the quiet old man; and, as the mist from the mountain top, he vanished away and disappeared. And the story of the year was finished.

"This is all very fine, no doubt," said the sparrows, "and it is very beautiful; but it is not according to the calendar, therefore, it must be all wrong."

The Pea Blossom

THERE WERE ONCE five peas in one shell, they were green, the shell was green, and so they believed that the whole world must be green also, which was a very natural conclusion. The shell grew, and the peas grew, they accommodated themselves to their position, and sat all in a row. The sun shone without and warmed the shell, and the rain made it clear and transparent; it was mild and agreeable in broad daylight, and dark at night, as it generally is; and the peas as they sat there grew bigger and bigger, and more thoughtful as they mused, for they felt there must be something else for them to do.

"Are we to sit here forever?" asked one; "shall we not become hard by sitting so long? It seems to me there must be something outside, and I feel sure of it."

And as weeks passed by, the peas became yellow, and the shell became yellow.

"All the world is turning yellow, I suppose," said they, – and perhaps they were right.

Suddenly they felt a pull at the shell; it was torn off, and held in human hands, then slipped into the pocket of a jacket in company with other full pods.

"Now we shall soon be opened," said one, – just what they all wanted.

"I should like to know which of us will travel furthest," said the smallest of the five; "we shall soon see now."

"What is to happen will happen," said the largest pea.

"Crack" went the shell as it burst, and the five peas rolled out into the bright sunshine. There they lay in a child's hand. A little boy was holding them tightly, and said they were fine peas for his pea-shooter. And immediately he put one in and shot it out.

"Now I am flying out into the wide world," said he; "catch me if you can;" and he was gone in a moment.

"I," said the second, "intend to fly straight to the sun, that is a shell that lets itself be seen, and it will suit me exactly;" and away he went.

"We will go to sleep wherever we find ourselves," said the two next, "we shall still be rolling onwards;" and they did certainly fall on the floor, and roll about before they got into the pea-shooter; but they were put in for all that. "We shall go farther than the others," said they.

"What is to happen will happen," exclaimed the last, as he was shot out of the pea-shooter; and as he spoke he flew up against an old board under a garret-window, and fell into a little crevice, which was almost filled up with moss and soft earth. The moss closed itself round him, and there he lay, a captive indeed, but not unnoticed by God.

"What is to happen will happen," said he to himself.

Within the little garret lived a poor woman, who went out to clean stoves, chop wood into small pieces and perform such-like hard work, for she was strong and industrious. Yet she remained always poor, and at home in the garret lay her only daughter, not quite grown up, and very delicate and weak. For a whole year she had kept her bed, and it seemed as if she could neither live nor die.

"She is going to her little sister," said the woman; "I had but the two children, and it was not an easy thing to support both of them; but the good God helped me in my work, and took one of them to Himself and provided for her. Now I would gladly keep the other that was left to me, but I suppose they are not to be separated, and my sick girl will very soon go to her sister above." But the sick girl still remained where she was, quietly and patiently she lay all the day long, while her mother was away from home at her work.

Spring came, and one morning early the sun shone brightly through the little window, and threw its rays over the floor of the room. just as the mother was going to her work, the sick girl fixed her gaze on the lowest pane of the window – "Mother," she exclaimed, "what can that little green thing be that peeps in at the window? It is moving in the wind."

The mother stepped to the window and half opened it. "Oh!" she said, "there is actually a little pea which has taken root and is putting out its green leaves. How could it have got into this crack? Well now, here is a little garden for you to amuse yourself with." So the bed of the sick girl was drawn nearer to the window, that she might see the budding plant; and the mother went out to her work.

"Mother, I believe I shall get well," said the sick child in the evening, "the sun has shone in here so brightly and warmly to-day, and the little pea is thriving so well: I shall get on better, too, and go out into the warm sunshine again."

"God grant it!" said the mother, but she did not believe it would be so. But she propped up with the little stick the green plant which had given her child such pleasant hopes of life, so that it might not be broken by the winds; she tied the piece of string to the window-sill and to the upper part of the frame, so that the pea-tendrils might twine round it when it shot up. And it did shoot up, indeed it might almost be seen to grow from day to day.

"Now really here is a flower coming," said the old woman one morning, and now at last she began to encourage the hope that her sick daughter might really recover. She remembered that for some time the child had spoken more cheerfully, and during the last few days had raised herself in bed in the morning to look with sparkling eyes at her little garden which contained only a single pea-plant. A week after, the invalid sat up for the first time a whole hour, feeling quite happy by the open window in the warm sunshine, while outside grew the little plant, and on it a pink pea-blossom in full bloom. The little maiden bent down and gently kissed the delicate leaves. This day was to her like a festival.

"Our heavenly Father Himself has planted that pea, and made it grow and flourish, to bring joy to you and hope to me, my blessed child," said the happy mother, and she smiled at the flower, as if it had been an angel from God.

But what became of the other peas? Why the one who flew out into the wide world, and said, "Catch me if you can," fell into a gutter on the roof of a house, and ended his travels in the crop of a pigeon. The two lazy ones were carried quite as far, for they also were eaten by pigeons, so they were at least of some use; but the fourth, who wanted to reach the sun, fell into a sink and lay there in the dirty water for days and weeks, till he had swelled to a great size.

"I am getting beautifully fat," said the pea, "I expect I shall burst at last; no pea could do more that that, I think; I am the most remarkable of all the five which were in the shell." And the sink confirmed the opinion.

But the young maiden stood at the open garret window, with sparkling eyes and the rosy hue of health on her cheeks, she folded her thin hands over the pea-blossom, and thanked God for what He had done.

"I," said the sink, "shall stand up for my pea."

The Goloshes of Fortune

A Beginning

IN A HOUSE in Copenhagen, not far from the king's new market, a very large party had assembled, the host and his family expecting, no doubt, to receive invitations in return. One half of the company were already seated at the card-tables, the other half seemed to be waiting the result of their hostess's question, "Well, how shall we amuse ourselves?"

Conversation followed, which, after a while, began to prove very entertaining. Among other subjects, it turned upon the events of the middle ages, which some persons maintained were more full of interest than our own times. Counsellor Knapp defended this opinion so warmly that the lady of the house immediately went over to his side, and both exclaimed against Oersted's Essays on Ancient and Modern Times, in which the preference is given to our own. The counsellor considered the times of the Danish king, Hans, as the noblest and happiest.

The conversation on this topic was only interrupted for a moment by the arrival of a newspaper, which did not, however, contain much worth reading, and while it is still going on we will pay a visit to the ante-room, in which cloaks, sticks, and goloshes were carefully placed. Here sat two maidens, one young, and the other old, as if they had come and were waiting to accompany their mistresses home; but on looking at them more closely, it could easily be seen that they were no common servants. Their shapes were too graceful, their complexions too delicate, and the cut of their dresses much too elegant. They were two fairies. The younger was not Fortune herself, but the chambermaid of one of Fortune's attendants, who carries about her more trifling gifts. The elder one, who was named Care, looked rather gloomy; she always goes about to perform her own business in person; for then she knows it is properly done. They were telling each other where they had been during the day. The messenger of Fortune had only transacted a few unimportant matters; for instance, she had preserved a new bonnet from a shower of rain, and obtained for an honest man a bow from a titled nobody, and so on; but she had something extraordinary to relate, after all.

"I must tell you," said she, "that to-day is my birthday; and in honor of it I have been intrusted with a pair of goloshes, to introduce amongst mankind. These goloshes have the property of making every one who puts them on imagine himself in any place he wishes, or that he exists at any period. Every wish is fulfilled at the moment it is expressed, so that for once mankind have the chance of being happy."

"No," replied Care; "you may depend upon it that whoever puts on those goloshes will be very unhappy, and bless the moment in which he can get rid of them."

"What are you thinking of?" replied the other. "Now see; I will place them by the door; some one will take them instead of his own, and he will be the happy man."

This was the end of their conversation.

What Happened to the Counsellor

It was late when Counsellor Knapp, lost in thought about the times of King Hans, desired to return home; and fate so ordered it that he put on the goloshes of Fortune instead of his own, and walked out into the East Street. Through the magic power of the goloshes, he was at once carried back three hundred years, to the times of King Hans, for which he had been longing when he put them on. Therefore he immediately set his foot into the mud and mire of the street, which in those days possessed no pavement.

"Why, this is horrible; how dreadfully dirty it is!" said the counsellor; "and the whole pavement has vanished, and the lamps are all out."

The moon had not yet risen high enough to penetrate the thick foggy air, and all the objects around him were confused together in the darkness. At the nearest corner, a lamp hung before a picture of the Madonna; but the light it gave was almost useless, for he only perceived it when he came quite close and his eyes fell on the painted figures of the Mother and Child.

"That is most likely a museum of art," thought he, "and they have forgotten to take down the sign."

Two men, in the dress of olden times, passed by him.

"What odd figures!" thought he; "they must be returning from some masquerade."

Suddenly he heard the sound of a drum and fifes, and then a blazing light from torches shone upon him. The counsellor stared with astonishment as he beheld a most strange procession pass before him. First came a whole troop of drummers, beating their drums very cleverly; they were followed by life-guards, with longbows and crossbows. The principal person in the procession was a clerical-looking gentleman. The astonished counsellor asked what it all meant, and who the gentleman might be.

"That is the bishop of Zealand."

"Good gracious!" he exclaimed; "what in the world has happened to the bishop? what can he be thinking about?" Then he shook his head and said, "It cannot possibly be the bishop himself."

While musing on this strange affair, and without looking to the right or left, he walked on through East Street and over Highbridge Place. The bridge, which he supposed led to Palace Square, was nowhere to be found; but instead, he saw a bank and some shallow water, and two people, who sat in a boat.

"Does the gentleman wish to be ferried over the Holm?" asked one.

"To the Holm!" exclaimed the counsellor, not knowing in what age he was now existing; "I want to go to Christian's Haven, in Little Turf Street." The men stared at him. "Pray tell me where the bridge is!" said he. "It is shameful that the lamps are not lighted here, and it is as muddy as if one were walking in a marsh." But the more he talked with the boatmen the less they could understand each other.

"I don't understand your outlandish talk," he cried at last, angrily turning his back upon them. He could not, however, find the bridge nor any railings.

"What a scandalous condition this place is in," said he; never, certainly, had he found his own times so miserable as on this evening. "I think it will be better for me to take a coach; but where are they?" There was not one to be seen! "I shall be obliged to go back to the king's new market," said he, "where there are plenty of carriages standing, or I shall never reach Christian's Haven." Then he went towards East Street, and had nearly passed through it, when the moon burst forth from a cloud.

"Dear me, what have they been erecting here?" he cried, as he caught sight of the East gate, which in olden times used to stand at the end of East Street. However, he found an opening through which he passed, and came out upon where he expected to find the new market. Nothing was to be seen but an open meadow, surrounded by a few bushes, through which ran a broad canal or stream. A few miserable-looking wooden booths, for the accommodation of Dutch watermen, stood on the opposite shore.

"Either I behold a fata morgana, or I must be tipsy," groaned the counsellor. "What can it be? What is the matter with me?" He turned back in the full conviction that he must be ill. In walking through the street this time, he examined the houses more closely; he found that most of them were built of lath and plaster, and many had only a thatched roof.

"I am certainly all wrong," said he, with a sigh; "and yet I only drank one glass of punch. But I cannot bear even that, and it was very foolish to give us punch and hot salmon; I shall speak about it to our hostess, the agent's lady. Suppose I were to go back now and say how ill I feel, I fear it would look so ridiculous, and it is not very likely that I should find any one up." Then he looked for the house, but it was not in existence.

"This is really frightful; I cannot even recognize East Street. Not a shop to be seen; nothing but old, wretched, tumble-down houses, just as if I were at Roeskilde or Ringstedt. Oh, I really must be ill! It is no use to stand upon ceremony. But where in the world is the agent's house. There is a house, but it is not his; and people still up in it, I can hear. Oh dear! I certainly am very queer." As he reached the half-open door, he saw a light and went in. It was a tavern of the olden times, and seemed a kind of beershop. The room had the appearance of a Dutch interior. A number of people, consisting of seamen, Copenhagen citizens, and a few scholars, sat in deep conversation over their mugs, and took very little notice of the new comer.

"Pardon me," said the counsellor, addressing the landlady, "I do not feel quite well, and I should be much obliged if you will send for a fly to take me to Christian's Haven." The woman stared at him and shook her head. Then she spoke to him in German. The counsellor supposed from this that she did not understand Danish; he therefore repeated his request in German. This, as well as his singular dress, convinced the woman that he was a foreigner. She soon understood, however, that he did not find himself quite well, and therefore brought him a mug of water. It had something of the taste of seawater, certainly, although it had been drawn from the well outside. Then the counsellor leaned his head on his hand, drew a deep breath, and pondered over all the strange things that had happened to him.

"Is that to-day's number of the Day?" he asked, quite mechanically, as he saw the woman putting by a large piece of paper. She did not understand what he meant, but she handed him the sheet; it was a woodcut, representing a meteor, which had appeared in the town of Cologne.

"That is very old," said the counsellor, becoming quite cheerful at the sight of this antique drawing. "Where did you get this singular sheet? It is very interesting, although the whole affair is a fable. Meteors are easily explained in these days; they are northern lights, which are often seen, and are no doubt caused by electricity."

Those who sat near him, and heard what he said, looked at him in great astonishment, and one of them rose, took off his hat respectfully, and said in a very serious manner, "You must certainly be a very learned man, monsieur."

"Oh no," replied the counsellor; "I can only discourse on topics which every one should understand."

"Modestia is a beautiful virtue," said the man. "Moreover, I must add to your speech mihi secus videtur; yet in this case I would suspend my judicium."

"May I ask to whom I have the pleasure of speaking?"

"I am a Bachelor of Divinity," said the man. This answer satisfied the counsellor. The title agreed with the dress.

"This is surely," thought he, "an old village schoolmaster, a perfect original, such as one meets with sometimes even in Jutland."

"This is not certainly a locus docendi," began the man; "still I must beg you to continue the conversation. You must be well read in ancient lore."

"Oh yes," replied the counsellor; "I am very fond of reading useful old books, and modern ones as well, with the exception of every-day stories, of which we really have more than enough."

"Every-day stories?" asked the bachelor.

"Yes, I mean the new novels that we have at the present day."

"Oh," replied the man, with a smile; "and yet they are very witty, and are much read at Court. The king likes especially the romance of Messeurs Iffven and Gaudian, which describes King Arthur and his knights of the round table. He has joked about it with the gentlemen of his Court."

"Well, I have certainly not read that," replied the counsellor. "I suppose it is quite new, and published by Heiberg."

"No," answered the man, "it is not by Heiberg; Godfred von Gehman brought it out."

"Oh, is he the publisher? That is a very old name," said the counsellor; "was it not the name of the first publisher in Denmark?"

"Yes; and he is our first printer and publisher now," replied the scholar.

So far all had passed off very well; but now one of the citizens began to speak of a terrible pestilence which had been raging a few years before, meaning the plague of 1484. The counsellor thought he referred to the cholera, and they could discuss this without finding out the mistake. The war in 1490 was spoken of as quite recent. The English pirates had taken some ships in the Channel in 1801, and the counsellor, supposing they referred to these, agreed with them in finding fault with the English. The rest of the talk, however, was not so agreeable; every moment one contradicted the other. The good bachelor appeared very ignorant, for the simplest remark of the counsellor seemed to him either too bold or too fantastic. They stared at each other, and when it became worse the bachelor spoke in Latin, in the hope of being better understood; but it was all useless.

"How are you now?" asked the landlady, pulling the counsellor's sleeve.

Then his recollection returned to him. In the course of conversation he had forgotten all that had happened previously.

"Goodness me! where am I?" said he. It bewildered him as he thought of it.

"We will have some claret, or mead, or Bremen beer," said one of the guests; "will you drink with us?"

Two maids came in. One of them had a cap on her head of two colors. They poured out the wine, bowed their heads, and withdrew.

The counsellor felt a cold shiver run all over him. "What is this? what does it mean?" said he; but he was obliged to drink with them, for they overpowered the good man with their politeness. He became at last desperate; and when one of them said he was tipsy, he did not doubt the man's word in the least – only begged them to get a droschky; and then they thought he was speaking the Muscovite language. Never before had he been in such rough and vulgar company. "One might believe that the country was going back to heathenism," he observed. "This is the most terrible moment of my life."

Just then it came into his mind that he would stoop under the table, and so creep to the door. He tried it; but before he reached the entry, the rest discovered what he was about, and seized him by the feet, when, luckily for him, off came the goloshes, and with them vanished the whole enchantment. The counsellor now saw quite plainly a lamp, and a large building behind it; everything looked familiar and beautiful. He was in East Street, as it now appears; he lay with his legs turned towards a porch, and just by him sat the watchman asleep.

"Is it possible that I have been lying here in the street dreaming?" said he. "Yes, this is East Street; how beautifully bright and gay it looks! It is quite shocking that one glass of punch should have upset me like this."

Two minutes afterwards he sat in a droschky, which was to drive him to Christian's Haven. He thought of all the terror and anxiety which he had undergone, and felt thankful from his heart for the reality and comfort of modern times, which, with all their errors, were far better than those in which he so lately found himself.

The Watchman's Adventures

"Well, I declare, there lies a pair of goloshes," said the watchman. "No doubt, they belong to the lieutenant who lives up stairs. They are lying just by his door." Gladly would the honest man have rung, and given them in, for a light was still burning, but he did not wish to disturb the other people in the house; so he let them lie. "These things must keep the feet very warm," said he; "they are of such nice soft leather." Then he tried them on, and they fitted his feet exactly. "Now," said he, "how droll things are in this world! There's that man can lie down in his warm bed, but he does not do so. There he goes pacing up and down the room. He ought to be a happy man. He has neither wife nor children, and he goes out into company every evening. Oh, I wish I were he; then I should be a happy man."

As he uttered this wish, the goloshes which he had put on took effect, and the watchman at once became the lieutenant. There he stood in his room, holding a little piece of pink paper between his fingers, on which was a poem, – a poem written by the lieutenant himself. Who has not had, for once in his life, a moment of poetic inspiration? and at such a moment, if the thoughts are written down, they flow in poetry. The following verses were written on the pink paper: –

"OH WERE I RICH!

"Oh were I rich! How oft, in youth's bright hour,
When youthful pleasures banish every care,
I longed for riches but to gain a power,
The sword and plume and uniform to wear!
The riches and the honor came for me;
Yet still my greatest wealth was poverty:
Ah, help and pity me!

"Once in my youthful hours, when gay and free,
A maiden loved me; and her gentle kiss,

Rich in its tender love and purity,
Taught me, alas! too much of earthly bliss.
Dear child! She only thought of youthful glee;
She loved no wealth, but fairy tales and me.
Thou knowest: ah, pity me!

"Oh were I rich! again is all my prayer:
That child is now a woman, fair and free,
As good and beautiful as angels are.
Oh, were I rich in lovers' poetry,
To tell my fairy tale, love's richest lore!
But no; I must be silent – I am poor.
Ah, wilt thou pity me?

"Oh were I rich in truth and peace below,
I need not then my poverty bewail.
To thee I dedicate these lines of woe;
Wilt thou not understand the mournful tale?
A leaf on which my sorrows I relate –
Dark story of a darker night of fate.
Ah, bless and pity me!"

"Well, yes; people write poems when they are in love, but a wise man will not print them. A lieutenant in love, and poor. This is a triangle, or more properly speaking, the half of the broken die of fortune." The lieutenant felt this very keenly, and therefore leaned his head against the window-frame, and sighed deeply. "The poor watchman in the street," said he, "is far happier than I am. He knows not what I call poverty. He has a home, a wife and children, who weep at his sorrow and rejoice at his joy. Oh, how much happier I should be could I change my being and position with him, and pass through life with his humble expectations and hopes! Yes, he is indeed happier than I am."

At this moment the watchman again became a watchman; for having, through the goloshes of Fortune, passed into the existence of the lieutenant, and found himself less contented than he expected, he had preferred his former condition, and wished himself again a watchman. "That was an ugly dream," said he, "but droll enough. It seemed to me as if I were the lieutenant up yonder, but there was no happiness for me. I missed my wife and the little ones, who are always ready to smother me with kisses." He sat down again and nodded, but he could not get the dream out of his thoughts, and he still had the goloshes on his feet. A falling star gleamed across the sky. "There goes one!" cried he. "However, there are quite enough left; I should very much like to examine these a little nearer, especially the moon, for that could not slip away under one's hands. The student, for whom my wife washes, says that when we die we shall fly from one star to another. If that were true, it would be very delightful, but I don't believe it. I wish I could make a little spring up there now; I would willingly let my body lie here on the steps."

There are certain things in the world which should be uttered very cautiously; doubly so when the speaker has on his feet the goloshes of Fortune. Now we shall hear what happened to the watchman.

Nearly every one is acquainted with the great power of steam; we have proved it by the rapidity with which we can travel, both on a railroad or in a steamship across the sea. But this speed is like the movements of the sloth, or the crawling march of the snail, when compared to the swiftness with which light travels; light flies nineteen million times faster than the fleetest race-horse, and electricity is more rapid still. Death is an electric shock which we receive in our hearts, and on the wings of electricity the liberated soul flies away swiftly, the light from the sun travels to our earth ninety-five millions of miles in eight minutes and a few seconds; but on the wings of electricity, the mind requires only a second to accomplish the same distance. The space between the heavenly bodies is, to thought, no farther than the distance which we may have to walk from one friend's house to another in the same town; yet this electric shock obliges us to use our bodies here below, unless, like the watchman, we have on the goloshes of Fortune.

In a very few seconds the watchman had travelled more than two hundred thousand miles to the moon, which is formed of a lighter material than our earth, and may be said to be as soft as new fallen snow. He found himself on one of the circular range of mountains which we see represented in Dr. Madler's large map of the moon. The interior had the appearance of a large hollow, bowl-shaped, with a depth about half a mile from the brim. Within this hollow stood a large town; we may form some idea of its appearance by pouring the white of an egg into a glass of water. The materials of which it was built seemed just as soft, and pictured forth cloudy turrets and sail-like terraces, quite transparent, and floating in the thin air. Our earth hung over his head like a great dark red ball. Presently he discovered a number of beings, which might certainly be called men, but were very different to ourselves. A more fantastical imagination than Herschel's must have discovered these. Had they been placed in groups, and painted, it might have been said, "What beautiful foliage!" They had also a language of their own. No one could have expected the soul of the watchman to understand it, and yet he did understand it, for our souls have much greater capabilities then we are inclined to believe. Do we not, in our dreams, show a wonderful dramatic talent? each of our acquaintance appears to us then in his own character, and with his own voice; no man could thus imitate them in his waking hours. How clearly, too, we are reminded of persons whom we have not seen for many years; they start up suddenly to the mind's eye with all their peculiarities as living realities. In fact, this memory of the soul is a fearful thing; every sin, every sinful thought it can bring back, and we may well ask how we are to give account of "every idle word" that may have been whispered in the heart or uttered with the lips. The spirit of the watchman therefore understood very well the language of the inhabitants of the moon. They were disputing about our earth, and doubted whether it could be inhabited. The atmosphere, they asserted, must be too dense for any inhabitants of the moon to exist there. They maintained that the moon alone was inhabited, and was really the heavenly body in which the old world people lived. They likewise talked politics.

But now we will descend to East Street, and see what happened to the watchman's body. He sat lifeless on the steps. His staff had fallen out of his hand, and his eyes stared at the moon, about which his honest soul was wandering.

"What is it o'clock, watchman?" inquired a passenger. But there was no answer from the watchman.

The man then pulled his nose gently, which caused him to lose his balance. The body fell forward, and lay at full length on the ground as one dead.

All his comrades were very much frightened, for he seemed quite dead; still they allowed him to remain after they had given notice of what had happened; and at dawn the body was carried to the hospital. We might imagine it to be no jesting matter if the soul of the man should chance to return to him, for most probably it would seek for the body in East Street without being able to find it. We might fancy the soul inquiring of the police, or at the address office, or among the missing parcels, and then at length finding it at the hospital. But we may comfort ourselves by the certainty that the soul, when acting upon its own impulses, is wiser than we are; it is the body that makes it stupid.

As we have said, the watchman's body had been taken to the hospital, and here it was placed in a room to be washed. Naturally, the first thing done here was to take off the goloshes, upon which the soul was instantly obliged to return, and it took the direct road to the body at once, and in a few seconds the man's life returned to him. He declared, when he quite recovered himself, that this had been the most dreadful night he had ever passed; not for a hundred pounds would he go through such feelings again. However, it was all over now.

The same day he was allowed to leave, but the goloshes remained at the hospital.

The Eventful Moment – a Most Unusual Journey

Every inhabitant of Copenhagen knows what the entrance to Frederick's Hospital is like; but as most probably a few of those who read this little tale may not reside in Copenhagen, we will give a short description of it.

The hospital is separated from the street by an iron railing, in which the bars stand so wide apart that, it is said, some very slim patients have squeezed through, and gone to pay little visits in the town. The most difficult part of the body to get through was the head; and in this case, as it often happens in the world, the small heads were the most fortunate. This will serve as sufficient introduction to our tale. One of the young volunteers, of whom, physically speaking, it might be said that he had a great head, was on guard that evening at the hospital. The rain was pouring down, yet, in spite of these two obstacles, he wanted to go out just for a quarter of an hour; it was not worth while, he thought, to make a confidant of the porter, as he could easily slip through the iron railings. There lay the goloshes, which the watchman had forgotten. It never occurred to him that these could be goloshes of Fortune. They would be very serviceable to him in this rainy weather, so he drew them on. Now came the question whether he could squeeze through the palings; he certainly had never tried, so he stood looking at them. "I wish to goodness my head was through," said he, and instantly, though it was so thick and large, it slipped through quite easily. The goloshes answered that purpose very well, but his body had to follow, and this was impossible. "I am too fat," he said; "I thought my head would be the worst, but I cannot get my body through, that is certain." Then he tried to pull his head back again, but without success; he could move his neck about easily enough, and that was all. His first feeling was one of anger, and then his spirits sank below zero. The goloshes of Fortune had placed him in this terrible position, and unfortunately it never occurred to him to wish himself free. No, instead of wishing he kept twisting about, yet did not stir from the spot. The rain poured, and not a creature could be seen in the street. The porter's bell he was unable to reach, and however was he to get loose! He foresaw that he should have to stay there till morning, and then they must send for a smith to file away the iron bars, and that would be a work of time. All the charity children would just be going to school: and all the sailors who inhabited that quarter of the town would be there to see him standing in the pillory. What a crowd there would be. "Ha," he cried, "the blood is rushing to my head, and I shall go mad. I believe I am crazy already; oh, I wish I were free, then all these sensations would pass off." This is just what he ought to have said at first. The moment he had expressed the thought his head was free. He started back, quite bewildered with the fright which the goloshes of Fortune had caused him. But we must not suppose it was all over; no, indeed, there was worse to come yet. The night passed, and the whole of the following day; but no one sent for the goloshes. In the evening a declamatory performance was to take place at the amateur theatre in a distant street. The house was crowded; among the audience was the young volunteer from the hospital, who seemed to have quite forgotten his adventures of the previous evening. He had on the goloshes; they had not been sent for, and as the streets were still very dirty, they were of great service to him. A new poem, entitled "My Aunt's Spectacles," was being recited. It described these spectacles as possessing a wonderful power; if any one put them on in a large assembly the people appeared like cards, and the future events of ensuing years could be easily foretold by them. The idea struck him that he should very much like to have such a pair of spectacles; for, if used rightly, they would perhaps enable him to see into the hearts of people, which he thought would be more interesting than to know what was going to happen next year; for future events would be sure to show themselves, but the hearts of people never. "I can fancy what I should see in the whole row of ladies and gentlemen on the first seat, if I could only look into their hearts; that lady, I imagine, keeps a store for things of all descriptions; how my eyes would wander about in that collection; with many ladies I should no doubt find a large millinery establishment. There is another that is perhaps empty, and would be all the better for cleaning out. There may be some well stored with good articles. Ah, yes," he sighed, "I know one, in which everything is solid, but a servant is there already, and that is the only thing against it. I dare say from many I should hear the words, 'Please to walk in.' I only wish I could slip into the hearts like a little tiny thought." This was the word of command for the goloshes. The volunteer shrunk up together, and commenced a most unusual journey through the hearts of the spectators in the first row. The first heart he entered was that of a lady, but he thought he must have got into one of the rooms of an orthopedic institution where plaster casts of deformed limbs were hanging on the walls, with this difference, that the casts in the institution are formed when the patient enters, but here they were formed and preserved after the good people had left. These were casts of the bodily and mental deformities of the lady's female friends carefully preserved. Quickly he passed into another heart, which had the appearance of a spacious, holy church, with the white dove of innocence fluttering over the altar. Gladly would he have fallen on his knees in such a sacred place; but he was carried on to another heart, still, however, listening to the tones of the organ, and feeling himself that he had become another and a better man. The next heart was also a sanctuary, which he felt almost unworthy to enter; it represented a mean garret, in which lay a sick mother; but the warm sunshine streamed through the window, lovely roses bloomed in a little flowerbox on the roof, two blue birds sang of childlike joys, and the sick mother prayed for a blessing on her daughter. Next he crept on his hands and knees through an overfilled butcher's shop; there was meat, nothing but meat, wherever he stepped; this was the heart of a rich, respectable man, whose name is doubtless in the directory. Then he entered the heart of this man's wife; it was an old, tumble-down pigeon-house; the husband's portrait served as a weather-cock; it was connected with all the doors, which opened and shut just as the husband's decision turned. The next heart was a complete cabinet of mirrors, such as can be seen in the Castle of Rosenberg. But these mirrors magnified in an astonishing degree; in the middle of the floor sat, like the Grand Lama, the insignificant I of the owner, astonished at the contemplation of his own features. At his next visit he fancied he must have got into a narrow needlecase, full of sharp needles: "Oh," thought he, "this must be the heart of an old maid;" but such was not the fact; it belonged to a young officer, who wore several orders, and was said to be a man of intellect and heart.

The poor volunteer came out of the last heart in the row quite bewildered. He could not collect his thoughts, and imagined his foolish fancies had carried him away. "Good gracious!" he sighed, "I must have a tendency to softening of the brain, and here it is so exceedingly hot that the blood is rushing to my head." And then suddenly recurred to him the strange event of the evening before, when his head had been fixed between the iron railings in front of the hospital. "That is the cause of it all!" he exclaimed, "I must do something in time. A Russian bath would be a very good thing to begin with. I wish I were lying on one of the highest shelves." Sure enough, there he lay on an upper shelf of a vapor bath, still in his evening costume, with his boots and goloshes on, and the hot drops from the ceiling falling on his face. "Ho!" he cried, jumping down and rushing towards the plunging bath. The attendant stopped him with a loud cry, when he saw a man with all his clothes on. The volunteer had, however, presence of mind enough to whisper, "It is for a wager;" but the first thing he did, when he reached his own room, was to put a large blister on his neck, and another on his back, that his crazy fit might be cured. The next morning his back was very sore, which was all he gained by the goloshes of Fortune.

The Clerk's Transformation

The watchman, whom we of course have not forgotten, thought, after a while, of the goloshes which he had found and taken to the hospital; so he went and fetched them. But neither the lieutenant nor any one in the street could recognize them as their own, so he gave them up to the police. "They look exactly like my own goloshes," said one of the clerks, examining the unknown articles, as they stood by the side of his own. "It would require even more than the eye of a shoemaker to know one pair from the other."

"Master clerk," said a servant who entered with some papers. The clerk turned and spoke to the man; but when he had done with him, he turned to look at the goloshes again, and now he was in greater doubt than ever as to whether the pair on the right or on the left belonged to him. "Those that are wet must be mine," thought he; but he thought wrong, it was just the reverse. The goloshes of Fortune were the wet pair; and, besides, why should not a clerk in a police office be wrong sometimes? So he drew them on, thrust his papers into his pocket, placed a few manuscripts under his arm, which he had to take with him, and to make abstracts from at home. Then, as it was Sunday morning and the weather very fine, he said to himself, "A walk to Fredericksburg will do me good:" so away he went.

There could not be a quieter or more steady young man than this clerk. We will not grudge him this little walk, it was just the thing to do him good after sitting so much. He went on at first like a mere automaton, without thought or wish; therefore the goloshes had no opportunity to display their magic power. In the avenue he met with an acquaintance, one of our young poets, who told him that he intended to start on the following day on a summer excursion. "Are you really going away so soon?" asked the clerk. "What a free, happy man you are. You can roam about where you will, while such as we are tied by the foot."

"But it is fastened to the bread-tree," replied the poet. "You need have no anxiety for the morrow; and when you are old there is a pension for you."

"Ah, yes; but you have the best of it," said the clerk; "it must be so delightful to sit and write poetry. The whole world makes itself agreeable to you, and then you are your own master. You should try how you would like to listen to all the trivial things in a court of justice." The poet shook his head, so also did the clerk; each retained his own opinion, and so they parted. "They are strange people, these poets," thought the clerk. "I should like to try what it is to have a poetic taste, and to become a poet myself. I am sure I should not write such mournful verses as they do. This is a splendid spring day for a poet, the air is so remarkably clear, the clouds are so beautiful, and the green grass has such a sweet smell. For many years I have not felt as I do at this moment."

We perceive, by these remarks, that he had already become a poet. By most poets what he had said would be considered common-place, or as the Germans call it, "insipid." It is a foolish fancy to look upon poets as different to other men. There are many who are more the poets of nature than those who are professed poets. The difference is this, the poet's intellectual memory is better; he seizes upon an idea or a sentiment, until he can embody it, clearly and plainly in words, which the others cannot do. But the transition from a character of every-day life to one of a more gifted nature is a great transition; and so the clerk became aware of the change after a time. "What a delightful perfume," said he; "it reminds me of the violets at Aunt Lora's. Ah, that was when I was a little boy. Dear me, how long it seems since I thought of those days! She was a good old maiden lady! she lived yonder, behind the Exchange. She always had a sprig or a few blossoms in water, let the winter be ever so severe. I could smell the violets, even while I was placing warm penny pieces against the frozen panes to make peep-holes, and a pretty view it was on which I peeped. Out in the river lay the ships, icebound, and forsaken by their crews; a screaming crow represented the only living creature on board. But when the breezes of spring came, everything started into life. Amidst shouting and cheers the ships were tarred and rigged, and then they sailed to foreign lands."

"I remain here, and always shall remain, sitting at my post at the police office, and letting others take passports to distant lands. Yes, this is my fate," and he sighed deeply. Suddenly he paused. "Good gracious, what has come over me? I never felt before as I do now; it must be the air of spring. It is overpowering, and yet it is delightful."

He felt in his pockets for some of his papers. "These will give me something else to think of," said he. Casting his eyes on the first page of one, he read, "'Mistress Sigbirth; an original Tragedy, in Five Acts.' What is this? – in my own handwriting, too! Have I written this tragedy?" He read again, "'The Intrigue on the Promenade; or, the Fast-Day. A Vaudeville.' However did I get all this? Some one must have put them into my pocket. And here is a letter!" It was from the manager of a theatre; the pieces were rejected, not at all in polite terms.

"Hem, hem!" said he, sitting down on a bench; his thoughts were very elastic, and his heart softened strangely. Involuntarily he seized one of the nearest flowers; it was a little, simple daisy. All that botanists can say in many lectures was explained in a moment by this little flower. It spoke of the glory of its birth; it told of the strength of the sunlight, which had caused its delicate leaves to expand, and given to it such sweet perfume. The struggles of life which arouse sensations in the bosom have their type in the tiny flowers. Air and light are the lovers of the flowers, but light is the favored one; towards light it turns, and only when light vanishes does it fold its leaves together, and sleep in the embraces of the air."

"It is light that adorns me," said the flower.

"But the air gives you the breath of life," whispered the poet.

Just by him stood a boy, splashing with his stick in a marshy ditch. The water-drops spurted up among the green twigs, and the clerk thought of the millions of animalculae which were thrown into the air with every drop of water, at a height which must be the same to them as it would be to us if we were hurled beyond the clouds. As the clerk thought of all these things, and became conscious of the great change in his own feelings, he smiled, and said to himself, "I must be asleep and dreaming; and yet, if so, how wonderful for a dream to be so natural and real, and to know at the same time too that it is but a dream. I hope I shall be able to remember it all when I wake tomorrow. My sensations seem most unaccountable. I have a clear perception of everything as if I were wide awake. I am quite sure if I recollect all this tomorrow, it will appear utterly ridiculous and absurd. I have had this happen to me before. It is with the clever or wonderful things we say or hear in dreams, as with the gold which comes from under the earth, it is rich and beautiful when we possess it, but when seen in a true light it is but as stones and withered leaves."

"Ah!" he sighed mournfully, as he gazed at the birds singing merrily, or hopping from branch to branch, "they are much better off than I. Flying is a glorious power. Happy is he who is born with wings. Yes, if I could change myself into anything I would be a little lark." At the same moment his coat-tails and sleeves grew together and formed wings, his clothes changed to feathers, and his goloshes to claws. He felt what was taking place, and laughed to himself. "Well, now it is evident I must be dreaming; but I never had such a wild dream as this." And then he flew up into the green boughs and sang, but there was no poetry in the song, for his poetic nature had left him. The goloshes, like all persons who wish to do a thing thoroughly, could only attend to one thing at a time. He wished to be a poet, and he became one. Then he wanted to be a little bird, and in this change he lost the characteristics of the former one. "Well," thought he, "this is charming; by day I sit in a police-office, amongst the dryest law papers, and at night I can dream that I am a lark, flying about in the gardens of Fredericksburg. Really a complete comedy could be written about it." Then he flew down into the grass, turned his head about in every direction, and tapped his beak on the bending blades of grass, which, in proportion to his size, seemed to him as long as the palm-leaves in northern Africa.

In another moment all was darkness around him. It seemed as if something immense had been thrown over him. A sailor boy had flung his large cap over the bird, and a hand came underneath and caught the clerk by the back and wings so roughly, that he squeaked, and then cried out in his alarm, "You impudent rascal, I am a clerk in the police-office!" but it only sounded to the boy like "tweet, tweet;" so he tapped the bird on the beak, and walked away with him. In the avenue he met two school-boys, who appeared to belong to a better class of society, but whose inferior abilities kept them in the lowest class at school. These boys bought the bird for eightpence, and so the clerk returned to Copenhagen. "It is well for me that I am dreaming," he thought; "otherwise

I should become really angry. First I was a poet, and now I am a lark. It must have been the poetic nature that changed me into this little creature. It is a miserable story indeed, especially now I have fallen into the hands of boys. I wonder what will be the end of it." The boys carried him into a very elegant room, where a stout, pleasant-looking lady received them, but she was not at all gratified to find that they had brought a lark – a common field-bird as she called it. However, she allowed them for one day to place the bird in an empty cage that hung near the window. "It will please Polly perhaps," she said, laughing at a large gray parrot, who was swinging himself proudly on a ring in a handsome brass cage. "It is Polly's birthday," she added in a simpering tone, "and the little field-bird has come to offer his congratulations."

Polly did not answer a single word, he continued to swing proudly to and fro; but a beautiful canary, who had been brought from his own warm, fragrant fatherland, the summer previous, began to sing as loud as he could.

"You screamer!" said the lady, throwing a white handkerchief over the cage.

"Tweet, tweet," sighed he, "what a dreadful snowstorm!" and then he became silent.

The clerk, or as the lady called him the field-bird, was placed in a little cage close to the canary, and not far from the parrot. The only human speech which Polly could utter, and which she sometimes chattered forth most comically, was "Now let us be men." All besides was a scream, quite as unintelligible as the warbling of the canary-bird, excepting to the clerk, who being now a bird, could understand his comrades very well.

"I flew beneath green palm-trees, and amidst the blooming almond-trees," sang the canary. "I flew with my brothers and sisters over beautiful flowers, and across the clear, bright sea, which reflected the waving foliage in its glittering depths; and I have seen many gay parrots, who could relate long and delightful stories."

"They were wild birds," answered the parrot, "and totally uneducated. Now let us be men. Why do you not laugh? If the lady and her visitors can laugh at this, surely you can. It is a great failing not to be able to appreciate what is amusing. Now let us be men."

"Do you remember," said the canary, "the pretty maidens who used to dance in the tents that were spread out beneath the sweet blossoms? Do you remember the delicious fruit and the cooling juice from the wild herbs?"

"Oh, yes," said the parrot; "but here I am much better off. I am well fed, and treated politely. I know that I have a clever head; and what more do I want? Let us be men now. You have a soul for poetry. I have deep knowledge and wit. You have genius, but no discretion. You raise your naturally high notes so much, that you get covered over. They never serve me so. Oh, no; I cost them something more than you. I keep them in order with my beak, and fling my wit about me. Now let us be men."

"O my warm, blooming fatherland," sang the canary bird, "I will sing of thy dark-green trees and thy quiet streams, where the bending branches kiss the clear, smooth water. I will sing of the joy of my brothers and sisters, as their shining plumage flits among the dark leaves of the plants which grow wild by the springs."

"Do leave off those dismal strains," said the parrot; "sing something to make us laugh; laughter is the sign of the highest order of intellect. Can a dog or a horse laugh? No, they can cry; but to man alone is the power of laughter given. Ha! ha! ha!" laughed Polly, and repeated his witty saying, "Now let us be men."

"You little gray Danish bird," said the canary, "you also have become a prisoner. It is certainly cold in your forests, but still there is liberty there. Fly out! they have forgotten to close the cage, and the window is open at the top. Fly, fly!"

Instinctively, the clerk obeyed, and left the cage; at the same moment the half-opened door leading into the next room creaked on its hinges, and, stealthily, with green fiery eyes, the cat crept in and chased the lark round the room. The canary-bird fluttered in his cage, and the parrot flapped his wings and cried, "Let us be men;" the poor clerk, in the most deadly terror, flew through the window, over the houses, and through the streets, till at length he was obliged to seek a resting-place. A house opposite to him had a look of home. A window stood open; he flew in, and perched upon the table. It was his own room. "Let us be men now," said he, involuntarily imitating the parrot; and at the same moment he became a clerk again, only that he was sitting on the table. "Heaven preserve us!" said he; "How did I get up here and fall asleep in this way? It was an uneasy dream too that I had. The whole affair appears most absurd."

The Best Thing the Goloshes Did

Early on the following morning, while the clerk was still in bed, his neighbor, a young divinity student, who lodged on the same storey, knocked at his door, and then walked in. "Lend me your goloshes," said he; "it is so wet in the garden, but the sun is shining brightly. I should like to go out there and smoke my pipe." He put on the goloshes, and was soon in the garden, which contained only one plum-tree and one apple-tree; yet, in a town, even a small garden like this is a great advantage.

The student wandered up and down the path; it was just six o'clock, and he could hear the sound of the post-horn in the street. "Oh, to travel, to travel!" cried he; "there is no greater happiness in the world: it is the height of my ambition. This restless feeling would be stilled, if I could take a journey far away from this country. I should like to see beautiful Switzerland, to travel through Italy, and," – It was well for him that the goloshes acted immediately, otherwise he might have been carried too far for himself as well as for us. In a moment he found himself in Switzerland, closely packed with eight others in the diligence. His head ached, his back was stiff, and the blood had ceased to circulate, so that his feet were swelled and pinched by his boots. He wavered in a condition between sleeping and waking. In his right-hand pocket he had a letter of credit; in his left-hand pocket was his passport; and a few louis d'ors were sewn into a little leather bag which he carried in his breast-pocket. Whenever he dozed, he dreamed that he had lost one or another of these possessions; then he would awake with a start, and the first movements of his hand formed a triangle from his right-hand pocket to his breast, and from his breast to his left-hand pocket, to feel whether they were all safe. Umbrellas, sticks, and hats swung in the net before him, and almost obstructed the prospect, which was really very imposing; and as he glanced at it, his memory recalled the words of one poet at least, who has sung of Switzerland, and whose poems have not yet been printed: –

> *"How lovely to my wondering eyes*
> *Mont Blanc's fair summits gently rise;*
> *'Tis sweet to breathe the mountain air, –*
> *If you have gold enough to spare."*

Grand, dark, and gloomy appeared the landscape around him. The pine-forests looked like little groups of moss on high rocks, whose summits were lost in clouds of mist. Presently it began to snow, and the wind blew keen and cold. "Ah," he sighed, "if I were only on the other side of the Alps now, it would be summer, and I should be able to get money on my letter of credit. The anxiety I feel on this matter prevents me from enjoying myself in Switzerland. Oh, I wish I was on the other side of the Alps."

And there, in a moment, he found himself, far away in the midst of Italy, between Florence and Rome, where the lake Thrasymene glittered in the evening sunlight like a sheet of molten gold between the dark blue mountains. There, where Hannibal defeated Flaminius, the grape vines clung to each other with the friendly grasp of their green tendril fingers; while, by the wayside, lovely half-naked children were watching a herd of coal-black swine under the blossoms of fragrant laurel. Could we rightly describe this picturesque scene, our readers would exclaim, "Delightful Italy!"

But neither the student nor either of his travelling companions felt the least inclination to think of it in this way. Poisonous flies and gnats flew into the coach by thousands. In vain they drove them away with a myrtle branch, the flies stung them notwithstanding. There was not a man in the coach whose face was not swollen and disfigured with the stings. The poor horses looked wretched; the flies settled on their backs in swarms, and they were only relieved when the coachmen got down and drove the creatures off.

As the sun set, an icy coldness filled all nature, not however of long duration. It produced the feeling which we experience when we enter a vault at a funeral, on a summer's day; while the hills and the clouds put on that singular green hue which we often notice in old paintings, and look upon as unnatural until we have ourselves seen nature's coloring in the south. It was a glorious spectacle; but the stomachs of the travellers were empty, their bodies exhausted with fatigue, and all the longings of their heart turned towards a resting-place for the night; but where to find one they knew not. All the eyes were too eagerly seeking for this resting-place, to notice the beauties of nature.

The road passed through a grove of olive-trees; it reminded the student of the willow-trees at home. Here stood a lonely inn, and close by it a number of crippled beggars had placed themselves; the brightest among them looked, to quote the words of Marryat, "like the eldest son of Famine who had just come of age." The others were either blind, or had withered legs, which obliged them to creep about on their hands and knees, or they had shrivelled arms and hands without fingers. It was indeed poverty arrayed in rags. "Eccellenza, miserabili!" they exclaimed, stretching forth their diseased limbs. The hostess received the travellers with bare feet, untidy hair, and a dirty blouse. The doors were fastened together with string; the floors of the rooms were of brick, broken in many places; bats flew about under the roof; and as to the odor within –

"Let us have supper laid in the stable," said one of the travellers; "then we shall know what we are breathing."

The windows were opened to let in a little fresh air, but quicker than air came in the withered arms and the continual whining sounds, "Miserabili, eccellenza". On the walls were inscriptions, half of them against "la bella Italia."

The supper made its appearance at last. It consisted of watery soup, seasoned with pepper and rancid oil. This last delicacy played a principal part in the salad. Musty eggs and roasted cocks'-combs were the best dishes on the table; even the wine had a strange taste, it was certainly a mixture. At night, all the boxes were placed against the doors, and one of the travellers watched while the others slept. The student's turn came to watch. How close the air felt in that room; the heat overpowered him. The gnats were buzzing about and stinging, while the miserabili, outside, moaned in their dreams.

"Travelling would be all very well," said the student of divinity to himself, "if we had no bodies, or if the body could rest while the soul is flying. Wherever I go I feel a want which oppresses my heart, for something better presents itself at the moment; yes, something better, which shall be the best of all; but where is that to be found? In fact, I know in my heart very well what I want. I wish to attain the greatest of all happiness."

No sooner were the words spoken than he was at home. Long white curtains shaded the windows of his room, and in the middle of the floor stood a black coffin, in which he now lay in the still sleep of death; his wish was fulfilled, his body was at rest, and his spirit travelling.

"Esteem no man happy until he is in his grave," were the words of Solon. Here was a strong fresh proof of their truth. Every corpse is a sphinx of immortality. The sphinx in this sarcophagus might unveil its own mystery in the words which the living had himself written two days before –

> *"Stern death, thy chilling silence waketh dread;*
> *Yet in thy darkest hour there may be light.*
> *Earth's garden reaper! from the grave's cold bed*
> *The soul on Jacob's ladder takes her flight.*
>
> *Man's greatest sorrows often are a part*
> *Of hidden griefs, concealed from human eyes,*
> *Which press far heavier on the lonely heart*
> *Than now the earth that on his coffin lies."*

Two figures were moving about the room; we know them both. One was the fairy named Care, the other the messenger of Fortune. They bent over the dead.

"Look!" said Care; "what happiness have your goloshes brought to mankind?"

"They have at least brought lasting happiness to him who slumbers here," she said.

"Not so," said Care, "he went away of himself, he was not summoned. His mental powers were not strong enough to discern the treasures which he had been destined to discover. I will do him a favor now." And she drew the goloshes from his feet.

The sleep of death was ended, and the recovered man raised himself. Care vanished, and with her the goloshes; doubtless she looked upon them as her own property.

The Metal Pig

IN THE CITY of Florence, not far from the Piazza del Granduca, runs a little street called Porta Rosa. In this street, just in front of the market-place where vegetables are sold, stands a pig, made of brass and curiously formed. The bright color has been changed by age to dark green; but clear, fresh water pours from the snout, which shines as if it had been polished, and so indeed it has, for hundreds of poor people and children seize it in their hands as they place their mouths close to the mouth of the animal, to drink. It is quite a picture to see a half-naked boy clasping the well-formed creature by the head, as he presses his rosy lips against its jaws. Every one who visits Florence can very quickly find the place; he has only to ask the first beggar he meets for the Metal Pig, and he will be told where it is.

It was late on a winter evening; the mountains were covered with snow, but the moon shone brightly, and moonlight in Italy is like a dull winter's day in the north; indeed it is better, for clear air seems to raise us above the earth, while in the north a cold, gray, leaden sky appears to press us down to earth, even as the cold damp earth shall one day press on us in the grave. In the garden of the grand duke's palace, under the roof of one of the wings, where a thousand roses bloom in winter, a little ragged boy had been sitting the whole day long; a boy, who might serve as a type of Italy, lovely and smiling, and yet still suffering. He was hungry and thirsty, yet no one gave him anything; and when it became dark, and they were about to close the gardens, the porter turned him out. He stood a long time musing on the bridge which crosses the Arno, and looking at the glittering stars, reflected in the water which flowed between him and the elegant marble bridge Della Trinità. He then walked away towards the Metal Pig, half knelt down, clasped it with his arms, and then put his mouth to the shining snout and drank deep draughts of the fresh water. Close by, lay a few salad-leaves and two chestnuts, which were to serve for his supper. No one was in the street but himself; it belonged only to him, so he boldly seated himself on the pig's back, leaned forward so that his curly head could rest on the head of the animal, and, before he was aware, he fell asleep.

It was midnight. The Metal Pig raised himself gently, and the boy heard him say quite distinctly, "Hold tight, little boy, for I am going to run;" and away he started for a most wonderful ride. First, they arrived at the Piazza del Granduca, and the metal horse which bears the duke's statue, neighed aloud. The painted coats-of-arms on the old council-house shone like transparent pictures, and Michael Angelo's David tossed his sling; it was as if everything had life. The metallic groups of figures, among which were Perseus and the Rape of the Sabines, looked like living persons, and cries of terror sounded from them all across the noble square. By the Palazzo degli Uffizi, in the arcade, where the nobility assemble for the carnival, the Metal Pig stopped. "Hold fast," said the animal; "hold fast, for I am going up stairs."

The little boy said not a word; he was half pleased and half afraid. They entered a long gallery, where the boy had been before. The walls were resplendent with paintings; here stood statues and busts, all in a clear light as if it were day. But the grandest appeared when the door of a side room opened; the little boy could remember what beautiful things he had seen there, but to-night everything shone in its brightest colors. Here stood the figure of a beautiful woman, as beautifully sculptured as possible by one of the great masters. Her graceful limbs appeared to move; dolphins sprang at her feet, and immortality shone from her eyes. The world called her the Venus de' Medici. By her side were statues, in which the spirit of life breathed in stone; figures of men, one of whom whetted his sword, and was named the Grinder; wrestling gladiators formed another group, the sword had been sharpened for them, and they strove for the goddess of beauty. The boy was dazzled by so much glitter; for the walls were gleaming with bright colors, all appeared living reality.

As they passed from hall to hall, beauty everywhere showed itself; and as the Metal Pig went step by step from one picture to the other, the little boy could see it all plainly. One glory eclipsed another; yet there was one picture that fixed itself on the little boy's memory, more especially because of the happy children it represented, for these the little boy had seen in daylight. Many pass this picture by with indifference, and yet it contains a treasure of poetic feeling; it represents Christ descending into Hades. They are not the lost whom the spectator sees, but the heathen of olden times. The Florentine, Angiolo Bronzino, painted this picture; most beautiful is the expression on the face of the two children, who appear to have full confidence that they shall reach heaven at last. They are embracing each other, and one little one stretches out his hand towards another who stands below him, and points to himself, as if he were saying, "I am going to heaven." The older people stand as if uncertain, yet hopeful, and they bow in humble adoration to the Lord Jesus. On this picture the boy's eyes rested longer than on any other: the Metal Pig stood still before it. A low sigh was heard. Did it come from the picture or from the animal? The boy raised his hands towards the smiling children, and then the Pig ran off with him through the open vestibule.

"Thank you, thank you, you beautiful animal," said the little boy, caressing the Metal Pig as it ran down the steps.

"Thanks to yourself also," replied the Metal Pig; "I have helped you and you have helped me, for it is only when I have an innocent child on my back that I receive the power to run. Yes; as you see, I can even venture under the rays of the lamp, in front of the picture of the Madonna, but I may not enter the church; still from without, and while you are upon my back, I may look in through the open door. Do not get down yet, for if you do, then I shall be lifeless, as you have seen me in the Porta Rosa."

"I will stay with you, my dear creature," said the little boy. So then they went on at a rapid pace through the streets of Florence, till they came to the square before the church of Santa Croce. The folding-doors flew open, and light streamed from the altar through the church into the deserted square. A wonderful blaze of light streamed from one of the monuments in the left-side aisle, and a thousand moving stars seemed to form a glory round it; even the coat-of-arms on the tomb-stone shone, and a red ladder on a blue field gleamed like fire. It was the grave of Galileo. The monument is unadorned, but the red ladder is an emblem of art, signifying that the way to glory leads up a shining ladder, on which the prophets of mind rise to heaven, like Elias of old. In the right aisle of the church every statue on the richly carved sarcophagi seemed endowed with life. Here stood Michael Angelo; there Dante, with the laurel wreath round his brow; Alfieri and Machiavelli; for here side by side rest the great men – the pride of Italy. The church itself is very beautiful, even more beautiful than the marble cathedral at Florence, though not so large. It seemed as if the carved vestments stirred, and as if the marble figures they covered raised their heads higher, to gaze upon the brightly colored glowing altar where the white-robed boys swung the golden censers, amid music and song, while the strong fragrance of incense filled the church, and streamed forth into the square. The boy stretched forth his hands towards the light, and at the same moment the Metal Pig started again so rapidly that he was obliged to cling tightly to him. The wind whistled in his ears, he heard the church door creak on its hinges as it closed, and it seemed to him as if he had lost his senses – then a cold shudder passed over him, and he awoke.

It was morning; the Metal Pig stood in its old place on the Porta Rosa, and the boy found he had slipped nearly off its back. Fear and trembling came upon him as he thought of his mother; she had sent him out the day before to get some money, he had not done so, and now he was hungry and thirsty. Once more he clasped the neck of his metal horse, kissed its nose, and nodded farewell to it. Then he wandered away into one of the narrowest streets, where there was scarcely room for a loaded donkey to pass. A great iron-bound door stood ajar; he passed through, and climbed up a brick staircase, with dirty walls and a rope for a balustrade, till he came to an open gallery hung with rags. From here a flight of steps led down to a court, where from a well water was drawn up by iron rollers to the different stories of the house, and where the water-buckets hung side by side. Sometimes the roller and the bucket danced in the air, splashing the water all over the court. Another broken-down staircase led from the gallery, and two Russian sailors running down it almost upset the poor boy. They were coming from their nightly carousal. A woman not very young, with an unpleasant face and a quantity of black hair, followed them. "What have you brought home?" she asked. when she saw the boy.

"Don't be angry," he pleaded; "I received nothing, I have nothing at all;" and he seized his mother's dress and would have kissed it. Then they went into a little room. I need not describe it, but only say that there stood in it an earthen pot with handles, made for holding fire, which in Italy is called a marito. This pot she took in her lap, warmed her fingers, and pushed the boy with her elbow.

"Certainly you must have some money," she said. The boy began to cry, and then she struck him with her foot till he cried out louder.

"Will you be quiet? or I'll break your screaming head;" and she swung about the fire-pot which she held in her hand, while the boy crouched to the earth and screamed.

Then a neighbor came in, and she had also a marito under her arm. "Felicita," she said, "what are you doing to the child?"

"The child is mine," she answered; "I can murder him if I like, and you too, Giannina." And then she swung about the fire-pot. The other woman lifted up hers to defend herself, and the two pots clashed together so violently that they were dashed to pieces, and fire and ashes flew about the room. The boy rushed out at the sight, sped across the courtyard, and fled from the house. The poor child ran till he was quite out of breath; at last he stopped at the church, the doors of which were opened to him the night before, and went in. Here everything was bright, and the boy knelt down by the first tomb on his right, the grave of Michael Angelo, and sobbed as if his heart would break. People came and went, mass was performed, but no one noticed the boy, excepting an elderly citizen, who stood still and looked at him for a moment, and then went away like the rest. Hunger and thirst overpowered the child, and he became quite faint and ill. At last he crept into a corner behind the marble monuments, and went to sleep. Towards evening he was awakened by a pull at his sleeve; he started up, and the same old citizen stood before him.

"Are you ill? where do you live? have you been here all day?" were some of the questions asked by the old man. After hearing his answers, the old man took him home to a small house close by, in a back street. They entered a glovemaker's shop, where a woman sat sewing busily. A little white poodle, so closely shaven that his pink skin could plainly be seen, frisked about the room, and gambolled upon the boy.

"Innocent souls are soon intimate," said the woman, as she caressed both the boy and the dog. These good people gave the child food and drink, and said he should stay with them all night, and that the next day the old man, who was called Giuseppe, would go and speak to his mother. A little homely bed was prepared for him, but to him who had so often slept on the hard stones it was a royal couch, and he slept sweetly and dreamed of the splendid pictures and of the Metal Pig. Giuseppe went out the next morning, and the poor child was not glad to see him go, for he knew that the old man was gone to his mother, and that, perhaps, he would have to go back. He wept at the thought, and then he played with the little, lively dog, and kissed it, while the old woman looked kindly at him to encourage him. And what news did Giuseppe bring back? At first the boy could not hear, for he talked a great deal to his wife, and she nodded and stroked the boy's cheek.

Then she said, "He is a good lad, he shall stay with us, he may become a clever glovemaker, like you. Look what delicate fingers he has got; Madonna intended him for a glovemaker." So the boy stayed with them, and the woman herself taught him to sew; and he ate well, and slept well, and became very merry. But at last he began to tease Bellissima, as the little dog was called. This made the woman angry, and she scolded him and threatened him, which made him very unhappy, and he went and sat in his own room full of sad thoughts. This chamber looked upon the street, in which hung skins to dry, and there were thick iron bars across his window. That night he lay awake, thinking of the Metal Pig; indeed, it was always in his thoughts. Suddenly he fancied he heard feet outside going pit-a-pat. He sprung out of bed and went to the window. Could it be the Metal Pig? But there was nothing to be seen; whatever he had heard had passed already. Next morning, their neighbor, the artist, passed by, carrying a paint-box and a large roll of canvas.

"Help the gentleman to carry his box of colors," said the woman to the boy; and he obeyed instantly, took the box, and followed the painter. They walked on till they reached the picture gallery, and mounted the same staircase up which he had ridden that night on the Metal Pig. He remembered all the statues and pictures, the beautiful marble Venus, and again he looked at the Madonna with the Saviour and St. John. They stopped before the picture by Bronzino, in which Christ is represented as standing in the lower world, with the children smiling before Him, in the sweet expectation of entering heaven; and the poor boy smiled, too, for here was his heaven.

"You may go home now," said the painter, while the boy stood watching him, till he had set up his easel.

"May I see you paint?" asked the boy; "may I see you put the picture on this white canvas?"

"I am not going to paint yet," replied the artist; then he brought out a piece of chalk. His hand moved quickly, and his eye measured the great picture; and though nothing appeared but a faint line, the figure of the Saviour was as clearly visible as in the colored picture.

"Why don't you go?" said the painter. Then the boy wandered home silently, and seated himself on the table, and learned to sew gloves. But all day long his thoughts were in the picture gallery; and so he pricked his fingers and was awkward. But he did not tease Bellissima. When evening came, and the house door stood open, he slipped out. It was a bright, beautiful, starlight evening, but rather cold. Away he went through the already-deserted streets, and soon came to the Metal Pig; he stooped down and kissed its shining nose, and then seated himself on its back.

"You happy creature," he said; "how I have longed for you! we must take a ride to-night."

But the Metal Pig lay motionless, while the fresh stream gushed forth from its mouth. The little boy still sat astride on its back, when he felt something pulling at his clothes. He looked down, and there was Bellissima, little smooth-shaven Bellissima, barking as if she would have said, "Here I am too; why are you sitting there?"

A fiery dragon could not have frightened the little boy so much as did the little dog in this place. "Bellissima in the street, and not dressed!" as the old lady called it; "what would be the end of this?"

The dog never went out in winter, unless she was attired in a little lambskin coat which had been made for her; it was fastened round the little dog's neck and body with red ribbons, and was decorated with rosettes and little bells. The dog looked almost like a little kid when she was allowed to go out in winter, and trot after her mistress. And now here she was in the cold, and not dressed. Oh, how would it end? All his fancies were quickly put to flight; yet he kissed the Metal Pig once more, and then took Bellissima in his arms. The poor little thing trembled so with cold, that the boy ran homeward as fast as he could.

"What are you running away with there?" asked two of the police whom he met, and at whom the dog barked. "Where have you stolen that pretty dog?" they asked; and they took it away from him.

"Oh, I have not stolen it; do give it to me back again," cried the boy, despairingly.

"If you have not stolen it, you may say at home that they can send to the watch-house for the dog." Then they told him where the watch-house was, and went away with Bellissima.

Here was a dreadful trouble. The boy did not know whether he had better jump into the Arno, or go home and confess everything. They would certainly kill him, he thought.

"Well, I would gladly be killed," he reasoned; "for then I shall die, and go to heaven:" and so he went home, almost hoping for death.

The door was locked, and he could not reach the knocker. No one was in the street; so he took up a stone, and with it made a tremendous noise at the door.

"Who is there?" asked somebody from within.

"It is I," said he. "Bellissima is gone. Open the door, and then kill me."

Then indeed there was a great panic. Madame was so very fond of Bellissima. She immediately looked at the wall where the dog's dress usually hung; and there was the little lambskin.

"Bellissima in the watch-house!" she cried. "You bad boy! how did you entice her out? Poor little delicate thing, with those rough policemen! and she'll be frozen with cold."

Giuseppe went off at once, while his wife lamented, and the boy wept. Several of the neighbors came in, and amongst them the painter. He took the boy between his knees, and questioned him; and, in broken sentences, he soon heard the whole story, and also about the Metal Pig, and the wonderful ride to the picture-gallery, which was certainly rather incomprehensible. The painter, however, consoled the little fellow, and tried to soften the lady's anger; but she would not be pacified till her husband returned with Bellissima, who had been with the police. Then there was great rejoicing, and the painter caressed the boy, and gave him a number of pictures. Oh, what beautiful pictures these were! – figures with funny heads; and, above all, the Metal Pig was there too. Oh, nothing could be more delightful. By means of a few strokes, it was made to appear on the paper; and even the house that stood behind it had been sketched in. Oh, if he could only draw and paint! He who could do this could conjure all the world before him. The first leisure moment during the next day, the boy got a pencil, and on the back of one of the other drawings he attempted to copy the drawing of the Metal Pig, and he succeeded. Certainly it was rather crooked, rather up and down, one leg thick, and another thin; still it was like the copy, and he was overjoyed at what he had done. The pencil would not go quite as it ought, – he had found that out; but the next day he tried again. A second pig was drawn by the side of the first, and this looked a hundred times better; and the third attempt was so good, that everybody might know what it was meant to represent.

And now the glovemaking went on but slowly. The orders given by the shops in the town were not finished quickly; for the Metal Pig had taught the boy that all objects may be drawn upon paper; and Florence is a picture-book in itself for any one who chooses to turn over its pages. On the Piazza dell Trinita stands a slender pillar, and upon it is the goddess of Justice, blindfolded, with her scales in her hand. She was soon represented on paper, and it was the glovemaker's boy who placed her there. His collection of pictures increased; but as yet they were only copies of lifeless objects, when one day Bellissima came gambolling before him: "Stand still," cried he, "and I will draw you beautifully, to put amongst my collection."

But Bellissima would not stand still, so she must be bound fast in one position. He tied her head and tail; but she barked and jumped, and so pulled and tightened the string, that she was nearly strangled; and just then her mistress walked in.

"You wicked boy! the poor little creature!" was all she could utter.

She pushed the boy from her, thrust him away with her foot, called him a most ungrateful, good-for-nothing, wicked boy, and forbade him to enter the house again. Then she wept, and kissed her little half-strangled Bellissima. At this moment the painter entered the room. In the year 1834 there was an exhibition in the Academy of Arts at Florence. Two pictures, placed side by side, attracted a large number of spectators. The smaller of the two represented a little boy sitting at a table, drawing; before him was a little white poodle, curiously shaven; but as the animal would not stand still, it had been fastened with a string to its head and tail, to keep it in one position. The truthfulness and life in this picture interested every one. The painter was said to be a young Florentine, who had been found in the streets, when a child, by an old glovemaker, who had brought him up. The boy had taught himself to draw: it was also said that a young artist, now famous, had discovered talent in the child just as he was about to be sent away for having tied up madame's favorite little dog, and using it as a model. The glovemaker's boy had also become a great painter, as the picture proved; but the larger picture by its side was a still greater proof of his talent. It represented a handsome boy, clothed in rags, lying asleep, and leaning against the Metal Pig in the street of the Porta Rosa. All the spectators knew the spot well. The child's arms were round the neck of the Pig, and he was in a deep sleep. The lamp before the picture of the Madonna threw a strong, effective light on the pale, delicate face of the child. It was a beautiful picture. A large gilt frame surrounded it, and on one corner of the frame a laurel wreath had been hung; but a black band, twined unseen among the green leaves, and a streamer of crape, hung down from it; for within the last few days the young artist had – died.

Everything in the Right Place

IT IS MORE than a hundred years ago! At the border of the wood, near a large lake, stood the old mansion: deep ditches surrounded it on every side, in which reeds and bulrushes grew. Close by the drawbridge, near the gate, there was an old willow tree, which bent over the reeds.

From the narrow pass came the sound of bugles and the trampling of horses' feet; therefore a little girl who was watching the geese hastened to drive them away from the bridge, before the whole hunting party came galloping up; they came, however, so quickly, that the girl, in order to avoid being run over, placed herself on one of the high corner-stones of the bridge. She was still half a child and very delicately built; she had bright blue eyes, and a gentle, sweet expression. But such things the baron did not notice; while he was riding past the little goose-girl, he reversed his hunting crop, and in rough play gave her such a push with it that she fell backward into the ditch.

"Everything in the right place!" he cried. "Into the ditch with you."

Then he burst out laughing, for that he called fun; the others joined in – the whole party shouted and cried, while the hounds barked.

While the poor girl was falling she happily caught one of the branches of the willow tree, by the help of which she held herself over the water, and as soon as the baron with his company and the dogs had disappeared through the gate, the girl endeavoured to scramble up, but the branch broke off, and she would have fallen backward among the rushes, had not a strong hand from above seized her at this moment. It was the hand of a pedlar; he had witnessed what had happened from a short distance, and now hastened to assist her.

"Everything in the right place," he said, imitating the noble baron, and pulling the little maid up to the dry ground. He wished to put the branch back in the place it had been broken off, but it is not possible to put everything in the right place; therefore he stuck the branch into the soft ground.

"Grow and thrive if you can, and produce a good flute for them yonder at the mansion," he said; it would have given him great pleasure to see the noble baron and his companions well thrashed. Then he entered the castle – but not the banqueting hall; he was too humble for that. No; he went to the servants' hall. The men-servants and maids looked over his stock of articles and bargained with him; loud crying and screaming were heard from the master's table above: they called it singing – indeed, they did their best. Laughter and the howls of dogs were heard through the open windows: there they were feasting and revelling; wine and strong old ale were foaming in the glasses and jugs; the favorite dogs ate with their masters; now and then the squires kissed one of these animals, after having wiped its mouth first with the tablecloth. They ordered the pedlar to come up, but only to make fun of him. The wine had got into their heads, and reason had left them. They poured beer into a stocking that he could drink with them, but quick. That's what they called fun, and it made them laugh. Then meadows, peasants, and farmyards were staked on one card and lost.

"Everything in the right place!" the pedlar said when he had at last safely got out of Sodom and Gomorrah, as he called it. "The open high road is my right place; up there I did not feel at ease."

The little maid, who was still watching the geese, nodded kindly to him as he passed through the gate.

Days and weeks passed, and it was seen that the broken willow-branch which the peddlar had stuck into the ground near the ditch remained fresh and green – nay, it even put forth fresh twigs; the little goose-girl saw that the branch had taken root, and was very pleased; the tree, so she said, was now her tree. While the tree was advancing, everything else at the castle was going backward, through feasting and gambling, for these are two rollers upon which nobody stands safely. Less than six years afterwards the baron passed out of his castle-gate a poor beggar, while the baronial seat had been bought by a rich tradesman. He was the very pedlar they had made fun of and poured beer into a stocking for him to drink; but honesty and industry bring one forward, and now the pedlar was the possessor of the baronial estate. From that time forward no card-playing was permitted there.

"That's a bad pastime," he said; "when the devil saw the Bible for the first time he wanted to produce a caricature in opposition to it, and invented card-playing."

The new proprietor of the estate took a wife, and whom did he take? – The little goose-girl, who had always remained good and kind, and who looked as beautiful in her new clothes as if she had been a lady of high birth. And how did all this come about? That would be too long a tale to tell in our busy time, but it really happened, and the most important events have yet to be told.

It was pleasant and cheerful to live in the old place now: the mother superintended the household, and the father looked after things out-of-doors, and they were indeed very prosperous.

Where honesty leads the way, prosperity is sure to follow. The old mansion was repaired and painted, the ditches were cleaned and fruit-trees planted; all was homely and pleasant, and the floors were as white and shining as a pasteboard. In the long winter evenings the mistress and her maids sat at the spinning-wheel in the large hall; every Sunday the counsellor – this title the pedlar had obtained, although only in his old days – read aloud a portion from the Bible. The children (for they had children) all received the best education, but they were not all equally clever, as is the case in all families.

In the meantime the willow tree near the drawbridge had grown up into a splendid tree, and stood there, free, and was never clipped. "It is our genealogical tree," said the old people to their children, "and therefore it must be honoured."

A hundred years had elapsed. It was in our own days; the lake had been transformed into marsh land; the whole baronial seat had, as it were, disappeared. A pool of water near some ruined walls was the only remainder of the deep ditches; and here stood a magnificent old tree with overhanging branches – that was the genealogical tree. Here it stood, and showed how beautiful a willow can look if one does not interfere with it. The trunk, it is true, was cleft in the middle from the root to the crown; the storms had bent it a little, but it still stood there, and out of every crevice and cleft, in which wind and weather had carried mould, blades of grass and flowers sprang forth. Especially above, where the large boughs parted, there was quite a hanging garden, in which wild raspberries and hart's-tongue ferns throve, and even a little mistletoe had taken root, and grew gracefully in the old willow branches, which were reflected in the dark water beneath when the wind blew the chickweed into the corner of the pool. A footpath which led across the fields passed close by the old tree. High up, on the woody hillside, stood the new mansion. It had a splendid view, and was large and magnificent; its window panes were so clear that one might have thought there were none there at all. The large flight of steps which led to the entrance looked like a bower covered with roses and broad-leaved plants. The lawn was as green as if each blade of grass was cleaned separately morning and evening. Inside, in the hall, valuable oil paintings were hanging on the walls. Here stood chairs and sofas covered with silk and velvet, which could be easily rolled about on castors; there were tables with polished marble tops, and books bound in morocco with gilt edges. Indeed, well-to-do and distinguished people lived here; it was the dwelling of the baron and his family. Each article was in keeping with its surroundings. "Everything in the right place" was the motto according to which they also acted here, and therefore all the paintings which had once been the honour and glory of the old mansion were now hung up in the passage which led to the servants' rooms. It was all old lumber, especially two portraits – one representing a man in a scarlet coat with a wig, and the other a lady with powdered and curled hair holding a rose in her hand, each of them being surrounded by a large wreath of willow branches. Both portraits had many holes in them, because the baron's sons used the two old people as targets for their crossbows. They represented the counsellor and his wife, from whom the whole family descended. "But they did not properly belong to our family," said one of the boys; "he was a pedlar and she kept the geese. They were not like papa and mamma." The portraits were old lumber, and "everything in its right place." That was why the great-grandparents had been hung up in the passage leading to the servants' rooms.

The son of the village pastor was tutor at the mansion. One day he went for a walk across the fields with his young pupils and their elder sister, who had lately been confirmed. They walked along the road which passed by the old willow tree, and while they were on the road she picked a bunch of field-flowers. "Everything in the right place," and indeed the bunch looked very beautiful. At the same time she listened to all that was said, and she very much liked to hear the pastor's son speak about the elements and of the great men and women in history. She had a healthy mind, noble in thought and deed, and with a heart full of love for everything that God had created. They stopped at the old willow tree, as the youngest of the baron's sons wished very much to have a flute from it, such as had been cut for him from other willow trees; the pastor's son broke a branch off. "Oh, pray do not do it!" said the young lady; but it was already done. "That is our famous old tree. I love it very much. They often laugh at me at home about it, but that does not matter. There is a story attached to this tree." And now she told him all that we already know about the tree – the old mansion, the pedlar and the goose-girl who had met there for the first time, and had become the ancestors of the noble family to which the young lady belonged.

"They did not like to be knighted, the good old people," she said; "their motto was 'everything in the right place,' and it would not be right, they thought, to purchase a title for money. My grandfather, the first baron, was their son. They say he was a very learned man, a great favorite with the princes and princesses, and was invited to all court festivities. The others at home love him best; but, I do not know why, there seemed to me to be something about the old couple that attracts my heart! How homely, how patriarchal, it must have been in the old mansion, where the mistress sat at the spinning-wheel with her maids, while her husband read aloud out of the Bible!"

"They must have been excellent, sensible people," said the pastor's son. And with this the conversation turned naturally to noblemen and commoners; from the manner in which the tutor spoke about the significance of being noble, it seemed almost as if he did not belong to a commoner's family.

"It is good fortune to be of a family who have distinguished themselves, and to possess as it were a spur in oneself to advance to all that is good. It is a splendid thing to belong to a noble family, whose name serves as a card of admission to the highest circles. Nobility is a distinction; it is a gold coin that bears the stamp of its own value. It is the fallacy of the time, and many poets express it, to say that all that is noble is bad and stupid, and that, on the contrary, the lower one goes among the poor, the more brilliant virtues one finds. I do not share this opinion, for it is wrong. In the upper classes one sees many touchingly beautiful traits; my own mother has told me of such, and I could mention several. One day she was visiting a nobleman's house in town; my grandmother, I believe, had been the lady's nurse when she was a child. My mother and the nobleman were alone in the room, when he suddenly noticed an old woman on crutches come limping into the courtyard; she came every Sunday to carry a gift away with her.

"'There is the poor old woman,' said the nobleman; 'it is so difficult for her to walk.'

"My mother had hardly understood what he said before he disappeared from the room, and went downstairs, in order to save her the troublesome walk for the gift she came to fetch. Of course this is only a little incident, but it has its good sound like the poor widow's two mites in the Bible, the sound which echoes in the depth of every human heart; and this is what the poet ought to show and point out – more especially in our own time he ought to sing of this; it does good, it mitigates and reconciles! But when a man, simply because he is of noble birth and possesses a genealogy, stands on his hind legs and neighs in the street like an Arabian horse, and says when a commoner has been in a room: 'Some people from the street have been here,' there nobility is decaying; it has become a mask of the kind that Thespis created, and it is amusing when such a person is exposed in satire."

Such was the tutor's speech; it was a little long, but while he delivered it he had finished cutting the flute.

There was a large party at the mansion; many guests from the neighborhood and from the capital had arrived. There were ladies with tasteful and with tasteless dresses; the big hall was quite crowded with people. The clergymen stood humbly together in a corner, and looked as if they were preparing for a funeral, but it was a festival – only the amusement had not yet begun. A great concert was to take place, and that is why the baron's young son had brought his willow flute with him; but he could not make it sound, nor could his father, and therefore the flute was good for nothing.

There was music and songs of the kind which delight most those that perform them; otherwise quite charming!

"Are you an artist?" said a cavalier, the son of his father; "you play on the flute, you have made it yourself; it is genius that rules – the place of honour is due to you."

"Certainly not! I only advance with the time, and that of course one can't help."

"I hope you will delight us all with the little instrument – will you not?" Thus saying he handed to the tutor the flute which had been cut from the willow tree by the pool; and then announced in a loud voice that the tutor wished to perform a solo on the flute. They wished to tease him – that was evident, and therefore the tutor declined to play, although he could do so very well. They urged and requested him, however, so long, that at last he took up the flute and placed it to his lips.

That was a marvellous flute! Its sound was as thrilling as the whistle of a steam engine; in fact it was much stronger, for it sounded and was heard in the yard, in the garden, in the wood, and many miles round in the country; at the same time a storm rose and roared; "Everything in the right place." And with this the baron, as if carried by the wind, flew out of the hall straight into the shepherd's cottage, and the shepherd flew – not into the hall, thither he could not come – but into the servants' hall, among the smart footmen who were striding about in silk stockings; these haughty menials looked horror-struck that such a person ventured to sit at table with them. But in the hall the baron's daughter flew to the place of honour at the end of the table – she was worthy to sit there; the pastor's son had the seat next to her; the two sat there as if they were a bridal pair. An old Count, belonging to one of the oldest families of the country, remained untouched in his place of honour; the flute was just, and it is one's duty to be so. The sharp-tongued cavalier who had caused the flute to be played, and who was the child of his parents, flew headlong into the fowl-house, but not he alone.

The flute was heard at the distance of a mile, and strange events took place. A rich banker's family, who were driving in a coach and four, were blown out of it, and could not even find room behind it with their footmen. Two rich farmers who had in our days shot up higher than their own corn-fields, were flung into the ditch; it was a dangerous flute. Fortunately it burst at the first sound, and that was a good thing, for then it was put back into its owner's pocket – "its right place."

The next day, nobody spoke a word about what had taken place; thus originated the phrase, "to pocket the flute." Everything was again in its usual order, except that the two old pictures of the peddlar and the goose-girl were hanging in the banqueting-hall. There they were on the wall as if blown up there; and as a real expert said that they were painted by a master's hand, they remained there and were restored. "Everything in the right place," and to this it will come. Eternity is long, much longer indeed than this story.

The Goblin and the Huckster

THERE WAS ONCE a regular student, who lived in a garret, and had no possessions. And there was also a regular huckster, to whom the house belonged, and who occupied the ground floor. A goblin lived with the huckster, because at Christmas he always had a large dish full of jam, with a great piece of butter in the middle. The huckster could afford this; and therefore the goblin remained with the huckster, which was very cunning of him.

One evening the student came into the shop through the back door to buy candles and cheese for himself, he had no one to send, and therefore he came himself; he obtained what he wished, and then the huckster and his wife nodded good evening to him, and she was a woman who could do more than merely nod, for she had usually plenty to say for herself. The student nodded in return as he turned to leave, then suddenly stopped, and began reading the piece of paper in which the cheese was wrapped. It was a leaf torn out of an old book, a book that ought not to have been torn up, for it was full of poetry.

"Yonder lies some more of the same sort," said the huckster: "I gave an old woman a few coffee berries for it; you shall have the rest for sixpence, if you will."

"Indeed I will," said the student; "give me the book instead of the cheese; I can eat my bread and butter without cheese. It would be a sin to tear up a book like this. You are a clever man; and a practical man; but you understand no more about poetry than that cask yonder."

This was a very rude speech, especially against the cask; but the huckster and the student both laughed, for it was only said in fun. But the goblin felt very angry that any man should venture to say such things to a huckster who was a householder and sold the best butter. As soon as it was night, and the shop closed, and every one in bed except the student, the goblin stepped softly into the bedroom where the huckster's wife slept, and took away her tongue, which of course, she did not then want. Whatever object in the room he placed his tongue upon immediately received voice and speech, and was able to express its thoughts and feelings as readily as the lady herself could do. It could only be used by one object at a time, which was a good thing, as a number speaking at once would have caused great confusion. The goblin laid the tongue upon the cask, in which lay a quantity of old newspapers.

"Is it really true," he asked, "that you do not know what poetry is?"

"Of course I know," replied the cask: "poetry is something that always stand in the corner of a newspaper, and is sometimes cut out; and I may venture to affirm that I have more of it in me than the student has, and I am only a poor tub of the huckster's."

Then the goblin placed the tongue on the coffee mill; and how it did go to be sure! Then he put it on the butter tub and the cash box, and they all expressed the same opinion as the waste-paper tub; and a majority must always be respected.

"Now I shall go and tell the student," said the goblin; and with these words he went quietly up the back stairs to the garret where the student lived. He had a candle burning still, and the goblin peeped through the keyhole and saw that he was reading in the torn book, which he had brought out of the shop. But how light the room was! From the book shot forth a ray of light which grew broad and full, like the stem of a tree, from which bright rays spread upward and over the student's head. Each leaf was fresh, and each flower was like a beautiful female head; some with dark and sparkling eyes, and others with eyes that were wonderfully blue and clear. The fruit gleamed like stars, and the room was filled with sounds of beautiful music. The little goblin had never imagined, much less seen or heard of, any sight so glorious as this. He stood still on tiptoe, peeping in, till the light went out in the garret. The student no doubt had blown out his candle and gone to bed; but the little goblin remained standing there nevertheless, and listening to the music which still sounded on, soft and beautiful, a sweet cradle-song for the student, who had lain down to rest.

"This is a wonderful place," said the goblin; "I never expected such a thing. I should like to stay here with the student;" and the little man thought it over, for he was a sensible little spirit. At last he sighed, "but the student has no jam!" So he went down stairs again into the huckster's shop, and it was a good thing he got back when he did, for the cask had almost worn out the lady's tongue; he had given a description of all that he contained on one side, and was just about to turn himself over to the other side to describe what was there, when the goblin entered and restored the tongue to the lady. But from that time forward, the whole shop, from the cash box down to the pinewood logs, formed their opinions from that of the cask; and they all had such confidence in him, and treated him with so much respect, that when the huckster read the criticisms on theatricals and art of an evening, they fancied it must all come from the cask.

But after what he had seen, the goblin could no longer sit and listen quietly to the wisdom and understanding down stairs; so, as soon as the evening light glimmered in the garret, he took courage, for it seemed to him as if the rays of light were strong cables, drawing him up, and obliging him to go and peep through the keyhole; and, while there, a feeling of vastness came over him such as we experience by the ever-moving sea, when the storm breaks forth; and it brought tears into his eyes. He did not himself know why he wept, yet a kind of pleasant feeling mingled with his tears. "How wonderfully glorious it would be to sit with the student under such a tree;" but that was out of the question, he must be content to look through the keyhole, and be thankful for even that.

There he stood on the old landing, with the autumn wind blowing down upon him through the trap-door. It was very cold; but the little creature did not really feel it, till the light in the garret went out, and the tones of music died away. Then how he shivered, and crept down stairs again to his warm corner, where it felt home-like and comfortable. And when Christmas came again, and brought the dish of jam and the great lump of butter, he liked the huckster best of all.

Soon after, in the middle of the night, the goblin was awoke by a terrible noise and knocking against the window shutters and the house doors, and by the sound of the watchman's horn; for a great fire had broken out, and the whole street appeared full of flames. Was it in their house, or a neighbor's? No one could tell, for terror had seized upon all. The huckster's wife was so bewildered that she took her gold ear-rings out of her ears and put them in her pocket, that she might save something at least. The huckster ran to get his business papers, and the servant resolved to save her blue silk mantle, which she had managed to buy. Each wished to keep the best things they had. The goblin had the same wish; for, with one spring, he was up stairs and in the student's room, whom he found standing by the open window, and looking quite calmly at the fire, which was raging at the house of a neighbor opposite. The goblin caught up the wonderful book which lay on the table, and popped it into his red cap, which he held tightly with both hands. The greatest treasure in the house was saved; and he ran away with it to the roof, and seated himself on the chimney. The flames of the burning house opposite illuminated him as he sat, both hands pressed tightly over his cap, in which the treasure lay; and then he found out what feelings really reigned in his heart, and knew exactly which way they tended. And yet, when the fire was extinguished, and the goblin again began to reflect, he hesitated, and said at last, "I must divide myself between the two; I cannot quite give up the huckster, because of the jam."

And this is a representation of human nature. We are like the goblin; we all go to visit the huckster "because of the jam."

The Puppet-Show Man

ON BOARD A steamer I once met an elderly man, with such a merry face that, if it was really an index of his mind, he must have been the happiest fellow in creation; and indeed he considered himself so, for I heard it from his own mouth. He was a Dane, the owner of a travelling theatre. He had all his company with him in a large box, for he was the proprietor of a puppet-show. His inborn cheerfulness, he said, had been tested by a member of the Polytechnic Institution, and the experiment had made him completely happy. I did not at first understand all this, but afterwards he explained the whole story to me; and here it is: –

"I was giving a representation," he said, "in the hall of the posting-house in the little town of Slagelse; there was a splendid audience, entirely juvenile excepting two respectable matrons. All at once, a person in black, of student-like appearance, entered the room, and sat down; he laughed aloud at the telling points, and applauded quite at the proper time. This was a very unusual spectator for me, and I felt anxious to know who he was. I heard that he was a member of the Polytechnic Institution in Copenhagen, who had been sent out to lecture to the people in the provinces. Punctually at eight o'clock my performance closed, for children must go early to bed, and a manager must also consult the convenience of the public.

"At nine o'clock the lecturer commenced his lecture and his experiments, and then I formed a part of his audience. It was wonderful both to hear and to see. The greater part of it was beyond my comprehension, but it led me to think that if we men can acquire so much, we must surely be intended to last longer than the little span which extends only to the time when we are hidden away under the earth. His experiments were quite miracles on a small scale, and yet the explanations flowed as naturally as water from his lips. At the time of Moses and the prophets, such a man would have been placed among the sages of the land; in the middle ages they would have burnt him at the stake.

"All night long I could not sleep; and the next evening when I gave another performance and the lecturer was present, I was in one of my best moods.

"I once heard of an actor, who, when he had to act the part of a lover, always thought of one particular lady in the audience; he only played for her, and forgot all the rest of the house, and now the Polytechnic lecturer was my she, my only auditor, for whom alone I played.

"When the performance was over, and the puppets removed behind the curtain, the Polytechnic lecturer invited me into his room to take a glass of wine. He talked of my comedies, and I of his science, and I believe we were both equally pleased. But I had the best of it, for there was much in what he did that he could not always explain to me. For instance, why a piece of iron which is rubbed on a cylinder, should become magnetic. How does this happen? The magnetic sparks come to it, – but how? It is the same with people in the world; they are rubbed about on this spherical globe till the electric spark comes upon them, and then we have a Napoleon, or a Luther, or some one of the kind.

"'The whole world is but a series of miracles,' said the lecturer, 'but we are so accustomed to them that we call them everyday matters.' And he went on explaining things to me till my skull seemed lifted from my brain, and I declared that were I not such an old fellow, I would at once become a member of the Polytechnic Institution, that I might learn to look at the bright side of everything, although I was one of the happiest of men.

"'One of the happiest!' said the lecturer, as if the idea pleased him; 'are you really happy?'

"'Yes,' I replied; 'for I am welcomed in every town, when I arrive with my company; but I certainly have one wish which sometimes weighs upon my cheerful temper like a mountain of lead. I should like to become the manager of a real theatre, and the director of a real troupe of men and women.'

"'I understand,' he said; 'you would like to have life breathed into your puppets, so that they might be living actors, and you their director. And would you then be quite happy?'

"I said I believed so. But he did not; and we talked it over in all manner of ways, yet could not agree on the subject. However, the wine was excellent, and we clanked our glasses together as we drank. There must have been magic in it, or I should most certainly become tipsy; but that did not happen, for my mind seemed quite clear; and, indeed, a kind of sunshine filled the room, and beamed from the eyes of the Polytechnic lecturer. It made me think of the old stories when the gods, in their immortal youth, wandered upon this earth, and paid visits to mankind. I said so to him, and he smiled; and I could have sworn that he was one of these ancient deities in disguise, or, at all events, that he belonged to the race of the gods. The result seemed to prove I was right in my suspicions; for it was arranged that my highest wish should be granted, that my puppets were to be gifted with life, and that I was to be the manager of a real company. We drank to my success, and clanked our glasses. Then he packed all my dolls into the box, and fastened it on my back, and I felt as if I were spinning round in a circle, and presently found myself lying on the floor. I remember that quite well. And then the whole company sprang from the box. The spirit had come upon us all; the puppets had become distinguished actors – at least, so they said themselves – and I was their director.

"When all was ready for the first representation, the whole company requested permission to speak to me before appearing in public. The dancing lady said the house could not be supported unless she stood on one leg; for she was a great genius, and begged to be treated as such. The lady who acted the part of the queen expected to be treated as a queen off the stage, as well as on it, or else she said she should get out of practice. The man whose duty it was to deliver a letter gave himself as many airs as he who took the part of first lover in the piece; he declared that the inferior parts were as important as the great ones, and deserving equal consideration, as parts of an artistic whole. The hero of the piece would only play in a part containing points likely to bring down the applause of the house. The 'prima donna' would only act when the lights were red, for she declared that a blue light did not suit her complexion. It was like a company of flies in a bottle, and I was in the bottle with them; for I was their director. My breath was taken away, my head whirled, and I was as miserable as a man could be. It was quite a novel, strange set of beings among whom I now found myself. I only wished I had them all in my box again, and that I had never been their director. So I told them roundly that, after all, they were nothing but puppets; and then they killed me. After a while I found myself lying on my bed in my room; but how I got there, or how I got away at all from the Polytechnic professor, he may perhaps know, I don't. The moon shone upon the floor, the box lay open, and the dolls were all scattered about in great confusion; but I was not idle. I jumped off the bed, and into the box they all had to go, some on their heads, some on their feet. Then I shut down the lid, and seated myself upon the box. 'Now you'll have to stay,' said I, 'and I shall be cautious how I wish you flesh and blood again.'

"I felt quite light, my cheerfulness had returned, and I was the happiest of mortals. The Polytechnic professor had fully cured me. I was as happy as a king, and went to sleep on the box. Next morning – correctly speaking, it was noon, for I slept remarkably late that day – I found myself still sitting there, in happy consciousness that my former wish had been a foolish one. I inquired for the Polytechnic professor; but he had disappeared like the Greek and Roman gods; from that time I have been the happiest man in the world. I am a happy director; for none of my company ever grumble, nor the public either, for I always make them merry. I can arrange my pieces just as I please. I choose out of every comedy what I like best, and no one is offended. Plays that are neglected now-a-days by the great public were ran after thirty years ago, and listened to till the tears ran down the cheeks of the audience. These are the pieces I bring forward. I place them before the little ones, who cry over them as papa and mamma used to cry thirty years ago. But I make them shorter, for the youngsters don't like long speeches; and if they have anything mournful, they like it to be over quickly."

In the Uttermost Parts of the Sea

SOME YEARS AGO, large ships were sent towards the north pole, to explore the distant coasts, and to try how far men could penetrate into those unknown regions. For more than a year one of these ships had been pushing its way northward, amid snow and ice, and the sailors had endured many hardships; till at length winter set in, and the sun entirely disappeared; for many weeks there would be constant night. All around, as far as the eye could reach, nothing could be seen but fields of ice, in which the ship remained stuck fast. The snow lay piled up in great heaps, and of these the sailors made huts, in the form of bee-hives, some of them as large and spacious as one of the "Huns' graves," and others only containing room enough to hold three or four men. It was not quite dark; the northern lights shot forth red and blue flames, like continuous fireworks, and the snow glittered, and reflected back the light, so that the night here was one long twilight. When the moon was brightest, the natives came in crowds to see the sailors. They had a very singular appearance in their rough, hairy dresses of fur, and riding in sledges over the ice. They brought with them furs and skins in great abundance, so that the snow-houses were soon provided with warm carpets, and the furs also served for the sailors to wrap themselves in, when they slept under the roofs of snow, while outside it was freezing with a cold far more severe than in the winter with us. In our country it was still autumn, though late in the season; and they thought of that in their distant exile, and often pictured to themselves the yellow leaves on the trees at home. Their watches pointed to the hours of evening, and time to go to sleep, although in these regions it was now always night.

In one of the huts, two of the men laid themselves down to rest. The younger of these men had brought with him from home his best, his dearest treasure – a Bible, which his grandmother had given him on his departure. Every night the sacred volume rested under his head, and he had known from his childhood what was written in it. Every day he read in the book, and while stretched on his cold couch, the holy words he had learnt would come into his mind: "If I take the wings of the morning, and fly to the uttermost parts of the sea, even there Thou art with me, and Thy right hand shall uphold me;" and under the influence of that faith which these holy words inspired, sleep came upon him, and dreams, which are the manifestations of God to the spirit. The soul lives and acts, while the body is at rest. He felt this life in him, and it was as if he heard the sound of dear, well-known melodies, as if the breezes of summer floated around him; and over his couch shone a ray of brightness, as if it were shining through the covering of his snow-roof. He lifted his head, and saw that the bright gleaming was not the reflection of the glittering snow, but the dazzling brightness of the pinions of a mighty angel, into whose beaming face he was gazing. As from the cup of a lily, the angel rose from amidst the leaves of the Bible; and, stretching out his arm, the walls of the hut sunk down, as though they had been formed of a light, airy veil of mist, and the green hills and meadows of home, with its ruddy woods, lay spread around him in the quiet sunshine of a lovely autumn day. The nest of the stork was empty, but ripe fruit still hung on the wild apple-tree, although the leaves had fallen. The red hips gleamed on the hedges, and the starling which hung in the green cage outside the window of the peasant's hut, which was his home, whistled the tune which he had taught him. His grandmother hung green birds'-food around the cage, as he, her grandson, had been accustomed to do. The daughter of the village blacksmith, who was young and fair, stood at the well, drawing water. She nodded to the grandmother, and the old woman nodded to her, and pointed to a letter which had come from a long way off. That very morning the letter had arrived from the cold regions of the north; there, where the absent one was sweetly sleeping under the protecting hand of God. They laughed and wept over the letter; and he, far away, amid ice and snow, under the shadow of the angel's wings, wept and smiled with them in spirit; for he saw and heard it all in his dream. From the letter they read aloud the words of Holy Writ: "In the uttermost parts of the sea, Thy right hand shall uphold me." And as the angel spread his wings like a veil over the sleeper, there was the sound of beautiful music and a hymn. Then the vision fled. It was dark again in the snow-hut: but the Bible still rested beneath his head, and faith and hope dwelt in his heart. God was with him, and he carried home in his heart, even "in the uttermost parts of the sea."

The Marsh King's Daughter

THE STORKS RELATE to their little ones a great many stories, and they are all about moors and reed banks, and suited to their age and capacity. The youngest of them are quite satisfied with "kribble, krabble," or such nonsense, and think it very grand; but the elder ones want something with a deeper meaning, or at least something about their own family.

We are only acquainted with one of the two longest and oldest stories which the storks relate – it is about Moses, who was exposed by his mother on the banks of the Nile, and was found by the king's daughter, who gave him a good education, and he afterwards became a great man; but where he was buried is still unknown.

Every one knows this story, but not the second; very likely because it is quite an inland story. It has been repeated from mouth to mouth, from one stork-mamma to another, for thousands of years; and each has told it better than the last; and now we mean to tell it better than all.

The first stork pair who related it lived at the time it happened, and had their summer residence on the rafters of the Viking's house, which stood near the wild moorlands of Wendsyssell; that is, to speak more correctly, the great moorheath, high up in the north of Jutland, by the Skjagen peak. This wilderness is still an immense wild heath of marshy ground, about which we can read in the "Official Directory." It is said that in olden times the place was a lake, the ground of which had heaved up from beneath, and now the moorland extends for miles in every direction, and is surrounded by damp meadows, trembling, undulating swamps, and marshy ground covered with turf, on which grow bilberry bushes and stunted trees. Mists are almost always hovering over this region, which, seventy years ago, was overrun with wolves. It may well be called the Wild Moor; and one can easily imagine, with such a wild expanse of marsh and lake, how lonely and dreary it must have been a thousand years ago. Many things may be noticed now that existed then. The reeds grow to the same height, and bear the same kind of long, purple-brown leaves, with their feathery tips. There still stands the birch, with its white bark and its delicate, loosely hanging leaves; and with regard to the living beings who frequented this spot, the fly still wears a gauzy dress of the same cut, and the favorite colors of the stork are white, with black and red for stockings. The people, certainly, in those days, wore very different dresses to those they now wear, but if any of them, be he huntsman or squire, master or servant, ventured on the wavering, undulating, marshy ground of the moor, they met with the same fate a thousand years ago as they would now. The wanderer sank, and went down to the Marsh King, as he is named, who rules in the great moorland empire beneath. They also called him "Gunkel King," but we like the name of "Marsh King" better, and we will give him that name as the storks do. Very little is known of the Marsh King's rule, but that, perhaps, is a good thing.

In the neighborhood of the moorlands, and not far from the great arm of the North Sea and the Cattegat which is called the Lumfjorden, lay the castle of the Viking, with its water-tight stone cellars, its tower, and its three projecting storeys. On the ridge of the roof the stork had built his nest, and there the stork-mamma sat on her eggs and felt sure her hatching would come to something.

One evening, stork-papa stayed out rather late, and when he came home he seemed quite busy, bustling, and important. "I have something very dreadful to tell you," said he to the stork-mamma.

"Keep it to yourself then," she replied. "Remember that I am hatching eggs; it may agitate me, and will affect them."

"You must know it at once," said he. "The daughter of our host in Egypt has arrived here. She has ventured to take this journey, and now she is lost."

"She who sprung from the race of the fairies, is it?" cried the mother stork. "Oh, tell me all about it; you know I cannot bear to be kept waiting at a time when I am hatching eggs."

"Well, you see, mother," he replied, "she believed what the doctors said, and what I have heard you state also, that the moor-flowers which grow about here would heal her sick father; and she has flown to the north in swan's plumage, in company with some other swan-princesses, who come to these parts every year to renew their youth. She came, and where is she now!"

"You enter into particulars too much," said the mamma stork, "and the eggs may take cold; I cannot bear such suspense as this."

"Well," said he, "I have kept watch; and this evening I went among the rushes where I thought the marshy ground would bear me, and while I was there three swans came. Something in their manner of flying seemed to say to me, 'Look carefully now; there is one not all swan, only swan's feathers.' You know, mother, you have the same intuitive feeling that I have; you know whether a thing is right or not immediately."

"Yes, of course," said she; "but tell me about the princess; I am tired of hearing about the swan's feathers."

"Well, you know that in the middle of the moor there is something like a lake," said the stork-papa. "You can see the edge of it if you raise yourself a little. Just there, by the reeds and the green banks, lay the trunk of an elder-tree; upon this the three swans stood flapping their wings, and looking about them; one of them threw off her plumage, and I immediately recognized her as one of the princesses of our home in Egypt. There she sat, without any covering but her long, black hair. I heard her tell the two others to take great care of the swan's plumage, while she dipped down into the water to pluck the flowers which she fancied she saw there. The others nodded, and picked up the feather dress, and took possession of it. I wonder what will become of it? thought I, and she most likely asked herself the same question. If so, she received an answer, a very practical one; for the two swans rose up and flew away with her swan's plumage. 'Dive down now!' they cried; 'thou shalt never more fly in the swan's plumage, thou shalt never again see Egypt; here, on the moor, thou wilt remain.' So saying, they tore the swan's plumage into a thousand pieces, the feathers drifted about like a snow-shower, and then the two deceitful princesses flew away."

"Why, that is terrible," said the stork-mamma; "I feel as if I could hardly bear to hear any more, but you must tell me what happened next."

"The princess wept and lamented aloud; her tears moistened the elder stump, which was really not an elder stump but the Marsh King himself, he who in marshy ground lives and rules. I saw myself how the stump of the tree turned round, and was a tree no more, while long, clammy branches like arms, were extended from it. Then the poor child was terribly frightened, and started up to run away. She hastened to cross the green, slimy ground; but it will not bear any weight, much less hers. She quickly sank, and the elder stump dived immediately after her; in fact, it was he who drew her down. Great black bubbles rose up out of the moor-slime, and with these every trace of the two vanished. And now the princess is buried in the wild marsh, she will never now carry flowers to Egypt to cure her father. It would have broken your heart, mother, had you seen it."

"You ought not to have told me," said she, "at such a time as this; the eggs might suffer. But I think the princess will soon find help; some one will rise up to help her. Ah! if it had been you or I, or one of our people, it would have been all over with us."

"I mean to go every day," said he, "to see if anything comes to pass;" and so he did.

A long time went by, but at last he saw a green stalk shooting up out of the deep, marshy ground. As it reached the surface of the marsh, a leaf spread out, and unfolded itself broader and broader, and close to it came forth a bud.

One morning, when the stork-papa was flying over the stem, he saw that the power of the sun's rays had caused the bud to open, and in the cup of the flower lay a charming child – a little maiden, looking as if she had just come out of a bath. The little one was so like the Egyptian princess, that the stork, at the first moment, thought it must be the princess herself, but after a little reflection he decided that it was much more likely to be the daughter of the princess and the Marsh King; and this explained also her being placed in the cup of a water-lily. "But she cannot be left to lie here," thought the stork, "and in my nest there are already so many. But stay, I have thought of something: the wife of the Viking has no children, and how often she has wished for a little one. People always say the stork brings the little ones; I will do so in earnest this time. I shall fly with the child to the Viking's wife; what rejoicing there will be!"

And then the stork lifted the little girl out of the flower-cup, flew to the castle, picked a hole with his beak in the bladder-covered, window, and laid the beautiful child in the bosom of the Viking's wife. Then he flew back quickly to the stork-mamma and told her what he had seen and done; and the little storks listened to it all, for they were then quite old enough to do so. "So you see," he continued, "that the princess is not dead, for she must have sent her little one up here; and now I have found a home for her."

"Ah, I said it would be so from the first," replied the stork-mamma; "but now think a little of your own family. Our travelling time draws near, and I sometimes feel a little irritation already under the wings. The cuckoos and the nightingale are already gone, and I heard the quails say they should go too as soon as the wind was favorable. Our youngsters will go through all the manoeuvres at the review very well, or I am much mistaken in them."

The Viking's wife was above measure delighted when she awoke the next morning and found the beautiful little child lying in her bosom. She kissed it and caressed it; but it cried terribly, and struck out with its arms and legs, and did not seem to be pleased at all. At last it cried itself to sleep; and as it lay there so still and quiet, it was a most beautiful sight to see. The Viking's wife was so delighted, that body and soul were full of joy. Her heart felt so light within her, that it seemed as if her husband and his soldiers, who were absent, must come home as suddenly and unexpectedly as the little child had done. She and her whole household therefore busied themselves in preparing everything for the reception of her lord. The long, colored tapestry, on which she and her maidens had worked pictures of their idols, Odin, Thor, and Friga, was hung up. The slaves polished the old shields that served as ornaments; cushions were placed on the seats, and dry wood laid on the fireplaces in the centre of the hall, so that the flames might be fanned up at a moment's notice. The Viking's wife herself assisted in the work, so that at night she felt very tired, and quickly fell into a sound sleep. When she awoke, just before morning, she was terribly alarmed to find that the infant had vanished. She sprang from her couch, lighted a pine-chip, and searched all round the room, when, at last, in that part of the bed where her feet had been, lay, not the child, but a great, ugly frog. She was quite disgusted at this sight, and seized a heavy stick to kill the frog; but the creature looked at her with such strange, mournful eyes, that she was unable to strike the blow. Once more she searched round the room; then she started at hearing the frog utter a low, painful croak. She sprang from the couch and opened the window hastily; at the same moment the sun rose, and threw its beams through the window, till it rested on the couch where the great frog lay. Suddenly it appeared as if the frog's broad mouth contracted, and became small and red. The limbs moved and stretched out and extended themselves till they took a beautiful shape; and behold there was the pretty child lying before her, and the ugly frog was gone. "How is this?" she cried, "have I had a wicked dream? Is it not my own lovely cherub that lies there." Then she kissed it and fondled it; but the child struggled and fought, and bit as if she had been a little wild cat.

The Viking did not return on that day, nor the next; he was, however, on the way home; but the wind, so favorable to the storks, was against him; for it blew towards the south. A wind in favor of one is often against another.

After two or three days had passed, it became clear to the Viking's wife how matters stood with the child; it was under the influence of a powerful sorcerer. By day it was charming in appearance as an angel of light, but with a temper wicked and wild; while at night, in the form of an ugly frog, it was quiet and mournful, with eyes full of sorrow. Here were two natures, changing inwardly and outwardly with the absence and return of sunlight. And so it happened that by day the child, with the actual form of its mother, possessed the fierce disposition of its father; at night, on the contrary, its outward appearance plainly showed its descent on the father's side, while inwardly it had the heart and mind of its mother. Who would be able to loosen this wicked charm which the sorcerer had worked upon it? The wife of the Viking lived in constant pain and sorrow about it. Her heart clung to the little creature, but she could not explain to her husband the circumstances in which it was placed. He was expected to return shortly; and were she to tell him, he would very likely, as was the custom at that time, expose the poor child in the public highway, and let any one take it away who would. The good wife of the Viking could not let that happen, and she therefore resolved that the Viking should never see the child excepting by daylight.

One morning there sounded a rushing of storks' wings over the roof. More than a hundred pair of storks had rested there during the night, to recover themselves after their excursion; and now they soared aloft, and prepared for the journey southward.

"All the husbands are here, and ready!" they cried; "wives and children also!"

"How light we are!" screamed the young storks in chorus. "Something pleasant seems creeping over us, even down to our toes, as if we were full of live frogs. Ah, how delightful it is to travel into foreign lands!"

"Hold yourselves properly in the line with us," cried papa and mamma. "Do not use your beaks so much; it tries the lungs." And then the storks flew away.

About the same time sounded the clang of the warriors' trumpets across the heath. The Viking had landed with his men. They were returning home, richly laden with spoil from the Gallic coast, where the people, as did also the inhabitants of Britain, often cried in alarm, "Deliver us from the wild northmen."

Life and noisy pleasure came with them into the castle of the Viking on the moorland. A great cask of mead was drawn into the hall, piles of wood blazed, cattle were slain and served up, that they might feast in reality, The priest who offered the sacrifice sprinkled the devoted parishioners with the warm blood; the fire crackled, and the smoke rolled along beneath the roof; the soot fell upon them from the beams; but they were used to all these things. Guests were invited, and received handsome presents. All wrongs and unfaithfulness were forgotten. They drank deeply, and threw in each other's faces the bones that were left, which was looked upon as a sign of good feeling amongst them. A bard, who was a kind of musician as well as warrior, and who had been with the Viking in his expedition, and knew what to sing about, gave them one of his best songs, in which they heard all their warlike deeds praised, and every wonderful action brought forward with honor. Every verse ended with this refrain, –

> "Gold and possessions will flee away,
> Friends and foes must die one day;
> Every man on earth must die,
> But a famous name will never die."

And with that they beat upon their shields, and hammered upon the table with knives and bones, in a most outrageous manner.

The Viking's wife sat upon a raised cross seat in the open hall. She wore a silk dress, golden bracelets, and large amber beads. She was in costly attire, and the bard named her in his song, and spoke of the rich treasure of gold which she had brought to her husband. Her husband had already seen the wonderfully beautiful child in the daytime, and was delighted with her beauty; even her wild ways pleased him. He said the little maiden would grow up to be a heroine, with the strong will and determination of a man. She would never wink her eyes, even if, in joke, an expert hand should attempt to cut off her eye-brows with a sharp sword.

The full cask of mead soon became empty, and a fresh one was brought in; for these were people who liked plenty to eat and drink. The old proverb, which every one knows, says that "the cattle know when to leave their pasture, but a foolish man knows not the measure of his own appetite." Yes, they all knew this; but men may know what is right, and yet often do wrong. They also knew "that even the welcome guest becomes wearisome when he sits too long in the house." But there they remained; for pork and mead are good things. And so at the Viking's house they stayed, and enjoyed themselves; and at night the bondmen slept in the ashes, and dipped their fingers in the fat, and licked them. Oh, it was a delightful time!

Once more in the same year the Viking went forth, though the storms of autumn had already commenced to roar. He went with his warriors to the coast of Britain; he said that it was but an excursion of pleasure across the water, so his wife remained at home with the little girl. After a while, it is quite certain the foster-mother began to love the poor frog, with its gentle eyes and its deep sighs, even better than the little beauty who bit and fought with all around her.

The heavy, damp mists of autumn, which destroy the leaves of the wood, had already fallen upon forest and heath. Feathers of plucked birds, as they call the snow, flew about in thick showers, and winter was coming. The sparrows took possession of the stork's nest, and conversed about the absent owners in their own fashion; and they, the stork pair and all their young ones, where were they staying now? The storks might have been found in the land of Egypt, where the sun's rays shone forth bright and warm, as it does here at midsummer. Tamarinds and acacias were in full bloom all over the country, the crescent of Mahomet glittered brightly from the cupolas of the mosques, and on the slender pinnacles sat many of the storks, resting after their long journey. Swarms of them took divided possession of the nests – nests which lay close to each other between the venerable columns, and crowded the arches of temples in forgotten cities. The date and the palm lifted themselves as a screen or as a sun-shade over them. The gray pyramids looked like broken shadows in the clear air and the far-off desert, where the ostrich wheels his rapid flight, and the lion, with his subtle eyes, gazes at the marble sphinx which lies half buried in sand. The waters of the Nile had retreated, and the whole bed of the river was covered with frogs, which was a most acceptable prospect for the stork families. The young storks thought their eyes deceived them, everything around appeared so beautiful.

"It is always like this here, and this is how we live in our warm country," said the stork-mamma; and the thought made the young ones almost beside themselves with pleasure.

"Is there anything more to see?" they asked; "are we going farther into the country?"

"There is nothing further for us to see," answered the stork-mamma. "Beyond this delightful region there are immense forests, where the branches of the trees entwine round each other, while prickly, creeping plants cover the paths, and only an elephant could force a passage for himself with his great feet. The snakes are too large, and the lizards too lively for us to catch. Then there is the desert; if you went there, your eyes would soon be full of sand with the lightest breeze, and if it should blow great guns, you would most likely find yourself in a sand-drift. Here is the best place for you, where there are frogs and locusts; here I shall remain, and so must you." And so they stayed.

The parents sat in the nest on the slender minaret, and rested, yet still were busily employed in cleaning and smoothing their feathers, and in sharpening their beaks against their red stockings; then they would stretch out their necks, salute each other, and gravely raise their heads with the high-polished forehead, and soft, smooth feathers, while their brown eyes shone with intelligence. The female young ones strutted about amid the moist rushes, glancing at the other young storks and making acquaintances, and swallowing a frog at every third step, or tossing a little snake about with their beaks, in a way they considered very becoming, and besides it tasted very good. The young male storks soon began to quarrel; they struck at each other with their wings, and pecked with their beaks till the blood came. And in this manner many of the young ladies and gentlemen were betrothed to each other: it was, of course, what they wanted, and indeed what they lived for. Then they returned to a nest, and there the quarrelling began afresh; for in hot countries people are almost all violent and passionate. But for all that it was pleasant, especially for the old people, who watched them with great joy: all that their young ones did suited them. Every day here there was sunshine, plenty to eat, and nothing to think of but pleasure. But in the rich castle of their Egyptian host, as they called him, pleasure was not to be found. The rich and mighty lord of the castle lay on his couch, in the midst of the great hall, with its many colored walls looking like the centre of a great tulip; but he was stiff and powerless in all his limbs, and lay stretched out like a mummy. His family and servants stood round him; he was not dead, although he could scarcely be said to live. The healing moor-flower from the north, which was to have been found and brought to him by her who loved him so well, had not arrived. His young and beautiful daughter who, in swan's plumage, had flown over land and seas to the distant north, had never returned. She is dead, so the two swan-maidens had said when they came home; and they made up quite a story about her, and this is what they told, –

"We three flew away together through the air," said they: "a hunter caught sight of us, and shot at us with an arrow. The arrow struck our young friend and sister, and slowly singing her farewell song she sank down, a dying swan, into the forest lake. On the shores of the lake, under a spreading birch-tree, we laid her in the cold earth. We had our revenge; we bound fire under the wings of a swallow, who had a nest on the thatched roof of the huntsman. The house took fire, and burst into flames; the hunter was burnt with the house, and the light was reflected over the sea as far as the spreading birch, beneath which we laid her sleeping dust. She will never return to the land of Egypt." And then they both wept. And stork-papa, who heard the story, snapped with his beak so that it might be heard a long way off.

"Deceit and lies!" cried he; "I should like to run my beak deep into their chests."

"And perhaps break it off," said the mamma stork, "then what a sight you would be. Think first of yourself, and then of your family; all others are nothing to us."

"Yes, I know," said the stork-papa; "but to-morrow I can easily place myself on the edge of the open cupola, when the learned and wise men assemble to consult on the state of the sick man; perhaps they may come a little nearer to the truth." And the learned and wise men assembled together, and talked a great deal on every point; but the stork could make no sense out of anything they said; neither were there any good results from their consultations, either for the sick man, or for his daughter in the marshy heath. When we listen to what people say in this world, we shall hear a great deal; but it is an advantage to know what has been said and done before, when we listen to a conversation. The stork did, and we know at least as much as he, the stork.

"Love is a life-giver. The highest love produces the highest life. Only through love can the sick man be cured." This had been said by many, and even the learned men acknowledged that it was a wise saying.

"What a beautiful thought!" exclaimed the papa stork immediately.

"I don't quite understand it," said the mamma stork, when her husband repeated it; "however, it is not my fault, but the fault of the thought; whatever it may be, I have something else to think of."

Now the learned men had spoken also of love between this one and that one; of the difference of the love which we have for our neighbor, to the love that exists between parents and children; of the love of the plant for the light, and how the germ springs forth when the sunbeam kisses the ground. All these things were so elaborately and learnedly explained, that it was impossible for stork-papa to follow it, much less to talk about it. His thoughts on the subject quite weighed him down; he stood the whole of the following day on one leg, with half-shut eyes, thinking deeply. So much learning was quite a heavy weight for him to carry. One thing, however, the papa stork could understand. Every one, high and low, had from their inmost hearts expressed their opinion that it was a great misfortune for so many thousands of people – the whole country indeed – to have this man so sick, with no hopes of his recovery. And what joy and blessing it would spread around if he could by any means be cured! But where bloomed the flower that could bring him health? They had searched for it everywhere; in learned writings, in the shining stars, in the weather and wind. Inquiries had been made in every by-way that could be thought of, until at last the wise and learned men has asserted, as we have been already told, that "love, the life-giver, could alone give new life to a father;" and in saying this, they had overdone it, and said more than they understood themselves. They repeated it, and wrote it down as a recipe, "Love is a life-giver." But how could such a recipe be prepared – that was a difficulty they could not overcome. At last it was decided that help could only come from the princess herself, whose whole soul was wrapped up in her father, especially as a plan had been adopted by her to enable her to obtain a remedy.

More than a year had passed since the princess had set out at night, when the light of the young moon was soon lost beneath the horizon. She had gone to the marble sphinx in the desert, shaking the sand from her sandals, and then passed through the long passage, which leads to the centre of one of the great pyramids, where the mighty kings of antiquity, surrounded with pomp and splendor, lie veiled in the form of mummies. She had been told by the wise men, that if she laid her head on the breast of one of them, from the head she would learn where to find life and recovery for her father. She had performed all this, and in a dream had learnt that she must bring home to her father the lotus flower, which grows in the deep sea, near the moors and heath in the Danish land. The very place and situation had been pointed out to her, and she was told that the flower would restore her father to health and strength. And, therefore, she had gone forth from the land of Egypt, flying over to the open marsh and the wild moor in the plumage of a swan.

The papa and mamma storks knew all this, and we also know it now. We know, too, that the Marsh King has drawn her down to himself, and that to the loved ones at home she is forever dead. One of the wisest of them said, as the stork-mamma also said, "That in some way she would, after all, manage to succeed;" and so at last they comforted themselves with this hope, and would wait patiently; in fact, they could do nothing better.

"I should like to get away the swan's feathers from those two treacherous princesses," said the papa stork; "then, at least, they would not be able to fly over again to the wild moor, and do more wickedness. I can hide the two suits of feathers over yonder, till we find some use for them."

"But where will you put them?" asked the mamma stork.

"In our nest on the moor. I and the young ones will carry them by turns during our flight across; and as we return, should they prove too heavy for us, we shall be sure to find plenty of places on the way in which we can conceal them till our next journey. Certainly one suit of swan's feathers would be enough for the princess, but two are always better. In those northern countries no one can have too many travelling wrappers."

"No one will thank you for it," said stork-mamma; "but you are master; and, excepting at breeding time, I have nothing to say."

In the Viking's castle on the wild moor, to which the storks directed their flight in the following spring, the little maiden still remained. They had named her Helga, which was rather too soft a name for a child with a temper like hers, although her form was still beautiful. Every month this temper showed itself in sharper outlines; and in the course of years, while the storks still made the same journeys in autumn to the hill, and in spring to the moors, the child grew to be almost a woman, and before any one seemed aware of it, she was a wonderfully beautiful maiden of sixteen. The casket was splendid, but the contents were worthless. She was, indeed, wild and savage even in those hard, uncultivated times. It was a pleasure to her to splash about with her white hands in the warm blood of the horse which had been slain for sacrifice. In one of her wild moods she bit off the head of the black cock, which the priest was about to slay for the sacrifice. To her foster-father she said one day, "If thine enemy were to pull down thine house about thy ears, and thou shouldest be sleeping in unconscious security, I would not wake thee; even if I had the power I would never do it, for my ears still tingle with the blow that thou gavest me years ago. I have never forgotten it." But the Viking treated her words as a joke; he was, like every one else, bewitched with her beauty, and knew nothing of the change in the form and temper of Helga at night. Without a saddle, she would sit on a horse as if she were a part of it, while it rushed along at full speed; nor would she spring from its back, even when it quarrelled with other horses and bit them. She would often leap from the high shore into the sea with all her clothes on, and swim to meet the Viking, when his boat was steering home towards the shore. She once cut off a long lock of her beautiful hair, and twisted it into a string for her bow. "If a thing is to be done well," said she, "I must do it myself."

The Viking's wife was, for the time in which she lived, a woman of strong character and will; but, compared to her daughter, she was a gentle, timid woman, and she knew that a wicked sorcerer had the terrible child in his power. It was sometimes as if Helga acted from sheer wickedness; for often when her mother stood on the threshold of the door, or stepped into the yard, she would seat herself on the brink of the well, wave her arms and legs in the air, and suddenly fall right in. Here she was able, from her frog nature, to dip and dive about in the water of the deep well, until at last she would climb forth like a cat, and come back into the hall dripping with water, so that the green leaves that were strewed on the floor were whirled round, and carried away by the streams that flowed from her.

But there was one time of the day which placed a check upon Helga. It was the evening twilight; when this hour arrived she became quiet and thoughtful, and allowed herself to be advised and led; then also a secret feeling seemed to draw her towards her mother. And as usual, when the sun set, and the transformation took place, both in body and mind, inwards and outwards, she would remain quiet and mournful, with her form shrunk together in the shape of a frog. Her body was much larger than those animals ever are, and on this account it was much more hideous in appearance; for she looked like a wretched dwarf, with a frog's head, and webbed fingers. Her eyes had a most piteous expression; she was without a voice, excepting a hollow, croaking sound, like the smothered sobs of a dreaming child.

Then the Viking's wife took her on her lap, and forgot the ugly form, as she looked into the mournful eyes, and often said, "I could wish that thou wouldst always remain my dumb frog child, for thou art too terrible when thou art clothed in a form of beauty." And the Viking woman wrote Runic characters against sorcery and spells of sickness, and threw them over the wretched child; but they did no good.

"One can scarcely believe that she was ever small enough to lie in the cup of the water-lily," said the papa stork; "and now she is grown up, and the image of her Egyptian mother, especially about the eyes. Ah, we shall never see her again; perhaps she has not discovered how to help herself, as you and the wise men said she would. Year after year have I flown across and across the moor, but there was no sign of her being still alive. Yes, and I may as well tell you that you that each year, when I arrived a few days before you to repair the nest, and put everything in its place, I have spent a whole night flying here and there over the marshy lake, as if I had been an owl or a bat, but all to no purpose. The two suit of swan's plumage, which I and the young ones dragged over here from the land of the Nile, are of no use; trouble enough it was to us to bring them here in three journeys, and now they are lying at the bottom of the nest; and if a fire should happen to break out, and the wooden house be burnt down, they would be destroyed."

"And our good nest would be destroyed, too," said the mamma stork; "but you think less of that than of your plumage stuff and your moor-princess. Go and stay with her in the marsh if you like. You are a bad father to your own children, as I have told you already, when I hatched my first brood. I only hope neither we nor our children may have an arrow sent through our wings, owing to that wild girl. Helga does not know in the least what she is about. We have lived in this house longer than she has, she should think of that, and we have never forgotten our duty. We have paid every year our toll of a feather, an egg, and a young one, as it is only right we should do. You don't suppose I can wander about the court-yard, or go everywhere as I used to do in old times. I can do it in Egypt, where I can be a companion of the people, without forgetting myself. But here I cannot go and peep into the pots and kettles as I do there. No, I can only sit up here and feel angry with that girl, the little wretch; and I am angry with you, too; you should have left her lying in the water lily, then no one would have known anything about her."

"You are far better than your conversation," said the papa stork; "I know you better than you know yourself." And with that he gave a hop, and flapped his wings twice, proudly; then he stretched his neck and flew, or rather soared away, without moving his outspread wings. He went on for some distance, and then he gave a great flap with his wings and flew on his course at a rapid rate, his head and neck bending proudly before him, while the sun's rays fell on his glossy plumage.

"He is the handsomest of them all," said the mamma stork, as she watched him; "but I won't tell him so."

Early in the autumn, the Viking again returned home laden with spoil, and bringing prisoners with him. Among them was a young Christian priest, one of those who contemned the gods of the north. Often lately there had been, both in hall and chamber, a talk of the new faith which was spreading far and wide in the south, and which, through the means of the holy Ansgarius, had already reached as far as Hedeby on the Schlei. Even Helga had heard of this belief in the teachings of One who was named Christ, and who for the love of mankind, and for their redemption, had given up His life. But to her all this had, as it were, gone in one ear and out the other. It seemed that she only understood the meaning of the word "love," when in the form of a miserable frog she crouched together in the corner of the sleeping chamber; but the Viking's wife had listened to the wonderful story, and had felt herself strangely moved by it.

On their return, after this voyage, the men spoke of the beautiful temples built of polished stone, which had been raised for the public worship of this holy love. Some vessels, curiously formed of massive gold, had been brought home among the booty. There was a peculiar fragrance about them all, for they were incense vessels, which had been swung before the altars in the temples by the Christian priests. In the deep stony cellars of the castle, the young Christian priest was immured, and his hands and feet tied together with strips of bark. The Viking's wife considered him as beautiful as Baldur, and his distress raised her pity; but Helga said he ought to have ropes fastened to his heels, and be tied to the tails of wild animals.

"I would let the dogs loose after him" she said; "over the moor and across the heath. Hurrah! that would be a spectacle for the gods, and better still to follow in its course."

But the Viking would not allow him to die such a death as that, especially as he was the disowned and despiser of the high gods. In a few days, he had decided to have him offered as a sacrifice on the blood-stone in the grove. For the first time, a man was to be sacrificed here. Helga begged to be allowed to sprinkle the assembled people with the blood of the priest. She sharpened her glittering knife; and when one of the great, savage dogs, who were running about the Viking's castle in great numbers, sprang towards her, she thrust the knife into his side, merely, as she said, to prove its sharpness.

The Viking's wife looked at the wild, badly disposed girl, with great sorrow; and when night came on, and her daughter's beautiful form and disposition were changed, she spoke in eloquent words to Helga of the sorrow and deep grief that was in her heart. The ugly frog, in its monstrous shape, stood before her, and raised its brown mournful eyes to her face, listening to her words, and seeming to understand them with the intelligence of a human being.

"Never once to my lord and husband has a word passed my lips of what I have to suffer through you; my heart is full of grief about you," said the Viking's wife. "The love of a mother is greater and more powerful than I ever imagined. But love never entered thy heart; it is cold and clammy, like the plants on the moor."

Then the miserable form trembled; it was as if these words had touched an invisible bond between body and soul, for great tears stood in the eyes.

"A bitter time will come for thee at last," continued the Viking's wife; "and it will be terrible for me too. It had been better for thee if thou hadst been left on the high-road, with the cold night wind to lull thee to sleep." And the Viking's wife shed bitter tears, and went away in anger and sorrow, passing under the partition of furs, which hung loose over the beam and divided the hall.

The shrivelled frog still sat in the corner alone. Deep silence reigned around. At intervals, a half-stifled sigh was heard from its inmost soul; it was the soul of Helga. It seemed in pain, as if a new life were arising in her heart. Then she took a step forward and listened; then stepped again forward, and seized with her clumsy hands the heavy bar which was laid across the door. Gently, and with much trouble, she pushed back the bar, as silently lifted the latch, and then took up the glimmering lamp which stood in the ante-chamber of the hall. It seemed as if a stronger will than her own gave her strength. She removed the iron bolt from the closed cellar-door, and slipped in to the prisoner. He was slumbering. She touched him with her cold, moist hand, and as he awoke and caught sight of the hideous form, he shuddered as if he beheld a wicked apparition. She drew her knife, cut through the bonds which confined his hands and feet, and beckoned to him to follow her. He uttered some holy names and made the sign of the cross, while the form remained motionless by his side.

"Who art thou?" he asked, "whose outward appearance is that of an animal, while thou willingly performest acts of mercy?"

The frog-figure beckoned to him to follow her, and led him through a long gallery concealed by hanging drapery to the stables, and then pointed to a horse. He mounted upon it, and she sprang up also before him, and held tightly by the animal's mane. The prisoner understood her, and they rode on at a rapid trot, by a road which he would never have found by himself, across the open heath. He forgot her ugly form, and only thought how the mercy and loving-kindness of the Almighty was acting through this hideous apparition. As he offered pious prayers and sang holy songs of praise, she trembled. Was it the effect of prayer and praise that caused this? or, was she shuddering in the cold morning air at the thought of approaching twilight? What were her feelings? She raised herself up, and wanted to stop the horse and spring off, but the Christian priest held her back with all his might, and then sang a pious song, as if this could loosen the wicked charm that had changed her into the semblance of a frog.

And the horse galloped on more wildly than before. The sky painted itself red, the first sunbeam pierced through the clouds, and in the clear flood of sunlight the frog became changed. It was Helga again, young and beautiful, but with a wicked demoniac spirit. He held now a beautiful young woman in his arms, and he was horrified at the sight. He stopped the horse, and sprang from its back. He imagined that some new sorcery was at work. But Helga also leaped from the horse and stood on the ground. The child's short garment reached only to her knee. She snatched the sharp knife from her girdle, and rushed like lightning at the astonished priest. "Let me get at thee!" she cried; "let me get at thee, that I may plunge this knife into thy body. Thou art pale as ashes, thou beardless slave." She pressed in upon him. They struggled with each other in heavy combat, but it was as if an invisible power had been given to the Christian in the struggle. He held her fast, and the old oak under which they stood seemed to help him, for the loosened roots on the ground became entangled in the maiden's feet, and held them fast. Close by rose a bubbling spring, and he sprinkled Helga's face and neck with the water, commanded the unclean spirit to come forth, and pronounced upon her a Christian blessing. But the water of faith has no power unless the well-spring of faith flows within. And yet even here its power was shown; something more than the mere strength of a man opposed itself, through his means, against the evil which struggled within her. His holy action seemed to overpower her. She dropped her arms, glanced at him with pale cheeks and looks of amazement. He appeared to her a mighty magician skilled in secret arts; his language was the darkest magic to her, and the movements of his hands in the air were as the secret signs of a magician's wand. She would not have blinked had he waved over her head a sharp knife or a glittering axe; but she shrunk from him as he signed her with the sign of the cross on her forehead and breast, and sat before him like a tame bird, with her head bowed down. Then he spoke to her, in gentle words, of the deed of love she had performed for him during the night, when she had come to him in the form of an ugly frog, to loosen his bonds, and to lead him forth to life and light; and he told her that she was bound in closer fetters than he had been, and that she could recover also life and light by his means. He would take her to Hedeby to St. Ansgarius, and there, in that Christian town, the spell of the sorcerer would be removed. But he would not let her sit before him on the horse, though of her own free will she wished to do so. "Thou must sit behind me, not before me," said he. "Thy magic beauty has a magic power which comes from an evil origin, and I fear it; still I am sure to overcome through my faith in Christ." Then he knelt down, and prayed with pious fervor. It was as if the quiet woodland were a holy church consecrated by his worship. The birds sang as if they were also of this new congregation; and the fragrance of the wild flowers was as the ambrosial perfume of incense; while, above all, sounded the words of Scripture, "A light to them that sit in darkness and in the shadow of death, to guide their feet into the way of peace." And he spoke these words with the deep longing of his whole nature.

Meanwhile, the horse that had carried them in wild career stood quietly by, plucking at the tall bramble-bushes, till the ripe young berries fell down upon Helga's hands, as if inviting her to eat. Patiently she allowed herself to be lifted on the horse, and sat there like a somnambulist – as one who walked in his sleep. The Christian bound two branches together with bark, in the form of a cross, and held it on high as they rode through the forest. The way gradually grew thicker of brushwood, as they rode along, till at last it became a trackless wilderness. Bushes of the wild sloe here and there blocked up the path, so that they had to ride over them. The bubbling spring formed not a stream, but a marsh, round which also they were obliged to guide the horse; still there were strength and refreshment in the cool forest breeze, and no trifling power in the gentle words spoken in faith and Christian love by the young priest, whose inmost heart yearned to lead this poor lost one into the way of light and life. It is said that rain-drops can make a hollow in the hardest stone, and the waves of the sea can smooth and round the rough edges of the rocks; so did the dew of mercy fall upon Helga, softening what was hard, and smoothing what was rough in her character. These effects did not yet appear; she was not herself aware of them; neither does the seed in the lap of earth know, when the refreshing dew and the warm sunbeams fall upon it, that it contains within itself power by which it will flourish and bloom. The song of the mother sinks into the heart of the child, and the little one prattles the words after her, without understanding their meaning; but after a time the thoughts expand, and what has been heard in childhood seems to the mind clear and bright. So now the "Word," which is all-powerful to create, was working in the heart of Helga.

They rode forth from the thick forest, crossed the heath, and again entered a pathless wood. Here, towards evening, they met with robbers.

"Where hast thou stolen that beauteous maiden?" cried the robbers, seizing the horse by the bridle, and dragging the two riders from its back.

The priest had nothing to defend himself with, but the knife he had taken from Helga, and with this he struck out right and left. One of the robbers raised his axe against him; but the young priest sprang on one side, and avoided the blow, which fell with great force on the horse's neck, so that the blood gushed forth, and the animal sunk to the ground. Then Helga seemed suddenly to awake from her long, deep reverie; she threw herself hastily upon the dying animal. The priest placed himself before her, to defend and shelter her; but one of the robbers swung his iron axe against the Christian's head with such force that it was dashed to pieces, the blood and brains were scattered about, and he fell dead upon the ground. Then the robbers seized beautiful Helga by her white arms and slender waist; but at that moment the sun went down, and as its last ray disappeared, she was changed into the form of a frog. A greenish white mouth spread half over her face; her arms became thin and slimy; while broad hands, with webbed fingers, spread themselves out like fans. Then the robbers, in terror, let her go, and she stood among them, a hideous monster; and as is the nature of frogs to do, she hopped up as high as her own size, and disappeared in the thicket. Then the robbers knew that this must be the work of an evil spirit or some secret sorcery, and, in a terrible fright, they ran hastily from the spot.

The full moon had already risen, and was shining in all her radiant splendor over the earth, when from the thicket, in the form of a frog, crept poor Helga. She stood still by the corpse of the Christian priest, and the carcase of the dead horse. She looked at them with eyes that seemed to weep, and from the frog's head came forth a croaking sound, as when a child bursts into tears. She threw herself first upon one, and then upon the other; brought water in her hand, which, from being webbed, was large and hollow, and poured it over them; but they were dead, and dead they would remain. She understood that at last. Soon wild animals would come and tear their dead bodies; but no, that must not happen. Then she dug up the earth, as deep as she was able, that she might prepare a grave for them. She had nothing but a branch of a tree and her two hands, between the fingers of which the webbed skin stretched, and they were torn by the work, while the blood ran down her hands. She saw at last that her work would be useless, more than she could accomplish; so she fetched more water, and washed the face of the dead, and then covered it with fresh green leaves; she also brought large boughs and spread over him, and scattered dried leaves between the branches. Then she brought the heaviest stones that she could carry, and laid them over the dead body, filling up the crevices with moss, till she thought she had fenced in his resting-place strongly enough. The difficult task had employed her the whole night; and as the sun broke forth, there stood the beautiful Helga in all her loveliness, with her bleeding hands, and, for the first time, with tears on her maiden cheeks. It was, in this transformation, as if two natures were striving together within her; her whole frame trembled, and she looked around her as if she had just awoke from a painful dream. She leaned for support against the trunk of a slender tree, and at last climbed to the topmost branches, like a cat, and seated herself firmly upon them. She remained there the whole day, sitting alone, like a frightened squirrel, in the silent solitude of the wood, where the rest and stillness is as the calm of death.

Butterflies fluttered around her, and close by were several ant-hills, each with its hundreds of busy little creatures moving quickly to and fro. In the air, danced myriads of gnats, swarm upon swarm, troops of buzzing flies, ladybirds, dragon-flies with golden wings, and other little winged creatures. The worm crawled forth from the moist ground, and the moles crept out; but, excepting these, all around had the stillness of death: but when people say this, they do not quite understand themselves what they mean. None noticed Helga but a flock of magpies, which flew chattering round the top of the tree on which she sat. These birds hopped close to her on the branches with bold curiosity. A glance from her eyes was a signal to frighten them away, and they were not clever enough to find out who she was; indeed she hardly knew herself.

When the sun was near setting, and the evening's twilight about to commence, the approaching transformation aroused her to fresh exertion. She let herself down gently from the tree, and, as the last sunbeam vanished, she stood again in the wrinkled form of a frog, with the torn, webbed skin on her hands, but her eyes now gleamed with more radiant beauty than they had ever possessed in her most beautiful form of loveliness; they were now pure, mild maidenly eyes that shone forth in the face of a frog. They showed the existence of deep feeling and a human heart, and the beauteous eyes overflowed with tears, weeping precious drops that lightened the heart.

On the raised mound which she had made as a grave for the dead priest, she found the cross made of the branches of a tree, the last work of him who now lay dead and cold beneath it. A sudden thought came to Helga, and she lifted up the cross and planted it upon the grave, between the stones that covered him and the dead horse. The sad recollection brought the tears to her eyes, and in this gentle spirit she traced the same sign in the sand round the grave; and as she formed, with both her hands, the sign of the cross, the web skin fell from them like a torn glove. She washed her hands in the water of the spring, and gazed with astonishment at their delicate whiteness. Again she made the holy sign in the air, between herself and the dead man; her lips trembled, her tongue moved, and the name which she in her ride through the forest had so often heard spoken, rose to her lips, and she uttered the words, "Jesus Christ." Then the frog skin fell from her; she was once more a lovely maiden. Her head bent wearily, her tired limbs required rest, and then she slept.

Her sleep, however, was short. Towards midnight, she awoke; before her stood the dead horse, prancing and full of life, which shone forth from his eyes and from his wounded neck. Close by his side appeared the murdered Christian priest, more beautiful than Baldur, as the Viking's wife had said; but now he came as if in a flame of fire. Such gravity, such stern justice, such a piercing glance shone from his large, gentle eyes, that it seemed to penetrate into every corner of her heart. Beautiful Helga trembled at the look, and her memory returned with a power as if it had been the day of judgment. Every good deed that had been done for her, every loving word that had been said, were vividly before her mind. She understood now that love had kept her here during the day of her trial; while the creature formed of dust and clay, soul and spirit, had wrestled and struggled with evil. She acknowledged that she had only followed the impulses of an evil disposition, that she had done nothing to cure herself; everything had been given her, and all had happened as it were by the ordination of Providence. She bowed herself humbly, confessed her great imperfections in the sight of Him who can read every fault of the heart, and then the priest spoke. "Daughter of the moorland, thou hast come from the swamp and the marshy earth, but from this thou shalt arise. The sunlight shining into thy inmost soul proves the origin from which thou hast really sprung, and has restored the body to its natural form. I am come to thee from the land of the dead, and thou also must pass through the valley to reach the holy mountains where mercy and perfection dwell. I cannot lead thee to Hedeby that thou mayst receive Christian baptism, for first thou must remove the thick veil with which the waters of the moorland are shrouded, and bring forth from its depths the living author of thy being and thy life. Till this is done, thou canst not receive consecration."

Then he lifted her on the horse and gave her a golden censer, similar to those she had already seen at the Viking's house. A sweet perfume arose from it, while the open wound in the forehead of the slain priest, shone with the rays of a diamond. He took the cross from the grave, and held it aloft, and now they rode through the air over the rustling trees, over the hills where warriors lay buried each by his dead war-horse; and the brazen monumental figures rose up and galloped forth, and stationed themselves on the summits of the hills. The golden crescent on their foreheads, fastened with golden knots, glittered in the moonlight, and their mantles floated in the wind. The dragon, that guards buried treasure, lifted his head and gazed after them. The goblins and the satyrs peeped out from beneath the hills, and flitted to and fro in the fields, waving blue, red, and green torches, like the glowing sparks in burning paper. Over woodland and heath, flood and fen, they flew on, till they reached the wild moor, over which they hovered in broad circles. The Christian priest held the cross aloft, and it glittered like gold, while from his lips sounded pious prayers. Beautiful Helga's voice joined with his in the hymns he sung, as a child joins in her mother's song. She swung the censer, and a wonderful fragrance of incense arose from it; so powerful, that the reeds and rushes of the moor burst forth into blossom. Each germ came forth from the deep ground: all that had life raised itself. Blooming water-lilies spread themselves forth like a carpet of wrought flowers, and upon them lay a slumbering woman, young and beautiful. Helga fancied that it was her own image she saw reflected in the still water. But it was her mother she beheld, the wife of the Marsh King, the princess from the land of the Nile.

The dead Christian priest desired that the sleeping woman should be lifted on the horse, but the horse sank beneath the load, as if he had been a funeral pall fluttering in the wind. But the sign of the cross made the airy phantom strong, and then the three rode away from the marsh to firm ground.

At the same moment the cock crew in the Viking's castle, and the dream figures dissolved and floated away in the air, but mother and daughter stood opposite to each other.

"Am I looking at my own image in the deep water?" said the mother.

"Is it myself that I see represented on a white shield?" cried the daughter.

Then they came nearer to each other in a fond embrace. The mother's heart beat quickly, and she understood the quickened pulses. "My child!" she exclaimed, "the flower of my heart – my lotus flower of the deep water!" and she embraced her child again and wept, and the tears were as a baptism of new life and love for Helga. "In swan's plumage I came here," said the mother, "and here I threw off my feather dress. Then I sank down through the wavering ground, deep into the marsh beneath, which closed like a wall around me; I found myself after a while in fresher water; still a power drew me down deeper and deeper. I felt the weight of sleep upon my eyelids. Then I slept, and dreams hovered round me. It seemed to me as if I were again in the pyramids of Egypt, and yet the waving elder trunk that had frightened me on the moor stood ever before me. I observed the clefts and wrinkles in the stem; they shone forth in strange colors, and took the form of hieroglyphics. It was the mummy case on which I gazed. At last it burst, and forth stepped the thousand years' old king, the mummy form, black as pitch, black as the shining wood-snail, or the slimy mud of the swamp. Whether it was really the mummy or the Marsh King I know not. He seized me in his arms, and I felt as if I must die. When I recovered myself, I found in my bosom a little bird, flapping its wings, twittering and fluttering. The bird flew away from my bosom, upwards towards the dark, heavy canopy above me, but a long, green band kept it fastened to me. I heard and understood the tenor of its longings. Freedom! sunlight! to my father! Then I thought of my father, and the sunny land of my birth, my life, and my love. Then I loosened the band, and let the bird fly away to its home – to a father. Since that hour I have ceased to dream; my sleep has been long and heavy, till in this very hour, harmony and fragrance awoke me, and set me free."

The green band which fastened the wings of the bird to the mother's heart, where did it flutter now? whither had it been wafted? The stork only had seen it. The band was the green stalk, the cup of the flower the cradle in which lay the child, that now in blooming beauty had been folded to the mother's heart.

And while the two were resting in each other's arms, the old stork flew round and round them in narrowing circles, till at length he flew away swiftly to his nest, and fetched away the two suits of swan's feathers, which he had preserved there for many years. Then he returned to the mother and daughter, and threw the swan's plumage over them; the feathers immediately closed around them, and they rose up from the earth in the form of two white swans.

"And now we can converse with pleasure," said the stork-papa; "we can understand one another, although the beaks of birds are so different in shape. It is very fortunate that you came to-night. To-morrow we should have been gone. The mother, myself and the little ones, we're about to fly to the south. Look at me now: I am an old friend from the Nile, and a mother's heart contains more than her beak. She always said that the princess would know how to help herself. I and the young ones carried the swan's feathers over here, and I am glad of it now, and how lucky it is that I am here still. When the day dawns we shall start with a great company of other storks. We'll fly first, and you can follow in our track, so that you cannot miss your way. I and the young ones will have an eye upon you."

"And the lotus-flower which I was to take with me," said the Egyptian princess, "is flying here by my side, clothed in swan's feathers. The flower of my heart will travel with me; and so the riddle is solved. Now for home! now for home!"

But Helga said she could not leave the Danish land without once more seeing her foster-mother, the loving wife of the Viking. Each pleasing recollection, each kind word, every tear from the heart which her foster-mother had wept for her, rose in her mind, and at that moment she felt as if she loved this mother the best.

"Yes, we must go to the Viking's castle," said the stork; "mother and the young ones are waiting for me there. How they will open their eyes and flap their wings! My wife, you see, does not say much; she is short and abrupt in her manner; but she means well, for all that. I will flap my wings at once, that they may hear us coming." Then stork-papa flapped his wings in first-rate style, and he and the swans flew away to the Viking's castle.

In the castle, every one was in a deep sleep. It had been late in the evening before the Viking's wife retired to rest. She was anxious about Helga, who, three days before, had vanished with the Christian priest. Helga must have helped him in his flight, for it was her horse that was missed from the stable; but by what power had all this been accomplished? The Viking's wife thought of it with wonder, thought on the miracles which they said could be performed by those who believed in the Christian faith, and followed its teachings. These passing thoughts formed themselves into a vivid dream, and it seemed to her that she was still lying awake on her couch, while without darkness reigned. A storm arose; she heard the lake dashing and rolling from east and west, like the waves of the North Sea or the Cattegat. The monstrous snake which, it is said, surrounds the earth in the depths of the ocean, was trembling in spasmodic convulsions. The night of the fall of the gods was come, "Ragnorock," as the heathens call the judgment-day, when everything shall pass away, even the high gods themselves. The war trumpet sounded; riding upon the rainbow, came the gods, clad in steel, to fight their last battle on the last battle-field. Before them flew the winged vampires, and the dead warriors closed up the train. The whole firmament was ablaze with the northern lights, and yet the darkness triumphed. It was a terrible hour. And, close to the terrified woman, Helga seemed to be seated on the floor, in the hideous form of a frog, yet trembling, and clinging to her foster-mother, who took her on her lap, and lovingly caressed her, hideous and frog-like as she was. The air was filled with the clashing of arms and the hissing of arrows, as if a storm of hail was descending upon the earth. It seemed to her the hour when earth and sky would burst asunder, and all things be swallowed up in Saturn's fiery lake; but she knew that a new heaven and a new earth would arise, and that corn-fields would wave where now the lake rolled over desolate sands, and the ineffable God reign. Then she saw rising from the region of the dead, Baldur the gentle, the loving, and as the Viking's wife gazed upon him, she recognized his countenance. It was the captive Christian priest. "White Christian!" she exclaimed aloud, and with the words, she pressed a kiss on the forehead of the hideous frog-child. Then the frog-skin fell off, and Helga stood before her in all her beauty, more lovely and gentle-looking, and with eyes beaming with love. She kissed the hands of her foster-mother, blessed her for all her fostering love and care during the days of her trial and misery, for the thoughts she had suggested and awoke in her heart, and for naming the Name which she now repeated. Then beautiful Helga rose as a mighty swan, and spread her wings with the rushing sound of troops of birds of passage flying through the air.

Then the Viking's wife awoke, but she still heard the rushing sound without. She knew it was the time for the storks to depart, and that it must be their wings which she heard. She felt she should like to see them once more, and bid them farewell. She rose from her couch, stepped out on the threshold, and beheld, on the ridge of the roof, a party of storks ranged side by side. Troops of the birds were flying in circles over the castle and the highest trees; but just before her, as she stood on the threshold and close to the well where Helga had so often sat and alarmed her with her wildness, now stood two swans, gazing at her with intelligent eyes. Then she remembered her dream, which still appeared to her as a reality. She thought of Helga in the form of a swan. She thought of a Christian priest, and suddenly a wonderful joy arose in her heart. The swans flapped their wings and arched their necks as if to offer her a greeting, and the Viking's wife spread out her arms towards them, as if she accepted it, and smiled through her tears. She was roused from deep thought by a rustling of wings and snapping of beaks; all the storks arose, and started on their journey towards the south.

"We will not wait for the swans," said the mamma stork; "if they want to go with us, let them come now; we can't sit here till the plovers start. It is a fine thing after all to travel in families, not like the finches and the partridges. There the male and the female birds fly in separate flocks, which, to speak candidly, I consider very unbecoming."

"What are those swans flapping their wings for?"

"Well, every one flies in his own fashion," said the papa stork. "The swans fly in an oblique line; the cranes, in the form of a triangle; and the plovers, in a curved line like a snake."

"Don't talk about snakes while we are flying up here," said stork-mamma. "It puts ideas into the children's heads that can not be realized."

"Are those the high mountains I have heard spoken of?" asked Helga, in the swan's plumage.

"They are storm-clouds driving along beneath us," replied her mother.

"What are yonder white clouds that rise so high?" again inquired Helga.

"Those are mountains covered with perpetual snows, that you see yonder," said her mother. And then they flew across the Alps towards the blue Mediterranean.

"Africa's land! Egyptia's strand!" sang the daughter of the Nile, in her swan's plumage, as from the upper air she caught sight of her native land, a narrow, golden, wavy strip on the shores of the Nile; the other birds espied it also and hastened their flight.

"I can smell the Nile mud and the wet frogs," said the stork-mamma, "and I begin to feel quite hungry. Yes, now you shall taste something nice, and you will see the marabout bird, and the ibis, and the crane. They all belong to our family, but they are not nearly so handsome as we are. They give themselves great airs, especially the ibis. The Egyptians have spoilt him. They make a mummy of him, and stuff him with spices. I would rather be stuffed with live frogs, and so would you, and so you shall. Better have something in your inside while you are alive, than to be made a parade of after you are dead. That is my opinion, and I am always right."

"The storks are come," was said in the great house on the banks of the Nile, where the lord lay in the hall on his downy cushions, covered with a leopard skin, scarcely alive, yet not dead, waiting and hoping for the lotus-flower from the deep moorland in the far north. Relatives and servants were standing by his couch, when the two beautiful swans who had come with the storks flew into the hall. They threw off their soft white plumage, and two lovely female forms approached the pale, sick old man, and threw back their long hair, and when Helga bent over her grandfather, redness came back to his cheeks, his eyes brightened, and life returned to his benumbed limbs. The old man rose up with health and energy renewed; daughter and grandchild welcomed him as joyfully as if with a morning greeting after a long and troubled dream.

Joy reigned through the whole house, as well as in the stork's nest; although there the chief cause was really the good food, especially the quantities of frogs, which seemed to spring out of the ground in swarms.

Then the learned men hastened to note down, in flying characters, the story of the two princesses, and spoke of the arrival of the health-giving flower as a mighty event, which had been a blessing to the house and the land. Meanwhile, the stork-papa told the story to his family in his own way; but not till they had eaten and were satisfied; otherwise they would have had something else to do than to listen to stories.

"Well," said the stork-mamma, when she had heard it, "you will be made something of at last; I suppose they can do nothing less."

"What could I be made?" said stork-papa; "what have I done? – just nothing."

"You have done more than all the rest," she replied. "But for you and the youngsters the two young princesses would never have seen Egypt again, and the recovery of the old man would not have been effected. You will become something. They must certainly give you a doctor's hood, and our young ones will inherit it, and their children after them, and so on. You already look like an Egyptian doctor, at least in my eyes."

"I cannot quite remember the words I heard when I listened on the roof," said stork-papa, while relating the story to his family; "all I know is, that what the wise men said was so complicated and so learned, that they received not only rank, but presents; even the head cook at the great house was honored with a mark of distinction, most likely for the soup."

"And what did you receive?" said the stork-mamma. "They certainly ought not to forget the most important person in the affair, as you really are. The learned men have done nothing at all but use their tongues. Surely they will not overlook you."

Late in the night, while the gentle sleep of peace rested on the now happy house, there was still one watcher. It was not stork-papa, who, although he stood on guard on one leg, could sleep soundly. Helga alone was awake. She leaned over the balcony, gazing at the sparkling stars that shone clearer and brighter in the pure air than they had done in the north, and yet they were the same stars. She thought of the Viking's wife in the wild moorland, of the gentle eyes of her foster-mother, and of the tears she had shed over the poor frog-child that now lived in splendor and starry beauty by the waters of the Nile, with air balmy and sweet as spring. She thought of the love that dwelt in the breast of the heathen woman, love that had been shown to a wretched creature, hateful as a human being, and hideous when in the form of an animal. She looked at the glittering stars, and thought of the radiance that had shone forth on the forehead of the dead man, as she had fled with him over the woodland and moor. Tones were awakened in her memory; words which she had heard him speak as they rode onward, when she was carried, wondering and trembling, through the air; words from the great Fountain of love, the highest love that embraces all the human race. What had not been won and achieved by this love?

Day and night beautiful Helga was absorbed in the contemplation of the great amount of her happiness, and lost herself in the contemplation, like a child who turns hurriedly from the giver to examine the beautiful gifts. She was over-powered with her good fortune, which seemed always increasing, and therefore what might it become in the future? Had she not been brought by a wonderful miracle to all this joy and happiness? And in these thoughts she indulged, until at last she thought no more of the Giver. It was the over-abundance of youthful spirits unfolding its wings for a daring flight. Her eyes sparkled with energy, when suddenly arose a loud noise in the court below, and the daring thought vanished. She looked down, and saw two large ostriches running round quickly in narrow circles; she had never seen these creatures before, – great, coarse, clumsy-looking birds with curious wings that looked as if they had been clipped, and the birds themselves had the appearance of having been roughly used. She inquired about them, and for the first time heard the legend which the Egyptians relate respecting the ostrich.

Once, say they, the ostriches were a beautiful and glorious race of birds, with large, strong wings. One evening the other large birds of the forest said to the ostrich, "Brother, shall we fly to the river to-morrow morning to drink, God willing?" and the ostrich answered, "I will."

With the break of day, therefore, they commenced their flight; first rising high in the air, towards the sun, which is the eye of God; still higher and higher the ostrich flew, far above the other birds, proudly approaching the light, trusting in its own strength, and thinking not of the Giver, or saying, "if God will." When suddenly the avenging angel drew back the veil from the flaming ocean of sunlight, and in a moment the wings of the proud bird were scorched and shrivelled, and they sunk miserably to the earth. Since that time the ostrich and his race have never been able to rise in the air; they can only fly terror-stricken along the ground, or run round and round in narrow circles. It is a warning to mankind, that in all our thoughts and schemes, and in every action we undertake, we should say, "if God will."

Then Helga bowed her head thoughtfully and seriously, and looked at the circling ostrich, as with timid fear and simple pleasure it glanced at its own great shadow on the sunlit walls. And the story of the ostrich sunk deeply into the heart and mind of Helga: a life of happiness, both in the present and in the future, seemed secure for her, and what was yet to come might be the best of all, God willing.

Early in the spring, when the storks were again about to journey northward, beautiful Helga took off her golden bracelets, scratched her name on them, and beckoned to the stork-father. He came to her, and she placed the golden circlet round his neck, and begged him to deliver it safely to the Viking's wife, so that she might know that her foster-daughter still lived, was happy, and had not forgotten her.

"It is rather heavy to carry," thought stork-papa, when he had it on his neck; "but gold and honor are not to be flung into the street. The stork brings good fortune – they'll be obliged to acknowledge that at last."

"You lay gold, and I lay eggs," said stork-mamma; "with you it is only once in a way, I lay eggs every year But no one appreciates what we do; I call it very mortifying."

"But then we have a consciousness of our own worth, mother," replied stork-papa.

"What good will that do you?" retorted stork-mamma; "it will neither bring you a fair wind, nor a good meal."

"The little nightingale, who is singing yonder in the tamarind grove, will soon be going north, too." Helga said she had often heard her singing on the wild moor, so she determined to send a message by her. While flying in the swan's plumage she had learnt the bird language; she had often conversed with the stork and the swallow, and she knew that the nightingale would understand. So she begged the nightingale to fly to the beechwood, on the peninsula of Jutland, where a mound of stone and twigs had been raised to form the grave, and she begged the nightingale to persuade all the other little birds to build their nests round the place, so that evermore should resound over that grave music and song. And the nightingale flew away, and time flew away also.

In the autumn, an eagle, standing upon a pyramid, saw a stately train of richly laden camels, and men attired in armor on foaming Arabian steeds, whose glossy skins shone like silver, their nostrils were pink, and their thick, flowing manes hung almost to their slender legs. A royal prince of Arabia, handsome as a prince should be, and accompanied by distinguished guests, was on his way to the stately house, on the roof of which the storks' empty nests might be seen. They were away now in the far north, but expected to return very soon. And, indeed, they returned on a day that was rich in joy and gladness.

A marriage was being celebrated, in which the beautiful Helga, glittering in silk and jewels, was the bride, and the bridegroom the young Arab prince. Bride and bridegroom sat at the upper end of the table, between the bride's mother and grandfather. But her gaze was not on the bridegroom, with his manly, sunburnt face, round which curled a black beard, and whose dark fiery eyes were fixed upon her; but away from him, at a twinkling star, that shone down upon her from the sky. Then was heard the sound of rushing wings beating the air. The storks were coming home; and the old stork pair, although tired with the journey and requiring rest, did not fail to fly down at once to the balustrades of the verandah, for they knew already what feast was being celebrated. They had heard of it on the borders of the land, and also that Helga had caused their figures to be represented on the walls, for they belonged to her history.

"I call that very sensible and pretty," said stork-papa.

"Yes, but it is very little," said mamma stork; "they could not possibly have done less."

But, when Helga saw them, she rose and went out into the verandah to stroke the backs of the storks. The old stork pair bowed their heads, and curved their necks, and even the youngest among the young ones felt honored by this reception.

Helga continued to gaze upon the glittering star, which seemed to glow brighter and purer in its light; then between herself and the star floated a form, purer than the air, and visible through it. It floated quite near to her, and she saw that it was the dead Christian priest, who also was coming to her wedding feast – coming from the heavenly kingdom.

"The glory and brightness, yonder, outshines all that is known on earth," said he.

Then Helga the fair prayed more gently, and more earnestly, than she had ever prayed in her life before, that she might be permitted to gaze, if only for a single moment, at the glory and brightness of the heavenly kingdom. Then she felt herself lifted up, as it were, above the earth, through a sea of sound and thought; not only around her, but within her, was there light and song, such as words cannot express.

"Now we must return;" he said; "you will be missed."

"Only one more look," she begged; "but one short moment more."

"We must return to earth; the guests will have all departed. Only one more look! – the last!"

Then Helga stood again in the verandah. But the marriage lamps in the festive hall had been all extinguished, and the torches outside had vanished. The storks were gone; not a guest could be seen; no bridegroom – all in those few short moments seemed to have died. Then a great dread fell upon her. She stepped from the verandah through the empty hall into the next chamber, where slept strange warriors. She opened a side door, which once led into her own apartment, but now, as she passed through, she found herself suddenly in a garden which she had never before seen here, the sky blushed red, it was the dawn of morning. Three minutes only in heaven, and a whole night on earth had passed away! Then she saw the storks, and called to them in their own language.

Then stork-papa turned his head towards here, listened to her words, and drew near. "You speak our language," said he, "what do you wish? Why do you appear, – you – a strange woman?"

"It is I – it is Helga! Dost thou not know me? Three minutes ago we were speaking together yonder in the verandah."

"That is a mistake," said the stork, "you must have dreamed all this."

"No, no," she exclaimed. Then she reminded him of the Viking's castle, of the great lake, and of the journey across the ocean.

Then stork-papa winked his eyes, and said, "Why that's an old story which happened in the time of my grandfather. There certainly was a princess of that kind here in Egypt once, who came from the Danish land, but she vanished on the evening of her wedding day, many hundred years ago, and never came back. You may read about it yourself yonder, on a monument in the garden. There you will find swans and storks sculptured, and on the top is a figure of the princess Helga, in marble."

And so it was; Helga understood it all now, and sank on her knees. The sun burst forth in all its glory, and, as in olden times, the form of the frog vanished in his beams, and the beautiful form stood forth in all its loveliness; so now, bathed in light, rose a beautiful form, purer, clearer than air – a ray of brightness – from the Source of light Himself. The body crumbled into dust, and a faded lotus-flower lay on the spot on which Helga had stood.

"Now that is a new ending to the story," said stork-papa; "I really never expected it would end in this way, but it seems a very good ending."

"And what will the young ones say to it, I wonder?" said stork-mamma.

"Ah, that is a very important question," replied the stork.

The Garden of Paradise

THERE WAS ONCE a king's son who had a larger and more beautiful collection of books than any one else in the world, and full of splendid copper-plate engravings. He could read and obtain information respecting every people of every land; but not a word could he find to explain the situation of the garden of paradise, and this was just what he most wished to know. His grandmother had told him when he was quite a little boy, just old enough to go to school, that each flower in the garden of paradise was a sweet cake, that the pistils were full of rich wine, that on one flower history was written, on another geography or tables; so those who wished to learn their lessons had only to eat some of the cakes, and the more they ate, the more history, geography, or tables they knew. He believed it all then; but as he grew older, and learnt more and more, he became wise enough to understand that the splendor of the garden of paradise must be very different to all this. "Oh, why did Eve pluck the fruit from the tree of knowledge? why did Adam eat the forbidden fruit?" thought the king's son: "if I had been there it would never have happened, and there would have been no sin in the world." The garden of paradise occupied all his thoughts till he reached his seventeenth year.

One day he was walking alone in the wood, which was his greatest pleasure, when evening came on. The clouds gathered, and the rain poured down as if the sky had been a waterspout; and it was as dark as the bottom of a well at midnight; sometimes he slipped over the smooth grass, or fell over stones that projected out of the rocky ground. Every thing was dripping with moisture, and the poor prince had not a dry thread about him. He was obliged at last to climb over great blocks of stone, with water spurting from the thick moss. He began to feel quite faint, when he heard a most singular rushing noise, and saw before him a large cave, from which came a blaze of light. In the middle of the cave an immense fire was burning, and a noble stag, with its branching horns, was placed on a spit between the trunks of two pine-trees. It was turning slowly before the fire, and an elderly woman, as large and strong as if she had been a man in disguise, sat by, throwing one piece of wood after another into the flames.

"Come in," she said to the prince; "sit down by the fire and dry yourself."

"There is a great draught here," said the prince, as he seated himself on the ground.

"It will be worse when my sons come home," replied the woman; "you are now in the cavern of the Winds, and my sons are the four Winds of heaven: can you understand that?"

"Where are your sons?" asked the prince.

"It is difficult to answer stupid questions," said the woman. "My sons have plenty of business on hand; they are playing at shuttlecock with the clouds up yonder in the king's hall," and she pointed upwards.

"Oh, indeed," said the prince; "but you speak more roughly and harshly and are not so gentle as the women I am used to."

"Yes, that is because they have nothing else to do; but I am obliged to be harsh, to keep my boys in order, and I can do it, although they are so head-strong. Do you see those four sacks hanging on the wall? Well, they are just as much afraid of those sacks, as you used to be of the rat behind the looking-glass. I can bend the boys together, and put them in the sacks without any resistance on their parts, I can tell you. There they stay, and dare not attempt to come out until I allow them to do so. And here comes one of them."

It was the North Wind who came in, bringing with him a cold, piercing blast; large hailstones rattled on the floor, and snowflakes were scattered around in all directions. He wore a bearskin dress and cloak. His sealskin cap was drawn over his ears, long icicles hung from his beard, and one hailstone after another rolled from the collar of his jacket.

"Don't go too near the fire," said the prince, "or your hands and face will be frost-bitten."

"Frost-bitten!" said the North Wind, with a loud laugh; "why frost is my greatest delight. What sort of a little snip are you, and how did you find your way to the cavern of the Winds?"

"He is my guest," said the old woman, "and if you are not satisfied with that explanation you can go into the sack. Do you understand me?"

That settled the matter. So the North Wind began to relate his adventures, whence he came, and where he had been for a whole month. "I come from the polar seas," he said; "I have been on the Bear's Island with the Russian walrus-hunters. I sat and slept at the helm of their ship, as they sailed away from North Cape. Sometimes when I woke, the storm-birds would fly about my legs. They are curious birds; they give one flap with their wings, and then on their outstretched pinions soar far away."

"Don't make such a long story of it," said the mother of the winds; "what sort of a place is Bear's Island?"

"A very beautiful place, with a floor for dancing as smooth and flat as a plate. Half-melted snow, partly covered with moss, sharp stones, and skeletons of walruses and polar-bears, lie all about, their gigantic limbs in a state of green decay. It would seem as if the sun never shone there. I blew gently, to clear away the mist, and then I saw a little hut, which had been built from the wood of a wreck, and was covered with the skins of the walrus, the fleshy side outwards; it looked green and red, and on the roof sat a growling bear. Then I went to the sea shore, to look after birds' nests, and saw the unfledged nestlings opening their mouths and screaming for food. I blew into the thousand little throats, and quickly stopped their screaming. Farther on were the walruses with pig's heads, and teeth a yard long, rolling about like great worms."

"You relate your adventures very well, my son," said the mother, "it makes my mouth water to hear you.

"After that," continued the North Wind, "the hunting commenced. The harpoon was flung into the breast of the walrus, so that a smoking stream of blood spurted forth like a fountain, and besprinkled the ice. Then I thought of my own game; I began to blow, and set my own ships, the great icebergs sailing, so that they might crush the boats. Oh, how the sailors howled and cried out! but I howled louder than they. They were obliged to unload their cargo, and throw their chests and the dead walruses on the ice. Then I sprinkled snow over them, and left them in their crushed boats to drift southward, and to taste salt water. They will never return to Bear's Island."

"So you have done mischief," said the mother of the Winds.

"I shall leave others to tell the good I have done," he replied. "But here comes my brother from the West; I like him best of all, for he has the smell of the sea about him, and brings in a cold, fresh air as he enters."

"Is that the little Zephyr?" asked the prince.

"Yes, it is the little Zephyr," said the old woman; "but he is not little now. In years gone by he was a beautiful boy; now that is all past."

He came in, looking like a wild man, and he wore a slouched hat to protect his head from injury. In his hand he carried a club, cut from a mahogany tree in the American forests, not a trifle to carry.

"Whence do you come?" asked the mother.

"I come from the wilds of the forests, where the thorny brambles form thick hedges between the trees; where the water-snake lies in the wet grass, and mankind seem to be unknown."

"What were you doing there?"

"I looked into the deep river, and saw it rushing down from the rocks. The water drops mounted to the clouds and glittered in the rainbow. I saw the wild buffalo swimming in the river, but the strong tide carried him away amidst a flock of wild ducks, which flew into the air as the waters dashed onwards, leaving the buffalo to be hurled over the waterfall. This pleased me; so I raised a storm, which rooted up old trees, and sent them floating down the river."

"And what else have you done?" asked the old woman.

"I have rushed wildly across the savannahs; I have stroked the wild horses, and shaken the cocoa-nuts from the trees. Yes, I have many stories to relate; but I need not tell everything I know. You know it all very well, don't you, old lady?" And he kissed his mother so roughly, that she nearly fell backwards. Oh, he was, indeed, a wild fellow.

Now in came the South Wind, with a turban and a flowing Bedouin cloak.

"How cold it is here!" said he, throwing more wood on the fire. "It is easy to feel that the North Wind has arrived here before me."

"Why it is hot enough here to roast a bear," said the North Wind.

"You are a bear yourself," said the other.

"Do you want to be put in the sack, both of you?" said the old woman. "Sit down, now, on that stone, yonder, and tell me where you have been."

"In Africa, mother. I went out with the Hottentots, who were lion-hunting in the Kaffir land, where the plains are covered with grass the color of a green olive; and here I ran races with the ostrich, but I soon outstripped him in swiftness. At last I came to the desert, in which lie the golden sands, looking like the bottom of the sea. Here I met a caravan, and the travellers had just killed their last camel, to obtain water; there was very little for them, and they continued their painful journey beneath the burning sun, and over the hot sands, which stretched before them a vast, boundless desert. Then I rolled myself in the loose sand, and whirled it in burning columns over their heads. The dromedarys stood still in terror, while the merchants drew their caftans over their heads, and threw themselves on the ground before me, as they do before Allah, their god. Then I buried them beneath a pyramid of sand, which covers them all. When I blow that away on my next visit, the sun will bleach their bones, and travellers will see that others have been there before them; otherwise, in such a wild desert, they might not believe it possible."

"So you have done nothing but evil," said the mother. "Into the sack with you;" and, before he was aware, she had seized the South Wind round the body, and popped him into the bag. He rolled about on the floor, till she sat herself upon him to keep him still.

"These boys of yours are very lively," said the prince.

"Yes," she replied, "but I know how to correct them, when necessary; and here comes the fourth." In came the East Wind, dressed like a Chinese.

"Oh, you come from that quarter, do you?" said she; "I thought you had been to the garden of paradise."

"I am going there to-morrow," he replied; "I have not been there for a hundred years. I have just come from China, where I danced round the porcelain tower till all the bells jingled again. In the streets an official flogging was taking place, and bamboo canes were being broken on the shoulders of men of every high position, from the first to the ninth grade. They cried, 'Many thanks, my fatherly benefactor;' but I am sure the words did not come from their hearts, so I rang the bells till they sounded, 'ding, ding-dong.'"

"You are a wild boy," said the old woman; "it is well for you that you are going to-morrow to the garden of paradise; you always get improved in your education there. Drink deeply from the fountain of wisdom while you are there, and bring home a bottleful for me."

"That I will," said the East Wind; "but why have you put my brother South in a bag? Let him out; for I want him to tell me about the phoenix-bird. The princess always wants to hear of this bird when I pay her my visit every hundred years. If you will open the sack, sweetest mother, I will give you two pocketfuls of tea, green and fresh as when I gathered it from the spot where it grew."

"Well, for the sake of the tea, and because you are my own boy, I will open the bag."

She did so, and the South Wind crept out, looking quite cast down, because the prince had seen his disgrace.

"There is a palm-leaf for the princess," he said. "The old phoenix, the only one in the world, gave it to me himself. He has scratched on it with his beak the whole of his history during the hundred years he has lived. She can there read how the old phoenix set fire to his own nest, and sat upon it while it was burning, like a Hindoo widow. The dry twigs around the nest crackled and smoked till the flames burst forth and consumed the phoenix to ashes. Amidst the fire lay an egg, red hot, which presently burst with a loud report, and out flew a young bird. He is the only phoenix in the world, and the king over all the other birds. He has bitten a hole in the leaf which I give you, and that is his greeting to the princess."

"Now let us have something to eat," said the mother of the Winds. So they all sat down to feast on the roasted stag; and as the prince sat by the side of the East Wind, they soon became good friends.

"Pray tell me," said the prince, "who is that princess of whom you have been talking! and where lies the garden of paradise?"

"Ho! ho!" said the East Wind, "would you like to go there? Well, you can fly off with me to-morrow; but I must tell you one thing – no human being has been there since the time of Adam and Eve. I suppose you have read of them in your Bible."

"Of course I have," said the prince.

"Well," continued the East Wind, "when they were driven out of the garden of paradise, it sunk into the earth; but it retained its warm sunshine, its balmy air, and all its splendor. The fairy queen lives there, in the island of happiness, where death never comes, and all is beautiful. I can manage to take you there to-morrow, if you will sit on my back. But now don't talk any more, for I want to go to sleep;" and then they all slept.

When the prince awoke in the early morning, he was not a little surprised at finding himself high up above the clouds. He was seated on the back of the East Wind, who held him faithfully; and they were so high in the air that woods and fields, rivers and lakes, as they lay beneath them, looked like a painted map.

"Good morning," said the East Wind. "You might have slept on a while; for there is very little to see in the flat country over which we are passing unless you like to count the churches; they look like spots of chalk on a green board." The green board was the name he gave to the green fields and meadows.

"It was very rude of me not to say good-bye to your mother and your brothers," said the prince.

"They will excuse you, as you were asleep," said the East Wind; and then they flew on faster than ever.

The leaves and branches of the trees rustled as they passed. When they flew over seas and lakes, the waves rose higher, and the large ships dipped into the water like diving swans. As darkness came on, towards evening, the great towns looked charming; lights were sparkling, now seen now hidden, just as the sparks go out one after another on a piece of burnt paper. The prince clapped his hands with pleasure; but the East Wind advised him not to express his admiration in that manner, or he might fall down, and find himself hanging on a church steeple. The eagle in the dark forests flies swiftly; but faster than he flew the East Wind. The Cossack, on his small horse, rides lightly o'er the plains; but lighter still passed the prince on the winds of the wind.

"There are the Himalayas, the highest mountains in Asia," said the East Wind. "We shall soon reach the garden of paradise now."

Then, they turned southward, and the air became fragrant with the perfume of spices and flowers. Here figs and pomegranates grew wild, and the vines were covered with clusters of blue and purple grapes. Here they both descended to the earth, and stretched themselves on the soft grass, while the flowers bowed to the breath of the wind as if to welcome it. "Are we now in the garden of paradise?" asked the prince.

"No, indeed," replied the East Wind; "but we shall be there very soon. Do you see that wall of rocks, and the cavern beneath it, over which the grape vines hang like a green curtain? Through that cavern we must pass. Wrap your cloak round you; for while the sun scorches you here, a few steps farther it will be icy cold. The bird flying past the entrance to the cavern feels as if one wing were in the region of summer, and the other in the depths of winter."

"So this then is the way to the garden of paradise?" asked the prince, as they entered the cavern. It was indeed cold; but the cold soon passed, for the East Wind spread his wings, and they gleamed like the brightest fire. As they passed on through this wonderful cave, the prince could see great blocks of stone, from which water trickled, hanging over their heads in fantastic shapes. Sometimes it was so narrow that they had to creep on their hands and knees, while at other times it was lofty and wide, like the free air. It had the appearance of a chapel for the dead, with petrified organs and silent pipes. "We seem to be passing through the valley of death to the garden of paradise," said the prince.

But the East Wind answered not a word, only pointed forwards to a lovely blue light which gleamed in the distance. The blocks of stone assumed a misty appearance, till at last they looked like white clouds in moonlight. The air was fresh and balmy, like a breeze from the mountains perfumed with flowers from a valley of roses. A river, clear as the air itself, sparkled at their feet, while in its clear depths could be seen gold and silver fish sporting in the bright water, and purple eels emitting sparks of fire at every moment, while the broad leaves of the water-lilies, that floated on its surface, flickered with all the colors of the rainbow. The flower in its color of flame seemed to receive its nourishment from the water, as a lamp is sustained by oil. A marble bridge, of such exquisite workmanship that it appeared as if formed of lace and pearls, led to the island of happiness, in which bloomed the garden of paradise. The East Wind took the prince in his arms, and carried him over, while the flowers and the leaves sang the sweet songs of his childhood in tones so full and soft that no human voice could venture to imitate. Within the garden grew large trees, full of sap; but whether they were palm-trees or gigantic water-plants, the prince knew not. The climbing plants hung in garlands of green and gold, like the illuminations on the margins of old missals or twined among the initial letters. Birds, flowers, and festoons appeared intermingled in seeming confusion. Close by, on the grass, stood a group of peacocks, with radiant tails outspread to the sun. The prince touched them, and found, to his surprise, that they were not really birds, but the leaves of the burdock tree, which shone with the colors of a peacock's tail. The lion and the tiger, gentle and tame, were springing about like playful cats among the green bushes, whose perfume was like the fragrant blossom of the olive. The plumage of the wood-pigeon glistened like pearls as it struck the lion's mane with its wings; while the antelope, usually so shy, stood near, nodding its head as if it wished to join in the frolic. The fairy of paradise next made her appearance. Her raiment shone like the sun, and her serene countenance beamed with happiness like that of a mother rejoicing over her child. She was young and beautiful, and a train of lovely maidens followed her, each wearing a bright star in her hair. The East Wind gave her the palm-leaf, on which was written the history of the phoenix; and her eyes sparkled with joy. She then took the prince by the hand, and led him into her palace, the walls of which were richly colored, like a tulip-leaf when it is turned to the sun. The roof had the appearance of an inverted flower, and the colors grew deeper and brighter to the gazer. The prince walked to a window, and saw what appeared to be the tree of knowledge of good and evil, with Adam and Eve standing by, and the serpent near them. "I thought they were banished from paradise," he said.

The princess smiled, and told him that time had engraved each event on a window-pane in the form of a picture; but, unlike other pictures, all that it represented lived and moved, – the leaves rustled, and the persons went and came, as in a looking-glass. He looked through another pane, and saw the ladder in Jacob's dream, on which the angels were ascending and descending with outspread wings. All that had ever happened in the world here lived and moved on the panes of glass, in pictures such as time alone could produce. The fairy now led the prince into a large, lofty room with transparent walls, through which the light shone. Here were portraits, each one appearing more beautiful than the other – millions of happy beings, whose laughter and song mingled in one sweet melody: some of these were in such an elevated position that they appeared smaller than the smallest rosebud, or like pencil dots on paper. In the centre of the hall stood a tree, with drooping branches, from which hung golden apples, both great and small, looking like oranges amid the green leaves. It was the tree of knowledge of good and evil, from which Adam and Eve had plucked and eaten the forbidden fruit, and from each leaf trickled a bright red dewdrop, as if the tree were weeping tears of blood for their sin. "Let us now take the boat," said the fairy: "a sail on the cool waters will refresh us. But we shall not move from the spot, although the boat may rock on the swelling water; the countries of the world will glide before us, but we shall remain still."

It was indeed wonderful to behold. First came the lofty Alps, snow-clad, and covered with clouds and dark pines. The horn resounded, and the shepherds sang merrily in the valleys. The banana-trees bent their drooping branches over the boat, black swans floated on the water, and singular animals and flowers appeared on the distant shore. New Holland, the fifth division of the world, now glided by, with mountains in the background, looking blue in the distance. They heard the song of the priests, and saw the wild dance of the savage to the sound of the drums and trumpets of bone; the pyramids of Egypt rising to the clouds; columns and sphinxes, overthrown and buried in the sand, followed in their turn; while the northern lights flashed out over the extinguished volcanoes of the north, in fireworks none could imitate.

The prince was delighted, and yet he saw hundreds of other wonderful things more than can be described. "Can I stay here forever?" asked he.

"That depends upon yourself," replied the fairy. "If you do not, like Adam, long for what is forbidden, you can remain here always."

"I should not touch the fruit on the tree of knowledge," said the prince; there is abundance of fruit equally beautiful."

"Examine your own heart," said the princess, "and if you do not feel sure of its strength, return with the East Wind who brought you. He is about to fly back, and will not return here for a hundred years. The time will not seem to you more than a hundred hours, yet even that is a long time for temptation and resistance. Every evening, when I leave you, I shall be obliged to say, 'Come with me,' and to beckon to you with my hand. But you must not listen, nor move from your place to follow me; for with every step you will find your power to resist weaker. If once you attempted to follow me, you would soon find yourself in the hall, where grows the tree of knowledge, for I sleep beneath its perfumed branches. If you stooped over me, I should be forced to smile. If you then kissed my lips, the garden of paradise would sink into the earth, and to you it would be lost. A keen wind from the desert would howl around you; cold rain fall on your head, and sorrow and woe be your future lot."

"I will remain," said the prince.

So the East Wind kissed him on the forehead, and said, "Be firm; then shall we meet again when a hundred years have passed. Farewell, farewell." Then the East Wind spread his broad pinions, which shone like the lightning in harvest, or as the northern lights in a cold winter.

"Farewell, farewell," echoed the trees and the flowers.

Storks and pelicans flew after him in feathery bands, to accompany him to the boundaries of the garden.

"Now we will commence dancing," said the fairy; "and when it is nearly over at sunset, while I am dancing with you, I shall make a sign, and ask you to follow me: but do not obey. I shall be obliged to repeat the same thing for a hundred years; and each time, when the trial is past, if you resist, you will gain strength, till resistance becomes easy, and at last the temptation will be quite overcome. This evening, as it will be the first time, I have warned you."

After this the fairy led him into a large hall, filled with transparent lilies. The yellow stamina of each flower formed a tiny golden harp, from which came forth strains of music like the mingled tones of flute and lyre. Beautiful maidens, slender and graceful in form, and robed in transparent gauze, floated through the dance, and sang of the happy life in the garden of paradise, where death never entered, and where all would bloom forever in immortal youth. As the sun went down, the whole heavens became crimson and gold, and tinted the lilies with the hue of roses. Then the beautiful maidens offered to the prince sparkling wine; and when he had drank, he felt happiness greater than he had ever known before. Presently the background of the hall opened and the tree of knowledge appeared, surrounded by a halo of glory that almost blinded him. Voices, soft and lovely as his mother's sounded in his ears, as if she were singing to him, "My child, my beloved child." Then the fairy beckoned to him, and said in sweet accents, "Come with me, come with me." Forgetting his promise, forgetting it even on the very first evening, he rushed towards her, while she continued to beckon to him and to smile. The fragrance around him overpowered his senses, the music from the harps sounded more entrancing, while around the tree appeared millions of smiling faces, nodding and singing. "Man should know everything; man is the lord of the earth." The tree of knowledge no longer wept tears of blood, for the dewdrops shone like glittering stars.

"Come, come," continued that thrilling voice, and the prince followed the call. At every step his cheeks glowed, and the blood rushed wildly through his veins. "I must follow," he cried; "it is not a sin, it cannot be, to follow beauty and joy. I only want to see her sleep, and nothing will happen unless I kiss her, and that I will not do, for I have strength to resist, and a determined will."

The fairy threw off her dazzling attire, bent back the boughs, and in another moment was hidden among them.

"I have not sinned yet," said the prince, "and I will not;" and then he pushed aside the boughs to follow the princess. She was lying already asleep, beautiful as only a fairy in the garden of paradise could be. She smiled as he bent over her, and he saw tears trembling out of her beautiful eyelashes. "Do you weep for me?" he whispered. "Oh weep not, thou loveliest of women. Now do I begin to understand the happiness of paradise; I feel it to my inmost soul, in every thought. A new life is born within me. One moment of such happiness is worth an eternity of darkness and woe." He stooped and kissed the tears from her eyes, and touched her lips with his.

A clap of thunder, loud and awful, resounded through the trembling air. All around him fell into ruin. The lovely fairy, the beautiful garden, sunk deeper and deeper. The prince saw it sinking down in the dark night till it shone only like a star in the distance beneath him. Then he felt a coldness, like death, creeping over him; his eyes closed, and he became insensible.

When he recovered, a chilling rain was beating upon him, and a sharp wind blew on his head. "Alas! what have I done?" he sighed; "I have sinned like Adam, and the garden of paradise has sunk into the earth." He opened his eyes, and saw the star in the distance, but it was the morning star in heaven which glittered in the darkness.

Presently he stood up and found himself in the depths of the forest, close to the cavern of the Winds, and the mother of the Winds sat by his side. She looked angry, and raised her arm in the air as she spoke. "The very first evening!" she said. "Well, I expected it! If you were my son, you should go into the sack."

"And there he will have to go at last," said a strong old man, with large black wings, and a scythe in his hand, whose name was Death. "He shall be laid in his coffin, but not yet. I will allow him to wander about the world for a while, to atone for his sin, and to give him time to become better. But I shall return when he least expects me. I shall lay him in a black coffin, place it on my head, and fly away with it beyond the stars. There also blooms a garden of paradise, and if he is good and pious he will be admitted; but if his thoughts are bad, and his heart is full of sin, he will sink with his coffin deeper than the garden of paradise has sunk. Once in every thousand years I shall go and fetch him, when he will either be condemned to sink still deeper, or be raised to a happier life in the world beyond the stars."

The Shadow

IN VERY HOT climates, where the heat of the sun has great power, people are usually as brown as mahogany; and in the hottest countries they are negroes, with black skins. A learned man once travelled into one of these warm climates, from the cold regions of the north, and thought he would roam about as he did at home; but he soon had to change his opinion. He found that, like all sensible people, he must remain in the house during the whole day, with every window and door closed, so that it looked as if all in the house were asleep or absent. The houses of the narrow street in which he lived were so lofty that the sun shone upon them from morning till evening, and it became quite unbearable. This learned man from the cold regions was young as well as clever; but it seemed to him as if he were sitting in an oven, and he became quite exhausted and weak, and grew so thin that his shadow shrivelled up, and became much smaller than it had been at home. The sun took away even what was left of it, and he saw nothing of it till the evening, after sunset. It was really a pleasure, as soon as the lights were brought into the room, to see the shadow stretch itself against the wall, even to the ceiling, so tall was it; and it really wanted a good stretch to recover its strength. The learned man would sometimes go out into the balcony to stretch himself also; and as soon as the stars came forth in the clear, beautiful sky, he felt revived. People at this hour began to make their appearance in all the balconies in the street; for in warm climates every window has a balcony, in which they can breathe the fresh evening air, which is very necessary, even to those who are used to a heat that makes them as brown as mahogany; so that the street presented a very lively appearance. Here were shoemakers, and tailors, and all sorts of people sitting. In the street beneath, they brought out tables and chairs, lighted candles by hundreds, talked and sang, and were very merry. There were people walking, carriages driving, and mules trotting along, with their bells on the harness, "tingle, tingle," as they went. Then the dead were carried to the grave with the sound of solemn music, and the tolling of the church bells. It was indeed a scene of varied life in the street. One house only, which was just opposite to the one in which the foreign learned man lived, formed a contrast to all this, for it was quite still; and yet somebody dwelt there, for flowers stood in the balcony, blooming beautifully in the hot sun; and this could not have been unless they had been watered carefully. Therefore some one must be in the house to do this. The doors leading to the balcony were half opened in the evening; and although in the front room all was dark, music could be heard from the interior of the house. The foreign learned man considered this music very delightful; but perhaps he fancied it; for everything in these warm countries pleased him, excepting the heat of the sun. The foreign landlord said he did not know who had taken the opposite house – nobody was to be seen there; and as to the music, he thought it seemed very tedious, to him most uncommonly so.

"It is just as if some one was practising a piece that he could not manage; it is always the same piece. He thinks, I suppose, that he will be able to manage it at last; but I do not think so, however long he may play it."

Once the foreigner woke in the night. He slept with the door open which led to the balcony; the wind had raised the curtain before it, and there appeared a wonderful brightness over all in the balcony of the opposite house. The flowers seemed like flames of the most gorgeous colors, and among the flowers stood a beautiful slender maiden. It was to him as if light streamed from her, and dazzled his eyes; but then he had only just opened them, as he awoke from his sleep. With one spring he was out of bed, and crept softly behind the curtain. But she was gone – the brightness had disappeared; the flowers no longer appeared like flames, although still as beautiful as ever. The door stood ajar, and from an inner room sounded music so sweet and so lovely, that it produced the most enchanting thoughts, and acted on the senses with magic power. Who could live there? Where was the real entrance? for, both in the street and in the lane at the side, the whole ground floor was a continuation of shops; and people could not always be passing through them.

One evening the foreigner sat in the balcony. A light was burning in his own room, just behind him. It was quite natural, therefore, that his shadow should fall on the wall of the opposite house; so that, as he sat amongst the flowers on his balcony, when he moved, his shadow moved also.

"I think my shadow is the only living thing to be seen opposite," said the learned man; "see how pleasantly it sits among the flowers. The door is only ajar; the shadow ought to be clever enough to step in and look about him, and then to come back and tell me what he has seen. You could make yourself useful in this way," said he, jokingly; "be so good as to step in now, will you?" and then he nodded to the shadow, and the shadow nodded in return. "Now go, but don't stay away altogether."

Then the foreigner stood up, and the shadow on the opposite balcony stood up also; the foreigner turned round, the shadow turned; and if any one had observed, they might have seen it go straight into the half-opened door of the opposite balcony, as the learned man re-entered his own room, and let the curtain fall. The next morning he went out to take his coffee and read the newspapers.

"How is this?" he exclaimed, as he stood in the sunshine. "I have lost my shadow. So it really did go away yesterday evening, and it has not returned. This is very annoying."

And it certainly did vex him, not so much because the shadow was gone, but because he knew there was a story of a man without a shadow. All the people at home, in his country, knew this story; and when he returned, and related his own adventures, they would say it was only an imitation; and he had no desire for such things to be said of him. So he decided not to speak of it at all, which was a very sensible determination.

In the evening he went out again on his balcony, taking care to place the light behind him; for he knew that a shadow always wants his master for a screen; but he could not entice him out. He made himself little, and he made himself tall; but there was no shadow, and no shadow came. He said, "Hem, a-hem;" but it was all useless. That was very vexatious; but in warm countries everything grows very quickly; and, after a week had passed, he saw, to his great joy, that a new shadow was growing from his feet, when he walked in the sunshine; so that the root must have remained. After three weeks, he had quite a respectable shadow, which, during his return journey to northern lands, continued to grow, and became at last so large that he might very well have spared half of it. When this learned man arrived at home, he wrote books about the true, the good, and the beautiful, which are to be found in this world; and so days and years passed – many, many years.

One evening, as he sat in his study, a very gentle tap was heard at the door. "Come in," said he; but no one came. He opened the door, and there stood before him a man so remarkably thin that he felt seriously troubled at his appearance. He was, however, very well dressed, and looked like a gentleman. "To whom have I the honor of speaking?" said he.

"Ah, I hoped you would recognize me," said the elegant stranger; "I have gained so much that I have a body of flesh, and clothes to wear. You never expected to see me in such a condition. Do you not recognize your old shadow? Ah, you never expected that I should return to you again. All has been prosperous with me since I was with you last; I have become rich in every way, and, were I inclined to purchase my freedom from service, I could easily do so." And as he spoke he rattled between his fingers a number of costly trinkets which hung to a thick gold watch-chain he wore round his neck. Diamond rings sparkled on his fingers, and it was all real.

"I cannot recover from my astonishment," said the learned man. "What does all this mean?"

"Something rather unusual," said the shadow; "but you are yourself an uncommon man, and you know very well that I have followed in your footsteps ever since your childhood. As soon as you found that I have travelled enough to be trusted alone, I went my own way, and I am now in the most brilliant circumstances. But I felt a kind of longing to see you once more before you die, and I wanted to see this place again, for there is always a clinging to the land of one's birth. I know that you have now another shadow; do I owe you anything? If so, have the goodness to say what it is."

"No! Is it really you?" said the learned man. "Well, this is most remarkable; I never supposed it possible that a man's old shadow could become a human being."

"Just tell me what I owe you," said the shadow, "for I do not like to be in debt to any man."

"How can you talk in that manner?" said the learned man. "What question of debt can there be between us? You are as free as any one. I rejoice exceedingly to hear of your good fortune. Sit down, old friend, and tell me a little of how it happened, and what you saw in the house opposite to me while we were in those hot climates."

"Yes, I will tell you all about it," said the shadow, sitting down; "but then you must promise me never to tell in this city, wherever you may meet me, that I have been your shadow. I am thinking of being married, for I have more than sufficient to support a family."

"Make yourself quite easy," said the learned man; "I will tell no one who you really are. Here is my hand, – I promise, and a word is sufficient between man and man."

"Between man and a shadow," said the shadow; for he could not help saying so.

It was really most remarkable how very much he had become a man in appearance. He was dressed in a suit of the very finest black cloth, polished boots, and an opera crush hat, which could be folded together so that nothing could be seen but the crown and the rim, besides the trinkets, the gold chain, and the diamond rings already spoken of. The shadow was, in fact, very well dressed, and this made a man of him. "Now I will relate to you what you wish to know," said the shadow, placing his foot with the polished leather boot as firmly as possible on the arm of the new shadow of the learned man, which lay at his feet like a poodle dog. This was done, it might be from pride, or perhaps that the new shadow might cling to him, but the prostrate shadow remained quite quiet and at rest, in order that it might listen, for it wanted to know how a shadow could be sent away by its master, and become a man itself. "Do you know," said the shadow, "that in the house opposite to you lived the most glorious creature in the world? It was poetry. I remained there three weeks, and it was more like three thousand years, for I read all that has ever been written in poetry or prose; and I may say, in truth, that I saw and learnt everything."

"Poetry!" exclaimed the learned man. "Yes, she lives as a hermit in great cities. Poetry! Well, I saw her once for a very short moment, while sleep weighed down my eyelids. She flashed upon me from the balcony like the radiant aurora borealis, surrounded with flowers like flames of fire. Tell me, you were on the balcony that evening; you went through the door, and what did you see?"

"I found myself in an ante-room," said the shadow. "You still sat opposite to me, looking into the room. There was no light, or at least it seemed in partial darkness, for the door of a whole suite of rooms stood open, and they were brilliantly lighted. The blaze of light would have killed me, had I approached too near the maiden myself, but I was cautious, and took time, which is what every one ought to do."

"And what didst thou see?" asked the learned man.

"I saw everything, as you shall hear. But – it really is not pride on my part, as a free man and possessing the knowledge that I do, besides my position, not to speak of my wealth – I wish you would say you to me instead of thou."

"I beg your pardon," said the learned man; "it is an old habit, which it is difficult to break. You are quite right; I will try to think of it. But now tell me everything that you saw."

"Everything," said the shadow; "for I saw and know everything."

"What was the appearance of the inner rooms?" asked the scholar. "Was it there like a cool grove, or like a holy temple? Were the chambers like a starry sky seen from the top of a high mountain?"

"It was all that you describe," said the shadow; "but I did not go quite in – I remained in the twilight of the ante-room – but I was in a very good position, – I could see and hear all that was going on in the court of poetry."

"But what did you see? Did the gods of ancient times pass through the rooms? Did old heroes fight their battles over again? Were there lovely children at play, who related their dreams?"

"I tell you I have been there, and therefore you may be sure that I saw everything that was to be seen. If you had gone there, you would not have remained a human being, whereas I became one; and at the same moment I became aware of my inner being, my inborn affinity to the nature of poetry. It is true I did not think much about it while I was with you, but you will remember that I was always much larger at sunrise and sunset, and in the moonlight even more visible than yourself, but I did not then understand my inner existence. In the ante-room it was revealed to me. I became a man; I came out in full maturity. But you had left the warm countries. As a man, I felt ashamed to go about without boots or clothes, and that exterior finish by which man is known. So I went my own way; I can tell you, for you will not put it in a book. I hid myself under the cloak of a cake woman, but she little thought who she concealed. It was not till evening that I ventured out. I ran about the streets in the moonlight. I drew myself up to my full height upon the walls, which tickled my back very pleasantly. I ran here and there, looked through the highest windows into the rooms, and over the roofs. I looked in, and saw what nobody else could see, or indeed ought to see; in fact, is a bad world, and I would not care to be a man, but that men are of some importance.

I saw the most miserable things going on between husbands and wives, parents and children, – sweet, incomparable children. I have seen what no human being has the power of knowing, although they would all be very glad to know – the evil conduct of their neighbors. Had I written a newspaper, how eagerly it would have been read! Instead of which, I wrote directly to the persons themselves, and great alarm arose in all the town I visited. They had so much fear of me, and yet how dearly they loved me. The professor made me a professor. The tailor gave me new clothes; I am well provided for in that way. The overseer of the mint struck coins for me. The women declared that I was handsome, and so I became the man you now see me. And now I must say adieu. Here is my card. I live on the sunny side of the street, and always stay at home in rainy weather." And the shadow departed.

"This is all very remarkable," said the learned man.

Years passed, days and years went by, and the shadow came again. "How are you going on now?" he asked.

"Ah!" said the learned man; "I am writing about the true, the beautiful, and the good; but no one cares to hear anything about it. I am quite in despair, for I take it to heart very much."

"That is what I never do," said the shadow; "I am growing quite fat and stout, which every one ought to be. You do not understand the world; you will make yourself ill about it; you ought to travel; I am going on a journey in the summer, will you go with me? I should like a travelling companion; will you travel with me as my shadow? It would give me great pleasure, and I will pay all expenses."

"Are you going to travel far?" asked the learned man.

"That is a matter of opinion," replied the shadow. "At all events, a journey will do you good, and if you will be my shadow, then all your journey shall be paid."

"It appears to me very absurd," said the learned man.

"But it is the way of the world," replied the shadow, "and always will be." Then he went away.

Everything went wrong with the learned man. Sorrow and trouble pursued him, and what he said about the good, the beautiful, and the true, was of as much value to most people as a nutmeg would be to a cow. At length he fell ill. "You really look like a shadow," people said to him, and then a cold shudder would pass over him, for he had his own thoughts on the subject.

"You really ought to go to some watering-place," said the shadow on his next visit. "There is no other chance for you. I will take you with me, for the sake of old acquaintance. I will pay the expenses of your journey, and you shall write a description of it to amuse us by the way. I should like to go to a watering-place; my beard does not grow as it ought, which is from weakness, and I must have a beard. Now do be sensible and accept my proposal; we shall travel as intimate friends."

And at last they started together. The shadow was master now, and the master became the shadow. They drove together, and rode and walked in company with each other, side by side, or one in front and the other behind, according to the position of the sun. The shadow always knew when to take the place of honor, but the learned man took no notice of it, for he had a good heart, and was exceedingly mild and friendly.

One day the master said to the shadow, "We have grown up together from our childhood, and now that we have become travelling companions, shall we not drink to our good fellowship, and say thee and thou to each other?"

"What you say is very straightforward and kindly meant," said the shadow, who was now really master. "I will be equally kind and straightforward. You are a learned man, and know how wonderful human nature is. There are some men who cannot endure the smell of brown paper; it makes them ill. Others will feel a shuddering sensation to their very marrow, if a nail is scratched on a pane of glass. I myself have a similar kind of feeling when I hear any one say thou to me. I feel crushed by it, as I used to feel in my former position with you. You will perceive that this is a matter of feeling, not pride. I cannot allow you to say thou to me; I will gladly say it to you, and therefore your wish will be half fulfilled." Then the shadow addressed his former master as thou.

"It is going rather too far," said the latter, "that I am to say you when I speak to him, and he is to say thou to me." However, he was obliged to submit.

They arrived at length at the baths, where there were many strangers, and among them a beautiful princess, whose real disease consisted in being too sharp-sighted, which made every one very uneasy. She saw at once that the new comer was very different to every one else. "They say he is here to make his beard grow," she thought; "but I know the real cause, he is unable to cast a shadow." Then she became very curious on the matter, and one day, while on the promenade, she entered into conversation with the strange gentleman. Being a princess, she was not obliged to stand upon much ceremony, so she said to him without hesitation, "Your illness consists in not being able to cast a shadow."

"Your royal highness must be on the high road to recovery from your illness," said he. "I know your complaint arose from being too sharp-sighted, and in this case it has entirely failed. I happen to have a most unusual shadow. Have you not seen a person who is always at my side? Persons often give their servants finer cloth for their liveries than for their own clothes, and so I have dressed out my shadow like a man; nay, you may observe that I have even given him a shadow of his own; it is rather expensive, but I like to have things about me that are peculiar."

"How is this?" thought the princess; "am I really cured? This must be the best watering-place in existence. Water in our times has certainly wonderful power. But I will not leave this place yet, just as it begins to be amusing. This foreign prince – for he must be a prince – pleases me above all things. I only hope his beard won't grow, or he will leave at once."

In the evening, the princess and the shadow danced together in the large assembly rooms. She was light, but he was lighter still; she had never seen such a dancer before. She told him from what country she had come, and found he knew it and had been there, but not while she was at home. He had looked into the windows of her father's palace, both the upper and the lower windows; he had seen many things, and could therefore answer the princess, and make allusions which quite astonished her. She thought he must be the cleverest man in all the world, and felt the greatest respect for his knowledge. When she danced with him again she fell in love with him, which the shadow quickly discovered, for she had with her eyes looked him through and through. They danced once more, and she was nearly telling him, but she had some discretion; she thought of her country, her kingdom, and the number of people over whom she would one day have to rule. "He is a clever man," she thought to herself, "which is a good thing, and he dances admirably, which is also good. But has he well-grounded knowledge? that is an important question, and I must try him." Then she asked him a most difficult question, she herself could not have answered it, and the shadow made a most unaccountable grimace.

"You cannot answer that," said the princess.

"I learnt something about it in my childhood," he replied; "and believe that even my very shadow, standing over there by the door, could answer it."

"Your shadow," said the princess; "indeed that would be very remarkable."

"I do not say so positively," observed the shadow; "but I am inclined to believe that he can do so. He has followed me for so many years, and has heard so much from me, that I think it is very likely. But your royal highness must allow me to observe, that he is very proud of being considered a man, and to put him in a good humor, so that he may answer correctly, he must be treated as a man."

"I shall be very pleased to do so," said the princess. So she walked up to the learned man, who stood in the doorway, and spoke to him of the sun, and the moon, of the green forests, and of people near home and far off; and the learned man conversed with her pleasantly and sensibly.

"What a wonderful man he must be, to have such a clever shadow!" thought she. "If I were to choose him it would be a real blessing to my country and my subjects, and I will do it." So the princess and the shadow were soon engaged to each other, but no one was to be told a word about it, till she returned to her kingdom.

"No one shall know," said the shadow; "not even my own shadow;" and he had very particular reasons for saying so.

After a time, the princess returned to the land over which she reigned, and the shadow accompanied her.

"Listen my friend," said the shadow to the learned man; "now that I am as fortunate and as powerful as any man can be, I will do something unusually good for you. You shall live in my palace, drive with me in the royal carriage, and have a hundred thousand dollars a year; but you must allow every one to call you a shadow, and never venture to say that you have been a man. And once a year, when I sit in my balcony in the sunshine, you must lie at my feet as becomes a shadow to do; for I must tell you I am going to marry the princess, and our wedding will take place this evening."

"Now, really, this is too ridiculous," said the learned man. "I cannot, and will not, submit to such folly. It would be cheating the whole country, and the princess also. I will disclose everything, and say that I am the man, and that you are only a shadow dressed up in men's clothes."

"No one would believe you," said the shadow; "be reasonable, now, or I will call the guards."

"I will go straight to the princess," said the learned man.

"But I shall be there first," replied the shadow, "and you will be sent to prison." And so it turned out, for the guards readily obeyed him, as they knew he was going to marry the king's daughter.

"You tremble," said the princess, when the shadow appeared before her. "Has anything happened? You must not be ill to-day, for this evening our wedding will take place."

"I have gone through the most terrible affair that could possibly happen," said the shadow; "only imagine, my shadow has gone mad; I suppose such a poor, shallow brain, could not bear much; he fancies that he has become a real man, and that I am his shadow."

"How very terrible," cried the princess; "is he locked up?"

"Oh yes, certainly; for I fear he will never recover."

"Poor shadow!" said the princess; "it is very unfortunate for him; it would really be a good deed to free him from his frail existence; and, indeed, when I think how often people take the part of the lower class against the higher, in these days, it would be policy to put him out of the way quietly."

"It is certainly rather hard upon him, for he was a faithful servant," said the shadow; and he pretended to sigh.

"Yours is a noble character," said the princess, and bowed herself before him.

In the evening the whole town was illuminated, and cannons fired "boom," and the soldiers presented arms. It was indeed a grand wedding. The princess and the shadow stepped out on the balcony to show themselves, and to receive one cheer more. But the learned man heard nothing of all these festivities, for he had already been executed.

The Sunbeam and the Captive

IT IS AUTUMN. We stand on the ramparts, and look out over the sea. We look at the numerous ships, and at the Swedish coast on the opposite side of the sound, rising far above the surface of the waters which mirror the glow of the evening sky. Behind us the wood is sharply defined; mighty trees surround us, and the yellow leaves flutter down from the branches. Below, at the foot of the wall, stands a gloomy looking building enclosed in palisades. The space between is dark and narrow, but still more dismal must it be behind the iron gratings in the wall which cover the narrow loopholes or windows, for in these dungeons the most depraved of the criminals are confined. A ray of the setting sun shoots into the bare cells of one of the captives, for God's sun shines upon the evil and the good. The hardened criminal casts an impatient look at the bright ray. Then a little bird flies towards the grating, for birds twitter to the just as well as to the unjust. He only cries, "Tweet, tweet," and then perches himself near the grating, flutters his wings, pecks a feather from one of them, puffs himself out, and sets his feathers on end round his breast and throat. The bad, chained man looks at him, and a more gentle expression comes into his hard face. In his breast there rises a thought which he himself cannot rightly analyze, but the thought has some connection with the sunbeam, with the bird, and with the scent of violets, which grow luxuriantly in spring at the foot of the wall. Then there comes the sound of the hunter's horn, merry and full. The little bird starts, and flies away, the sunbeam gradually vanishes, and again there is darkness in the room and in the heart of that bad man. Still the sun has shone into that heart, and the twittering of the bird has touched it.

Sound on, ye glorious strains of the hunter's horn; continue your stirring tones, for the evening is mild, and the surface of the sea, heaving slowly and calmly, is smooth as a mirror.

Little Wonders

Little Tiny

THERE WAS ONCE a woman who wished very much to have a little child, but she could not obtain her wish. At last she went to a fairy, and said, "I should so very much like to have a little child; can you tell me where I can find one?"

"Oh, that can be easily managed," said the fairy. "Here is a barleycorn of a different kind to those which grow in the farmer's fields, and which the chickens eat; put it into a flower-pot, and see what will happen."

"Thank you," said the woman, and she gave the fairy twelve shillings, which was the price of the barleycorn. Then she went home and planted it, and immediately there grew up a large handsome flower, something like a tulip in appearance, but with its leaves tightly closed as if it were still a bud. "It is a beautiful flower," said the woman, and she kissed the red and golden-colored leaves, and while she did so the flower opened, and she could see that it was a real tulip. Within the flower, upon the green velvet stamens, sat a very delicate and graceful little maiden. She was scarcely half as long as a thumb, and they gave her the name of "Thumbelina," or Tiny, because she was so small. A walnut-shell, elegantly polished, served her for a cradle; her bed was formed of blue violet-leaves, with a rose-leaf for a counterpane. Here she slept at night, but during the day she amused herself on a table, where the woman had placed a plateful of water. Round this plate were wreaths of flowers with their stems in the water, and upon it floated a large tulip-leaf, which served Tiny for a boat. Here the little maiden sat and rowed herself from side to side, with two oars made of white horse-hair. It really was a very pretty sight. Tiny could, also, sing so softly and sweetly that nothing like her singing had ever before been heard. One night, while she lay in her pretty bed, a large, ugly, wet toad crept through a broken pane of glass in the window, and leaped right upon the table where Tiny lay sleeping under her rose-leaf quilt. "What a pretty little wife this would make for my son," said the toad, and she took up the walnut-shell in which little Tiny lay asleep, and jumped through the window with it into the garden.

In the swampy margin of a broad stream in the garden lived the toad, with her son. He was uglier even than his mother, and when he saw the pretty little maiden in her elegant bed, he could only cry, "Croak, croak, croak."

"Don't speak so loud, or she will wake," said the toad, "and then she might run away, for she is as light as swan's down. We will place her on one of the water-lily leaves out in the stream; it will be like an island to her, she is so light and small, and then she cannot escape; and, while she is away, we will make haste and prepare the state-room under the marsh, in which you are to live when you are married."

Far out in the stream grew a number of water-lilies, with broad green leaves, which seemed to float on the top of the water. The largest of these leaves appeared farther off than the rest, and the old toad swam out to it with the walnut-shell, in which little Tiny lay still asleep. The tiny little creature woke very early in the morning, and began to cry bitterly when she found where she was, for she could see nothing but water on every side of the large green leaf, and no way of reaching the land. Meanwhile the old toad was very busy under the marsh, decking her room with rushes and wild yellow flowers, to make it look pretty for her new daughter-in-law. Then she swam out with her ugly son to the leaf on which she had placed poor little Tiny. She wanted to fetch the pretty bed, that she might put it in the bridal chamber to be ready for her. The old toad bowed low to her in the water, and said, "Here is my son, he will be your husband, and you will live happily in the marsh by the stream."

"Croak, croak, croak," was all her son could say for himself; so the toad took up the elegant little bed, and swam away with it, leaving Tiny all alone on the green leaf, where she sat and wept. She could not bear to think of living with the old toad, and having her ugly son for a husband. The little fishes, who swam about in the water beneath, had seen the toad, and heard what she said, so they lifted their heads above the water to look at the little maiden. As soon as they caught sight of her, they saw she was very pretty, and it made them very sorry to think that she must go and live with the ugly toads. "No, it must never be!" so they assembled together in the water, round the green stalk which held the leaf on which the little maiden stood, and gnawed it away at the root with their teeth. Then the leaf floated down the stream, carrying Tiny far away out of reach of land.

Tiny sailed past many towns, and the little birds in the bushes saw her, and sang, "What a lovely little creature;" so the leaf swam away with her farther and farther, till it brought her to other lands. A graceful little white butterfly constantly fluttered round her, and at last alighted on the leaf. Tiny pleased him, and she was glad of it, for now the toad could not possibly reach her, and the country through which she sailed was beautiful, and the sun shone upon the water, till it glittered like liquid gold. She took off her girdle and tied one end of it round the butterfly, and the other end of the ribbon she fastened to the leaf, which now glided on much faster than ever, taking little Tiny with it as she stood. Presently a large cockchafer flew by; the moment he caught sight of her, he seized her round her delicate waist with his claws, and flew with her into a tree. The green leaf floated away on the brook, and the butterfly flew with it, for he was fastened to it, and could not get away.

Oh, how frightened little Tiny felt when the cockchafer flew with her to the tree! But especially was she sorry for the beautiful white butterfly which she had fastened to the leaf, for if he could not free himself he would die of hunger. But the cockchafer did not trouble himself at all about the matter. He seated himself by her side on a large green leaf, gave her some honey from the flowers to eat, and told her she was very pretty, though not in the least like a cockchafer. After a time, all the cockchafers turned up their feelers, and said, "She has only two legs! how ugly that looks." "She has no feelers," said another. "Her waist is quite slim. Pooh! she is like a human being."

"Oh! she is ugly," said all the lady cockchafers, although Tiny was very pretty. Then the cockchafer who had run away with her, believed all the others when they said she was ugly, and would have nothing more to say to her, and told her she might go where she liked. Then he flew down with her from the tree, and placed her on a daisy, and she wept at the thought that she was so ugly that even the cockchafers would have nothing to say to her. And all the while she was really the loveliest creature that one could imagine, and as tender and delicate as a beautiful rose-leaf. During the whole summer poor little Tiny lived quite alone in the wide forest. She wove herself a bed with blades of grass, and hung it up under a broad leaf, to protect herself from the rain. She sucked the honey from the flowers for food, and drank the dew from their leaves every morning. So passed away the summer and the autumn, and then came the winter, – the long, cold winter. All the birds who had sung to her so sweetly were flown away, and the trees and the flowers had withered. The large clover leaf under the shelter of which she had lived, was now rolled together and shrivelled up, nothing remained but a yellow withered stalk. She felt dreadfully cold, for her clothes were torn, and she was herself so frail and delicate, that poor little Tiny was nearly frozen to death. It began to snow too; and the snow-flakes, as they fell upon her, were like a whole shovelful falling upon one of us, for we are tall, but she was only an inch high. Then she wrapped herself up in a dry leaf, but it cracked in the middle and could not keep her warm, and she shivered with cold. Near the wood in which she had been living lay a corn-field, but the corn had been cut a long time; nothing remained but the bare dry stubble standing up out of the frozen ground. It was to her like struggling through a large wood. Oh! how she shivered with the cold. She came at last to the door of a field-mouse, who had a little den under the corn-stubble. There dwelt the field-mouse in warmth and comfort, with a whole roomful of corn, a kitchen, and a beautiful dining room. Poor little Tiny stood before the door just like a little beggar-girl, and begged for a small piece of barley-corn, for she had been without a morsel to eat for two days.

"You poor little creature," said the field-mouse, who was really a good old field-mouse, "come into my warm room and dine with me." She was very pleased with Tiny, so she said, "You are quite welcome to stay with me all the winter, if you like; but you must keep my rooms clean and neat, and tell me stories, for I shall like to hear them very much." And Tiny did all the field-mouse asked her, and found herself very comfortable.

"We shall have a visitor soon," said the field-mouse one day; "my neighbor pays me a visit once a week. He is better off than I am; he has large rooms, and wears a beautiful black velvet coat. If you could only have him for a husband, you would be well provided for indeed. But he is blind, so you must tell him some of your prettiest stories."

But Tiny did not feel at all interested about this neighbor, for he was a mole. However, he came and paid his visit dressed in his black velvet coat.

"He is very rich and learned, and his house is twenty times larger than mine," said the field-mouse.

He was rich and learned, no doubt, but he always spoke slightingly of the sun and the pretty flowers, because he had never seen them. Tiny was obliged to sing to him, "Lady-bird, lady-bird, fly away home," and many other pretty songs. And the mole fell in love with her because she had such a sweet voice; but he said nothing yet, for he was very cautious. A short time before, the mole had dug a long passage under the earth, which led from the dwelling of the field-mouse to his own, and here she had permission to walk with Tiny whenever she liked. But he warned them not to be alarmed at the sight of a dead bird which lay in the passage. It was a perfect bird, with a beak and feathers, and could not have been dead long, and was lying just where the mole had made his passage. The mole took a piece of phosphorescent wood in his mouth, and it glittered like fire in the dark; then he went before them to light them through the long, dark passage. When they came to the spot where lay the dead bird, the mole pushed his broad nose through the ceiling, the earth gave way, so that there was a large hole, and the daylight shone into the passage. In the middle of the floor lay a dead swallow, his beautiful wings pulled close to his sides, his feet and his head drawn up under his feathers; the poor bird had evidently died of the cold. It made little Tiny very sad to see it, she did so love the little birds; all the summer they had sung and twittered for her so beautifully. But the mole pushed it aside with his crooked legs, and said, "He will sing no more now. How miserable it must be to be born a little bird! I am thankful that none of my children will ever be birds, for they can do nothing but cry, 'Tweet, tweet,' and always die of hunger in the winter."

"Yes, you may well say that, as a clever man!" exclaimed the field-mouse, "What is the use of his twittering, for when winter comes he must either starve or be frozen to death. Still birds are very high bred."

Tiny said nothing; but when the two others had turned their backs on the bird, she stooped down and stroked aside the soft feathers which covered the head, and kissed the closed eyelids. "Perhaps this was the one who sang to me so sweetly in the summer," she said; "and how much pleasure it gave me, you dear, pretty bird."

The mole now stopped up the hole through which the daylight shone, and then accompanied the lady home. But during the night Tiny could not sleep; so she got out of bed and wove a large, beautiful carpet of hay; then she carried it to the dead bird, and spread it over him; with some down from the flowers which she had found in the field-mouse's room. It was as soft as wool, and she spread some of it on each side of the bird, so that he might lie warmly in the cold earth. "Farewell, you pretty little bird," said she, "farewell; thank you for your delightful singing during the summer, when all the trees were green, and the warm sun shone upon us." Then she laid her head on the bird's breast, but she was alarmed immediately, for it seemed as if something inside the bird went "thump, thump." It was the bird's heart; he was not really dead, only benumbed with the cold, and the warmth had restored him to life. In autumn, all the swallows fly away into warm countries, but if one happens to linger, the cold seizes it, it becomes frozen, and falls down as if dead; it remains where it fell, and the cold snow covers it. Tiny trembled very much; she was quite frightened, for the bird was large, a great deal larger than herself, – she was only an inch high. But she took courage, laid the wool more thickly over the poor swallow, and then took a leaf which she had used for her own counterpane, and laid it over the head of the poor bird. The next morning she again stole out to see him. He was alive but very weak; he could only open his eyes for a moment to look at Tiny, who stood by holding a piece of decayed wood in her hand, for she had no other lantern. "Thank you, pretty little maiden," said the sick swallow; "I have been so nicely warmed, that I shall soon regain my strength, and be able to fly about again in the warm sunshine."

"Oh," said she, "it is cold out of doors now; it snows and freezes. Stay in your warm bed; I will take care of you."

Then she brought the swallow some water in a flower-leaf, and after he had drank, he told her that he had wounded one of his wings in a thorn-bush, and could not fly as fast as the others, who were soon far away on their journey to warm countries. Then at last he had fallen to the earth, and could remember no more, nor how he came to be where she had found him. The whole winter the swallow remained underground, and Tiny nursed him with care and love. Neither the mole nor the field-mouse knew anything about it, for they did not like swallows. Very soon the spring time came, and the sun warmed the earth. Then the swallow bade farewell to Tiny, and she opened the hole in the ceiling which the mole had made. The sun shone in upon them so beautifully, that the swallow asked her if she would go with him; she could sit on his back, he said, and he would fly away with her into the green woods. But Tiny knew it would make the field-mouse very grieved if she left her in that manner, so she said, "No, I cannot."

"Farewell, then, farewell, you good, pretty little maiden," said the swallow; and he flew out into the sunshine.

Tiny looked after him, and the tears rose in her eyes. She was very fond of the poor swallow.

"Tweet, tweet," sang the bird, as he flew out into the green woods, and Tiny felt very sad. She was not allowed to go out into the warm sunshine. The corn which had been sown in the field over the house of the field-mouse had grown up high into the air, and formed a thick wood to Tiny, who was only an inch in height.

"You are going to be married, Tiny," said the field-mouse. "My neighbor has asked for you. What good fortune for a poor child like you. Now we will prepare your wedding clothes. They must be both woollen and linen. Nothing must be wanting when you are the mole's wife."

Tiny had to turn the spindle, and the field-mouse hired four spiders, who were to weave day and night. Every evening the mole visited her, and was continually speaking of the time when the summer would be over. Then he would keep his wedding-day with Tiny; but now the heat of the sun was so great that it burned the earth, and made it quite hard, like a stone. As soon, as the summer was over, the wedding should take place. But Tiny was not at all pleased; for she did not like the tiresome mole. Every morning when the sun rose, and every evening when it went down, she would creep out at the door, and as the wind blew aside the ears of corn, so that she could see the blue sky, she thought how beautiful and bright it seemed out there, and wished so much to see her dear swallow again. But he never returned; for by this time he had flown far away into the lovely green forest.

When autumn arrived, Tiny had her outfit quite ready; and the field-mouse said to her, "In four weeks the wedding must take place."

Then Tiny wept, and said she would not marry the disagreeable mole.

"Nonsense," replied the field-mouse. "Now don't be obstinate, or I shall bite you with my white teeth. He is a very handsome mole; the queen herself does not wear more beautiful velvets and furs. His kitchen and cellars are quite full. You ought to be very thankful for such good fortune."

So the wedding-day was fixed, on which the mole was to fetch Tiny away to live with him, deep under the earth, and never again to see the warm sun, because he did not like it. The poor child was very unhappy at the thought of saying farewell to the beautiful sun, and as the field-mouse had given her permission to stand at the door, she went to look at it once more.

"Farewell bright sun," she cried, stretching out her arm towards it; and then she walked a short distance from the house; for the corn had been cut, and only the dry stubble remained in the fields. "Farewell, farewell," she repeated, twining her arm round a little red flower that grew just by her side. "Greet the little swallow from me, if you should see him again."

"Tweet, tweet," sounded over her head suddenly. She looked up, and there was the swallow himself flying close by. As soon as he spied Tiny, he was delighted; and then she told him how unwilling she felt to marry the ugly mole, and to live always beneath the earth, and never to see the bright sun any more. And as she told him she wept.

"Cold winter is coming," said the swallow, "and I am going to fly away into warmer countries. Will you go with me? You can sit on my back, and fasten yourself on with your sash. Then we can fly away from the ugly mole and his gloomy rooms, – far away, over the mountains, into warmer countries, where the sun shines more brightly – than here; where it is always summer, and the flowers bloom in greater beauty. Fly now with me, dear little Tiny; you saved my life when I lay frozen in that dark passage."

"Yes, I will go with you," said Tiny; and she seated herself on the bird's back, with her feet on his outstretched wings, and tied her girdle to one of his strongest feathers.

Then the swallow rose in the air, and flew over forest and over sea, high above the highest mountains, covered with eternal snow. Tiny would have been frozen in the cold air, but she crept under the bird's warm feathers, keeping her little head uncovered, so that she might admire the beautiful lands over which they passed. At length they reached the warm countries, where the sun shines brightly, and the sky seems so much higher above the earth. Here, on the hedges, and by the wayside, grew purple, green, and white grapes; lemons and oranges hung from trees in the woods; and the air was fragrant with myrtles and orange blossoms. Beautiful children ran along the country lanes, playing with large gay butterflies; and as the swallow flew farther and farther, every place appeared still more lovely.

At last they came to a blue lake, and by the side of it, shaded by trees of the deepest green, stood a palace of dazzling white marble, built in the olden times. Vines clustered round its lofty pillars, and at the top were many swallows' nests, and one of these was the home of the swallow who carried Tiny.

"This is my house," said the swallow; "but it would not do for you to live there – you would not be comfortable. You must choose for yourself one of those lovely flowers, and I will put you down upon it, and then you shall have everything that you can wish to make you happy."

"That will be delightful," she said, and clapped her little hands for joy.

A large marble pillar lay on the ground, which, in falling, had been broken into three pieces. Between these pieces grew the most beautiful large white flowers; so the swallow flew down with Tiny, and placed her on one of the broad leaves. But how surprised she was to see in the middle of the flower, a tiny little man, as white and transparent as if he had been made of crystal! He had a gold crown on his head, and delicate wings at his shoulders, and was not much larger than Tiny herself. He was the angel of the flower; for a tiny man and a tiny woman dwell in every flower; and this was the king of them all.

"Oh, how beautiful he is!" whispered Tiny to the swallow.

The little prince was at first quite frightened at the bird, who was like a giant, compared to such a delicate little creature as himself; but when he saw Tiny, he was delighted, and thought her the prettiest little maiden he had ever seen. He took the gold crown from his head, and placed it on hers, and asked her name, and if she would be his wife, and queen over all the flowers.

This certainly was a very different sort of husband to the son of a toad, or the mole, with my black velvet and fur; so she said, "Yes," to the handsome prince. Then all the flowers opened, and out of each came a little lady or a tiny lord, all so pretty it was quite a pleasure to look at them. Each of them brought Tiny a present; but the best gift was a pair of beautiful wings, which had belonged to a large white fly and they fastened them to Tiny's shoulders, so that she might fly from flower to flower. Then there was much rejoicing, and the little swallow who sat above them, in his nest, was asked to sing a wedding song, which he did as well as he could; but in his heart he felt sad for he was very fond of Tiny, and would have liked never to part from her again.

"You must not be called Tiny any more," said the spirit of the flowers to her. "It is an ugly name, and you are so very pretty. We will call you Maia."

"Farewell, farewell," said the swallow, with a heavy heart as he left the warm countries to fly back into Denmark. There he had a nest over the window of a house in which dwelt the writer of fairy tales. The swallow sang, "Tweet, tweet," and from his song came the whole story.

The Ugly Duckling

IT WAS LOVELY summer weather in the country, and the golden corn, the green oats, and the haystacks piled up in the meadows looked beautiful. The stork walking about on his long red legs chattered in the Egyptian language, which he had learnt from his mother. The corn-fields and meadows were surrounded by large forests, in the midst of which were deep pools. It was, indeed, delightful to walk about in the country. In a sunny spot stood a pleasant old farm-house close by a deep river, and from the house down to the water side grew great burdock leaves, so high, that under the tallest of them a little child could stand upright. The spot was as wild as the centre of a thick wood. In this snug retreat sat a duck on her nest, watching for her young brood to hatch; she was beginning to get tired of her task, for the little ones were a long time coming out of their shells, and she seldom had any visitors. The other ducks liked much better to swim about in the river than to climb the slippery banks, and sit under a burdock leaf, to have a gossip with her. At length one shell cracked, and then another, and from each egg came a living creature that lifted its head and cried, "Peep, peep." "Quack, quack," said the mother, and then they all quacked as well as they could, and looked about them on every side at the large green leaves. Their mother allowed them to look as much as they liked, because green is good for the eyes. "How large the world is," said the young ducks, when they found how much more room they now had than while they were inside the egg-shell. "Do you imagine this is the whole world?" asked the mother; "Wait till you have seen the garden; it stretches far beyond that to the parson's field, but I have never ventured to such a distance. Are you all out?" she continued, rising; "No, I declare, the largest egg lies there still. I wonder how long this is to last, I am quite tired of it;" and she seated herself again on the nest.

"Well, how are you getting on?" asked an old duck, who paid her a visit.

"One egg is not hatched yet," said the duck, "it will not break. But just look at all the others, are they not the prettiest little ducklings you ever saw? They are the image of their father, who is so unkind, he never comes to see."

"Let me see the egg that will not break," said the duck; "I have no doubt it is a turkey's egg. I was persuaded to hatch some once, and after all my care and trouble with the young ones, they were afraid of the water. I quacked and clucked, but all to no purpose. I could not get them to venture in. Let me look at the egg. Yes, that is a turkey's egg; take my advice, leave it where it is and teach the other children to swim."

"I think I will sit on it a little while longer," said the duck; "as I have sat so long already, a few days will be nothing."

"Please yourself," said the old duck, and she went away.

At last the large egg broke, and a young one crept forth crying, "Peep, peep." It was very large and ugly. The duck stared at it and exclaimed, "It is very large and not at all like the others. I wonder if it really is a turkey. We shall soon find it out, however when we go to the water. It must go in, if I have to push it myself."

On the next day the weather was delightful, and the sun shone brightly on the green burdock leaves, so the mother duck took her young brood down to the water, and jumped in with a splash. "Quack, quack," cried she, and one after another the little ducklings jumped in. The water closed over their heads, but they came up again in an instant, and swam about quite prettily with their legs paddling under them as easily as possible, and the ugly duckling was also in the water swimming with them.

"Oh," said the mother, "that is not a turkey; how well he uses his legs, and how upright he holds himself! He is my own child, and he is not so very ugly after all if you look at him properly. Quack, quack! come with me now, I will take you into grand society, and introduce you to the farmyard, but you must keep close to me or you may be trodden upon; and, above all, beware of the cat."

When they reached the farmyard, there was a great disturbance, two families were fighting for an eel's head, which, after all, was carried off by the cat. "See, children, that is the way of the world," said the mother duck, whetting her beak, for she would have liked the eel's head herself. "Come, now, use your legs, and let me see how well you can behave. You must bow your heads prettily to that old duck yonder; she is the highest born of them all, and has Spanish blood, therefore, she is well off. Don't you see she has a red flag tied to her leg, which is something very grand, and a great honor for a duck; it shows that every one is anxious not to lose her, as she can be recognized both by man and beast. Come, now, don't turn your toes, a well-bred duckling spreads his feet wide apart, just like his father and mother, in this way; now bend your neck, and say 'quack.'"

The ducklings did as they were bid, but the other duck stared, and said, "Look, here comes another brood, as if there were not enough of us already! and what a queer looking object one of them is; we don't want him here," and then one flew out and bit him in the neck.

"Let him alone," said the mother; "he is not doing any harm."

"Yes, but he is so big and ugly," said the spiteful duck "and therefore he must be turned out."

"The others are very pretty children," said the old duck, with the rag on her leg, "all but that one; I wish his mother could improve him a little."

"That is impossible, your grace," replied the mother; "he is not pretty; but he has a very good disposition, and swims as well or even better than the others. I think he will grow up pretty, and perhaps be smaller; he has remained too long in the egg, and therefore his figure is not properly formed;" and then she stroked his neck and smoothed the feathers, saying, "It is a drake, and therefore not of so much consequence. I think he will grow up strong, and able to take care of himself."

"The other ducklings are graceful enough," said the old duck. "Now make yourself at home, and if you can find an eel's head, you can bring it to me."

And so they made themselves comfortable; but the poor duckling, who had crept out of his shell last of all, and looked so ugly, was bitten and pushed and made fun of, not only by the ducks, but by all the poultry. "He is too big," they all said, and the turkey cock, who had been born into the world with spurs, and fancied himself really an emperor, puffed himself out like a vessel in full sail, and flew at the duckling, and became quite red in the head with passion, so that the poor little thing did not know where to go, and was quite miserable because he was so ugly and laughed at by the whole farmyard. So it went on from day to day till it got worse and worse. The poor duckling was driven about by every one; even his brothers and sisters were unkind to him, and would say, "Ah, you ugly creature, I wish the cat would get you," and his mother said she wished he had never been born. The ducks pecked him, the chickens beat him, and the girl who fed the poultry kicked him with her feet. So at last he ran away, frightening the little birds in the hedge as he flew over the palings.

"They are afraid of me because I am ugly," he said. So he closed his eyes, and flew still farther, until he came out on a large moor, inhabited by wild ducks. Here he remained the whole night, feeling very tired and sorrowful.

In the morning, when the wild ducks rose in the air, they stared at their new comrade. "What sort of a duck are you?" they all said, coming round him.

He bowed to them, and was as polite as he could be, but he did not reply to their question. "You are exceedingly ugly," said the wild ducks, "but that will not matter if you do not want to marry one of our family."

Poor thing! he had no thoughts of marriage; all he wanted was permission to lie among the rushes, and drink some of the water on the moor. After he had been on the moor two days, there came two wild geese, or rather goslings, for they had not been out of the egg long, and were very saucy. "Listen, friend," said one of them to the duckling, "you are so ugly, that we like you very well. Will you go with us, and become a bird of passage? Not far from here is another moor, in which there are some pretty wild geese, all unmarried. It is a chance for you to get a wife; you may be lucky, ugly as you are."

"Pop, pop," sounded in the air, and the two wild geese fell dead among the rushes, and the water was tinged with blood. "Pop, pop," echoed far and wide in the distance, and whole flocks of wild geese rose up from the rushes. The sound continued from every direction, for the sportsmen surrounded the moor, and some were even seated on branches of trees, overlooking the rushes. The blue smoke from the guns rose like clouds over the dark trees, and as it floated away across the water, a number of sporting dogs bounded in among the rushes, which bent beneath them wherever they went. How they terrified the poor duckling! He turned away his head to hide it under his wing, and at the same moment a large terrible dog passed quite near him. His jaws were open, his tongue hung from his mouth, and his eyes glared fearfully. He thrust his nose close to the duckling, showing his sharp teeth, and then, "splash, splash," he went into the water without touching him, "Oh," sighed the duckling, "how thankful I am for being so ugly; even a dog will not bite me." And so he lay quite still, while the shot rattled through the rushes, and gun after gun was fired over him. It was late in the day before all became quiet, but even then the poor young thing did not dare to move. He waited quietly for several hours, and then, after looking carefully around him, hastened away from the moor as fast as he could. He ran over field and meadow till a storm arose, and he could hardly struggle against it. Towards evening, he reached a poor little cottage that seemed ready to fall, and only remained standing because it could not decide on which side to fall first. The storm continued so violent, that the duckling could go no farther; he sat down by the cottage, and then he noticed that the door was not quite closed in consequence of one of the hinges having given way. There was therefore a narrow opening near the bottom large enough for him to slip through, which he did very quietly, and got a shelter for the night. A woman, a tom cat, and a hen lived in this cottage. The tom cat, whom the mistress called, "My little son," was a great favorite; he could raise his back, and purr, and could even throw out sparks from his fur if it were stroked the wrong way. The hen had very short legs, so she was called "Chickie short legs." She laid good eggs, and her mistress loved her as if she had been her own child. In the morning, the strange visitor was discovered, and the tom cat began to purr, and the hen to cluck.

"What is that noise about?" said the old woman, looking round the room, but her sight was not very good; therefore, when she saw the duckling she thought it must be a fat duck, that had strayed from home. "Oh what a prize!" she exclaimed, "I hope it is not a drake, for then I shall have some duck's eggs. I must wait and see." So the duckling was allowed to remain on trial for three weeks, but there were no eggs. Now the tom cat was the master of the house, and the hen was mistress, and they always said, "We and the world," for they believed themselves to be half the world, and the better half too. The duckling thought that others might hold a different opinion on the subject, but the hen would not listen to such doubts. "Can you lay eggs?" she asked. "No." "Then have the goodness to hold your tongue." "Can you raise your back, or purr, or throw out sparks?" said the tom cat. "No." "Then you have no right to express an opinion when sensible people are speaking." So the duckling sat in a corner, feeling very low spirited, till the sunshine and the fresh air came into the room through the open door, and then he began to feel such a great longing for a swim on the water, that he could not help telling the hen.

"What an absurd idea," said the hen. "You have nothing else to do, therefore you have foolish fancies. If you could purr or lay eggs, they would pass away."

"But it is so delightful to swim about on the water," said the duckling, "and so refreshing to feel it close over your head, while you dive down to the bottom."

"Delightful, indeed!" said the hen, "why you must be crazy! Ask the cat, he is the cleverest animal I know, ask him how he would like to swim about on the water, or to dive under it, for I will not speak of my own opinion; ask our mistress, the old woman – there is no one in the world more clever than she is. Do you think she would like to swim, or to let the water close over her head?"

"You don't understand me," said the duckling.

"We don't understand you? Who can understand you, I wonder? Do you consider yourself more clever than the cat, or the old woman? I will say nothing of myself. Don't imagine such nonsense, child, and thank your good fortune that you have been received here. Are you not in a warm room, and in society from which you may learn something. But you are a chatterer, and your company is not very agreeable. Believe me, I speak only for your own good. I may tell you unpleasant truths, but that is a proof of my friendship. I advise you, therefore, to lay eggs, and learn to purr as quickly as possible."

"I believe I must go out into the world again," said the duckling.

"Yes, do," said the hen. So the duckling left the cottage, and soon found water on which it could swim and dive, but was avoided by all other animals, because of its ugly appearance. Autumn came, and the leaves in the forest turned to orange and gold. then, as winter approached, the wind caught them as they fell and whirled them in the cold air. The clouds, heavy with hail and snow-flakes, hung low in the sky, and the raven stood on the ferns crying, "Croak, croak." It made one shiver with cold to look at him. All this was very sad for the poor little duckling. One evening, just as the sun set amid radiant clouds, there came a large flock of beautiful birds out of the bushes. The duckling had never seen any like them before. They were swans, and they curved their graceful necks, while their soft plumage shown with dazzling whiteness. They uttered a singular cry, as they spread their glorious wings and flew away from those cold regions to warmer countries across the sea. As they mounted higher and higher in the air, the ugly little duckling felt quite a strange sensation as he watched them. He whirled himself in the water like a wheel, stretched out his neck towards them, and uttered a cry so strange that it frightened himself. Could he ever forget those beautiful, happy birds; and when at last they were out of his sight, he dived under the water, and rose again almost beside himself with excitement. He knew not the names of these birds, nor where they had flown, but he felt towards them as he had never felt for any other bird in the world. He was not envious of these beautiful creatures, but wished to be as lovely as they. Poor ugly creature, how gladly he would have lived even with the ducks had they only given him encouragement. The winter grew colder and colder; he was obliged to swim about on the water to keep it from freezing, but every night the space on which he swam became smaller and smaller. At length it froze so hard that the ice in the water crackled as he moved, and the duckling had to paddle with his legs as well as he could, to keep the space from closing up. He became exhausted at last, and lay still and helpless, frozen fast in the ice.

Early in the morning, a peasant, who was passing by, saw what had happened. He broke the ice in pieces with his wooden shoe, and carried the duckling home to his wife. The warmth revived the poor little creature; but when the children wanted to play with him, the duckling thought they would do him some harm; so he started up in terror, fluttered into the milk-pan, and splashed the milk about the room. Then the woman clapped her hands, which frightened him still more. He flew first into the butter-cask, then into the meal-tub, and out again. What a condition he was in! The woman screamed, and struck at him with the tongs; the children laughed and screamed, and tumbled over each other, in their efforts to catch him; but luckily he escaped. The door stood open; the poor creature could just manage to slip out among the bushes, and lie down quite exhausted in the newly fallen snow.

It would be very sad, were I to relate all the misery and privations which the poor little duckling endured during the hard winter; but when it had passed, he found himself lying one morning in a moor, amongst the rushes. He felt the warm sun shining, and heard the lark singing, and saw that all around was beautiful spring. Then the young bird felt that his wings were strong, as he flapped them against his sides, and rose high into the air. They bore him onwards, until he found himself in a large garden, before he well knew how it had happened. The apple-trees were in full blossom, and the fragrant elders bent their long green branches down to the stream which wound round a smooth lawn. Everything looked beautiful, in the freshness of early spring. From a thicket close by came three beautiful white swans, rustling their feathers, and swimming lightly over the smooth water. The duckling remembered the lovely birds, and felt more strangely unhappy than ever.

"I will fly to those royal birds," he exclaimed, "and they will kill me, because I am so ugly, and dare to approach them; but it does not matter: better be killed by them than pecked by the ducks, beaten by the hens, pushed about by the maiden who feeds the poultry, or starved with hunger in the winter."

Then he flew to the water, and swam towards the beautiful swans. The moment they espied the stranger, they rushed to meet him with outstretched wings.

"Kill me," said the poor bird; and he bent his head down to the surface of the water, and awaited death.

But what did he see in the clear stream below? His own image; no longer a dark, gray bird, ugly and disagreeable to look at, but a graceful and beautiful swan. To be born in a duck's nest, in a farmyard, is of no consequence to a bird, if it is hatched from a swan's egg. He now felt glad at having suffered sorrow and trouble, because it enabled him to enjoy so much better all the pleasure and happiness around him; for the great swans swam round the new-comer, and stroked his neck with their beaks, as a welcome.

Into the garden presently came some little children, and threw bread and cake into the water.

"See," cried the youngest, "there is a new one;" and the rest were delighted, and ran to their father and mother, dancing and clapping their hands, and shouting joyously, "There is another swan come; a new one has arrived."

Then they threw more bread and cake into the water, and said, "The new one is the most beautiful of all; he is so young and pretty." And the old swans bowed their heads before him.

Then he felt quite ashamed, and hid his head under his wing; for he did not know what to do, he was so happy, and yet not at all proud. He had been persecuted and despised for his ugliness, and now he heard them say he was the most beautiful of all the birds. Even the elder-tree bent down its bows into the water before him, and the sun shone warm and bright. Then he rustled his feathers, curved his slender neck, and cried joyfully, from the depths of his heart, "I never dreamed of such happiness as this, while I was an ugly duckling."

Little Ida's Flowers

"MY POOR FLOWERS are quite dead," said little Ida, "they were so pretty yesterday evening, and now all the leaves are hanging down quite withered. What do they do that for," she asked, of the student who sat on the sofa; she liked him very much, he could tell the most amusing stories, and cut out the prettiest pictures; hearts, and ladies dancing, castles with doors that opened, as well as flowers; he was a delightful student. "Why do the flowers look so faded to-day?" she asked again, and pointed to her nosegay, which was quite withered.

"Don't you know what is the matter with them?" said the student. "The flowers were at a ball last night, and therefore, it is no wonder they hang their heads."

"But flowers cannot dance?" cried little Ida.

"Yes indeed, they can," replied the student. "When it grows dark, and everybody is asleep, they jump about quite merrily. They have a ball almost every night."

"Can children go to these balls?"

"Yes," said the student, "little daisies and lilies of the valley."

"Where do the beautiful flowers dance?" asked little Ida.

"Have you not often seen the large castle outside the gates of the town, where the king lives in summer, and where the beautiful garden is full of flowers? And have you not fed the swans with bread when they swam towards you? Well, the flowers have capital balls there, believe me."

"I was in the garden out there yesterday with my mother," said Ida, "but all the leaves were off the trees, and there was not a single flower left. Where are they? I used to see so many in the summer."

"They are in the castle," replied the student. "You must know that as soon as the king and all the court are gone into the town, the flowers run out of the garden into the castle, and you should see how merry they are. The two most beautiful roses seat themselves on the throne, and are called the king and queen, then all the red cockscombs range themselves on each side, and bow, these are the lords-in-waiting. After that the pretty flowers come in, and there is a grand ball. The blue violets represent little naval cadets, and dance with hyacinths and crocuses which they call young ladies. The tulips and tiger-lilies are the old ladies who sit and watch the dancing, so that everything may be conducted with order and propriety."

"But," said little Ida, "is there no one there to hurt the flowers for dancing in the king's castle?"

"No one knows anything about it," said the student. "The old steward of the castle, who has to watch there at night, sometimes comes in; but he carries a great bunch of keys, and as soon as the flowers hear the keys rattle, they run and hide themselves behind the long curtains, and stand quite still, just peeping their heads out. Then the old steward says, 'I smell flowers here,' but he cannot see them."

"Oh how capital," said little Ida, clapping her hands. "Should I be able to see these flowers?"

"Yes," said the student, "mind you think of it the next time you go out, no doubt you will see them, if you peep through the window. I did so to-day, and I saw a long yellow lily lying stretched out on the sofa. She was a court lady."

"Can the flowers from the Botanical Gardens go to these balls?" asked Ida. "It is such a distance!"

"Oh yes," said the student "whenever they like, for they can fly. Have you not seen those beautiful red, white. and yellow butterflies, that look like flowers? They were flowers once. They have flown off their stalks into the air, and flap their leaves as if they were little wings to make them fly. Then, if they behave well, they obtain permission to fly about during the day, instead of being obliged to sit still on their stems at home, and so in time their leaves become real wings. It may be, however, that the flowers in the Botanical Gardens have never been to the king's palace, and, therefore, they know nothing of the merry doings at night, which take place there. I will tell you what to do, and the botanical professor, who lives close by here, will be so surprised. You know him very well, do you not? Well, next time you go into his garden, you must tell one of the flowers that there is going to be a grand ball at the castle, then that flower will tell all the others, and they will fly away to the castle as soon as possible. And when the professor walks into his garden, there will not be a single flower left. How he will wonder what has become of them!"

"But how can one flower tell another? Flowers cannot speak?"

"No, certainly not," replied the student; "but they can make signs. Have you not often seen that when the wind blows they nod at one another, and rustle all their green leaves?"

"Can the professor understand the signs?" asked Ida.

"Yes, to be sure he can. He went one morning into his garden, and saw a stinging nettle making signs with its leaves to a beautiful red carnation. It was saying, 'You are so pretty, I like you very much.' But the professor did not approve of such nonsense, so he clapped his hands on the nettle to stop it. Then the leaves, which are its fingers, stung him so sharply that he has never ventured to touch a nettle since."

"Oh how funny!" said Ida, and she laughed.

"How can anyone put such notions into a child's head?" said a tiresome lawyer, who had come to pay a visit, and sat on the sofa. He did not like the student, and would grumble when he saw him cutting out droll or amusing pictures. Sometimes it would be a man hanging on a gibbet and holding a heart in his hand as if he had been stealing hearts. Sometimes it was an old witch riding through the air on a broom and carrying her husband on her nose. But the lawyer did not like such jokes, and he would say as he had just said, "How can anyone put such nonsense into a child's head! what absurd fancies there are!"

But to little Ida, all these stories which the student told her about the flowers, seemed very droll, and she thought over them a great deal. The flowers did hang their heads, because they had been dancing all night, and were very tired, and most likely they were ill. Then she took them into the room where a number of toys lay on a pretty little table, and the whole of the table drawer besides was full of beautiful things. Her doll Sophy lay in the doll's bed asleep, and little Ida said to her, "You must really get up Sophy, and be content to lie in the drawer to-night; the poor flowers are ill, and they must lie in your bed, then perhaps they will get well again." So she took the doll out, who looked quite cross, and said not a single word, for she was angry at being turned out of her bed. Ida placed the flowers in the doll's bed, and drew the quilt over them. Then she told them to lie quite still and be good, while she made some tea for them, so that they might be quite well and able to get up the next morning. And she drew the curtains close round the little bed, so that the sun might not shine in their eyes. During the whole evening she could not help thinking of what the student had told her. And before she went to bed herself, she was obliged to peep behind the curtains into the garden where all her mother's beautiful flowers grew, hyacinths and tulips, and many others. Then she whispered to them quite softly, "I know you are going to a ball to-night." But the flowers appeared as if they did not understand, and not a leaf moved; still Ida felt quite sure she knew all about it. She lay awake a long time after she was in bed, thinking how pretty it must be to see all the beautiful flowers dancing in the king's garden. "I wonder if my flowers have really been there," she said to herself, and then she fell asleep. In the night she awoke; she had been dreaming of the flowers and of the student, as well as of the tiresome lawyer who found fault with him. It was quite still in Ida's bedroom; the night-lamp burnt on the table, and her father and mother were asleep. "I wonder if my flowers are still lying in Sophy's bed," she thought to herself; "how much I should like to know." She raised herself a little, and glanced at the door of the room where all her flowers and playthings lay; it was partly open, and as she listened, it seemed as if some one in the room was playing the piano, but softly and more prettily than she had ever before heard it. "Now all the flowers are certainly dancing in there," she thought, "oh how much I should like to see them," but she did not dare move for fear of disturbing her father and mother. "If they would only come in here," she thought; but they did not come, and the music continued to play so beautifully, and was so pretty, that she could resist no longer. She crept out of her little bed, went softly to the door and looked into the room. Oh what a splendid sight there was to be sure! There was no night-lamp burning, but the room appeared quite light, for the moon shone through the window upon the floor, and made it almost like day. All the hyacinths and tulips stood in two long rows down the room, not a single flower remained in the window, and the flower-pots were all empty. The flowers were dancing gracefully on the floor, making turns and holding each other by their long green leaves as they swung round. At the piano sat a large yellow lily which little Ida was sure she had seen in the summer, for she remembered the student saying she was very much like Miss Lina, one of Ida's friends. They all laughed at him then, but now it seemed to little Ida as if the tall, yellow flower was really like the young lady. She had just the same manners while playing, bending her long yellow face from side to side, and nodding in time to the beautiful music. Then she saw a large purple crocus jump into the middle of the table where the playthings stood, go up to the doll's bedstead and draw back the curtains; there lay the sick flowers, but they got up directly, and nodded to the others as a sign that they wished to dance with them. The old rough doll, with the broken mouth, stood up and bowed to the pretty flowers. They did not look ill at all now, but jumped about and were very merry, yet none of them noticed little Ida. Presently it seemed as if something fell from the table. Ida looked that way, and saw a slight carnival rod jumping down among the flowers as if it belonged to them; it was, however, very smooth and neat, and a little wax doll with a broad brimmed hat on her head, like the one worn by the lawyer, sat upon it. The carnival rod hopped about among the flowers on its three red stilted feet, and stamped quite loud when it danced the Mazurka; the flowers could not perform this dance, they were too light to stamp in that manner. All at once the wax doll which rode on the carnival rod seemed to grow larger and taller, and it turned round and said to the paper flowers, "How can you put such things in a child's head? they are all foolish fancies;" and then the doll was exactly like the lawyer with the broad brimmed hat, and looked as yellow and as cross as he did; but the paper dolls struck him on his thin legs, and he shrunk up again and became quite a little wax doll. This was very amusing, and Ida could not help laughing. The carnival rod went on dancing, and the lawyer was obliged to dance also. It was no use, he might make himself great and tall, or remain a little wax doll with a large black hat; still he must dance. Then at last the other flowers interceded for him, especially those who had lain in the doll's bed, and the carnival rod gave up his dancing. At the same moment a loud knocking was heard in the drawer, where Ida's doll Sophy lay with many other toys. Then the rough doll ran to the end of the table, laid himself flat down upon it, and began to pull the drawer out a little way.

Then Sophy raised himself, and looked round quite astonished, "There must be a ball here to-night," said Sophy. "Why did not somebody tell me?"

"Will you dance with me?" said the rough doll.

"You are the right sort to dance with, certainly," said she, turning her back upon him.

Then she seated herself on the edge of the drawer, and thought that perhaps one of the flowers would ask her to dance; but none of them came. Then she coughed, "Hem, hem, a-hem;" but for all that not one came. The shabby doll now danced quite alone, and not very badly, after all. As none of the flowers seemed to notice Sophy, she let herself down from the drawer to the floor, so as to make a very great noise. All the flowers came round her directly, and asked if she had hurt herself, especially those who had lain in her bed. But she was not hurt at all, and Ida's flowers thanked her for the use of the nice bed, and were very kind to her. They led her into the middle of the room, where the moon shone, and danced with her, while all the other flowers formed a circle round them. Then Sophy was very happy, and said they might keep her bed; she did not mind lying in the drawer at all. But the flowers thanked her very much, and said, –

"We cannot live long. To-morrow morning we shall be quite dead; and you must tell little Ida to bury us in the garden, near to the grave of the canary; then, in the summer we shall wake up and be more beautiful than ever."

"No, you must not die," said Sophy, as she kissed the flowers.

Then the door of the room opened, and a number of beautiful flowers danced in. Ida could not imagine where they could come from, unless they were the flowers from the king's garden. First came two lovely roses, with little golden crowns on their heads; these were the king and queen. Beautiful stocks and carnations followed, bowing to every one present. They had also music with them. Large poppies and peonies had pea-shells for instruments, and blew into them till they were quite red in the face. The bunches of blue hyacinths and the little white snowdrops jingled their bell-like flowers, as if they were real bells. Then came many more flowers: blue violets, purple heart's-ease, daisies, and lilies of the valley, and they all danced together, and kissed each other. It was very beautiful to behold.

At last the flowers wished each other good-night. Then little Ida crept back into her bed again, and dreamt of all she had seen. When she arose the next morning, she went quickly to the little table, to see if the flowers were still there. She drew aside the curtains of the little bed. There they all lay, but quite faded; much more so than the day before. Sophy was lying in the drawer where Ida had placed her; but she looked very sleepy.

"Do you remember what the flowers told you to say to me?" said little Ida. But Sophy looked quite stupid, and said not a single word.

"You are not kind at all," said Ida; "and yet they all danced with you."

Then she took a little paper box, on which were painted beautiful birds, and laid the dead flowers in it.

"This shall be your pretty coffin," she said; "and by and by, when my cousins come to visit me, they shall help me to bury you out in the garden; so that next summer you may grow up again more beautiful than ever."

Her cousins were two good-tempered boys, whose names were James and Adolphus. Their father had given them each a bow and arrow, and they had brought them to show Ida. She told them about the poor flowers which were dead; and as soon as they obtained permission, they went with her to bury them. The two boys walked first, with their crossbows on their shoulders, and little Ida followed, carrying the pretty box containing the dead flowers. They dug a little grave in the garden. Ida kissed her flowers and then laid them, with the box, in the earth. James and Adolphus then fired their crossbows over the grave, as they had neither guns nor cannons.

The Old House

A VERY OLD house stood once in a street with several that were quite new and clean. The date of its erection had been carved on one of the beams, and surrounded by scrolls formed of tulips and hop-tendrils; by this date it could be seen that the old house was nearly three hundred years old. Verses too were written over the windows in old-fashioned letters, and grotesque faces, curiously carved, grinned at you from under the cornices. One story projected a long way over the other, and under the roof ran a leaden gutter, with a dragon's head at the end. The rain was intended to pour out at the dragon's mouth, but it ran out of his body instead, for there was a hole in the gutter. The other houses in the street were new and well built, with large window panes and smooth walls. Any one could see they had nothing to do with the old house. Perhaps they thought, "How long will that heap of rubbish remain here to be a disgrace to the whole street. The parapet projects so far forward that no one can see out of our windows what is going on in that direction. The stairs are as broad as the staircase of a castle, and as steep as if they led to a church-tower. The iron railing looks like the gate of a cemetery, and there are brass knobs upon it. It is really too ridiculous."

Opposite to the old house were more nice new houses, which had just the same opinion as their neighbors.

At the window of one of them sat a little boy with fresh rosy cheeks, and clear sparkling eyes, who was very fond of the old house, in sunshine or in moonlight. He would sit and look at the wall from which the plaster had in some places fallen off, and fancy all sorts of scenes which had been in former times. How the street must have looked when the houses had all gable roofs, open staircases, and gutters with dragons at the spout. He could even see soldiers walking about with halberds. Certainly it was a very good house to look at for amusement.

An old man lived in it, who wore knee-breeches, a coat with large brass buttons, and a wig, which any one could see was a real wig. Every morning an old man came to clean the rooms, and to wait upon him, otherwise the old man in the knee-breeches would have been quite alone in the house. Sometimes he came to one of the windows and looked out; then the little boy nodded to him, and the old man nodded back again, till they became acquainted, and were friends, although they had never spoken to each other; but that was of no consequence.

The little boy one day heard his parents say, "The old man opposite is very well off, but is terribly lonely." The next Sunday morning the little boy wrapped something in a piece of paper and took it to the door of the old house, and said to the attendant who waited upon the old man, "Will you please give this from me to the gentleman who lives here; I have two tin soldiers, and this is one of them, and he shall have it, because I know he is terribly lonely."

And the old attendant nodded and looked very pleased, and then he carried the tin soldier into the house.

Afterwards he was sent over to ask the little boy if he would not like to pay a visit himself. His parents gave him permission, and so it was that he gained admission to the old house.

The brassy knobs on the railings shone more brightly than ever, as if they had been polished on account of his visit; and on the door were carved trumpeters standing in tulips, and it seemed as if they were blowing with all their might, their cheeks were so puffed out. "Tanta-ra-ra, the little boy is coming; Tanta-ra-ra, the little boy is coming."

Then the door opened. All round the hall hung old portraits of knights in armor, and ladies in silk gowns; and the armor rattled, and the silk dresses rustled. Then came a staircase which went up a long way, and then came down a little way and led to a balcony, which was in a very ruinous state. There were large holes and long cracks, out of which grew grass and leaves, indeed the whole balcony, the courtyard, and the walls were so overgrown with green that they looked like a garden. In the balcony stood flower-pots, on which were heads having asses' ears, but the flowers in them grew just as they pleased. In one pot pinks were growing all over the sides, at least the green leaves were shooting forth stalk and stem, and saying as plainly as they could speak, "The air has fanned me, the sun has kissed me, and I am promised a little flower for next Sunday – really for next Sunday."

Then they entered a room in which the walls were covered with leather, and the leather had golden flowers stamped upon it.

> "Gilding will fade in damp weather,
> To endure, there is nothing like leather,"

said the walls. Chairs handsomely carved, with elbows on each side, and with very high backs, stood in the room, and as they creaked they seemed to say, "Sit down. Oh dear, how I am creaking. I shall certainly have the gout like the old cupboard. Gout in my back, ugh."

And then the little boy entered the room where the old man sat.

"Thank you for the tin soldier my little friend," said the old man, "and thank you also for coming to see me."

"Thanks, thanks," or "Creak, creak," said all the furniture.

There was so much that the pieces of furniture stood in each other's way to get a sight of the little boy.

On the wall near the centre of the room hung the picture of a beautiful lady, young and gay, dressed in the fashion of the olden times, with powdered hair, and a full, stiff skirt. She said neither "thanks" nor "creak," but she looked down upon the little boy with her mild eyes; and then he said to the old man,

"Where did you get that picture?"

"From the shop opposite," he replied. "Many portraits hang there that none seem to trouble themselves about. The persons they represent have been dead and buried long since. But I knew this lady many years ago, and she has been dead nearly half a century."

Under a glass beneath the picture hung a nosegay of withered flowers, which were no doubt half a century old too, at least they appeared so.

And the pendulum of the old clock went to and fro, and the hands turned round; and as time passed on, everything in the room grew older, but no one seemed to notice it.

"They say at home," said the little boy, "that you are very lonely."

"Oh," replied the old man, "I have pleasant thoughts of all that has passed, recalled by memory; and now you are come to visit me, and that is very pleasant."

Then he took from the book-case, a book full of pictures representing long processions of wonderful coaches, such as are never seen at the present time. Soldiers like the knave of clubs, and citizens with waving banners. The tailors had a flag with a pair of scissors supported by two lions, and on the shoemakers' flag there were not boots, but an eagle with two heads, for the shoemakers must have everything arranged so that they can say, "This is a pair." What a picture-book it was; and then the old man went into another room to fetch apples and nuts. It was very pleasant, certainly, to be in that old house.

"I cannot endure it," said the tin soldier, who stood on a shelf, "it is so lonely and dull here. I have been accustomed to live in a family, and I cannot get used to this life. I cannot bear it. The whole day is long enough, but the evening is longer. It is not here like it was in your house opposite, when your father and mother talked so cheerfully together, while you and all the dear children made such a delightful noise. No, it is all lonely in the old man's house. Do you think he gets any kisses? Do you think he ever has friendly looks, or a Christmas tree? He will have nothing now but the grave. Oh, I cannot bear it."

"You must not look only on the sorrowful side," said the little boy; "I think everything in this house is beautiful, and all the old pleasant thoughts come back here to pay visits."

"Ah, but I never see any, and I don't know them," said the tin soldier, "and I cannot bear it."

"You must bear it," said the little boy. Then the old man came back with a pleasant face; and brought with him beautiful preserved fruits, as well as apples and nuts; and the little boy thought no more of the tin soldier. How happy and delighted the little boy was; and after he returned home, and while days and weeks passed, a great deal of nodding took place from one house to the other, and then the little boy went to pay another visit. The carved trumpeters blew "Tanta-ra-ra. There is the little boy. Tanta-ra-ra." The swords and armor on the old knight's pictures rattled. The silk dresses rustled, the leather repeated its rhyme, and the old chairs had the gout in their backs, and cried, "Creak;" it was all exactly like the first time; for in that house, one day and one hour were just like another. "I cannot bear it any longer," said the tin soldier; "I have wept tears of tin, it is so melancholy here. Let me go to the wars, and lose an arm or a leg, that would be some change; I cannot bear it. Now I know what it is to have visits from one's old recollections, and all they bring with them. I have had visits from mine, and you may believe me it is not altogether pleasant. I was very nearly jumping from the shelf. I saw you all in your house opposite, as if you were really present. It was Sunday morning, and you children stood round the table, singing the hymn that you sing every morning. You were standing quietly, with your hands folded, and your father and mother. You were standing quietly, with your hands folded, and your father and mother were looking just as serious, when the door opened, and your little sister Maria, who is not two years old, was brought into the room. You know she always dances when she hears music and singing of any sort; so she began to dance immediately, although she ought not to have done so, but she could not get into the right time because the tune was so slow; so she stood first on one leg and then on the other, and bent her head very low, but it would not suit the music. You all stood looking very grave, although it was very difficult to do so, but I laughed so to myself that I fell down from the table, and got a bruise, which is there still; I know it was not right to laugh. So all this, and everything else that I have seen, keeps running in my head, and these must be the old recollections that bring so many thoughts with them.

Tell me whether you still sing on Sundays, and tell me about your little sister Maria, and how my old comrade is, the other tin soldier. Ah, really he must be very happy; I cannot endure this life."

"You are given away," said the little boy; "you must stay. Don't you see that?" Then the old man came in, with a box containing many curious things to show him. Rouge-pots, scent-boxes, and old cards, so large and so richly gilded, that none are ever seen like them in these days. And there were smaller boxes to look at, and the piano was opened, and inside the lid were painted landscapes. But when the old man played, the piano sounded quite out of tune. Then he looked at the picture he had bought at the broker's, and his eyes sparkled brightly as he nodded at it, and said, "Ah, she could sing that tune."

"I will go to the wars! I will go to the wars!" cried the tin soldier as loud as he could, and threw himself down on the floor. Where could he have fallen? The old man searched, and the little boy searched, but he was gone, and could not be found. "I shall find him again," said the old man, but he did not find him. The boards of the floor were open and full of holes. The tin soldier had fallen through a crack between the boards, and lay there now in an open grave. The day went by, and the little boy returned home; the week passed, and many more weeks. It was winter, and the windows were quite frozen, so the little boy was obliged to breathe on the panes, and rub a hole to peep through at the old house. Snow drifts were lying in all the scrolls and on the inscriptions, and the steps were covered with snow as if no one were at home. And indeed nobody was home, for the old man was dead. In the evening, a hearse stopped at the door, and the old man in his coffin was placed in it. He was to be taken to the country to be buried there in his own grave; so they carried him away; no one followed him, for all his friends were dead; and the little boy kissed his hand to the coffin as the hearse moved away with it. A few days after, there was an auction at the old house, and from his window the little boy saw the people carrying away the pictures of old knights and ladies, the flower-pots with the long ears, the old chairs, and the cup-boards. Some were taken one way, some another. Her portrait, which had been bought at the picture dealer's, went back again to his shop, and there it remained, for no one seemed to know her, or to care for the old picture. In the spring; they began to pull the house itself down; people called it complete rubbish. From the street could be seen the room in which the walls were covered with leather, ragged and torn, and the green in the balcony hung straggling over the beams; they pulled it down quickly, for it looked ready to fall, and at last it was cleared away altogether. "What a good riddance," said the neighbors' houses. Very shortly, a fine new house was built farther back from the road; it had lofty windows and smooth walls, but in front, on the spot where the old house really stood, a little garden was planted, and wild vines grew up over the neighboring walls; in front of the garden were large iron railings and a great gate, which looked very stately. People used to stop and peep through the railings. The sparrows assembled in dozens upon the wild vines, and chattered all together as loud as they could, but not about the old house; none of them could remember it, for many years had passed by, so many indeed, that the little boy was now a man, and a really good man too, and his parents were very proud of him. He was just married, and had come, with his young wife, to reside in the new house with the garden in front of it, and now he stood there by her side while she planted a field flower that she thought very pretty. She was planting it herself with her little hands, and pressing down the earth with her fingers. "Oh dear, what was that?" she exclaimed, as something pricked her. Out of the soft earth something was sticking up. It was – only think! – it was really the tin soldier, the very same which had been lost up in the old man's room, and had been hidden among old wood and rubbish for a long time, till it sunk into the earth, where it must have been for many years. And the young wife wiped the soldier, first with a green leaf, and then with her fine pocket-handkerchief, that smelt of such beautiful perfume. And the tin soldier felt as if he was recovering from a fainting fit. "Let me see him," said the young man, and then he smiled and shook his head, and said, "It can scarcely be the same, but it reminds me of something that happened to one of my tin soldiers when I was a little boy." And then he told his wife about the old house and the old man, and of the tin soldier which he had sent across, because he thought the old man was lonely; and he related the story so clearly that tears came into the eyes of the young wife for the old house and the old man. "It is very likely that this is really the same soldier," said she, and I will take care of him, and always remember what you have told me; but some day you must show me the old man's grave."

"I don't know where it is," he replied; "no one knows. All his friends are dead; no one took care of him, and I was only a little boy."

"Oh, how dreadfully lonely he must have been," said she.

"Yes, terribly lonely," cried the tin soldier; "still it is delightful not to be forgotten."

"Delightful indeed," cried a voice quite near to them; no one but the tin soldier saw that it came from a rag of the leather which hung in tatters; it had lost all its gilding, and looked like wet earth, but it had an opinion, and it spoke it thus: –

> *"Gilding will fade in damp weather,*
> *To endure, there is nothing like leather."*

But the tin soldier did not believe any such thing.

The Happy Family

THE LARGEST GREEN leaf in this country is certainly the burdock-leaf. If you hold it in front of you, it is large enough for an apron; and if you hold it over your head, it is almost as good as an umbrella, it is so wonderfully large. A burdock never grows alone; where it grows, there are many more, and it is a splendid sight; and all this splendor is good for snails. The great white snails, which grand people in olden times used to have made into fricassees; and when they had eaten them, they would say, "O, what a delicious dish!" for these people really thought them good; and these snails lived on burdock-leaves, and for them the burdock was planted.

There was once an old estate where no one now lived to require snails; indeed, the owners had all died out, but the burdock still flourished; it grew over all the beds and walks of the garden – its growth had no check – till it became at last quite a forest of burdocks. Here and there stood an apple or a plum-tree; but for this, nobody would have thought the place had ever been a garden. It was burdock from one end to the other; and here lived the last two surviving snails. They knew not themselves how old they were; but they could remember the time when there were a great many more of them, and that they were descended from a family which came from foreign lands, and that the whole forest had been planted for them and theirs. They had never been away from the garden; but they knew that another place once existed in the world, called the Duke's Palace Castle, in which some of their relations had been boiled till they became black, and were then laid on a silver dish; but what was done afterwards they did not know. Besides, they could not imagine exactly how it felt to be boiled and placed on a silver dish; but no doubt it was something very fine and highly genteel. Neither the cockchafer, nor the toad, nor the earth-worm, whom they questioned about it, would give them the least information; for none of their relations had ever been cooked or served on a silver dish. The old white snails were the most aristocratic race in the world, – they knew that. The forest had been planted for them, and the nobleman's castle had been built entirely that they might be cooked and laid on silver dishes.

They lived quite retired and very happily; and as they had no children of their own, they had adopted a little common snail, which they brought up as their own child. The little one would not grow, for he was only a common snail; but the old people, particularly the mother-snail, declared that she could easily see how he grew; and when the father said he could not perceive it, she begged him to feel the little snail's shell, and he did so, and found that the mother was right.

One day it rained very fast. "Listen, what a drumming there is on the burdock-leaves; turn, turn, turn; turn, turn, turn," said the father-snail.

"There come the drops," said the mother; "they are trickling down the stalks. We shall have it very wet here presently. I am very glad we have such good houses, and that the little one has one of his own. There has been really more done for us than for any other creature; it is quite plain that we are the most noble people in the world.

We have houses from our birth, and the burdock forest has been planted for us. I should very much like to know how far it extends, and what lies beyond it."

"There can be nothing better than we have here," said the father-snail; "I wish for nothing more."

"Yes, but I do," said the mother; "I should like to be taken to the palace, and boiled, and laid upon a silver dish, as was done to all our ancestors; and you may be sure it must be something very uncommon."

"The nobleman's castle, perhaps, has fallen to decay," said the snail-father, "or the burdock wood may have grown out. You need not be in a hurry; you are always so impatient, and the youngster is getting just the same. He has been three days creeping to the top of that stalk. I feel quite giddy when I look at him."

"You must not scold him," said the mother-snail; "he creeps so very carefully. He will be the joy of our home; and we old folks have nothing else to live for. But have you ever thought where we are to get a wife for him? Do you think that farther out in the wood there may be others of our race?"

"There may be black snails, no doubt," said the old snail; "black snails without houses; but they are so vulgar and conceited too. But we can give the ants a commission; they run here and there, as if they all had so much business to get through. They, most likely, will know of a wife for our youngster."

"I certainly know a most beautiful bride," said one of the ants; "but I fear it would not do, for she is a queen."

"That does not matter," said the old snail; "has she a house?"

"She has a palace," replied the ant, – "a most beautiful ant-palace with seven hundred passages."

"Thank-you," said the mother-snail; "but our boy shall not go to live in an ant-hill. If you know of nothing better, we will give the commission to the white gnats; they fly about in rain and sunshine; they know the burdock wood from one end to the other."

"We have a wife for him," said the gnats; "a hundred man-steps from here there is a little snail with a house, sitting on a gooseberry-bush; she is quite alone, and old enough to be married. It is only a hundred man-steps from here."

"Then let her come to him," said the old people. "He has the whole burdock forest; she has only a bush."

So they brought the little lady-snail. She took eight days to perform the journey; but that was just as it ought to be; for it showed her to be one of the right breeding. And then they had a wedding. Six glow-worms gave as much light as they could; but in other respects it was all very quiet; for the old snails could not bear festivities or a crowd. But a beautiful speech was made by the mother-snail. The father could not speak; he was too much overcome. Then they gave the whole burdock forest to the young snails as an inheritance, and repeated what they had so often said, that it was the finest place in the world, and that if they led upright and honorable lives, and their family increased, they and their children might some day be taken to the nobleman's palace, to be boiled black, and laid on a silver dish. And when they had finished speaking, the old couple crept into their houses, and came out no more; for they slept.

The young snail pair now ruled in the forest, and had a numerous progeny. But as the young ones were never boiled or laid in silver dishes, they concluded that the castle had fallen into decay, and that all the people in the world were dead; and as nobody contradicted them, they thought they must be right. And the rain fell upon the burdock-leaves, to play the drum for them, and the sun shone to paint colors on the burdock forest for them, and they were very happy; the whole family were entirely and perfectly happy.

The Elf of the Rose

IN THE MIDST of a garden grew a rose-tree, in full blossom, and in the prettiest of all the roses lived an elf. He was such a little wee thing, that no human eye could see him. Behind each leaf of the rose he had a sleeping chamber. He was as well formed and as beautiful as a little child could be, and had wings that reached from his shoulders to his feet. Oh, what sweet fragrance there was in his chambers! and how clean and beautiful were the walls! for they were the blushing leaves of the rose.

During the whole day he enjoyed himself in the warm sunshine, flew from flower to flower, and danced on the wings of the flying butterflies. Then he took it into his head to measure how many steps he would have to go through the roads and cross-roads that are on the leaf of a linden-tree. What we call the veins on a leaf, he took for roads; ay, and very long roads they were for him; for before he had half finished his task, the sun went down: he had commenced his work too late. It became very cold, the dew fell, and the wind blew; so he thought the best thing he could do would be to return home. He hurried himself as much as he could; but he found the roses all closed up, and he could not get in; not a single rose stood open. The poor little elf was very much frightened. He had never before been out at night, but had always slumbered secretly behind the warm rose-leaves. Oh, this would certainly be his death. At the other end of the garden, he knew there was an arbor, overgrown with beautiful honey-suckles. The blossoms looked like large painted horns; and he thought to himself, he would go and sleep in one of these till the morning. He flew thither; but "hush!" two people were in the arbor, – a handsome young man and a beautiful lady. They sat side by side, and wished that they might never be obliged to part. They loved each other much more than the best child can love its father and mother.

"But we must part," said the young man; "your brother does not like our engagement, and therefore he sends me so far away on business, over mountains and seas. Farewell, my sweet bride; for so you are to me."

And then they kissed each other, and the girl wept, and gave him a rose; but before she did so, she pressed a kiss upon it so fervently that the flower opened. Then the little elf flew in, and leaned his head on the delicate, fragrant walls. Here he could plainly hear them say, "Farewell, farewell;" and he felt that the rose had been placed on the young man's breast. Oh, how his heart did beat! The little elf could not go to sleep, it thumped so loudly. The young man took it out as he walked through the dark wood alone, and kissed the flower so often and so violently, that the little elf was almost crushed. He could feel through the leaf how hot the lips of the young man were, and the rose had opened, as if from the heat of the noonday sun.

There came another man, who looked gloomy and wicked. He was the wicked brother of the beautiful maiden. He drew out a sharp knife, and while the other was kissing the rose, the wicked man stabbed him to death; then he cut off his head, and buried it with the body in the soft earth under the linden-tree.

"Now he is gone, and will soon be forgotten," thought the wicked brother; "he will never come back again. He was going on a long journey over mountains and seas; it is easy for a man to lose his life in such a journey. My sister will suppose he is dead; for he cannot come back, and she will not dare to question me about him."

Then he scattered the dry leaves over the light earth with his foot, and went home through the darkness; but he went not alone, as he thought, – the little elf accompanied him. He sat in a dry rolled-up linden-leaf, which had fallen from the tree on to the wicked man's head, as he was digging the grave. The hat was on the head now, which made it very dark, and the little elf shuddered with fright and indignation at the wicked deed.

It was the dawn of morning before the wicked man reached home; he took off his hat, and went into his sister's room. There lay the beautiful, blooming girl, dreaming of him whom she loved so, and who was now, she supposed, travelling far away over mountain and sea. Her wicked brother stopped over her, and laughed hideously, as fiends only can laugh. The dry leaf fell out of his hair upon the counterpane; but he did not notice it, and went to get a little sleep during the early morning hours. But the elf slipped out of the withered leaf, placed himself by the ear of the sleeping girl, and told her, as in a dream, of the horrid murder; described the place where her brother had slain her lover, and buried his body; and told her of the linden-tree, in full blossom, that stood close by.

"That you may not think this is only a dream that I have told you," he said, "you will find on your bed a withered leaf."

Then she awoke, and found it there. Oh, what bitter tears she shed! and she could not open her heart to any one for relief.

The window stood open the whole day, and the little elf could easily have reached the roses, or any of the flowers; but he could not find it in his heart to leave one so afflicted. In the window stood a bush bearing monthly roses. He seated himself in one of the flowers, and gazed on the poor girl. Her brother often came into the room, and would be quite cheerful, in spite of his base conduct; so she dare not say a word to him of her heart's grief.

As soon as night came on, she slipped out of the house, and went into the wood, to the spot where the linden-tree stood; and after removing the leaves from the earth, she turned it up, and there found him who had been murdered. Oh, how she wept and prayed that she also might die! Gladly would she have taken the body home with her; but that was impossible; so she took up the poor head with the closed eyes, kissed the cold lips, and shook the mould out of the beautiful hair.

"I will keep this," said she; and as soon as she had covered the body again with the earth and leaves, she took the head and a little sprig of jasmine that bloomed in the wood, near the spot where he was buried, and carried them home with her. As soon as she was in her room, she took the largest flower-pot she could find, and in this she placed the head of the dead man, covered it up with earth, and planted the twig of jasmine in it.

"Farewell, farewell," whispered the little elf. He could not any longer endure to witness all this agony of grief, he therefore flew away to his own rose in the garden. But the rose was faded; only a few dry leaves still clung to the green hedge behind it.

"Alas! how soon all that is good and beautiful passes away," sighed the elf.

After a while he found another rose, which became his home, for among its delicate fragrant leaves he could dwell in safety. Every morning he flew to the window of the poor girl, and always found her weeping by the flower pot. The bitter tears fell upon the jasmine twig, and each day, as she became paler and paler, the sprig appeared to grow greener and fresher. One shoot after another sprouted forth, and little white buds blossomed, which the poor girl fondly kissed. But her wicked brother scolded her, and asked her if she was going mad. He could not imagine why she was weeping over that flower-pot, and it annoyed him. He did not know whose closed eyes were there, nor what red lips were fading beneath the earth. And one day she sat and leaned her head against the flower-pot, and the little elf of the rose found her asleep. Then he seated himself by her ear, talked to her of that evening in the arbor, of the sweet perfume of the rose, and the loves of the elves. Sweetly she dreamed, and while she dreamt, her life passed away calmly and gently, and her spirit was with him whom she loved, in heaven. And the jasmine opened its large white bells, and spread forth its sweet fragrance; it had no other way of showing its grief for the dead. But the wicked brother considered the beautiful blooming plant as his own property, left to him by his sister, and he placed it in his sleeping room, close by his bed, for it was very lovely in appearance, and the fragrance sweet and delightful. The little elf of the rose followed it, and flew from flower to flower, telling each little spirit that dwelt in them the story of the murdered young man, whose head now formed part of the earth beneath them, and of the wicked brother and the poor sister. "We know it," said each little spirit in the flowers, "we know it, for have we not sprung from the eyes and lips of the murdered one. We know it, we know it," and the flowers nodded with their heads in a peculiar manner. The elf of the rose could not understand how they could rest so quietly in the matter, so he flew to the bees, who were gathering honey, and told them of the wicked brother. And the bees told it to their queen, who commanded that the next morning they should go and kill the murderer. But during the night, the first after the sister's death, while the brother was sleeping in his bed, close to where he had placed the fragrant jasmine, every flower cup opened, and invisibly the little spirits stole out, armed with poisonous spears. They placed themselves by the ear of the sleeper, told him dreadful dreams and then flew across his lips, and pricked his tongue with their poisoned spears. "Now have we revenged the dead," said they, and flew back into the white bells of the jasmine flowers. When the morning came, and as soon as the window was opened, the rose elf, with the queen bee, and the whole swarm of bees, rushed in to kill him. But he was already dead. People were standing round the bed, and saying that the scent of the jasmine had killed him. Then the elf of the rose understood the revenge of the flowers, and explained it to the queen bee, and she, with the whole swarm, buzzed about the flower-pot. The bees could not be driven away. Then a man took it up to remove it, and one of the bees stung him in the hand, so that he let the flower-pot fall, and it was broken to pieces. Then every one saw the whitened skull, and they knew the dead man in the bed was a murderer. And the queen bee hummed in the air, and sang of the revenge of the flowers, and of the elf of the rose and said that behind the smallest leaf dwells One, who can discover evil deeds, and punish them also.

The Beetle Who Went on His Travels

THERE WAS ONCE an Emperor who had a horse shod with gold. He had a golden shoe on each foot, and why was this? He was a beautiful creature, with slender legs, bright, intelligent eyes, and a mane that hung down over his neck like a veil. He had carried his master through fire and smoke in the battle-field, with the bullets whistling round him; he had kicked and bitten, and taken part in the fight, when the enemy advanced; and, with his master on his back, he had dashed over the fallen foe, and saved the golden crown and the Emperor's life, which was of more value than the brightest gold. This is the reason of the Emperor's horse wearing golden shoes.

A beetle came creeping forth from the stable, where the farrier had been shoeing the horse. "Great ones, first, of course," said he, "and then the little ones; but size is not always a proof of greatness." He stretched out his thin leg as he spoke.

"And pray what do you want?" asked the farrier.

"Golden shoes," replied the beetle.

"Why, you must be out of your senses," cried the farrier. "Golden shoes for you, indeed!"

"Yes, certainly; golden shoes," replied the beetle. "Am I not just as good as that great creature yonder, who is waited upon and brushed, and has food and drink placed before him? And don't I belong to the royal stables?"

"But why does the horse have golden shoes?" asked the farrier; "of course you understand the reason?"

"Understand! Well, I understand that it is a personal slight to me," cried the beetle. "It is done to annoy me, so I intend to go out into the world and seek my fortune."

"Go along with you," said the farrier.

"You're a rude fellow," cried the beetle, as he walked out of the stable; and then he flew for a short distance, till he found himself in a beautiful flower-garden, all fragrant with roses and lavender. The lady-birds, with red and black shells on their backs, and delicate wings, were flying about, and one of them said, "Is it not sweet and lovely here? Oh, how beautiful everything is."

"I am accustomed to better things," said the beetle. "Do you call this beautiful? Why, there is not even a dung-heap." Then he went on, and under the shadow of a large haystack he found a caterpillar crawling along. "How beautiful this world is!" said the caterpillar. "The sun is so warm, I quite enjoy it. And soon I shall go to sleep, and die as they call it, but I shall wake up with beautiful wings to fly with, like a butterfly."

"How conceited you are!" exclaimed the beetle. "Fly about as a butterfly, indeed! what of that. I have come out of the Emperor's stable, and no one there, not even the Emperor's horse, who, in fact, wears my cast-off golden shoes, has any idea of flying, excepting myself. To have wings and fly! why, I can do that already;" and so saying, he spread his wings and flew away. "I don't want to be disgusted," he said to himself, "and yet I can't help it." Soon after, he fell down upon an extensive lawn, and for a time pretended to sleep, but at last fell asleep in earnest. Suddenly a heavy shower of rain came falling from the clouds. The beetle woke up with the noise and would have been glad to creep into the earth for shelter, but he could not. He was tumbled over and over with the rain, sometimes swimming on his stomach and sometimes on his back; and as for flying, that was out of the question. He began to doubt whether he should escape with his life, so he remained, quietly lying where he was. After a while the weather cleared up a little, and the beetle was able to rub the water from his eyes, and look about him. He saw something gleaming, and he managed to make his way up to it. It was linen which had been laid to bleach on the grass. He crept into a fold of the damp linen, which certainly was not so comfortable a place to lie in as the warm stable, but there was nothing better, so he remained lying there for a whole day and night, and the rain kept on all the time. Towards morning he crept out of his hiding-place, feeling in a very bad temper with the climate. Two frogs were sitting on the linen, and their bright eyes actually glistened with pleasure.

"Wonderful weather this," cried one of them, "and so refreshing. This linen holds the water together so beautifully, that my hind legs quiver as if I were going to swim."

"I should like to know," said another, "If the swallow who flies so far in her many journeys to foreign lands, ever met with a better climate than this. What delicious moisture! It is as pleasant as lying in a wet ditch. I am sure any one who does not enjoy this has no love for his fatherland."

"Have you ever been in the Emperor's stable?" asked the beetle. "There the moisture is warm and refreshing; that's the climate for me, but I could not take it with me on my travels. Is there not even a dunghill here in this garden, where a person of rank, like myself, could take up his abode and feel at home?" But the frogs either did not or would not understand him.

"I never ask a question twice," said the beetle, after he had asked this one three times, and received no answer. Then he went on a little farther and stumbled against a piece of broken crockery-ware, which certainly ought not to have been lying there. But as it was there, it formed a good shelter against wind and weather to several families of earwigs who dwelt in it. Their requirements were not many, they were very sociable, and full of affection for their children, so much so that each mother considered her own child the most beautiful and clever of them all.

"Our dear son has engaged himself," said one mother, "dear innocent boy; his greatest ambition is that he may one day creep into a clergyman's ear. That is a very artless and loveable wish; and being engaged will keep him steady. What happiness for a mother!"

"Our son," said another, "had scarcely crept out of the egg, when he was off on his travels. He is all life and spirits, I expect he will wear out his horns with running. How charming this is for a mother, is it not Mr. Beetle?" for she knew the stranger by his horny coat.

"You are both quite right," said he; so they begged him to walk in, that is to come as far as he could under the broken piece of earthenware.

"Now you shall also see my little earwigs," said a third and a fourth mother, "they are lovely little things, and highly amusing. They are never ill-behaved, except when they are uncomfortable in their inside, which unfortunately often happens at their age."

Thus each mother spoke of her baby, and their babies talked after their own fashion, and made use of the little nippers they have in their tails to nip the beard of the beetle.

"They are always busy about something, the little rogues," said the mother, beaming with maternal pride; but the beetle felt it a bore, and he therefore inquired the way to the nearest dung-heap.

"That is quite out in the great world, on the other side of the ditch," answered an earwig, "I hope none of my children will ever go so far, it would be the death of me."

"But I shall try to get so far," said the beetle, and he walked off without taking any formal leave, which is considered a polite thing to do.

When he arrived at the ditch, he met several friends, all them beetles; "We live here," they said, "and we are very comfortable. May we ask you to step down into this rich mud, you must be fatigued after your journey."

"Certainly," said the beetle, "I shall be most happy; I have been exposed to the rain, and have had to lie upon linen, and cleanliness is a thing that greatly exhausts me; I have also pains in one of my wings from standing in the draught under a piece of broken crockery. It is really quite refreshing to be with one's own kindred again."

"Perhaps you came from a dung-heap," observed the oldest of them.

"No, indeed, I came from a much grander place," replied the beetle; "I came from the emperor's stable, where I was born, with golden shoes on my feet. I am travelling on a secret embassy, but you must not ask me any questions, for I cannot betray my secret."

Then the beetle stepped down into the rich mud, where sat three young-lady beetles, who tittered, because they did not know what to say.

"None of them are engaged yet," said their mother, and the beetle maidens tittered again, this time quite in confusion.

"I have never seen greater beauties, even in the royal stables," exclaimed the beetle, who was now resting himself.

"Don't spoil my girls," said the mother; "and don't talk to them, pray, unless you have serious intentions."

But of course the beetle's intentions were serious, and after a while our friend was engaged. The mother gave them her blessing, and all the other beetles cried "hurrah."

Immediately after the betrothal came the marriage, for there was no reason to delay. The following day passed very pleasantly, and the next was tolerably comfortable; but on the third it became necessary for him to think of getting food for his wife, and, perhaps, for children.

"I have allowed myself to be taken in," said our beetle to himself, "and now there's nothing to be done but to take them in, in return."

No sooner said than done. Away he went, and stayed away all day and all night, and his wife remained behind a forsaken widow.

"Oh," said the other beetles, "this fellow that we have received into our family is nothing but a complete vagabond. He has gone away and left his wife a burden upon our hands."

"Well, she can be unmarried again, and remain here with my other daughters," said the mother. "Fie on the villain that forsook her!"

In the mean time the beetle, who had sailed across the ditch on a cabbage leaf, had been journeying on the other side. In the morning two persons came up to the ditch. When they saw him they took him up and turned him over and over, looking very learned all the time, especially one, who was a boy. "Allah sees the black beetle in the black stone, and the black rock. Is not that written in the Koran?" he asked.

Then he translated the beetle's name into Latin, and said a great deal upon the creature's nature and history. The second person, who was older and a scholar, proposed to carry the beetle home, as they wanted just such good specimens as this. Our beetle considered this speech a great insult, so he flew suddenly out of the speaker's hand. His wings were dry now, so they carried him to a great distance, till at last he reached a hothouse, where a sash of the glass roof was partly open, so he quietly slipped in and buried himself in the warm earth. "It is very comfortable here," he said to himself, and soon after fell asleep. Then he dreamed that the emperor's horse was dying, and had left him his golden shoes, and also promised that he should have two more. All this was very delightful, and when the beetle woke up he crept forth and looked around him. What a splendid place the hothouse was! At the back, large palm-trees were growing; and the sunlight made the leaves – look quite glossy; and beneath them what a profusion of luxuriant green, and of flowers red like flame, yellow as amber, or white as new-fallen snow! "What a wonderful quantity of plants," cried the beetle; "how good they will taste when they are decayed! This is a capital store-room. There must certainly be some relations of mine living here; I will just see if I can find any one with whom I can associate. I'm proud, certainly; but I'm also proud of being so. Then he prowled about in the earth, and thought what a pleasant dream that was about the dying horse, and the golden shoes he had inherited. Suddenly a hand seized the beetle, and squeezed him, and turned him round and round. The gardener's little son and his playfellow had come into the hothouse, and, seeing the beetle, wanted to have some fun with him. First, he was wrapped, in a vine-leaf, and put into a warm trousers' pocket. He twisted and turned about with all his might, but he got a good squeeze from the boy's hand, as a hint for him to keep quiet. Then the boy went quickly towards a lake that lay at the end of the garden. Here the beetle was put into an old broken wooden shoe, in which a little stick had been fastened upright for a mast, and to this mast the beetle was bound with a piece of worsted. Now he was a sailor, and had to sail away. The lake was not very large, but to the beetle it seemed an ocean, and he was so astonished at its size that he fell over on his back, and kicked out his legs. Then the little ship sailed away; sometimes the current of the water seized it, but whenever it went too far from the shore one of the boys turned up his trousers, and went in after it, and brought it back to land. But at last, just as it went merrily out again, the two boys were called, and so angrily, that they hastened to obey, and ran away as fast as they could from the pond, so that the little ship was left to its fate. It was carried away farther and farther from the shore, till it reached the open sea. This was a terrible prospect for the beetle, for he could not escape in consequence of being bound to the mast. Then a fly came and paid him a visit. "What beautiful weather," said the fly; "I shall rest here and sun myself. You must have a pleasant time of it."

"You speak without knowing the facts," replied the beetle; "don't you see that I am a prisoner?"

"Ah, but I'm not a prisoner," remarked the fly, and away he flew.

"Well, now I know the world," said the beetle to himself; "it's an abominable world; I'm the only respectable person in it. First, they refuse me my golden shoes; then I have to lie on damp linen, and to stand in a draught; and to crown all, they fasten a wife upon me. Then, when I have made a step forward in the world, and found out a comfortable position, just as I could wish it to be, one of these human boys comes and ties me up, and leaves me to the mercy of the wild waves, while the emperor's favorite horse goes prancing about proudly on his golden shoes. This vexes me more than anything. But it is useless to look for sympathy in this world. My career has been very interesting, but what's the use of that if nobody knows anything about it? The world does not deserve to be made acquainted with my adventures, for it ought to have given me golden shoes when the emperor's horse was shod, and I stretched out my feet to be shod, too. If I had received golden shoes I should have been an ornament to the stable; now I am lost to the stable and to the world. It is all over with me."

But all was not yet over. A boat, in which were a few young girls, came rowing up. "Look, yonder is an old wooden shoe sailing along," said one of the younger girls.

"And there's a poor little creature bound fast in it," said another.

The boat now came close to our beetle's ship, and the young girls fished it out of the water. One of them drew a small pair of scissors from her pocket, and cut the worsted without hurting the beetle, and when she stepped on shore she placed him on the grass. "There," she said, "creep away, or fly, if thou canst. It is a splendid thing to have thy liberty." Away flew the beetle, straight through the open window of a large building; there he sank down, tired and exhausted, exactly on the mane of the emperor's favorite horse, who was standing in his stable; and the beetle found himself at home again. For some time he clung to the mane, that he might recover himself. "Well," he said, "here I am, seated on the emperor's favorite horse, – sitting upon him as if I were the emperor himself. But what was it the farrier asked me? Ah, I remember now, – that's a good thought, – he asked me why the golden shoes were given to the horse. The answer is quite clear to me, now. They were given to the horse on my account." And this reflection put the beetle into a good temper. The sun's rays also came streaming into the stable, and shone upon him, and made the place lively and bright. "Travelling expands the mind very much," said the beetle. "The world is not so bad after all, if you know how to take things as they come.

The Pen and the Inkstand

IN A POET'S room, where his inkstand stood on the table, the remark was once made, "It is wonderful what can be brought out of an inkstand. What will come next? It is indeed wonderful."

"Yes, certainly," said the inkstand to the pen, and to the other articles that stood on the table; "that's what I always say. It is wonderful and extraordinary what a number of things come out of me. It's quite incredible, and I really don't know what is coming next when that man dips his pen into me. One drop out of me is enough for half a page of paper, and what cannot half a page contain? From me, all the works of a poet are produced; all those imaginary characters whom people fancy they have known or met. All the deep feeling, the humor, and the vivid pictures of nature. I myself don't understand how it is, for I am not acquainted with nature, but it is certainly in me. From me have gone forth to the world those wonderful descriptions of troops of charming maidens, and of brave knights on prancing steeds; of the halt and the blind, and I know not what more, for I assure you I never think of these things."

"There you are right," said the pen, "for you don't think at all; if you did, you would see that you can only provide the means. You give the fluid that I may place upon the paper what dwells in me, and what I wish to bring to light. It is the pen that writes: no man doubts that; and, indeed, most people understand as much about poetry as an old inkstand."

"You have had very little experience," replied the inkstand. "You have hardly been in service a week, and are already half worn out. Do you imagine you are a poet? You are only a servant, and before you came I had many like you, some of the goose family, and others of English manufacture. I know a quill pen as well as I know a steel one. I have had both sorts in my service, and I shall have many more when he comes – the man who performs the mechanical part – and writes down what he obtains from me. I should like to know what will be the next thing he gets out of me."

"Inkpot!" exclaimed the pen contemptuously.

Late in the evening the poet came home. He had been to a concert, and had been quite enchanted with the admirable performance of a famous violin player whom he had heard there. The performer had produced from his instrument a richness of tone that sometimes sounded like tinkling waterdrops or rolling pearls; sometimes like the birds twittering in chorus, and then rising and swelling in sound like the wind through the fir-trees. The poet felt as if his own heart were weeping, but in tones of melody like the sound of a woman's voice. It seemed not only the strings, but every part of the instrument from which these sounds were produced. It was a wonderful performance and a difficult piece, and yet the bow seemed to glide across the strings so easily that it was as if any one could do it who tried. Even the violin and the bow appeared to perform independently of their master who guided them; it was as if soul and spirit had been breathed into the instrument, so the audience forgot the performer in the beautiful sounds he produced. Not so the poet; he remembered him, and named him, and wrote down his thoughts on the subject. "How foolish it would be for the violin and the bow to boast of their performance, and yet we men often commit that folly. The poet, the artist, the man of science in his laboratory, the general, – we all do it; and yet we are only the instruments which the Almighty uses; to Him alone the honor is due. We have nothing of ourselves of which we should be proud." Yes, this is what the poet wrote down. He wrote it in the form of a parable, and called it "The Master and the Instruments."

"That is what you have got, madam," said the pen to the inkstand, when the two were alone again. "Did you hear him read aloud what I had written down?"

"Yes, what I gave you to write," retorted the inkstand. "That was a cut at you because of your conceit. To think that you could not understand that you were being quizzed. I gave you a cut from within me. Surely I must know my own satire."

"Ink-pitcher!" cried the pen.

"Writing-stick!" retorted the inkstand. And each of them felt satisfied that he had given a good answer. It is pleasing to be convinced that you have settled a matter by your reply; it is something to make you sleep well, and they both slept well upon it. But the poet did not sleep. Thoughts rose up within him like the tones of the violin, falling like pearls, or rushing like the strong wind through the forest. He understood his own heart in these thoughts; they were as a ray from the mind of the Great Master of all minds.

"To Him be all the honor."

The Butterfly

THERE WAS ONCE a butterfly who wished for a bride, and, as may be supposed, he wanted to choose a very pretty one from among the flowers. He glanced, with a very critical eye, at all the flower-beds, and found that the flowers were seated quietly and demurely on their stalks, just as maidens should sit before they are engaged; but there was a great number of them, and it appeared as if his search would become very wearisome. The butterfly did not like to take too much trouble, so he flew off on a visit to the daisies. The French call this flower "Marguerite," and they say that the little daisy can prophesy. Lovers pluck off the leaves, and as they pluck each leaf, they ask a question about their lovers; thus: "Does he or she love me? – Ardently? Distractedly? Very much? A little? Not at all?" and so on. Every one speaks these words in his own language. The butterfly came also to Marguerite to inquire, but he did not pluck off her leaves; he pressed a kiss on each of them, for he thought there was always more to be done by kindness.

"Darling Marguerite daisy," he said to her, "you are the wisest woman of all the flowers. Pray tell me which of the flowers I shall choose for my wife. Which will be my bride? When I know, I will fly directly to her, and propose."

But Marguerite did not answer him; she was offended that he should call her a woman when she was only a girl; and there is a great difference. He asked her a second time, and then a third; but she remained dumb, and answered not a word. Then he would wait no longer, but flew away, to commence his wooing at once. It was in the early spring, when the crocus and the snowdrop were in full bloom.

"They are very pretty," thought the butterfly; "charming little lasses; but they are rather formal."

Then, as the young lads often do, he looked out for the elder girls. He next flew to the anemones; these were rather sour to his taste. The violet, a little too sentimental. The lime-blossoms, too small, and besides, there was such a large family of them. The apple-blossoms, though they looked like roses, bloomed to-day, but might fall off to-morrow, with the first wind that blew; and he thought that a marriage with one of them might last too short a time. The pea-blossom pleased him most of all; she was white and red, graceful and slender, and belonged to those domestic maidens who have a pretty appearance, and can yet be useful in the kitchen. He was just about to make her an offer, when, close by the maiden, he saw a pod, with a withered flower hanging at the end.

"Who is that?" he asked.

"That is my sister," replied the pea-blossom.

"Oh, indeed; and you will be like her some day," said he; and he flew away directly, for he felt quite shocked.

A honeysuckle hung forth from the hedge, in full bloom; but there were so many girls like her, with long faces and sallow complexions. No; he did not like her. But which one did he like?

Spring went by, and summer drew towards its close; autumn came; but he had not decided. The flowers now appeared in their most gorgeous robes, but all in vain; they had not the fresh, fragrant air of youth. For the heart asks for fragrance, even when it is no longer young; and there is very little of that to be found in the dahlias or the dry chrysanthemums; therefore the butterfly turned to the mint on the ground. You know, this plant has no blossom; but it is sweetness all over, – full of fragrance from head to foot, with the scent of a flower in every leaf.

"I will take her," said the butterfly; and he made her an offer. But the mint stood silent and stiff, as she listened to him. At last she said, –

"Friendship, if you please; nothing more. I am old, and you are old, but we may live for each other just the same; as to marrying – no; don't let us appear ridiculous at our age."

And so it happened that the butterfly got no wife at all. He had been too long choosing, which is always a bad plan. And the butterfly became what is called an old bachelor.

It was late in the autumn, with rainy and cloudy weather. The cold wind blew over the bowed backs of the willows, so that they creaked again. It was not the weather for flying about in summer clothes; but fortunately the butterfly was not out in it. He had got a shelter by chance. It was in a room heated by a stove, and as warm as summer. He could exist here, he said, well enough.

"But it is not enough merely to exist," said he, "I need freedom, sunshine, and a little flower for a companion."

Then he flew against the window-pane, and was seen and admired by those in the room, who caught him, and stuck him on a pin, in a box of curiosities. They could not do more for him.

"Now I am perched on a stalk, like the flowers," said the butterfly. "It is not very pleasant, certainly; I should imagine it is something like being married; for here I am stuck fast." And with this thought he consoled himself a little.

"That seems very poor consolation," said one of the plants in the room, that grew in a pot.

"Ah," thought the butterfly, "one can't very well trust these plants in pots; they have too much to do with mankind."

Soup from a Sausage Skewer

"Soup from a Sausage Skewer"

WE HAD SUCH an excellent dinner yesterday," said an old mouse of the female sex to another who had not been present at the feast. "I sat number twenty-one below the mouse-king, which was not a bad place. Shall I tell you what we had? Everything was first rate. Mouldy bread, tallow candle, and sausage. And then, when we had finished that course, the same came on all over again; it was as good as two feasts. We were very sociable, and there was as much joking and fun as if we had been all of one family circle. Nothing was left but the sausage skewers, and this formed a subject of conversation, till at last it turned to the proverb, 'Soup from sausage skins;' or, as the people in the neighboring country call it, 'Soup from a sausage skewer.' Every one had heard the proverb, but no one had ever tasted the soup, much less prepared it. A capital toast was drunk to the inventor of the soup, and some one said he ought to be made a relieving officer to the poor. Was not that witty? Then the old mouse-king rose and promised that the young lady-mouse who should learn how best to prepare this much-admired and savory soup should be his queen, and a year and a day should be allowed for the purpose."

"That was not at all a bad proposal," said the other mouse; "but how is the soup made?"

"Ah, that is more than I can tell you. All the young lady mice were asking the same question. They wished very much to be queen, but they did not want to take the trouble of going out into the world to learn how to make soup, which was absolutely necessary to be done first. But it is not every one who would care to leave her family, or her happy corner by the fire-side at home, even to be made queen. It is not always easy to find bacon and cheese-rind in foreign lands every day, and it is not pleasant to have to endure hunger, and be perhaps, after all, eaten up alive by the cat."

Most probably some such thoughts as these discouraged the majority from going out into the world to collect the required information. Only four mice gave notice that they were ready to set out on the journey. They were young and lively, but poor. Each of them wished to visit one of the four divisions of the world, so that it might be seen which was the most favored by fortune. Every one took a sausage skewer as a traveller's staff, and to remind them of the object of their journey. They left home early in May, and none of them returned till the first of May in the following year, and then only three of them. Nothing was seen or heard of the fourth, although the day of decision was close at hand. "Ah, yes, there is always some trouble mixed up with the greatest pleasure," said the mouse-king; but he gave orders that all the mice within a circle of many miles should be invited at once. They were to assemble in the kitchen, and the three travelled mice were to stand in a row before them, while a sausage skewer, covered with crape, was to be stuck up instead of the missing mouse. No one dared to express an opinion until the king spoke, and desired one of them to go on with her story. And now we shall hear what she said.

What the First Little Mouse
Saw and Heard on Her Travels

"When I first went out into the world," said the little mouse, "I fancied, as so many of my age do, that I already knew everything, but it was not so. It takes years to acquire great knowledge. I went at once to sea in a ship bound for the north. I had been told that the ship's cook must know how to prepare every dish at sea, and it is easy enough to do that with plenty of sides of bacon, and large tubs of salt meat and mouldy flour. There I found plenty of delicate food, but no opportunity for learning how to make soup from a sausage skewer. We sailed on for many days and nights; the ship rocked fearfully, and we did not escape without a wetting. As soon as we arrived at the port to which the ship was bound, I left it, and went on shore at a place far towards the north. It is a wonderful thing to leave your own little corner at home, to hide yourself in a ship where there are sure to be some nice snug corners for shelter, then suddenly to find yourself thousands of miles away in a foreign land. I saw large pathless forests of pine and birch trees, which smelt so strong that I sneezed and thought of sausage. There were great lakes also which looked as black as ink at a distance, but were quite clear when I came close to them. Large swans were floating upon them, and I thought at first they were only foam, they lay so still; but when I saw them walk and fly, I knew what they were directly. They belong to the goose species, one can see that by their walk. No one can attempt to disguise family descent. I kept with my own kind, and associated with the forest and field mice, who, however, knew very little, especially about what I wanted to know, and which had actually made me travel abroad. The idea that soup could be made from a sausage skewer was to them such an out-of-the-way, unlikely thought, that it was repeated from one to another through the whole forest. They declared that the problem would never be solved, that the thing was an impossibility. How little I thought that in this place, on the very first night, I should be initiated into the manner of its preparation.

"It was the height of summer, which the mice told me was the reason that the forest smelt so strong, and that the herbs were so fragrant, and the lakes with the white swimming swans so dark, and yet so clear. On the margin of the wood, near to three or four houses, a pole, as large as the mainmast of a ship, had been erected, and from the summit hung wreaths of flowers and fluttering ribbons; it was the Maypole. Lads and lasses danced round the pole, and tried to outdo the violins of the musicians with their singing. They were as merry as ever at sunset and in the moonlight, but I took no part in the merry-making. What has a little mouse to do with a Maypole dance? I sat in the soft moss, and held my sausage skewer tight. The moon threw its beams particularly on one spot where stood a tree covered with exceedingly fine moss. I may almost venture to say that it was as fine and soft as the fur of the mouse-king, but it was green, which is a color very agreeable to the eye. All at once I saw the most charming little people marching towards me. They did not reach higher than my knee; they looked like human beings, but were better proportioned, and they called themselves elves. Their clothes were very delicate and fine, for they were made of the leaves of flowers, trimmed with the wings of flies and gnats, which had not a bad effect. By their manner, it appeared as if they were seeking for something. I knew not what, till at last one of them espied me and came towards me, and the foremost pointed to my sausage skewer, and said, 'There, that is just what we want; see, it is pointed at the top; is it not capital?' and the longer he looked at my pilgrim's staff, the more delighted he became. 'I will lend it to you,' said I, 'but not to keep.'

"'Oh no, we won't keep it!' they all cried; and then they seized the skewer, which I gave up to them, and danced with it to the spot where the delicate moss grew, and set it up in the middle of the green. They wanted a maypole, and the one they now had seemed cut out on purpose for them. Then they decorated it so beautifully that it was quite dazzling to look at. Little spiders spun golden threads around it, and then it was hung with fluttering veils and flags so delicately white that they glittered like snow in the moonshine. After that they took colors from the butterfly's wing, and sprinkled them over the white drapery which gleamed as if covered with flowers and diamonds, so that I could not recognize my sausage skewer at all. Such a maypole had never been seen in all the world as this. Then came a great company of real elves. Nothing could be finer than their clothes, and they invited me to be present at the feast; but I was to keep at a certain distance, because I was too large for them. Then commenced such music that it sounded like a thousand glass bells, and was so full and strong that I thought it must be the song of the swans. I fancied also that I heard the voices of the cuckoo and the black-bird, and it seemed at last as if the whole forest sent forth glorious melodies – the voices of children, the tinkling of bells, and the songs of the birds; and all this wonderful melody came from the elfin maypole. My sausage peg was a complete peal of bells. I could scarcely believe that so much could have been produced from it, till I remembered into what hands it had fallen. I was so much affected that I wept tears such as a little mouse can weep, but they were tears of joy. The night was far too short for me; there are no long nights there in summer, as we often have in this part of the world. When the morning dawned, and the gentle breeze rippled the glassy mirror of the forest lake, all the delicate veils and flags fluttered away into thin air; the waving garlands of the spider's web, the hanging bridges and galleries, or whatever else they may be called, vanished away as if they had never been. Six elves brought me back my sausage skewer, and at the same time asked me to make any request, which they would grant if in their power; so I begged them, if they could, to tell me how to make soup from a sausage skewer.

"'How do we make it?' said the chief of the elves with a smile. 'Why you have just seen it; you scarcely knew your sausage skewer again, I am sure.'

"They think themselves very wise, thought I to myself. Then I told them all about it, and why I had travelled so far, and also what promise had been made at home to the one who should discover the method of preparing this soup. 'What use will it be,' I asked, 'to the mouse-king or to our whole mighty kingdom that I have seen all these beautiful things? I cannot shake the sausage peg and say, Look, here is the skewer, and now the soup will come. That would only produce a dish to be served when people were keeping a fast.'

"Then the elf dipped his finger into the cup of a violet, and said to me, 'Look here, I will anoint your pilgrim's staff, so that when you return to your own home and enter the king's castle, you have only to touch the king with your staff, and violets will spring forth and cover the whole of it, even in the coldest winter time; so I think I have given you really something to carry home, and a little more than something.'"

But before the little mouse explained what this something more was, she stretched her staff out to the king, and as it touched him the most beautiful bunch of violets sprang forth and filled the place with perfume. The smell was so powerful that the mouse-king ordered the mice who stood nearest the chimney to thrust their tails into the fire, that there might be a smell of burning, for the perfume of the violets was overpowering, and not the sort of scent that every one liked.

"But what was the something more of which you spoke just now?" asked the mouse-king.

"Why," answered the little mouse, "I think it is what they call 'effect;'" and thereupon she turned the staff round, and behold not a single flower was to be seen upon it! She now only held the naked skewer, and lifted it up as a conductor lifts his baton at a concert. "Violets, the elf told me," continued the mouse, "are for the sight, the smell, and the touch; so we have only now to produce the effect of hearing and tasting;" and then, as the little mouse beat time with her staff, there came sounds of music, not such music as was heard in the forest, at the elfin feast, but such as is often heard in the kitchen – the sounds of boiling and roasting. It came quite suddenly, like wind rushing through the chimneys, and seemed as if every pot and kettle were boiling over. The fire-shovel clattered down on the brass fender; and then, quite as suddenly, all was still, – nothing could be heard but the light, vapory song of the tea-kettle, which was quite wonderful to hear, for no one could rightly distinguish whether the kettle was just beginning to boil or going to stop. And the little pot steamed, and the great pot simmered, but without any regard for each; indeed there seemed no sense in the pots at all. And as the little mouse waved her baton still more wildly, the pots foamed and threw up bubbles, and boiled over; while again the wind roared and whistled through the chimney, and at last there was such a terrible hubbub, that the little mouse let her stick fall.

"That is a strange sort of soup," said the mouse-king; "shall we not now hear about the preparation?"

"That is all," answered the little mouse, with a bow.

"That all!" said the mouse-king; "then we shall be glad to hear what information the next may have to give us."

What the Second Mouse Had to Tell

"I was born in the library, at a castle," said the second mouse. "Very few members of our family ever had the good fortune to get into the dining-room, much less the store-room. On my journey, and here to-day, are the only times I have ever seen a kitchen. We were often obliged to suffer hunger in the library, but then we gained a great deal of knowledge. The rumor reached us of the royal prize offered to those who should be able to make soup from a sausage skewer. Then my old grandmother sought out a manuscript which, however, she could not read, but had heard it read, and in it was written, 'Those who are poets can make soup of sausage skewers.' She then asked me if I was a poet. I felt myself quite innocent of any such pretensions. Then she said I must go out and make myself a poet. I asked again what I should be required to do, for it seemed to me quite as difficult as to find out how to make soup of a sausage skewer. My grandmother had heard a great deal of reading in her day, and she told me three principal qualifications were necessary – understanding, imagination, and feeling. 'If you can manage to acquire these three, you will be a poet, and the sausage-skewer soup will be quite easy to you.'

"So I went forth into the world, and turned my steps towards the west, that I might become a poet. Understanding is the most important matter in everything. I knew that, for the two other qualifications are not thought much of; so I went first to seek for understanding. Where was I to find it? 'Go to the ant and learn wisdom,' said the great Jewish king. I knew that from living in a library. So I went straight on till I came to the first great ant-hill, and then I set myself to watch, that I might become wise. The ants are a very respectable people, they are wisdom itself. All they do is like the working of a sum in arithmetic, which comes right. 'To work and to lay eggs,' say they, 'and to provide for posterity, is to live out your time properly;' and that they truly do. They are divided into the clean and the dirty ants, their rank is pointed out by a number, and the ant-queen is number ONE; and her opinion is the only correct one on everything; she seems to have the whole wisdom of the world in her, which was just the important matter I wished to acquire. She said a great deal which was no doubt very clever; yet to me it sounded like nonsense. She said the ant-hill was the loftiest thing in the world, and yet close to the mound stood a tall tree, which no one could deny was loftier, much loftier, but no mention was made of the tree. One evening an ant lost herself on this tree; she had crept up the stem, not nearly to the top, but higher than any ant had ever ventured; and when at last she returned home she said that she had found something in her travels much higher than the ant-hill. The rest of the ants considered this an insult to the whole community; so she was condemned to wear a muzzle and to live in perpetual solitude. A short time afterwards another ant got on the tree, and made the same journey and the same discovery, but she spoke of it cautiously and indefinitely, and as she was one of the superior ants and very much respected, they believed her, and when she died they erected an eggshell as a monument to her memory, for they cultivated a great respect for science. I saw," said the little mouse, "that the ants were always running to and fro with her burdens on their backs. Once I saw one of them drop her load; she gave herself a great deal of trouble in trying to raise it again, but she could not succeed. Then two others came up and tried with all their strength to help her, till they nearly dropped their own burdens in doing so; then they were obliged to stop for a moment in their help, for every one must think of himself first. And the ant-queen remarked that their conduct that day showed that they possessed kind hearts and good understanding. 'These two qualities,' she continued, 'place us ants in the highest degree above all other reasonable beings. Understanding must therefore be seen among us in the most prominent manner, and my wisdom is greater than all.' And so saying she raised herself on her two hind legs, that no one else might be mistaken for her. I could not therefore make an error, so I ate her up. We are to go to the ants to learn wisdom, and I had got the queen.

"I now turned and went nearer to the lofty tree already mentioned, which was an oak. It had a tall trunk with a wide-spreading top, and was very old. I knew that a living being dwelt here, a dryad as she is called, who is born with the tree and dies with it. I had heard this in the library, and here was just such a tree, and in it an oak-maiden. She uttered a terrible scream when she caught sight of me so near to her; like many women, she was very much afraid of mice. And she had more real cause for fear than they have, for I might have gnawed through the tree on which her life depended. I spoke to her in a kind and friendly manner, and begged her to take courage. At last she took me up in her delicate hand, and then I told her what had brought me out into the world, and she promised me that perhaps on that very evening she should be able to obtain for me one of the two treasures for which I was seeking. She told me that Phantaesus was her very dear friend, that he was as beautiful as the god of love, that he remained often for many hours with her under the leafy boughs of the tree which then rustled and waved more than ever over them both. He called her his dryad, she said, and the tree his tree; for the grand old oak, with its gnarled trunk, was just to his taste. The root, spreading deep into the earth, the top rising high in the fresh air, knew the value of the drifted snow, the keen wind, and the warm sunshine, as it ought to be known. 'Yes,' continued the dryad, 'the birds sing up above in the branches, and talk to each other about the beautiful fields they have visited in foreign lands; and on one of the withered boughs a stork has built his nest, – it is beautifully arranged, and besides it is pleasant to hear a little about the land of the pyramids. All this pleases Phantaesus, but it is not enough for him; I am obliged to relate to him of my life in the woods; and to go back to my childhood, when I was little, and the tree so small and delicate that a stinging-nettle could overshadow it, and I have to tell everything that has happened since then till now that the tree is so large and strong. Sit you down now under the green bindwood and pay attention, when Phantaesus comes I will find an opportunity to lay hold of his wing and to pull out one of the little feathers. That feather you shall have; a better was never given to any poet, it will be quite enough for you.'

"And when Phantaesus came the feather was plucked, and," said the little mouse, "I seized and put it in water, and kept it there till it was quite soft. It was very heavy and indigestible, but I managed to nibble it up at last. It is not so easy to nibble one's self into a poet, there are so many things to get through. Now, however, I had two of them, understanding and imagination; and through these I knew that the third was to be found in the library. A great man has said and written that there are novels whose sole and only use appeared to be that they might relieve mankind of overflowing tears – a kind of sponge, in fact, for sucking up feelings and emotions. I remembered a few of these books, they had always appeared tempting to the appetite; they had been much read, and were so greasy, that they must have absorbed no end of emotions in themselves. I retraced my steps to the library, and literally devoured a whole novel, that is, properly speaking, the interior or soft part of it; the crust, or binding, I left. When I had digested not only this, but a second, I felt a stirring within me; then I ate a small piece of a third romance, and felt myself a poet. I said it to myself, and told others the same. I had head-ache and back-ache, and I cannot tell what aches besides. I thought over all the stories that may be said to be connected with sausage pegs, and all that has ever been written about skewers, and sticks, and staves, and splinters came to my thoughts; the ant-queen must have had a wonderfully clear understanding. I remembered the man who placed a white stick in his mouth by which he could make himself and the stick invisible. I thought of sticks as hobby-horses, staves of music or rhyme, of breaking a stick over a man's back, and heaven knows how many more phrases of the same sort relating to sticks, staves, and skewers. All my thoughts rein on skewers, sticks of wood, and staves; and as I am, at last, a poet, and I have worked terribly hard to make myself one, I can of course make poetry on anything. I shall therefore be able to wait upon you every day in the week with a poetical history of a skewer. And that is my soup."

"In that case," said the mouse-king, "we will hear what the third mouse has to say."

"Squeak, squeak," cried a little mouse at the kitchen door; it was the fourth, and not the third, of the four who were contending for the prize, one whom the rest supposed to be dead. She shot in like an arrow, and overturned the sausage peg that had been covered with crape. She had been running day and night. She had watched an opportunity to get into a goods train, and had travelled by the railway; and yet she had arrived almost too late. She pressed forward, looking very much ruffled. She had lost her sausage skewer, but not her voice; for she began to speak at once as if they only waited for her, and would hear her only, and as if nothing else in the world was of the least consequence. She spoke out so clearly and plainly, and she had come in so suddenly, that no one had time to stop her or to say a word while she was speaking. And now let us hear what she said.

What the Fourth Mouse, Who Spoke Before the Third, Had to Tell

"I started off at once to the largest town," said she, "but the name of it has escaped me. I have a very bad memory for names. I was carried from the railway, with some forfeited goods, to the jail, and on arriving I made my escape, and ran into the house of the turnkey. The turnkey was speaking of his prisoners, especially of one who had uttered thoughtless words. These words had given rise to other words, and at length they were written down and registered: 'The whole affair is like making soup of sausage skewers,' said he, 'but the soup may cost him his neck.'

"Now this raised in me an interest for the prisoner," continued the little mouse, "and I watched my opportunity, and slipped into his apartment, for there is a mouse-hole to be found behind every closed door. The prisoner looked pale; he had a great beard and large, sparkling eyes. There was a lamp burning, but the walls were so black that they only looked the blacker for it. The prisoner scratched pictures and verses with white chalk on the black walls, but I did not read the verses. I think he found his confinement wearisome, so that I was a welcome guest. He enticed me with bread-crumbs, with whistling, and with gentle words, and seemed so friendly towards me, that by degrees I gained confidence in him, and we became friends; he divided his bread and water with me, gave me cheese and sausage, and I really began to love him. Altogether, I must own that it was a very pleasant intimacy. He let me run about on his hand, and on his arm, and into his sleeve; and I even crept into his beard, and he called me his little friend. I forgot what I had come out into the world for; forgot my sausage skewer which I had laid in a crack in the floor – it is lying there still. I wished to stay with him always where I was, for I knew that if I went away the poor prisoner would have no one to be his friend, which is a sad thing. I stayed, but he did not. He spoke to me so mournfully for the last time, gave me double as much bread and cheese as usual, and kissed his hand to me. Then he went away, and never came back. I know nothing more of his history.

"The jailer took possession of me now. He said something about soup from a sausage skewer, but I could not trust him. He took me in his hand certainly, but it was to place me in a cage like a tread-mill. Oh how dreadful it was! I had to run round and round without getting any farther in advance, and only to make everybody laugh. The jailer's granddaughter was a charming little thing. She had curly hair like the brightest gold, merry eyes, and such a smiling mouth.

"'You poor little mouse,' said she, one day as she peeped into my cage, 'I will set you free.' She then drew forth the iron fastening, and I sprang out on the window-sill, and from thence to the roof. Free! free! that was all I could think of; not of the object of my journey. It grew dark, and as night was coming on I found a lodging in an old tower, where dwelt a watchman and an owl. I had no confidence in either of them, least of all in the owl, which is like a cat, and has a great failing, for she eats mice. One may however be mistaken sometimes; and so was I, for this was a respectable and well-educated old owl, who knew more than the watchman, and even as much as I did myself. The young owls made a great fuss about everything, but the only rough words she would say to them were, 'You had better go and make some soup from sausage skewers.' She was very indulgent and loving to her children. Her conduct gave me such confidence in her, that from the crack where I sat I called out 'squeak.' This confidence of mine pleased her so much that she assured me she would take me under her own protection, and that not a creature should do me harm. The fact was, she wickedly meant to keep me in reserve for her own eating in winter, when food would be scarce. Yet she was a very clever lady-owl; she explained to me that the watchman could only hoot with the horn that hung loose at his side; and then she said he is so terribly proud of it, that he imagines himself an owl in the tower; – wants to do great things, but only succeeds in small; all soup on a sausage skewer. Then I begged the owl to give me the recipe for this soup. 'Soup from a sausage skewer,' said she, 'is only a proverb amongst mankind, and may be understood in many ways. Each believes his own way the best, and after all, the proverb signifies nothing.' 'Nothing!' I exclaimed. I was quite struck. Truth is not always agreeable, but truth is above everything else, as the old owl said. I thought over all this, and saw quite plainly that if truth was really so far above everything else, it must be much more valuable than soup from a sausage skewer. So I hastened to get away, that I might be home in time, and bring what was highest and best, and above everything – namely, the truth. The mice are an enlightened people, and the mouse-king is above them all. He is therefore capable of making me queen for the sake of truth."

"Your truth is a falsehood," said the mouse who had not yet spoken; "I can prepare the soup, and I mean to do so."

How It Was Prepared

"I did not travel," said the third mouse; "I stayed in this country: that was the right way. One gains nothing by travelling – everything can be acquired here quite as easily; so I stayed at home. I have not obtained what I know from supernatural beings. I have neither swallowed it, nor learnt it from conversing with owls. I have got it all from my reflections and thoughts. Will you now set the kettle on the fire – so? Now pour the water in – quite full – up to the brim; place it on the fire; make up a good blaze; keep it burning, that the water may boil; it must boil over and over. There, now I throw in the skewer. Will the mouse-king be pleased now to dip his tail into the boiling water, and stir it round with the tail. The longer the king stirs it, the stronger the soup will become. Nothing more is necessary, only to stir it."

"Can no one else do this?" asked the king.

"No," said the mouse; "only in the tail of the mouse-king is this power contained."

And the water boiled and bubbled, as the mouse-king stood close beside the kettle. It seemed rather a dangerous performance; but he turned round, and put out his tail, as mice do in a dairy, when they wish to skim the cream from a pan of milk with their tails and afterwards lick it off. But the mouse-king's tail had only just touched the hot steam, when he sprang away from the chimney in a great hurry, exclaiming, "Oh, certainly, by all means, you must be my queen; and we will let the soup question rest till our golden wedding, fifty years hence; so that the poor in my kingdom, who are then to have plenty of food, will have something to look forward to for a long time, with great joy."

And very soon the wedding took place. But many of the mice, as they were returning home, said that the soup could not be properly called "soup from a sausage skewer," but "soup from a mouse's tail." They acknowledged also that some of the stories were very well told; but that the whole could have been managed differently. "I should have told it so – and so – and so." These were the critics who are always so clever afterwards.

When this story was circulated all over the world, the opinions upon it were divided; but the story remained the same. And, after all, the best way in everything you undertake, great as well as small, is to expect no thanks for anything you may do, even when it refers to "soup from a sausage skewer."

A Rose from Homer's Grave

ALL THE SONGS of the east speak of the love of the nightingale for the rose in the silent starlight night. The winged songster serenades the fragrant flowers.

Not far from Smyrna, where the merchant drives his loaded camels, proudly arching their long necks as they journey beneath the lofty pines over holy ground, I saw a hedge of roses. The turtle-dove flew among the branches of the tall trees, and as the sunbeams fell upon her wings, they glistened as if they were mother-of-pearl. On the rose-bush grew a flower, more beautiful than them all, and to her the nightingale sung of his woes; but the rose remained silent, not even a dewdrop lay like a tear of sympathy on her leaves. At last she bowed her head over a heap of stones, and said, "Here rests the greatest singer in the world; over his tomb will I spread my fragrance, and on it I will let my leaves fall when the storm scatters them. He who sung of Troy became earth, and from that earth I have sprung. I, a rose from the grave of Homer, am too lofty to bloom for a nightingale." Then the nightingale sung himself to death. A camel-driver came by, with his loaded camels and his black slaves; his little son found the dead bird, and buried the lovely songster in the grave of the great Homer, while the rose trembled in the wind.

The evening came, and the rose wrapped her leaves more closely round her, and dreamed: and this was her dream.

It was a fair sunshiny day; a crowd of strangers drew near who had undertaken a pilgrimage to the grave of Homer. Among the strangers was a minstrel from the north, the home of the clouds and the brilliant lights of the aurora borealis. He plucked the rose and placed it in a book, and carried it away into a distant part of the world, his fatherland. The rose faded with grief, and lay between the leaves of the book, which he opened in his own home, saying, "Here is a rose from the grave of Homer."

Then the flower awoke from her dream, and trembled in the wind. A drop of dew fell from the leaves upon the singer's grave. The sun rose, and the flower bloomed more beautiful than ever. The day was hot, and she was still in her own warm Asia. Then footsteps approached, strangers, such as the rose had seen in her dream, came by, and among them was a poet from the north; he plucked the rose, pressed a kiss upon her fresh mouth, and carried her away to the home of the clouds and the northern lights. Like a mummy, the flower now rests in his "Iliad," and, as in her dream, she hears him say, as he opens the book, "Here is a rose from the grave of Homer."

The Flax

THE FLAX WAS in full bloom; it had pretty little blue flowers as delicate as the wings of a moth, or even more so. The sun shone, and the showers watered it; and this was just as good for the flax as it is for little children to be washed and then kissed by their mother. They look much prettier for it, and so did the flax.

"People say that I look exceedingly well," said the flax, "and that I am so fine and long that I shall make a beautiful piece of linen. How fortunate I am; it makes me so happy, it is such a pleasant thing to know that something can be made of me. How the sunshine cheers me, and how sweet and refreshing is the rain; my happiness overpowers me, no one in the world can feel happier than I am."

"Ah, yes, no doubt," said the fern, "but you do not know the world yet as well as I do, for my sticks are knotty;" and then it sung quite mournfully –

> *"Snip, snap, snurre,*
> *Basse lurre:*
> *The song is ended."*

"No, it is not ended," said the flax. "To-morrow the sun will shine, or the rain descend. I feel that I am growing. I feel that I am in full blossom. I am the happiest of all creatures."

Well, one day some people came, who took hold of the flax, and pulled it up by the roots; this was painful; then it was laid in water as if they intended to drown it; and, after that, placed near a fire as if it were to be roasted; all this was very shocking. "We cannot expect to be happy always," said the flax; "by experiencing evil as well as good, we become wise." And certainly there was plenty of evil in store for the flax. It was steeped, and roasted, and broken, and combed; indeed, it scarcely knew what was done to it. At last it was put on the spinning wheel. "Whirr, whirr," went the wheel so quickly that the flax could not collect its thoughts. "Well, I have been very happy," he thought in the midst of his pain, "and must be contented with the past;" and contented he remained till he was put on the loom, and became a beautiful piece of white linen. All the flax, even to the last stalk, was used in making this one piece. "Well, this is quite wonderful; I could not have believed that I should be so favored by fortune. The fern was not wrong with its song of

> '*Snip, snap, snurre,*
> *Basse lurre.*'

But the song is not ended yet, I am sure; it is only just beginning. How wonderful it is, that after all I have suffered, I am made something of at last; I am the luckiest person in the world – so strong and fine; and how white, and what a length! This is something different to being a mere plant and bearing flowers. Then I had no attention, nor any water unless it rained; now, I am watched and taken care of. Every morning the maid turns me over, and I have a shower-bath from the watering-pot every evening. Yes, and the clergyman's wife noticed me, and said I was the best piece of linen in the whole parish. I cannot be happier than I am now."

After some time, the linen was taken into the house, placed under the scissors, and cut and torn into pieces, and then pricked with needles. This certainly was not pleasant; but at last it was made into twelve garments of that kind which people do not like to name, and yet everybody should wear one. "See, now, then," said the flax; "I have become something of importance. This was my destiny; it is quite a blessing. Now I shall be of some use in the world, as everyone ought to be; it is the only way to be happy. I am now divided into twelve pieces, and yet we are all one and the same in the whole dozen. It is most extraordinary good fortune."

Years passed away, and at last the linen was so worn it could scarcely hold together. "It must end very soon," said the pieces to each other; "we would gladly have held together a little longer, but it is useless to expect impossibilities." And at length they fell into rags and tatters, and thought it was all over with them, for they were torn to shreds, and steeped in water, and made into a pulp, and dried, and they knew not what besides, till all at once they found themselves beautiful white paper. "Well, now, this is a surprise; a glorious surprise too," said the paper. "I am now finer than ever, and I shall be written upon, and who can tell what fine things I may have written upon me. This is wonderful luck!" And sure enough the most beautiful stories and poetry were written upon it, and only once was there a blot, which was very fortunate. Then people heard the stories and poetry read, and it made them wiser and better; for all that was written had a good and sensible meaning, and a great blessing was contained in the words on this paper.

"I never imagined anything like this," said the paper, "when I was only a little blue flower, growing in the fields. How could I fancy that I should ever be the means of bringing knowledge and joy to man? I cannot understand it myself, and yet it is really so. Heaven knows that I have done nothing myself, but what I was obliged to do with my weak powers for my own preservation; and yet I have been promoted from one joy and honor to another. Each time I think that the song is ended; and then something higher and better begins for me. I suppose now I shall be sent on my travels about the world, so that people may read me. It cannot be otherwise; indeed, it is more than probable; for I have more splendid thoughts written upon me, than I had pretty flowers in olden times. I am happier than ever."

But the paper did not go on its travels; it was sent to the printer, and all the words written upon it were set up in type, to make a book, or rather, many hundreds of books; for so many more persons could derive pleasure and profit from a printed book, than from the written paper; and if the paper had been sent around the world, it would have been worn out before it had got half through its journey.

"This is certainly the wisest plan," said the written paper; "I really did not think of that. I shall remain at home, and be held in honor, like some old grandfather, as I really am to all these new books. They will do some good. I could not have wandered about as they do. Yet he who wrote all this has looked at me, as every word flowed from his pen upon my surface. I am the most honored of all."

Then the paper was tied in a bundle with other papers, and thrown into a tub that stood in the washhouse.

"After work, it is well to rest," said the paper, "and a very good opportunity to collect one's thoughts. Now I am able, for the first time, to think of my real condition; and to know one's self is true progress. What will be done with me now, I wonder? No doubt I shall still go forward. I have always progressed hitherto, as I know quite well."

Now it happened one day that all the paper in the tub was taken out, and laid on the hearth to be burnt. People said it could not be sold at the shop, to wrap up butter and sugar, because it had been written upon. The children in the house stood round the stove; for they wanted to see the paper burn, because it flamed up so prettily, and afterwards, among the ashes, so many red sparks could be seen running one after the other, here and there, as quick as the wind. They called it seeing the children come out of school, and the last spark was the schoolmaster. They often thought the last spark had come; and one would cry, "There goes the schoolmaster;" but the next moment another spark would appear, shining so beautifully. How they would like to know where the sparks all went to! Perhaps we shall find out some day, but we don't know now.

The whole bundle of paper had been placed on the fire, and was soon alight. "Ugh," cried the paper, as it burst into a bright flame; "ugh." It was certainly not very pleasant to be burning; but when the whole was wrapped in flames, the flames mounted up into the air, higher than the flax had ever been able to raise its little blue flower, and they glistened as the white linen never could have glistened. All the written letters became quite red in a moment, and all the words and thoughts turned to fire.

"Now I am mounting straight up to the sun," said a voice in the flames; and it was as if a thousand voices echoed the words; and the flames darted up through the chimney, and went out at the top. Then a number of tiny beings, as many in number as the flowers on the flax had been, and invisible to mortal eyes, floated above them. They were even lighter and more delicate than the flowers from which they were born; and as the flames were extinguished, and nothing remained of the paper but black ashes, these little beings danced upon it; and whenever they touched it, bright red sparks appeared.

"The children are all out of school, and the schoolmaster was the last of all," said the children. It was good fun, and they sang over the dead ashes, –

> *"Snip, snap, snurre,*
> *Basse lure:*
> *The song is ended."*

But the little invisible beings said, "The song is never ended; the most beautiful is yet to come."

But the children could neither hear nor understand this, nor should they; for children must not know everything.

The Shirt-Collar

THERE WAS ONCE a fine gentleman who possessed among other things a boot-jack and a hair-brush; but he had also the finest shirt-collar in the world, and of this collar we are about to hear a story. The collar had become so old that he began to think about getting married; and one day he happened to find himself in the same washing-tub as a garter. "Upon my word," said the shirt-collar, "I have never seen anything so slim and delicate, so neat and soft before. May I venture to ask your name?"

"I shall not tell you," replied the garter.

"Where do you reside when you are at home?" asked the shirt-collar. But the garter was naturally shy, and did not know how to answer such a question.

"I presume you are a girdle," said the shirt-collar, "a sort of under girdle. I see that you are useful, as well as ornamental, my little lady."

"You must not speak to me," said the garter; "I do not think I have given you any encouragement to do so."

"Oh, when any one is as beautiful as you are," said the shirt-collar, "is not that encouragement enough?"

"Get away; don't come so near me," said the garter, "you appear to me quite like a man."

"I am a fine gentleman certainly," said the shirt-collar, "I possess a boot-jack and a hair-brush." This was not true, for these things belonged to his master; but he was a boaster.

"Don't come so near me," said the garter; "I am not accustomed to it."

"Affectation!" said the shirt-collar.

Then they were taken out of the wash-tub, starched, and hung over a chair in the sunshine, and then laid on the ironing-board. And now came the glowing iron. "Mistress widow," said the shirt-collar, "little mistress widow, I feel quite warm. I am changing, I am losing all my creases. You are burning a hole in me. Ugh! I propose to you."

"You old rag," said the flat-iron, driving proudly over the collar, for she fancied herself a steam-engine, which rolls over the railway and draws carriages. "You old rag!" said she.

The edges of the shirt-collar were a little frayed, so the scissors were brought to cut them smooth. "Oh!" exclaimed the shirt-collar, "what a first-rate dancer you would make; you can stretch out your leg so well. I never saw anything so charming; I am sure no human being could do the same."

"I should think not," replied the scissors.

"You ought to be a countess," said the shirt collar; "but all I possess consists of a fine gentleman, a boot-jack, and a comb. I wish I had an estate for your sake."

"What! is he going to propose to me?" said the scissors, and she became so angry that she cut too sharply into the shirt collar, and it was obliged to be thrown by as useless.

"I shall be obliged to propose to the hair-brush," thought the shirt collar; so he remarked one day, "It is wonderful what beautiful hair you have, my little lady. Have you never thought of being engaged?"

"You might know I should think of it," answered the hair brush; "I am engaged to the boot-jack."

"Engaged!" cried the shirt collar, "now there is no one left to propose to;" and then he pretended to despise all love-making.

A long time passed, and the shirt collar was taken in a bag to the paper-mill. Here was a large company of rags, the fine ones lying by themselves, separated from the coarser, as it ought to be. They had all many things to relate, especially the shirt collar, who was a terrible boaster. "I have had an immense number of love affairs," said the shirt collar, "no one left me any peace. It is true I was a very fine gentleman; quite stuck up. I had a boot-jack and a brush that I never used. You should have seen me then, when I was turned down. I shall never forget my first love; she was a girdle, so charming, and fine, and soft, and she threw herself into a washing tub for my sake. There was a widow too, who was warmly in love with me, but I left her alone, and she became quite black. The next was a first-rate dancer; she gave me the wound from which I still suffer, she was so passionate. Even my own hair-brush was in love with me, and lost all her hair through neglected love. Yes, I have had great experience of this kind, but my greatest grief was for the garter – the girdle I meant to say – that jumped into the wash-tub. I have a great deal on my conscience, and it is really time I should be turned into white paper."

And the shirt collar came to this at last. All the rags were made into white paper, and the shirt collar became the very identical piece of paper which we now see, and on which this story is printed. It happened as a punishment to him, for having boasted so shockingly of things which were not true. And this is a warning to us, to be careful how we act, for we may some day find ourselves in the rag-bag, to be turned into white paper, on which our whole history may be written, even its most secret actions. And it would not be pleasant to have to run about the world in the form of a piece of paper, telling everything we have done, like the boasting shirt collar.

The Races

A PRIZE, OR rather two prizes, a great one and a small one, had been awarded for the greatest swiftness in running, – not in a single race, but for the whole year.

"I obtained the first prize," said the hare. "Justice must still be carried out, even when one has relations and good friends among the prize committee; but that the snail should have received the second prize, I consider almost an insult to myself."

"No," said the fence-rail, who had been a witness at the distribution of prizes; "there should be some consideration for industry and perseverance. I have heard many respectable people say so, and I can quite understand it. The snail certainly took half a year to get over the threshold of the door; but he injured himself, and broke his collar-bone by the haste he made. He gave himself up entirely to the race, and ran with his house on his back, which was all, of course, very praiseworthy; and therefore he obtained the second prize."

"I think I ought to have had some consideration too," said the swallow. "I should imagine no one can be swifter in soaring and flight than I am; and how far I have been! far, far away."

"Yes, that is your misfortune," said the fence-rail; "you are so fickle, so unsettled; you must always be travelling about into foreign lands when the cold commences here. You have no love of fatherland in you. There can be no consideration for you."

"But now, if I have been lying the whole winter in the moor," said the swallow, "and suppose I slept the whole time, would that be taken into account?"

"Bring a certificate from the old moor-hen," said he, "that you have slept away half your time in fatherland; then you will be treated with some consideration."

"I deserved the first prize, and not the second," said the snail. "I know so much, at least, that the hare only ran from cowardice, and because he thought there was danger in delay. I, on the other hand, made running the business of my life, and have become a cripple in the service. If any one had a first prize, it ought to have been myself. But I do not understand chattering and boasting; on the contrary, I despise it." And the snail spat at them with contempt.

"I am able to affirm with word of oath, that each prize – at least, those for which I voted – was given with just and proper consideration," said the old boundary post in the wood, who was a member of the committee of judges. "I always act with due order, consideration, and calculation. Seven times have I already had the honor to be present at the distribution of the prizes, and to vote; but to-day is the first time I have been able to carry out my will. I always reckon the first prize by going through the alphabet from the beginning, and the second by going through from the end. Be so kind as to give me your attention, and I will explain to you how I reckon from the beginning. The eighth letter from A is H, and there we have H for hare; therefore I awarded to the hare the first prize. The eighth letter from the end of the alphabet is S, and therefore the snail received the second prize. Next year, the letter I will have its turn for the first prize, and the letter R for the second."

"I should really have voted for myself," said the mule, "if I had not been one of the judges on the committee. Not only the rapidity with which advance is made, but every other quality should have due consideration; as, for instance, how much weight a candidate is able to draw; but I have not brought this quality forward now, nor the sagacity of the hare in his flight, nor the cunning with which he suddenly springs aside and doubles, to lead people on a false track, thinking he has concealed himself. No; there is something else on which more stress should be laid, and which ought not be left unnoticed. I mean that which mankind call the beautiful. It is on the beautiful that I particularly fix my eyes. I observed the well-grown ears of the hare; it is a pleasure to me to observe how long they are. It seemed as if I saw myself again in the days of my childhood; and so I voted for the hare."

"Buz," said the fly; "there, I'm not going to make a long speech; but I wish to say something about hares. I have really overtaken more than one hare, when I have been seated on the engine in front of a railway train. I often do so. One can then so easily judge of one's own swiftness. Not long ago, I crushed the hind legs of a young hare. He had been running a long time before the engine; he had no idea that I was travelling there. At last he had to stop in his career, and the engine ran over his hind legs, and crushed them; for I set upon it. I left him lying there, and rode on farther. I call that conquering him; but I do not want the prize."

"It really seems to me," thought the wild rose, though she did not express her opinion aloud – it is not in her nature to do so, – though it would have been quite as well if she had; "it certainly seems to me that the sunbeam ought to have had the honor of receiving the first prize. The sunbeam flies in a few minutes along the immeasurable path from the sun to us. It arrives in such strength, that all nature awakes to loveliness and beauty; we roses blush and exhale fragrance in its presence. Our worshipful judges don't appear to have noticed this at all. Were I the sunbeam, I would give each one of them a sun stroke; but that would only make them mad, and they are mad enough already. I only hope," continued the rose, "that peace may reign in the wood. It is glorious to bloom, to be fragrant, and to live; to live in story and in song. The sunbeam will outlive us all."

"What is the first prize?" asked the earthworm, who had overslept the time, and only now came up.

"It contains a free admission to a cabbage-garden," replied the mule. "I proposed that as one of the prizes. The hare most decidedly must have it; and I, as an active and thoughtful member of the committee, took especial care that the prize should be one of advantage to him; so now he is provided for. The snail can now sit on the fence, and lick up moss and sunshine. He has also been appointed one of the first judges of swiftness in racing. It is worth much to know that one of the members is a man of talent in the thing men call a 'committee.' I must say I expect much in the future; we have already made such a good beginning."

The Nightingale

IN CHINA, YOU know, the emperor is a Chinese, and all those about him are Chinamen also. The story I am going to tell you happened a great many years ago, so it is well to hear it now before it is forgotten. The emperor's palace was the most beautiful in the world. It was built entirely of porcelain, and very costly, but so delicate and brittle that whoever touched it was obliged to be careful. In the garden could be seen the most singular flowers, with pretty silver bells tied to them, which tinkled so that every one who passed could not help noticing the flowers. Indeed, everything in the emperor's garden was remarkable, and it extended so far that the gardener himself did not know where it ended. Those who travelled beyond its limits knew that there was a noble forest, with lofty trees, sloping down to the deep blue sea, and the great ships sailed under the shadow of its branches. In one of these trees lived a nightingale, who sang so beautifully that even the poor fishermen, who had so many other things to do, would stop and listen. Sometimes, when they went at night to spread their nets, they would hear her sing, and say, "Oh, is not that beautiful?" But when they returned to their fishing, they forgot the bird until the next night. Then they would hear it again, and exclaim "Oh, how beautiful is the nightingale's song!"

Travellers from every country in the world came to the city of the emperor, which they admired very much, as well as the palace and gardens; but when they heard the nightingale, they all declared it to be the best of all. And the travellers, on their return home, related what they had seen; and learned men wrote books, containing descriptions of the town, the palace, and the gardens; but they did not forget the nightingale, which was really the greatest wonder. And those who could write poetry composed beautiful verses about the nightingale, who lived in a forest near the deep sea. The books travelled all over the world, and some of them came into the hands of the emperor; and he sat in his golden chair, and, as he read, he nodded his approval every moment, for it pleased him to find such a beautiful description of his city, his palace, and his gardens. But when he came to the words, "the nightingale is the most beautiful of all," he exclaimed, "What is this? I know nothing of any nightingale. Is there such a bird in my empire? and even in my garden? I have never heard of it. Something, it appears, may be learnt from books."

Then he called one of his lords-in-waiting, who was so high-bred, that when any in an inferior rank to himself spoke to him, or asked him a question, he would answer, "Pooh," which means nothing.

"There is a very wonderful bird mentioned here, called a nightingale," said the emperor; "they say it is the best thing in my large kingdom. Why have I not been told of it?"

"I have never heard the name," replied the cavalier; "she has not been presented at court."

"It is my pleasure that she shall appear this evening." said the emperor; "the whole world knows what I possess better than I do myself."

"I have never heard of her," said the cavalier; "yet I will endeavor to find her."

But where was the nightingale to be found? The nobleman went up stairs and down, through halls and passages; yet none of those whom he met had heard of the bird. So he returned to the emperor, and said that it must be a fable, invented by those who had written the book. "Your imperial majesty," said he, "cannot believe everything contained in books; sometimes they are only fiction, or what is called the black art."

"But the book in which I have read this account," said the emperor, "was sent to me by the great and mighty emperor of Japan, and therefore it cannot contain a falsehood. I will hear the nightingale, she must be here this evening; she has my highest favor; and if she does not come, the whole court shall be trampled upon after supper is ended."

"Tsing-pe!" cried the lord-in-waiting, and again he ran up and down stairs, through all the halls and corridors; and half the court ran with him, for they did not like the idea of being trampled upon. There was a great inquiry about this wonderful nightingale, whom all the world knew, but who was unknown to the court.

At last they met with a poor little girl in the kitchen, who said, "Oh, yes, I know the nightingale quite well; indeed, she can sing. Every evening I have permission to take home to my poor sick mother the scraps from the table; she lives down by the sea-shore, and as I come back I feel tired, and I sit down in the wood to rest, and listen to the nightingale's song. Then the tears come into my eyes, and it is just as if my mother kissed me."

"Little maiden," said the lord-in-waiting, "I will obtain for you constant employment in the kitchen, and you shall have permission to see the emperor dine, if you will lead us to the nightingale; for she is invited for this evening to the palace." So she went into the wood where the nightingale sang, and half the court followed her. As they went along, a cow began lowing.

"Oh," said a young courtier, "now we have found her; what wonderful power for such a small creature; I have certainly heard it before."

"No, that is only a cow lowing," said the little girl; "we are a long way from the place yet."

Then some frogs began to croak in the marsh.

"Beautiful," said the young courtier again. "Now I hear it, tinkling like little church bells."

"No, those are frogs," said the little maiden; "but I think we shall soon hear her now:" and presently the nightingale began to sing.

"Hark, hark! there she is," said the girl, "and there she sits," she added, pointing to a little gray bird who was perched on a bough.

"Is it possible?" said the lord-in-waiting, "I never imagined it would be a little, plain, simple thing like that. She has certainly changed color at seeing so many grand people around her."

"Little nightingale," cried the girl, raising her voice, "our most gracious emperor wishes you to sing before him."

"With the greatest pleasure," said the nightingale, and began to sing most delightfully.

"It sounds like tiny glass bells," said the lord-in-waiting, "and see how her little throat works. It is surprising that we have never heard this before; she will be a great success at court."

"Shall I sing once more before the emperor?" asked the nightingale, who thought he was present.

"My excellent little nightingale," said the courtier, "I have the great pleasure of inviting you to a court festival this evening, where you will gain imperial favor by your charming song."

"My song sounds best in the green wood," said the bird; but still she came willingly when she heard the emperor's wish.

The palace was elegantly decorated for the occasion. The walls and floors of porcelain glittered in the light of a thousand lamps. Beautiful flowers, round which little bells were tied, stood in the corridors: what with the running to and fro and the draught, these bells tinkled so loudly that no one could speak to be heard. In the centre of the great hall, a golden perch had been fixed for the nightingale to sit on. The whole court was present, and the little kitchen-maid had received permission to stand by the door. She was not installed as a real court cook. All were in full dress, and every eye was turned to the little gray bird when the emperor nodded to her to begin. The nightingale sang so sweetly that the tears came into the emperor's eyes, and then rolled down his cheeks, as her song became still more touching and went to every one's heart. The emperor was so delighted that he declared the nightingale should have his gold slipper to wear round her neck, but she declined the honor with thanks: she had been sufficiently rewarded already. "I have seen tears in an emperor's eyes," she said, "that is my richest reward. An emperor's tears have wonderful power, and are quite sufficient honor for me;" and then she sang again more enchantingly than ever.

"That singing is a lovely gift;" said the ladies of the court to each other; and then they took water in their mouths to make them utter the gurgling sounds of the nightingale when they spoke to any one, so that they might fancy themselves nightingales. And the footmen and chambermaids also expressed their satisfaction, which is saying a great deal, for they are very difficult to please. In fact the nightingale's visit was most successful. She was now to remain at court, to have her own cage, with liberty to go out twice a day, and once during the night. Twelve servants were appointed to attend her on these occasions, who each held her by a silken string fastened to her leg. There was certainly not much pleasure in this kind of flying.

The whole city spoke of the wonderful bird, and when two people met, one said "nightin," and the other said "gale," and they understood what was meant, for nothing else was talked of. Eleven peddlers' children were named after her, but not of them could sing a note.

One day the emperor received a large packet on which was written "The Nightingale." "Here is no doubt a new book about our celebrated bird," said the emperor. But instead of a book, it was a work of art contained in a casket, an artificial nightingale made to look like a living one, and covered all over with diamonds, rubies, and sapphires. As soon as the artificial bird was wound up, it could sing like the real one, and could move its tail up and down, which sparkled with silver and gold. Round its neck hung a piece of ribbon, on which was written "The Emperor of Japan's nightingale is poor compared with that of the Emperor of China's."

"This is very beautiful," exclaimed all who saw it, and he who had brought the artificial bird received the title of "Imperial nightingale-bringer-in-chief."

"Now they must sing together," said the court, "and what a duet it will be." But they did not get on well, for the real nightingale sang in its own natural way, but the artificial bird sang only waltzes.

"That is not a fault," said the music-master, "it is quite perfect to my taste," so then it had to sing alone, and was as successful as the real bird; besides, it was so much prettier to look at, for it sparkled like bracelets and breast-pins. Three and thirty times did it sing the same tunes without being tired; the people would gladly have heard it again, but the emperor said the living nightingale ought to sing something. But where was she? No one had noticed her when she flew out at the open window, back to her own green woods.

"What strange conduct," said the emperor, when her flight had been discovered; and all the courtiers blamed her, and said she was a very ungrateful creature.

"But we have the best bird after all," said one, and then they would have the bird sing again, although it was the thirty-fourth time they had listened to the same piece, and even then they had not learnt it, for it was rather difficult. But the music-master praised the bird in the highest degree, and even asserted that it was better than a real nightingale, not only in its dress and the beautiful diamonds, but also in its musical power. "For you must perceive, my chief lord and emperor, that with a real nightingale we can never tell what is going to be sung, but with this bird everything is settled. It can be opened and explained, so that people may understand how the waltzes are formed, and why one note follows upon another."

"This is exactly what we think," they all replied, and then the music-master received permission to exhibit the bird to the people on the following Sunday, and the emperor commanded that they should be present to hear it sing. When they heard it they were like people intoxicated; however it must have been with drinking tea, which is quite a Chinese custom. They all said "Oh!" and held up their forefingers and nodded, but a poor fisherman, who had heard the real nightingale, said, "it sounds prettily enough, and the melodies are all alike; yet there seems something wanting, I cannot exactly tell what."

And after this the real nightingale was banished from the empire, and the artificial bird placed on a silk cushion close to the emperor's bed. The presents of gold and precious stones which had been received with it were round the bird, and it was now advanced to the title of "Little Imperial Toilet Singer," and to the rank of No. 1 on the left hand; for the emperor considered the left side, on which the heart lies, as the most noble, and the heart of an emperor is in the same place as that of other people.

The music-master wrote a work, in twenty-five volumes, about the artificial bird, which was very learned and very long, and full of the most difficult Chinese words; yet all the people said they had read it, and understood it, for fear of being thought stupid and having their bodies trampled upon.

So a year passed, and the emperor, the court, and all the other Chinese knew every little turn in the artificial bird's song; and for that same reason it pleased them better. They could sing with the bird, which they often did. The street-boys sang, "Zi-zi-zi, cluck, cluck, cluck," and the emperor himself could sing it also. It was really most amusing.

One evening, when the artificial bird was singing its best, and the emperor lay in bed listening to it, something inside the bird sounded "whizz." Then a spring cracked. "Whir-r-r-r" went all the wheels, running round, and then the music stopped. The emperor immediately sprang out of bed, and called for his physician; but what could he do? Then they sent for a watchmaker; and, after a great deal of talking and examination, the bird was put into something like order; but he said that it must be used very carefully, as the barrels were worn, and it would be impossible to put in new ones without injuring the music. Now there was great sorrow, as the bird could only be allowed to play once a year; and even that was dangerous for the works inside it. Then the music-master made a little speech, full of hard words, and declared that the bird was as good as ever; and, of course no one contradicted him.

Five years passed, and then a real grief came upon the land. The Chinese really were fond of their emperor, and he now lay so ill that he was not expected to live. Already a new emperor had been chosen and the people who stood in the street asked the lord-in-waiting how the old emperor was; but he only said, "Pooh!" and shook his head.

Cold and pale lay the emperor in his royal bed; the whole court thought he was dead, and every one ran away to pay homage to his successor. The chamberlains went out to have a talk on the matter, and the ladies'-maids invited company to take coffee. Cloth had been laid down on the halls and passages, so that not a footstep should be heard, and all was silent and still. But the emperor was not yet dead, although he lay white and stiff on his gorgeous bed, with the long velvet curtains and heavy gold tassels. A window stood open, and the moon shone in upon the emperor and the artificial bird. The poor emperor, finding he could scarcely breathe with a strange weight on his chest, opened his eyes, and saw Death sitting there. He had put on the emperor's golden crown, and held in one hand his sword of state, and in the other his beautiful banner. All around the bed and peeping through the long velvet curtains, were a number of strange heads, some very ugly, and others lovely and gentle-looking. These were the emperor's good and bad deeds, which stared him in the face now Death sat at his heart.

"Do you remember this?" "Do you recollect that?" they asked one after another, thus bringing to his remembrance circumstances that made the perspiration stand on his brow.

"I know nothing about it," said the emperor. "Music! music!" he cried; "the large Chinese drum! that I may not hear what they say." But they still went on, and Death nodded like a Chinaman to all they said. "Music! music!" shouted the emperor. "You little precious golden bird, sing, pray sing! I have given you gold and costly presents; I have even hung my golden slipper round your neck. Sing! sing!" But the bird remained silent. There was no one to wind it up, and therefore it could not sing a note.

Death continued to stare at the emperor with his cold, hollow eyes, and the room was fearfully still. Suddenly there came through the open window the sound of sweet music. Outside, on the bough of a tree, sat the living nightingale. She had heard of the emperor's illness, and was therefore come to sing to him of hope and trust. And as she sung, the shadows grew paler and paler; the blood in the emperor's veins flowed more rapidly, and gave life to his weak limbs; and even Death himself listened, and said, "Go on, little nightingale, go on."

"Then will you give me the beautiful golden sword and that rich banner? and will you give me the emperor's crown?" said the bird.

So Death gave up each of these treasures for a song; and the nightingale continued her singing. She sung of the quiet churchyard, where the white roses grow, where the elder-tree wafts its perfume on the breeze, and the fresh, sweet grass is moistened by the mourners' tears. Then Death longed to go and see his garden, and floated out through the window in the form of a cold, white mist.

"Thanks, thanks, you heavenly little bird. I know you well. I banished you from my kingdom once, and yet you have charmed away the evil faces from my bed, and banished Death from my heart, with your sweet song. How can I reward you?"

"You have already rewarded me," said the nightingale. "I shall never forget that I drew tears from your eyes the first time I sang to you. These are the jewels that rejoice a singer's heart. But now sleep, and grow strong and well again. I will sing to you again."

And as she sung, the emperor fell into a sweet sleep; and how mild and refreshing that slumber was! When he awoke, strengthened and restored, the sun shone brightly through the window; but not one of his servants had returned – they all believed he was dead; only the nightingale still sat beside him, and sang.

"You must always remain with me," said the emperor. "You shall sing only when it pleases you; and I will break the artificial bird into a thousand pieces."

"No; do not do that," replied the nightingale; "the bird did very well as long as it could. Keep it here still. I cannot live in the palace, and build my nest; but let me come when I like. I will sit on a bough outside your window, in the evening, and sing to you, so that you may be happy, and have thoughts full of joy. I will sing to you of those who are happy, and those who suffer; of the good and the evil, who are hidden around you. The little singing bird flies far from you and your court to the home of the fisherman and the peasant's cot. I love your heart better than your crown; and yet something holy lingers round that also. I will come, I will sing to you; but you must promise me one thing."

"Everything," said the emperor, who, having dressed himself in his imperial robes, stood with the hand that held the heavy golden sword pressed to his heart.

"I only ask one thing," she replied; "let no one know that you have a little bird who tells you everything. It will be best to conceal it." So saying, the nightingale flew away.

The servants now came in to look after the dead emperor; when, lo! there he stood, and, to their astonishment, said, "Good morning."

The Elfin Hill

A FEW LARGE lizards were running nimbly about in the clefts of an old tree; they could understand one another very well, for they spoke the lizard language.

"What a buzzing and a rumbling there is in the elfin hill," said one of the lizards; "I have not been able to close my eyes for two nights on account of the noise; I might just as well have had the toothache, for that always keeps me awake."

"There is something going on within there," said the other lizard; "they propped up the top of the hill with four red posts, till cock-crow this morning, so that it is thoroughly aired, and the elfin girls have learnt new dances; there is something."

"I spoke about it to an earth-worm of my acquaintance," said a third lizard; "the earth-worm had just come from the elfin hill, where he has been groping about in the earth day and night. He has heard a great deal; although he cannot see, poor miserable creature, yet he understands very well how to wriggle and lurk about. They expect friends in the elfin hill, grand company, too; but who they are the earth-worm would not say, or, perhaps, he really did not know. All the will-o'-the-wisps are ordered to be there to hold a torch dance, as it is called. The silver and gold which is plentiful in the hill will be polished and placed out in the moonlight."

"Who can the strangers be?" asked the lizards; "what can the matter be? Hark, what a buzzing and humming there is!"

Just at this moment the elfin hill opened, and an old elfin maiden, hollow behind, came tripping out; she was the old elf king's housekeeper, and a distant relative of the family; therefore she wore an amber heart on the middle of her forehead. Her feet moved very fast, "trip, trip;" good gracious, how she could trip right down to the sea to the night-raven.

"You are invited to the elf hill for this evening," said she; "but will you do me a great favor and undertake the invitations? you ought to do something, for you have no housekeeping to attend to as I have. We are going to have some very grand people, conjurors, who have always something to say; and therefore the old elf king wishes to make a great display."

"Who is to be invited?" asked the raven.

"All the world may come to the great ball, even human beings, if they can only talk in their sleep, or do something after our fashion. But for the feast the company must be carefully selected; we can only admit persons of high rank; I have had a dispute myself with the elf king, as he thought we could not admit ghosts. The merman and his daughter must be invited first, although it may not be agreeable to them to remain so long on dry land, but they shall have a wet stone to sit on, or perhaps something better; so I think they will not refuse this time. We must have all the old demons of the first class, with tails, and the hobgoblins and imps; and then I think we ought not to leave out the death-horse, or the grave-pig, or even the church dwarf, although they do belong to the clergy, and are not reckoned among our people; but that is merely their office, they are nearly related to us, and visit us very frequently."

"Croak," said the night-raven as he flew away with the invitations.

The elfin maidens we're already dancing on the elf hill, and they danced in shawls woven from moonshine and mist, which look very pretty to those who like such things. The large hall within the elf hill was splendidly decorated; the floor had been washed with moonshine, and the walls had been rubbed with magic ointment, so that they glowed like tulip-leaves in the light. In the kitchen were frogs roasting on the spit, and dishes preparing of snail skins, with children's fingers in them, salad of mushroom seed, hemlock, noses and marrow of mice, beer from the marsh woman's brewery, and sparkling salt-petre wine from the grave cellars. These were all substantial food. Rusty nails and church-window glass formed the dessert. The old elf king had his gold crown polished up with powdered slate-pencil; it was like that used by the first form, and very difficult for an elf king to obtain. In the bedrooms, curtains were hung up and fastened with the slime of snails; there was, indeed, a buzzing and humming everywhere.

"Now we must fumigate the place with burnt horse-hair and pig's bristles, and then I think I shall have done my part," said the elf man-servant.

"Father, dear," said the youngest daughter, "may I now hear who our high-born visitors are?"

"Well, I suppose I must tell you now," he replied; "two of my daughters must prepare themselves to be married, for the marriages certainly will take place. The old goblin from Norway, who lives in the ancient Dovre mountains, and who possesses many castles built of rock and freestone, besides a gold mine, which is better than all, so it is thought, is coming with his two sons, who are both seeking a wife. The old goblin is a true-hearted, honest, old Norwegian graybeard; cheerful and straightforward. I knew him formerly, when we used to drink together to our good fellowship: he came here once to fetch his wife, she is dead now. She was the daughter of the king of the chalk-hills at Moen. They say he took his wife from chalk; I shall be delighted to see him again. It is said that the boys are ill-bred, forward lads, but perhaps that is not quite correct, and they will become better as they grow older. Let me see that you know how to teach them good manners."

"And when are they coming?" asked the daughter.

"That depends upon wind and weather," said the elf king; "they travel economically. They will come when there is the chance of a ship. I wanted them to come over to Sweden, but the old man was not inclined to take my advice. He does not go forward with the times, and that I do not like."

Two will-o'-the-wisps came jumping in, one quicker than the other, so of course, one arrived first. "They are coming! they are coming!" he cried.

"Give me my crown," said the elf king, "and let me stand in the moonshine."

The daughters drew on their shawls and bowed down to the ground. There stood the old goblin from the Dovre mountains, with his crown of hardened ice and polished fir-cones. Besides this, he wore a bear-skin, and great, warm boots, while his sons went with their throats bare and wore no braces, for they were strong men.

"Is that a hill?" said the youngest of the boys, pointing to the elf hill, "we should call it a hole in Norway."

"Boys," said the old man, "a hole goes in, and a hill stands out; have you no eyes in your heads?"

Another thing they wondered at was, that they were able without trouble to understand the language.

"Take care," said the old man, "or people will think you have not been well brought up."

Then they entered the elfin hill, where the select and grand company were assembled, and so quickly had they appeared that they seemed to have been blown together. But for each guest the neatest and pleasantest arrangement had been made. The sea folks sat at table in great water-tubs, and they said it was just like being at home. All behaved themselves properly excepting the two young northern goblins; they put their legs on the table and thought they were all right.

"Feet off the table-cloth!" said the old goblin. They obeyed, but not immediately. Then they tickled the ladies who waited at table, with the fir-cones, which they carried in their pockets. They took off their boots, that they might be more at ease, and gave them to the ladies to hold. But their father, the old goblin, was very different; he talked pleasantly about the stately Norwegian rocks, and told fine tales of the waterfalls which dashed over them with a clattering noise like thunder or the sound of an organ, spreading their white foam on every side. He told of the salmon that leaps in the rushing waters, while the water-god plays on his golden harp. He spoke of the bright winter nights, when the sledge bells are ringing, and the boys run with burning torches across the smooth ice, which is so transparent that they can see the fishes dart forward beneath their feet. He described everything so clearly, that those who listened could see it all; they could see the saw-mills going, the men-servants and the maidens singing songs, and dancing a rattling dance, – when all at once the old goblin gave the old elfin maiden a kiss, such a tremendous kiss, and yet they were almost strangers to each other.

Then the elfin girls had to dance, first in the usual way, and then with stamping feet, which they performed very well; then followed the artistic and solo dance. Dear me, how they did throw their legs about! No one could tell where the dance begun, or where it ended, nor indeed which were legs and which were arms, for they were all flying about together, like the shavings in a saw-pit! And then they spun round so quickly that the death-horse and the grave-pig became sick and giddy, and were obliged to leave the table.

"Stop!" cried the old goblin, "is that the only house-keeping they can perform? Can they do anything more than dance and throw about their legs, and make a whirlwind?"

"You shall soon see what they can do," said the elf king. And then he called his youngest daughter to him. She was slender and fair as moonlight, and the most graceful of all the sisters. She took a white chip in her mouth, and vanished instantly; this was her accomplishment. But the old goblin said he should not like his wife to have such an accomplishment, and thought his boys would have the same objection. Another daughter could make a figure like herself follow her, as if she had a shadow, which none of the goblin folk ever had. The third was of quite a different sort; she had learnt in the brew-house of the moor witch how to lard elfin puddings with glow-worms.

"She will make a good housewife," said the old goblin, and then saluted her with his eyes instead of drinking her health; for he did not drink much.

Now came the fourth daughter, with a large harp to play upon; and when she struck the first chord, every one lifted up the left leg (for the goblins are left-legged), and at the second chord they found they must all do just what she wanted.

"That is a dangerous woman," said the old goblin; and the two sons walked out of the hill; they had had enough of it. "And what can the next daughter do?" asked the old goblin.

"I have learnt everything that is Norwegian," said she; "and I will never marry, unless I can go to Norway."

Then her youngest sister whispered to the old goblin, "That is only because she has heard, in a Norwegian song, that when the world shall decay, the cliffs of Norway will remain standing like monuments; and she wants to get there, that she may be safe; for she is so afraid of sinking."

"Ho! ho!" said the old goblin, "is that what she means? Well, what can the seventh and last do?"

"The sixth comes before the seventh," said the elf king, for he could reckon; but the sixth would not come forward.

"I can only tell people the truth," said she. "No one cares for me, nor troubles himself about me; and I have enough to do to sew my grave clothes."

So the seventh and last came; and what could she do? Why, she could tell stories, as many as you liked, on any subject.

"Here are my five fingers," said the old goblin; "now tell me a story for each of them."

So she took him by the wrist, and he laughed till he nearly choked; and when she came to the fourth finger, there was a gold ring on it, as if it knew there was to be a betrothal. Then the old goblin said, "Hold fast what you have: this hand is yours; for I will have you for a wife myself."

Then the elfin girl said that the stories about the ring-finger and little Peter Playman had not yet been told.

"We will hear them in the winter," said the old goblin, "and also about the fir and the birch-trees, and the ghost stories, and of the tingling frost. You shall tell your tales, for no one over there can do it so well; and we will sit in the stone rooms, where the pine logs are burning, and drink mead out of the golden drinking-horn of the old Norwegian kings. The water-god has given me two; and when we sit there, Nix comes to pay us a visit, and will sing you all the songs of the mountain shepherdesses. How merry we shall be! The salmon will be leaping in the waterfalls, and dashing against the stone walls, but he will not be able to come in. It is indeed very pleasant to live in old Norway. But where are the lads?"

Where indeed were they? Why, running about the fields, and blowing out the will-o'-the-wisps, who so good-naturedly came and brought their torches.

"What tricks have you been playing?" said the old goblin. "I have taken a mother for you, and now you may take one of your aunts."

But the youngsters said they would rather make a speech and drink to their good fellowship; they had no wish to marry. Then they made speeches and drank toasts, and tipped their glasses, to show that they were empty. Then they took off their coats, and lay down on the table to sleep; for they made themselves quite at home. But the old goblin danced about the room with his young bride, and exchanged boots with her, which is more fashionable than exchanging rings.

"The cock is crowing," said the old elfin maiden who acted as housekeeper; "now we must close the shutters, that the sun may not scorch us."

Then the hill closed up. But the lizards continued to run up and down the riven tree; and one said to the other, "Oh, how much I was pleased with the old goblin!"

"The boys pleased me better," said the earth-worm. But then the poor miserable creature could not see.

The Silver Shilling

THERE WAS ONCE a shilling, which came forth from the mint springing and shouting, "Hurrah! now I am going out into the wide world." And truly it did go out into the wide world. The children held it with warm hands, the miser with a cold and convulsive grasp, and the old people turned it about, goodness knows how many times, while the young people soon allowed it to roll away from them. The shilling was made of silver, it contained very little copper, and considered itself quite out in the world when it had been circulated for a year in the country in which it had been coined. One day, it really did go out into the world, for it belonged to a gentleman who was about to travel in foreign lands. This gentleman was not aware that the shilling lay at the bottom of his purse when he started, till he one day found it between his fingers. "Why," cried he, "here is a shilling from home; well, it must go on its travels with me now!" and the shilling jumped and rattled for joy, when it was put back again into the purse.

Here it lay among a number of foreign companions, who were always coming and going, one taking the place of another, but the shilling from home was always put back, and had to remain in the purse, which was certainly a mark of distinction. Many weeks passed, during which the shilling had travelled a long distance in the purse, without in the least knowing where he was. He had found out that the other coins were French and Italian; and one coin said they were in this town, and another said they were in that, but the shilling was unable to make out or imagine what they meant. A man certainly cannot see much of the world if he is tied up in a bag, and this was really the shilling's fate. But one day, as he was lying in the purse, he noticed that it was not quite closed, and so he slipped near to the opening to have a little peep into society. He certainly had not the least idea of what would follow, but he was curious, and curiosity often brings its own punishment. In his eagerness, he came so near the edge of the purse that he slipped out into the pocket of the trousers; and when, in the evening, the purse was taken out, the shilling was left behind in the corner to which it had fallen. As the clothes were being carried into the hall, the shilling fell out on the floor, unheard and unnoticed by any one. The next morning the clothes were taken back to the room, the gentleman put them on, and started on his journey again; but the shilling remained behind on the floor. After a time it was found, and being considered a good coin, was placed with three other coins. "Ah," thought the shilling, "this is pleasant; I shall now see the world, become acquainted with other people, and learn other customs."

"Do you call that a shilling?" said some one the next moment. "That is not a genuine coin of the country, – it is false; it is good for nothing."

Now begins the story as it was afterwards related by the shilling himself.

"'False! good for nothing!' said he. That remark went through and through me like a dagger. I knew that I had a true ring, and that mine was a genuine stamp. These people must at all events be wrong, or they could not mean me. But yes, I was the one they called 'false, and good for nothing.'

"'Then I must pay it away in the dark,' said the man who had received me. So I was to be got rid of in the darkness, and be again insulted in broad daylight.

"'False! good for nothing!' Oh, I must contrive to get lost, thought I. And I trembled between the fingers of the people every time they tried to pass me off slyly as a coin of the country. Ah! unhappy shilling that I was! Of what use were my silver, my stamp, and my real value here, where all these qualities were worthless. In the eyes of the world, a man is valued just according to the opinion formed of him. It must be a shocking thing to have a guilty conscience, and to be sneaking about on account of wicked deeds. As for me, innocent as I was, I could not help shuddering before their eyes whenever they brought me out, for I knew I should be thrown back again up the table as a false pretender. At length I was paid away to a poor old woman, who received me as wages for a hard day's work. But she could not again get rid of me; no one would take me. I was to the woman a most unlucky shilling. 'I am positively obliged to pass this shilling to somebody,' said she; 'I cannot, with the best intentions, lay by a bad shilling. The rich baker shall have it, – he can bear the loss better than I can. But, after all, it is not a right thing to do.'

"'Ah!' sighed I to myself, 'am I also to be a burden on the conscience of this poor woman? Am I then in my old days so completely changed?' The woman offered me to the rich baker, but he knew the current money too well, and as soon as he received me he threw me almost in the woman's face. She could get no bread for me, and I felt quite grieved to the heart that I should be cause of so much trouble to another, and be treated as a cast-off coin. I who, in my young days, felt so joyful in the certainty of my own value, and knew so well that I bore a genuine stamp. I was as sorrowful now as a poor shilling can be when nobody will have him. The woman took me home again with her, and looking at me very earnestly, she said, 'No, I will not try to deceive any one with thee again. I will bore a hole through thee, that everyone may know that thou art a false and worthless thing; and yet, why should I do that? Very likely thou art a lucky shilling. A thought has just struck me that it is so, and I believe it. Yes, I will make a hole in the shilling,' said she, 'and run a string through it, and then give it to my neighbor's little one to hang round her neck, as a lucky shilling.' So she drilled a hole through me.

"It is really not at all pleasant to have a hole bored through one, but we can submit to a great deal when it is done with a good intention. A string was drawn through the hole, and I became a kind of medal. They hung me round the neck of a little child, and the child laughed at me and kissed me, and I rested for one whole night on the warm, innocent breast of a child.

"In the morning the child's mother took me between her fingers, and had certain thoughts about me, which I very soon found out. First, she looked for a pair of scissors, and cut the string.

"'Lucky shilling!' said she, 'certainly this is what I mean to try.' Then she laid me in vinegar till I became quite green, and after that she filled up the hole with cement, rubbed me a little to brighten me up, and went out in the twilight hour to the lottery collector, to buy herself a ticket, with a shilling that should bring luck. How everything seemed to cause me trouble. The lottery collector pressed me so hard that I thought I should crack. I had been called false, I had been thrown away, – that I knew; and there were many shillings and coins with inscriptions and stamps of all kinds lying about. I well knew how proud they were, so I avoided them from very shame. With the collector were several men who seemed to have a great deal to do, so I fell unnoticed into a chest, among several other coins.

"Whether the lottery ticket gained a prize, I know not; but this I know, that in a very few days after, I was recognized as a bad shilling, and laid aside. Everything that happened seemed always to add to my sorrow. Even if a man has a good character, it is of no use for him to deny what is said of him, for he is not considered an impartial judge of himself.

"A year passed, and in this way I had been changed from hand to hand; always abused, always looked at with displeasure, and trusted by no one; but I trusted in myself, and had no confidence in the world. Yes, that was a very dark time.

"At length one day I was passed to a traveller, a foreigner, the very same who had brought me away from home; and he was simple and true-hearted enough to take me for current coin. But would he also attempt to pass me? and should I again hear the outcry, 'False! good-for-nothing!' The traveller examined me attentively, 'I took thee for good coin,' said he; then suddenly a smile spread all over his face. I have never seen such a smile on any other face as on his. 'Now this is singular,' said he, 'it is a coin from my own country; a good, true, shilling from home. Some one has bored a hole through it, and people have no doubt called it false. How curious that it should come into my hands. I will take it home with me to my own house.'

"Joy thrilled through me when I heard this. I had been once more called a good, honest shilling, and I was to go back to my own home, where each and all would recognize me, and know that I was made of good silver, and bore a true, genuine stamp. I should have been glad in my joy to throw out sparks of fire, but it has never at any time been my nature to sparkle. Steel can do so, but not silver. I was wrapped up in fine, white paper, that I might not mix with the other coins and be lost; and on special occasions, when people from my own country happened to be present, I was brought forward and spoken of very kindly. They said I was very interesting, and it was really quite worth while to notice that those who are interesting have often not a single word to say for themselves.

"At length I reached home. All my cares were at an end. Joy again overwhelmed me; for was I not good silver, and had I not a genuine stamp? I had no more insults or disappointments to endure; although, indeed, there was a hole through me, as if I were false; but suspicions are nothing when a man is really true, and every one should persevere in acting honestly, for all will be made right in time. That is my firm belief," said the shilling.

The Conceited Apple-Branch

IT WAS THE month of May. The wind still blew cold; but from bush and tree, field and flower, came the welcome sound, "Spring is come." Wild-flowers in profusion covered the hedges. Under the little apple-tree, Spring seemed busy, and told his tale from one of the branches which hung fresh and blooming, and covered with delicate pink blossoms that were just ready to open. The branch well knew how beautiful it was; this knowledge exists as much in the leaf as in the blood; I was therefore not surprised when a nobleman's carriage, in which sat the young countess, stopped in the road just by. She said that an apple-branch was a most lovely object, and an emblem of spring in its most charming aspect. Then the branch was broken off for her, and she held it in her delicate hand, and sheltered it with her silk parasol. Then they drove to the castle, in which were lofty halls and splendid drawing-rooms. Pure white curtains fluttered before the open windows, and beautiful flowers stood in shining, transparent vases; and in one of them, which looked as if it had been cut out of newly fallen snow, the apple-branch was placed, among some fresh, light twigs of beech. It was a charming sight. Then the branch became proud, which was very much like human nature.

People of every description entered the room, and, according to their position in society, so dared they to express their admiration. Some few said nothing, others expressed too much, and the apple-branch very soon got to understand that there was as much difference in the characters of human beings as in those of plants and flowers. Some are all for pomp and parade, others have a great deal to do to maintain their own importance, while the rest might be spared without much loss to society. So thought the apple-branch, as he stood before the open window, from which he could see out over gardens and fields, where there were flowers and plants enough for him to think and reflect upon; some rich and beautiful, some poor and humble indeed.

"Poor, despised herbs," said the apple-branch; "there is really a difference between them and such as I am. How unhappy they must be, if they can feel as those in my position do! There is a difference indeed, and so there ought to be, or we should all be equals."

And the apple-branch looked with a sort of pity upon them, especially on a certain little flower that is found in fields and in ditches. No one bound these flowers together in a nosegay; they were too common; they were even known to grow between the paving-stones, shooting up everywhere, like bad weeds; and they bore the very ugly name of "dog-flowers" or "dandelions."

"Poor, despised plants," said the apple-bough, "it is not your fault that you are so ugly, and that you have such an ugly name; but it is with plants as with men, – there must be a difference."

"A difference!" cried the sunbeam, as he kissed the blooming apple-branch, and then kissed the yellow dandelion out in the fields. All were brothers, and the sunbeam kissed them – the poor flowers as well as the rich.

The apple-bough had never thought of the boundless love of God, which extends over all the works of creation, over everything which lives, and moves, and has its being in Him; he had never thought of the good and beautiful which are so often hidden, but can never remain forgotten by Him, – not only among the lower creation, but also among men. The sunbeam, the ray of light, knew better.

"You do not see very far, nor very clearly," he said to the apple-branch. "Which is the despised plant you so specially pity?"

"The dandelion," he replied. "No one ever places it in a nosegay; it is often trodden under foot, there are so many of them; and when they run to seed, they have flowers like wool, which fly away in little pieces over the roads, and cling to the dresses of the people. They are only weeds; but of course there must be weeds. O, I am really very thankful that I was not made like one of these flowers."

There came presently across the fields a whole group of children, the youngest of whom was so small that it had to be carried by the others; and when he was seated on the grass, among the yellow flowers, he laughed aloud with joy, kicked out his little legs, rolled about, plucked the yellow flowers, and kissed them in childlike innocence. The elder children broke off the flowers with long stems, bent the stalks one round the other, to form links, and made first a chain for the neck, then one to go across the shoulders, and hang down to the waist, and at last a wreath to wear round the head, so that they looked quite splendid in their garlands of green stems and golden flowers. But the eldest among them gathered carefully the faded flowers, on the stem of which was grouped together the seed, in the form of a white feathery coronal. These loose, airy wool-flowers are very beautiful, and look like fine snowy feathers or down. The children held them to their mouths, and tried to blow away the whole coronal with one puff of the breath. They had been told by their grandmothers that who ever did so would be sure to have new clothes before the end of the year. The despised flower was by this raised to the position of a prophet or foreteller of events.

"Do you see," said the sunbeam, "do you see the beauty of these flowers? do you see their powers of giving pleasure?"

"Yes, to children," said the apple-bough.

By-and-by an old woman came into the field, and, with a blunt knife without a handle, began to dig round the roots of some of the dandelion-plants, and pull them up. With some of these she intended to make tea for herself; but the rest she was going to sell to the chemist, and obtain some money.

"But beauty is of higher value than all this," said the apple-tree branch; "only the chosen ones can be admitted into the realms of the beautiful. There is a difference between plants, just as there is a difference between men."

Then the sunbeam spoke of the boundless love of God, as seen in creation, and over all that lives, and of the equal distribution of His gifts, both in time and in eternity.

"That is your opinion," said the apple-bough.

Then some people came into the room, and, among them, the young countess, – the lady who had placed the apple-bough in the transparent vase, so pleasantly beneath the rays of the sunlight. She carried in her hand something that seemed like a flower. The object was hidden by two or three great leaves, which covered it like a shield, so that no draught or gust of wind could injure it, and it was carried more carefully than the apple-branch had ever been. Very cautiously the large leaves were removed, and there appeared the feathery seed-crown of the despised dandelion. This was what the lady had so carefully plucked, and carried home so safely covered, so that not one of the delicate feathery arrows of which its mist-like shape was so lightly formed, should flutter away. She now drew it forth quite uninjured, and wondered at its beautiful form, and airy lightness, and singular construction, so soon to be blown away by the wind.

"See," she exclaimed, "how wonderfully God has made this little flower. I will paint it with the apple-branch together. Every one admires the beauty of the apple-bough; but this humble flower has been endowed by Heaven with another kind of loveliness; and although they differ in appearance, both are the children of the realms of beauty."

Then the sunbeam kissed the lowly flower, and he kissed the blooming apple-branch, upon whose leaves appeared a rosy blush.

The Darning-Needle

THERE WAS ONCE a darning-needle who thought herself so fine that she fancied she must be fit for embroidery. "Hold me tight," she would say to the fingers, when they took her up, "don't let me fall; if you do I shall never be found again, I am so very fine."

"That is your opinion, is it?" said the fingers, as they seized her round the body.

"See, I am coming with a train," said the darning-needle, drawing a long thread after her; but there was no knot in the thread.

The fingers then placed the point of the needle against the cook's slipper. There was a crack in the upper leather, which had to be sewn together.

"What coarse work!" said the darning-needle, "I shall never get through. I shall break! – I am breaking!" and sure enough she broke. "Did I not say so?" said the darning-needle, "I know I am too fine for such work as that."

"This needle is quite useless for sewing now," said the fingers; but they still held it fast, and the cook dropped some sealing-wax on the needle, and fastened her handkerchief with it in front.

"So now I am a breast-pin," said the darning-needle; "I knew very well I should come to honor some day: merit is sure to rise;" and she laughed, quietly to herself, for of course no one ever saw a darning-needle laugh. And there she sat as proudly as if she were in a state coach, and looked all around her. "May I be allowed to ask if you are made of gold?" she inquired of her neighbor, a pin; "you have a very pretty appearance, and a curious head, although you are rather small. You must take pains to grow, for it is not every one who has sealing-wax dropped upon him;" and as she spoke, the darning-needle drew herself up so proudly that she fell out of the handkerchief right into the sink, which the cook was cleaning. "Now I am going on a journey," said the needle, as she floated away with the dirty water, "I do hope I shall not be lost." But she really was lost in a gutter. "I am too fine for this world," said the darning-needle, as she lay in the gutter; "but I know who I am, and that is always some comfort." So the darning-needle kept up her proud behavior, and did not lose her good humor. Then there floated over her all sorts of things, – chips and straws, and pieces of old newspaper. "See how they sail," said the darning-needle; "they do not know what is under them. I am here, and here I shall stick. See, there goes a chip, thinking of nothing in the world but himself – only a chip. There's a straw going by now; how he turns and twists about! Don't be thinking too much of yourself, or you may chance to run against a stone. There swims a piece of newspaper; what is written upon it has been forgotten long ago, and yet it gives itself airs. I sit here patiently and quietly. I know who I am, so I shall not move."

One day something lying close to the darning-needle glittered so splendidly that she thought it was a diamond; yet it was only a piece of broken bottle. The darning-needle spoke to it, because it sparkled, and represented herself as a breast-pin. "I suppose you are really a diamond?" she said.

"Why yes, something of the kind," he replied; and so each believed the other to be very valuable, and then they began to talk about the world, and the conceited people in it.

"I have been in a lady's work-box," said the darning-needle, "and this lady was the cook. She had on each hand five fingers, and anything so conceited as these five fingers I have never seen; and yet they were only employed to take me out of the box and to put me back again."

"Were they not high-born?"

"High-born!" said the darning-needle, "no indeed, but so haughty. They were five brothers, all born fingers; they kept very proudly together, though they were of different lengths. The one who stood first in the rank was named the thumb, he was short and thick, and had only one joint in his back, and could therefore make but one bow; but he said that if he were cut off from a man's hand, that man would be unfit for a soldier. Sweet-tooth, his neighbor, dipped himself into sweet or sour, pointed to the sun and moon, and formed the letters when the fingers wrote. Longman, the middle finger, looked over the heads of all the others. Gold-band, the next finger, wore a golden circle round his waist. And little Playman did nothing at all, and seemed proud of it. They were boasters, and boasters they will remain; and therefore I left them."

"And now we sit here and glitter," said the piece of broken bottle.

At the same moment more water streamed into the gutter, so that it overflowed, and the piece of bottle was carried away.

"So he is promoted," said the darning-needle, "while I remain here; I am too fine, but that is my pride, and what do I care?" And so she sat there in her pride, and had many such thoughts as these, – "I could almost fancy that I came from a sunbeam, I am so fine. It seems as if the sunbeams were always looking for me under the water. Ah! I am so fine that even my mother cannot find me. Had I still my old eye, which was broken off, I believe I should weep; but no, I would not do that, it is not genteel to cry."

One day a couple of street boys were paddling in the gutter, for they sometimes found old nails, farthings, and other treasures. It was dirty work, but they took great pleasure in it. "Hallo!" cried one, as he pricked himself with the darning-needle, "here's a fellow for you."

"I am not a fellow, I am a young lady," said the darning-needle; but no one heard her.

The sealing-wax had come off, and she was quite black; but black makes a person look slender, so she thought herself even finer than before.

"Here comes an egg-shell sailing along," said one of the boys; so they stuck the darning-needle into the egg-shell.

"White walls, and I am black myself," said the darning-needle, "that looks well; now I can be seen, but I hope I shall not be sea-sick, or I shall break again." She was not sea-sick, and she did not break. "It is a good thing against sea-sickness to have a steel stomach, and not to forget one's own importance. Now my sea-sickness has past: delicate people can bear a great deal."

Crack went the egg-shell, as a waggon passed over it. "Good heavens, how it crushes!" said the darning-needle. "I shall be sick now. I am breaking!" but she did not break, though the waggon went over her as she lay at full length; and there let her lie.

The Bottle Neck

CLOSE TO THE corner of a street, among other abodes of poverty, stood an exceedingly tall, narrow house, which had been so knocked about by time that it seemed out of joint in every direction. This house was inhabited by poor people, but the deepest poverty was apparent in the garret lodging in the gable. In front of the little window, an old bent bird-cage hung in the sunshine, which had not even a proper water-glass, but instead of it the broken neck of a bottle, turned upside down, and a cork stuck in to make it hold the water with which it was filled. An old maid stood at the window; she had hung chickweed over the cage, and the little linnet which it contained hopped from perch to perch and sang and twittered merrily.

"Yes, it's all very well for you to sing," said the bottle neck: that is, he did not really speak the words as we do, for the neck of a bottle cannot speak; but he thought them to himself in his own mind, just as people sometimes talk quietly to themselves.

"Yes, you may sing very well, you have all your limbs uninjured; you should feel what it is like to lose your body, and only have a neck and a mouth left, with a cork stuck in it, as I have: you wouldn't sing then, I know. After all, it is just as well that there are some who can be happy. I have no reason to sing, nor could I sing now if I were ever so happy; but when I was a whole bottle, and they rubbed me with a cork, didn't I sing then? I used to be called a complete lark. I remember when I went out to a picnic with the furrier's family, on the day his daughter was betrothed, – it seems as if it only happened yesterday. I have gone through a great deal in my time, when I come to recollect: I have been in the fire and in the water, I have been deep in the earth, and have mounted higher in the air than most other people, and now I am swinging here, outside a bird-cage, in the air and the sunshine. Oh, indeed, it would be worth while to hear my history; but I do not speak it aloud, for a good reason – because I cannot."

Then the bottle neck related his history, which was really rather remarkable; he, in fact, related it to himself, or, at least, thought it in his own mind. The little bird sang his own song merrily; in the street below there was driving and running to and fro, every one thought of his own affairs, or perhaps of nothing at all; but the bottle neck thought deeply. He thought of the blazing furnace in the factory, where he had been blown into life; he remembered how hot it felt when he was placed in the heated oven, the home from which he sprang, and that he had a strong inclination to leap out again directly; but after a while it became cooler, and he found himself very comfortable. He had been placed in a row, with a whole regiment of his brothers and sisters all brought out of the same furnace; some of them had certainly been blown into champagne bottles, and others into beer bottles, which made a little difference between them. In the world it often happens that a beer bottle may contain the most precious wine, and a champagne bottle be filled with blacking, but even in decay it may always be seen whether a man has been well born. Nobility remains noble, as a champagne bottle remains the same, even with blacking in its interior. When the bottles were packed our bottle was packed amongst them; it little expected then to finish its career as a bottle neck, or to be used as a water-glass to a bird's-cage, which is, after all, a place of honor, for it is to be of some use in the world. The bottle did not behold the light of day again, until it was unpacked with the rest in the wine merchant's cellar, and, for the first time, rinsed with water, which caused some very curious sensations. There it lay empty, and without a cork, and it had a peculiar feeling, as if it wanted something it knew not what. At last it was filled with rich and costly wine, a cork was placed in it, and sealed down. Then it was labelled "first quality," as if it had carried off the first prize at an examination; besides, the wine and the bottle were both good, and while we are young is the time for poetry. There were sounds of song within the bottle, of things it could not understand, of green sunny mountains, where the vines grow and where the merry vine-dressers laugh, sing, and are merry. "Ah, how beautiful is life." All these tones of joy and song in the bottle were like the working of a young poet's brain, who often knows not the meaning of the tones which are sounding within him. One morning the bottle found a purchaser in the furrier's apprentice, who was told to bring one of the best bottles of wine. It was placed in the provision basket with ham and cheese and sausages. The sweetest fresh butter and the finest bread were put into the basket by the furrier's daughter herself, for she packed it. She was young and pretty; her brown eyes laughed, and a smile lingered round her mouth as sweet as that in her eyes. She had delicate hands, beautifully white, and her neck was whiter still. It could easily be seen that she was a very lovely girl, and as yet she was not engaged. The provision basket lay in the lap of the young girl as the family drove out to the forest, and the neck of the bottle peeped out from between the folds of the white napkin. There was the red wax on the cork, and the bottle looked straight at the young girl's face, and also at the face of the young sailor who sat near her. He was a young friend, the son of a portrait painter. He had lately passed his examination with honor, as mate, and the next morning he was to sail in his ship to a distant coast. There had been a great deal of talk on this subject while the basket was being packed, and during this conversation the eyes and the mouth of the furrier's daughter did not wear a very joyful expression. The young people wandered away into the green wood, and talked together. What did they talk about? The bottle could not say, for he was in the provision basket. It remained there a long time; but when at last it was brought forth it appeared as if something pleasant had happened, for every one was laughing; the furrier's daughter laughed too, but she said very little, and her cheeks were like two roses. Then her father took the bottle and the cork-screw into his hands. What a strange sensation it was to have the cork drawn for the first time! The bottle could never after that forget the performance of that moment; indeed there was quite a convulsion within him as the cork flew out, and a gurgling sound as the wine was poured forth into the glasses.

"Long life to the betrothed," cried the papa, and every glass was emptied to the dregs, while the young sailor kissed his beautiful bride.

"Happiness and blessing to you both," said the old people-father and mother, and the young man filled the glasses again.

"Safe return, and a wedding this day next year," he cried; and when the glasses were empty he took the bottle, raised it on high, and said, "Thou hast been present here on the happiest day of my life; thou shalt never be used by others!" So saying, he hurled it high in the air.

The furrier's daughter thought she should never see it again, but she was mistaken. It fell among the rushes on the borders of a little woodland lake. The bottle neck remembered well how long it lay there unseen. "I gave them wine, and they gave me muddy water," he had said to himself, "but I suppose it was all well meant." He could no longer see the betrothed couple, nor the cheerful old people; but for a long time he could hear them rejoicing and singing. At length there came by two peasant boys, who peeped in among the reeds and spied out the bottle. Then they took it up and carried it home with them, so that once more it was provided for. At home in their wooden cottage these boys had an elder brother, a sailor, who was about to start on a long voyage. He had been there the day before to say farewell, and his mother was now very busy packing up various things for him to take with him on his voyage. In the evening his father was going to carry the parcel to the town to see his son once more, and take him a farewell greeting from his mother. A small bottle had already been filled with herb tea, mixed with brandy, and wrapped in a parcel; but when the boys came in they brought with them a larger and stronger bottle, which they had found. This bottle would hold so much more than the little one, and they all said the brandy would be so good for complaints of the stomach, especially as it was mixed with medical herbs. The liquid which they now poured into the bottle was not like the red wine with which it had once been filled; these were bitter drops, but they are of great use sometimes-for the stomach. The new large bottle was to go, not the little one: so the bottle once more started on its travels. It was taken on board (for Peter Jensen was one of the crew) the very same ship in which the young mate was to sail. But the mate did not see the bottle: indeed, if he had he would not have known it, or supposed it was the one out of which they had drunk to the felicity of the betrothed and to the prospect of a marriage on his own happy return. Certainly the bottle no longer poured forth wine, but it contained something quite as good; and so it happened that whenever Peter Jensen brought it out, his messmates gave it the name of "the apothecary," for it contained the best medicine to cure the stomach, and he gave it out quite willingly as long as a drop remained. Those were happy days, and the bottle would sing when rubbed with a cork, and it was called a "great lark," "Peter Jensen's lark."

Long days and months rolled by, during which the bottle stood empty in a corner, when a storm arose – whether on the passage out or home it could not tell, for it had never been ashore. It was a terrible storm, great waves arose, darkly heaving and tossing the vessel to and fro. The main mast was split asunder, the ship sprang a leak, and the pumps became useless, while all around was black as night. At the last moment, when the ship was sinking, the young mate wrote on a piece of paper, "We are going down: God's will be done." Then he wrote the name of his betrothed, his own name, and that of the ship. Then he put the leaf in an empty bottle that happened to be at hand, corked it down tightly, and threw it into the foaming sea. He knew not that it was the very same bottle from which the goblet of joy and hope had once been filled for him, and now it was tossing on the waves with his last greeting, and a message from the dead. The ship sank, and the crew sank with her; but the bottle flew on like a bird, for it bore within it a loving letter from a loving heart. And as the sun rose and set, the bottle felt as at the time of its first existence, when in the heated glowing stove it had a longing to fly away. It outlived the storms and the calm, it struck against no rocks, was not devoured by sharks, but drifted on for more than a year, sometimes towards the north, sometimes towards the south, just as the current carried it. It was in all other ways its own master, but even of that one may get tired. The written leaf, the last farewell of the bridegroom to his bride, would only bring sorrow when once it reached her hands; but where were those hands, so soft and delicate, which had once spread the table-cloth on the fresh grass in the green wood, on the day of her betrothal? Ah, yes! where was the furrier's daughter? and where was the land which might lie nearest to her home?

The bottle knew not, it travelled onward and onward, and at last all this wandering about became wearisome; at all events it was not its usual occupation. But it had to travel, till at length it reached land – a foreign country. Not a word spoken in this country could the bottle understand; it was a language it had never before heard, and it is a great loss not to be able to understand a language. The bottle was fished out of the water, and examined on all sides. The little letter contained within it was discovered, taken out, and turned and twisted in every direction; but the people could not understand what was written upon it. They could be quite sure that the bottle had been thrown overboard from a vessel, and that something about it was written on this paper: but what was written? that was the question, – so the paper was put back into the bottle, and then both were put away in a large cupboard of one of the great houses of the town. Whenever any strangers arrived, the paper was taken out and turned over and over, so that the address, which was only written in pencil, became almost illegible, and at last no one could distinguish any letters on it at all. For a whole year the bottle remained standing in the cupboard, and then it was taken up to the loft, where it soon became covered with dust and cobwebs. Ah! how often then it thought of those better days – of the times when in the fresh, green wood, it had poured forth rich wine; or, while rocked by the swelling waves, it had carried in its bosom a secret, a letter, a last parting sigh. For full twenty years it stood in the loft, and it might have stayed there longer but that the house was going to be rebuilt. The bottle was discovered when the roof was taken off; they talked about it, but the bottle did not understand what they said – a language is not to be learnt by living in a loft, even for twenty years. "If I had been down stairs in the room," thought the bottle, "I might have learnt it." It was now washed and rinsed, which process was really quite necessary, and afterwards it looked clean and transparent, and felt young again in its old age; but the paper which it had carried so faithfully was destroyed in the washing. They filled the bottle with seeds, though it scarcely knew what had been placed in it. Then they corked it down tightly, and carefully wrapped it up. There not even the light of a torch or lantern could reach it, much less the brightness of the sun or moon. "And yet," thought the bottle, "men go on a journey that they may see as much as possible, and I can see nothing." However, it did something quite as important; it travelled to the place of its destination, and was unpacked.

"What trouble they have taken with that bottle over yonder!" said one, "and very likely it is broken after all." But the bottle was not broken, and, better still, it understood every word that was said: this language it had heard at the furnaces and at the wine merchant's; in the forest and on the ship, – it was the only good old language it could understand. It had returned home, and the language was as a welcome greeting. For very joy, it felt ready to jump out of people's hands, and scarcely noticed that its cork had been drawn, and its contents emptied out, till it found itself carried to a cellar, to be left there and forgotten. "There's no place like home, even if it's a cellar." It never occurred to him to think that he might lie there for years, he felt so comfortable. For many long years he remained in the cellar, till at last some people came to carry away the bottles, and ours amongst the number.

Out in the garden there was a great festival. Brilliant lamps hung in festoons from tree to tree; and paper lanterns, through which the light shone till they looked like transparent tulips. It was a beautiful evening, and the weather mild and clear. The stars twinkled; and the new moon, in the form of a crescent, was surrounded by the shadowy disc of the whole moon, and looked like a gray globe with a golden rim: it was a beautiful sight for those who had good eyes. The illumination extended even to the most retired of the garden walks, at least not so retired that any one need lose himself there. In the borders were placed bottles, each containing a light, and among them the bottle with which we are acquainted, and whose fate it was, one day, to be only a bottle neck, and to serve as a water-glass to a bird's-cage. Everything here appeared lovely to our bottle, for it was again in the green wood, amid joy and feasting; again it heard music and song, and the noise and murmur of a crowd, especially in that part of the garden where the lamps blazed, and the paper lanterns displayed their brilliant colors. It stood in a distant walk certainly, but a place pleasant for contemplation; and it carried a light; and was at once useful and ornamental. In such an hour it is easy to forget that one has spent twenty years in a loft, and a good thing it is to be able to do so. Close before the bottle passed a single pair, like the bridal pair – the mate and the furrier's daughter – who had so long ago wandered in the wood. It seemed to the bottle as if he were living that time over again. Not only the guests but other people were walking in the garden, who were allowed to witness the splendor and the festivities. Among the latter came an old maid, who seemed to be quite alone in the world. She was thinking, like the bottle, of the green wood, and of a young betrothed pair, who were closely connected with herself; she was thinking of that hour, the happiest of her life, in which she had taken part, when she had herself been one of that betrothed pair; such hours are never to be forgotten, let a maiden be as old as she may. But she did not recognize the bottle, neither did the bottle notice the old maid. And so we often pass each other in the world when we meet, as did these two, even while together in the same town.

The bottle was taken from the garden, and again sent to a wine merchant, where it was once more filled with wine, and sold to an aeronaut, who was to make an ascent in his balloon on the following Sunday. A great crowd assembled to witness the sight; military music had been engaged, and many other preparations made. The bottle saw it all from the basket in which he lay close to a live rabbit. The rabbit was quite excited because he knew that he was to be taken up, and let down again in a parachute. The bottle, however, knew nothing of the "up," or the "down;" he saw only that the balloon was swelling larger and larger till it could swell no more, and began to rise and be restless. Then the ropes which held it were cut through, and the aerial ship rose in the air with the aeronaut and the basket containing the bottle and the rabbit, while the music sounded and all the people shouted "Hurrah."

"This is a wonderful journey up into the air," thought the bottle; "it is a new way of sailing, and here, at least, there is no fear of striking against anything."

Thousands of people gazed at the balloon, and the old maid who was in the garden saw it also; for she stood at the open window of the garret, by which hung the cage containing the linnet, who then had no water-glass, but was obliged to be contented with an old cup. In the window-sill stood a myrtle in a pot, and this had been pushed a little on one side, that it might not fall out; for the old maid was leaning out of the window, that she might see. And she did see distinctly the aeronaut in the balloon, and how he let down the rabbit in the parachute, and then drank to the health of all the spectators in the wine from the bottle. After doing this, he hurled it high into the air. How little she thought that this was the very same bottle which her friend had thrown aloft in her honor, on that happy day of rejoicing, in the green wood, in her youthful days. The bottle had no time to think, when raised so suddenly; and before it was aware, it reached the highest point it had ever attained in its life. Steeples and roofs lay far, far beneath it, and the people looked as tiny as possible. Then it began to descend much more rapidly than the rabbit had done, made somersaults in the air, and felt itself quite young and unfettered, although it was half full of wine. But this did not last long. What a journey it was! All the people could see the bottle; for the sun shone upon it. The balloon was already far away, and very soon the bottle was far away also; for it fell upon a roof, and broke in pieces. But the pieces had got such an impetus in them, that they could not stop themselves. They went jumping and rolling about, till at last they fell into the court-yard, and were broken into still smaller pieces; only the neck of the bottle managed to keep whole, and it was broken off as clean as if it had been cut with a diamond.

"That would make a capital bird's glass," said one of the cellar-men; but none of them had either a bird or a cage, and it was not to be expected they would provide one just because they had found a bottle neck that could be used as a glass. But the old maid who lived in the garret had a bird, and it really might be useful to her; so the bottle neck was provided with a cork, and taken up to her; and, as it often happens in life, the part that had been uppermost was now turned downwards, and it was filled with fresh water. Then they hung it in the cage of the little bird, who sang and twittered more merrily than ever.

"Ah, you have good reason to sing," said the bottle neck, which was looked upon as something very remarkable, because it had been in a balloon; nothing further was known of its history. As it hung there in the bird's-cage, it could hear the noise and murmur of the people in the street below, as well as the conversation of the old maid in the room within. An old friend had just come to visit her, and they talked, not about the bottle neck, but of the myrtle in the window.

"No, you must not spend a dollar for your daughter's bridal bouquet," said the old maid; "you shall have a beautiful little bunch for a nosegay, full of blossoms. Do you see how splendidly the tree has grown? It has been raised from only a little sprig of myrtle that you gave me on the day after my betrothal, and from which I was to make my own bridal bouquet when a year had passed: but that day never came; the eyes were closed which were to have been my light and joy through life. In the depths of the sea my beloved sleeps sweetly; the myrtle has become an old tree, and I am a still older woman. Before the sprig you gave me faded, I took a spray, and planted it in the earth; and now, as you see, it has become a large tree, and a bunch of the blossoms shall at last appear at a wedding festival, in the bouquet of your daughter."

There were tears in the eyes of the old maid, as she spoke of the beloved of her youth, and of their betrothal in the wood. Many thoughts came into her mind; but the thought never came, that quite close to her, in that very window, was a remembrance of those olden times, – the neck of the bottle which had, as it were shouted for joy when the cork flew out with a bang on the betrothal day. But the bottle neck did not recognize the old maid; he had not been listening to what she had related, perhaps because he was thinking so much about her.

The Old Street Lamp

DID YOU EVER hear the story of the old street lamp? It is not remarkably interesting, but for once in a way you may as well listen to it. It was a most respectable old lamp, which had seen many, many years of service, and now was to retire with a pension. It was this evening at its post for the last time, giving light to the street. His feelings were something like those of an old dancer at the theatre, who is dancing for the last time, and knows that on the morrow she will be in her garret, alone and forgotten. The lamp had very great anxiety about the next day, for he knew that he had to appear for the first time at the town hall, to be inspected by the mayor and the council, who were to decide if he were fit for further service or not; – whether the lamp was good enough to be used to light the inhabitants of one of the suburbs, or in the country, at some factory; and if not, it would be sent at once to an iron foundry, to be melted down. In this latter case it might be turned into anything, and he wondered very much whether he would then be able to remember that he had once been a street lamp, and it troubled him exceedingly. Whatever might happen, one thing seemed certain, that he would be separated from the watchman and his wife, whose family he looked upon as his own. The lamp had first been hung up on that very evening that the watchman, then a robust young man, had entered upon the duties of his office. Ah, well, it was a very long time since one became a lamp and the other a watchman. His wife had a little pride in those days; she seldom condescended to glance at the lamp, excepting when she passed by in the evening, never in the daytime. But in later years, when all these, – the watchman, the wife, and the lamp – had grown old, she had attended to it, cleaned it, and supplied it with oil. The old people were thoroughly honest, they had never cheated the lamp of a single drop of the oil provided for it.

This was the lamp's last night in the street, and to-morrow he must go to the town-hall, – two very dark things to think of. No wonder he did not burn brightly. Many other thoughts also passed through his mind. How many persons he had lighted on their way, and how much he had seen; as much, very likely, as the mayor and corporation themselves! None of these thoughts were uttered aloud, however; for he was a good, honorable old lamp, who would not willingly do harm to any one, especially to those in authority. As many things were recalled to his mind, the light would flash up with sudden brightness; he had, at such moments, a conviction that he would be remembered. "There was a handsome young man once," thought he; "it is certainly a long while ago, but I remember he had a little note, written on pink paper with a gold edge; the writing was elegant, evidently a lady's hand: twice he read it through, and kissed it, and then looked up at me, with eyes that said quite plainly, 'I am the happiest of men!' Only he and I know what was written on this his first letter from his lady-love. Ah, yes, and there was another pair of eyes that I remember, – it is really wonderful how the thoughts jump from one thing to another! A funeral passed through the street; a young and beautiful woman lay on a bier, decked with garlands of flowers, and attended by torches, which quite overpowered my light. All along the street stood the people from the houses, in crowds, ready to join the procession. But when the torches had passed from before me, and I could look round, I saw one person alone, standing, leaning against my post, and weeping. Never shall I forget the sorrowful eyes that looked up at me." These and similar reflections occupied the old street lamp, on this the last time that his light would shine. The sentry, when he is relieved from his post, knows at least who will succeed him, and may whisper a few words to him, but the lamp did not know his successor, or he could have given him a few hints respecting rain, or mist, and could have informed him how far the moon's rays would rest on the pavement, and from which side the wind generally blew, and so on.

On the bridge over the canal stood three persons, who wished to recommend themselves to the lamp, for they thought he could give the office to whomsoever he chose. The first was a herring's head, which could emit light in the darkness. He remarked that it would be a great saving of oil if they placed him on the lamp-post. Number two was a piece of rotten wood, which also shines in the dark. He considered himself descended from an old stem, once the pride of the forest. The third was a glow-worm, and how he found his way there the lamp could not imagine, yet there he was, and could really give light as well as the others. But the rotten wood and the herring's head declared most solemnly, by all they held sacred, that the glow-worm only gave light at certain times, and must not be allowed to compete with themselves. The old lamp assured them that not one of them could give sufficient light to fill the position of a street lamp; but they would believe nothing he said. And when they discovered that he had not the power of naming his successor, they said they were very glad to hear it, for the lamp was too old and worn-out to make a proper choice.

At this moment the wind came rushing round the corner of the street, and through the air-holes of the old lamp. "What is this I hear?" said he; "that you are going away to-morrow? Is this evening the last time we shall meet? Then I must present you with a farewell gift. I will blow into your brain, so that in future you shall not only be able to remember all that you have seen or heard in the past, but your light within shall be so bright, that you shall be able to understand all that is said or done in your presence."

"Oh, that is really a very, very great gift," said the old lamp; "I thank you most heartily. I only hope I shall not be melted down."

"That is not likely to happen yet," said the wind; "and I will also blow a memory into you, so that should you receive other similar presents your old age will pass very pleasantly."

"That is if I am not melted down," said the lamp. "But should I in that case still retain my memory?"

"Do be reasonable, old lamp," said the wind, puffing away.

At this moment the moon burst forth from the clouds. "What will you give the old lamp?" asked the wind.

"I can give nothing," she replied; "I am on the wane, and no lamps have ever given me light while I have frequently shone upon them." And with these words the moon hid herself again behind the clouds, that she might be saved from further importunities. Just then a drop fell upon the lamp, from the roof of the house, but the drop explained that he was a gift from those gray clouds, and perhaps the best of all gifts. "I shall penetrate you so thoroughly," he said, "that you will have the power of becoming rusty, and, if you wish it, to crumble into dust in one night."

But this seemed to the lamp a very shabby present, and the wind thought so too. "Does no one give any more? Will no one give any more?" shouted the breath of the wind, as loud as it could. Then a bright falling star came down, leaving a broad, luminous streak behind it.

"What was that?" cried the herring's head. "Did not a star fall? I really believe it went into the lamp. Certainly, when such high-born personages try for the office, we may as well say 'Good-night,' and go home."

And so they did, all three, while the old lamp threw a wonderfully strong light all around him.

"This is a glorious gift," said he; "the bright stars have always been a joy to me, and have always shone more brilliantly than I ever could shine, though I have tried with my whole might; and now they have noticed me, a poor old lamp, and have sent me a gift that will enable me to see clearly everything that I remember, as if it still stood before me, and to be seen by all those who love me. And herein lies the truest pleasure, for joy which we cannot share with others is only half enjoyed."

"That sentiment does you honor," said the wind; "but for this purpose wax lights will be necessary. If these are not lighted in you, your particular faculties will not benefit others in the least. The stars have not thought of this; they suppose that you and every other light must be a wax taper: but I must go down now." So he laid himself to rest.

"Wax tapers, indeed!" said the lamp, "I have never yet had these, nor is it likely I ever shall. If I could only be sure of not being melted down!"

The next day. Well, perhaps we had better pass over the next day. The evening had come, and the lamp was resting in a grandfather's chair, and guess where! Why, at the old watchman's house. He had begged, as a favor, that the mayor and corporation would allow him to keep the street lamp, in consideration of his long and faithful service, as he had himself hung it up and lit it on the day he first commenced his duties, four-and-twenty years ago. He looked upon it almost as his own child; he had no children, so the lamp was given to him. There it lay in the great arm-chair near to the warm stove. It seemed almost as if it had grown larger, for it appeared quite to fill the chair. The old people sat at their supper, casting friendly glances at the old lamp, whom they would willingly have admitted to a place at the table. It is quite true that they dwelt in a cellar, two yards deep in the earth, and they had to cross a stone passage to get to their room, but within it was warm and comfortable and strips of list had been nailed round the door. The bed and the little window had curtains, and everything looked clean and neat. On the window seat stood two curious flower-pots which a sailor, named Christian, had brought over from the East or West Indies. They were of clay, and in the form of two elephants, with open backs; they were hollow and filled with earth, and through the open space flowers bloomed. In one grew some very fine chives or leeks; this was the kitchen garden. The other elephant, which contained a beautiful geranium, they called their flower garden. On the wall hung a large colored print, representing the congress of Vienna, and all the kings and emperors at once. A clock, with heavy weights, hung on the wall and went "tick, tick," steadily enough; yet it was always rather too fast, which, however, the old people said was better than being too slow. They were now eating their supper, while the old street lamp, as we have heard, lay in the grandfather's arm-chair near the stove. It seemed to the lamp as if the whole world had turned round; but after a while the old watchman looked at the lamp, and spoke of what they had both gone through together, – in rain and in fog; during the short bright nights of summer, or in the long winter nights, through the drifting snow-storms, when he longed to be at home in the cellar. Then the lamp felt it was all right again. He saw everything that had happened quite clearly, as if it were passing before him. Surely the wind had given him an excellent gift. The old people were very active and industrious, they were never idle for even a single hour. On Sunday afternoons they would bring out some books, generally a book of travels which they were very fond of. The old man would read aloud about Africa, with its great forests and the wild elephants, while his wife would listen attentively, stealing a glance now and then at the clay elephants, which served as flower-pots.

"I can almost imagine I am seeing it all," she said; and then how the lamp wished for a wax taper to be lighted in him, for then the old woman would have seen the smallest detail as clearly as he did himself. The lofty trees, with their thickly entwined branches, the naked negroes on horseback, and whole herds of elephants treading down bamboo thickets with their broad, heavy feet.

"What is the use of all my capabilities," sighed the old lamp, "when I cannot obtain any wax lights; they have only oil and tallow here, and these will not do." One day a great heap of wax-candle ends found their way into the cellar. The larger pieces were burnt, and the smaller ones the old woman kept for waxing her thread. So there were now candles enough, but it never occurred to any one to put a little piece in the lamp.

"Here I am now with my rare powers," thought the lamp, "I have faculties within me, but I cannot share them; they do not know that I could cover these white walls with beautiful tapestry, or change them into noble forests, or, indeed, to anything else they might wish for." The lamp, however, was always kept clean and shining in a corner where it attracted all eyes. Strangers looked upon it as lumber, but the old people did not care for that; they loved the lamp. One day – it was the watchman's birthday – the old woman approached the lamp, smiling to herself, and said, "I will have an illumination to-day in honor of my old man." And the lamp rattled in his metal frame, for he thought, "Now at last I shall have a light within me," but after all no wax light was placed in the lamp, but oil as usual. The lamp burned through the whole evening, and began to perceive too clearly that the gift of the stars would remain a hidden treasure all his life. Then he had a dream; for, to one with his faculties, dreaming was no difficulty. It appeared to him that the old people were dead, and that he had been taken to the iron foundry to be melted down. It caused him quite as much anxiety as on the day when he had been called upon to appear before the mayor and the council at the town-hall. But though he had been endowed with the power of falling into decay from rust when he pleased, he did not make use of it. He was therefore put into the melting-furnace and changed into as elegant an iron candlestick as you could wish to see, one intended to hold a wax taper. The candlestick was in the form of an angel holding a nosegay, in the centre of which the wax taper was to be placed. It was to stand on a green writing table, in a very pleasant room; many books were scattered about, and splendid paintings hung on the walls. The owner of the room was a poet, and a man of intellect; everything he thought or wrote was pictured around him. Nature showed herself to him sometimes in the dark forests, at others in cheerful meadows where the storks were strutting about, or on the deck of a ship sailing across the foaming sea with the clear, blue sky above, or at night the glittering stars. "What powers I possess!" said the lamp, awaking from his dream; "I could almost wish to be melted down; but no, that must not be while the old people live. They love me for myself alone, they keep me bright, and supply me with oil. I am as well off as the picture of the congress, in which they take so much pleasure." And from that time he felt at rest in himself, and not more so than such an honorable old lamp really deserved to be.

The Bell, or Nature's Music

IN THE NARROW streets of a large town people often heard in the evening, when the sun was setting, and his last rays gave a golden tint to the chimney-pots, a strange noise which resembled the sound of a church bell; it only lasted an instant, for it was lost in the continual roar of traffic and hum of voices which rose from the town. "The evening bell is ringing," people used to say; "the sun is setting!" Those who walked outside the town, where the houses were less crowded and interspersed by gardens and little fields, saw the evening sky much better, and heard the sound of the bell much more clearly. It seemed as though the sound came from a church, deep in the calm, fragrant wood, and thither people looked with devout feelings.

A considerable time elapsed: one said to the other, "I really wonder if there is a church out in the wood. The bell has indeed a strange sweet sound! Shall we go there and see what the cause of it is?" The rich drove, the poor walked, but the way seemed to them extraordinarily long, and when they arrived at a number of willow trees on the border of the wood they sat down, looked up into the great branches and thought they were now really in the wood. A confectioner from the town also came out and put up a stall there; then came another confectioner who hung a bell over his stall, which was covered with pitch to protect it from the rain, but the clapper was wanting.

When people came home they used to say that it had been very romantic, and that really means something else than merely taking tea. Three persons declared that they had gone as far as the end of the wood; they had always heard the strange sound, but there it seemed to them as if it came from the town. One of them wrote verses about the bell, and said that it was like the voice of a mother speaking to an intelligent and beloved child; no tune, he said, was sweeter than the sound of the bell.

The emperor of the country heard of it, and declared that he who would really find out where the sound came from should receive the title of "Bellringer to the World," even if there was no bell at all.

Now many went out into the wood for the sake of this splendid berth; but only one of them came back with some sort of explanation. None of them had gone far enough, nor had he, and yet he said that the sound of the bell came from a large owl in a hollow tree. It was a wisdom owl, which continually knocked its head against the tree, but he was unable to say with certainty whether its head or the hollow trunk of the tree was the cause of the noise.

He was appointed "Bellringer to the World," and wrote every year a short dissertation on the owl, but by this means people did not become any wiser than they had been before.

It was just confirmation-day. The clergyman had delivered a beautiful and touching sermon, the candidates were deeply moved by it; it was indeed a very important day for them; they were all at once transformed from mere children to grown-up people; the childish soul was to fly over, as it were, into a more reasonable being.

The sun shone most brightly; and the sound of the great unknown bell was heard more distinctly than ever. They had a mind to go thither, all except three. One of them wished to go home and try on her ball dress, for this very dress and the ball were the cause of her being confirmed this time, otherwise she would not have been allowed to go. The second, a poor boy, had borrowed a coat and a pair of boots from the son of his landlord to be confirmed in, and he had to return them at a certain time. The third said that he never went into strange places if his parents were not with him; he had always been a good child, and wished to remain so, even after being confirmed, and they ought not to tease him for this; they, however, did it all the same. These three, therefore did not go; the others went on. The sun was shining, the birds were singing, and the confirmed children sang too, holding each other by the hand, for they had no position yet, and they were all equal in the eyes of God. Two of the smallest soon became tired and returned to the town; two little girls sat down and made garlands of flowers, they, therefore, did not go on. When the others arrived at the willow trees, where the confectioner had put up his stall, they said: "Now we are out here; the bell does not in reality exist – it is only something that people imagine!"

Then suddenly the sound of the bell was heard so beautifully and solemnly from the wood that four or five made up their minds to go still further on. The wood was very thickly grown. It was difficult to advance: wood lilies and anemones grew almost too high; flowering convolvuli and brambles were hanging like garlands from tree to tree; while the nightingales were singing and the sunbeams played. That was very beautiful! But the way was unfit for the girls; they would have torn their dresses. Large rocks, covered with moss of various hues, were lying about; the fresh spring water rippled forth with a peculiar sound. "I don't think that can be the bell," said one of the confirmed children, and then he lay down and listened. "We must try to find out if it is!" And there he remained, and let the others walk on.

They came to a hut built of the bark of trees and branches; a large crab-apple tree spread its branches over it, as if it intended to pour all its fruit on the roof, upon which roses were blooming; the long boughs covered the gable, where a little bell was hanging. Was this the one they had heard? All agreed that it must be so, except one who said that the bell was too small and too thin to be heard at such a distance, and that it had quite a different sound to that which had so touched men's hearts.

He who spoke was a king's son, and therefore the others said that such a one always wishes to be cleverer than other people.

Therefore they let him go alone; and as he walked on, the solitude of the wood produced a feeling of reverence in his breast; but still he heard the little bell about which the others rejoiced, and sometimes, when the wind blew in that direction, he could hear the sounds from the confectioner's stall, where the others were singing at tea. But the deep sounds of the bell were much stronger; soon it seemed to him as if an organ played an accompaniment – the sound came from the left, from the side where the heart is. Now something rustled among the bushes, and a little boy stood before the king's son, in wooden shoes and such a short jacket that the sleeves did not reach to his wrists. They knew each other: the boy was the one who had not been able to go with them because he had to take the coat and boots back to his landlord's son. That he had done, and had started again in his wooden shoes and old clothes, for the sound of the bell was too enticing – he felt he must go on.

"We might go together," said the king's son. But the poor boy with the wooden shoes was quite ashamed; he pulled at the short sleeves of his jacket, and said that he was afraid he could not walk so fast; besides, he was of opinion that the bell ought to be sought at the right, for there was all that was grand and magnificent.

"Then we shall not meet," said the king's son, nodding to the poor boy, who went into the deepest part of the wood, where the thorns tore his shabby clothes and scratched his hands, face, and feet until they bled. The king's son also received several good scratches, but the sun was shining on his way, and it is he whom we will now follow, for he was a quick fellow. "I will and must find the bell," he said, "if I have to go to the end of the world."

Ugly monkeys sat high in the branches and clenched their teeth. "Shall we beat him?" they said. "Shall we thrash him? He is a king's son!"

But he walked on undaunted, deeper and deeper into the wood, where the most wonderful flowers were growing; there were standing white star lilies with blood-red stamens, sky-blue tulips shining when the wind moved them; apple-trees covered with apples like large glittering soap bubbles: only think how resplendent these trees were in the sunshine! All around were beautiful green meadows, where hart and hind played in the grass. There grew magnificent oaks and beech-trees; and if the bark was split of any of them, long blades of grass grew out of the clefts; there were also large smooth lakes in the wood, on which the swans were swimming about and flapping their wings. The king's son often stood still and listened; sometimes he thought that the sound of the bell rose up to him out of one of these deep lakes, but soon he found that this was a mistake, and that the bell was ringing still farther in the wood. Then the sun set, the clouds were as red as fire; it became quiet in the wood; he sank down on his knees, sang an evening hymn and said: "I shall never find what I am looking for! Now the sun is setting, and the night, the dark night, is approaching. Yet I may perhaps see the round sun once more before he disappears beneath the horizon. I will climb up these rocks, they are as high as the highest trees!" And then, taking hold of the creepers and roots, he climbed up on the wet stones, where water-snakes were wriggling and the toads, as it were, barked at him: he reached the top before the sun, seen from such a height, had quite set. "Oh, what a splendor!" The sea, the great majestic sea, which was rolling its long waves against the shore, stretched out before him, and the sun was standing like a large bright altar and there where sea and heaven met – all melted together in the most glowing colors; the wood was singing, and his heart too. The whole of nature was one large holy church, in which the trees and hovering clouds formed the pillars, the flowers and grass the woven velvet carpet, and heaven itself was the great cupola; up there the flame color vanished as soon as the sun disappeared, but millions of stars were lighted; diamond lamps were shining, and the king's son stretched his arms out towards heaven, towards the sea, and towards the wood. Then suddenly the poor boy with the short-sleeved jacket and the wooden shoes appeared; he had arrived just as quickly on the road he had chosen. And they ran towards each other and took one another's hand, in the great cathedral of nature and poesy, and above them sounded the invisible holy bell; happy spirits surrounded them, singing hallelujahs and rejoicing.

The Last Pearl

WE ARE IN a rich, happy house, where the master, the servants, the friends of the family are full of joy and felicity. For on this day a son and heir has been born, and mother and child are doing well. The lamp in the bed-chamber had been partly shaded, and the windows were covered with heavy curtains of some costly silken material. The carpet was thick and soft, like a covering of moss. Everything invited to slumber, everything had a charming look of repose; and so the nurse had discovered, for she slept; and well she might sleep, while everything around her told of happiness and blessing. The guardian angel of the house leaned against the head of the bed; while over the child was spread, as it were, a net of shining stars, and each star was a pearl of happiness. All the good stars of life had brought their gifts to the newly born; here sparkled health, wealth, fortune, and love; in short, there seemed to be everything for which man could wish on earth.

"Everything has been bestowed here," said the guardian angel.

"No, not everything," said a voice near him – the voice of the good angel of the child; "one fairy has not yet brought her gift, but she will, even if years should elapse, she will bring her gift; it is the last pearl that is wanting."

"Wanting!" cried the guardian angel; "nothing must be wanting here; and if it is so, let us fetch it; let us seek the powerful fairy; let us go to her."

"She will come, she will come some day unsought!"

"Her pearl must not be missing; it must be there, that the crown, when worn, may be complete. Where is she to be found? Where does she dwell?" said the guardian angel. "Tell me, and I will procure the pearl."

"Will you do that?" replied the good angel of the child. "Then I will lead you to her directly, wherever she may be. She has no abiding place; she rules in the palace of the emperor, sometimes she enters the peasant's humble cot; she passes no one without leaving a trace of her presence. She brings her gift with her, whether it is a world or a bauble. To this child she must come. You think that to wait for this time would be long and useless. Well, then, let us go for this pearl – the only one lacking amidst all this wealth."

Then hand-in-hand they floated away to the spot where the fairy was now lingering. It was in a large house with dark windows and empty rooms, in which a peculiar stillness reigned. A whole row of windows stood open, so that the rude wind could enter at its pleasure, and the long white curtains waved to and fro in the current of air. In the centre of one of the rooms stood an open coffin, in which lay the body of a woman, still in the bloom of youth and very beautiful. Fresh roses were scattered over her. The delicate folded hands and the noble face glorified in death by the solemn, earnest look, which spoke of an entrance into a better world, were alone visible. Around the coffin stood the husband and children, a whole troop, the youngest in the father's arms. They were come to take a last farewell look of their mother. The husband kissed her hand, which now lay like a withered leaf, but which a short time before had been diligently employed in deeds of love for them all. Tears of sorrow rolled down their cheeks, and fell in heavy drops on the floor, but not a word was spoken. The silence which reigned here expressed a world of grief. With silent steps, still sobbing, they left the room. A burning light remained in the room, and a long, red wick rose far above the flame, which fluttered in the draught of air. Strange men came in and placed the lid of the coffin over the dead, and drove the nails firmly in; while the blows of the hammer resounded through the house, and echoed in the hearts that were bleeding.

"Whither art thou leading me?" asked the guardian angel. "Here dwells no fairy whose pearl could be counted amongst the best gifts of life."

"Yes, she is here; here in this sacred hour," replied the angel, pointing to a corner of the room; and there, – where in her life-time, the mother had taken her seat amidst flowers and pictures: in that spot, where she, like the blessed fairy of the house, had welcomed husband, children, and friends, and, like a sunbeam, had spread joy and cheerfulness around her, the centre and heart of them all, – there, in that very spot, sat a strange woman, clothed in long, flowing garments, and occupying the place of the dead wife and mother. It was the fairy, and her name was "Sorrow." A hot tear rolled into her lap, and formed itself into a pearl, glowing with all the colors of the rainbow. The angel seized it: the, pearl glittered like a star with seven-fold radiance. The pearl of Sorrow, the last, which must not be wanting, increases the lustre, and explains the meaning of all the other pearls.

"Do you see the shimmer of the rainbow, which unites earth to heaven?" So has there been a bridge built between this world and the next. Through the night of the grave we gaze upwards beyond the stars to the end of all things. Then we glance at the pearl of Sorrow, in which are concealed the wings which shall carry us away to eternal happiness.

Biographies

Hans Christian Andersen

Hans Christian Andersen was born in Denmark in 1805. When he was fourteen years old, he moved to Copenhagen with the intention of becoming an actor, but it was his writing that would earn him success. Although he published poetry, plays and sketches based on his travels, he is now most remembered for his fairy tales, which have influenced generations of children's authors. The first two volumes of *Fairy Tales Told for Children* were published in 1835, and when his fairy tales were translated a decade later he received long-lasting recognition in the field.

Mrs. H. B. Paull

Susannah Mary Paull (1812–88) was born in St James Parish, Middlesex, England as Suzannah Mary Peakome, the daughter of the saddler William Peakome. She married Henry Hugh Beams Paull (hence the "H. B.") and we know little else about her other than that she seems to have become a fairly prolific writer of religious and children's fiction, possibly to support herself after her husband got into financial difficulties. She began in 1855 with *The Doctor's Vision: An Allegory* and her last fiction work appears to have been *Mabel Berrington's Faith: and Other Stories* (1886). She also of course successfully translated the fairy tales of Hans Christian Andersen (the first edition of which was published in 1867), as well as those of the brothers Grimm.

Maria Tatar

(Foreword: *Hans Christian Andersen Fairy Tales*)
Maria Tatar is the John L. Loeb Research Professor of Germanic Languages & Literatures and Folklore & Mythology at Harvard University, where she is also a Senior Fellow at the Society of Fellows. Her books include *Enchanted Hunters: The Power of Stories in Childhood*, *The Annotated Hans Christian Andersen*, and *The Annotated Brothers Grimm*.

Sources

The tales in this book are based mainly on the edition entitled *Hans Andersen's Fairy Tales*, translated by Mrs. Henry H. B. Paull (Susannah Mary Paull), London: Frederick Warne & Co., 1872/1883.

FLAME TREE PUBLISHING
Epic, Dark, Thrilling & Gothic
New & Classic Writing

Flame Tree's Gothic Fantasy books offer a carefully curated series of new titles, each with combinations of original and classic writing:

*Chilling Horror • Chilling Ghost • Science Fiction
Murder Mayhem • Crime & Mystery • Swords & Steam
Dystopia Utopia • Supernatural Horror • Lost Worlds
Time Travel • Heroic Fantasy • Pirates & Ghosts • Agents & Spies
Endless Apocalypse • Alien Invasion • Robots & AI • Lost Souls
Haunted House • Cosy Crime • Urban Crime • American Gothic
Epic Fantasy • Detective Mysteries • Detective Thrillers • A Dying Planet
Bodies in the Library • Footsteps in the Dark • Strange Lands • Lovecraft Mythos*

**Also, new companion titles offer rich collections of
classic fiction, myths and tales in the gothic fantasy tradition:**

*George Orwell Visions of Dystopia • H.G. Wells • Lovecraft • Sherlock Holmes
Bram Stoker • Edgar Allan Poe • Mary Shelley • Charles Dickens Supernatural
African Myths & Tales • Celtic Myths & Tales • Greek Myths & Tales
Norse Myths & Tales • Chinese Myths & Tales • Japanese Myths & Tales
Native American Myths & Tales • Irish Fairy Tales • Heroes & Heroines Myths & Tales
Witches, Wizards, Seers & Healers Myths & Tales • Gods & Monsters Myths & Tales
One Thousand and One Arabian Nights • Alice's Adventures in Wonderland
King Arthur & The Knights of the Round Table • The Divine Comedy
Brothers Grimm • The Wonderful Wizard of Oz • The Age of Queen Victoria*

Available from all good bookstores, worldwide, and online at
flametreepublishing.com

See our new fiction imprint
FLAME TREE PRESS | FICTION WITHOUT FRONTIERS
New and original writing in Horror, Crime, SF and Fantasy

And join our monthly newsletter with offers and more stories:
FLAME TREE FICTION NEWSLETTER
flametreepress.com

GOTHIC FANTASY

For our books, calendars, blog
and latest special offers please see:
flametreepublishing.com